Working under a Carnegie grant in association with the Harvard Graduate School of Education, James Moffett developed a new rationale for an English curriculum for public schools. The concept of *Points of View* stemmed directly from his acclaimed pioneering program, and this newly Revised and Updated Edition has been designed by him and his co-editor, Kenneth R. McElheny, to retain the instructive power of its original approach while dramatically enchancing its relevance by including more modern and multicultural voices.

JAMES MOFFETT has served on the faculties of Phillips Exeter Academy, Harvard, U.C. Berkeley, San Diego State, and Middlebury College's Bread Loaf School of English as well as on the consulting Faculty of the National Endowment for the Humanities. The author of ground-breaking, prize-winning books in education, he currently gives talks and workshops internationally and lives in Mariposa, California.

KENNETH R. McELHENY taught English at Arlington School, Belmont, Massachusetts, for a number of years and continues there as Dean. Earlier, after acquiring B.A. and M.A. degrees at San Francisco State College, he was Chairman of the Language Arts Department of Pacifica High School, Pittsburg, California, and taught at Phillips Exeter Academy. He lives in Brookline, Massachusetts.

POINTS OF VIEW:
AN ANTHOLOGY
OF SHORT STORIES

REVISED EDITION

James Moffett

and

Kenneth R. McElheny

A MENTOR BOOK

In memory of George Bennett.

Special thanks to Judy Moffett
for suggestions and consultation.

MENTOR
Published by the Penguin Group
Penguin Books USA Inc., 375 Hudson Street, New York,
New York 10014, U.S.A.
Penguin Books Ltd, 27 Wrights Lane, London W8 5TZ, England
Penguin Books Australia Ltd, Ringwood, Victoria, Australia
Penguin Books Canada Ltd, 10 Alcorn Avenue, Toronto,
Ontario, Canada M4V 3B2
Penguin Books (N.Z.) Ltd, 182–190 Wairau Road, Auckland 10,
New Zealand

Penguin Books Ltd., Registered Offices: Harmondsworth,
Middlesex, England

First published by Mentor, an imprint of Dutton Signet,
a division of Penguin Books USA Inc.

First Printing, June, 1966
First Printing, Revised Edition, August, 1995

10 9 8 7 6 5 4 3

 REGISTERED TRADEMARK—MARCA REGISTRADA

Library of Congress Cataloging Card Number: 94–79667

Contents

DIARY NARRATION

SUBJECTIVE NARRATION

DETACHED AUTOBIOGRAPHY

ANONYMOUS NARRATION— DUAL CHARACTER POINT OF VIEW

ANONYMOUS NARRATION— MULTIPLE CHARACTER POINT OF VIEW

ANONYMOUS NARRATION— NO CHARACTER POINT OF VIEW

Preface

These stories could have been arranged in random sequence to make the usual heterogeneous collection; each stands on its own merits as an appealing, artistic short story. But the originality of this long-popular anthology has been that, in addition to their individual worth, these stories enrich each other by forming together a continuum of narrative technique. Whether you read the book front to back or back to front, the especially arranged sequence creates a growing context from which each story gains. Between one cover and the other, the vantage point of the storyteller continually shifts, making the whole book tell a super story of its own.

Twenty-eight years have passed since this collection first appeared in 1966. We selected the original stories during the Fifties and early Sixties on the basis of trials we were carrying out in our classes with students at Phillips Exeter Academy (now, but not then, coeducational and ethnically diverse). Still avoiding excerpts but taking advantage of today's wealth of ethnic and gender authorship, this edition replaces over half of those first selections and accommodates the interests of a far more varied readership.

The first edition survived long enough to become dated because it was based on a unique concept of anthologizing that teachers and other readers came to value most highly. The stories are selected and arrayed so as to create a continuum of first- and third-person fictional techniques or "points of view." The very order of placement illuminates the stories, readers have felt, because the juxtapositions make one aware of which technique an author chose and of why it suited that story's particular subject. Readers thus more readily appreciate for themselves the interplay between form and content that makes fiction work its spell.

In 1985 a companion volume appeared, also under the Mentor imprint. *Points of Departure: An Anthology of Nonfiction* again presents texts on a scale of first- and third-person points of view but emphasizes the real sources of the subject matter. This time the letters and diaries, autobiography and memoir, biography and chronicle don't *pose* as real documents, like the short stories modeled on them, but are actual. Together, the two collections allow readers to appreciate both the similarities and the differences between fiction and nonfiction. While sharing narrative forms, imaginative and actual discourse start and end in different places, as befits their different purposes and methods. Fiction begins in the infra range of interior and dramatic monologues, in drama, whereas nonfiction passes completely beyond stories to the ultra realm of statements, to essay.

Just as some teachers made the very structure of *Points of View* the outline of a course in literature or creative writing, some teachers of nonfiction or expository writing have used *Points of Departure* to organize a program of reading and writing. By bringing fiction and nonfiction into a felicitous juncture, these companion volumes enhance one another wherever they are read together in an integrated course or in interrelated courses. Both are part of a body of work on discourse analysis and teaching rationale that has played a part in changing the teaching of school and college English since the late 1960s. (See Related Works by James Moffett at the end.)

Besides the impact of feminism and ethnicity, English education has undergone revolution in pedagogy and literary criticism. Today's curriculum is arranged for students to see more for themselves rather than merely be told. The spectrum comprising *Points of View* originated from precisely this principle of self-teaching. Much extended by postmodern theory, today's competing approaches to literature vary in the emphasis they place on the *author*'s intentions, the *reader*'s responses, or the cultural grounds of the *subject*. The shifting relations among these first, second, and third persons—storyteller, audience, and story—constitute the very basis of the sequence in *Points of View*. What happened is a factor of who's telling the story, to whom, and in what circumstances.

Asserting ethnic and gender identity, taking charge of one's own learning, acknowledging the multiple meanings of texts according to contexts and subtexts—all represent a new pluralism and populism that reflects the relativity of life both in and out of books.

More on rationale in the Afterword. But first the stories themselves.

INTERIOR MONOLOGUE

In these first two stories the reader tunes in to somebody's train of thought or stream of consciousness. The situation is like that of soliloquies in the theater: the audience overhears the inner life because the character gives it voice. Reading such a story is like listening to a soliloquy.

Though limited in point of view, interior monologues can vary considerably, because each bespeaks a particular mind in particular circumstances. If the character is soliloquizing about the here and now, as in "A Telephone Call," the story features the movement of thought and feeling itself—the inner drama. The more the character dwells in the past and reflects at large, as in the second story, the more the monologue may resemble familiar narrative. But always the telling is as much the story as the told.

Interior monologue thrives in poetry as well as in drama, because rendering the ongoing inner life often demands extraordinary uses of language. Such poems as Amy Lowell's "Patterns," Robert Browning's "Soliloquy of the Spanish Cloister," T. S. Eliot's "The Love Song of J. Alfred Prufrock," and John Keats' "Ode to a Nightingale" are interior monologues. The technique arrived late in fiction and is rarely used to tell a story all by itself. Édouard Dujardin is generally credited with having invented interior monologue as a fictional device in his 1887 novel We'll to the Woods No More. *Like most modern novelists, James Joyce and William Faulkner don't try to sustain it throughout an entire novel, as Dujardin did, but rather weave it in and out of other techniques. An exception is Virginia Woolf's* The Waves, *which rotates among interior monologues of its main characters. All three novelists stylize the stream of con-*

13

sciousness through special structure and language, especially when it may be subverbal or subconscious. Claude Mauriac's The Dinner Party *consists entirely of alternated interior and dramatic monologues.*

A Telephone Call
Dorothy Parker

Please God, let him telephone me now. Dear God, let him call me now. I won't ask anything else of You, truly I won't. It isn't very much to ask. It would be so little to You, God, such a little, little thing. Only let him telephone now. Please, God. Please, please, please.

If I didn't think about it, maybe the telephone might ring. Sometimes it does that. If I could think of something else. If I could think of something else. Maybe if I counted five hundred by fives, it might ring by that time. I'll count slowly. I won't cheat. And if it rings when I get to three hundred, I won't stop; I won't answer it until I get to five hundred. Five, ten, fifteen, twenty, twenty-five, thirty, thirty-five, forty, forty-five, fifty.... Oh, please ring. Please.

This is the last time I'll look at the clock. I will not look at it again. It's ten minutes past seven. He said he would telephone at five o'clock. "I'll call you at five, darling." I think that's where he said "darling." I'm almost sure he said it there. I know he called me "darling" twice, and the other time was when he said good-bye. "Good-bye, darling." He was busy, and he can't say much in the office, but he called me "darling" twice. He couldn't have minded my calling him up. I know you shouldn't keep telephoning them—I know they don't like that. When you do that, they know you are thinking about them and wanting them, and that makes them hate you. But I hadn't talked to him in three days—not in three days. And all I did was ask him how he was; it was just the way anybody might have called him up. He couldn't have minded that. He couldn't have thought I was bothering him. "No, of course you're not," he said. And he said he'd telephone me. He didn't have to say that. I didn't ask him to, truly I didn't. I'm sure I didn't.

15

I don't think he would say he'd telephone me, and then just never do it. Please don't let him do that, God. Please don't.

"I'll call you at five, darling." "Good-bye, darling." He was busy, and he was in a hurry, and there were people around him, but he called me "darling" twice. That's mine, that's mine. I have that, even if I never see him again. Oh, but that's so little. That isn't enough. Nothing's enough, if I never see him again. Please let me see him again, God. Please, I want him so much. I want him so much. I'll be good, God. I will try to be better, I will, if You will let me see him again. If You will let him telephone me. Oh, let him telephone me now.

Ah, don't let my prayer seem too little to You, God. You sit up there, so white and old, with all the angels about You and the stars slipping by. And I come to You with a prayer about a telephone call. Ah, don't laugh, God. You see, You don't know how it feels. You're so safe, there on Your throne, with the blue swirling under You. Nothing can touch You; no one can twist Your heart in his hands. This is suffering, God, this is bad, bad suffering. Won't You help me? For Your Son's sake, help me. You said You would do whatever was asked of You in His name. Oh, God, in the name of Thine only beloved Son, Jesus Christ, our Lord, let him telephone me now.

I must stop this. I mustn't be this way. Look. Suppose a young man says he'll call a girl up, and then something happens, and he doesn't. That isn't so terrible, is it? Why, it's going on all over the world, right this minute. Oh, what do I care what's going on all over the world? Why can't that telephone ring? Why can't it, why can't it? Couldn't you ring? Ah, please, couldn't you? You damned, ugly, shiny thing. It would hurt you to ring, wouldn't it? Oh, that would hurt you. Damn you, I'll pull your filthy roots out of the wall, I'll smash your smug black face in little bits. Damn you to hell.

No, no, no. I must stop. I must think about something else. This is what I'll do. I'll put the clock in the other room. Then I can't look at it. If I do have to look at it, then I'll have to walk into the bedroom, and that will be something to do. Maybe, before I look at it again, he will call me. I'll be so sweet to him, if he calls me. If he says he can't see me tonight, I'll say, "Why, that's all right, dear. Why, of course it's all right." I'll be the way I was when I first met him. Then maybe he'll like me again. I was always sweet, at first. Oh, it's so easy to be sweet to people before you love them.

I think he must still like me a little. He couldn't have called me "darling" twice today, if he didn't still like me a little. It isn't all gone, if he still likes me a little; even if it's only a little, little bit. You see, God, if You would just let him telephone me, I wouldn't have to ask You anything more. I would be sweet to him, I would be gay, I would be just the way I used to be, and then he would love me again. And then I would never have to ask You for anything more. Don't You see, God? So won't You please let him telephone me? Won't You please, please, please?

Are You punishing me, God, because I've been bad? Are You angry with me because I did that? Oh, but, God, there are so many bad people—You could not be hard only to me. And it wasn't very bad; it couldn't have been bad. We didn't hurt anybody, God. Things are only bad when they hurt people. We didn't hurt one single soul; You know that. You know it wasn't bad, don't You, God? So won't You let him telephone me now?

If he doesn't telephone me, I'll know God is angry with me. I'll count five hundred by fives, and if he hasn't called me then, I will know God isn't going to help me, ever again. That will be the sign. Five, ten, fifteen, twenty, twenty-five, thirty, thirty-five, forty, forty-five, fifty, fifty-five. . . . It was bad. I knew it was bad. All right, God, send me to hell. You think You're frightening me with Your hell, don't You? You think Your hell is worse than mine.

I mustn't. I mustn't do this. Suppose he's a little late calling me up—that's nothing to get hysterical about. Maybe he isn't going to call—maybe he's coming straight up here without telephoning. He'll be cross if he sees I have been crying. They don't like you to cry. He doesn't cry. I wish to God I could make him cry. I wish I could make him cry and tread the floor and feel his heart heavy and big and festering in him. I wish I could hurt him like hell.

He doesn't wish that about me. I don't think he even knows how he makes me feel. I wish he could know, without my telling him. They don't like you to tell them they've made you cry. They don't like you to tell them you're unhappy because of them. If you do, they think you're possessive and exacting. And then they hate you. They hate you whenever you say anything you really think. You always have to keep playing little games. Oh, I thought we didn't have to; I thought this was so big I could say whatever I meant. I guess you can't, ever. I guess there isn't ever anything big enough for that. Oh, if he would just telephone, I wouldn't tell him I had been sad about him. They hate sad people. I would be so sweet and so gay, he couldn't help but like me. If he would only telephone. If he would only telephone.

Maybe that's what he is doing. Maybe he is coming up here without calling me up. Maybe he's on his way now. Something might have happened to him. No, nothing could ever happen to him. I can't picture anything happening to him. I never picture him run over. I never see him lying still and long and dead. I wish he were dead. That's a terrible wish. That's a lovely wish. If he were dead, he would be mine. If he were dead, I would never think of now and the last few weeks. I would remember only the lovely times. It would be all beautiful. I wish he were dead. I wish he were dead, dead, dead.

This is silly. It's silly to go wishing people were dead just because they don't call you up the very minute they said they would. Maybe the clock's fast; I don't know whether it's right. Maybe he's hardly late at all. Anything could have made him a little late. Maybe he had to stay at his office. Maybe he went home, to call me up from there, and somebody came in. He doesn't like to telephone me in front of people. Maybe he's worried, just a little, little bit, about keeping me waiting. He might even hope that I would call him up. I could do that. I could telephone him.

I mustn't. I mustn't, I mustn't. Oh, God, please don't let me telephone him. Please keep me from doing that. I know, God, just as well as You do, that if he were worried about me, he'd telephone no matter where he was or how many people there were around him. Please

make me know that, God. I don't ask You to make it
easy for me—You can't do that, for all that You could
make a world. Only let me know it, God. Don't let me
go on hoping. Don't let me say comforting things to
myself. Please don't let me hope, dear God. Please don't.

I won't telephone him. I'll never telephone him again
as long as I live. He'll rot in hell, before I'll call him up.
You don't have to give me strength, God; I have it myself. If he wanted me, he could get me. He knows where
I am. He knows I'm waiting here. He's so sure of me,
so sure. I wonder why they hate you, as soon as they
are sure of you. I should think it would be so sweet to
be sure.

It would be so easy to telephone him. Then I'd know.
Maybe it wouldn't be a foolish thing to do. Maybe he
wouldn't mind. Maybe he'd like it. Maybe he has been
trying to get me. Sometimes people try and try to get
you on the telephone, and they say the number doesn't
answer. I'm not just saying that to help myself; that really happens. You know that really happens, God. Oh,
God, keep me away from that telephone. Keep me away.
Let me still have just a little bit of pride. I think I'm
going to need it, God. I think it will be all I'll have.

Oh, what does pride matter, when I can't stand it if I
don't talk to him? Pride like that is such a silly, shabby
little thing. The real pride, the big pride, is in having no
pride. I'm not saying that just because I want to call
him. I am not. That's true, I know that's true. I will be
big. I will be beyond little prides.

Please, God, keep me from telephoning him. Please,
God.

I don't see what pride has to do with it. This is such
a little thing, for me to be bringing in pride, for me to
be making such a fuss about. I may have misunderstood
him. Maybe he said for me to call him up, at five. "Call
me at five, darling." He could have said that, perfectly
well. It's so possible that I didn't hear him right. "Call
me at five, darling." I'm almost sure that's what he said.
God, don't let me talk this way to myself. Make me
know, please make me know.

I'll think about something else. I'll just sit quietly. If
I could sit still. If I could sit still. Maybe I could read.
Oh, all the books are about people who love each other,

truly and sweetly. What do they want to write about that for? Don't they know it isn't true? Don't they know it's a lie, it's a God damned lie? What do they have to tell about that for, when they know how it hurts? Damn them, damn them, damn them.

I won't. I'll be quiet. This is nothing to get excited about. Look. Suppose he were someone I didn't know very well. Suppose he were another girl. Then I'd just telephone and say, "Well, for goodness' sake, what happened to you?" That's what I'd do, and I'd never even think about it. Why can't I be casual and natural, just because I love him? I can be. Honestly, I can be. I'll call him up, and be so easy and pleasant. You see if I won't, God. Oh, don't let me call him. Don't, don't, don't.

God, aren't You really going to let him call me? Are You sure, God? Couldn't you please relent? Couldn't You? I don't even ask You to let him telephone me now, God; only let him do it in a little while. I'll count five hundred by fives. I'll do it so slowly and so fairly. If he hasn't telephoned then, I'll call him. I will. Oh, please, dear God, dear kind God, my blessed Father in Heaven, let him call before then. Please, God. Please.

Five, ten, fifteen, twenty, twenty-five, thirty, thirty-five. . . .

I Stand Here Ironing

Tillie Olsen

I stand here ironing, and what you asked me moves
tormented back and forth with the iron.

"I wish you would manage the time to come in and
talk with me about your daughter. I'm sure you can help
me understand her. She's a youngster who needs help
and whom I'm deeply interested in helping."

"Who needs help?" Even if I came what good would
it do? You think because I am her mother I have a key,
or that in some way you could use me as a key? She
has lived for nineteen years. There is all that life that
has happened outside of me, beyond me.

And when is there time to remember, to sift, to weigh,
to estimate, to total? I will start and there will be an
interruption and I will have to gather it all together
again. Or I will become engulfed with all I did or did
not do, with what should have been and what cannot
be helped.

She was a beautiful baby. The first and only one of
our five that was beautiful at birth. You do not guess
how new and uneasy her tenancy in her now loveliness.
You did not know her all those years she was thought
homely, or seeing her poring over her baby pictures,
making me tell her over and over how beautiful she had
been—and would be, I would tell her—and was now, to
the seeing eye. But the seeing eyes were few or nonexis-
tent. Including mine.

I nursed her. They feel that's important nowadays. I
nursed all the children, but with her, with all the fierce
rigidity of first motherhood, I did like the books said.
Though her cries battered me to trembling and my
breasts ached with swollenness, I waited till the clock
decreed.

Why do I put that first? I do not even know if it matters, or if it explains anything.

She was a beautiful baby. She blew shining bubbles of sound. She loved motion, loved light, loved color and music and textures. She would lie on the floor in her blue overalls patting the surface so hard in ecstasy her hands and feet would blur. She was a miracle to me, but when she was eight months old I had to leave her daytimes with the woman downstairs to whom she was no miracle at all, for I worked or looked for work and for Emily's father, who "could no longer endure" (he wrote in his good-by note) "sharing want with us."

I was nineteen. It was the pre-relief, pre-WPA world of the depression. I would start running as soon as I got off the streetcar, running up the stairs, the place smelling sour, and awake or asleep to startle awake, when she saw me she would break into a clogged weeping that could not be comforted, a weeping I can yet hear.

After a while I found a job hashing at night so I could be with her days, and it was better. But it came to where I had to bring her to his family and leave her.

It took a long time to raise the money for her fare back. Then she got chicken pox and I had to wait longer. When she finally came, I hardly knew her, walking quick and nervous like her father, looking like her father, thin, and dressed in a shoddy red that yellowed her skin and glared at the pock marks. All the baby loveliness was gone.

She was two. Old enough for nursery school they said, and I did not know then what I know now—the fatigue of the long day, and the lacerations of group life in nurseries that are only parking places for children.

Except that it would have made no difference if I had known. It was the only place there was. It was the only way we could be together, the only way I could hold a job.

And even without knowing, I knew. I knew the teacher that was evil because all these years it has curdled into my memory, the little boy hunched in the corner, her rasp, "why aren't you outside, because Alvin hits you? that's no reason, go out coward." I knew Emily hated it even if she did not clutch and implore "don't go Mommy" like the other children, mornings.

She always had a reason why we should stay home. Momma, you look sick, Momma. I feel sick. Momma, the teachers aren't there today, they're sick. Momma there was a fire there last night. Momma it's a holiday today, no school, they told me.

But never a direct protest, never rebellion. I think of our others in their three-, four-year-oldness—the explosions, the tempers, the denunciations, the demands—and I feel suddenly ill. I stop the ironing. What in me demanded that goodness in her? And what was the cost, the cost to her of such goodness?

The old man living in the back once said in his gentle way: "You should smile at Emily more when you look at her." What *was* in my face when I looked at her? I loved her. There were all the acts of love.

It was only with the others I remembered what he said, so that it was the face of joy, and not of care or tightness or worry I turned to them—but never to Emily. She does not smile easily, let alone almost always as her brothers and sisters do. Her face is closed and somber, but when she wants, how fluid. You must have seen it in her pantomimes, you spoke of her rare gift for comedy on the stage that rouses a laughter out of the audience so dear they applaud and applaud and do not want to let her go.

Where does it come from, that comedy? There was none of it in her when she came back to me that second time, after I had had to send her away again. She had a new daddy now to learn to love, and I think perhaps it was a better time. Except when we left her alone nights, telling ourselves she was old enough.

"Can't you go some other time Mommy, like tomorrow?" she would ask. "Will it be just a little while you'll be gone?"

The time we came back, the front door open, the clock on the floor in the hall. She rigid awake. "It wasn't just a little while. I didn't cry. I called you a little, just three times, and then I went downstairs to open the door so you could come faster. The clock talked loud, I threw it away, it scared me what it talked."

She said the clock talked loud that night I went to the hospital to have Susan. She was delirious with the fever that comes before red measles, but she was fully con-

scious all the week I was gone and the week after we
were home when she could not come near the baby or
me.

She did not get well. She stayed skeleton thin, not
wanting to eat, and night after night she had nightmares.
She would call for me, and I would sleepily call back,
"you're all right, darling, go to sleep, it's just a dream,"
and if she still called, in a sterner voice, "now go to
sleep Emily, there's nothing to hurt you." Twice, only
twice, when I had to get up for Susan anyhow, I went
in to sit with her.

Now when it is too late (as if she would let me hold
and comfort her like I do the others) I get up and go
to her at her moan or restless stirring. "Are you awake?
Can I get you something?" And the answer is always
the same: "No, I'm all right, go back to sleep Mother."

They persuaded me at the clinic to send her away to
a convalescent home in the country where "she can have
the kind of food and care you can't manage for her, and
you'll be free to concentrate on the new baby." They
still send children to that place. I see pictures on the
society page of sleek young women planning affairs to
raise money for it, or dancing at the affairs, or decorat-
ing Easter eggs or filling Christmas stockings for the
children.

They never have a picture of the children so I do not
know if they still wear those gigantic red bows and the
ravaged looks on the every other Sunday when parents
can come to visit "unless otherwise notified"—as we
were notified the first six weeks.

Oh it is a handsome place, green lawns and tall trees
and fluted flower beds. High up on the balconies of each
cottage the children stand, the girls in their red bows
and white dresses, the boys in white suits and giant red
ties. The parents stand below shrieking up to be heard
and the children shriek down to be heard, and between
them the invisible wall "Not To Be Contaminated by
Parental Germs or Physical Affection."

There was a tiny girl who always stood hand in hand
with Emily. Her parents never came. One visit she was
gone. "They moved her to Rose Cottage," Emily
shouted in explanation. "They don't like you to love
anybody here."

She wrote once a week, the labored writing of a seven-year-old. "I am fine. How is the baby. If I write my leter nicly I will have a star. Love." There never was a star. We wrote every other day, letters she could never hold or keep but only hear read—once. "We simply do not have room for children to keep any personal possessions," they patiently explained when we pieced one Sunday's shrieking together to plead how much it would mean to Emily to keep her letters and cards.

Each visit she looked frailer. "She isn't eating," they told us. (They had runny eggs for breakfast or mush with lumps, Emily said later, I'd hold it in my mouth and not swallow. Nothing ever tasted good, just when they had chicken.)

It took us eight months to get her released home, and only the fact that she gained back so little of her seven lost pounds convinced the social worker.

I used to try to hold and love her after she came back, but her body would stay stiff, and after a while she'd push away. She ate little. Food sickened her, and I think much of life too. Oh she had physical lightness and brightness, twinkling by on skates, bouncing like a ball up and down up and down over the jump rope, skimming over the hill; but these were momentary.

She fretted about her appearance, thin and dark and foreign-looking at a time when every little girl was supposed to look or thought she should look a chubby blond replica of Shirley Temple. The doorbell sometimes rang for her, but no one seemed to come and play in the house or be a best friend. Maybe because we moved so much.

There was a boy she loved painfully through two school semesters. Months later she told me how she had taken pennies from my purse to buy him candy. "Licorice was his favorite and I brought him some every day, but he still liked Jennifer better'n me. Why Mommy why?" A question I could never answer.

School was a worry to her. She was not glib or quick in a world where glibness and quickness were easily confused with ability to learn. To her overworked and exasperated teachers she was an overconscientious "slow learner" who kept trying to catch up and was absent entirely too often.

I let her be absent, though sometimes the illness was imaginary. How different from my now-strictness about attendance with the others. I wasn't working. We had a new baby, I was home anyhow. Sometimes, after Susan grew old enough, I would keep her home from school, too, to have them all together.

Mostly Emily had asthma, and her breathing, harsh and labored, would fill the house with a curiously tranquil sound. I would bring the two old dresser mirrors and her boxes of collections to her bed. She would select beads and single earrings, bottle tops and shells, dried flowers and pebbles, old postcards and scraps, all sorts of oddments; then she and Susan would play Kingdom, setting up landscapes and furniture, peopling them with action.

Those were the only times of peaceful companionship between her and Susan. I have edged away from it, that poisonous feeling between them, that terrible balancing of hurts and needs I had to do between the two, and did so badly, those earlier years.

Oh there are conflicts between the others too, each one human, needing, demanding, hurting, taking—but only between Emily and Susan, no, Emily toward Susan that corroding resentment. It seems so obvious on the surface, yet it is not obvious. Susan, the second child, Susan, golden and curly haired and chubby, quick and articulate and assured, everything in appearance and manner Emily was not; Susan, not able to resist Emily's precious things, losing or sometimes clumsily breaking them; Susan telling jokes and riddles to company for applause while Emily sat silent (to say to me later: that was *my* riddle, Mother, I told it to Susan); Susan, who for all the five years' difference in age was just a year behind Emily in developing physically.

I am glad for that slow physical development that widened the difference between her and her contemporaries, though she suffered over it. She was too vulnerable for that terrible world of youthful competition, of preening and parading, of constant measuring of yourself against every other, of envy, "If I had that copper hair," or "If I had that skin . . ." She tormented herself enough about not looking like the others, there was enough of the unsureness, the having to be conscious of words before you speak, the constant caring—what are they thinking of me? what kind of an impression am I making—there was enough without having it all magnified unendurably by the merciless physical drives.

Ronnie is calling. He is wet and I change him. It is rare there is such a cry now. That time of motherhood is almost behind me when the ear is not one's own but must always be racked and listening for the child cry, the child call. We sit for a while and I hold him, looking out over the city spread in charcoal with its soft aisles of light. "Shuggily" he breathes. A funny word, a family word, inherited from Emily, invented by her to say comfort.

In this and other ways she leaves her seal, I say aloud. And startle at my saying it. What do I mean? What did I start to gather together, to try and make coherent? I was at the terrible, growing years. War years. I do not remember them well. I was working, there were four smaller ones now, there was not time for her. She had to help be a mother, and housekeeper, and shopper. She had to set her seal. Mornings of crisis and near hysteria trying to get lunches packed, hair combed, coats and shoes found, everyone to school or Child Care on time, the baby ready for transportation. And always the paper scribbled on by a smaller one, the book looked at by Susan then mislaid, the homework not done. Running out to that huge school where she was one, she was lost, she was a drop; suffering over the unpreparedness, stammering and unsure in her classes.

There was so little time left at night after the kids were bedded down. She would struggle over books, always eating (it was in those years she developed her enormous appetite that is legendary in our family) and I would be ironing, or preparing food for the next day, or writing V-mail to Bill, or tending the baby. Sometimes, to make me laugh, or out of her despair, she would imitate happenings or types at school.

I think I said once: "Why don't you do something like this in the school amateur show?" One morning she phoned me at work, hardly understandable through the weeping: "Mother, I did it. I won, I won; they gave me first prize; they clapped and clapped and wouldn't let me go."

Now suddenly she was Somebody, and as imprisoned in her difference as in anonymity.

She began to be asked to perform at other high schools, even in colleges, then at city and state-wide affairs. The first one we went to, I only recognized her the first moment when thin, shy, she almost drowned herself into the curtains. Then: Was this Emily? the control, the command, the convulsing and deadly clowning, the spell, then the roaring, stamping audience, unwilling to let this rare and precious laughter out of their lives.

Afterwards: You ought to do something about her with a gift like that—but without money or knowing how, what does one do? We have left it all to her, and the gift has as often eddied inside, clogged and clotted, as been used and growing.

She is coming. She runs up the stairs two at a time with her light graceful step, and I know she is happy tonight. Whatever it was that occasioned your call did not happen today.

"Aren't you ever going to finish the ironing, Mother? Whistler painted his mother in a rocker. I'd have to paint mine standing over an ironing board." This is one of her communicative nights and she tells me everything and nothing as she fixes herself a plate of food out of the icebox.

She is so lovely. Why did you want me to come in at all? Why were you concerned? She will find her way.

She starts up the stairs to bed. "Don't get me up with the rest in the morning." "But I thought you were having midterms." "Oh, those," she comes back in and says quite lightly, "in a couple of years when we'll all be atom-dead they won't matter a bit."

She has said it before. She believes it. But because I have been dredging the past, and all that compounds a human being is so heavy and meaningful in me, I cannot endure it tonight.

I will never total it all now. I will never come in to say: She was a child seldom smiled at. Her father left me before she was a year old. I worked her first six years when there was work, or I sent her home and to his relatives. There were years she had care she hated. She was dark and thin and foreign-looking in a world where the prestige went to blondness and curly hair and dimples, slow where glibness was prized. She was a child of anxious, not proud, love. We were poor and could not afford for her the soil of easy growth. I was a young mother, I was a distracted mother. There were the other children pushing up, demanding. Her younger sister was all that she was not. She did not like me to touch her. She kept too much in herself, her life was such she had to keep too much in herself. My wisdom came too late. She has much in her and probably nothing will come of it. She is a child of her age, of depression, of war, of fear.

Let her be. So all that is in her will not bloom—but in how many does it? There is still enough left to live by. Only help her to believe—help make it so there is cause for her to believe that she is more than this dress on the ironing board, helpless before the iron.

DRAMATIC MONOLOGUE

Now the reader overhears somebody speaking aloud to another person. The monologuist has a particular reason for telling a particular story to a particular audience, and his or her speech, as in real life, is spontaneous and unrehearsed. We can learn who the speaker and listener are, and their circumstances, only from references within the monologue itself. And as also in real life, we have to make sense of what we witness without benefit of a narrative guide. This is a no-host show.

This kind of monologue too has a counterpart in the theater, whenever one character takes over the stage and talks for a long time uninterruptedly. From the Greeks on, playwrights have used dramatic monologues, as in the case of the sergeant reporting near the opening of Macbeth, *to recount offstage action. But besides narrating, monologuists may explain themselves, reveal themselves, or betray themselves. Along with soliloquies and colloquies, dramatic monologues are one of the staple components of plays.*

Many poems, like Robert Browning's "My Last Duchess," John Donne's "The Flea," and the bulk of Samuel Taylor Coleridge's "The Rime of the Ancient Mariner" are dramatic monologues inasmuch as they are uttered by one character to another in a stipulated scene. Many other poems may lack a definite listener or setting but are uttered by an identified speaker, like Alfred Tennyson's "Ulysses" or A. E. Housman's "The Carpenter's Son."

Novelists have always, through monologues, let their characters share the narration and reveal themselves, and whole chapters of Samuel Fielding's and Fyodor Dostoevsky's novels are told by one character to another. Likewise framed by the author's narrative, Chaucer's Canterbury Tales *comprise some superb dramatic mono-*

*logues. But it is really to American vernacular writers of
the twentieth century, inspired by* Huck Finn, *that we owe
the exploitation of this technique for whole fictional
works. Eudora Welty sustained it throughout an entire
novel,* The Ponder Heart, *as did Albert Camus in* The
Fall.

*Since a monologue naturally occurs within the frame-
work of a dialogue, short stories of this sort frequently
indicate interaction between the monologuist and a re-
sponsive listener. The art here is to reflect such responses
in the monologue. The following three stories progress
from least to most interaction.*

Straight Pool

John O'Hara

I'll shoot you fifty points if you spot me ten balls. Isn't that a laugh? You spotting me. Snowball! Rack 'em up for straight pool. *I'll play it safe.*

It sure is a laugh, you spotting me, when I used to beat you fifty to thirty-five. For a while there—*I'll play the four-ball, cross sides*—for a while there I could beat you fifty to thirty-five without any trouble, but now I'm lucky if I can beat you with you spotting me fifty to forty. *Eleven-ball. Your shot, and there they are, all open for you.* You know, I'm not making any alibi, Jack, but this is the first time I've had a cue in my hand in over a month. Oh, geez, way over a month. I bet it's two months. I had to practically pack up a suitcase and join the Army or something to get out tonight. Mae and one of her crying spells again. Damn it, Jack—*oh, nice shot, atta working in there*—you know I'm not a hard guy to get along with. At least I don't think I am, but Mae gets these crying spells, and honest to God, I can't stay in the house another minute. And then if I say I'm going out, even if it's only for a pack of cigarettes, why, she suddenly all of a sudden stops crying and sits there looking at me, not saying a word, and it's worse than her crying. I don't know what makes her do that. If I stay, she cries all the time I'm there, and if I make a move to go out of the house—honest, I'm afraid to leave her alone. When she gets in one of these spells, she's liable to do anything, so I very seldom leave. But I can stand only so much. I'm only human, just like anybody else; and you go around fixing refrigerators all day long, getting up and sitting down and answering dumb questions, and any man would want some peace when he gets home. But not me. I mean, do I get it? No. I come home and it's an even chance she's going to have a crying

32

spell. I never can tell how it's going to be till I'm home a while, and then all of a sudden she's liable to get up from the table and be gone a half an hour, and I eat by myself and finally I have to do the dishes. And when I go to the bedroom, it's always the same story. She's lying there on the bed and when I come in the room she won't even look at me. She says, "Did you do the dishes?" and I say, "Yes," and she says I shouldn't of. Then I tell her if she feels lousy she ought to go to bed, but I know damn well it isn't that she feels sick or anything. I mean there's nothing wrong with her. I had her go to the doctor to see if there was anything really wrong with her, but there wasn't. She had an aunt that died of cancer, and I thought maybe she was afraid of that, but no. She was O.K., according to the doctor.

That was a tough one to miss, Jack. Play the ten, in the side. Now the one-ball in the corner. That makes it ten to four this frame, and look at that break shot. Hey, Snowball, rack 'em up. I'll play it off the pile.... Keeripes! What a miss! There you are, all yours.

So after she went to see the doctor and he said there was nothing wrong, I thought maybe it was just something that would wear off. You know how women are. They get these funny ideas in their heads and all they need is a little attention. So I stayed home a lot and took her to the pictures and I didn't go out of the house except to go to work, and it looked for a while as if she was all right. So one night I said I was going down and shoot a game of pool. "Who with?" she said. And I said I didn't know, just going down to the Olympic and see if there was anybody there. "No, you're not," she said. "You're going down there and talk about me. You're going to talk about me with Jack McMorrow," she said. "No, I wasn't," I told her. I said maybe I'd shoot a game with you, but I said I wasn't going to talk about her to you, and that was the last time I was down here. I guess that must of been close to two months ago.

Nice run, boy. I don't see how you missed that one. It was dead for the corner. You're not giving me any breaks, are you? ... Well, there's my high run. Three balls. You'll be out in five frames the way I'm playing.

Well, when I got home that night, the last time I was down here, the first thing she wanted to know was did

I talk to you about her, and I told her I didn't even see you. She has some kind of a fear about us talking about her, I guess. It must of been that, because every time since then, every time I wanted to come down here she put on that stare act and I'd be afraid to leave her.

Nice shot.

I'd be afraid to leave her on account of I didn't know what would happen while I was gone. She was nuts on the subject of you. Not about you, exactly, but about us talking about her. Jack McMorrow! Jack McMorrow! For some reason I can't fathom out she had this idea that when you and me get together we'd always talk about her. She'd say, "I know men. They always talk about girls that way." I said to her, "Listen," I said, "a man doesn't go to a poolroom to talk about his wife. At least I don't," I said. I said, "I go to a poolroom to shoot pool." But I couldn't convince her.

Well, you left me safe enough. Play the five.

Well, I decided I had to humor her. There was something wrong that she wouldn't tell me about, and I decided to humor her for a while and maybe it'd come out all right. She was always talking about you, always you, and you were the one she had this idea about, so I said to her, I told her I wouldn't see you any more. I said I'd stop going down to the Olympic, and she knew I wouldn't see you anywhere else, and that made her feel all right, I think, because the crying spells slackened off and stopped altogether. So she seemed to be all right again and when I had to go to Waterbury, Connecticut, two weeks ago, to attend the funeral of my aunt, I asked her if she wanted to go along but she said no, and then I said I wouldn't go, and she said she was all right, and she sounded all right, so I went to Waterbury to this funeral and stayed overnight. Well, I guess that's where I made my mistake. I shouldn't of left her alone overnight. When I came back from Waterbury, I could see she was all upset and nervous, and she had one of her crying spells and so on, and then the day before yesterday I came home and she was cockeyed drunk with a bottle of gin. I never saw her so drunk. We had a big fight and all. A hell of a fight, and yesterday she didn't get up for breakfast, and last night when I came home from work she wouldn't say a word. And then tonight when I came home, the same story over again. Cockeyed again. "What's the idea?" I said, and we had it out hot and heavy, but she didn't want me to leave, so I said I'd leave all right, and she was lucky if I came back. I got the hell out of the house as sore as a boil. I guess I oughtn't to be talking about her like this, especially to you, because you're the one she thinks is always talking about her, but I have to talk to somebody. I think I'll go to Brooklyn and get drunk. How about it? ...

What's the matter? You quitting? ... Oh! If I'd of known you had a date, we could of made it twenty-five points. You're ahead anyhow, and I don't feel like shooting much. Guess I'll go to Brooklyn. My brother just got a gallon of apple....

The Lady's Maid

Katherine Mansfield

Eleven o'clock. A knock at the door.... I hope I haven't disturbed you, madam. You weren't asleep—were you? But I've just given my lady her tea, and there was such a nice cup over, I thought, perhaps ...

... Not at all, madam. I always make a cup of tea last thing. She drinks it in bed after her prayers to warm her up. I put the kettle on when she kneels down and I say to it, "Now you needn't be in too much of a hurry to say *your* prayers." But it's always boiling before my lady is half through. You see, madam, we know such a lot of people, and they've all got to be prayed for—every one. My lady keeps a list of the names in a little red book. Oh dear! whenever someone new has been to see us and my lady says afterwards, "Ellen, give me my little red book," I feel quite wild, I do. "There's another," I think, "keeping her out of her bed in all weathers." And she won't have a cushion, you know, madam; she kneels on the hard carpet. It fidgets me something dreadful to see her, knowing her as I do. I've tried to cheat her; I've spread out the eiderdown. But the first time I did it—oh, she gave me such a look—holy it was, madam. "Did our Lord have an eiderdown, Ellen?" she said. But—I was younger at the time—I felt inclined to say, "No, but our Lord wasn't your age, and he didn't know what it was to have your lumbago." Wicked—wasn't it? But she's *too* good, you know, madam. When I tucked her up just now and seen—saw her lying back, her hands outside and her head on the pillow—so pretty—I couldn't help thinking, "Now you look just like your dead mother when I laid her out!"

... Yes, madam, it was all left to me. Oh, she did look sweet. I did her hair, softlike, round her forehead, all in dainty curls, and just to one side of her neck I put a

36

bunch of the most beautiful purple pansies. Those pansies made a picture of her, madam! I shall never forget them. I thought tonight, when I looked at my lady, "Now, if only the pansies was there no one could tell the difference."

... Only the last year, madam. Only after she'd got a little—well—feeble as you might say. Of course, she was never dangerous; she was the sweetest old lady. But how it took her was—she thought she'd lost something. She couldn't keep still, she couldn't settle. All day long she'd be up and down, up and down; you'd meet her everywhere—on the stairs, in the porch, making for the kitchen. And she'd look up at you, and she'd say—just like a child, "I've lost it, I've lost it." "Come along," I'd say, "come along, and I'll lay out your patience for you." But she'd catch me by the hand—I was a favorite of hers—and whisper, "Find it for me, Ellen. Find it for me." Sad, wasn't it?

... No, she never recovered, madam. She had a stroke at the end. Last words she ever said was—very slow, "Look in—the—Look—in—" And then she was gone.

... No, madam, I can't say I noticed it. Perhaps some girls. But you see, it's like this, I've got nobody but my lady. My mother died of consumption when I was four, and I lived with my grandfather, who kept a hairdresser's shop. I used to spend all my time in the shop under a table dressing my doll's hair—copying the assistants, I suppose. They were ever so kind to me. Used to make me little wigs, all colors, the latest fashions and all. And there I'd sit all day, quiet as quiet—the customers never knew. Only now and again I'd take my peep from under the tablecloth.

... But one day I managed to get a pair of scissors and—would you believe it, madam? I cut off all my hair; snipped it off all in bits, like the little monkey I was. Grandfather was *furious!* He caught hold of the tongs—I shall never forget it—grabbed me by the hand and shut my fingers in them. "That'll teach you!" he said. It was a fearful burn. I've got the mark of it today.

... Well, you see, madam, he'd taken such pride in my hair. He used to sit me up on the counter, before the customers came, and do it something beautiful—big, soft curls and waved over the top. I remember the assistants standing round, and me ever so solemn with the penny grandfather gave me to hold while it was being done. . . . But he always took the penny back afterwards. Poor grandfather! Wild, he was, at the fright I'd made of myself. But he frightened me that time. Do you know what I did, madam? I ran away. Yes, I did, round the corners, in and out, I don't know how far I didn't run. Oh, dear, I must have looked a sight, with my hand rolled up in my pinny and my hair sticking out. People must have laughed when they saw me. . . .

. . . No, madam, grandfather never got over it. He couldn't bear the sight of me after. Couldn't eat his dinner, even, if I was there. So my aunt took me. She was a cripple, an upholstress. Tiny! She had to stand on the sofas when she wanted to cut out the backs. And it was helping her I met my lady. . . .

. . . Not so very, madam. I was thirteen, turned. And I don't remember ever feeling—well—a child, as you might say. You see there was my uniform, and one thing and another. My lady put me into collars and cuffs from the first. Oh yes—once I did! That was—funny! It was like this. My lady had her two little nieces staying with her—we were at Sheldon at the time—and there was a fair on the common.

"Now, Ellen," she said, "I want you to take the two young ladies for a ride on the donkeys." Off we went; solemn little loves they were; each had a hand. But when we came to the donkeys they were too shy to go on. So we stood and watched instead. Beautiful those donkeys were! They were the first I'd seen out of a cart—for pleasure as you might say. They were a lovely silver-gray, with little red saddles and blue bridles and bells jing-a-jingling on their ears. And quite big girls—older than me, even—were riding them, ever so gay. Not at all common, I don't mean, madam, just enjoying themselves. And I don't know what it was, but the way the little feet went, and the eyes—so gentle—and the soft ears—made me want to go on a donkey more than anything in the world!

. . . Of course, I couldn't. I had my young ladies. And what would I have looked like perched up there in my uniform? But all the rest of the day it was donkeys—donkeys on the brain with me. I felt I should have burst if I didn't tell someone; and who was there to tell? But when I went to bed—I was sleeping in Mrs. James's bedroom, our cook that was, at the time—as soon as the light was out, there they were, my donkeys, jingling along, with their neat little feet and sad eyes. . . . Well, madam, would you believe it, I waited for a long time and pretended to be asleep, and then suddenly I sat up and called out as loud as I could, *"I do want to go on a donkey. I do want a donkey ride!"* You see, I had to say it, and I thought they wouldn't laugh at me if they knew I was only dreaming. Artful—wasn't it? Just what a silly child would think. . . .

. . . No, madam, never now. Of course, I did think of it at one time. But it wasn't to be. He had a little flower shop just down the road and across from where we was living. Funny—wasn't it? And me such a one for flowers. We were having a lot of company at the time, and I was in and out of the shop more often than not, as the saying is. And Harry and I (his name was Harry) got to quarreling about how things ought to be arranged—and that began it. Flowers! you wouldn't believe it, madam, the flowers he used to bring me. He'd stop at nothing. It was lilies of the valley more than once, and I'm not exaggerating! Well, of course, we were going to be married and live over the shop, and it was all going to be just so, and I was to have the window to arrange. . . . Oh, how I've done that window of a Saturday! Not really, of course, madam, just dreaming, as you might say. I've done it for Christmas—motto in holly, and all—and I've had my Easter lilies with a gorgeous star all daffodils in the middle. I've hung—well, that's enough of that. The day came he was to call for me to choose the furniture. Shall I ever forget it? It was a Tuesday. My lady wasn't quite herself that afternoon. Not that she'd said anything, of course; she never does or will. But I knew by the way that she kept wrapping herself up and asking me if it was cold—and her little nose looked . . . pinched. I didn't like leaving her; I knew I'd be worrying all the time. At last I asked her if she'd rather I put it off. "Oh no, Ellen," she said, "you mustn't mind about me. You mustn't disappoint your young man." And so cheerful, you know, madam, never thinking about herself. It made me feel worse than ever. I began to wonder . . . then she dropped her handkerchief and began to stoop down to pick it up herself—a thing she never did. "Whatever are you doing!" I cried, running to stop her. "Well," she said, smiling, you know, madam, "I shall have to begin to practice." Oh, it was all I could do not to burst out crying. I went over to the dressing table and made believe to rub up the silver, and I couldn't keep myself in, and I asked her if she'd rather I . . . didn't get married. "No, Ellen," she said—that was her voice, madam, like I'm giving you—"No, Ellen, not for the *wide world!*" But while she said it, madam—I was looking in her glass; of course, she didn't know I could see her—she put her little hand on her heart just like her dear mother used to, and lifted her eyes. . . . Oh, *madam!*

When Harry came I had his letters all ready, and the ring and a ducky little brooch he'd given me—a silver bird it was, with a chain in its beak, and on the end of the chain a heart with a dagger. Quite the thing! I opened the door to him. I never gave him time for a word. "There you are," I said. "Take them all back," I said, "it's all over. I'm not going to marry you," I said, "I can't leave my lady." White! he turned as white as a woman. I had to slam the door, and there I stood, all of a tremble, till I knew he had gone. When I opened the door—believe me or not, madam—that man *was* gone! I ran out into the road just as I was, in my apron and my house shoes, and there I stayed in the middle of the road . . . staring. People must have laughed if they saw me. . . .

. . . Goodness gracious!—What's that? It's the clock striking! And here I've been keeping you awake. Ah, madam, you ought to have stopped me. . . . Can I tuck in your feet? I always tuck in my lady's feet, every night, just the same. And she says, "Good night, Ellen. Sleep sound and wake early!" I don't know what I should do if she didn't say that, now.

. . . Oh dear, I sometimes think . . . whatever should I do if anything were to . . . But, there, thinking's no good to anyone—is it, madam? Thinking won't help. Not that I do it often. And if ever I do I pull myself up sharp, "Now, then, Ellen. At it again—you silly girl! If you can't find anything better to do than to start thinking! . . ."

... & Answers

Joyce Carol Oates

I remember the car, yes. I can still see it. It swerved off the road, it crashed through the guard rail, down the cliff and into the water.... I remember seeing the guard rail collapse. I don't think I could hear anything, except screaming. It was my own screaming. And hers.... I remember that guard rail. Yes, it had been painted white recently. The weeds near it were splattered with white paint, they must have sprayed the paint on, and I—

This was just before my own accident. Yes. Seconds before. I was staring at that other car, at the broken rail and the edge of the cliff—I was screaming, and—I lost control of the car—

I have never understood it. I don't believe it. I did see that other car—it crashed just ahead of me, around the turn in the road. I don't believe the car wasn't found.

How? Maybe it belonged to someone who was so important, they wouldn't allow him to die. I mean the newspapers, the government.... Deaths can be kept secret, can't they? Anything is possible.

I don't want to talk about it again. My life isn't interesting.

I hate to repeat it, my life; I've answered so many questions, yes, I know you are being very patient and courteous, yes.... My life is an ordinary life. It isn't interesting. Nobody would write about it. I was born in San Diego and lived around here all my life.... What kind of events? I don't know what you mean by "events." I grew up without thinking about it, like a plant up through the soil—or a weed—just pushing its way through. I tried not to think about it. I never thought that I was unusual.... Which tests? High school? Did you look up those old records? Why did you do that?

But it didn't mean anything. I didn't believe it, I didn't allow it to change my life. We were tested one afternoon, all afternoon, complicated questions with multiple-choice answers, very confusing questions, some of them involving little shapes and designs and symbols, not the kind of questions we were used to answering in school. Very confusing, yes ... some of the kids gave up and started fooling around and were asked to leave.... I was afraid to give up. I remember how strange the questions were, and exciting in a way, because they made me think about things I hadn't thought of before.... Yes, I was always afraid of tests and questions. There are so many questions to be answered! I used to be afraid of giving the wrong answers....

But now I'm not. Why should I be?

Well, that was years ago, I don't think it means anything now. A week after the test we were called down to the principal's office, a few of us, called out of our first-period class by an announcement over the loudspeaker; you know how frightening that can be, to hear your name over a loud-speaker.... Two boys and myself. Everyone knew the boys were very smart. But the principal told us we had all done well on the tests. He was very pleased. I think he looked at me strangely. I was embarrassed. He said we were in the upper percentile of something, one percentile ... ? I don't remember the terminology.

No, I didn't really believe it. It must have been a mistake.

How should I know? Someone else's score might have gotten mixed up with mine, how should I know? My life has been completely ordinary. I wanted it to be ordinary.

I was married when I was nineteen and my husband is a very ... well, you've met my husband ... he is a very nice man, very kind. I prefer his parents to my own, in fact.

A little weak, maybe. But very kind. I've never regretted my marriage, no, not at all. We live in a very nice apartment, we moved there five years ago, right after Linda was born. It's a high-rise apartment building, the Northumberland, in the San Fernando Valley.... The ninth floor. It has a very nice view. It's a little small, so my husband would sit at the table in the dining alcove to go over work he brought home, and I'd sit there with him and do something, oh, I don't know, anything, mending or anything, and sometimes he'd ask me to check some figures for him ... his work is very complicated, he's an income tax specialist ... and I'd help him a little, the best I could. I can add up columns of figures quickly, in my head. And Linda would sit with us until it was her bedtime, playing, cutting out paper dresses to fit over cardboard dolls. Sometimes she would have trouble cutting them out carefully and I'd help her. Children get frustrated very easily when things don't go right....

I don't want to talk about her.

I did see the other car. It wasn't a hallucination. No, I couldn't exactly see who was driving it, everything happened so fast, he was swerving off the road when I came around the turn ... or she was, it might have been a woman.... The road is very dangerous all along the coast. They should do something about it.

Because I wanted to go for a drive. I wanted to show Linda how pretty it was, the northern part of the state. The ocean, and the rocks, and the sky ... all those little flowers along the side of the road....

From Sunday until Wednesday Linda had been sick in bed with the flu. I caught it from her. I didn't go to bed, of course. The week before, my husband had had sinus trouble, very bad headaches, so the apartment smelled of sick people—you know, Kleenex stuffed in

paper bags, in wastebaskets, and the feeling of germs in
the air, a sense of thickness. . . . When she was in bed
Linda needed attention all the time, conversation, she
was always asking questions . . . a thousand questions. . . .
She was very quick, very curious. All the questions she
could think of to ask! She was very smart for her age.
We are very proud of her. . . . So she was better that
morning, and I was going to take her down to the playground the way I always did when it didn't rain; there's
a nice little playground by the apartment building, a concrete square with a pond and some swings and benches,
where all the children play. I've gotten to know a lot of
the other mothers there. It's a very friendly place. But a
number of men have begun using the square, just sitting
around. Not bums, no. I don't know how to describe
them. They're not bums or alcoholics, the kind of men
you might see in downtown squares, but ordinary men,
middle-aged, in suits and neckties, just sitting around.
Maybe they lost their jobs . . . ? I began to be afraid of
going there with Linda. So when she got over the flu
and we were going down in the elevator I asked her if
she would like to go for a ride; I thought of it just in a
second, it came to me out of nowhere. It wasn't anything
I had planned. No. No, my husband didn't know about
it. How could he . . . ? I just thought of it going down in
the elevator. Of course Linda wanted to go. We were
both very excited, very happy. I don't know why I felt
so happy. . . . Linda was so pleased she began to jump
around the way she does, a little feverish, the way children are when they open presents, almost as if they're
afraid of the presents. Of course they want them, but
still they're afraid. I was like that myself. Linda gets very
excited over surprises, even good ones. She's only . . .
she was only . . . five years old. Surprises are disturbing
to children, good surprises as well as bad ones.

No. Not really. I don't remember much of my own
childhood.

If you could only understand how ordinary I am, and
how simple, you'd see what a waste of time it is for you
to construct these theories. . . . It makes me embarrassed.
I'm not equal to you.

I said: I'm not equal to you.

Because you imagine something that isn't there. I did see the other car when I came around the turn. The other driver was speeding. I saw his car crash into the railing and go over the side, and I heard the screaming, and my mind went blank with fear, and all the confusion—do you know what it's like to feel your car go out of control . . . ? I don't remember anything after that.

I already told you: he was a famous man, maybe a politician, an important man, and his death was to be kept secret. So the police are keeping it a secret, out of the newspapers. *You* wouldn't know about it either. Isn't that possible? There are many secrets in the world. I know that. Even when I was a child I knew that. The world is held together by secrets.

. . . Then nothing. Nothing. I don't remember my own car going over the side, I don't remember the water. I woke up and someone was lifting me onto a cot—the ambulance stretcher—a Negro boy in a white outfit was yelling for someone to grab my legs before I slipped off. He was one of the ambulance attendants. But I remember this the way you remember flashes from a movie, without any emotion, because they don't have anything to do with you personally. I don't remember being hurt. No. I don't remember the water, or anyone screaming, either one of us screaming. . . .

What? Did I say that? . . . Then maybe I do remember it, it's all so confusing and. . . .

If my husband says that, it must be true. I believe him. I wake up and he's shaking me, he's frightened and seems ready to cry, he says, *Wake up! You're having a nightmare!* He says that I scream at night sometimes. I don't know I'm screaming, I don't remember what I dream about that could make me cry out. . . . Once my husband began crying himself. I stared at him, I didn't know that men could cry. I didn't think they could cry. My father certainly never cried, he was a very hard, secretive man. Not big. But he gave the impression of

being big. He had many secrets he kept from all of us,
about work, and money ... even from my mother, he
kept secrets. When he died, he tried to keep it a secret.
He lied about how sick he was and why he was going
to the hospital. ...

I'm not upset!

He told my mother he was going on a fishing trip with
some men from work. He worked in a factory. He said
he'd be gone a few days, but he was really going to the
hospital. He died during the operation. None of us knew
where he was. It was just after Labor Day, when school
started, and my brothers and I were all confused and
frightened. That was the kind of man he was: very hard,
very tough. He joked a lot, but if you listened closely
you discovered that he never said anything. You could
never imagine him, what was in his mind; he liked to
keep everyone guessing. I was afraid of him. But I loved
him. Then a year ago I first began to notice, in my
daughter, something strange ... when she was very excited she would get nervous, fluttery, her eyes would
narrow as if she were afraid of something, the way I had
been with my father. As if she had inherited it from me.
Is that possible, that children can inherit fear? Can you
inherit fear, does it come along with physical characteristics like the color of hair and eyes?

I would never risk that. No. Not another child. Never.

Because of the fear that can be passed on. And all
the questions that must be met, and answered, during a
lifetime. ... It's a terrible thing to turn a child loose into
that, a world of people asking questions and poking and
examining ... asking questions, not believing the answers, taking notes, asking more questions. ...

I'm not upset. I'm not angry. Is my face strange, do
you see something in it that I don't know about? I used
to be a pretty woman. But now my face is strange.

Yes, my face is strange.

I believe what you say, but it hasn't anything to do with me. I trust you. I know you want to help me, you have that goal in mind, yes, I trust you, I know you don't want to deceive me, and—

I'm not angry. I'm not upset. Sometimes my mouth turns up at the corners, sharply, but it doesn't mean anything, it isn't a sarcastic smile, it isn't any kind of smile at all. I only smile when people smile at me. That way I can be sure that a smile is appropriate. I wasn't being sarcastic. I know you're paid to help me or someone else like me, and I don't want to disappoint you the way I've disappointed everyone else. So when I say that I believe you I mean that it's easy for me to believe you, on the surface. I believe anything men tell me and I always did. On the surface. What men say to me, what they said to me before my marriage—when I was involved with several men—goes along the surface of my skin, like the passing of hands over my skin, caresses, but it doesn't affect me. So I do believe you. I trust you just as I would trust any man.

I don't discuss that kind of thing, not with anyone. Not even a doctor.

But I am an ordinary woman, an average woman. That doesn't mean normal, I suppose. I know I'm not normal because of the concussion—my headaches, the way my vision gets blurred at night—I'm not normal now—but I will be normal sometime soon. And through it all I've been an ordinary woman, because you can't change that. My soul is ordinary. It's just that I can't remember the accident. The baby is gone but I have to keep living. . . . No, I don't want to move to another building, it's all right where we are. One building is like another where we live. I have to keep living there.

I'm not crying. This isn't what I would call crying. I feel a strange vibration in my head, as if things were rattling. Or is that from trucks outside on the street? My father used to drive a truck before he went to work in the factory. He was gone a lot. He hated driving. After he quit that job he went to work in a factory that made precision tools or parts of tools, for one of the aircraft companies. But he hated that too.

No, I didn't know him at all. In fact, I never think about him.

Since the accident. People are always asking me questions. . . . They are obsessed with making me remember certain things. The way teachers want children to learn and remember certain facts, but not others. The facts in books. *Learn what we tell you and nothing else!* . . . But you are like that, aren't you? You want me to remember certain things, the events of two or three minutes in my life, that are all over with and will never come back again. But I can't remember. And what I do remember you don't believe.

Yes, I want to be well.

According to your standards, and other people's standards. Yes. I want to be well again. My husband wants me to be well. I want to please you both. Women do want to please men, that's why they remember things that are important to men . . . they learn what is important, and after a while it becomes automatic.

Because of a certain fear. I don't know what it is.

. . . I told you: it came to me in the elevator, the thought of taking a drive. Instead of sitting in the square. Linda was very excited about it. Once I mentioned it to her, of course I couldn't go back on my word. You know how children are. And she needed fresh air, she was pale and restless and I had the idea that. . . .

That she was an unhappy child.

That we were failing her—I told my husband that once, I don't remember when. That her childhood was a failure.

The opposite of "success," I suppose.

Yes, I admit it's a strange thing to say, I suppose it is. But maybe I got it out of a magazine I had happened to read . . . ? You don't read those magazines. But there are many articles in women's magazines that help women, housewives, to organize their lives. They make you think seriously about your life. How to bake little cakes that can be fashioned into a train, for a child's party . . . or weaving rugs out of fluffy wool . . . or assessing your success as a mother, on a scale of ten. Maybe I got the vocabulary from one of those articles.

I'm not being ironic.

It might be that sick people sound ironic, because they're weak. Their voices are weak. But they're not ironic at all. They only want to please other people and be considered well again.

. . . So I asked him if he thought her childhood was a failure. If he noticed how frightened she was. . . . Of the street, of other children in the playground, of trucks . . . television shows, some of them . . . bad dreams . . . I don't know, what are children afraid of? Being lost, or kidnapped. I hated to see her so fearful. If we went shopping she was always afraid of getting lost; she stayed right with me. But my husband said he hadn't noticed.

No, no reason. There was no reason for her to be afraid. I would never have left her.

Yes, it's working out better at home now. Did he tell you that? I think it's better. I think I'll be able to sleep with him again soon, and eat breakfast with him again . . . it's just the early hour, the way he eats. . . . He didn't say anything? No, he doesn't eat noisily, he's a very neat, careful man. It's just the idea of it.

Of sitting close to someone who is eating; moving his mouth.

Sometimes I stay in the bathroom as long as I can. Or I say I'm not hungry. I don't want to hurt his feelings. Sometimes I make his breakfast, then take as long as I can to make my own. That way he might be finished before I sit down.

He doesn't believe me. No.

He just doesn't talk about it, none of it. He would never ask me about the other car. But I know he doesn't believe there was another car.

I don't have to answer that.

I resent that. I have never been suicidal.

I believe in God.

Yes, but I don't think about Him. I wouldn't know what to think about Him.

I believe in God the way I believe ... in certain things ... the way I believe in books I will never read, in their facts, in maps I will never see, in parts of the world I will never see. The way I believe in you; what you tell me. Because none of it is important.

You're angry ... ?

Yes, you are angry. I think you're angry.

Because you expect something from me that I can't give you. But there isn't anything inside me, I don't go down that deep. I can't remember much about the accident because there isn't much to me. . . . One morning when Linda and I went to the playground we sat with another mother, her name is Mollie, a very nice girl I got to know, and while our children were playing we noticed a man watching us. He was really staring at us. I became very nervous and wanted to get Linda and leave, and I was terrified that Mollie would walk away and leave me there, and we kept talking and trying not to notice him, and finally I started to laugh, I told Mollie that we had an admirer; so it turned into a joke and Mollie and I laughed about it. We whispered and laughed. The man kept staring at us, maybe he didn't know what was going on or didn't care. Mollie and I laughed together because it struck us—*what did he want?* What could we give him? Women can't give men much of anything. A body isn't very important, it doesn't last, it isn't like God, and yet men expect something like God. They expect something. Then when they discover there's nothing there, nothing inside, they get angry. Like you. I think you're angry with me because you expect something from me that—

I don't want to talk about her.

She was only five. You know that. What could I expect from her? She was very pretty, with hair lighter than mine. She looked like me when I was that age. Looked like snapshots of me. She could read a little, story books and things, she was very curious and asked a lot of questions. She was always asking me questions: like what made cars run, why can you see through glass, how much water could come out of a faucet. I don't want to talk about her. . . .

No.

. . . Except once, in the playground. She was playing with some other children and they started fighting. Over a toy, I don't know what. I ran over to get her, and she was fighting with a little boy, the two of them punching each other hard and crying, and I grabbed hold of her to pull her away . . . and . . . she was still angry. . . . I thought for a moment that I didn't know her. That this child was not mine.

The moment passed. I never thought it again.

I told you: that this little girl, who was struggling and screaming, wasn't mine. But the moment passed and I never had that thought again, not once.

No. In fact, I don't know what you mean by that.

But to be depressed you have to be happy too. Like a valley between two mountains . . . ? You have to be happy first. Then it changes and you're depressed.

I'm not being ironic.

Yes, I did request a change. Because I think a woman would be more tolerant.

When I say that there is nothing in me, nothing mysterious, she wouldn't be disappointed. Men expect too much. And yet even while I tell you this, and you nod your head, you're looking at me in a certain way.... I hate that look. I don't want it. I hate it.

When you were an intern you must have stuck your fingers inside women, didn't you? You wore rubber gloves! You did those things! You must have turned women upside down and inside out; you must have poked them and listened to their hearts and smelled their smells, which they couldn't help; you must have cut up the bodies of dead women; yet you still believe in the mystery, don't you? You still believe. But I don't. I looked at my daughter and it was like looking at myself in a mirror, but the mirror was dwarfed, and I could stare right into her eyes but I couldn't stare into my own in a mirror, but only at them. Because of the surface ... the rounded surface.... I can't explain. Because of the opaque part of the eye.... I don't know.

I said I wasn't depressed. What does my husband tell you? It isn't necessary to move. I avoid the park, the playground, the other mothers; so they can't feel sorry for me. I don't think about it. We keep the door to her room shut, we avoid the subject of her, it isn't necessary to move. Linda would have left home sometime in the future. I knew I would lose her sometime.

Not a hard birth, no. You're the third person to ask me that. An ordinary labor and an ordinary birth. I was under all the time. I don't remember much. No pain, no. Sometimes a bulk like a mountain, the way a mountain towers over a small village, you know, taking up most of the sky ... sometimes I see or feel a bulk like that when I remember giving birth to her, but I couldn't explain what it is. Maybe pain or the memory of pain. The fear of pain. I don't know.

Are you asking me if I killed her?

My pulse is always normal, like this. Check it. Check my head, my brain—wire me up again—go through all the tests again, those complicated little gauges! What can they tell you? Anything that I couldn't tell you myself? . . . You can't claim anything of the past except a few bodies and some crumpled metal. And you never found the first car and the first body! Where is that other driver? Why don't you look for him? All I did was follow him off the cliff; I lost control of the car and went right after him. When I woke up in the hospital that was the first thing I asked them—I didn't even remember about Linda—I asked about that other car. "Did he drown? Did he get out of the car in time? Is he safe?" I asked them. They'll tell you. Maybe it's written down. Because I wanted that other driver to live, didn't I? Because why else would I ask about him, when I had forgotten my own daughter? Why else would I ask? I must have wanted him to live, didn't I?

LETTER NARRATION

A letter is a written monologue, still relatively spontaneous, still addressed to a certain person for a certain reason. But of course the writer is not face-to-face with a listener, and that makes all the difference between speech and writing. A two-way correspondence is like a dialogue at a distance; feedback is delayed, and one composes more deliberately.

The first story here is a single letter mocking an office memorandum, that pale corporate vestige of the dying art of letter writing (which Rosellen Brown certainly revives for a moment). The next story is a "bundle of letters" by several crisscrossing correspondents that gradually builds up and fills out a mosaic of a story. Readers are still on their own without a cozy host to make connections for them and to pull the assorted points of view together into a coherent account. The last two stories add other documents to letters—a memoir or deposition—to complete the mosaic.

The epistolary novel enjoyed its greatest vogue in the eighteenth century, when it was used to make the new genre of prose fiction more plausible by grafting it onto a familiar domestic sort of writing (Samuel Richardson's Clarissa Harlowe, Tobias Smollett's Humphry Clinker, Fanny Burney's Evelina, Madame de Staël's Corinne, Jean-Jacques Rousseau's La Nouvelle Héloïse, and Choderlos de Laclos's Les Liaisons Dangereuses). As the following stories by James and Bierce show, nineteenth-century authors tended to use the technique more selectively and for shorter fiction. Within the last few decades, novelists as well as short story writers have found new reasons to tell their stories partially or entirely through letters and other documents (Mark Harris's Wake Up, Stupid, Bel Kaufman's Up the Down Staircase, and Alice

Walker's The Color Purple*). As in our examples here, modern authors often like to make readers figure out for themselves "what's the story" from the personal and sometimes conflicting evidence that characters supply.*

A story told through a multiplicity of writers anticipates the later technique of third-person narration with multiple character points of view, which also builds not just through the addition of incidents but through the accumulation of different people's points of view. A single character writing letters to a listening post whose responses are not given anticipates the next technique, diary narration.

Inter-Office

Rosellen Brown

TO: The Mayor

FROM: Sid R.

These are not the promised notes from the Transit Authority meeting—sorry. I will not give them to Gail to type. She shocks and worries and mothers me enough already.

I have a couple of stories to tell you, Mr. Mayor, to drink down with your morning optimism. I am not going nuts, I am not trying to extort more pay or make the evening headlines or any damn thing. It's only that I came to work today, over the beautiful bridge with its purple castles, from the Fourth Largest Fun City in the U.S.A. And I parked my car in its usual towable place, right in the cold shadow of City Hall, and walked down the corridors, turned, walked, turned, walked to my desk, listening to my heels click on the polished floor and they sounded for all the world, Mr. Mayor, like the heels of a significant man: a man who manages, or better. Has an office fairly near your right hand (how things are measured here, of course; leaving aside take-home-after-taxes, literal distance=figurative distance, space=trust). *Likes* his work, considers it basic to change in the city, to things that are real palpable entities to him, like justice and opportunity. Change. (Today the word clanks and jangles, echoes, what does it sound like? Change, chains, chance, chase ...) Has a more than adequate home life, when he's there long enough, home from this double-time work, to remember everybody's name.

And this morning I am here with my hands shaking, near to shouting with pain at every noise, cracking the way a man truly, cosmically, hung over, no kid stuff, cracks whenever anyone comes within touching distance. Gail took my arm when I came in, probably green, and said, "Sid?" to which I nastily countered, "Gail?" and slammed the door to my inner office. She appears to be holding all calls. Smart girl. (For the mayor's sake or mine?)

I promised you some stories. One: Couple of months ago a neighbor of mine took off. Fellow by the name of Tom. Just split. The day of our street fair where I live, a day I was proud of: the city as it ought to be, the rainbow city. His wife swore to me they had had no fight, nothing had been bothering him that very morning. He had left a strange note alluding to some money that had disappeared from one of the stands to the fair. None of it made sense. Now this particular neighbor of mine, no close friend, was a sort of flamboyant type who called himself a radical because his wife was black, who bitched a lot but didn't do much; who mugged for the camera, as it were. Nobody knew him really, the way you realize you never knew a suicide. But it occurs to me that he was serious under that motley, those bells. I knew him well enough to say he was no thief. I thought he was crazy when he left, but I think I understand him better this morning, or understand how quickly things come together or fall apart, without much warning, and I wish I knew where he went. I comb his children's faces for clues, but they comb mine. I comb the papers for signs. Is he taking evening courses at Columbia? Frequenting massage parlors? Floating belly-up on the Hudson like a perch?

The second story gets us closer to the point. Months ago—four? six? ten, maybe?—I was witness to an open-and-shut case of police brutality. I was on my way home early from work, coming up from the subway. (Dock my pay, I don't remember why.) Up the block is the junior high, a gray wall of a building, a monument to the absolutely uninflected boredom of its architect, and right in front is this kid Wilbert from up my block, getting his arm tied, snapped, broken smack off behind him like a branch, a stick of grass—just like that—and the cop who's applying the pressure is shouting *Kid had a knife! Kid had a knife!* to keep the civilian review freaks off his head. But never fear, there is no Lone Ranger to ride up for the dirt-brown boy to say, O hold there! What knife? O how? O where? Sheee-it. Instead, the fat cat who stands in the parking lot down on the corner, he's got nothing to do all day but back up cars eighty miles an hour, he joins in shouting and dancing. Yeah, I seen it shining, must be a knife! Maybe they'll make him a deputy sheriff. But he didn't need a knife, not above or below ground anywhere that side of the damn cafeteria. He'd come running out the wrong door of the school at the wrong time and stepped too close to this very edgy cop, who grabbed his shirt as he spun by.

Well, the crowd broke and the cop got Wilbert in the car, none too sweetly, and I kept walking. Down around the corner comes the patrol car headed for the jail, and what do I see in the back but a true comic-book skirmish—you could just about hear the pow! and whack! and see the puffs of pain go up in black rays. Trust me, it's funnier in "Blondie." They could have scooped his brains out in a drinking cup. All the force of these dark-blue shoulders bending over Wilbert, who's invisible, and up front the other cop's driving and I can see his mouth puckered up to whistle.

Well, what could I do but join that battle? I, who have a dim memory of having worked so fervently right here at this cluttered desk to create a civilian review board, trying to love the deformed bastard that got born—that same day I went up to Wilbert's rooming house to find him out on a bail bond, getting his lip, his ear, his chest bathed by his mother, who just kept crying with no let-up while we talked. I assume she saves up, waiting for this kind of occasion. He was actually feeling relieved: he knew he could have waited one hell of a long time to get out, and a thousand bucks in his pocket wouldn't have helped him. Luck, his bruises, I don't know what got him home so soon. Sure I convinced him. What's it to him—we file suit, we don't file suit. He doesn't expect to win a damn thing that matters. If he wins this one, then it couldn't have mattered—it's a pretty simple kind of accounting. All he says is, "Ever see a cop on the inside of the House of D?" And expects to go to jail himself.

We brought suit—for me, then. The courts, of course, tried to bugger us. We sit and sit through postponements, nonappearances (that maggoty cop is wearing us down, waiting us out). One time the judge forgot we

were on his calendar; *forgot*, while we sat on slats outside, and paced and sat some more. Well, I've got time—
no boss but you bossing over me—and he's got time,
God knows, that's the best he's got, all he's inherited is
the damn empty hours of his life. He does incredible
monologues while we sit there twitching. They shock his
churchy mama but they keep me fluid: dances around,
sings "The old *su*preme court of Brooklyn, the Kings
County slave court, *cucaracha* court, dead-of-night court,
and what do who care if we sit and get covered with
cobwebs and snow and shit, flowers grow out our ears,
our eyes fall in, our dicks fall off, our hearts get cavities
and the dentist say pull. Pull! Who give one creeping
crawling bleeding damn?"

So it took forever but I thought of all people I've got
to hang in there, and we WON. The kid was acquitted,
the cop was disciplined. (They probably tickled him to
death.) We made two inches on page 83 of the *Times*.
Me and Wilbert, in that order. He muttered a little
thanks, his mother stopped crying a while. Well, I didn't
do it for his thanks. But then I notice he's crossing the
street when he sees me coming. "Hey Wilbert!" He
ducks his head, "Hey man," and edges on past.

Well. Last night we were ripped off. I can't even tell
you the details, they are so gross. I mean it was not your
ordinary daily rip-off, no one is exempt from that, not
on our block, not even professional cop-haters and
pinkos like myself. Our fame only travels so far. No, this
one was surrogate murder. There too, just take my word
for it. Rape and murder. Let me merely say that the
gism on the bodice (is bodice the proper word? I don't
have much occasion) of my wife's best cocktail dress, so
thick it will never dry, was the most delicate and subtle
of the violations.

Imagine them discussing us. I mean, these are the boys
who went to a house on Caspian when the family was
out at a funeral. Hey ster-e-os, man, pow-er tools! We
cream them while they over to the graveyard crying they
honky eyes bloodshot. So what would they say of the
likes of me—Sid Rosenberg, *amicus curiae?* You think?
My man—they say, that four-floor house with the big
gold knocker and that orange tree in a box shitting oranges big as jawbreakers. Empty the desk drawers. Cut

up the shirts. Pour ink on the rugs. Fuck the dresses, once, twice. Break glass in the bed. Blood on the mirrors. Write LAY OFF and HELP and WHO THE HELL YOU ARE. So much for *amicae* ...

Because I know who did it and I even know why. Subtle, it all is, the policers of police, the judgers of the judges—we all look alike. I know, I know. His fingerprints are unique. He wanted me to know. This too is an old story: so says Mrs. Olsen down the way a few doors, a round and sunny social-working lady who has devoted all her twenty-hour days to a gallant paint-chipped youth center around the corner, which appears to have succeeded over the years chiefly in training up its kids, in their rinky-dink hats, to steal her TVs and rob the clubhouse strongbox.

We are ready for welfare, Mr. Mayor. Overnight I have sprouted an ulcer, my arteries are clogging like drains. My wife is moving, she tells me, with or without my company. She could have been *in* that dress, she said, sinking down on the littered bed, covering her secret parts with stiff hands.

Gail has lost patience only because I won't explain. She is finally trying to distract me with urgent phone calls: long distance, transatlantic, you yourself from down the hall. So I've done half a day's work. The sanitation men are nearing insurrection. The firemen (fire-*fighters*—is there something demeaning about being men? Too unprofessional?) have begun to throw bricks and bottles *back* and are making bombs in the firehouse. The district lines for judgeships are redrawn so that everyone who likes you has disappeared into a single garbage bag, tied with a twist-em donated by the governor, and they are on their way, with the watered-down garbage, to the city dump. To think I desperately fought to defend this job just this last year from internecine madmen jealous of it, or me, who wanted to sit here amid this rubble themselves. I remember it, smiling: the chicanery and backbiting, the memos and head counts and bottomless promises in return for support, quite ordinary warfare that keeps one in shape, I suppose, and keeps me sitting here in your funny city with my feet in a backed-up sewer....

And the price of a b.l.t. has gone up to $1.95. Mr.

Mayor, I am sitting in this well-upholstered chair dreaming of French Connection roadblocks on the Brooklyn Bridge and Roebling's foot smashed, with what kind of bellow, under a caisson, to make such a royal roadblock possible. What was I doing in 1960 or thereabouts when my friend, barely pubescent but who can come at will—how many times?—on my Doree's yellow dress, was born in some bleak bedroom, his mother shouting her pentecostal prayers? I was running for senior class treasurer, planning a career in world-saving, which has since been Jewed-down, as they say in some circles, to city-saving. Well, if I don't save this one, then it will be some other. Can I be cured of it? Can you? With all my household smashed can I afford a b.l.t.? It's a real question. Grown men who pity themselves to tears are disgusting; the civil service, like the military, would never allow such a display. But I never took that test.

Your Honor, Your Highness, they could do this to you, you know. Were it not for paid security, Gracie Mansion would be trashed. With your wife in that dress. I sound like the synagogues and church basements I go to harangue, South Ozone Park, Mill Basin, Tremont Avenue. I sound like the men who give me bad dreams, the bozos with the lip who say, Lock them up, they forage on our lawns, they feed on our daughters. But I see the way it is: Only one *macho* at a time, us or them. Them or us. Where was I when my little friend began? He must have hurt his hands, I mean the slug-white cop. While Wilbert slumped maybe thinking, The Lord is my (German) shepherd: I want Him on my leash, the cop was bleeding too, his tender knuckles raked. He didn't know Wilbert's head is stone, layers of scar, old ringed prepubescent tree. . . .

I'm taking the afternoon off, Mr. Mayor. Not quitting, just maybe walking home. Fuck the car, let them tow it, city plates and all. I hope they take it, seventy-five bucks worth. I can't wait to get angry again, it's a state I know better and prefer to abjectness. But meanwhile, yes, these are tears. I'll say to Gail. Why not.

A Bundle of Letters

Henry James

I

*From Miss Miranda Hope, in Paris,
to Mrs. Abraham C. Hope,
at Bangor, Maine*

September 5th, 1879

MY DEAR MOTHER

I have kept you posted as far as Tuesday week last, and, although my letter will not have reached you yet, I will begin another, before my news accumulates too much. I am glad you show my letters round in the family, for I like them all to know what I am doing, and I can't write to everyone, though I try to answer all reasonable expectations. But there are a great many unreasonable ones, as I suppose you know—not yours, dear mother, for I am bound to say that you never required of me more than was natural. You see you are reaping your reward: I write to you before I write to anyone else.

There is one thing, I hope—that you don't show any of my letters to William Platt. If he wants to see any of my letters, he knows the right way to go to work. I wouldn't have him see one of these letters, written for circulation in the family, for anything in the world. If he wants one for himself, he has got to write to me first. Let him write to me first, and then I will see about answering him. You can show him this if you like; but if you show him anything more, I will never write to you again.

I told you in my last about my farewell to England, my crossing the channel, and my first impressions of Paris. I have thought a great deal about that lovely England since I left it, and all the famous historic scenes I visited; but I have come to the conclusion that it is not a country in which I should care to reside. The position of woman does not seem to me at all satisfactory, and that is a point, you know, on which I feel very strongly. It seems to me that in England they play a very faded-out part, and those with whom I conversed had a kind of depressed and humiliated tone; a little dull, tame look, as if they were used to being snubbed and bullied, which made me want to give them a good shaking. There are a great many people—and a great many things, too—over here that I should like to perform that operation upon. I should like to shake the starch out of some of them, and the dust out of the others. I know fifty girls in Bangor that come much more up to my notion of the stand a truly noble woman should take, than those young ladies in England. But they had a most lovely way of speaking (in England), and the men are *remarkably handsome*. (You can show this to William Platt, if you like.)

I gave you my first impressions of Paris, which quite came up to my expectations, much as I had heard and read about it. The objects of interest are extremely numerous, and the climate is remarkably cheerful and sunny. I should say the position of woman here was considerably higher, though by no means coming up to the American standard. The manners of the people are in some respects extremely peculiar, and I feel at last that I am indeed in *foreign parts*. It is, however, a truly elegant city (very superior to New York), and I have spent a great deal of time in visiting the various monuments and palaces. I won't give you an account of all my wanderings, though I have been most indefatigable; for I am keeping, as I told you before, a most *exhaustive* journal, which I will allow you the *privilege* of reading on my return to Bangor. I am getting on remarkably well, and I must say I am sometimes surprised at my universal good fortune. It only shows what a little energy and common sense will accomplish. I have discovered none of these objections to a young lady traveling in Europe by herself, of which we heard so much before I left, and I don't expect I ever shall, for I certainly don't mean to look for them. I know what I want and I always manage to get it.

I have received a great deal of politeness—some of it really most pressing, and I have experienced no drawbacks whatever. I have made a great many pleasant acquaintances in traveling round (both ladies and gentlemen), and had a great many most interesting talks. I have collected a great deal of information, for which I refer you to my journal. I assure you my journal is going to be a splendid thing. I do just exactly as I do in Bangor, and I find I do perfectly right; and at any rate, I don't care if I don't. I didn't come to Europe to lead a merely conventional life; I could do that at Bangor. You know I never *would* do it at Bangor, so it isn't likely I am going to make myself miserable over here. So long as I accomplish what I desire, and make my money hold out, I shall regard the thing as a success. Sometimes I feel rather lonely, especially in the evening; but I generally manage to interest myself in something or in someone. In the evening I usually read up about the objects of interest I have visited during the day, or I post up my journal. Sometimes I go to the theater; or else I play the piano in the public parlor. The public parlor at the hotel isn't much; but the piano is better than that fearful old thing at the Sebago House. Sometimes I go downstairs and talk to the lady who keeps the books—a French lady, who is remarkably polite. She is very pretty, and always wears a black dress, with the most beautiful fit; she speaks a little English; she tells me she had to learn it in order to converse with the Americans who come in such numbers to this hotel. She has given me a great deal of information about the position of woman in France, and much of it is very encouraging. But she has told me at the same time some things that I should not like to write to you (I am hesitating even about putting them into my journal), especially if my letters are to be handed round in the family. I assure you they appear to talk about things here that we never think of mentioning at Bangor, or even of thinking about. She seems to think she can tell me everything, because I told her I was traveling for general culture. Well, I *do* want to know so much that it seems sometimes as if I wanted to know everything; and yet there are some things that I think I don't want to know. But, as a general thing, everything is intensely interesting; I don't mean only everything that this French lady tells me, but everything

I see and hear for myself. I feel really as if I should gain all I desire.

I meet a great many Americans, who, as a general thing, I must say, are not as polite to me as the people over here. The people over here—especially the gentlemen—are much more what I should call *attentive.* I don't know whether Americans are more *sincere;* I haven't yet made up my mind about that. The only drawback I experience is when Americans sometimes express surprise that I should be traveling round alone; so you see it doesn't come from Europeans. I always have my answer ready: "For general culture, to acquire the languages, and to see Europe for myself"; and that generally seems to satisfy them. Dear mother, my money holds out very well, and it *is* real interesting.

II

From the Same to the Same

September 16th

Since I last wrote to you I have left that hotel, and come to live in a French family. It's a kind of boardinghouse combined with a kind of school; only it's not like an American boardinghouse, nor like an American school either. There are four or five people here that have come to learn the language—not to take lessons, but to have an opportunity for conversation. I was very glad to come to such a place, for I had begun to realize that I was not making much progress with the French. It seemed to me that I should feel ashamed to have spent two months in Paris, and not to have acquired more insight into the language. I had always heard so much of French conversation, and I found I was having no more opportunity to practice it than if I had remained at Bangor. In fact, I used to hear a great deal more at Bangor, from those French Canadians that came down to cut the ice, than I saw I should ever hear at that hotel. The lady that kept the books seemed to want so much to talk to me in English (for the sake of practice, too, I suppose), that I couldn't bear to let her know I didn't like it. The chambermaid was Irish, and all the waiters were German, so that I never heard a word of French spoken. I suppose you might hear a great deal in the shops; only, as I don't buy anything—I prefer to spend my money for purposes of culture—I don't have that advantage.

I have been thinking some of taking a teacher, but I am well acquainted with the grammar already, and teachers always keep you bothering over the verbs. I was a good deal troubled, for I felt as if I didn't want to go away without having, at least, got a general idea of French conversation. The theater gives you a good deal of insight, and, as I told you in my last, I go a good deal to places of amusement. I find no difficulty whatever in going to such places alone, and am always treated with the politeness which, as I told you before, I encounter everywhere. I see plenty of other ladies alone (mostly French), and they generally seem to be enjoying themselves as much as I. But, at the theater, everyone talks so fast that I can scarcely make out what they say; and, besides, there are a great many vulgar expressions which it is unnecessary to learn. But it was the theater, nevertheless, that put me on the track. The very next day after I wrote you last, I went to the Palais Royal, which is one of the principal theaters in Paris. It is very small, but it is very celebrated, and in my guidebook it is marked with *two stars*, which is a sign of importance attached only to *first-class* objects of interest. But after I had been there half an hour I found I couldn't understand a single word of the play, they gabbled it off so fast, and they made use of such peculiar expressions. I felt a good deal disappointed and troubled—I was afraid I shouldn't gain all I had come for. But while I was thinking it over—thinking what I *should* do—I heard two gentlemen talking behind me. It was between the acts, and I couldn't help listening to what they said. They were talking English, but I guess they were Americans.

"Well," said one of them, "it all depends on what you are after. I'm after French; that's what I'm after."

"Well," said the other, "I'm after Art."

"Well," said the first, "I'm after Art too; but I'm after French most."

Then, dear mother, I am sorry to say the second one swore a little. He said, "Oh, damn French!"

"No, I won't damn French," said his friend. "I'll acquire it—that's what I'll do with it. I'll go right into a family."

"What family'll you go into?"

"Into some French family. That's the only way to do—to go to some place where you can talk. If you're after Art, you want to stick to the galleries; you want to go right through the Louvre, room by room; you want to take a room a day, or something of that sort. But, if you want to acquire French, the thing is to look out for a family. There are lots of French families here that take you to board and teach you. My second cousin—that young lady I told you about—she got in with a crowd like that, and they booked her right up in three months. They just took her right in and they talked to her. That's what they do to you; they set you right down and they talk *at* you. You've got to understand them; you can't help yourself. That family my cousin was with has moved away somewhere, or I should try and get in with them. They were very smart people, that family; after she left, my cousin corresponded with them in French. But I mean to find some other crowd, if it takes a lot of trouble!"

I listened to all this with great interest, and when he spoke about his cousin I was on the point of turning around to ask him the address of the family that she was with; but the next moment he said they had moved away; so I sat still. The other gentleman, however, didn't seem to be affected in the same way as I was.

"Well," he said, "you may follow up that if you like; I mean to follow up the pictures. I don't believe there is ever going to be any considerable demand in the United States for French; but I can promise you that in about ten years there'll be a big demand for Art! And it won't be temporary either."

That remark may be very true, but I don't care anything about the demand; I want to know French for its own sake. I don't want to think I have been all this while without having gained an insight. . . . The very next day, I asked the lady who kept the books at the hotel whether she knew of any family that could take me to board and give me the benefit of their conversation. She instantly threw up her hands, with several little shrill cries (in their French way, you know), and told me that her dearest friend kept a regular place of that kind. If she had known I was looking out for such a place she would have told me before; she had not spoken of it

herself, because she didn't wish to injure the hotel by
being the cause of my going away. She told me this was
a charming family, who had often received American
ladies (and others as well) who wished to follow up the
language, and she was sure I should be delighted with
them. So she gave me their address, and offered to go
with me to introduce me. But I was in such a hurry that
I went off by myself, and I had no trouble in finding
these good people. They were delighted to receive me,
and I was very much pleased with what I saw of them.
They seemed to have plenty of conversation, and there
will be no trouble about that.

I came here to stay about three days ago, and by this
time I have seen a great deal of them. The price of
board struck me as rather high; but I must remember
that a quantity of conversation is thrown in. I have a
very pretty little room—without any carpet, but with
seven mirrors, two clocks, and five curtains. I was rather
disappointed after I arrived to find that there are several
other Americans here for the same purpose as myself.
At least there are three Americans and two English people; and also a German gentleman. I am afraid, therefore, our conversation will be rather mixed, but I have
not yet time to judge. I try to talk with Madame de
Maisonrouge all I can (she is the lady of the house, and
the *real* family consists only of herself and her two
daughters). They are all most elegant, interesting
women, and I am sure we shall become intimate friends.
I will write you more about them in my next. Tell William Platt I don't care what he does.

III

From Miss Violet Ray, in Paris,
to Miss Agnes Rich, in New York

September 21st

We had hardly got here when father received a telegram
saying he would have to come right back to New York.
It was for something about his business—I don't know
exactly what; you know I never understand those things,
never want to. We had just got settled at the hotel, in
some charming rooms, and mother and I, as you may
imagine, were greatly annoyed. Father is extremely

fussy, as you know, and his first idea, as soon as he found he should have to go back, was that we should go back with him. He declared he would never leave us in Paris alone, and that we must return and come out again. I don't know what he thought would happen to us; I suppose he thought we should be too extravagant. It's father's theory that we are always running up bills, whereas a little observation would show him that we wear the same old *rags* FOR MONTHS. But father has no observation; he has nothing but theories. Mother and I, however, have, fortunately, a great deal of *practice,* and we succeeded in making him understand that we wouldn't budge from Paris, and that we would rather be chopped into small pieces than cross that dreadful ocean again. So, at last, he decided to go back alone, and to leave us here for three months. But, to show you how fussy he is, he refused to let us stay at the hotel, and insisted that we should go into a *family.* I don't know what put such an idea into his head, unless it was some advertisement that he saw in one of the American papers that are published here.

There are families here who receive American and English people to live with them, under the pretense of teaching them French. You may imagine what people they are—I mean the families themselves. But the Americans who choose this peculiar manner of seeing Paris must be actually just as bad. Mother and I were horrified, and declared that *main force* should not remove us from the hotel. But father has a way of arriving at his ends which is more efficient than violence. He worries and fusses; he "nags," as we used to say at school; and, when mother and I are quite worn out, his triumph is assured. Mother is usually worn out more easily than I, and she ends by siding with father; so that, at last, when they combine their forces against poor little me, I have to succumb. You should have heard the way father went on about this "family" plan; he talked to everyone he saw about it; he used to go round to the banker's and talk to the people there—the people in the post office; he used to try and exchange ideas about it with the waiters at the hotel. He said it would be more safe, more respectable, more economical; that I should perfect my French; that mother would learn how a French household is conducted; that he should feel more easy, and five hundred reasons more. They were none of them good, but that made no difference. It's all humbug, his talking about economy, when every one knows that business in America has completely recovered, that the prostration is all over, and that *immense fortunes* are being made. We have been economizing for the last five years, and I supposed we came abroad to reap the benefits of it.

As for my French, it is quite as perfect as I want it to be. (I assure you I am often surprised at my own fluency, and, when I get a little more practice in the genders and the idioms, I shall do very well in this respect.) To make a long story short, however, father carried his point, as usual; mother basely deserted me at the last moment, and, after holding out alone for three days, I told them to do with me what they pleased! Father lost three steamers in succession by remaining in Paris to argue with me. You know he is like the schoolmaster in Goldsmith's "Deserted Village"—"e'en though vanquished, he would argue still." He and mother went to look at some seventeen families (they had got the addresses somewhere), while I retired to my sofa, and would have nothing to do with it. At last they made arrangements, and I was transported to the establishment from which I now write you. I write you from the bosom of a Parisian ménage—from the depths of a second-rate boardinghouse.

Father only left Paris after he had seen us what he calls comfortably settled here, and had informed Madame de Maisonrouge (the mistress of the establishment—the head of the "family") that he wished my French pronunciation especially attended to. The pronunciation, as it happens, is just what I am most at home in; if he had said my genders or my idioms there would have been some sense. But poor father has no tact, and this defect is especially marked since he has been in Europe. He will be absent, however, for three months, and mother and I shall breathe more freely; the situation will be less intense. I must confess that we breathe more freely than I expected, in this place, where we have been for about a week. I was sure, before we came, that it would prove to be an establishment of the *lowest description*; but I must say that, in this respect, I am agreeably disappointed. The French are so clever that they know even how to manage a place of this kind. Of course it is very disagreeable to live with strangers, but as, after all, if I were not staying with Madame de Maisonrouge I should not be living in the Faubourg St. Germain, I don't know that from the point of view of exclusiveness it is any great loss to be here.

Our rooms are very prettily arranged, and the table is remarkably good. Mamma thinks the whole thing—the place and the people, the manners and customs—very amusing; but mamma is very easily amused. As for me, you know, all that I ask is to be let alone, and not to have people's society *forced upon me*. I have never wanted for society of my own choosing, and, so long as I retain possession of my faculties, I don't suppose I ever shall. As I said, however, the place is very well managed, and I succeed in doing as I please, which, you know, is my most cherished pursuit. Madame de Maisonrouge has a great deal of tact—much more than poor father. She is what they call here a *belle femme*, which means that she is a tall, ugly woman, with style. She dresses very well, and has a great deal of talk; but, though she is a very good imitation of a lady, I never see her behind the dinner table, in the evening, smiling and bowing, as the people come in, and looking all the while at the dishes and the servants, without thinking of a *dame de comptoir* blooming in a corner of a shop or a restaurant. I am sure that, in spite of her fine name, she was once a *dame de comptoir*. I am also sure that, in spite of her smiles and the pretty things she says to everyone, she hates us all, and would like to murder us. She is a hard, clever Frenchwoman, who would like to amuse herself and enjoy her Paris, and she must be bored to death at passing all her time in the midst of stupid English people who mumble broken French at her. Some day she will poison the soup or the *vin rouge*; but I hope that will not be until after mother and I shall have left her. She has two daughters, who, except that one is decidedly pretty, are meager imitations of herself.

The "family," for the rest, consists altogether of our beloved compatriots, and of still more beloved Englanders. There is an Englishman here, with his sister, and they seem to be rather nice people. He is remarkably handsome, but excessively affected and patronizing, es-

pecially to us Americans; and I hope to have a chance
of biting his head off before long. The sister is very
pretty, and, apparently, very nice; but, in costume, she
is Britannia incarnate. There is a very pleasant little
Frenchman—when they are nice they are charming—and
a German doctor, a big, blond man, who looks like a
great white bull; and two Americans, besides mother and
me. One of them is a young man from Boston,—an
æsthetic young man, who talks about its being "a real
Corot day," etc., and a young woman—a girl, a female,
I don't know what to call her—from Vermont, or Minnesota, or some such place. This young woman is the most
extraordinary specimen of artless Yankeeism that I ever
encountered; she is really too horrible, I have been three
times to Clémentine about your underskirt, etc.

IV

From Louis Leverett, in Paris,
to Harvard Trement, in Boston

September 25th

MY DEAR HARVARD

I have carried out my plan, of which I gave you a hint
in my last, and I only regret that I should not have done
it before. It is human nature, after all, that is the most
interesting thing in the world, and it only reveals itself
to the truly earnest seeker. There is a want of earnest-
ness in that life of hotels and railroad trains, which so
many of our countrymen are content to lead in this
strange Old World, and I was distressed to find how far
I, myself, had been led along the dusty, beaten track. I
had, however, constantly wanted to turn aside into more
unfrequented ways; to plunge beneath the surface and
see what I should discover. But the opportunity had always been missing; somehow, I never meet those opportunities that we hear about and read about—the things
that happen to people in novels and biographies. And
yet I am always on the watch to take advantage of any
opening that may present itself; I am always looking out
for experiences, for sensations—I might almost say for
adventures.

The great thing is to *live*, you know—to feel, to be
conscious of one's possibilities; not to pass through life

mechanically and insensibly, like a letter through the post office. There are times, my dear Harvard, when I feel as if I were really capable of everything—*capable de tout,* as they say here—of the greatest excesses as well as the greatest heroism. Oh, to be able to say that one has lived—*qu'on a vécu,* as they say here—that idea exercises an indefinable attraction for me. You will, perhaps, reply, it is easy to say it; but the thing is to make people believe you! And, then, I don't want any second-hand, spurious sensations; I want the knowledge that leaves a trace—that leaves strange scars and stains and reveries behind it! But I am afraid I shock you, perhaps even frighten you.

If you repeat my remarks to any of the West Cedar Street circle, be sure you tone them down as your discretion will suggest. For yourself, you will know that I have always had an intense desire to see something of *real French life.* You are acquainted with my great sympathy with the French; with my natural tendency to enter into the French way of looking at life. I sympathize with the artistic temperament; I remember you used sometimes to hint to me that you thought my own temperament too artistic. I don't think that in Boston there is any real sympathy with the artistic temperament; we tend to make everything a matter of right and wrong. And in Boston one can't *live—on ne peut pas vivre,* as they say here. I don't mean one can't reside—for a great many people manage that; but one can't live, æsthetically—I may almost venture to say, sensuously. This is why I have always been so much drawn to the French, who are so æsthetic, so sensuous. I am so sorry that Théophile Gautier has passed away; I should have liked so much to go and see him, and tell him all that I owe him. He was living when I was here before; but, you know, at that time I was traveling with the Johnsons, who are not æsthetic, and who used to make me feel rather ashamed of my artistic temperament. If I had gone to see the great apostle of beauty, I should have had to go clandestinely—*en cachette,* as they say here; and that is not my nature; I like to do everything frankly, freely, *naïvement, au grand jour.* This is the great thing—to be free, to be frank, to be *naïf.* Doesn't Matthew Arnold say that somewhere—or is it Swinburne, or Pater?

When I was with the Johnsons everything was superficial; and, as regards life, everything was brought down
to the question of right and wrong. They were too didactic; art should never be didactic; and what is life but an
art? Pater has said that so well, somewhere. With the
Johnsons I am afraid I lost many opportunities; the tone
was gray and cottony, I might almost say woolly. But
now, as I tell you, I have determined to take right hold
for myself; to look right into European life, and judge
it without Johnsonian prejudices. I have taken up my
residence in a French family, in a real Parisian house.
You see I have the courage of my opinions; I don't
shrink from carrying out my theory that the great thing
is to *live*.

You know I have always been intensely interested in
Balzac, who never shrank from the reality, and whose
almost *lurid* pictures of Parisian life have often haunted
me in my wanderings through the old wicked-looking
streets on the other side of the river. I am only sorry
that my new friends—my French family—do not live in
the old city—*au cœur du vieux Paris*, as they say here.
They live only in the Boulevard Haussman, which is less
picturesque; but in spite of this they have a great deal
of the Balzac tone. Madame de Maisonrouge belongs to
one of the oldest and proudest families in France; but
she has had reverses which have compelled her to open
an establishment in which a limited number of travelers,
who are weary of the beaten track, who have the sense
of local color—she explains it herself, she expresses it
so well—in short, to open a sort of boardinghouse. I
don't see why I should not, after all, use that expression,
for it is the correlative of the term *pension bourgeoise*,
employed by Balzac in the *Père Goriot*. Do you remember the *pension bourgeoise* of Madame Vacquer *née* de
Conflans? But this establishment is not at all like that:
and indeed it is not at all *bourgeois*; there is something
distinguished, something aristocratic, about it. The Pension Vauquer was dark, brown, sordid, *graisseuse*; but
this is in quite a different tone, with high, clear, lightly-
draped windows, tender, subtle, almost morbid, colors,
and furniture in elegant, studied, reed-like lines. Madame de Maisonrouge reminds me of Madame Hulot—
do you remember "la belle Madame Hulot?"—in *Les*

Parents Pauvres. She has a great charm; a little artificial, a little fatigued, with a little suggestion of hidden things in her life; but I have always been sensitive to the charm of fatigue, of duplicity.

I am rather disappointed, I confess, in the society I find here; it is not so local, so characteristic, as I could have desired. Indeed, to tell the truth, it is not local at all; but, on the other hand, it is cosmopolitan, and there is a great advantage in that. We are French, we are English, we are American, we are German: and, I believe, there are some Russians and Hungarians expected. I am much interested in the study of national types; in comparing, contrasting, seizing the strong points, the weak points, the point of view of each. It is interesting to shift one's point of view—to enter into strange, exotic ways of looking at life.

The American types here are not, I am sorry to say, so interesting as they might be, and, excepting myself, are exclusively feminine. We are *thin,* my dear Harvard; we are pale, we are sharp. There is something meager about us; our line is wanting in roundness, our composition in richness. We lack temperament; we don't know how to live; *nous ne savons pas vivre,* as they say here. The American temperament is represented (putting myself aside, and I often think that my temperament is not at all American) by a young girl and her mother, and another young girl without her mother—without her mother or any attendant or appendage whatever. These young girls are rather curious types; they have a certain interest, they have a certain grace, but they are disappointing too; they don't go far; they don't keep all they promise; they don't satisfy the imagination. They are cold, slim, sexless; the physique is not generous, not abundant; it is only the drapery, the skirts and furbelows (that is, I mean in the young lady who has her mother) that are abundant. They are very different: one of them all elegance, all expensiveness, with an air of high fashion, from New York; the other a plain, pure, clear-eyed, straight-waisted, straight-stepping maiden from the heart of New England. And yet they are very much alike too—more alike than they would care to think themselves; for they eye each other with cold, mistrustful, deprecating looks. They are both specimens of the emancipated young American girl—practical, positive, passionless, subtle, and knowing, as you please, either too much or too little. And yet, as I say, they have a certain stamp, a certain grace; I like to talk with them, to study them.

The fair New Yorker is, sometimes, very amusing; she asks me if every one in Boston talks like me—if every one is as "intellectual" as your poor correspondent. She is for ever throwing Boston up at me; I can't get rid of Boston. The other one rubs it into me too; but in a different way; she seems to feel about it as a good Mahommedan feels toward Mecca, and regards it as a kind of focus of light for the whole human race. Poor little Boston, what nonsense is talked in thy name! But this New England maiden is, in her way, a strange type: she is traveling all over Europe alone—"to see it," she says, "for herself." For herself! What can that stiff, slim self of hers do with such sights, such visions! She looks at everything, goes everywhere, passes her way, with her clear, quiet eyes wide open; skirting the edge of obscene abysses without suspecting them; pushing through brambles without tearing her robe; exciting, without knowing it, the most injurious suspicions; and always holding her course, passionless, stainless, fearless, charmless! It is a little figure in which, after all, if you can get the right point of view, there is something rather striking.

By way of contrast, there is a lovely English girl, with eyes as shy as violets, and a voice as sweet! She has a sweet Gainsborough head, and a great Gainsborough hat, with a mighty plume in front of it, which makes shadow over her quiet English eyes. Then she has a sage-green robe, "mystic, wonderful," all embroidered with subtle devices and flowers, and birds of tender tint; very straight and tight in front, and adorned behind, along the spine, with large, strange, iridescent buttons. The revival of taste, of the sense of beauty, in England, interests me deeply; what is there in a simple row of spinal buttons to make one dream—to *donner à rêver,* as they say here? I think that a great æsthetic renaissance is at hand, and that a great light will be kindled in England, for all the world to see. There are spirits there that I should like to commune with; I think they would understand me.

This gracious English maiden, with her clinging robes, her amulets and girdles, with something quaint and angular in her step, her carriage, something medieval and Gothic in the details of her person and dress, this lovely Evelyn Vane (isn't it a beautiful name?) is deeply, delightfully picturesque. She is much a woman—*elle est bien femme,* as they say here; simpler, softer, rounder, richer than the young girls I spoke of just now. Not much talk—a great, sweet silence. Then the violet eye—the very eye itself seems to blush; the great shadowy hat, making the brow so quiet; the strange, clinging, clutching, pictured raiment! As I say, it is a very gracious, tender type. She has her brother with her, who is a beautiful, fair-haired, gray-eyed young Englishman. He is purely objective; and he, too, is very plastic.

V

From Miranda Hope to her Mother
September 26th

You must not be frightened at not hearing from me oftener; it is not because I am in any trouble, but because I am getting on so well. If I were in any trouble I don't think I should write to you; I should just keep quiet and see it through myself. But that is not the case at present; and, if I don't write to you, it is because I am so deeply interested over here that I don't seem to find time. It was a real providence that brought me to this house, where, in spite of all obstacles, I am able to do much good work. I wonder how I find the time for all I do; but when I think that I have only got a year in Europe, I feel as if I wouldn't sacrifice a single hour.

The obstacles I refer to are the disadvantages I have in learning French, there being so many persons around me speaking English, and that, as you may say, in the very bosom of a French family. It seems as if you heard English everywhere; but I certainly didn't expect to find it in a place like this. I am not discouraged, however, and I talk French all I can, even with the other English boarders. Then I have a lesson every day from Miss Maisonrouge (the elder daughter of the lady of the house), and French conversation every evening in the *salon,* from eight to eleven, with Madame herself, and some friends of hers that often come in. Her cousin, Mr. Verdier, a young French gentleman, is fortunately staying with her, and I make a point of talking with him as much as possible. I have *extra private lessons* from him, and I often go out to walk with him. Some night, soon, he is to accompany me to the opera. We have also a most interesting plan of visiting all the galleries in Paris together. Like most of the French, he converses with great fluency, and I feel as if I should really gain from him. He is remarkably handsome, and extremely polite—paying a great many compliments, which, I am afraid, are not always *sincere*. When I return to Bangor I will tell you some of the things he has said to me. I think you will consider them extremely curious, and very beautiful *in their way*.

The conversation in the parlor (from eight to eleven) is often remarkably brilliant, and I often wish that you, or some of the Bangor folks, could be there to enjoy it. Even though you couldn't understand it I think you would like to hear the way they go on; they seem to express so much. I sometimes think that at Bangor they don't express enough (but it seems as if over there, there was less to express). It seems as if, at Bangor, there were things that folks never *tried* to say; but here, I have learned from studying French that you have no idea what you *can* say, before you try. At Bangor they seem to give it up beforehand; they don't make any effort. (I don't say this in the least for William Platt, *in particular*.)

I am sure I don't know what they will think of me when I get back. It seems as if, over here, I had learned to come out with everything. I suppose they will think I am not sincere; but isn't it more sincere to come out with things than to conceal them? I have become very good friends with everyone in the house—that is (you see, I *am* sincere), with *almost* everyone. It is the most interesting circle I ever was in. There's a girl here, an American, that I don't like so much as the rest; but that is only because she won't let me. I should like to like her, ever so much, because she is most lovely and most attractive; but she doesn't seem to want to know me or to like me. She comes from New York, and she is remarkably pretty, with beautiful eyes and the most delicate features; she is also remarkably elegant—in this respect would bear comparison with anyone I have seen over here. But it seems as if she didn't want to recognize me, or associate with me; as if she wanted to make a difference between us. It is like people they call "haughty" in books. I have never seen anyone like that before—anyone that wanted to make a difference; and at first I was right down interested, she seemed to me so like a proud young lady in a novel. I kept saying to myself all day, "haughty, haughty," and I wished she would keep on so. But she did keep on; she kept on too long; and then I began to feel hurt. I couldn't think what I have done, and I can't think yet. It's as if she had got some idea about me, or had heard someone say something. If some girls should behave like that I shouldn't make any account of it; but this one is so refined, and looks as if she might be so interesting if I once got to know her, that I think about it a good deal. I am bound to find out what her reason is—for of course she has got some reason; I am right down curious to know.

I went up to her to ask her the day before yesterday; I thought that was the best way. I told her I wanted to know her better, and would like to come and see her in her room—they tell me she has got a lovely room—and that if she had heard anything against me, perhaps she would tell me when I came. But she was more distant than ever, and she just turned it off; said that she had never heard me mentioned, and that her room was too small to receive visitors. I suppose she spoke the truth, but I am sure she has got some reason, all the same. She has got some idea, and I am bound to find out before I go, if I have to ask everybody in the house. I *am* right down curious. I wonder if she doesn't think me refined— or if she had ever heard anything against Bangor? I can't think it is that. Don't you remember when Clara Barnard went to visit in New York, three years ago, how much attention she received? And you know Clara *is* Bangor, to the soles of her shoes. Ask William Platt— so long as he isn't a native—if he doesn't consider Clara Barnard refined.

Apropos, as they say here, of refinement, there is another American in the house—a gentleman from Boston—who is just crowded with it. His name is Mr. Louis Leverett (such a beautiful name, I think), and he is

about thirty years old. He is rather small, and he looks
pretty sick; he suffers from some affection of the liver.
But his conversation is remarkably interesting, and I delight to listen to him—he has such beautiful ideas. I feel
as if it were hardly right, not being in French; but, fortunately, he uses a great many French expressions. It's in
a different style from the conversation of Mr. Verdier—
not so complimentary, but more intellectual. He is intensely fond of pictures, and has given me a great many
ideas about them which I should never have gained without him; I shouldn't have known where to look for such
ideas. He thinks everything of pictures; he thinks we
don't make near enough of them. They seem to make a
good deal of them here; but I couldn't help telling him
the other day that in Bangor I really don't think we do.
If I had any money to spend I would buy some and
take them back, to hang up. Mr. Leverett says it would
do them good—not the pictures, but the Bangor folks.
He thinks everything of the French, too, and says we
don't make nearly enough of *them*. I couldn't help telling
him the other day that at any rate they make enough of
themselves. But it is very interesting to hear him go on
about the French, and it is so much gain to me, so long
as that is what I came for. I talk to him as much as I
dare about Boston, but I do feel as if this were right
down wrong—a stolen pleasure.

I can get all the Boston culture I want when I go back,
if I carry out my plan, my happy vision, of going there
to reside. I ought to direct all my efforts to European
culture now, and keep Boston to finish off. But it seems
as if I couldn't help taking a peep now and then, in
advance—with a Bostonian. I don't know when I may
meet one again; but if there are many others like Mr.
Leverett there, I shall be certain not to want when I
carry out my dream. He is just as full of culture as he
can live. But it seems strange how many different sorts
there are.

There are two of the English who I suppose are very
cultivated too; but it doesn't seem as if I could enter
into theirs so easily, though I try all I can. I do love
their way of speaking, and sometimes I feel almost as if
it would be right to give up trying to learn French, and
just try to learn to speak our own tongue as these En-

glish speak it. It isn't the things they say so much, though these are often rather curious, but it is in the way they pronounce, and the sweetness of their voice. It seems as if they must *try* a good deal to talk like that; but these English that are here don't seem to try at all, either to speak or do anything else. They are a young lady and her brother. I believe they belong to some noble family. I have had a good deal of intercourse with them, because I have felt more free to talk to them than to the Americans—on account of the language. It seems as if in talking with them I was almost learning a new one.

I never supposed when I left Bangor, that I was coming to Europe to learn *English!* If I do learn it, I don't think you will understand me when I get back, and I don't think you'll like it much. I should be a good deal criticized if I spoke like that at Bangor. However, I verily believe Bangor is the most critical place on earth; I have seen nothing like it over here. Tell them all I have come to the conclusion that they are *a great deal too fastidious.* But I was speaking about this English young lady and her brother. I wish I could put them before you. She is lovely to look at; she seems so modest and retiring. In spite of this, however, she dresses in a way that attracts great attention, as I couldn't help noticing when one day I went out to walk with her. She was ever so much looked at; but she didn't seem to notice it, until at last I couldn't help calling attention to it. Mr. Leverett thinks everything of it; he calls it the "costume of the future." I should call it rather the costume of the past—you know the English have such an attachment to the past. I said this the other day to Madame de Maisonrouge—that Miss Vane dressed in the costume of the past. *De l'an passé, vous voulez dire?* said Madame, with her little French laugh (you can get William Platt to translate this, he used to tell me he knew so much French).

You know I told you, in writing some time ago, that I had tried to get some insight into the position of woman in England, and, being here with Miss Vane, it has seemed to me to be a good opportunity to get a little more. I have asked her a great deal about it; but she doesn't seem able to give me much information. The first time I asked her she told me the position of a lady depended upon the rank of her father, her eldest brother, her husband, etc. She told me her own position was very good, because her father was some relation— I forget what—to a lord. She thinks everything of this; and that proves to me that the position of woman in her country cannot be satisfactory; because, if it were, it wouldn't depend upon that of your relations, even your nearest. I don't know much about lords, and it does try my patience (though she is just as sweet as she can live) to hear her talk as if it were a matter of course that I should.

I feel as if it were right to ask her as often as I can if she doesn't consider everyone equal; but she always says she doesn't, and she confesses that she doesn't think she is equal to "Lady Something-or-other," who is the wife of that relation of her father. I try and persuade her all I can that she is; but it seems as if she didn't want to be persuaded; and when I ask her if Lady So-and-so is of the same opinion (that Miss Vane isn't her equal), she looks so soft and pretty with her eyes, and says, "Of course she is!" When I tell her that this is right down bad for Lady So-and-so, it seems as if she wouldn't believe me, and the only answer she will make is that Lady So-and-so is "extremely nice." I don't believe she is nice at all; if she were nice, she wouldn't have such ideas as that. I tell Miss Vane that at Bangor we think such ideas vulgar; but then she looks as though she had never heard of Bangor. I often want to shake her, though she *is* so sweet. If she isn't angry with the people who make her feel that way, I am angry for her. I am angry with her brother, too, for she is evidently very much afraid of him, and this gives me some further insight into the subject. She thinks everything of her brother, and thinks it natural that she should be afraid of him, not only physically (for this *is* natural as he is enormously tall and strong, and has very big fists), but morally and intellectually. She seems unable, however, to take in any argument, and she makes me realize what I have often heard—that if you are timid nothing will reason you out of it.

Mr. Vane, also (the brother), seems to have the same prejudices, and when I tell him, as I often think it right to do, that his sister is not his subordinate, even if she does think so, but his equal, and, perhaps in some respects his superior, and that if my brother, in Bangor, were to treat me as he treats this poor young girl, who has not spirit enough to see the question in its true light, there would be an indignation meeting of the citizens, to protest against such an outrage to the sanctity of womanhood—when I tell him all this, at breakfast or dinner, he bursts out laughing so loud that all the plates clatter on the table.

But at such a time as this there is always one person who seems interested in what I say—a German gentleman, a professor, who sits next to me at dinner, and whom I must tell you more about another time. He is very learned, and has a great desire for information; he appreciates a great many of my remarks, and, after dinner, in the salon, he often comes to me to ask me questions about them. I have to think a little, sometimes, to know what I did say, or what I do think. He takes you right up where you left off, and he is almost as fond of discussing as William Platt is. He is splendidly educated, in the German style, and he told me the other day that he was an "intellectual broom." Well, if he is, he sweeps clean; I told him that. After he has been talking to me I feel as if I hadn't got a speck of dust left in my mind anywhere. It's a most delightful feeling. He says he's an observer; and I am sure there is plenty over here to observe. But I have told you enough for today. I don't know how much longer I shall stay here; I am getting on so fast that it sometimes seems as if I shouldn't need all the time I have laid out. I suppose your cold weather has promptly begun, as usual; it sometimes makes me envy you. The fall weather here is very dull and damp, and I feel very much as if I should like to be braced up.

VI

From Miss Evelyn Vane, in Paris,
to the Lady Augusta Fleming, at Brighton
Paris, September 30th

DEAR LADY AUGUSTA

I am afraid I shall not be able to come to you on January 7th as you kindly proposed at Homburg. I am so very, very sorry; it is a great disappointment to me.

But I have just heard that it has been settled that mamma and the children are coming abroad for a part of the winter, and mamma wishes me to go with them to Hyères, where Georgina has been ordered for her lungs. She has not been at all well these three months, and now that the damp weather has begun she is very poorly indeed; so that last week papa decided to have a consultation, and he and mamma went with her up to town and saw some three or four doctors. They all of them ordered the south of France, but they didn't agree about the place; so that mamma herself decided for Hyères, because it is the most economical. I believe it is very dull, but I hope it will do Georgina good. I am afraid, however, that nothing will do her good until she consents to take more care of herself; I am afraid she is very wild and willful, and mamma tells me that all this month it has taken papa's positive orders to make her stop indoors. She is very cross (mamma writes me) about coming abroad, and doesn't seem at all to mind the expenses that papa has been put to,—talks very ill-naturedly about losing the hunting, etc. She expected to begin to hunt in December, and wants to know whether anybody keeps hounds at Hyères. Fancy a girl wanting to follow the hounds when her lungs are so bad! But I dare say that when she gets there she will be glad enough to keep quiet, as they say that the heat is intense. It may cure Georgina, but I am sure it will make the rest of us very ill.

Mamma, however, is only going to bring Mary and Gus and Fred and Adelaide abroad with her; the others will remain at Kingscote until February (about the 3d), when they will go to Eastbourne for a month with Miss Turnover, the new governess, who has turned out such a very nice person. She is going to take Miss Travers, who has been with us so long, but who is only qualified for the younger children, to Hyères, and I believe some of the Kingscote servants. She has perfect confidence in Miss T.; it is only a pity she has such an odd name. Mamma thought of asking her if she would mind taking another when she came; but papa thought she might object. Lady Battledown makes all her governesses take the same name; she gives £5 more a year for the purpose. I forget what it is she calls them; I think it's Johnson (which to me always suggests a lady's maid). Governesses shouldn't have too pretty a name; they shouldn't have a nicer name than the family.

I suppose you heard from the Desmonds that I did not go back to England with them. When it began to be talked about that Georgina should be taken abroad, mamma wrote to me that I had better stop in Paris for a month with Harold, so that she could pick me up on their way to Hyères. It saves the expense of my journey to Kingscote and back, and gives me the opportunity to "finish" a little, in French.

You know Harold came here six weeks ago, to get up his French for those dreadful examinations that he has to pass so soon. He came to live with some French people that take in young men (and others) for this purpose; it's a kind of coaching place, only kept by women. Mamma had heard it was very nice; so she wrote to me that I was to come and stop here with Harold. The Desmonds brought me and made the arrangement, or the bargain, or whatever you call it. Poor Harold was naturally not at all pleased; but he has been very kind, and has treated me like an angel. He is getting on beautifully with his French; for though I don't think the place is so good as papa supposed, yet Harold is so immensely clever that he can scarcely help learning. I am afraid I learn much less, but, fortunately, I have not to pass an examination—except if mamma takes it into her head to examine me. But she will have so much to think of with Georgina that I hope this won't occur to her. If it does, I shall be, as Harold says, in a dreadful funk.

This is not such a nice place for a girl as for a young man, and the Desmonds thought it *exceedingly odd* that mamma should wish me to come here. As Mrs. Desmond said, it is because she is so very unconventional. But you know Paris is so very amusing, and if only Harold remains good-natured about it, I shall be content to wait for the caravan (that's what he calls mamma and the children). The person who keeps the establishment, or whatever they call it, is rather odd, and *exceedingly foreign*; but she is wonderfully civil, and is perpetually sending to my door to see if I want anything. The servants are not at all like English servants, and come bursting in, the footman (they have only one) and the maids alike, at all sorts of hours, in the *most sudden way*. Then when one rings, it is half an hour before they come. All this is very uncomfortable, and I daresay it will be worse at Hyères. There, however, fortunately, we shall have our own people.

There are some very odd Americans here, who keep throwing Harold into fits of laughter. One is a dreadful little man who is always sitting over the fire, and talking about the color of the sky. I don't believe he ever saw the sky except through the windowpane. The other day he took hold of my frock (that green one you thought so nice at Homburg) and told me that it reminded him of the texture of the Devonshire turf. And then he talked for half an hour about the Devonshire turf, which I thought such a very extraordinary subject. Harold says he is mad. It is very strange to be living in this way, with people one doesn't know. I mean that one doesn't know as one knows them in England.

The other Americans (beside the madman) are two girls, about my own age, one of whom is rather nice. She has a mother; but the mother is always sitting in her bedroom which seems so very odd. I should like mamma to ask them to Kingscote, but I am afraid mamma wouldn't like the mother, who is rather vulgar. The other girl is rather vulgar too, and is traveling about quite alone. I think she is a kind of schoolmistress; but the other girl (I mean the nicer one, with the mother) tells me she is more respectable than she seems. She has, however, the most extraordinary opinions—wishes to do away with the aristocracy, thinks it wrong that Arthur should have Kingscote when papa dies, etc. I don't see what it signifies to her that poor Arthur should come into the property, which will be so delightful—except for papa dying. But Harold says she is mad. He chaffs her tremendously about her radicalism, and he is so immensely clever that she can't answer him, though she is rather clever, too.

There is also a Frenchman, a nephew, or cousin, or something, of the person of the house, who is extremely nasty; and a German professor, or doctor, who eats with his knife and is a great bore. I am so very sorry about giving up my visit. I am afraid you will never ask me again.

VII

From Léon Verdier in Paris,
to Prosper Gobain, at Lille

September 28th

MY DEAR PROSPER

It is a long time since I have given you of my news, and I don't know what puts it into my head tonight to recall myself to your affectionate memory. I suppose it is that when we are happy the mind reverts instinctively to those with whom formerly we shared our exaltations and depressions, and *je t'en ai trop dit, dans le bon temps, mon gros Prosper,* and you always listened to me too imperturbably, with your pipe in your mouth, your waist-coat unbuttoned, for me not to feel that I can count upon your sympathy today. *Nous en sommes nous flan-quées, des confidences*—in those happy days when my first thought in seeing an adventure *poindre à l'horizon* was of the pleasure I should have in relating it to the great Prosper. As I tell thee, I am happy; decidedly, I am happy, and from this affirmation I fancy you can construct the rest. Shall I help thee a little? Take three adorable girls ... three, my good Prosper—the mystic number—neither more nor less. Take them and place thy insatiable little Léon in the midst of them! Is the situation sufficiently indicated, and do you apprehend the motives of my felicity?

You expected, perhaps, I was going to tell you that I had made my fortune, or that the Uncle Blondeau had at last decided to return into the breast of nature, after having constituted me his universal legatee. But I needn't remind you that women are always for some-thing in the happiness of him who writes to thee—for something in his happiness, and for a good deal more in his misery. But don't let me talk of misery now; time enough when it comes; *ces demoiselles* have gone to join the serried ranks of their amiable predecessors. Excuse me—I comprehend your impatience. I will tell you of whom *ces demoiselles* consist.

You have heard me speak of my *cousine* de Maison-rouge, that *grande belle femme,* who, after having mar-ried, *en secondes noces*—there had been, to tell the truth, some irregularity about her first union—a venerable relic of the old noblesse of Poitou, was left, by the death of her husband, complicated by the indulgence of expensive tastes on an income of 17,000 francs, on the pavement of Paris, with two little demons of daughters to bring up in the path of virtue. She managed to bring them up; my little cousins are rigidly virtuous. If you ask me how she managed it, I can't tell you; it's no business of mine, and, *a fortiori,* none of yours. She is now fifty years old (she confesses to thirty-seven), and her daughters, whom she has never been able to marry, are respectively twenty-seven and twenty-three (they confess to twenty and to seventeen). Three years ago she had the thrice-blessed idea of opening a sort of *pension* for the entertainment and instruction of the blundering barbarians who come to Paris in the hope of picking up a few stray particles of the language of Voltaire—or of Zola. The idea *lui a porté bonheur;* the shop does a very good business. Until within a few months ago it was carried on by my cousins alone; but lately the need of a few extensions and embellishments has caused itself to be felt. My cousin has undertaken them, regardless of expense; she has asked me to come and stay with her—board and lodging gratis—and keep an eye on the grammatical eccentricities of her *pensionnaires.* I am the extension, my good Prosper; I am the embellishment! I live for nothing, and I straighten up the accent of the prettiest English lips. The English lips are not all pretty, heaven knows, but enough of them are so to make it a gaining bargain for me.

Just now, as I told you, I am in daily conversation with three separate pairs. The owner of one of them has private lessons; she pays extra. My cousin doesn't give me a sou of the money; but I make bold nevertheless, to say that my trouble is remunerated. But I am well, very well, with proprietors to the two other pairs. One of them is a little Anglaise, of about twenty—a little *figure de keepsake;* the most adorable miss that you ever, or at least that I ever, beheld. She is decorated all over with beads and bracelets and embroidered dandelions; but her principal decoration consists of the softest little gray eyes in the world, which rest upon you with a profundity of confidence—a confidence that I really feel some compunction in betraying. She has a tint as white as this sheet of paper, except just in the middle of each cheek, where it passes into the purest and most transparent, most liquid, carmine. Occasionally this rosy fluid overflows into the rest of her face—by which I mean that she blushes—as softly as the mark of your breath on the windowpane.

Like every Anglaise, she is rather pinched and prim in public; but it is very easy to see that when no one is looking *elle ne demande qu'à se laisser aller!* Whenever she wants it I am always there, and I have given her to understand that she can count upon me. I have every reason to believe that she appreciates the assurance, though I am bound in honesty to confess that with her the situation is a little less advanced than with the others. *Que voulez-vous?* The English are heavy, and the Anglaises move slowly, that's all. The movement, however, is perceptible, and once this fact is established I can let the pottage simmer. I can give her time to arrive, for I am over-well occupied with her *concurrentes. Celles-ci* don't keep me waiting, *par exemple!*

These young ladies are Americans, and you know that it is the national character to move fast. "All right—go ahead!" (I am learning a great deal of English, or, rather, a great deal of American.) They go ahead at a rate that sometimes makes it difficult for me to keep up. One of them is prettier than the other; but this latter (the one that takes the private lessons) is really *une fille prodigieuse. Ah, par exemple, elle brûle ses vaisseux celle-la!* She threw herself into my arms the very first day, and I almost owed her a grudge for having deprived me of that pleasure of gradation, of carrying the defenses, one by one, which is almost as great as that of entering the place.

Would you believe that at the end of exactly twelve minutes she gave me a rendezvous? It is true it was in the Galerie d'Apollon, at the Louvre; but that was respectable for a beginning, and since then we have had them by the dozen; I have ceased to keep the account. *Non, c'est une fille qui me dépasse.*

The little one (she has a mother somewhere, out of sight, shut up in a closet or a trunk) is a good deal prettier, and perhaps, on that account *elle y met plus de façons.* She doesn't knock about Paris with me by the hour; she contents herself with long interviews in the *petit salon,* with the curtains half-drawn, beginning at about three o'clock, when every one is *à la promenade.* She is admirable, this little one; a little too thin, the bones rather accentuated, but the detail, on the whole, most satisfactory. And you can say anything to her. She takes the trouble to appear not to understand, but her conduct, half an hour afterwards, reassures you completely—oh, completely!

However, it is the tall one, the one of the private lessons, that is the most remarkable. These private lessons, my good Prosper, are the most brilliant invention of the age, and a real stroke of genius on the part of Miss Miranda! They also take place in the *petit salon,* but with the doors tightly closed, and with explicit directions to every one in the house that we are not to be disturbed. And we are not, my good Prosper; we are not! Not a sound, not a shadow, interrupts our felicity. My *cousine* is really admirable; the shop deserves to succeed. Miss Miranda is tall and rather flat; she is too pale; she hasn't the adorable *rougeurs* of the little Anglaise. But she has bright, keen, inquisitive eyes, superb teeth, a nose modeled by a sculptor, and a way of holding up her head and looking everyone in the face, which is the most finished piece of impertinence I ever beheld. She is making the *tour du monde,* entirely alone, without even a soubrette to carry the ensign, for the purpose of seeing for herself *à quoi s'en tenir sur les hommes et les choses*—on *les hommes* particularly. *Dis donc,* Prosper, it must be a *drôle de pays* over there, where young persons animated by this ardent curiosity are manufactured! If we should turn the tables, some day, thou and I, and go over and see it for ourselves. It is as well that we should go and find them *chez elles,* as that they should come out here after us. *Dis donc, mon gros Prosper....*

VIII

From Dr. Rudolf Staub, in Paris,
to Dr. Julius Hirsch, at Göttingen

MY DEAR BROTHER IN SCIENCE

I resume my hasty notes, of which I sent you the first

installment some weeks ago. I mentioned then that I intended to leave my hotel, not finding it sufficiently local and national. It was kept by a Pomeranian, and the waiters, without exception, were from the Fatherland. I fancied myself at Berlin, Unter den Linden, and I reflected that, having taken the serious step of visiting the headquarters of the Gallic genius, I should try and project myself, as much as possible, into the circumstances which are in part the consequence and in part the cause of its irrepressible activity. It seemed to me that there could be no well-grounded knowledge without this preliminary operation of placing myself in relations, as slightly as possible modified by elements proceeding from a different combination of causes, with the spontaneous home life of the country.

I accordingly engaged a room in the house of a lady of pure French extraction and education, who supplements the shortcomings of an income insufficient to the ever-growing demands of the Parisian system of sense-gratification, by providing food and lodging for a limited number of distinguished strangers. I should have preferred to have my room alone in the house, and to take my meals in a brewery, of very good appearance, which I speedily discovered in the same street; but this arrangement, though very lucidly proposed by myself, was not acceptable to the mistress of the establishment (a woman with a mathematical head), and I have consoled myself for the extra expense by fixing my thoughts upon the opportunity that conformity to the customs of the house gives me of studying the table manners of my companions, and of observing the French nature at a peculiarly physiological moment, the moment when the satisfaction of the *taste,* which is the governing quality in its composition, produces a kind of exhalation, an intellectual transpiration, which, though light and perhaps invisible to a superficial spectator, is nevertheless appreciable by a properly adjusted instrument.

I have adjusted my instrument very satisfactorily (I mean the one I carry in my good, square German head), and I am not afraid of losing a single drop of this valuable fluid, as it condenses itself upon the plate of my observation. A prepared surface is what I need, and I have prepared my surface.

Unfortunately here, also, I find the individual native in the minority. There are only four French persons in the house—the individuals concerned in its management, three of whom are women, and one a man. This preponderance of the feminine element is, however, in itself characteristic, as I need not remind you what an abnormally-developed part this sex has played in French history. The remaining figure is apparently that of a man, but I hesitate to classify him so superficially. He appears to me less human than simian, and whenever I hear him talk I seem to myself to have paused in the street to listen to the shrill clatter of a hand organ, to which the gambols of a hairy *homunculus* form an accompaniment.

I mentioned to you before that my expectation of rough usage, in consequence of my German nationality, had proved completely unfounded. No one seems to know or to care what my nationality is, and I am treated, on the contrary, with the civility which is the portion of every traveler who pays the bill without scanning the items too narrowly. This, I confess, has been something of a surprise to me, and I have not yet made up my mind as to the fundamental cause of the anomaly. My determination to take up my abode in a French interior was largely dictated by the supposition that I should be substantially disagreeable to its inmates. I wished to observe the different forms taken by the irritation that I should naturally produce; for it is under the influence of irritation that the French character most completely expresses itself. My presence, however, does not appear to operate as a stimulus, and in this respect I am materially disappointed. They treat me as they treat everyone else; whereas, in order to be treated differently, I was resigned in advance to be treated worse. I have not, as I say, fully explained to myself this logical contradiction; but this is the explanation to which I tend. The French are so exclusively occupied with the idea of themselves, that in spite of the very definite image the German personality presented to them by the war of 1870, they have at present no distinct apprehension of its existence. They are not very sure that there are any Germans; they have already forgotten the convincing proofs of the fact that were presented to them nine years ago. A German was something disagreeable, which they determined to keep out of their conception of things. I therefore think that we are wrong to govern ourselves upon the hypothesis of the *revanche*; the French nature is too shallow for that large and powerful plant to bloom in it.

The English-speaking specimens, too, I have not been willing to neglect the opportunity to examine; and among these I have paid special attention to the American varieties, of which I find here several singular examples. The two most remarkable are a young man who presents all the characteristics of a period of national decadence; reminding me strongly of some diminutive Hellenized Roman of the third century. He is an illustration of the period of culture in which the faculty of appreciation has obtained such a preponderance over that of production that the latter sinks into a kind of rank sterility, and the mental condition becomes analogous to that of a malarious bog. I learn from him that there is an immense number of Americans exactly resembling him, and that the city of Boston, indeed, is almost exclusively composed of them. (He communicated this fact very proudly, as if it were greatly to the credit of his native country; little perceiving the truly sinister impression it made upon me.)

What strikes one in it is that it is a phenomenon to the best of my knowledge—and you know what my knowledge is—unprecedented and unique in the history of mankind; the arrival of a nation at an ultimate stage of evolution without having passed through the mediate one; the passage of the fruit, in other words, from crudity to rottenness, without the interposition of a period of useful (and ornamental) ripeness. With the Americans, indeed, the crudity and the rottenness are identical and simultaneous; it is impossible to say, as in the conversation of this deplorable young man, which is one and which is the other; they are inextricably mingled. I prefer the talk of the French *homunculus*; it is at least more amusing.

It is interesting in his manner to perceive, so largely developed, the germs of extinction in the so-called powerful Anglo-Saxon family. I find them in almost as recognizable a form in a young woman from the State of Maine, in the province of New England, with whom I have had a good deal of conversation. She differs somewhat from the young man I just mentioned, in that the faculty of production, of action, is, in her, less inanimate; she has more of the freshness and vigor that we suppose to belong to a young civilization. But unfortunately she produces nothing but evil, and her tastes and habits are similarly those of a Roman lady of the lower Empire. She makes no secret of them, and has, in fact, elaborated a complete system of licentious behavior. As the opportunities she finds in her own country do not satisfy her, she has come to Europe "to try," as she says, "for herself." It is the doctrine of universal experience professed with a cynicism that is really most extraordinary, and which, presenting itself in a young woman of considerable education, appears to me to be the judgment of a society.

Another observation which pushes me to the same induction—that of the premature vitiation of the American population—is the attitude of the Americans whom I have before me with regard to each other. There is another young lady here, who is less abnormally developed than the one I have just described, but who yet bears the stamp of this peculiar combination of incompleteness and effeteness. These three persons look with the greatest mistrust and aversion upon each other; and each has repeatedly taken me apart and assured me, secretly, that he or she only is the real, the genuine, the typical American. A type that has lost itself before it has been fixed—what can you look for from this?

Add to this that there are two young Englanders in the house, who hate all the Americans in a lump, making between them none of the distinctions and favorable comparisons which they insist upon, and you will, I think, hold me warranted in believing that, between precipitate decay and internecine enmities, the English-speaking family is destined to consume itself, and that with its decline the prospect of general pervasiveness, to which I alluded above, will brighten for the deep-lunged children of the Fatherland!

IX

Miranda Hope to her Mother

October 22nd

DEAR MOTHER

I am off in a day or two to visit some new country; I haven't yet decided which. I have satisfied myself with regard to France, and obtained a good knowledge of the language. I have enjoyed my visit to Madame de Maisonrouge deeply, and feel as if I were leaving a circle of real friends. Everything has gone on beautifully up to the end, and everyone has been as kind and attentive as if I were their own sister, especially Mr. Verdier, the French gentleman, from whom I have gained more than I ever expected (in six weeks), and with whom I have promised to *correspond*. So you can imagine me dashing off the most correct French letters; and, if you don't believe it, I will keep the rough draft to show you when I go back.

The German gentleman is also more interesting, the more you know him; it seems sometimes as if I could fairly drink in his ideas. I have found out why the young lady from New York doesn't like me! It is because I said one day at dinner that I *admired* to go to the Louvre. Well, when I first came, it seemed as if I *did* admire everything!

Tell William Platt his letter has come. I knew he would have to write, and I was bound I would make him! I haven't decided what country I will visit yet; it seems as if there were so many to choose from. But I shall take care to pick out a good one, and to meet plenty of fresh experiences.

Dearest mother, my money holds out, and it *is* most interesting!

A Wilderness Station

Alice Munro

Miss Margaret Cresswell, Matron,
House of Industry, Toronto,
to Mr. Simon Herron, North Huron, January 15, 1852.

Since your letter is accompanied by an endorsement from your minister, I am happy to reply. Requests of your sort are made to us frequently, but unless we have such an endorsement we cannot trust that they are made in good faith.

We do not have any girl at the Home who is of marriageable age, since we send our girls out to make a living usually around the age of fourteen or fifteen, but we do keep track of them for some years or usually until they are married. In cases such as yours we sometimes recommend one of these girls and will arrange a meeting, and then of course it is up to the two parties involved to see if they are suited.

There are two girls eighteen years of age that we are still in touch with. Both are apprenticed to a milliner and are good seamstresses, but a marriage to a likely man would probably be preferred to a lifetime of such work. Further than that cannot be said, it must be left to the girl herself and of course to your liking for her, or the opposite.

The two girls are a Miss Sadie Johnstone and a Miss Annie McKillop. Both were born legitimately of Christian parents and were placed in the Home due to parental deaths. Drunkenness or immorality was not a factor. In Miss Johnstone's case there is however the factor of consumption, and though she is the prettier of the two and a plump rosy girl, I feel I must warn you that perhaps she is not suited to the hard work of a life in the bush. The other girl, Miss McKillop, is of more durable constitution though of leaner frame and not so good a complexion. She has a waywardness about one eye but it does not interfere with her vision and her sewing is excellent. The darkness of her eyes and hair and brown tinge of her skin is no indication of mixed blood, as both parents were from Fife. She is a hardy girl and I think would be suited to such a life as you can offer, being also free from the silly timidness we often see in girls of her age. I will speak to her and acquaint her with the idea and will await your letter as to when you propose to meet her.

Carstairs Argus, Fiftieth Anniversary Edition, February 3, 1907. Recollections of Mr. George Herron.

On the first day of September, 1851, my brother Simon and I got a box of bedclothes and household utensils together and put them in a wagon with a horse to pull it, and set out from Halton County to try our fortunes in the wilds of Huron and Bruce, as wilds they were then thought to be. The goods were from Archie Frame that Simon worked for, and counted as part of his wages. Likewise we had to rent the horse off him, and his boy that was about my age came along to take it and the wagon back.

It ought to be said in the beginning that my brother and I were left alone, our father first and then our mother dying of fever within five weeks of landing in this country, when I was three years old and Simon eight. Simon was put to work for Archie Frame that was our mother's cousin, and I was taken on by the schoolteacher and his wife that had no child of their own. This was in Halton, and I would have been content to go on living there but Simon being only a few miles away continued to visit and say that as soon as we were old enough we would go and take up land and be on our own, not working for others, as this was what our father had intended. Archie Frame never sent Simon to school as I was sent, so Simon was always bound to get away. When I had come to be fourteen years of age and a husky lad, as was my brother, he said we should go and take up Crown land north of the Huron Tract.

We only got as far as Preston on the first day as the roads were rough and bad across Nassagaweya and Puslinch. Next day we got to Shakespeare and the third afternoon to Stratford. The roads were always getting worse as

we came west, so we thought best to get our box sent on
to Clinton by the stage. But the stage had quit running
due to rains, and they were waiting till the roads froze up,
so we told Archie Frame's boy to turn about and return
with horse and cart and goods back to Halton. Then we
took our axes on our shoulders, and walked to Carstairs.

Hardly a soul was there before us. Carstairs was just
under way, with a rough building that was store and inn
combined, and there was a German named Roem building a sawmill. One man who got there before us and
already had a fair-sized cabin built was Henry Treece,
who afterwards became my father-in-law.

We got ourselves boarded at the inn where we slept
on the bare floor with one blanket or quilt between us.
Winter was coming early with cold rains and everything
damp, but we were expecting hardship or at least Simon
was. I came from a softer place. He said we must put
up with it so I did.

We began to underbrush a road to our piece of land
and then we got it marked out and cut the logs for our
shanty and big scoops to roof it. We were able to borrow
an ox from Henry Treece to draw the logs. But Simon
was not of a mind to borrow or depend on anybody. He
was minded to try raising the shanty ourselves, but when
we saw we could not do it I made my way to the
Treeces' place and with Henry and two of his sons and
a fellow from the mill it was accomplished. We started
next day to fill up the cracks between the logs with mud
and we got some hemlock branches so we would not be
out money anymore for staying at the inn but could
sleep in our own place. We had a big slab of elm for
the door. My brother had heard from some French-
Canadian fellows that were at Archie Frame's that in
the lumber camps the fire was always in the middle of
the shanty. So he said that was the way we should have
ours, and we got four posts and were building the chimney on them, house-fashion, intending to plaster it with
mud inside and out. We went to our hemlock bed with
a good fire going but waking in the middle of the night
we saw our lumber was all ablaze and the scoops burning
away briskly also. We tore down the chimney and the
scoops being green basswood were not hard to put out.
As soon as it came day we started to build the chimney

in the ordinary way in the end of the house and I thought it best not to make any remark.

After the small trees and brush was cleared out a bit we set to chopping down the big trees. We cut down a big ash and split into slabs for our floor. Still our box had not come which was to be shipped from Halton, so Henry Treece sent us a very large and comfortable bearskin for our cover in bed but my brother would not take the favour and sent it back saying no need. Then after several weeks we got our box and had to ask for the ox to bring it on from Clinton, but my brother said that is the last we will need to ask, of any person's help.

We walked to Walley and brought back flour and salt fish on our backs. A man rowed us across the river at Manchester for a steep price. There were no bridges then, and all that winter not a good enough freeze to make it easy going over the rivers.

Around Christmastime my brother said to me that he thought we had the place in good enough shape now for him to be bringing in a wife, so we should have somebody to cook and do for us and milk a cow when we could afford one. This was the first I had heard of any wife and I said that I did not know he was acquainted with anybody. He said he was not but he had heard that you could write to the Orphanage Home and ask if they had a girl there that was willing to think about the prospect and that they would recommend, and if so he would go and see her. He wanted one between eighteen and twenty-two years of age, healthy and not afraid of work and raised in the Orphanage, not taken in lately, so that she would not be expecting any luxuries or to be waited on and would not be recalling about when things were easier for her. I do not doubt that to those hearing about this nowadays it seems a strange way to go about things. It was not that my brother could not have gone courting and got a wife on his own, because he was a good-looking fellow, but he did not have the time or the money or inclination, his mind was all occupied with establishing our holding. And if a girl had parents they would probably not want her to go far away where there was little in comforts and so much work.

That it was a respectable way of doing things is shown by the fact that the minister Mr. McBain, who was lately come into the district, helped Simon to write the letter and sent word on his own to vouch for him.

So a letter came back that there was a girl that might fit the bill and Simon went off to Toronto and got her. Her name was Annie but her maiden name I have forgotten. They had to ford the streams in Hullet and trudge through deep soft snow after leaving the stage in Clinton, and when they got back she was worn out and very surprised at what she saw, since she said she had never imagined so much bush. She had in her box some sheets and pots and dishes that ladies had given her and that made the place more comfortable.

Early in April my brother and I went out to chop down some trees in the bush at the farthest corner of our property. While Simon was away to get married I had done some chopping in the other direction towards Treece's, but Simon wanted to get all our boundaries cut clear around and not to go on chopping where I had been. The day started out mild and there was still a lot of soft snow in the bush. We were chopping down a tree where Simon wanted, and in some way, I cannot say how, a branch of it came crashing down where we didn't expect. We just heard the little branches cracking where it fell and looked up to see it and it hit Simon on the head and killed him instantly.

I had to drag his body back then to the shanty through the snow. He was a tall fellow, though not fleshy, and it was an awkward task and greatly wearying. It had got colder by this time and when I got to the clearing I saw snow on the wind like the start of a storm. Our footsteps were filled in that we had made earlier. By this time, Simon was all covered with snow that did not melt on him, and his wife coming to the door was greatly puzzled, thinking that I was dragging along a log.

In the shanty Annie washed him off and we sat still awhile not knowing what we should do. The preacher was at the inn as there was no church or house for him yet and the inn was only about four miles away, but the storm had come up very fierce so you could not even see the trees at the edge of the clearing. It had the look of a storm that would last two or three days, the wind being from the northwest. We knew we could not keep the body in the shanty and we could not set it out in the snow fearing the bobcats would get at it, so we had to set to work and bury him. The ground was not frozen under the snow so I dug out a grave near the shanty and Annie sewed him in a sheet and we laid him in his grave, not staying long in the wind but saying the Lord's Prayer and reading one Psalm out of the Bible. I am not sure which one but I remember it was near the end of the Book of Psalms and it was very short.

This was the third day of April, 1852.

That was our last snow of the year, and later the minister came and said the service and I put up a wooden marker. Later on we got our plot in the cemetery and put his stone there but he is not under it as it is a foolish useless thing in my opinion to cart a man's bones from one place to another when it is only bones and his soul has gone on to Judgment.

I was left to chop and clear by myself and soon I began to work side by side with the Treeces, who treated me with the greatest kindness. We worked all together on my land or their land, not minding if it was the one or the other. I started to take my meals and even to sleep at their place and got to know their daughter Jenny who was about of my age, and we made our plans to marry, which we did in due course. Our life together was a long one with many hardships but we were fortunate in the end and raised eight children. I have seen my sons take over my wife's father's land as well as my own since my two brothers-in-law went away and did well for themselves in the West.

My brother's wife did not continue in this place but went her own way to Walley.

Now there are gravel roads running north, south, east, and west and a railway not a half mile from my farm. Except for woodlots the bush is a thing of the past and I often think of the trees I have cut down and if I had them to cut down today I would be a wealthy man.

The Reverend Walter McBain, Minister of the Free
Presbyterian Church of North Huron,
to Mr. James Mullen, Clerk of the Peace, Walley,
United Counties of Huron and Bruce, September 10, 1852.

I write to inform you, sir, of the probable arrival in your town of a young woman of this district, by the name of Annie Herron, a widow and one of my congregation. This young person has left her home here in the vicinity of Carstairs in Holloway Township, I believe she intends to walk to Walley. She may appear at the Gaol there seeking to be admitted, so I think it my duty to tell you who and what she is and her history here since I have known her.

I came to this area in November of last year, being the first minister of any kind to venture. My parish is as yet mostly bush, and there is nowhere for me to lodge but at the Carstairs Inn. I was born in the west of Scotland and came to this country under the auspices of the Glasgow Mission. After applying to know God's will, I was directed by Him to go to preach wherever was most need of a minister. I tell you this so you may know what sort I am that bring you my account and my view of the affairs of this woman.

She came here late last winter as the bride of the young man Simon Herron. He had written on my advice to the House of Industry in Toronto that they might recommend to him a Christian, preferably Presbyterian, female suitable to his needs, and she was the one recommended. He married her straightaway and brought her here to the shanty he had built with his brother. These two young lads had come into the country to clear themselves a piece of land and get possession of it, being themselves orphans and without expectations. They were about this work one day at the end of winter when an accident befell. A branch was loosed while chopping down a tree and fell upon the elder brother so as to cause instant death. The younger lad succeeded in getting the body back to the shanty and since they were held prisoner by a heavy snowstorm they conducted their own funeral and burial.

The Lord is strict in His mercies and we are bound to receive His blows as signs of His care and goodness for so they will prove to be.

Deprived of his brother's help the lad found a place in a neighboring family, also members in good standing of my congregation, who have accepted him as a son, though he still works for title to his own land. This family would have taken in the young widow as well, but she would have nothing to do with their offer and seemed to develop an aversion to everyone who would help her. Particularly she seemed so towards her brother-in-law, who said that he had never had the least quarrel with her, and towards myself. When I talked to her she would not give any answer or sign that her soul was coming into submission. It is a fault of mine that I am not well equipped to talk to women. I have not the ease to win their trust. Their stubbornness is of another kind than a man's.

She stopped appearing at services, and the deterioration of her property showed the state of her mind and spirit. She would not plant peas and potatoes though they were given to her to grow among the stumps. She did not chop down the wild vines around her door. Most often she did not light a fire so she could have oatcake or porridge. Her brother-in-law being removed, there was no order imposed on her days. When I visited her the door was open and it was evident that animals came and went in her house. If she was there she hid herself, to mock me. Those who caught sight of her said that her clothing was filthy and torn from scrambling about in the bushes, and she was scratched by thorns and bitten by the mosquito insects and let her hair go uncombed and unplaited. I believe she lived on salt fish and bannock that the neighbours or her brother-in-law left for her.

Then while I was still puzzling how I might find a way to protect her body through the winter and deal with the more important danger to her soul, there comes word she is gone. She left the door open and went away without cloak or bonnet and wrote on the shanty floor with a burnt stick the two words: Walley, Gaol. I take this to mean she intends to go there and turn herself in. Her brother-in-law thinks it would be no use for him to go after her because of her unfriendly attitude to himself, and I cannot set out because of a deathbed I am attending. I ask you therefore to let me know if she has arrived and in what state and how you will deal with her. I consider her still as a soul in my charge, and I will try to visit her before winter if you keep her there. She is a child of the Free Church and the Covenant and as such she is entitled to a minister of her own faith and you must not think it sufficient that some priest of the

Church of England or Baptist or Methodist be sent to her.

In case she should not come to the Gaol but wander in the streets, I ought to tell you that she is dark-haired and tall, meagre in body, not comely but not ill-favoured except having one eye that goes to the side.

> *Mr. James Mullen, Clerk of the Peace, Walley,*
> *to the Reverend Walter McBain, Carstairs,*
> *North Huron,*
> *September 30, 1852.*

Your letter to me arrived most timely and appreciated, concerning the young woman Annie Herron. She completed her journey to Walley unharmed and with no serious damage though she was weak and hungry when she presented herself at the Gaol. On its being inquired what she did there, she said that she came to confess to a murder, and to be locked up. There was consultation round and about, I was sent for, and it being near to midnight, I agreed that she should spend the night in a cell. The next day I visited her and got all particulars I could.

Her story of being brought up in the Orphanage, her apprenticeship to a milliner, her marriage, and her coming to North Huron all accords pretty well with what you have told me. Events in her account begin to differ only with her husband's death. In that matter what she says is this:

On the day in early April when her husband and his brother went out to chop trees, she was told to provide them with food for their midday meal, and since she had not got it ready when they wanted to leave, she agreed to take it to them in the woods. Consequently she baked up some oatcakes and took some salt fish and followed their tracks and found them at work some distance away. But when her husband unwrapped his food he was very offended, because she had wrapped it in a way that the salty oil from the fish had soaked into the cakes, and they were all crumbled and unpleasant to eat. In his disappointment he became enraged and promised her a beating when he was more at leisure to do it. He then turned his back on her, being seated on a log, and she picked up a rock and threw it at him, hitting him on the

head so that he fell down unconscious and in fact dead.
She and his brother then carried and dragged the body
back to the house. By that time a blizzard had come up
and they were imprisoned within. The brother said that
they should not reveal the truth as she had not intended
murder, and she agreed. They then buried him—her
story agreeing again with yours—and that might have
been the end of it, but she became more and more troubled, convinced that she had surely been intending to
kill him. If she had not killed him, she says, it would
only have meant a worse beating, and why should she
have risked that? So she decided at last upon confession
and as if to prove something handed me a lock of hair
stiffened with blood.

This is her tale, and I do not believe it for a minute.
No rock that this girl could pick up, combined with the
force that she could summon to throw it, would serve to
kill a man. I questioned her about this, and she changed
her story, saying that it was a large rock that she had
picked up in both hands and that she had not thrown it
but smashed it down on his head from behind. I said
why did not the brother prevent you, and she said he
was looking the other way. Then I said there must indeed be a bloodied rock lying somewhere in the wood,
and she said she had washed it off with snow. (In fact
it is not likely a rock would come to hand so easily, with
all such depth of snow about.) I asked her to roll up her
sleeve that I might judge of the muscles in her arms, to
do such a job, and she said that she had been a huskier
woman some months since.

I conclude that she is lying, or self-deluded. But I see
nothing for it at the moment but to admit her to the
Gaol. I asked her what she thought would happen to
her now, and she said, well, you will try me and then
you will hang me. But you do not hang people in the
winter, she said, so I can stay here till spring. And if
you let me work here, maybe you will want me to go
on working and you will not want me hanged. I do not
know where she got this idea about people not being
hanged in the winter. I am in perplexity about her. As
you may know, we have a very fine new Gaol here
where the inmates are kept warm and dry and are
decently fed and treated with all humanity, and there

has been a complaint that some are not sorry—and at this time of year, even happy—to get into it. But it is obvious that she cannot wander about much longer, and from your account she is unwilling to stay with friends and unable to make a tolerable home for herself. The Gaol at present serves as a place of detention for the Insane as well as criminals, and if she is charged with Insanity, I could keep her here for the winter, perhaps with removal to Toronto in the spring. I have engaged for a doctor to visit her. I spoke to her of your letter and your hope of coming to see her, but I found her not at all agreeable to that. She asks that nobody be allowed to see her excepting a Miss Sadie Johnstone, who is not in this part of the country.

I am enclosing a letter I have written to her brother-in-law for you to pass on to him, so that he may know what she has said and tell me what he thinks about it. I thank you in advance for conveying the letter to him, also for the trouble you have been to, in informing me as fully as you have done. I am a member of the Church of England, but have a high regard for the work being done by other Protestant denominations in bringing an orderly life to this part of the world we find ourselves in. You may believe that I will do what is in my power to do, to put you in a position to deal with the soul of this young woman, but it might be better to wait until she is in favour of it.

The Reverend Walter McBain to Mr. James Mullen,
November 18, 1852.

I carried your letter at once to Mr. George Herron and believe that he has replied and given you his recollection of events. He was amazed at his sister-in-law's claim, since she had never said anything of this to him or to anybody else. He says that it is all her invention or fancy, since she was never in the woods when it happened and there was no need for her to be, as they had carried their food with them when they left the house. He says that there had been at another time some reproof from his brother to her, over the spoiling of some cakes by their proximity to fish, but it did not happen at this time. Nor were there any rocks about to do such a deed on impulse if she had been there and wished to do it.

My delay in answering your letter, for which I beg pardon, is due to a bout of ill health. I had an attack of the gravel and a rheumatism of the stomach worse than any misery that ever fell upon me before. I am somewhat improved at present and will be able to go about as usual by next week if all continues to mend.

As to the question of the young woman's sanity, I do not know what your Doctor will say but I have thought on this and questioned the Divinity and my belief is this. It may well be that so early in the marriage her submission to her husband was not complete and there would be carelessness about his comfort, and naughty words, and quarrelsome behaviour, as well as the hurtful sulks and silences her sex is prone to. His death occurring before any of this was put right, she would feel a natural and harrowing remorse, and this must have taken hold of her mind so strongly that she made herself out to be actually responsible for his death. In this way, I think many folk are driven mad. Madness is at first taken on by some as a kind of play, for which shallowness and audacity they are punished later on, by finding out that it is play no longer, and the Devil has blocked off every escape.

It is still my hope to speak to her and make her understand this. I am under difficulties at present not only of my wretched corpus but of being lodged in a foul and noisy place obliged to hear day and night such uproars as destroy sleep and study and intrude even on my prayers. The wind blows bitterly through the logs, but if I go down to the fire there is swilling of spirits and foulest insolence. And outside nothing but trees to choke off every exit and icy bog to swallow man and horse. There was a promise to build a church and lodging but those who made the promise have grown busy with their own affairs and it seems to have been put off. I have not however left off preaching even in my illness and in such barns and houses as are provided. I take heart remembering a great man, the great preacher and interpreter of God's will, Thomas Boston, who in the latter days of his infirmity preached the grandeur of God from his chamber window to a crowd of two thousand or so assembled in the yard below. So I mean to preach to the end though my congregation will be smaller.

Whatsoever crook there is in one's lot, it is of God's making. Thomas Boston.

This world is a wilderness, in which we may indeed get our station changed, but the move will be out of one wilderness station unto another. Ibid.

Mr. James Mullen to the Reverend Walter McBain, January 17, 1853.

I write to you that our young woman's health seems sturdy, and she no longer looks such a scarecrow, eating well and keeping herself clean and tidy. Also she seems quieter in her spirits. She has taken to mending the linen in the prison, which she does well. But I must tell you that she is firm as ever against a visit, and I cannot advise you to come here as I think your trouble might be for nothing. The journey is very hard in winter and it would do no good to your state of health.

Her brother-in-law has written me a very decent letter affirming that there is no truth to her story, so I am satisfied on that.

You may be interested in hearing what the doctor who visited her had to say about her case. His belief is that she is subject to a sort of delusion peculiar to females, for which the motive is a desire for self-importance, also a wish to escape the monotony of life or the drudgery they may have been born to. They may imagine themselves possessed by the forces of evil, to have committed various and hideous crimes, and so forth. Sometimes they may report that they have taken numerous lovers, but these lovers will be all imaginary and the woman who thinks herself a prodigy of vice will in fact be quite chaste and untouched. For all this he—the doctor—lays the blame on the sort of reading that is available to these females, whether it is of ghosts or demons or of love escapades with Lords and Dukes and suchlike.

With his questioning there did come to light something further that we did not know. On his saying to her, did she not fear hanging, she replied, no, for there is a reason you will not hang me. You mean that they will judge that you are mad? said he, and she said, oh, perhaps that, but is it not true also that they will never hang a woman that is with child? The doctor then examined her to find out if this were true, and she agreed to the examination, so she must have made the claim in good faith. He discovered however that she had deceived herself. The signs she took were simply the results of her going so long underfed and in such a reduced state. He told her of his findings, but it is hard to say whether she believes him.

The Gaol has become a much less peaceful shelter recently due to the admission of a genuinely insane female apparently driven mad by a rape. Her screams resound sometimes for hours at a stretch. Women are not made to stand this country.

I am sorry to hear of your bad health and miserable lodgings. The town has grown so civilized that we forget the hardship of the hinterlands. Those like yourself who choose to endure it deserve our admiration. But you must allow me to say that it seems pretty certain that a man not in robust health will be unable to bear up for long in your situation. Surely your Church would not consider it a defection were you to choose to serve it longer by removing to a more comfortable place.

I enclose a letter written by the young woman and sent to a Miss Sadie Johnstone, on King Street, Toronto. It was intercepted by us that we might know more of the state of her mind, but resealed and sent on. But it has come back marked "Unknown." We have not told the writer of this in hopes that she will write again and more fully, revealing to us something to help us decide whether or not she is a conscious liar.

Mrs. Annie Herron, Walley Gaol, United Counties
of Huron and Bruce, to Miss Sadie Johnstone,
49 King Street, Toronto,
December 20, 1852.

Sadie I am in here pretty well and safe and nothing to complain of either in food or blankets. It is a good stone building and something like the Home. If you could come and see me I would be very glad. I often talk to you a whole lot in my head, which I don't want to write because what if they are spies. I do the sewing here, the things was not in good repair when I came, but now they are pretty good. And I am making curtains for the Opera House, a job that was sent in. I hope to see you. You could come on the stage right to this place. Maybe you would not like to come in the winter but in the springtime you would like to come.

> *Mr. James Mullen to the Reverend Walter McBain,*
> *April 7, 1853.*

Not having had any reply to my last letter, I trust you are well and might still be interested in the case of Annie Herron. She is still here and busies herself at sewing jobs which I have undertaken to get her from outside. No more is said of being with child, or of hanging, or of her story. She has written once again to Sadie Johnstone but quite briefly and I enclose her letter here. Do you have an idea who this person Sadie Johnstone might be?

> *Mrs. Annie Herron, Walley Gaol, United Counties*
> *of Huron and Bruce, to Miss Sadie Johnstone,*
> *49 King Street, Toronto,*
> *April 1, 1853.*

I don't get any answer from you Sadie. I don't think they sent on my letter. Today is the First of April, 1853. But not April Fool like we used to fool each other. Please come and see me if you can. I am in Walley Gaol but safe and well.

> *Mr. James Mullen from Edward Hoy, Landlord,*
> *Carstairs Inn,*
> *April 19, 1853.*

Your letter to Mr. McBain sent back to you, he died here at the inn February 25. There is some books here, nobody wants them.

> *Annie Herron, Walley Gaol, to Sadie Johnstone,*
> *Toronto. Finder Please Post.*

George came dragging him across the snow, I thought it was a log he dragged. I didn't know it was him. George said, it's him. A branch fell out of a tree and hit him, he said. He didn't say he was dead. I looked for him to speak. His mouth was partway open with snow in it. Also his eyes partway open. We had to get inside because it was starting to storm like anything. We dragged him in by the one leg each. I pretended to myself when I took hold of his leg that it was still the log. Inside where I had the fire going it was warm and the snow started melting off him. His blood thawed and ran a little around his ear. I didn't know what to do and I was afraid to go near him. I thought his eyes were watching me.

George sat by the fire with his big heavy coat on and his boots on. He was turned away. I sat at the table, which was of half-cut logs. I said, how do you know if he is dead? George said, touch him if you want to know. But I would not. Outside there was terrible storming, the wind in the trees and over top of our roof. I said, Our Father who art in Heaven, and gradually I got my courage. I kept saying it every time I moved. I have to wash him off, I said. Help me. I got the bucket where I kept the snow melting. I started on his feet and had to pull his boots off, a heavy job. George never turned around or paid attention or helped me when I asked. I didn't take the trousers or coat off him, I couldn't manage. But I washed his hands and wrists. I always kept the rag between my hand and his skin. The blood and wet where the snow had melted off him was on the floor under his head and shoulders so I wanted to turn him over and clean it up. But I couldn't do it. So I went and pulled George by his arm. Help me, I said. What? he said. I said we had to turn him. So he came and helped me and we got him turned over, he was lying face down. And then I saw, I saw where the axe had cut.

Neither one of us said anything. I washed it out, blood and what else. I said to George, go and get me the sheet from my box. There was the good sheet I wouldn't put on the bed. I didn't see the use of trying to take off his clothes though they were good cloth. We would have had to cut them away where the blood was stuck and then what would we have but the rags. I cut off the one little piece of his hair because I remembered when Lila died in the Home they did that. Then I got George to help me roll him on to the sheet and I started to sew him up in the sheet. While I was sewing I said to George, go out in the lee of the house where the wood is piled and maybe you can get in enough shelter there to dig him a grave. Take the wood away and the ground is likely softer underneath.

I had to crouch down at the sewing so I was nearly lying on the floor beside him. I sewed his head in first, folding the sheet over it because I had to look in his eyes and mouth. George went out and I could hear through the storm that he was doing what I said and pieces of wood were thrown up sometimes hitting the wall of the house. I sewed on, and every bit of him I lost sight of I would say even out loud, there goes, there goes. I had got the fold neat over his head but down at the feet I didn't have material enough to cover him, so I sewed on my eyelet petticoat I made at the Home to learn the stitch and that way I got him all sewed in.

I went out to help George. He had got all the wood out of the way and was at the digging. The ground was soft enough, as I had thought. He had the spade so I got the broad shovel and we worked away, him digging and loosening and me shovelling.

Then we moved him out. We could not do it now one leg each so George got him at the head and me at the ankles where the petticoat was and we rolled him into the earth and set to work again to cover him up. George had the shovel and it seemed I could not get enough dirt onto the spade so I pushed it in with my hands and kicked it in with my feet any way at all. When it was all back in, George beat it down flat with the shovel as much as he could. Then we moved all the wood back searching where it was in the snow and we piled it up in the right way so it did not look as if it was disturbed. I think we had no hats on or scarves but the work kept us warm.

We took in more wood for the fire and put the bar across the door. I wiped up the floor and I said to George, take off your boots. Then, take off your coat. George did what I told him. He sat by the fire. I made the kind of tea from catnip leaves that Mrs. Treece showed me how to make and I put a piece of sugar in it. George did not want it. Is it too hot? I said. I let it cool off but then he didn't want it either. So I began, and talked to him.

You didn't mean to do it.

It was in anger, you didn't mean what you were doing.

I saw him other times what he would do to you. I saw him knock you down for a little thing and you would just get up and never say a word. The same way he did to me.

If you had not done it, someday he would have done it to you.

Listen George. Listen to me.

If you own up what do you think will happen? They will hang you. You will be dead, you will be no good to anybody. What will become of your land? Likely it will all go back to the Crown and somebody else will get it and all the work you have done will be for them.

What will become of me here if you are took away?

I got some oatcakes that were cold and I warmed them up. I set one on his knee. He took it and bit it and chewed it but he could not get it down and he spit it onto the fire.

I said, listen. I know things. I am older than you are. I am religious too. I pray to God every night and my prayers are answered. I know what God wants as well as any preacher knows and I know that he does not want a good lad like you to be hanged. All you have to do is say you are sorry. Say you are sorry and mean it well and God will forgive you. I will say the same thing, I am sorry too because when I saw he was dead I did not wish for him to be alive. I will say, God forgive me, and you do the same. Kneel down.

But he would not. He would not move out of his chair. And I said, all right. I have an idea. I am going to get the Bible. I asked him, do you believe in the Bible? Say you do. Nod your head.

I did not see whether he nodded or not but I said, there. There you did. Now. I am going to do what we all used to do in the Home when we wanted to know what would happen to us or what we should do in our life. We would open the Bible anyplace and poke our finger at a page and then open our eyes and read the verse where our finger was and that would tell you what you needed to know. To make double sure of it just say when you close your eyes, God guide my finger.

He would not raise a hand from his knee, so I said,

all right. All right, I'll do it for you. I did it, and I read where my finger stopped.

It was something about being old and gray-headed, *O God, forsake me not,* and I said, what that means is that you are supposed to live till you are old and gray-headed and nothing is supposed to happen to you before that. It says so, in the Bible.

Then the next verse was so-and-so went and took so-and-so and she conceived and bore him a son.

It says you will have a son, I said. You have to live and get older and get married and have a son.

But the next verse I remember so I can say it. *Neither can they prove the things whereof they now accuse me.*

George, I said, do you hear that? *Neither can they prove the things whereof they now accuse me.* That means that you are safe.

You are safe. Get up now. Get up and go and lie on the bed and go to sleep.

He could not do that by himself but I did it. I pulled on him and pulled on him until he was standing up and then I got him across the room to the bed which was not his bed in the corner but the bigger bed, and got him to sit on it then lie down. I rolled him over and back and got his clothes off down to his shirt. His teeth were chattering and I was afraid of a chill or the fever. I heated up the flat-irons and wrapped them in cloth and laid them down one on each side of him close to his skin. There was not whiskey or brandy in the house to use, only the catnip tea. I put more sugar in it and got him to take it from a spoon. I rubbed his feet with my hands, then his arms and his legs, and I wrung out clothes in hot water which I laid over his stomach and his heart. I talked to him then in a different way quite softly and told him to go to sleep and when he woke up his mind would be clear and all his horrors would be wiped away.

A tree branch fell on him. It was just what you told me. I can see it falling. I can see it coming down so fast like a streak and little branches and crackling all along the way, it hardly takes longer than a gun going off and you say, what is that? and it has hit him and he is dead.

When I got him to sleep I lay down on the bed beside him. I took off my smock and I could see the black and blue marks on my arms. I pulled up my skirt to see if they were still there high on my legs, and they were.

Nothing bad happened after I lay down and I did not sleep all night but listened to him breathing and kept touching him to see if he was warmed up. I got up in the earliest light and fixed the fire. When he heard me he waked up and was better.

He did not forget what had happened but talked as if he thought it was all right. He said, we ought to have had a prayer and read something out of the Bible. He got the door opened and there was a big drift of snow but the sky was clearing. It was the last snow of the winter.

We went out and said the Lord's Prayer. Then he said, where is the Bible? Why is it not on the shelf? When I got it from beside the fire he said, what is it doing there? I did not remind him of anything. He did not know what to read so I picked the 131st Psalm that we had to learn at the Home. *Lord my heart is not haughty nor mine eyes lofty, neither do I exercise myself in great matters, or in things too high for me. Surely I have behaved and quieted myself as a child that is weaned of his mother, my soul is even as a weaned child.* He read it. Then he said he would shovel out a path and go and tell the Treeces. I said I would cook him some food. He went out and shovelled and didn't get tired and come in to eat as I thought he would. He shovelled and shovelled a long path out of sight and then he was gone and didn't come back. He didn't come back until near dark and then he said he had eaten. I said, did you tell them about the tree? Then he looked at me for the first time in a bad way. It was the same bad way his brother used to look but worse. I never said anything more to him about what had happened or hinted at it in any way. And he never said anything to me, except he would come and say things in my dreams. But I knew the difference always between my dreams and when I was awake, and when I was awake it was never anything but the bad look.

Mrs. Treece came and tried to get me to go and live with them the way George was living. She said I could eat and sleep there, they had enough beds. I would not go. They thought I would not go because of my grief but I wouldn't go because somebody might see my black and blue, also they would be watching for me to cry. I said I was not frightened to stay alone.

I dreamed nearly every night that one or other of them came and chased me with the axe. It was him or it was George, one or the other. Or sometimes not the axe, it was a big rock lifted in both hands and one of them waiting with it behind the door. Dreams are sent to warn us.

I didn't stay in the house where he could find me and when I gave up sleeping inside and slept outside I didn't have the dream so often. It got warm quickly and the flies and mosquitoes came but they hardly bothered me. I would see their bites but not feel them, which was another sign that in the outside I was protected. I got down when I heard anybody coming. I ate berries both red and black and God protected me from any badness in them.

I had another kind of dream after a while. I dreamed George came and talked to me and he still had the bad look but was trying to cover it up and pretend that he was kind. He kept coming into my dreams and he kept lying to me. It was beginning to get colder out and I did not want to go back in the shanty and the dew was heavy so I would be soaking when I slept in the grass. I went and opened the Bible to find out what I should do.

And now I got my punishment for cheating because the Bible did not tell me anything that I could understand, what to do. The cheating was when I was looking to find something for George, and I did not read exactly where my finger landed but looked around quick and found something else that was more what I wanted. I used to do that too when we would be looking up our verses in the Home and I always got good things and nobody ever caught me or suspected me at it. You never did either, Sadie.

So now I had my punishment when I couldn't find anything to help me however I looked. But something put it into my head to come here and I did. I had heard them talking about how warm it was and tramps would be wanting to come and get locked up, so I thought, I will too, and it was put into my head to tell them what I did. I told them the very same lie that George told me so often in my dreams, trying to get me to believe it was me and not him. I am safe from George here is the main thing. If they think I am crazy and I know the difference I am safe. Only I would like for you to come and see me.

And I would like for that yelling to stop.

When I am finished writing this, I will put it in with the curtains that I am making for the Opera House. And I will put on it Finder Please Post. I trust that a lot better than giving it to them like the two letters I gave them already that they never have sent.

Miss Christena Mullen, Walley, to Mr. Leopold Henry,
Department of History, Queen's University, Kingston,
July 8, 1959

Yes, I am the Miss Mullen that Treece Herron's sister remembers coming to the farm, and it is very kind of her to say I was a pretty young lady in a hat and veil. That was my motoring veil. The old lady she mentions was Mr. Herron's grandfather's sister-in-law, if I have got it straight. As you are doing the biography you will have got the relationships worked out. I never voted for Treece Herron myself since I am a Conservative, but he was a colourful politician and as you say a biography of him will bring some attention to this part of the country—too often thought of as "deadly dull."

I am rather surprised the sister does not mention the car in particular. It was a Stanley Steamer. I bought it myself on my twenty-fifth birthday in 1907. It cost twelve hundred dollars, that being part of my inheritance from my grandfather James Mullen who was an early Clerk of the Peace in Walley. He made money buying and selling farms.

My father having died young, my mother moved into my grandfather's house with all us five girls. It was a big cut-stone house called Traquair, now a Home for Young Offenders. I sometimes say in joke that it always was!

When I was young we employed a gardener, a cook, and a sewing-woman. All of them were "characters," all prone to feuding with each other, and all owing their jobs to the fact that my grandfather had taken an inter- est in them when they were inmates at the County Gaol (as it used to be spelled) and eventually had brought them home.

By the time I bought the Steamer I was the only one of us sisters living at home, and the sewing-woman was the only one of these old servants who remained. The sewing-woman was called Old Annie and never objected to that name. She used it herself and would write notes to the cook that said, "Tea was not hot, did you warm the pot? Old Annie." The whole third floor was Old Annie's domain and one of my sisters—Dolly—said that whenever she dreamed of home, that is, of Traquair, she dreamed of Old Annie up at the top of the third-floor stairs brandishing her measuring stick and wearing a black dress with long fuzzy black arms like a spider.

She had one eye that slid off to the side and gave her the air of taking in more information than the ordinary person.

We were not supposed to pester the servants with questions about their personal lives, particularly those who had been in the Gaol, but of course we did. Sometimes Old Annie called the Gaol the Home. She said that a girl in the next bed screamed and screamed, and that was why she—Annie—ran away and lived in the woods. She said the girl had been beaten for letting the fire go out. Why were you in jail, we asked her, and she would say, "I told a fib!" So for quite a while we had the impression that you went to jail for telling lies!

Some days she was in a good mood and would play hide-the-thimble with us. Sometimes she was in a bad mood and would stick us with pins when she was evening our hems if we turned too quickly or stopped too soon. She knew a place, she said, where you could get bricks to put on children's heads to stop them growing. She hated making wedding dresses (she never had to make one for me!) and didn't think much of any of the men that my sisters married. She hated Dolly's beau so much that she made some kind of deliberate mistake with the sleeves, which had to be ripped out, and Dolly cried. But she made us all beautiful ball gowns to wear when the Governor-General and Lady Minto came to Walley.

About being married herself, she sometimes said she had been and sometimes not. She said a man had come to the Home and had all the girls paraded in front of him and said, "I'll take the one with the coal-black hair." That being Old Annie, but she refused to go with him, even though he was rich and came in a carriage. Rather like Cinderella but with a different ending. Then she said a bear killed her husband, in the woods, and my grandfather had killed the bear and wrapped her in its skin and taken her home from the Gaol.

My mother used to say, "Now, girls. Don't get Old Annie going. And don't believe a word she says."

I am going on at great length filling in the background, but you did say you were interested in details of the period. I am like most people my age and forget to buy milk but could tell you the color of the coat I had when I was eight.

So, when I got the Stanley Steamer, Old Annie asked to be taken for a ride. It turned out that what she had in mind was more of a trip. This was a surprise since she had never wanted to go on trips before and refused to go to Niagara Falls and would not even go down to the Harbour to see the fireworks on the First of July. Also she was leery of automobiles and of me as a driver. But the big surprise was that she had somebody she wanted to go and see. She wanted to drive to Carstairs to see the Herron family, who she said were her relatives. She had never received any visits or letters from these people, and when I asked if she had written to inquire if we might visit she said, "I can't write." This was ridiculous—she wrote those notes to the cooks and long lists for me of things she wanted me to pick up down on the Square or in the city. Braid, buckram, taffeta—she could spell all of that.

"And they don't need to know beforehand," she said. "In the country it's different."

Well, I loved taking jaunts in the Steamer. I had been driving since I was fifteen, but this was the first car of my own and possibly the only steam car in Huron County. Everybody would run to see it go by. It did not make a beastly loud noise coughing and clanking like other cars but rolled along silently, more or less like a ship with high sails over the lake waters, and it did not foul the air but left behind a plume of steam. Stanley Steamers were banned in Boston, because of steam fogging the

air. I always loved to tell people that I used to drive a
car that was banned in Boston!

We started out fairly early on a Sunday in June. It
took about twenty-five minutes to get the steam up, and
all that time Old Annie sat up straight in the front seat
as if the show were already on the road. We both had
our motoring veils on, and long dusters, but the dress
Old Annie was wearing underneath was of plum-
coloured silk. In fact it was made over from the one she
had made for my grandmother to meet the Prince of
Wales in.

The Steamer covered the miles like an angel. It would
do fifty miles an hour—great then—but I did not push
it. I was trying to consider Old Annie's nerves. People
were still in church when we started, but later on, the
roads were full of horses and buggies making the journey
home. I was polite as all getout, edging by them. But it
turned out Old Annie did not want to be so sedate and
she kept saying, "Give it a squeeze," meaning the horn,
which was worked by a bulb under a mudguard down
at my side.

She must not have been out of Walley for more years
than I had been alive. When we crossed the bridge at
Saltford (that old iron bridge where there used to be so
many accidents because of the turn at both ends) she
said that there didn't use to be a bridge there, you had
to pay a man to row you.

"I couldn't pay but I crossed on the stones and just
hiked up my skirts and waded," she said. "It was that
dry a summer."

Naturally I did not know what summer she was talking about.

Then it was, Look at the big fields, where are the
stumps gone, where is the bush? And look how straight
the road goes, and they're building their houses out of
brick! And what are those buildings as big as churches?

Barns, I said.

I knew my way to Carstairs all right but expected help
from Old Annie once we got there. None was forth-
coming. I drove up and down the main street waiting
for her to spot something familiar. "If I could just see
the inn," she said, "I'd know where the track goes off
behind it."

It was a factory town, not very pretty in my opinion. The Steamer of course got attention, and I was able to call out for directions to the Herron farm without stopping the engine. Shouts and gestures, and finally I was able to get us on the right road. I told Old Annie to watch the mailboxes but she was concerned with finding the creek. I spotted the name myself, and turned us in at a long lane with a red brick house at the end of it and a couple of those barns that had amazed Old Annie. Red brick houses with verandas and key windows were all the style then, they were going up everywhere.

"Look there!" Old Annie said, and I thought she meant where a herd of cows was tearing away from us in the pasture-field alongside the lane. But she was pointing at a mound pretty well covered with wild grape, a few logs sticking out of it. She said that was the shanty. I said, "Well, good—now let's hope you recognize one or two of the people."

There were enough people around. A couple of visiting buggies were pulled up in the shade, horses tethered and cropping grass. By the time the Steamer stopped at the side veranda, a number of people were lined up to look at it. They didn't come forward—not even the children ran out to look close up the way town children would have done. They all just stood in a row looking at it in a tight-lipped sort of way.

Old Annie was staring off in the other direction.

She told me to get down. Get down, she said, and ask them if there is a Mr. George Herron that lives here and is he alive yet, or dead.

I did what I was told. And one of the men said, that's right. He is. My father.

Well, I have brought somebody, I told them. I have brought Mrs. Annie Herron.

The man said, that so?

(A pause here due to a couple of fainting fits and a trip to the hospital. Lots of tests to use up the taxpayers' money. Now I'm back and have read this over, astounded at the rambling but too lazy to start again. I have not even got to Treece Herron, which is the part you are interested in, but hold on, I'm nearly there.)

These people were all dumbfounded about Old Annie, or so I gathered. They had not known where she was or

what she was doing or if she was alive. But you mustn't
think they surged out and greeted her in any excited
way. Just the one young man came out, very mannerly.
He said to me that Old Annie was his grandfather's
sister-in-law. It was too bad we hadn't come even a few
months sooner, he said, because his grandfather had
been quite well and his mind quite clear—he had even
written a piece for the paper about his early days here—
but then he had got sick. He had recovered but would
never be himself again. He could not talk, except now
and then a few words.

This mannerly young man was Treece Herron.

We must have arrived just after they finished their
dinner. The woman of the house came out and asked
him—Treece Herron—to ask us if we had eaten. You
would think she or we did not speak English. They were
all very shy—the women with their skinned-back hair
and men in dark-blue Sunday suits and tongue-tied children. I hope you do not think I am making fun of
them—it is just that I cannot understand for the life of
me why it is necessary to be so shy.

We were taken to the dining room, which had an un-
used smell—they must have had their dinner elsewhere—and were served a great deal of food, of which
I remember salted radishes and leaf lettuce and roast
chicken and strawberries and cream. Dishes from the
china cabinet, not their usual. Good old Indian Tree.
They had sets of everything. Plushy living-room suite,
walnut dining-room suite. It was going to take them a
while, I thought, to get used to being prosperous.

Old Annie enjoyed the fuss of being waited on and
ate a lot, picking up the chicken bones to work the last
shred of meat off them. Children lurked around the
doorways and the women talked in subdued, rather scan-
dalized voices out in the kitchen. The young man, Treece
Herron, had the grace to sit down with us and drink a
cup of tea while we ate. He chatted readily enough
about himself and told me he was a divinity student at
Knox College. He said he liked living in Toronto. I got
the feeling he wanted me to understand that divinity
students were not all such sticks as I supposed or led
such a stringent existence. He had been tobogganing in
High Park, he had been picnicking at Hanlan's Point, he

had seen the giraffe in the Riverdale Zoo. As he talked the children got a little bolder and started trickling into the room. I asked the usual idiocies: How old are you? What book are you in at school? Do you like your teacher? He urged them to answer or answered for them and told me which were his brothers and sisters and which his cousins.

Old Annie said, "Are you all fond of each other, then?" which brought on funny looks.

The woman of the house came back and spoke to me again through the divinity student. She told him that Grandpa was up now and sitting on the front porch. She looked at the children and said, "What did you let all them in here for?"

Out we trooped to the front porch, where two straight-backed chairs were set up and an old man was settled on one of them. He had a beautiful full white beard reaching down to the bottom of his waistcoat. He did not seem interested in us. He had a long, pale, obedient old face.

Old Annie said, "Well, George," as if this was about what she had expected. She sat on the other chair and said to one of the little girls, "Now bring me a cushion. Bring me a thin kind of cushion and put it at my back."

I spent the afternoon giving rides in the Stanley Steamer. I knew enough about them now not to start in asking who wanted a ride, or bombarding them with questions, such as were they interested in automobiles? I just went out and patted it here and there as if it was a horse, and I looked in the boiler. The divinity student came behind and read the name of the Steamer written on the side. "The Gentlemen's Speedy Roadster." He asked was it my father's.

Mine, I said. I explained how the water in the boiler was heated and how much steam-pressure the boiler could withstand. People always wondered about that—about explosions. The children were closer by that time, and I suddenly remarked that the boiler was nearly empty. I asked if there was any way I could get some water.

Great scurry to get pails and man the pump! I went and asked the men on the veranda if that was all right, and thanked them when they told me help yourself.

Once the boiler was filled it was natural for me to ask if they would like me to get the steam up, and a spokesman said, it wouldn't hurt. Nobody was impatient during the wait. The men stared at the boiler, concentrating. This was certainly not the first car they had seen but probably the first steam car.

I offered the men a ride first. It was proper to. We bumped down the lane at five, then ten miles an hour. I knew they suffered somewhat, being driven by a woman, but the novelty of the experience held them. Next I got a load of children, hoisted in by the divinity student telling them to sit still and hold on and not be scared and not fall out. I put up the speed a little, knowing now the ruts and puddle-holes, and their hoots of fear and triumph could not be held back.

I have left out something about how I was feeling but will leave it out no longer, due to the effects of a Martini I am drinking now, my late-afternoon pleasure. I had troubles then which I have not yet admitted to you, because they were love-troubles. But when I had set out that day with Old Annie, I had determined to enjoy myself as much as I could. It seemed it would be an insult to the Stanley Steamer not to. All my life I found this a good rule to follow—to get as much pleasure as you could out of things, even when you weren't likely to be happy.

I told one of the boys to run around to the front veranda and ask if his grandfather would care for a ride. He came back and said, "They've both gone to sleep."

I had to get the boiler filled up before we started back, and while this was being done Treece Herron came and stood close to me.

"You have given us all a day to remember," he said.

I wasn't above flirting with him. I actually had a long career as a flirt ahead of me. It's quite a natural behaviour, once the loss of love makes you give up your ideas of marriage. (Ask an old woman to reminisce and you get the whole ragbag, is what you must be thinking by now.)

I said he would forget all about it, once he got back to his friends in Toronto. He said no indeed, he would never forget, and he asked if he could write to me. I said nobody could stop him.

On the way home I thought about this exchange and how ridiculous it would be if he should get a serious crush on me. A divinity student. I had no idea then of course that he would be getting out of Divinity and into Politics.

"Too bad old Mr. Herron wasn't able to talk to you," I said to Old Annie.

She said, "Well. I could talk to him."

Actually Treece Herron did write to me, but he must have had a few misgivings as well, because he enclosed some pamphlets about Mission Schools. Something about raising money for Mission Schools. That put me off and I didn't write back. (Years later I would joke that I could have married him if I'd played my cards right.)

I asked Old Annie if Mr. Herron could understand her when she talked to him, and she said, "Enough." I asked if she was glad about seeing him again and she said yes. "And glad for him to get to see me," she said, not without some gloating that probably referred to her dress and the vehicle.

So we just puffed along in the Steamer under the high arching trees that lined the roads in those days. From miles away the Lake could be seen—just glimpses of it, held wide apart in the trees and hills so that Old Annie asked me if it could possibly be the same lake, all the same one that Walley was on?

There were lots of old people going around then with peculiar ideas in their heads, though I suppose Old Annie had more than most. I recall her telling me another time that a girl in the Home had a baby out of a big boil that burst on her stomach, and it was the size of a rat and had no life in it, but they put it in the oven and it puffed up to the right size and baked to a good colour and started to kick its legs.

I told her that wasn't possible, it must have been a dream.

She said, "They took it afterwards, anyway, I never got to see it anymore." Then she said, "I did used to have the terriblest dreams."

Jupiter Doke, Brigadier General

Ambrose Bierce

From the Secretary of War to the Hon. Jupiter Doke, Hardpan Crossroads, Posey County, Illinois.

WASHINGTON, November 3, 1861.

Having faith in your patriotism and ability, the President has been pleased to appoint you a brigadier general of volunteers. Do you accept?

From the Hon. Jupiter Doke to the Secretary of War.

HARDPAN, ILLINOIS, November 9, 1861.

It is the proudest moment of my life. The office is one which should be neither sought nor declined. In times that try men's souls the patriot knows no North, no South, no East, no West. His motto should be: "My country, my whole country and nothing but my country." I accept the great trust confided in me by a free and intelligent people, and with a firm reliance on the principles of constitutional liberty, and invoking the guidance of an all-wise Providence, Ruler of Nations, shall labor so to discharge it as to leave no blot upon my political escutcheon. Say to his Excellency, the successor of the immortal Washington in the Seat of Power, that the patronage of my office will be bestowed with an eye single to securing the greatest good to the greatest number, the stability of republican institutions and the triumph of the party in all elections; and to this I pledge my life, my fortune and my sacred honor. I shall at once prepare an appropriate response to the speech of the chairman of the committee deputed to inform me of my appointment, and I trust the sentiments therein expressed will strike a sympathetic chord in the public heart, as well as command the Executive approval.

From the Secretary of War to Major General Blount Wardorg, Commanding the Military Department of Eastern Kentucky.

WASHINGTON, November 14, 1861.
I have assigned to your department Brigadier General Jupiter Doke, who will soon proceed to Distilleryville, on the Little Buttermilk River, and take command of the Illinois Brigade at that point, reporting to you by letter for orders. Is the route from Covington by way of Bluegrass, Opossum Corners and Horsecave still infested with bushwackers, as reported in your last dispatch? I have a plan for cleaning them out.

From Major General Blount Wardorg to the Secretary of War.

LOUISVILLE, KENTUCKY, November 20, 1861.
The name and services of Brigadier General Doke are unfamiliar to me, but I shall be pleased to have the advantage of his skill. The route from Covington to Distilleryville via Opossum Corners and Horsecave I have been compelled to abandon to the enemy, whose guerilla warfare made it possible to keep it open without detaching too many troops from the front. The brigade at Distilleryville is supplied by steamboats up the Little Buttermilk.

From the Secretary of War to Brigadier General Jupiter Doke, Hardpan, Illinois.

WASHINGTON, November 26, 1861.
I deeply regret that your commission had been forwarded by mail before the receipt of your letter of acceptance; so we must dispense with the formality of official notification to you by a committee. The President is highly gratified by the noble and patriotic sentiments of your letter, and directs that you proceed at once to your command at Distilleryville, Kentucky, and there report by letter to Major General Wardorg at Louisville, for orders. It is important that the strictest secrecy be

observed regarding your movements until you have
passed Covington, as it is desired to hold the enemy in
front of Distilleryville until you are within three days of
him. Then if your approach is known it will operate as
a demonstration against his right and cause him to
strengthen it with his left now at Memphis, Tennessee,
which it is desirable to capture first. Go by way of Bluegrass, Opossum Corners and Horsecave. All officers are
expected to be in full uniform when en route to the
front.

From Brigadier General Jupiter Doke
to the Secretary of War.

COVINGTON, KENTUCKY, December 7, 1861.
I arrived yesterday at this point, and have given my
proxy to Joel Briller, Esq., my wife's cousin, and a
staunch Republican, who will worthily represent Posey
County in field and forum. He points with pride to a
stainless record in the halls of legislation, which have
often echoed to his soul-stirring eloquence on questions
which lie at the very foundation of popular government.
He has been called the Patrick Henry of Hardpan, where
he has done yeoman's service in the cause of civil and
religious liberty. Mr. Briller left for Distilleryville last
evening, and the standard bearer of the Democratic host
confronting that stronghold of freedom will find him a
lion in his path. I have been asked to remain here and
deliver some addresses to the people in a local contest
involving issues of paramount importance. That duty
being performed, I shall in person enter the arena of
armed debate and move in the direction of the heaviest
firing, burning my ships behind me. I forward by this
mail to his Excellency the President a request for the
appointment of my son, Jabez Leonidas Doke, as postmaster at Hardpan. I would take it, sir, as a great favor
if you would give the application a strong oral endorsement, as the appointment is in the line of reform. Be
kind enough to inform me what are the emoluments of
the office I hold in the military arm, and if they are by
salary or fees. Are there any perquisites? My mileage
account will be transmitted monthly.

*From Brigadier General Jupiter Doke
to Major General Blount Wardorg.*

DISTILLERYVILLE, KENTUCKY, January 12, 1862.
I arrived on the tented field yesterday by steamboat, the recent storms having inundated the landscape, covering, I understand, the greater part of a congressional district. I am pained to find that Joel Briller, Esq., a prominent citizen of Posey County, Illinois, and a farseeing statesman who held my proxy, and who a month ago should have been thundering at the gates of Disunion, has not been heard from, and has doubtless been sacrificed upon the altar of his country. In him the American people lose a bulwark of freedom. I would respectfully move that you designate a committee to draw up resolutions of respect to his memory, and that the officeholders and men under your command wear the usual badge of mourning for thirty days. I shall at once place myself at the head of affairs here, and am now ready to entertain any suggestions which you may make, looking to the better enforcement of the laws in this commonwealth. The militant Democrats on the other side of the river appear to be contemplating extreme measures. They have two large cannons facing this way, and yesterday morning, I am told, some of them came down to the water's edge and remained in session for some time, making infamous allegations.

*From the Diary of Brigadier General Jupiter Doke,
at Distilleryville, Kentucky.*

January 12, 1862.—On my arrival yesterday at the Henry Clay Hotel (named in honor of the late farseeing statesman) I was waited on by a delegation consisting of the three colonels entrusted with the command of the regiments of my brigade. It was an occasion that will be memorable in the political annals of America. Forwarded copies of the speeches to the Posey *Maverick,* to be spread upon the record of the ages. The gentlemen composing the delegation unanimously reaffirmed their devotion to the principles of national unity and the Republican party. Was gratified to recognize in them men of political prominence and untarnished escutcheons. At the subsequent banquet, sentiments of lofty patriotism were expressed. Wrote to Mr. Wardorg at Louisville for instructions.

January 13, 1862.—Leased a prominent residence (the former incumbent being absent in arms against his country) for the term of one year, and wrote at once for Mrs. Brigadier General Doke and the vital issues—excepting Jabez Leonidas. In the camp of treason opposite here there are supposed to be three thousand misguided men laying the ax at the root of the tree of liberty. They have a clear majority, many of our men having returned without leave to their constituents. We could probably not poll more than two thousand votes. Have advised my heads of regiments to make a canvass of those remaining, all bolters to be read out of the phalanx.

January 14, 1862.—Wrote to the President, asking for the contract to supply this command with firearms and regalia through my brother-in-law, prominently identified with the manufacturing interests of the country. Club of cannon soldiers arrived at Jayhawk, three miles back from here, on their way to join us in battle array. Marched my whole brigade to Jayhawk to escort them into town, but their chairman, mistaking us for the opposing party, opened fire on the head of the procession and by the extraordinary noise of the cannon balls (I had no conception of it!) so frightened my horse that I was unseated without a contest. The meeting adjourned in disorder and returning to camp I found that a deputation of the enemy had crossed the river in our absence and made a division of the loaves and fishes. Wrote to the President, applying for the Gubernatorial Chair of the Territory of Idaho.

From Editorial Article in the Posey, Illinois, "Maverick,"
January 20, 1862.

Brigadier General Doke's thrilling account, in another column, of the Battle of Distilleryville will make the heart of every loyal Illinoisian leap with exultation. The brilliant exploit marks an era in military history, and as General Doke says, "lays broad and deep the foundations of American prowess in arms." As none of the troops engaged, except the gallant author-chieftain (a host in himself) hails from Posey County, he justly considered that a list of the fallen would only occupy our valuable space to the exclusion of more important matter, but his account of the strategic ruse by which he apparently abandoned his camp and so inveigled a perfidious enemy into it for the purpose of murdering the sick, the unfortunate countertempus at Jayhawk, the subsequent dash upon a trapped enemy flushed with a supposed success, driving their terrified legions across an impassable river which precluded pursuit—all these "moving accidents by flood and field" are related with a pen of fire and have all the terrible interest of romance.

Verily, truth is stranger than fiction and the pen is mightier than the sword. When by the graphic power of the art preservative of all arts we are brought face to face with such glorious events as these, the *Maverick's* enterprise in securing for its thousands of readers the services of so distinguished a contributor as the Great Captain who made the history as well as wrote it seems a matter of almost secondary importance. For President in 1864 (subject to the decision of the Republican National Convention) Brigadier General Jupiter Doke, of Illinois!

From Major General Blount Wardorg to Brigadier General Jupiter Doke.

LOUISVILLE, January 22, 1862.
Your letter apprising me of your arrival at Distilleryville was delayed in transmission, having only just been received (open) through the courtesy of the Confederate department commander under a flag of truce. He begs me to assure you that he would consider it an act of cruelty to trouble you, and I think it would be. Maintain, however, a threatening attitude, but at the least pressure retire. Your position is simply an outpost which it is not intended to hold.

*From Major General Blount Wardorg
to the Secretary of War.*

LOUISVILLE, January 23, 1862.
I have certain information that the enemy has concentrated twenty thousand troops of all arms on the Little Buttermilk. According to your assignment, General Doke is in command of the small brigade of raw troops opposing them. It is no part of my plan to contest the enemy's advance at that point, but I cannot hold myself responsible for any reverses to the brigade mentioned, under its present commander. I think him a fool.

*From the Secretary of War
to Major General Blount Wardorg.*

WASHINGTON, February 1, 1862.
The President has great faith in General Doke. If your estimate of him is correct, however, he would seem to be singularly well placed where he now is, as your plans appear to contemplate a considerable sacrifice for whatever advantages you expect to gain.

*From Brigadier General Jupiter Doke
to Major General Blount Wardorg.*

DISTILLERYVILLE, February 1, 1862.
Tomorrow I shall remove my headquarters to Jayhawk in order to point the way whenever my brigade retires from Distilleryville, as foreshadowed by your letter of the 22d ult. I have appointed a committee on Retreat, the minutes of whose first meeting I transmit to you. You will perceive that the committee having been duly organized by the election of a chairman and secretary, a resolution (prepared by myself) was adopted, to the effect that in case treason again raises her hideous head on this side of the river every man of the brigade is to mount a mule, the procession to move promptly in the direction of Louisville and the loyal North. In preparation for such an emergency I have for some time been collecting mules from the resident Democracy, and have on hand 2300 in a field at Jayhawk. Eternal vigilance is the price of liberty!

*From Major General Gibeon J. Buxter, C. S. A.,
to the Confederate Secretary of War.*

BUNG STATION, KENTUCKY, February 4, 1862.
On the night of the 2d inst., our entire force, consisting of 25,000 men and thirty-two field pieces, under command of Major General Simmons B. Flood, crossed by a ford to the north side of Little Buttermilk River at a point three miles above Distilleryville and moved obliquely down and away from the stream, to strike the Covington turnpike at Jayhawk; the object being, as you know, to capture Covington, destroy Cincinnati and occupy the Ohio Valley. For some months there had been in our front only a small brigade of undisciplined troops, apparently without a commander, who were useful to us, for by not disturbing them we could create an impression of our weakness. But the movement on Jayhawk having isolated them, I was about to detach an Alabama regiment to bring them in, my division being the leading one, when an earth-shaking rumble was felt and heard, and suddenly the head-of-column was struck by one of the terrible tornadoes for which this region is famous, and utterly annihilated. The tornado, I believe, passed along the entire length of the road back to the ford, dispersing or destroying our entire army; but of this I cannot be sure, for I was lifted from the earth insensible and blown back to the south side of the river. Continuous firing all night on the north side and the reports of such of our men as have recrossed at the ford convince me that the Yankee brigade has exterminated the disabled survivors. Our loss has been uncommonly heavy. Of my own division of 15,000 infantry, the casualties—killed, wounded, captured, and missing—are 14,994. Of General Dolliver Billows' division, 11,200 strong, I can find but two officers and a nigger cook. Of the artillery, 800 men, none have reported on this side of the river. General Flood is dead. I have assumed command of the expeditionary force, but owing to the heavy losses have deemed it advisable to contract my line of supplies as rapidly as possible. I shall push southward tomorrow morning early. The purposes of the campaign have been as yet but partly accomplished.

*From Major General Dolliver Billows, C. S. A.,
to the Confederate Secretary of War.*

BUHAC, KENTUCKY, February 5, 1862.
... But during the 2d they had, unknown to us, been reinforced by fifty thousand cavalry, and being apprised of our movement by a spy, this vast body was drawn up in the darkness at Jayhawk, and as the head of our column reached that point at about 11 P.M., fell upon it with astonishing fury, destroying the division of General Buxter in an instant. General Baumschank's brigade of artillery, which was in the rear, may have escaped—I did not wait to see, but withdrew my division to the river at a point several miles above the ford, and at daylight ferried it across on two fence rails lashed together with a suspender. Its losses, from an effective strength of 11,200, are 11,199. General Buxter is dead. I am changing my base to Mobile, Alabama.

*From Brigadier General Schneddeker Baumschank, C. S. A.,
to the Confederate Secretary of War.*

IODINE, KENTUCKY, February 6, 1862.
... Yoost den somdings occur, I know nod vot it vos—somdings mackneefcent, but it vas nod vor—und I finds meinselluf, afder leedle viles, in dis blace, midout a hors und mit no men und goons. Sheneral Peelows is deadt. You will blease be so goot as to resign me—I vights no more in a dam gontry vere I gets vipped und knows nod how it vos done.

Resolutions of Congress, February 15, 1862.

Resolved, That the thanks of Congress are due, and hereby tendered, to Brigadier General Jupiter Doke and the gallant men under his command for their unparalleled feat of attacking—themselves only 2000 strong—an army of 25,000 men and utterly overthrowing it, killing 5327, making prisoners of 19,003, of whom more than half were wounded, taking 32 guns, 20,000 stand of small arms and, in short, the enemy's entire equipment.

Resolved, That for this unexampled victory the President be requested to designate a day of thanksgiving and public celebration of religious rites in the various churches.

Resolved, That he be requested, in further commemoration of the great event, and in reward of the gallant spirits whose deeds have added such imperishable luster to the American arms, to appoint, with the advice and consent of the Senate, the following officer:

One major general.

Statement of Mr. Hannibal Alcazar Peyton, of Jayhawk, Kentucky.

Dat wus a almighty dark night, sho', and dese yere ole eyes aint wuf shuks, but I's got a year like a sque'l, an' w'en I cotch de mummer o' v'ices I knowed dat gang b'long on de far side o' de ribber. So I jes' runs in de house an' wakes Marse Doke an' tells him: "Skin outer dis fo' yo' life!" An' de Lo'd bress my soul! ef dat man didn' go right fru de winder in his shir' tail an' break for to cross de mule patch! An' dem twenty-free hunerd mules dey jes' t'ink it is de debble hese'f wid de brandin' iron, an' dey bu'st outen dat patch like a yarthquake, an' pile inter de upper ford road, an' flash down it five deep, an' it full o' Confed'rates from en' to en'! ...

DIARY NARRATION

Like monologuists and correspondents, the diarists of the next three stories are recounting events almost as they happen. Like correspondents, they write on successive dates even though entries may not be dated. But as diarists they are addressing no one in particular. "Dear Diary" suggests a curious image of an audience that is somehow close to the writer—a confidant—and yet remote, even general.

"The Yellow Wallpaper" continues into this century a tradition established by de Maupassant ("Le Horla"), Nikolai Gogol ("Diary of a Madman"), and Fyodor Dostoevsky ("The Gambler") of using the diary form to register the main character's changing state of mind. More recently, Daniel Keyes renewed this tradition in "Flowers for Algernon," the diary of a retarded man who becomes for a time a genius. Which is the main story—the events the diarist records or the inner shifts revealed in the recording itself? Such double stories catch the interplay of inner and outer lives.

Part of Daniel Defoe's Robinson Crusoe *is a diary as is also his* Journal of the Plague Year. *Most of Johann Wolfgang von Goethe's* The Sorrows of Werther *is a diary. But modern novelists have used the technique most and best, especially the French, for whom it often becomes a sort of confessional (André Gide in* Pastoral Symphony, *Jean Paul Sartre in* Nausea, *Georges Bernanos in* Diary of a Country Priest, *and François Mauriac in* Nest of Vipers). *The diary form has appealed to American vernacular writers like Ring Lardner ("Diary of a Caddy" and "I Can't Breathe") as well as to "postmodern" sophisticates like Donald Barthelme ("Me and Miss Mandible").*

In our last story here, Lorrie Moore's diarist replaces

the dear-diary confiding with the use of the second person "you," which invites the reader to identify with the main character and thus crosses one sort of point-of-view technique with another. Moore crosses both of these in turn with yet another by narrating in the present tense, which increases the diary's feeling of immediacy and the second-person feeling of involvement. Naipaul's story replaces a diary with a log, a less personal record that accommodates Naipaul's social satire, like his inclusion of another's responses to some of the entries. These variations remind us not only that the persons and tenses of grammar are creative but that writers constantly tinker with the techniques they inherit.

The Yellow Wallpaper
Charlotte Perkins Gilman

It is very seldom that mere ordinary people like John and myself secure ancestral halls for the summer.

A colonial mansion, a hereditary estate, I would say a haunted house, and reach the height of romantic felicity—but that would be asking too much of fate!

Still I will proudly declare that there is something queer about it.

Else, why should it be let so cheaply? And why have stood so long untenanted?

John laughs at me, of course, but one expects that in marriage.

John is practical in the extreme. He has no patience with faith, an intense horror of superstition, and he scoffs openly at any talk of things not to be felt and seen and put down in figures.

John is a physician, and *perhaps*—(I would not say it to a living soul, of course, but this is dead paper and a great relief to my mind)—*perhaps* that is one reason I do not get well faster.

You see he does not believe I am sick!

And what can one do?

If a physician of high standing, and one's own husband, assures friends and relatives that there is really nothing the matter with one but temporary nervous depression—a slight hysterical tendency—what is one to do?

My brother is also a physician, and also of high standing, and he says the same thing.

So I take phosphates or phosphites—whichever it is, and tonics, and journeys, and air, and exercise, and am absolutely forbidden to "work" until I am well again.

Personally, I disagree with their ideas.

Personally, I believe that congenial work, with excitement and change, would do me good.

But what is one to do?

I did write for a while in spite of them; but it *does* exhaust me a good deal—having to be so sly about it, or else meet with heavy opposition.

I sometimes fancy that in my condition if I had less opposition and more society and stimulus—but John says the very worst thing I can do is to think about my condition, and I confess it always makes me feel bad.

So I will let it alone and talk about the house.

The most beautiful place! It is quite alone, standing well back from the road, quite three miles from the village. It makes me think of English places that you read about, for there are hedges and walls and gates that lock, and lots of separate little houses for the gardeners and people.

There is a *delicious* garden! I never saw such a garden—large and shady, full of box-bordered paths, and lined with long grape-covered arbors with seats under them.

There were greenhouses, too, but they are all broken now.

There was some legal trouble, I believe, something about the heirs and coheirs; anyhow, the place has been empty for years.

That spoils my ghostliness, I am afraid, but I don't care—there is something strange about the house—I can feel it.

I even said so to John one moonlight evening, but he said what I felt was a *draught*, and shut the window.

I get unreasonably angry with John sometimes. I'm sure I never used to be so sensitive. I think it is due to this nervous condition.

But John says if I feel so, I shall neglect proper self-control; so I take pains to control myself—before him, at least, and that makes me very tired.

I don't like our room a bit. I wanted one downstairs that opened on the piazza and had roses all over the window, and such pretty old-fashioned chintz hangings! but John would not hear of it.

He said there was only one window and not room for two beds, and no near room for him if he took another.

He is very careful and loving, and hardly lets me stir without special direction.

I have a schedule prescription for each hour in the day; he takes all care from me, and so I feel basely ungrateful not to value it more.

He said we came here solely on my account, that I was to have perfect rest and all the air I could get. "Your exercise depends on your strength, my dear," said he, "and your food somewhat on your appetite; but air you can absorb all the time." So we took the nursery at the top of the house.

It is a big, airy room, the whole floor nearly, with windows that look all ways, and air and sunshine galore. It was nursery first and then playroom and gymnasium, I should judge; for the windows are barred for little children, and there are rings and things in the walls.

The paint and paper look as if a boys' school had used it. It is stripped off—the paper—in great patches all around the head of my bed, about as far as I can reach, and in a great place on the other side of the room low down. I never saw a worse paper in my life.

One of those sprawling flamboyant patterns committing every artistic sin.

It is dull enough to confuse the eye in following, pronounced enough to constantly irritate and provoke study, and when you follow the lame uncertain curves for a little distance they suddenly commit suicide—plunge off at outrageous angles, destroy themselves in unheard of contradictions.

The color is repellent, almost revolting; a smouldering unclean yellow, strangely faded by the slow-turning sunlight.

It is a dull yet lurid orange in some places, a sickly sulphur tint in others.

No wonder the children hated it! I should hate it myself it I had to live in this room long.

There comes John, and I must put this away,—he hates to have me write a word.

We have been here two weeks, and I haven't felt like writing before, since that first day.

I am sitting by the window now, up in this atrocious

nursery, and there is nothing to hinder my writing as much as I please, save lack of strength.

John is away all day, and even some nights when his cases are serious.

I am glad my case is not serious!

But these nervous troubles are dreadfully depressing.

John does not know how much I really suffer. He knows there is no *reason* to suffer, and that satisfies him.

Of course it is only nervousness. It does weigh on me so not to do my duty in any way!

I meant to be such a help to John, such a real rest and comfort, and here I am a comparative burden already!

Nobody would believe what an effort it is to do what little I am able—to dress and entertain, and order things.

It is fortunate Mary is so good with the baby. Such a dear baby!

And yet I *cannot* be with him, it makes me so nervous.

I suppose John never was nervous in his life. He laughs at me so about this wallpaper!

At first he meant to repaper the room, but afterwards he said that I was letting it get the better of me, and that nothing was worse for a nervous patient than to give way to such fancies.

He said that after the wallpaper was changed it would be the heavy bedstead, and then the barred windows, and then that gate at the head of the stairs, and so on.

"You know the place is doing you good," he said, "and really, dear, I don't care to renovate the house just for a three months' rental."

"Then do let us go downstairs," I said, "there are such pretty rooms there."

Then he took me in his arms and called me a blessed little goose, and said he would go down to the cellar, if I wished, and have it whitewashed into the bargain.

But he is right enough about the beds and windows and things.

It is an airy and comfortable room as any one need wish, and, of course, I would not be so silly as to make him uncomfortable just for a whim.

I'm really getting quite fond of the big room, all but that horrid paper.

Out of one window I can see the garden, those mysterious deep-shaded arbors, the riotous old-fashioned flowers, and bushes and gnarly trees.

Out of another I get a lovely view of the bay and a little private wharf belonging to the estate. There is a beautiful shaded lane that runs down there from the house. I always fancy I see people walking in these numerous paths and arbors, but John has cautioned me not to give way to fancy in the least. He says that with my imaginative power and habit of story-making, a nervous weakness like mine is sure to lead to all manner of excited fancies, and that I ought to use my will and good sense to check the tendency. So I try.

I think sometimes that if I were only well enough to write a little it would relieve the press of ideas and rest me.

But I find I get pretty tired when I try.

It is so discouraging not to have any advice and companionship about my work. When I get really well, John says we will ask Cousin Henry and Julia down for a long visit; but he says he would as soon put fireworks in my pillowcase as to let me have those stimulating people about now.

I wish I could get well faster.

But I must not think about that. This paper looks to me as if it *knew* what a vicious influence it had!

There is a recurrent spot where the pattern lolls like a broken neck and two bulbous eyes stare at you upside down.

I get positively angry with the impertinence of it and the everlastingness. Up and down and sideways they crawl, and those absurd, unblinking eyes are everywhere. There is one place where two breadths didn't match, and the eyes go all up and down the line, one a little higher than the other.

I never saw so much expression in an inanimate thing before, and we all know how much expression they have! I used to lie awake as a child and get more entertainment and terror out of blank walls and plain furniture than most children could find in a toy-store.

I remember what a kindly wink the knobs of our big, old bureau used to have, and there was one chair that always seemed like a strong friend.

I used to feel that if any of the other things looked too fierce I could always hop into that chair and be safe.

The furniture in this room is no worse than inharmonious, however, for we had to bring it all from downstairs. I suppose when this was used as a playroom they had to take the nursery things out, and no wonder! I never saw such ravages as the children have made here.

The wallpaper, as I said before, is torn off in spots, and it sticketh closer than a brother—they must have had perseverance as well as hatred.

Then the floor is scratched and gouged and splintered, the plaster itself is dug out here and there, and this great heavy bed which is all we found in the room, looks as if it had been through the wars.

But I don't mind it a bit—only the paper.

There comes John's sister. Such a dear girl as she is, and so careful of me! I must not let her find me writing.

She is a perfect and enthusiastic housekeeper, and hopes for no better profession. I verily believe she thinks it is the writing which made me sick!

But I can write when she is out, and see her a long way off from these windows.

There is one that commands the road, a lovely shaded winding road, and one that just looks off over the country. A lovely country, too, full of great elms and velvet meadows.

This wallpaper has a kind of sub-pattern in a different shade, a particularly irritating one, for you can only see it in certain lights, and not clearly then.

But in the places where it isn't faded and where the sun is just so—I can see a strange, provoking, formless sort of figure, that seems to skulk about behind that silly and conspicuous front design.

There's sister on the stairs!

Well, the Fourth of July is over! The people are all gone and I am tired out. John thought it might do me good to see a little company, so we just had mother and Nellie and the children down for a week.

Of course I didn't do a thing. Jennie sees to everything now.

But it tired me all the same.

John says if I don't pick up faster he shall send me to Weir Mitchell in the fall.

But I don't want to go there at all. I had a friend who was in his hands once, and she says he is just like John and my brother, only more so!

Besides, it is such an undertaking to go so far.

I don't feel as if it was worth while to turn my hand over for anything, and I'm getting dreadfully fretful and querulous.

I cry at nothing, and cry most of the time.

Of course I don't when John is here, or anybody else, but when I am alone.

And I am alone a good deal just now. John is kept in town very often by serious cases, and Jennie is good and lets me alone when I want her to.

So I walk a little in the garden or down that lovely lane, sit on the porch under the roses, and lie down up here a good deal.

I'm getting really fond of the room in spite of the wallpaper. Perhaps *because* of the wallpaper.

It dwells in my mind so!

I lie here on this great immovable bed—it is nailed down, I believe—and follow that pattern about by the hour. It is as good as gymnastics, I assure you. I start, we'll say, at the bottom, down in the corner over there where it has not been touched, and I determine for the thousandth time that I *will* follow that pointless pattern to some sort of a conclusion.

I know a little of the principle of design, and I know this thing was not arranged on any laws of radiation, or alternation, or repetition, or symmetry, or anything else that I ever heard of.

It is repeated, of course, by the breadths, but not otherwise.

Looked at in one way each breadth stands alone, the bloated curves and flourishes—a kind of "debased Romanesque" with *delirium tremens*—go waddling up and down in isolated columns of fatuity.

But, on the other hand, they connect diagonally, and the sprawling outlines run off in great slanting waves of optic horror, like a lot of wallowing seaweeds in full chase.

The whole thing goes horizontally, too, at least it

seems so, and I exhaust myself in trying to distinguish the order of its going in that direction.

They have used a horizontal breadth for a frieze, and that adds wonderfully to the confusion.

There is one end of the room where it is almost intact, and there, when the crosslights fade and the low sun shines directly upon it, I can almost fancy radiation after all—the interminable grotesques seem to form around a common centre and rush off in headlong plunges of equal distraction.

It makes me tired to follow it. I will take a nap I guess.

I don't know why I should write this.

I don't want to.

I don't feel able.

And I know John would think it absurd. But I *must* say what I feel and think in some way—it is such a relief!

But the effort is getting to be greater than the relief.

Half the time now I am awfully lazy, and lie down ever so much.

John says I mustn't lose my strength, and has me take cod liver oil and lots of tonics and things, to say nothing of ale and wine and rare meat.

Dear John! He loves me very dearly, and hates to have me sick. I tried to have a real earnest reasonable talk with him the other day, and tell him how I wish he would let me go and make a visit to Cousin Henry and Julia.

But he said I wasn't able to go, nor able to stand it after I got there; and I did not make out a very good case for myself, for I was crying before I had finished.

It is getting to be a great effort for me to think straight. Just this nervous weakness I suppose.

And dear John gathered me up in his arms, and just carried me upstairs and laid me on the bed, and sat by me and read to me till it tired my head.

He said I was his darling and his comfort and all he had, and that I must take care of myself for his sake, and keep well.

He says no one but myself can help me out of it, that I must use my will and self-control and not let any silly fancies run away with me.

There's one comfort, the baby is well and happy, and

does not have to occupy this nursery with the horrid wallpaper.

If we had not used it, that blessed child would have! What a fortunate escape! Why, I wouldn't have a child of mine, an impressionable little thing, live in such a room for worlds.

I never thought of it before, but it is lucky that John kept me here after all, I can stand it so much easier than a baby, you see.

Of course I never mention it to them any more—I am too wise—but I keep watch of it all the same.

There are things in that paper that nobody knows but me, or ever will.

Behind that outside pattern the dim shapes get clearer every day.

It is always the same shape, only very numerous.

And it is like a woman stooping down and creeping about behind that pattern. I don't like it a bit. I wonder—I begin to think—I wish John would take me away from here!

It is so hard to talk with John about my case, because he is so wise, and because he loves me so.

But I tried it last night.

It was moonlight. The moon shines in all around just as the sun does.

I hate to see it sometimes, it creeps so slowly, and always comes in by one window or another.

John was asleep and I hated to waken him, so I kept still and watched the moonlight on that undulating wallpaper till I felt creepy.

The faint figure behind seemed to shake the pattern, just as if she wanted to get out.

I got up softly and went to feel and see if the paper *did* move, and when I came back John was awake.

"What is it, little girl?" he said. "Don't go walking about like that—you'll get cold."

I thought it was a good time to talk, so I told him that I really was not gaining here, and that I wished he would take me away.

"Why darling!" said he, "our lease will be up in three weeks, and I can't see how to leave before.

"The repairs are not done at home, and I cannot possibly leave town just now. Of course if you were in any danger, I could and would, but you really are better, dear, whether you can see it or not. I am a doctor, dear, and I know. You are gaining flesh and color, your appetite is better, I feel really much easier about you."

"I don't weigh a bit more," said I, "nor as much; and my appetite may be better in the evening when you are here, but it is worse in the morning when you are away!"

"Bless her little heart!" said he with a big hug, "she shall be as sick as she pleases! But now let's improve the shining hours by going to sleep, and talk about it in the morning!"

"And you won't go away?" I asked gloomily.

"Why, how can I, dear? It is only three weeks more and then we will take a nice little trip of a few days while Jennie is getting the house ready. Really, dear, you are better!"

"Better in body perhaps—" I began, and stopped short, for he sat up straight and looked at me with such a stern, reproachful look that I could not say another word.

"My darling," said he, "I beg of you, for my sake and for our child's sake, as well as for your own, that you will never for one instant let that idea enter your mind! There is nothing so dangerous, so fascinating, to a temperament like yours. It is a false and foolish fancy. Can you not trust me as a physician when I tell you so?"

So of course I said no more on that score, and we went to sleep before long. He thought I was asleep first, but I wasn't, and lay there for hours trying to decide whether that front pattern and the back pattern really did move together or separately.

On a pattern like this, by daylight, there is a lack of sequence, a defiance of law, that is a constant irritant to a normal mind.

The color is hideous enough, and unreliable enough, and infuriating enough, but the pattern is torturing.

You think you have mastered it, but just as you get well underway in following, it turns a back-somersault and there you are. It slaps you in the face, knocks you down, and tramples upon you. It is like a bad dream.

The outside pattern is a florid arabesque, reminding one of a fungus. If you can imagine a toadstool in joints, an interminable string of toadstools, budding and sprouting in endless convolutions—why, that is something like it.

That is, sometimes!

There is one marked peculiarity about this paper, a thing nobody seems to notice but myself, and that is that it changes as the light changes.

When the sun shoots in through the east window—I always watch for that first long, straight ray—it changes so quickly that I never can quite believe it.

That is why I watch it always.

By moonlight—the moon shines in all night when there is a moon—I wouldn't know it was the same paper.

At night in any kind of light, in twilight, candle light, lamplight, and worst of all by moonlight, it becomes bars! The outside pattern I mean, and the woman behind it is as plain as can be.

I didn't realize for a long time what the thing was that showed behind, that dim sub-pattern, but now I am quite sure it is a woman.

By daylight she is subdued, quiet. I fancy it is the pattern that keeps her so still. It is so puzzling. It keeps me quiet by the hour.

I lie down ever so much now. John says it is good for me, and to sleep all I can.

Indeed he started the habit by making me lie down for an hour after each meal.

It is a very bad habit I am convinced, for you see I don't sleep.

And that cultivates deceit, for I don't tell them I'm awake—O no!

The fact is I am getting a little afraid of John.

He seems very queer sometimes, and even Jennie has an inexplicable look.

It strikes me occasionally, just as a scientific hypothesis,—that perhaps it is the paper!

I have watched John when he did not know I was looking, and come into the room suddenly on the most innocent excuses, and I've caught him several times *looking at the paper!* And Jennie too. I caught Jennie with her hand on it once.

She didn't know I was in the room, and when I asked her in a quiet, a very quiet voice, with the most restrained manner possible, what she was doing with the paper—she turned around as if she had been caught stealing, and looked quite angry—asked me why I should frighten her so!

Then she said that the paper stained everything it touched, and that she had found yellow smooches on all my clothes and John's, and she wished we would be more careful!

Did not that sound innocent? But I know she was studying that pattern, and I am determined that nobody shall find it out but myself!

Life is very much more exciting now than it used to be. You see I have something more to expect, to look forward to, to watch. I really do eat better, and am more quiet than I was.

John is so pleased to see me improve! He laughed a little the other day, and said I seemed to be flourishing in spite of my wallpaper.

I turned it off with a laugh. I had no intention of telling him it was *because* of the wallpaper—he would make fun of me. He might even want to take me away.

I don't want to leave now until I have found it out. There is a week more, and I think that will be enough.

I'm feeling ever so much better! I don't sleep much at night, for it is so interesting to watch developments; but I sleep a good deal in the daytime.

In the daytime it is tiresome and perplexing.

There are always new shoots on the fungus, and new shades of yellow all over it. I cannot keep count of them, though I have tried conscientiously.

It is the strangest yellow, that wallpaper! It makes me think of all the yellow things I ever saw—not beautiful ones like buttercups, but old foul, bad yellow things.

But there is something else about that paper—the smell! I noticed it the moment we came into the room, but with so much air and sun it was not bad. Now we have had a week of fog and rain, and whether the windows are open or not, the smell is here.

It creeps all over the house.

I find it hovering in the dining-room, skulking in the

parlor, hiding in the hall, lying in wait for me on the stairs.

It gets into my hair.

Even when I go to ride, if I turn my head suddenly and surprise it—there is that smell!

Such a peculiar odor, too! I have spent hours in trying to analyze it, to find what it smelled like.

It is not bad—at first, and very gentle, but quite the subtlest, most enduring odor I ever met.

In this damp weather it is awful, I wake up in the night and find it hanging over me.

It used to disturb me at first. I thought seriously of burning the house—to reach the smell.

But now I am used to it. The only thing I can think of that it is like is the *color* of the paper! A yellow smell.

There is a very funny mark on this wall, low down, near the mopboard. A streak that runs round the room. It goes behind every piece of furniture, except the bed, a long, straight, even *smooch,* as if it had been rubbed over and over.

I wonder how it was done and who did it, and what they did it for. Round and round and round—round and round and round—it makes me dizzy!

I really have discovered something at last.

Through watching so much at night, when it changes so, I have finally found out.

The front pattern *does* move—and no wonder! The woman behind shakes it!

Sometimes I think there are a great many women behind, and sometimes only one, and she crawls around fast, and her crawling shakes it all over.

Then in the very bright spots she keeps still, and in the very shady spots she just takes hold of the bars and shakes them hard.

And she is all the time trying to climb through. But nobody could climb through that pattern—it strangles so: I think that is why it has so many heads.

They get through, and then the pattern strangles them off and turns them upside down, and makes their eyes white!

If those heads were covered or taken off it would not be half so bad.

*   *   *

I think that woman gets out in the daytime!

And I'll tell you why—privately—I've seen her!

I can see her out of every one of my windows!

It is the same woman, I know, for she is always creeping, and most women do not creep by daylight.

I see her on that long road under the tree, creeping along, and when a carriage comes she hides under the blackberry vines.

I don't blame her a bit. It must be very humiliating to be caught creeping by daylight.

I always lock the door when I creep by daylight. I can't do it at night, for I know John would suspect something at once.

And John is so queer now, that I don't want to irritate him. I wish he would take another room! Besides, I don't want anybody to get that woman out at night but myself.

I often wonder if I could see her out of all the windows at once.

But, turn as fast as I can, I can only see out of one at one time.

And though I always see her, she *may* be able to creep faster than I can turn!

I have watched her sometimes away off in the open country, creeping as fast as a cloud shadow in a high wind.

If only that top pattern could be gotten off from the under one! I mean to try it, little by little.

I have found out another funny thing, but I shan't tell it this time! It does not do to trust people too much.

There are only two more days to get this paper off, and I believe John is beginning to notice. I don't like the look in his eyes.

And I heard him ask Jennie a lot of professional questions about me. She had a very good report to give.

She said I slept a good deal in the daytime.

John knows I don't sleep very well at night, for all I'm so quiet!

He asked me all sorts of questions, too, and pretended to be very loving and kind.

As if I couldn't see through him!

Still, I don't wonder he acts so, sleeping under this paper for three months.

It only interests me, but I feel sure John and Jennie are secretly affected by it.

Hurrah! This is the last day, but it is enough. John to stay in town over night, and won't be out until this evening.

Jennie wanted to sleep with me—the sly thing! but I told her I should undoubtedly rest better for a night all alone.

That was clever, for really I wasn't alone a bit! As soon as it was moonlight and that poor thing began to crawl and shake the pattern, I got up and ran to help her.

I pulled and she shook, I shook and she pulled, and before morning we had peeled off yards of that paper.

A strip about as high as my head and half around the room.

And then when the sun came and that awful pattern began to laugh at me, I declared I would finish it to-day!

We go away to-morrow, and they are moving all my furniture down again to leave things as they were before.

Jennie looked at the wall in amazement, but I told her merrily that I did it out of pure spite at the vicious thing.

She laughed and said she wouldn't mind doing it herself, but I must not get tired.

How she betrayed herself that time!

But I am here, and no person touches this paper but me—not *alive!*

She tried to get me out of the room—it was too patent! But I said it was so quiet and empty and clean now that I believed I would lie down again and sleep all I could; and not to wake me even for dinner—I would call when I woke.

So now she is gone, and the servants are gone, and the things are gone, and there is nothing left but that great bedstead nailed down, with the canvas mattress we found on it.

We shall sleep downstairs to-night, and take the boat home to-morrow.

I quite enjoy the room, now it is bare again.

How those children did tear about here!

This bedstead is fairly gnawed!

But I must get to work.

I have locked the door and thrown the key down into the front path.

I don't want to go out, and I don't want to have anybody come in, till John comes.

I want to astonish him.

I've got a rope up here that even Jennie did not find. If that woman does get out, and tries to get away, I can tie her.

But I forgot I could not reach far without anything to stand on!

This bed will *not* move!

I tried to lift and push it until I was lame, and then I got so angry I bit off a little piece at one corner—but it hurt my teeth.

Then I peeled off all the paper I could reach standing on the floor. It sticks horribly and the pattern just enjoys it! All those strangled heads and bulbous eyes and waddling fungus growths just shriek with derision!

I am getting angry enough to do something desperate. To jump out of the window would be admirable exercise, but the bars are too strong even to try.

Besides I wouldn't do it. Of course not. I know well enough that a step like that is improper and might be misconstrued.

I don't like to *look* out of the windows even—there are so many of those creeping women, and they creep so fast.

I wonder if they all come out of that wallpaper as I did?

But I am securely fastened now by my well-hidden rope—you don't get *me* out in the road there!

I suppose I shall have to get back behind the pattern when it comes night, and that is hard!

It is so pleasant to be out in this great room and creep around as I please!

I don't want to go outside. I won't, even if Jennie asks me to.

For outside you have to creep on the ground, and everything is green instead of yellow.

But here I can creep smoothly on the floor, and my

shoulder just fits in that long smooch around the wall, so I cannot lose my way.

Why there's John at the door!

It is no use, young man, you can't open it!

How he does call and pound!

Now he's crying for an axe.

It would be a shame to break down that beautiful door!

"John dear!" said I in the gentlest voice, "the key is down by the front steps, under a plantain leaf!"

That silenced him for a few moments.

Then he said—very quietly indeed, "Open the door, my darling!"

"I can't," said I. "The key is down by the front door under a plantain leaf!"

And then I said it again, several times, very gently and slowly, and said it so often that he had to go and see, and he got it of course, and came in. He stopped short by the door.

"What is the matter?" he cried. "For God's sake, what are you doing?"

I kept on creeping just the same, but I looked at him over my shoulder.

"I've got out at last," said I, "in spite of you and Jennie. And I've pulled off most of the paper, so you can't put me back!"

Now why should that man have fainted? But he did, and right across my path by the wall, so that I had to creep over him every time!

The Night Watchman's Occurrence Book

V. S. Naipaul

November 21. 10:30 P.M. C. A. Cavander take over duty at C—Hotel all corrected. *Cesar Alwyn Cavander*

7 A.M. C. A. Cavander hand over duty to Mr. Vignales at C—Hotel no report. *Cesar Alwyn Cavander*

November 22. 10:30 P.M. C. A. Cavander take over duty at C—Hotel no report. *Cesar Alwyn Cavander*

7 A.M. C. A. Cavander hand over duty to Mr. Vignales at C—Hotel all corrected. *Cesar Alwyn Cavander*

This is the third occasion on which I have found C. A. Cavander, Night Watchman, asleep on duty. Last night, at 12:45 A.M., I found him sound asleep in a rocking chair in the hotel lounge. Night Watchman Cavander has therefore been dismissed.
Night Watchman Hillyard: This book is to be known in future as "The Night Watchman's Occurrence Book." In it I shall expect to find a detailed account of everything that happens in the hotel tonight. Be warned by the example of ex-Night Watchman Cavander. *W. A. G. Inskip, Manager.*

Mr. Manager, remarks noted. You have no worry where I am concern sir. *Charles Ethelbert Hillyard, Night Watchman*

November 23. 11 P.M. Night Watchman Hillyard take over duty at C—Hotel with one torch light 2 fridge keys

and room keys 1, 3, 6, 10 and 13. Also 25 cartoons Carib
Beer and 7 cartoons Heineken and 2 cartoons American
cigarettes. Beer cartoons intact Bar intact all corrected
no report. *Charles Ethelbert Hillyard*

7 A.M. Night Watchman Hillyard hand over duty to Mr.
Vignales at C—Hotel with one torch light 2 fridge keys
and room keys 1, 3, 6, 10 and 13. 32 cartoons beer. Bar
intact all corrected no report. *Charles Ethelbert Hillyard*

> Night Watchman Hillyard: Mr. Wills complained bit-
> terly to me this morning that last night he was denied
> entry to the bar by you. I wonder if you know exactly
> what the purpose of this hotel is. In future all hotel
> guests are to be allowed entry to the bar at whatever
> time they choose. It is your duty simply to note what
> they take. This is one reason why the hotel provides
> a certain number of beer cartons (please note the
> spelling of this word). *W. A. G. Inskip*

Mr. Manager, remarks noted. I sorry I didn't get the
chance to take some education sir. *Chas. Ethelbert
Hillyard*

November 24. 11 P.M. N. W. Hillyard take over duty with
one Torch, 1 Bar Key, 2 Fridge Keys, 23 cartoons Beer,
all intact. 12 Midnight Bar close and Barman left leaving
Mr. Wills and others in Bar, and they left at 1 A.M. Mr.
Wills took 16 Carib Beer, Mr. Wilson 8, Mr. Percy 8. At
2 A.M. Mr. Wills come back in the bar and take 4 Carib
and some bread, he cut his hand trying to cut the bread,
so please don't worry about the stains on the carpet sir.
At 6 A.M. Mr. Wills come back for some soda water. It
didn't have any so he take a ginger beer instead. Sir you
see it is my intention to do this job good sir I cant see
how Night Watchman Cavander could fall asleep on this
job sir. *Chas. Ethelbert Hillyard*

> You always seem sure of the time, and guests appear
> to be in the habit of entering the bar on the hour.
> You will kindly note the exact time. The clock from
> the kitchen is left on the window near the switches.

You can use this clock but you MUST replace it every morning before you go off duty. *W. A. G. Inskip*

Noted. *Chas. Ethelbert Hillyard*

November 25. Midnight Bar close and 12:23 A.M. Barman left leaving Mr. Wills and others in Bar. Mr. Owen take 5 bottles Carib, Mr. Wilson 6 bottles Heineken, Mr. Wills 18 Carib and they left at 2:52 A.M. Nothing unusual. Mr. Wills was helpless, I don't see how anybody could drink so much, eighteen one man alone, this work enough to turn anybody Seventh Day Adventist, and another man come in the bar, I dont know his name, I hear they call him Paul, he assist me because the others couldn't do much, and we take Mr. Wills up to his room and take off his boots and slack his other clothes and then we left. Don't know sir if they did take more while I was away, nothing was mark on the Pepsi Cola board, but they was drinking still, it look as if they come back and take some more, but with Mr. Wills I want some extra assistance sir.

Mr. Manager, the clock break I find it break when I come back from Mr. Wills room sir. It stop 3:19 sir. *Chas. E. Hillyard*

More than 2 lbs of veal were removed from the Fridge last night, and a cake that was left in the press was cut. It is your duty, Night Watchman Hillyard, to keep an eye on these things. I ought to warn you that I have also asked the Police to check on all employees leaving the hotel, to prevent such occurrences in the future. *W. A. G. Inskip*

Mr. Manager, I don't know why people so anxious to blame servants sir. About the cake, the press lock at night and I don't have the key sir, everything safe where I am concern sir. *Chas. Hillyard*

November 26. Midnight Bar close and Barman left. Mr. Wills didn't come, I hear he at the American base tonight, all quiet, nothing unusual.

Mr. Manager, I request one thing. Please inform the

Barman to let me know sir when there is a female guest
in the hotel sir. *C. E. Hillyard*

This morning I received a report from a guest that
there were screams in the hotel during the night. You
wrote All Quiet. Kindly explain in writing. *W. A. G.
Inskip* Write Explanation here:

EXPLANATION. Not long after midnight the telephone
ring and a woman ask for Mr. Jimminez. I try to tell her
where he was but she say she cant hear properly. Fifteen
minutes later she came in a car, she was looking vex and
sleepy, and I went up to call him. The door was not
lock, I went in and touch his foot and call him very soft,
and he jump up and begin to shout. When he come to
himself he said he had Night Mere, and then he come
down and went away with the woman, was not necessary
to mention.

Mr. Manager, I request you again, please inform the
Barman to let me know sir when there is a female guest
in the hotel. *C. Hillyard*

November 27. 1 A.M. Bar close, Mr. Wills and a American 19 Carib and 2:30 A.M. a Police come and ask for Mr.
Wills, he say the American report that he was robbed of
$200.00c, he was last drinking at the C—with Mr. Wills
and others. Mr. Wills and the Police ask to open the Bar
to search it, I told them I cannot open the Bar for you
like that, the Police must come with the Manager. Then
the American say it was only joke he was joking, and
they try to get the Police to laugh, but the Police looking
the way I feeling. Then laughing Mr. Wills left in a garage car as he couldn't drive himself and the American
was waiting outside and they both fall down as they was
getting in the car, and Mr. Wills saying any time you
want a overdraft you just come to my bank kiddo. The
Police left walking by himself. *C. Hillyard*

Night Watchman Hillyard: "Was not necessary to
mention!!" You are not to decide what is necessary
to mention in this night watchman's occurrence book.
Since when have you become sole owner of the hotel
as to determine what is necessary to mention? If the

guest did not mention it I would never have known that there were screams in the hotel during the night. Also will you kindly tell me who Mr. Jimminez is? And what rooms he occupied or occupies? And by what right? You have been told by me personally that the names of all hotel guests are on the slate next to the light switches. If you find Mr. Jimminez's name on this slate, or could give me some information about him, I will be most warmly obliged to you. The lady you ask about is Mrs. Roscoe, Room 12, as you very well know. It is your duty to see that guests are not pestered by unauthorized callers. You should give no information about guests to such people, and I would be glad if in future you could direct such callers straight to me. *W. A. G. Inskip*

Sir was what I ask you two times, I dont know what sort of work I take up, I always believe that nightwatchman work is a quiet work and I don't like meddling in white people business, but the gentleman occupy Room 12 also, was there that I went up to call him, I didn't think it necessary to mention because was none of my business sir. *C. E. H.*

November 28. 12 Midnight Bar close and Barman left at 12:20 A.M. leaving Mr. Wills and others, and they all left at 1:25 A.M. Mr. Wills 8 Carib, Mr. Wilson 12, Mr. Percy 8, and the man they call Paul 12. Mrs. Roscoe join the gentlemen at 12:33 A.M., four gins, everybody calling her Minnie from Trinidad, and then they start singing that song, and some others. Nothing unusual. Afterwards there were mild singing and guitar music in Room 12. A man come in and ask to use the phone at 2:17 A.M. and while he was using it about 7 men come in and wanted to beat him up, so he put down the phone and they all ran away. At 3 A.M. I notice the padlock not on the press, I look inside, no cake, but the padlock was not put on in the first place sir. Mr. Wills come down again at 6 A.M. to look for his sweet, he look in the Fridge and did not see any. He took a piece of pineapple. A plate was covered in the Fridge, but it didn't have anything in it. Mr. Wills put it out, the cat jump on it and it fall down and break. The garage bulb not burning. *C. E. H.*

You will please sign your name at the bottom of your report. You are in the habit of writing Nothing Unusual. Please take note and think before making such a statement. I want to know what is meant by nothing unusual. I gather, not from you, needless to say, that the police have fallen into the habit of visiting the hotel at night. I would be most grateful if you could find the time to note the times of these visits. *W. A. G. Inskip*

Sir, nothing unusual means everything usual. I dont know, nothing I writing you liking. I don't know what sort of work this night watchman work getting to be, since when people have to start getting Cambridge certificate to get night watchman job, I ain't educated and because of this everybody think they could insult me. *Charles Ethelbert Hillyard*

November 29. Midnight Bar close and 12:15 Barman left leaving Mr. Wills and Mrs. Roscoe and others in the Bar. Mr. Wills and Mrs. Roscoe left at 12:30 A.M. leaving Mr. Wilson and the man they call Paul, and they all left at 1:00 A.M. Twenty minutes to 2 Mr. Wills and party return and left again at 5 to 3. At 3:45 Mr. Wills return and take bread and milk and olives and cherries, he ask for nutmeg too, I said we had none, he drink 2 Carib, and left ten minutes later. He also collect Mrs. Roscoe bag. All the drinks, except the 2 Carib, was taken by the man they call Paul. I don't know sir I don't like this sort of work, you better hire a night barman. At 5:30 Mrs. Roscoe and the man they call Paul come back to the bar, they was having a quarrel, Mr. Paul saying you make me sick, Mrs. Roscoe saying I feel sick, and then she vomit all over the floor, shouting I didn't want that damned milk. I was cleaning up when Mr. Wills come down to ask for soda water, we got to lay in more soda for Mr. Wills, but I need extra assistance with Mr. Wills Paul and party sir.

The police come at 2, 3:48 and 4:52. They sit down in the bar a long time. Firearms discharge 2 times in the back yard. Detective making inquiries. I dont know sir, I thinking it would be better for me to go back to some other sort of job. At 3 I hear somebody shout Thief, and I see a man running out of the back, and Mr. London, Room 9, say he miss 80 cents and a pack of cigarettes which was on his dressing case. I don't know when the people in this place does sleep. *Chas. Ethelbert Hillyard*

Night Watchman Hillyard: A lot more than 80 cents was stolen. Several rooms were in fact entered during the night, including my own. You are employed to prevent such things occurring. Your interest in the morals of our guests seems to be distracting your attention from your duties. Save your preaching for your roadside prayer meetings. Mr. Pick, Room 7, reports that in spite of the most pressing and repeated requests, you did not awaken him at 5. He has missed his plane to British Guiana as a result. No newspapers were delivered to the rooms this morning. I am again notifying you that papers must be handed personally to Doorman Vignales. And the messenger's bicycle, which I must remind you is the property of the hotel, has been damaged. What do you *do* at nights? *W. A. G. Inskip*

Please don't ask me sir.
   Relating to the damaged bicycle: I left the bicycle the same place where I meet it, nothing took place so as to damage it. I always take care of all property sir. I don't know how you could think I have time to go out for bicycle rides. About the papers, sir, the police and them read it and leave them in such a state that I didn't think it would be nice to give them to guests. I wake up Mr. Pick, room 7, at 4:50 A.M. 5 A.M. 5:15 A.M. and 5:30. He told me to keep off, he would not get up, and one time he pelt a box of matches at me, matches scatter all over the place. I always do everything to the best of my ability sir but God is my Witness I never find a night watchman work like this, so much writing I don't have time to do anything else, I dont have four hands and six eyes and I want this extra assistance with Mr. Wills and party sir. I am a poor man and you could abuse me, but you must not abuse my religion sir because the good Lord

sees All and will have His revenge sir, I don't know
what sort of work and trouble I land myself in, all I
want is a little quiet night work and all I getting is abuse.
Chas. E. Hillyard

November 30. 12:25 A.M. Bar close and Barman left 1:00
A.M. leaving Mr. Wills and party in Bar. Mr. Wills take
12 Carib, Mr. Wilson 6, Mr. Percy 14. Mrs. Roscoe five
gins. At 1:30 A.M. Mrs. Roscoe left and there were a
little singing and mild guitar playing in Room 12. Nothing unusual. The police came at 1:35 and sit down in the
bar for a time, not drinking, not talking, not doing anything except watching. At 1:45 the man they call Paul
come in with Mr. McPherson of the SS Naparoni, they
was both falling down and laughing whenever anything
break and the man they call Paul say Fireworks about
to begin to tell Minnie Malcolm coming the ship just
dock. Mr. Wills and party scatter leaving one or two
bottles half empty and then the man they call Paul tell
me to go up to Room 12 and tell Minnie Roscoe that
Malcolm coming. I don't know how people could behave
so the thing enough to make anybody turn priest. I notice the padlock on the bar door break off it hanging on
only by a little piece of wood. And when I went up to
Room 12 and tell Mrs. Roscoe that Malcolm coming the
ship just dock the woman get sober straight away like
she dont want to hear no more guitar music and she
asking me where to hide where to go. I don't know, I
feel the day of reckoning is at hand, but she not listening
to what I saying, she busy straightening up the room one
minute packing the next, and then she run out into the
corridor and before I could stop she run straight down
the back stairs to the annexe. And then 5 past 2, still in
the corridor, I see a big red man running up to me and
he sober as a judge and he mad as a drunkard and he
asking me where she is where she is. I ask whether he
is a authorized caller, he say you don't give me any of
that crap now, where she is, where she is. So remembering about the last time and Mr. Jimminez I direct him
to the manager office in the annexe. He hear a little
scuffling inside Mr. Inskip room and I make out Mr.
Inskip sleepy voice and Mrs. Roscoe voice and the red
man run inside and all I hearing for the next five minutes

is bam bam bodow bodow bow and this woman screaming. I don't know what sort of work this night watchman getting I want something quiet like the police. In time things quiet down and the red man drag Mrs. Roscoe out of the annexe and they take a taxi, and the Police sitting down quiet in the bar. Then Mr. Percy and the others come back one by one to the bar and they talking quiet and they not drinking and they left 3 A.M. 3:15 Mr. Wills return and take one whisky and 2 Carib. He asked for pineapple or some sweet fruit but it had nothing.

6 A.M. Mr. Wills come in the bar looking for soda but it aint have none. We have to get some soda for Mr. Wills sir.

6:30 A.M. the papers come and I deliver them to Doorman Vignales at 7 A.M. *Chas. Hillyard*

Mr. Hillyard: In view of the unfortunate illness of Mr. Inskip, I am temporarily in charge of the hotel. I trust you will continue to make your nightly reports, but I would be glad if you could keep your entries as brief as possible. *Robt. Magnus, Acting Manager*

December 1. 10:30 P.M. C. E. Hillyard take over duty at C—Hotel all corrected 12 Midnight Bar close 2 A.M. Mr. Wills 2 Carib, 1 bread 6 A.M. Mr. Wills 1 soda 7 A.M. Night Watchman Hillyard hand over duty to Mr. Vignales with one torch light 2 Fridge keys and Room Keys 1, 3, 6 and 12. Bar intact all corrected no report. *C. E. H.*

Amahl and the Night Visitors

Lorrie Moore

11/30. Understand that your cat is a whore and can't
help you. She takes on love with the whiskery adjustments of a golddigger. She is a gorgeous nomad, an un-
friend. Recall how just last month when you got her
from Bob downstairs, after Bob had become suddenly
allergic, she leaped into your lap and purred, guttural as
a German chanteuse, familiar and furry as a mold. And
Bob, visibly heartbroken, still in the room, sneezing and
giving instructions, hoping for one last cat nuzzle, de-
scended to his hands and knees and jiggled his fingers
in the shag. The cat only blinked. For you, however, she
smiled, gave a fish-breath peep, and settled.

"Oh, well," said Bob, getting up off the floor. "Now
I'm just a thing of her kittenish past."

That's the way with Bob. He'll say to the cat, "You
be a good girl now, honey," and then just shrug, go back
downstairs to his apartment, play jagged, creepy jazz,
drink wine, stare out at the wintry scalp of the mountain.

12/1. Moss Watson, the man you truly love like no other,
is singing December 23 in the Owonta Opera production
of *Amahl and the Night Visitors.* He's playing Kaspar,
the partially deaf Wise Man. Wisdom, says Moss, arrives
in all forms. And you think, Yes, sometimes as a king
and sometimes as a hesitant phone call that says the
king'll be late at rehearsal don't wait up, and then when
you call back to tell him to be careful not to let the cat
out when he comes home, you discover there's been no
rehearsal there at all.

At three o'clock in the morning you hear his car in
the driveway, the thud of the front door. When he comes
into the bedroom, you see his huge height framed for a
minute in the doorway, his hair lit bright as curry. When

he stoops to take off his shoes, it is as if some small piece of his back has given way, allowing him this one slow bend. He is quiet. When he gets into bed he kisses one of your shoulders, then pulls the covers up to his chin. He knows you're awake. "I'm tired," he announces softly, to ward you off when you roll toward him. Say: "You didn't let the cat out, did you?"

He says no, but he probably should have. "You're turning into a cat mom. Cats, Trudy, are the worst sort of surrogates."

Tell him you've always wanted to run off and join the surrogates.

Tell him you love him.

Tell him you know he didn't have rehearsal tonight.

"We decided to hold rehearsal at the Montessori school, what are you now, *my* mother?"

In the dark, discern the fine hook of his nose. Smooth the hair off his forehead. Say: "I love you Moss are you having an affair with a sheep?" You saw a movie once where a man was having an affair with a sheep, and acted, with his girlfriend, the way Moss now acts with you: exhausted.

Moss's eyes close. "I'm a king, not a shepherd, remember? You're acting like my ex-wife."

His ex-wife is now an anchorwoman in Missouri.

"Are you having a regular affair? Like with a person?"

"Trudy," he sighs, turns away from you, taking more than his share of blanket. "You've got to stop this." Know you are being silly. Any second now he will turn and press against you, reassure you with kisses, tell you oh how much he loves you. "How on earth, Trudy," is what he finally says, "would I ever have the time for an affair?"

12/2. Your cat is growing, eats huge and sloppy as a racehorse. Bob named her Stardust Sweetheart, a bit much even for Bob, so you and Moss think up other names for her: Pudge, Pudgemuffin, Pooch, Poopster, Secretariat, Stephanie, Emily. Call her all of them. "She has to learn how to deal with confusion," says Moss. "And we've gotta start letting her outside."

Say: "No. She's still too little. Something could happen." Pick her up and away from Moss. Bring her into the bathroom with you. Hold her up to the mirror. Say:

"Whossat? Whossat pretty kitty?" Wonder if you could turn into Bob.

12/3. Sometimes Moss has to rehearse in the living room. King Kaspar has a large black jewelry box about which he must sing to the young, enthralled Amahl. He must open drawers and haul out beads, licorice, magic stones. The drawers, however, keep jamming when they're not supposed to. Moss finally tears off his fake beard and screams, "I can't do this shit! I can't sing about money and gewgaws. I'm the tenor of love!" Last year they'd done *La Bohème* and Moss had been Rodolfo.

This is the sort of thing he needs you for: to help him with his box. Kneel down beside him. Show him how one of the drawers is off its runner. Show him how to pull it out just so far. He smiles and thanks you in his berserk King Kaspar voice: "Oh, thank you, thank you, thank you!" He begins his aria again: " 'This is my box. This is my box. I never travel without my box.' "

All singing is, says Moss, is sculpted howling.

Say, "Bye." Wheel the TV into the kitchen. Watch MacNeil-Lehrer. Worry about Congress.

Listen to the goose-call of trains, all night, trundling by your house.

12/4. Sometimes the phone rings, but then the caller hangs up.

12/5. Your cat now sticks her paws right in the water dish while she drinks, then steps out from her short wade and licks them, washes her face with them, repeatedly, over the ears and down, like an itch. Take to observing her. On her feet the gray and pink configurations of pads and fur look like tiny baboon faces. She sees you watching, freezes, blinks at you, then busies herself again, her face in her belly, one leg up at a time, an intent ballerina in a hairy body stocking. And yet she's growing so quickly, she's clumsy. She'll walk along and suddenly her hip will fly out of whack and she'll stop and look at it, not comprehending. Or her feet will stumble, or it's difficult for her to move her new bulk along the edges of furniture, her body pushing itself out into the world before she's really ready. It puts a dent in her confidence. She looks at you inquiringly:

What is happening to me? She rubs against your ankles and bleats. You pick her up, tuck her under your chin, your teeth clenched in love, your voice cooey, gooey with maternity, you say things like, "How's my little dirt-nose, my little fuzz-face, my little honey-head?"

"Jesus, Trudy," Moss yells from the next room. "Listen to how you talk to that cat."

12/6. Though the Christmas shopping season is under way, the store you work at downtown, Owonta Flair, is not doing well. "The malls," groans Morgan, your boss. "Every Christmas the malls! We're doomed. These candy cane slippers. What am I gonna do with these?"

Tell her to put one slipper from each pair in the window along with a mammoth sign that says, MATES INSIDE. "People only see the sign. Thom McAn did it once. They got hordes."

"You're depressed," says Morgan.

12/7. You and Moss invite the principals, except Amahl, over to dinner one night before a rehearsal. You also invite Bob. Three kings, Amahl's unwed mother, you, and Bob: this way four people can tell cranky anecdotes about the production, and two people can listen.

"This really is a trashy opera," says Sonia, who plays Amahl's mother. "Sentimental as all get-out." Sonia is everything you've always wanted to be: smart, Jewish, friendly, full-haired as Easter basket grass. She speaks with a mouthful of your spinach pie. She says she likes it. When she has swallowed, a piece of spinach remains behind, wrapped like a gap around one of her front teeth. Other than that she is very beautiful. Nobody says anything about the spinach on her tooth.

Two rooms away the cat is playing with a marble in the empty bathtub. This is one of her favorite games. She bats the marble and it speeds around the porcelain like a stock car. The noise is rattley, continuous.

"What is that weird noise?" asks Sonia.

"It's the beast," says Moss. "We should put her outside, Trudy." He pours Sonia more wine, and she murmurs, "Thanks."

Jump up. Say: "I'll go take the marble away."

Behind you you can hear Bob: "She used to be mine. Her name is Stardust Sweetheart. I got allergic."

Melchior shouts after you: "Aw, leave the cat alone, Trudy. Let her have some fun." But you go into the bathroom and take the marble away anyhow. Your cat looks up at you from the tub, her head cocked to one side, sweet and puzzled as a child movie star. Then she turns and bats drips from the faucet. Scratch the scruff of her neck. Close the door when you leave. Put the marble in your pocket.

You can hear Balthazar making jokes about the opera. He calls it *Amyl and the Nitrates.*

"I've always found Menotti insipid," Melchior is saying when you return to the dining room.

"Written for NBC, what can you expect," Sonia says. Soon she is off raving about *La Bohème* and other operas. She uses words like *verismo, messa di voce,* Montserrat Caballé. She smiles. "An opera should be like contraception: about *sex, not* children."

Start clearing the plates. Tell people to keep their forks for dessert. Tell them that no matter what anyone says, you think *Amahl* is a beautiful opera and that the ending, when the mother sends her son off with the kings, always makes you cry. Moss gives you a wink. Get brave. Give your head a toss. Add: "Papa*geno,* Papa*gena*—to me, *La Bohème*'s just a lot of scarves."

There is some gulping of wine.

Only Bob looks at you and smiles. "Here. I'll help you with the plates," he says.

Moss stands and makes a diversionary announcement: "Sonia, you've got a piece of spinach on your tooth."

"Christ," she says, and her tongue tunnels beneath her lip like an elegant gopher.

12/8. Sometimes still Moss likes to take candlelight showers with you. You usually have ten minutes before the hot water runs out. Soap his back, the wide moguls of his shoulders registering in you like a hunger. Press yourself against him. Whisper: "I really do like *La Bohème,* you know."

"It's okay," Moss says, all forgiveness. He turns and grabs your buttocks.

"It's just that your friends make me nervous. Maybe

it's work, Morgan that forty-watt hysteric making me crazy." Actually you like Morgan.

Begin to hum a Dionne Warwick song, then grow self-conscious and stop. Moss doesn't like to sing in the shower. He has his operas, his church jobs, his weddings and bar mitzvahs—in the shower he is strictly off-duty. Say: "I mean, it *could* be Morgan."

Moss raises his head up under the spray, beatific, absent. His hair slicks back, like a baby's or a gangster's, dark with water, shiny as a record album. "Does Bob make you nervous?" he asks.

"Bob? Bob suffers from terminal sweetness. I like Bob."

"So do I. He's a real gem."

Say: "Yeah, he's a real chum."

"I said *gem*," says Moss. "Not *chum*." Things fall quiet. Lately you've been mishearing each other. Last night in bed you said, "Moss, I usually don't like discussing sex, but—" And he said, "I don't like disgusting sex either." And then he fell asleep, his snores scratching in the dark like zombies.

Take turns rinsing. don't tell him he's hogging the water. Ask finally, "Do you think Bob's gay?"

"Of course he's gay."

"How do you know?"

"Oh, I don't know. He hangs out at Sammy's in the mall."

"Is that a gay bar?"

"Bit of everything," Moss shrugs.

Think: Bit of everything. Just like a mall. "Have you ever been there?" Scrub vigorously between your breasts.

"A few times," says Moss, the water growing cooler.

Say: "Oh." Then turn off the faucet, step out onto the bath mat. Hand Moss a towel. "I guess because I work trying to revive our poor struggling downtown I don't get out to these places much."

"I guess not," says Moss, candle shadows wobbling on the shower curtains.

12/9. Two years ago when Moss first moved in, there was something exciting about getting up in the morning. You would rise, dress, and, knowing your lover was asleep in your bed, drive out into the early morning office and fac-

tory traffic, feeling that you possessed all things, Your
Man, like a Patsy Cline song, at home beneath your covers,
pumping blood through your day like a heart.

Now you have a morbid fascination with news shows.
You get up, dress, flick on the TV, sit in front of it with a
bowl of cereal in your lap, quietly curse all governments
everywhere, get into your car, drive to work, wonder
how the sun has the nerve to show its face, wonder why
the world seems to be picking up speed, even old ladies
pass you on the highway, why you don't have a single
erotic fantasy that Moss isn't in, whether there really are
such things as vitamins, and how would you rather die
cancer or a car accident, the man you love, at home,
asleep, like a heavy, heavy heart through your day.

"Goddamn slippers," says Morgan at work.

12/10. The cat now likes to climb into the bathtub and
stand under the dripping faucet in order to clean herself.
She lets the water bead up on her face, then wipes herself, neatly dislodging the gunk from her eyes.

"Isn't she wonderful?" you ask Moss.

"Yeah. Come here you little scumbucket," he says,
slapping the cat on the haunches, as if she were a dog.

"She's not a dog, Moss. She's a cat."

"That's right. She's a cat. Remember that, Trudy."

12/11. The phone again. The ringing and hanging up.

12/12. Moss is still getting in very late. He goes about
the business of fondling you, like someone very tired at
night having to put out the trash and bolt-lock the door.

He sleeps with his arms folded behind his head, elbows protruding, treacherous as daggers, like the enemy
chariot in *Ben-Hur*.

12/13. Buy a Christmas tree, decorations, a stand, and lug
them home to assemble for Moss. Show him your surprise.

"Why are the lights all in a clump in the back?" he
asks, closing the front door behind him.

Say: "I know. Aren't they great? Wait till you see me
do the tinsel." Place handfuls of silver icicles, matted together like alfalfa sprouts, at the end of all the branches.

"Very cute," says Moss, kissing you, then letting go.

Follow him into the bathroom. Ask how rehearsal went. He points to the kitty litter and sings: " 'This is my box. I never travel without my box.' "

Say: "You are not a well man, Moss." Play with his belt loops.

12/14. The white fur around the cat's neck is growing and looks like a stiff Jacobean collar. "A rabato," says Moss, who suddenly seems to know these things. "When are we going to let her go outside?"

"Someday when she's older." The cat has lately taken to the front window the way a hypochondriac takes to a bed. When she's there she's more interested in the cars, the burled fingers of the trees, the occasional squirrel, the train tracks like long fallen ladders, than she is in you. Call her: "Here pootchy-kootchy-honey." Ply her, bribe her with food.

12/15. There are movies in town: one about Brazil, and one about sexual abandonment in upstate New York. "What do you say, Moss. Wanna go to the movies this weekend?"

"I can't," says Moss. "You know how busy I am."

12/16. The evening news is full of death: young marines, young mothers, young children. By comparison you have already lived forever. In a kind of heaven.

12/17. Give your cat a potato and let her dribble it about soccer-style. She's getting more coordinated, conducts little dramas with the potato, pretends to have conquered it, strolls over it, then somersaults back after it again. She's not bombing around, crashing into the sideboards anymore. She's learning moves. She watches the potato by the dresser leg, stalks it, then pounces. When she gets bored she climbs up onto the sill and looks out, tail switching. Other cats have spotted her now, have started coming around at night. Though she will want to go, do not let her out the front door.

12/18. The phone rings. You say hello, and the caller hangs up. Two minutes later it rings again, only this time Moss answers it in the next room, speaks softly, cryptically, not the hearty phone voice of the Moss of yester-year. When he hangs up, wander in and say, blasé as paste, "So, who was that?"

"Stop," says Moss. "Just stop."

Ask him what's the big deal, it was Sonia wasn't it.

"Stop," says Moss. "You're being my wife. Things are repeating themselves."

Say that nothing repeats itself. Nothing, nothing, nothing. "Sonia, right?"

"Trudy, you've got to stop this. You've been listening to too much *Tosca.* I'm going out to get a hamburger. Do you want anything?"

Say: "I'm the only person in the whole world who knows you, Moss. And I don't know you at all anymore."

"That's a different opera," he says. "I'm going out to get a hamburger. Do you want anything?"

Do not cry. Stick to monosyllables. Say: "No. Fine. Go."

Say: "Please don't let the cat out."

Say: "You should wear a hat it's cold."

12/19. Actually what you've been listening to is Dionne Warwick's *Golden Hits*—musical open heart surgery enough for you. Sometimes you pick up the cat and waltz her around, her purr staticky and intermittent as a walkie-talkie.

On "Do You Know the Way to San Jose," you put her down, do an unfortunate charleston, while she attacks your stockinged feet, thinking them large rodents.

Sometimes you knock into the Christmas tree.

Sometimes you collapse into a chair and convince yourself that things are still okay.

When Robert MacNeil talks about mounting inflation, you imagine him checking into a hotel room with a life-size, blow-up doll. This is, once in a while, how you amuse yourself.

When Moss gets in at four in the morning, whisper: "There are lots of people in this world, Moss, but you can't be in love with them all."

"I'm not," he says, "in love with the mall."

12/20. The mall stores stay open late this last week before Christmas. Moss is supposed to be there, "in the gazebo next to the Santa gazebo," for an *Amahl and the Night Visitors* promotional. Decide to drive up there. Perhaps you can look around in the men's shops for a sweater for Moss, perhaps even one for Bob as well. Last year was a bad Christmas: you and Moss returned each other's gifts for cash. You want to do better this year. You want to buy: sweaters.

The mall parking lot, even at 7 P.M., is, as Moss would say, packed as a bag, though you do manage to find a space.

Inside the mall entranceway it smells of stale popcorn, dry heat, and three-day-old hobo urine. A drunk, slumped by the door, smiles and toasts you with nothing.

Say: "Cheers."

To make your journey down to the gazebos at the other end of the mall, first duck into all the single-item shops along the way. Compare prices with the prices at Owonta Flair: things are a little cheaper here. Buy stuff, mostly for Moss and the cat.

In the pet food store the cashier hands you your bagged purchase, smiles, and says, "Merry Christmas."

Say: "You, too."

In the men's sweater shop the cashier hands you your bagged purchase, smiles, and says, "Merry Christmas."

Say: "You, too."

In the belt shop the cashier hands you your bagged purchase, smiles, and says, "Come again."

Say: "You, too." Grow warm. Narrow your eyes to seeds.

In the gazebo next to the Santa gazebo there is only an older man in gray coveralls stacking some folding chairs.

Say: "Excuse me, wasn't *Amahl and the Night Visitors* supposed to be here?"

The man stops for a moment. "There's visitors," he says, pointing out and around, past the gazebo to all the shoppers. Shoppers moving slow as winter. Shoppers who haven't seen a crosswalk or a window in hours.

"I mean the opera promotional."

"The singers?" He looks at his watch. "They packed it in a while ago."

Say thank you, and wander over to Cinema 1-2-3 to
read the movie posters. It's when you turn to go that
you see Moss and Bob coming out together from the
bar by the theater. They look tired.

Adjust your packages. Walk over. Say: "Hi. I guess I
missed the promo, so I was thinking of going to a movie."

"We ended it early," says Moss. "Sonia wasn't feeling
well. Bob and I just went into Sammy's for a drink."

Look and see the sign that, of course, reads SAMMY'S.

Bob smiles and says, "Hello, Trudy." Because Bob
says *hello* and never *hi*, he always manages to sound a
little like Mister Rogers.

You can see some of Moss's makeup and glue lines.
His fake beard is sticking out from his coat pocket.
Smile. Say: "Well, Moss. Here all along I thought it was
Sonia, and it's really Bob." Chuck him under the chin.
Keep your smile steady. You are the only one smiling.
Not even Bob. You have clearly said the wrong thing.

"Fuck off, Trudy," Moss says finally, palming his hair
back off his forehead.

Bob squirms in his coat. "I believe I forgot something," he says. "I'll see you both later." And he touches
Moss's arm, turns, disappears back inside Sammy's.

"Jesus Christ, Trudy." Moss's voice suddenly booms
through the mall. You can see a few stores closing up, men
coming out to lower the metal night gates. Santa Claus has
gotten down from the gazebo and is eating an egg roll.

Moss turns from you, charges toward the exit, an
angry giant with a beard sticking out of his coat pocket.
Run after him and grab his sleeve, make him stop. Say:
"I'm sorry, Moss. What am I doing? Tell me. What am
I doing wrong?" You look up at his face, with the orange and brown lines and the glue patches, and realize:
He doesn't understand you've planned your lives together. That you have even planned your deaths together, not really deaths at all but more like a *pas de
deux*. Like Gene Kelly and Leslie Caron in *An American
in Paris,* only older.

"You just won't let people be," says Moss, each con-
sonant spit like a fish bone.

Say: "People be? I don't understand, Moss, what is
happening to us?" You want to help him, rescue him,
build houses and magnificent lawns around him.

"To *us?*"

Moss's voice is loud. He puts on his gloves. He tells you you are a child. He needs to get away. For him you have managed to reduce love, like weather, to a map and a girl, and he needs to get away from you, live someplace else for a while, and think.

The bag with the cat food slips and falls. "The opera's in three days, Moss. Where are you going to go?"

"Right now," he says, "I'm going to get a hamburger." And he storms toward the mall doors, pushes against all of them until he finds the one that's open.

Stare and mumble at the theater candy concession. "Good and Plenty. There's no Good and Plenty." Your bangs droop into your vision. You keep hearing "Jingle Bells," over and over.

In the downtown theaters of your childhood, everything was made of carved wood, and in the ladies' rooms there were framed photographs of Elizabeth Taylor and Ava Gardner. The theaters had names: The Rialto, The Paramount. There were ushers and Good and Plenty. Ushers with flashlights and bow ties. That's the difference now. No ushers. Now you have to do everything by yourself.

"Trudy," says a voice behind you. "Would you like to be accompanied to the movies?" The passive voice. It's Bob's. Turn to look at him, but as with the Good and Plenty, you don't really see, everything around you vague and blurry as glop in your eye.

Say: "Sure. Why not."

In Cinema 3, sit in seats close to the aisle. Listen to the Muzak. The air smells like airplane air.

"It's a strange thing about Moss," Bob is saying, looking straight ahead. "He's so busy with the opera, it pushes him up against certain things. He ends up feeling restless and smothered. But, Trudy, Moss is a good man. He really is."

Don't say anything, and then say, finally, "Moss who?"

Stare at the curtain with the rose-tinted lights on it. Try to concentrate on more important matters, things like acid rain.

Bob taps his fingers on the metal arm of the seat. Say: "Look, Bob. I'm no idiot. I was born in New York City.

I lived there until I was four. Come on. Tell me: Who's Moss sleeping with?"

"As far as I know," says Bob, sure and serious as a tested hypothesis, "Moss isn't sleeping with anyone."

Continue staring at the rose lights. Then say in a loud contralto: "He's sleeping with *me*, Bob. That's who he's sleeping with."

When the lights dim and the curtains part, there arrive little cigarette lighters on the screen telling you not to smoke. Then there are coming attractions. Bob leans toward you, says, "These previews are horrible."

Say: "Yeah. Nothing Coming Soon."

There are so many previews you forget what movie you've come to see. When the feature presentation comes on, it takes you by surprise. The images melt together like a headache. The movie seems to be about a woman whose lover, losing interest in her, has begun to do inexplicable things like yell about the cat, and throw scenes in shopping malls.

"What is this movie about?"

"Brazil," whispers Bob.

The audience has begun to laugh at something someone is doing; you are tense with comic exile. Whisper: "Bob, I'm gonna go. Wanna go?"

"Yes, in fact, I do," says Bob.

It's ten-thirty and cold. The small stores are finally closed. In the parking lot, cars are leaving. Say to Bob: "God, look how many people shop here." The whole world suddenly seems to you like a downtown dying slow.

Spot your car and begin to head toward it. Bob catches your sleeve. "My car's the other way. Listen. Trudy. About Moss: No matter what's going on with him, no matter what he decides he has to do, the man loves you. I know he does."

Gently pull your sleeve away. Take a step sideways toward your car. Headlights, everywhere headlights and tires crunching. Say: "Bob, you're a sweet person. But you're sentimental as all get-out." Turn on the nail of your boot and walk.

At home the cat refuses to dance to Dionne Warwick with you. She sits on the sill of the window, rumbling in her throat, her tail a pendulum of fluff. Outside, undoubtedly, there are suitors, begging her not to be so coldhearted. "Ya got friends out there?" When you turn off the stereo, she jumps down from the sill and snakes lovingly about your ankles. Say something you never thought you'd say. Say: "Wanna go out?" She looks at you, all hope and supplication, and follows you to the door, carefully watching your hand as it moves for the knob: she wants you to let her go, to let her go and be. Begin slowly, turn, pull. The suction of door and frame gives way, and the cold night insinuates itself like a kind of future. She doesn't leave immediately. But her whole body is electrified, surveying the yard for eyes and rustles, and just to the left of the streetlight she suddenly spots them—four, five, phosphorescent glints—and, without a nudge, without ever looking back, she scurries out, off the porch, down after, into some sweet unknown, some somehow known unknown, some new yet very old religion.

12/21. Every adoration is seasonal as Christmas.

Moss stops by to get some things. He's staying with Balthazar for a few days, then after the opera and Christmas and all, he'll look for an efficiency somewhere.

Nod. "Efficiency. Great. That's what hell is: efficient." You want to ask him if this is all some silly opera where he's leaving in order to spare you his tragic, bluish death by consumption.

He says, "It's just something I've got to do." He opens cupboards in the kitchen, closets in the hallway, pulls down boxes, cups, boots. He is slow about it, doesn't do it in a mean way, you are grateful for that.

"What have you been doing tonight?" he asks, not looking, but his voice is urgent as a touch.

"I watched two hours of MacNeil-Lehrer. You can get it on channel seven and then later on channel four."

"Right," says Moss. "I know."

Pause. Then say: "Last night I let the cat out. Finally." Moss looks at you and smiles.

Smile back and shrug, as if all the world were a comedy you were only just now appreciating. Moss begins to put a hand to your shoulder but then takes it back. "Congratulations, Trudy," he murmurs.

"But she hasn't come back yet. I haven't seen her since last night."

"She'll come back," says Moss. "It's only been a day."

"But it's been a whole day. Maybe I should put in ads."

"It's only been one day. She'll come back. You'll see."

Step away from him. Outside, in front of the street-light, something like snow is falling. Think back again to MacNeil-Lehrer. Say in a level tone: "You know, there are people who know more about it than we do, who say that there is no circumnavigating a nuclear war, we will certainly have one, it's just a matter of time. And when it happens, it's going to dissolve all our communications systems, melt silicon chips—"

"Trudy, please." He wants you to stop. He knows this edge in your voice, this MacNeil-Lehrer edge. All of the world knotted and failing on your tongue.

"And then if you're off living someplace else, in some efficiency, how will I be able to get in touch with you? There I'll be, Moss, all alone in my pink pom-pom slippers, the entire planet exploding all around, and I won't be able to talk to you, to say—" In fifth grade you learned the first words ever spoken on the telephone: *Mr. Watson, come here, I want you.* And suddenly, as you look at him, at the potatoey fists of his cheeks, at his broom-blonde hair, it hits you as it would a child: Someday, like everybody, this man you truly love like no other is going to die. No matter how much you love him, you cannot save him. No matter how much you love: nothing, no one, lasts.

"Moss, we're not safe."

And though there's no flutter of walls, or heave of the floor, above the frayed-as-panic rug, shoes move, and Moss seems to come unstuck, to float toward you, his features beginning to slide in downward diagonals, some chip in his back dissolving, allowing him to bend. His arms reach out to bring you close to his chest. The buttons of his shirt poke against you, and his chin hooks, locks around your neck. When he is gone, the world will grow dull as Mars.

"It's okay," he whispers, his lips moving against your hair. Things grow fuzzy around the edge like a less than brilliant lie. "It's okay," says Moss.

SUBJECTIVE NARRATION

The following stories are all told by one of the characters after the conclusion of the events, and the speakers are not talking to themselves, some particular listener, or "dear diary" but rather to a nebulous, more remote audience starting to resemble the general public. The first two of these stories indicate the particular time and place of their utterance—like monologues, letters, and diaries—whereas the others are vague about how removed in time and space the speaker may be from the conclusion of the events.

These stories all create in common an impression of subjectivity in the sense that the narrators seem unreliable, try to get us on their side, or assume values or views we don't share. Of course all stories are somewhat subjective; any storyteller is, after all, mortal and fallible—even authors themselves, as we all should have realized before deconstructionists undertook to point out biases of epoch, gender, and heritage. To question someone else's perspective is to expose our own to challenge. We can try to distinguish between a narrator who does not seem to be aware of his or her biases or assumptions, and is therefore telling a different story from the one he or she intends, and a narrator who consciously makes biases so obvious that we consider them merely personal flavor. In the end, however, all we can do is test the speaker's perspective against our own. This is exactly what these stories force us to do even though, in form, they resemble conventional first-person narrations we are accustomed to trust. None of the signs of monologues, letters, and diaries are here to alert us. Only differences between our value system and that of the narrator will signal to us that the story is "subjective." And readers may differ on this among themselves.

Only modern authors deliberately create narrations meant to stand alone uncorrected that are also meant to seem incomplete, immature, prejudiced, or self-serving. However winning or sensible, Huck Finn and Holden Caulfield of J. D. Salinger's Catcher in the Rye are meant to show themselves at times naive or immature, unaware or inexperienced, even when their values may appear superior to the society's.

In this respect, it is no doubt significant that the narrators of all but one of the following stories are adolescent. They behave and speak in ways that characterize a stage of growth more than a fixed personality. Such is not true of the adult narrator of the last story! But all use a vernacular rather than literary language and freely reveal their personal traits, often unwittingly, to a degree that usually distinguishes amateur from professional storytellers, character from author.

The Somebody
Danny Santiago

This is Chato talking, Chato de Shamrock, from the East Side of old L.A., and I want you to know this is a big day in my life because today I quit school and went to work as a writer. I write on fences or buildings or anything that comes along. I write *my* name, not the one I got from my father. I want no part of him. I write my gang name, Chato, which means Catface, because I have a flat nose like a cat. It's a Mexican word because that's what I am, a Mexican, and I'm not ashamed of it. I like that language too, man. It's way better than English to say what you mean. But German is the best, man. It's got a real rugged sound, and I'm going to learn to talk it someday.

After Chato I write "de Shamrock." That's the street where I live, and it's the name of the gang I belong to, but the others are all gone now. Their families had to move away, except Gorilla is in jail and Blackie joined the Navy because he liked swimming. But I still have our old arsenal. It's buried under the chickens, and I dig it up when I get bored. There's tire irons and chains and pick handles with spikes and two zip guns we made out of wood and they shoot real bullets but not very straight. In the good old days nobody cared to tangle with us. But now I'm the only one left.

Well, today started off like any other day. The toilet roars like a hot rod taking off. My father coughs and spits about nineteen times and hollers it's six thirty. So I holler back I'm quitting school. Things hit me like that—sudden.

"Don't you want to be a lawyer no more," he says in Spanish, "and defend the Mexican people?"

My father thinks he is very funny, and next time I get

an idea what I'm going to do in the world, he's sure not
going to know about it.

"Don't you want to be a doctor," he says, "and cut
off my leg for nothing someday when I ask you?"

"Due beast ine dumb cop," I tell him in German, but
not very loud.

"How will you support me," he says, "when I retire?
Or will you marry a rich old woman that owns a pool
hall?"

"I'm quitting this dump! You'll never see me again!"

I hollered it at him, but already he was in the kitchen
making a big noise in his coffee. I could be dead and he
wouldn't take me serious. So I laid there and waited for
him to go off to work. When I woke up again, it was
way past eleven. I can sleep forever these days. So I got
out of bed and put on my cleanest jeans and my denim
jacket and combed myself very careful because already
I had a feeling this was going to be a big day for me.

I had to wait for breakfast because the baby was sick
and throwing up milk on everything. There is always a
baby vomiting in my house. When they're born, everybody comes over and says: *"Qué* cute!" but nobody
passes any comments on the dirty way babies act or the
dirty way they were made either. Sometimes my mother
asks me to hold one for her but it always cries, maybe
because I squeeze it a little hard when nobody's looking.

When my mother finally served me, I had to hold my
breath, she smelled so bad of babies. I don't like to look
at her any more. Her legs got those dark-blue rivers
running all over them. I kept waiting for her to bawl me
out about not going to school, but I guess she forgot, or
something. So I said good-by and cut out.

Every time I go out my front door I have to cry for
what they've done to old Shamrock Street. It used to be
so fine, man, with solid homes on both sides and with
back yards too. Then that trucking company bought all
the land except my father's place and a couple of others.
They came in with their wrecking bars and their bulldoz-
ers. You could hear those homes scream when they
ripped them apart. So now Shamrock Street is just front
walks that lead to a hole in the ground, and piles of
busted cement. And Pelón's house and Blackie's and
Egghead's are just stacks of old boards waiting to get

hauled away. I hope that never happens to your street, man.

My first stop was the front gate and there was that sign again, a big *S* wrapped around a cross like a snake with rays coming out, which is the mark of the Sierra Street gang, as everybody knows. I rubbed it off, but tonight they'll come and put it back again. In the old days they wouldn't dare to come on our street, but without your gang you're nobody. And one of these fine days they're going to catch up with me in person and that will be the end of Chato de Shamrock.

So I cruised on down to Main Street like a ghost in a graveyard. Just to prove I'm alive, I wrote my name on the parking-lot fence at the corner. A lot of names you see in public places are written very sloppy. Not me. I take my time. Like my fifth-grade teacher used to say, if other people are going to see your work, you owe it to yourself to do it right. She was real nice. She walked me home one time when some guys were after me. I think she wanted to adopt me but she never said anything about it. I owe a lot to that lady, and especially my writing. You should see it, man—it's real smooth and mellow, and curvy like a girl in a bathing suit. Everybody says so. Except one time they had me in Juvenile by mistake and some doctor looked at it. He said it proved I had something wrong with me, some long word. That doctor was crazy, because I made him show me his writing and it was real ugly, man, like a barbed-wire fence with little chickens stuck on the points and all flopping their wings.

Anyway, I signed myself very clean and neat on that corner. And then I thought, Why not look for a job someplace? But I was more in the mood to write my name, so I went into the dime store and helped myself to two boxes of crayons and some chalk and cruised on down Main, writing all the way. I wondered should I write more than my name. Should I write, "Chato is a fine guy," or "Chato is wanted by the police"? Things like that. News. But I decided against it. Better to keep them guessing. Then I crossed over to Forney Playground. It used to be our territory, but now the Sierra have taken over there like everyplace else. Just to show them, I wrote on the tennis court and the swimming pool and the gym. I left a fine little trail of Chato de Shamrock in eight colors. Some places I used chalk, which works better on brick or plaster. But crayons are the thing for cement or anything smooth, like in the girls' rest room. On that wall I also drew a little picture the girls would be interested in and put down a phone number beside it. I bet a lot of them are going to call that number, but it isn't mine because we don't have a phone in the first place, and in the second place I'm probably never going home again.

I'm telling you, I was pretty famous at the Forney by the time I cut out, and from there I continued my travels till something hit me. You know how you put your name on something and that proves it belongs to you? Things like schoolbooks or gym shoes? So I thought, How about that, now? And I put my name on the Triple A Market and on Morrie's Liquor Store and on the Zócalo, which is a beer joint. And then I cruised on up Broadway, getting rich. I took over a barber shop and a furniture store and the Plymouth agency. And the firehouse for laughs, and the phone company so I could call all my girlfriends and keep my dimes. And then there I was at Webster and Garcia's Funeral Home with the big white columns. At first I thought that might be bad luck, but then I said, Oh, well, we all got to die sometime. So I signed myself, and now I can eat good and live in style and have a big time all my life and then kiss you all good-by and give myself the best damn funeral in L.A. for free.

And speaking of funerals, along came the Sierra right then, eight or ten of them down the street with that stupid walk which is their trade-mark. I ducked into the garage and hid behind the hearse. Not that I'm a coward. Getting beat up doesn't bother me. What I hate is those blades, man. They're like a piece of ice cutting into your belly. But the Sierra didn't see me and went on by. I couldn't hear what they were saying but I knew they had me on their mind. So I ducked into the Boys' Club, where they don't let anybody get you, no matter who you are. To pass the time I shot some baskets and played a little pool and watched the television, but the story was boring, so it came to me, Why not write my name on the screen? Which I did with one of those squeaky pens. The cowboys sure looked fine with Chato de Shamrock written all over them. Everybody got a kick out of it. But of course up comes Mr. Calderon and makes me wipe it off. They're always spying on you up there. And he takes me into his office and closes the door.

"Well," he says, "and how is the last of the dinosaurs?"

"What's that?" I ask him.

He shows me their picture in a book, giant lizards and real ugly, man, worse than octopus, but they're all dead now, and he explains he called me that because of the Shamrocks. Then he goes into that voice with the church music in it and I look out of the window.

"I know it's hard to lose your gang, Chato," he says, "but this is your chance to make new friends and straighten yourself out. Why don't you start coming to Boys' Club more?"

"It's boring here," I tell him.

"What about school?"

"I can't go," I said. "They'll get me."

"Who?"

"Who do you think?"

"The Sierra's forgotten you're alive," he tells me.

"Then how come they put their mark on my house every night?"

"Do they?"

He stares at me very hard. I hate those eyes of his. He thinks he knows everything. And what is he? Just a Mexican like everybody else.

"Maybe you put that mark there yourself," he says. "To make yourself big. Just like you wrote on the television."

"That was my name! I like to write my name!"

"So do dogs," he says. "On every lamppost they come to."

"You're a dog yourself," I told him, but I don't think he heard me. He just went on talking. Brother, how they love to talk up there! But I didn't bother to listen, and when he ran out of gas I left. From now on I'm scratching that Boys' Club off my list.

                          *   *   *

   Out on the street it was getting nice and dark, but I
could still follow my trail back toward Broadway. It felt
good seeing Chato written everyplace, but at the Zócalo
I stopped dead. Around my name there was a big red
heart done in lipstick with some initials I didn't recognize. To tell the truth, I didn't know how to feel. In one
way I was mad that anyone would fool with my name,
especially if it was some guy doing it for laughs. But
what guy carries lipstick? And if it was a girl, that could
be kind of exciting.
   A girl is what it turned out to be. I caught up with
her at the telephone company. There she is, standing in
the shadows, drawing her heart around my name. And
she has a very pretty shape on her, too. I sneak up behind her very quiet, thinking all kinds of crazy things
and my blood shooting around so fast it shakes me all
over. And then she turns around and it's only Crusader
Rabbit. That's what we called her in the third grade after
a television show they had then, on account of her teeth.
And she couldn't shed the name clear into high school.
   When she sees me, she takes off down the alley, but
in twenty feet I catch her. I grab for the lipstick, but she
whips it behind her. I reach around and try to pull her
fingers open, but her hand is sweaty and so is mine. And
there we are, stuck together all the way down. I can feel
everything she's got and her breath is on my cheek. She
twists up against me, kind of giggling. To tell the truth,
I don't like to wrestle with girls. They don't fight fair.
And then we lost balance and fell against some garbage
cans, so I woke up. After that I got the lipstick away
from her very easy.
   "What right you got to my name?" I tell her. "I never
gave you permission."
   "You sign yourself real fine," she says.
   I know that already.
   "Let's go writing together," she says.
   "The Sierra's after me."
   "I don't care," she says. "Come on, Chato—you and
me can have a lot of fun."
   She came up close and giggled that way. She put her
hand on my hand that had the lipstick in it. And you
know what? I'm ashamed to say I almost told her yes.

It would be a change to go writing with a girl. We could talk there in the dark. We could decide on the best places. And her handwriting wasn't too bad either. But then I remembered I had my reputation to think of. Somebody would be sure to see us, and they'd be laughing at me all over the East Side. So I pulled my hand away and told her off.

"Run along, Crusader," I told her. "I don't want no partners, and especially not you."

"Who are you calling Crusader?" she screamed. "You ugly, squash-nose runt."

She called me everything. And spit at my face but missed. I didn't argue. I just cut out. And when I got to the first sewer I threw away her lipstick. Then I drifted over to the banks at Broadway and Bailey, which is a good spot for writing because a lot of people pass by there.

I don't like to brag, but it was the best work I've ever done in all my life. Under the street lamp my name shone like pure gold. I stood to one side and checked the people as they walked past and inspected it. With some you can't tell just how they feel, but with others it rings out like a cash register. There was one man. He got out of his Cadillac to buy a paper and when he saw my name he smiled. He was the age to be my father. I bet he'd give me a job if I asked him. I bet he'd take me to his home and to his office in the morning. Pretty soon I'd be sitting at my own desk and signing my name on letters and checks and things. But I would never buy a Cadillac, man. They burn too much gas.

Later a girl came by. She was around eighteen, I think, with green eyes. Her face was so pretty I didn't dare to look at her shape. Do you want me to go crazy? That girl stopped and really studied my name like she fell in love with it. She wanted to know me, I could tell. She wanted to take my hand and we'd go off together just holding hands and nothing dirty. We'd go to Beverly Hills and nobody would look at us the wrong way. I almost said, "Hello" to that girl, and, "How do you like my writing?" But not quite.

So here I am, standing on this corner with my chalk all gone and only one crayon left and it's ugly brown.

My fingers are too cold besides. But I don't care because I just had a vision, man. Did they ever turn on the lights for you so you could see the whole world and everything in it? That's how it came to me right now. I don't need to be a movie star or a boxing champion to make my name in the world. All I need is plenty of chalk and crayons. And that's easy. L.A. is a big city, man, but give me a couple of months and I'll be famous all over town. Of course they'll try to stop me—the Sierra, the police and everybody. But I'll be like a ghost, man. I'll be real mysterious, and all they'll know is just my name, signed like I always sign it, with lights shooting out like from the Holy Cross.

My Side of the Matter

Truman Capote

I know what is being said about me and you can take my side or theirs, that's your own business. It's my word against Eunice's and Olivia-Ann's, and it should be plain enough to anyone with two good eyes which one of us has their wits about them. I just want the citizens of the U.S.A. to know the facts, that's all.

The facts: On Sunday, August 12, this year of our Lord, Eunice tried to kill me with her papa's Civil War sword and Olivia-Ann cut up all over the place with a fourteen-inch hog knife. This is not even to mention lots of other things.

It began six months ago when I married Marge. That was the first thing I did wrong. We were married in Mobile after an acquaintance of only four days. We were both sixteen and she was visiting my cousin Georgia. Now that I've had plenty of time to think it over, I can't for the life of me figure how I fell for the likes of her. She has no looks, no body, and no brains whatsoever. But Marge is a natural blonde and maybe that's the answer. Well, we were married going on three months when Marge ups and gets pregnant; the second thing I did wrong. Then she starts hollering that she's got to go home to Mama—only she hasn't got no mama, just these two aunts, Eunice and Olivia-Ann. So she makes me quit my perfectly swell position clerking at the Cash'n' Carry and move here to Admiral's Mill which is nothing but a damn gap in the road any way you care to consider it.

The day Marge and I got off the train at the L&N depot it was raining cats and dogs and do you think anyone came to meet us? I'd shelled out forty-one cents for a telegram, too! Here my wife's pregnant and we have to tramp seven miles in a downpour. It was bad on

189

Marge as I couldn't carry hardly any of our stuff on account of I have terrible trouble with my back. When I first caught sight of this house I must say I was impressed. It's big and yellow and has real columns out in front and japonica trees, both red and white, lining the yard.

Eunice and Olivia-Ann had seen us coming and were waiting in the hall. I swear I wish you could get a look at these two. Honest, you'd die! Eunice is this big old fat thing with a behind that must weigh a tenth of a ton. She troops around the house, rain or shine, in this real old-fashioned nighty, calls it a kimono, but it isn't anything in this world but a dirty flannel nighty. Futhermore she chews tobacco and tries to pretend so ladylike, spitting on the sly. She keeps gabbing about what a fine education she had, which is her way of attempting to make me feel bad, although, personally, it never bothers me so much as one whit as I know for a fact she can't even read the funnies without she spells out every single, solitary word. You've got to hand her one thing, though—she can add and subtract money so fast that there's no doubt but what she could be up in Washington, D.C., working where they make the stuff. Not that she hasn't got plenty of money! Naturally she says she hasn't but I know she has because one day, accidentally, I happened to find close to a thousand dollars hidden in a flower pot on the side porch. I didn't touch one cent, only Eunice says I stole a hundred-dollar bill which is a venomous lie from start to finish. Of course anything Eunice says is an order from headquarters as not a breathing soul in Admiral's Mill can stand up and say he doesn't owe her money and if she said Charlie Carson (a blind, ninety-year-old invalid who hasn't taken a step since 1896) threw her on her back and raped her everybody in this county would swear the same on a stack of Bibles.

Now Olivia-Ann is worse, and that's the truth! Only she's not so bad on the nerves as Eunice, for she is a natural-born half-wit and ought really to be kept in somebody's attic. She's real pale and skinny and has a mustache. She squats around most the time whittling on a stick with her fourteen-inch hog knife, otherwise she's up to some devilment, like what she did to Mrs. Harry

Steller Smith. I swore not ever to tell anyone that, but when a vicious attempt has been made on a person's life, I say the hell with promises.

Mrs. Harry Steller Smith was Eunice's canary named after a woman from Pensacola who makes homemade cure-all that Eunice takes for the gout. One day I heard this terrible racket in the parlor and upon investigating, what did I find but Olivia-Ann shooing Mrs. Harry Steller Smith out an open window with a broom and the door to the bird cage wide. If I hadn't walked in at exactly that moment she might never have been caught. She got scared that I would tell Eunice and blurted out the whole thing, said it wasn't fair to keep one of God's creatures locked up that way, besides which she couldn't stand Mrs. Harry Steller Smith's singing. Well, I felt kind of sorry for her and she gave me two dollars, so I helped her cook up a story for Eunice. Of course I wouldn't have taken the money except I thought it would ease her conscience.

The very *first* words Eunice said when I stepped inside this house were, "So this is what you ran off behind our backs and married, Marge?"

Marge says, "Isn't he the best-looking thing, Aunt Eunice?"

Eunice eyes me u-p and d-o-w-n and says, "Tell him to turn around."

While my back is turned, Eunice says, "You sure must've picked the runt of the litter. Why, this isn't any sort of man at all."

I've never been so taken back in my life! True, I'm slightly stocky, but then I haven't got my full growth yet.

"He is too," says Marge.

Olivia-Ann, who's been standing there with her mouth so wide the flies could buzz in and out, says, "You heard what Sister said. He's not any sort of a man whatsoever. The very idea of this little runt running around claiming to be a man! Why, he isn't even of the male sex!"

Marge says, "You seem to forget, Aunt Olivia-Ann, that this is my husband, the father of my unborn child."

Eunice made a nasty sound like only she can and said, "Well, all I can say is I most certainly wouldn't be bragging about it."

Isn't that a nice welcome? And after I gave up my perfectly swell position clerking at the Cash'n' Carry.

But it's not a drop in the bucket to what came later that same evening. After Bluebell cleared away the supper dishes, Marge asked, just as nice as she could, if we could borrow the car and drive over to the picture show at Phoenix City.

"You must be clear out of your head," says Eunice, and, honest, you'd think we'd asked for the kimono off her back.

"You must be clear out of your head," says Olivia-Ann.

"It's six o'clock," says Eunice, "and if you think I'd let that runt drive my just-as-good-as-brand-new 1934 Chevrolet as far as the privy and back you must've gone clear out of your head."

Naturally such language makes Marge cry.

"Never you mind, honey," I said, "I've driven pulenty of Cadillacs in my time."

"Humf," says Eunice.

"Yeah," says I.

Eunice says, "If he's ever so much as driven a plow I'll eat a dozen gophers fried in turpentine."

"I won't have you refer to my husband in any such manner," says Marge. "You're acting simply outlandish! Why, you'd think I'd picked up some absolutely strange man in some absolutely strange place."

"If the shoe fits, wear it!" says Eunice.

"Don't think you can pull the sheep over our eyes," says Olivia-Ann in that braying voice of hers so much like the mating call of a jackass you can't rightly tell the difference.

"We weren't born just around the corner, you know," says Eunice.

Marge says, "I'll give you to understand that I'm legally wed till death do us part to this man by a certified justice of the peace as of three and one-half months ago. Ask anybody. Futhermore, Aunt Eunice, he is free, white and sixteen. Futhermore, George Far Sylvester does not appreciate hearing his father referred to in any such manner."

George Far Sylvester is the name we've planned for the baby. Has a strong sound, don't you think? Only the way things stand I have positively no feelings in the matter now whatsoever.

"How can a girl have a baby with a girl?" says Olivia-Ann, which was a calculated attack on my manhood. "I do declare there's something new every day."

"Oh, shush up," says Eunice. "Let us hear no more about the picture show in Phoenix City."

Marge sobs. "Oh-h-h, but it's Judy Garland."

"Never mind, honey," I said, "I most likely saw the show in Mobile ten years ago."

"That's a deliberate falsehood," shouts Olivia-Ann. "Oh, you are a scoundrel, you are. Judy hasn't been in the pictures ten years." Olivia-Ann's never seen not even one picture show in her entire fifty-two years (she won't tell anybody how old she is but I dropped a card to the capitol in Montgomery and they were very nice about answering), but she subscribes to eight movie books. According to Postmistress Delancey it's the only mail she ever gets outside of the Sears & Roebuck. She has this positively morbid crush on Gary Cooper and has one trunk and two suitcases full of his photos.

So we got up from the table and Eunice lumbers over to the window and looks out to the chinaberry tree and says, "Birds settling in their roost—time we went to bed. You have your old room, Marge, and I've fixed a cot for this gentleman on the back porch."

It took a solid minute for that to sink in.

I said, "And what, if I'm not too bold to ask, is the objection to my sleeping with my lawful wife?"

Then they both started yelling at me.

So Marge threw a conniption fit right then and there. "Stop it, stop it, stop it! I can't stand any more. Go on, babydoll—go on and sleep wherever they say. Tomorrow we'll see. . . ."

Eunice says, "I swanee if the child hasn't got a grain of sense, after all."

"Poor dear," says Olivia-Ann, wrapping her arm around Marge's waist and herding her off, "poor dear, so young, so innocent. Let's us just go and have a good cry on Olivia-Ann's shoulder."

May, June, and July and the best part of August I've squatted and sweltered on that damn back porch without an ounce of screening. And Marge—she hasn't opened her mouth in protest, not once! This part of Alabama is swampy, with mosquitoes that could murder a buffalo, given half a chance, not to mention dangerous flying roaches and a posse of local rats big enough to haul a wagon train from here to Timbucktoo. Oh, if it wasn't for that little unborn George I would've been making dust tracks on the road, way before now. I mean to say I haven't had five seconds alone with Marge since that first night. One or the other is always chaperoning and last week they like to have blown their tops when Marge locked herself in her room and they couldn't find me nowhere. The truth is I'd been down watching the niggers bale cotton but just for spite I let on to Eunice like Marge and I'd been up to no good. After that they added Bluebell to the shift.

And all this time I haven't even had cigarette change.

Eunice has hounded me day in and day out about getting a job. "Why don't the little heathen go out and get some honest work?" says she. As you've probably noticed, she never speaks to me directly, though more often than not I am the only one in her royal presence. "If he was any sort of man you could call a man he'd be trying to put a crust of bread in that girl's mouth instead of stuffing his own off my vittles." I think you should know that I've been living almost exclusively on cold yams and leftover grits for three months and thirteen days and I've been down to consult Dr. A. N. Carter twice. He's not exactly sure whether I have the scurvy or not.

And as for my not working, I'd like to know what a man of my abilities, a man who held a perfectly swell position with the Cash'n' Carry would find to do in a flea-bag like Admiral's Mill? There is all of one store here and Mr. Tubberville, the proprietor, is actually so lazy it's painful for him to have to sell anything. Then we have the Morning Star Baptist Church but they already have a preacher, an awful old turd named Shell whom Eunice drug over one day to see about the salvation of my soul. I heard him with my own ears tell her I was too far gone.

But it's what Eunice has done to Marge that really takes the cake. She has turned that girl against me in the most villainous fashion that words could not describe. Why, she even reached the point where she was sassing me back, but I provided her with a couple of good slaps and put a stop to that. No wife of mine is ever going to be disrespectful to me, not on your life!

The enemy lines are stretched tight: Bluebell, Olivia-Ann, Eunice, Marge, and the whole rest of Admiral's Mill (pop, 342). Allies: none. Such was the situation as of Sunday, August 12, when the attempt was made upon my very life.

Yesterday was quiet and hot enough to melt rock. The trouble began at exactly two o'clock. I know because Eunice has one of those fool cuckoo contraptions and it scares the daylights out of me. I was minding my own personal business in the parlor, composing a song on the upright piano which Eunice bought for Olivia-Ann and hired her a teacher to come all the way from Columbus, Georgia, once a week. Postmistress Delancey, who was my friend till she decided that it was maybe not so wise, says that the fancy teacher tore out of this house one afternoon like old Adolf Hitler was on his tail and leaped in his Ford coupé, never to be heard from again. Like I say, I'm trying to keep cool in the parlor not bothering a living soul when Olivia-Ann trots in with her hair all twisted up in curlers and shrieks, "Cease that infernal racket this very instant! Can't you give a body a minute's rest? And get off my piano right smart. It's not your piano, it's my piano and if you don't get off it right smart I'll have you in court like a shot the first Monday in September."

She's not anything in this world but jealous on account of I'm a natural-born musician and the songs I make up out of my own head are absolutely marvelous.

"And just look what you've done to my genuine ivory keys, Mr. Sylvester," says she, trotting over to the piano, "torn nearly every one of them right off at roots for purentee meanness, that's what you've done."

She knows good and well that the piano was ready for the junk heap the moment I entered this house.

I said, "Seeing as you're such a know-it-all, Miss Olivia-Ann, maybe it would interest you to know that I'm in the possession of a few interesting tales myself. A few things that maybe other people would be very grateful to know. Like what happened to Mrs. Harry Steller Smith, as for instance."

Remember Mrs. Harry Steller Smith?

She paused and looked at the empty bird cage. "You gave me your oath," says she and turned the most terrifying shade of purple.

"Maybe I did and again maybe I didn't," says I. "You did an evil thing when you betrayed Eunice that way but if some people will leave other people alone then maybe I can overlook it."

Well, sir, she walked out of there just as *nice* and *quiet* as you please. So I went and stretched out on the sofa which is the most horrible piece of furniture I've ever seen and is part of a matched set Eunice bought in Atlanta in 1912 and paid two thousand dollars for, cash— or so she claims. This set is black and olive plush and smells like wet chicken feathers on a damp day. There is a big table in one corner of the parlor which supports two pictures of Miss E and O-A's mama and papa. Papa is kind of handsome but just between you and me I'm convinced he has black blood in him from somewhere. He was a captain in the Civil War and that is one thing I'll never forget on account of his sword which is displayed over the mantel and figures prominently in the action yet to come. Mama has that hang-dog, half-wit look like Olivia-Ann, though I must say Mama carries it better.

So I had just about dozed off when I heard Eunice bellowing, "Where is he? Where is he?" And the next thing I know she's framed in the doorway with her hands planted plump on those hippo hips and the whole pack scrunched up behind her: Bluebell, Olivia-Ann and Marge.

Several seconds passed with Eunice tapping her big old bare foot just as fast and furious as she could and fanning her fat face with this cardboard picture of Niagara Falls.

"Where is it?" says she. "Where's my hundred dollars that he made away with while my trusting back was turned?"

"This is the straw that broke the camel's back," says I, but I was too hot and tired to get up.

"That's not the only back that's going to be broke,"

says she, her bug eyes about to pop clear out of their sockets. "That was my funeral money and I want it back. Wouldn't you know he'd steal from the dead?"

"Maybe he didn't take it," says Marge.

"You keep your mouth out of this, missy," says Olivia-Ann.

"He stole my money sure as shooting," says Eunice. "Why, look at his eyes—black with guilt!"

I yawned and said, "Like they say in the courts—if the party of the first part falsely accuses the party of the second part then the party of the first part can be locked away in jail even if the State Home is where they rightfully belong for the protection of all concerned."

"God will punish him," says Eunice.

"Oh, Sister," says Olivia-Ann, "let us not wait for God."

Whereupon Eunice advances on me with this most peculiar look, her dirty flannel nighty jerking along the floor. And Olivia-Ann leeches after her and Bluebell lets forth this moan that must have been heard clear to Eufala and back while Marge stands there wringing her hands and whimpering.

"Oh-h-h," sobs Marge, "please give her back that money, babydoll."

I said, "Et tu Brute?" which is from William Shakespeare.

"Look at the likes of him," says Eunice, "lying around all day not doing so much as licking a postage stamp."

"Pitiful," clucks Olivia-Ann.

"You'd think he was having a baby instead of that poor child." Eunice speaking.

Bluebell tosses in her two cents, "Ain't it the truth?"

"Well, if it isn't the old pots calling the kettle black," says I.

"After loafing here for three months does this runt have the audacity to cast aspersions in my direction?" says Eunice.

I merely flicked a bit of ash from my sleeve and not the least bit fazed, said, "Dr. A. N. Carter has informed me that I am in a dangerous scurvy condition and can't stand the least excitement whatsoever—otherwise I'm liable to foam at the mouth and bite somebody."

Then Bluebell says, "Why don't he go back to that

trash in Mobile, Miss Eunice? I'se sick and tired of carryin' his ol' slop jar."

Naturally that coal-black nigger made me so mad I couldn't see straight.

So just as calm as a cucumber I arose and picked up this umbrella off the hat tree and rapped her across the head with it until it cracked smack in two.

"My real Japanese silk parasol!" shrieks Olivia-Ann.

Marge cries, "You've killed Bluebell, you've killed poor old Bluebell!"

Eunice shoves Olivia-Ann and says, "He's gone clear out of his head, Sister! Run! Run and get Mr. Tubberville!"

"I don't like Mr. Tubberville," says Olivia-Ann staunchly. "I'll go get my hog knife." And she makes a dash for the door but seeing as I care nothing for death I brought her down with a sort of tackle. It wrenched my back something terrible.

"He's going to kill her!" hollers Eunice loud enough to bring the house down. "He's going to murder us all! I warned you, Marge. Quick, child, get Papa's sword!"

So Marge gets Papa's sword and hands it to Eunice. Talk about wifely devotion! And, if that's not bad enough, Olivia-Ann gives me this terrific knee punch and I had to let go. The next thing you know we hear her out in the yard bellowing hymns.

*Mine eyes have seen the glory of the
        coming of the Lord;
He is trampling out the vintage where
        the grapes of wrath are stored....*

Meanwhile Eunice is sashaying all over the place wildly thrashing Papa's sword and somehow I've managed to clamber atop the piano. Then Eunice climbs up on the piano stool and how that rickety contraption survived a monster like her I'll never be the one to tell.

"Come down from there, you yellow coward, before I run you through," says she and takes a whack and I've got a half-inch cut to prove it.

By this time Bluebell has recovered and skittered away to join Olivia-Ann holding services in the front yard. I guess they were expecting my body and God knows it would've been theirs if Marge hadn't passed out cold.

That's the only good thing I've got to say for Marge.

What happened after that I can't rightly remember except for Olivia-Ann reappearing with her fourteen-inch hog knife and a bunch of the neighbors. But suddenly Marge was the star attraction and I suppose they carried her to her room. Anyway, as soon as they left I barricaded the parlor door.

I've got all those black and olive plush chairs pushed against it and that big mahogany table that must weigh a couple of tons and the hat tree and lots of other stuff. I've locked the windows and pulled down the shades. Also I've found a five-pound box of Sweet Love candy and this very minute I'm munching a juicy, creamy, chocolate cherry. Sometimes they come to the door and knock and yell and plead. Oh, yes, they've started singing a song of a very different color. But as for me—I give them a tune on the piano every now and then just to let them know I'm cheerful.

My Sister's Marriage

Cynthia Marshall Rich

When my mother died she left just Olive and me to take care of Father. Yesterday when I burned the package of Olive's letters that left only me. I know that you'll side with my sister in all of this because you're only outsiders, and strangers can afford to sympathize with young love, and with whatever sounds daring and romantic, without thinking what it does to all the other people involved. I don't want you to hate my sister—I don't hate her—but I do want you to see that we're happier this way, Father and I, and as for Olive, she made her choice.

But if you weren't strangers, all of you, I wouldn't be able to tell you about this. "Keep yourself to yourself," my father has always said. "If you ever have worries, Sarah Ann, you come to me and don't go sharing your problems around town." And that's what I've always done. So if I knew you I certainly wouldn't ever tell you about Olive throwing the hairbrush, or about finding the letters buried in the back of the drawer.

I don't know what made Olive the way she is. We grew up together like twins—there were people who thought we were—and every morning before we went to school she plaited my hair and I plaited hers before the same mirror, in the same little twist of ribbons and braids behind our heads. We wore the same dresses and there was never a strain on the hem or a rip in our stockings to say to a stranger that we had lost our mother. And although we have never been well-to-do—my father is a doctor and his patients often can't pay—I know that there are people here in Conkling today who think we're rich, just because of little things like candlelight at dinner and my father's cigarette holder and the piano lessons that Olive and I had and the reproduction of *The Anatomy Lesson* that hangs above the mantelpiece instead of botanical prints. "You don't have to be rich to be a gentleman," my father says, "or to live like one."

My father is a gentleman and he raised Olive and myself as ladies. I can hear you laughing, because people like to make fun of words like "gentleman" and "lady," but they are words with ideals and standards behind them, and I hope that I will always hold to those ideals as my father taught me to. If Olive has renounced them, at least we did all we could.

Perhaps the reason that I can't understand Olive is that I have never been in love. I know that if I had ever fallen in love it would not have been, like Olive, at first sight but only after a long acquaintance. My father knew my mother for seven years before he proposed—it is much the safest way. Nowadays people make fun of that too, and the magazines are full of stories about people meeting in the moonlight and marrying the next morning, but if you read those stories you know that they are not the sort of people you would want to be like.

Even today Olive couldn't deny that we had a happy childhood. She used to be very proud of being the lady of the house, of sitting across the candlelight from my father at dinner like a little wife. Sometimes my father would hold his carving knife poised above the roast to stand smiling at her and say: "Olive, every day you remind me more of your mother."

I think that although she liked the smile, she minded the compliment, because she didn't like to hear about Mother. Once when my father spoke of her she said: "Papa, you're missing Mother again. I can't bear it when you miss Mother. Don't I take care of you all right? Don't I make things happy for you?" It wasn't that she hadn't loved Mother but that she wanted my father to be completely happy.

To tell the truth, it was Olive Father loved best. There was a time when I couldn't have said that, it would have hurt me too much. Taking care of our father was like playing a long game of "let's pretend," and when little girls play family nobody wants to be the children. I thought it wasn't fair, just because Olive was three years older, that she should always be the mother. I wanted to sit opposite my father at dinner and have him smile at me like that.

I was glad when Olive first began walking out with young men in the summer evenings. Then I would make lemonade for my father ("Is it as good as Olive's?") and we would sit out on the screened porch together watching the fireflies. I asked him about the patients he had seen that day, trying to think of questions as intelligent as Olive's. I knew that he was missing her and frowning into the long twilight for the swing of her white skirts. When she came up the steps he said, "I missed my housewife tonight," just as though I hadn't made the lemonade right after all. She knew, too, that it wasn't the same for him in the evenings without her and for a while, instead of going out, she brought the young men to the house. But soon she stopped even that ("I never realized how silly and shallow they were until I saw them with Papa," she said. "I was ashamed to have him talk to them"). I know that he was glad, and when my turn came I didn't want to go out because I hated leaving them alone together. It all seems a very long time ago. I used to hate it when Olive "mothered" me. Now I feel a little like Olive's mother, and she is like my rebellious child.

In spite of everything, I loved Olive When we were children we used to play together. The other children disliked us because we talked like grown-ups and didn't like to get dirty, but we were happy playing by ourselves on the front lawn where my father, if he were home, could watch us from his study window. So it wasn't surprising that when we grew older we were still best friends. I loved Olive and I see now how she took advantage of that love. Sometimes I think she felt that if she was to betray my father she wanted me to betray him too.

I still believe that it all began, not really with Mr. Dixon, but with the foreign stamps. She didn't see many of them, those years after high school when she was working in the post office, because not very many people in Conkling have friends abroad, but the ones she saw— and even the postmarks from Chicago or California— made her dream. She told her dreams to Father, and of course he understood and said that perhaps some summer we could take a trip to New England as far as Boston. My father hasn't lived in Conkling all of his life. He went to Harvard, and that is one reason he is different from the other men here. He is a scholar and not bound to provincial ideas. People here respect him and come to him for advice.

Olive wasn't satisfied and she began to rebel. Even she admitted that there wasn't anything for her to rebel against. She told me about it, sitting on the window sill in her long white nightgown, braiding and unbraiding the hair that she had never cut.

"It's not, don't you see, that I don't love Father. And it certainly isn't that I'm not happy here. But what I mean is, how can I ever know whether or not I'm really happy here unless I go somewhere else? When you graduate from school you'll feel the same way. You'll want—you'll want to know."

"I like it here," I said from the darkness of the room, but she didn't hear me.

"You know what I'm going to do, Sarah Ann? Do you know what I'm going to do? I'm going to save some money and go on a little trip—it wouldn't have to be expensive, I could go by bus—and I'll just see things, and then maybe I'll know."

"Father promised he'd take us to New England."

"No," said Olive, "no, you don't understand. Anyhow, I'll save the money."

And still she wasn't satisfied. She began to read. Olive and I always did well in school, and our names were called out for Special Recognition on Class Day. Miss Singleton wanted Olive to go to drama school after she played the part of Miranda in *The Tempest*, but my father talked to her, and when he told her what an actress' life is like she realized it wasn't what she wanted. Aside from books for school, though, we never read very much. We didn't need to because my father has read everything you've heard of, and people in town have said that talking to him about anything is better than reading three books.

Still, Olive decided to read. She would choose a book from my father's library and go into the kitchen, where the air was still heavy and hot from dinner, and sit on the very edge of the tall, hard three-legged stool. She had an idea that if she sat in a comfortable chair in the parlor she would not be attentive or would skip the difficult passages. So she would sit like that for hours, under the hard light of the unshaded bulb that hangs from the ceiling, until her arms ached from holding the book.

"What do you want to find out about?" my father would ask.

"Nothing," Olive said. "I'm just reading."

My father hates evasion.

"Now, Olive, nobody reads without a purpose. If you're interested in something, maybe I can help you. I might even know something about it myself."

When she came into our bedroom she threw the book on the quilt and said: "Why does he have to pry, Sarah Ann? It's so simple—just wanting to read a book. Why does he have to make a fuss about it as though I were trying to hide something from him?"

That was the first time that I felt a little like Olive's mother.

"But he's only taking an interest," I said. "He just wants us to share things with him. Lots of fathers wouldn't even care. You don't know how lucky we are."

"You don't understand, Sarah Ann. You're too young to understand."

"Of course I understand," I said shortly. "Only I've outgrown feeling like that."

It was true. When I was a little girl I wrote something on a piece of paper, something that didn't matter much, but it mattered to me because it was a private thought. My father came into my room and saw me shove the paper under the blotter, and he wanted me to show it to him. So I quickly said, "No, it's private, I wrote it to myself, I didn't write it to be seen," but he said he wanted to see it. And I said, "No, no, no, it was silly anyway," and he said, "Sarah Ann, nothing you have to say would seem silly to me, you never give me credit for understanding, I can understand a great deal," but I said it wasn't just him, really it wasn't, because I hadn't written it for anyone at all to see. Then he was all sad and hurt and said this wasn't a family where we keep things hidden and there I was hiding this from him. I heard his voice, and it went on and on and he said I had no faith in him and that I shouldn't keep things from him—and I said it wasn't anything big or special, it was just some silly nonsense, but if it was nonsense, he said, why wouldn't I let him read it, since it would make him happy? And I cried and cried, because it was only a very little piece of paper and why did he have to see it anyway, but he was very solemn and said if you held back little things soon you would be holding back bigger things and the gap would grow wider and wider. So I gave him the paper. He read it and said nothing except that I was a good girl and he couldn't see what all the fuss had been about.

Of course now I know that he was only taking an interest and I shouldn't have minded that. But I was a little girl then and minded dreadfully, and that is why I understood how Olive felt, although she was grown-up then and should have known better.

She must have understood that she was being childish, because when my father came in a few minutes later and said, "Olive, you're our little mother. We mustn't quarrel. There should be only love between us," she rose and kissed him. She told him about the book she had been reading, and he said: "Well, as it happens, I do know something about that." They sat for a long time discussing the book, and I think he loved Olive better than ever. The next evening, instead of shutting herself in the bright, hot kitchen, Olive sat with us in the cool of the parlor until bedtime, hemming a slip. And it was just as always.

But I suppose that these things really had made a difference in Olive. For we had always been alike, and I cannot imagine allowing a perfect stranger to ask me personal questions before we had even been introduced. She told me about it afterward, how he had bought a book of three-cent stamps and stayed to chat through the half-open grilled window. Suddenly he said, quite seriously: "Why do you wear your hair like that?"

"Pardon me?" said Olive.

"Why do you wear your hair like that? You ought to shake it loose around your shoulders. It must be yards long."

That is when I would have remembered—if I had forgotten—that I was a lady. I would have closed the grill, not rudely but just firmly enough to show my displeasure, and gone back to my desk. Olive told me she thought of doing that but she looked at him and knew, she said, that he didn't mean to be impolite, that he really wanted to know.

And instead she said: "I only wear it down at night."

That afternoon he walked her home from the post office.

Olive told me everything long before my father knew anything. It was the beginning of an unwholesome deceit in her. And it was nearly a week later that she told even me. By that time he was meeting her every afternoon and they took long walks together, as far as Merton's Pond, before she came home to set the dinner table.

"Only don't tell Father," she said.

"Why not?"

"I think I'm afraid of him. I don't know why. I'm afraid of what he might say."

"He won't say anything," I said. "Unless there's something wrong. And if there's something wrong, wouldn't you want to know?"

Of course, I should have told Father myself right away. But that was how she played upon my love for her.

"I'm telling you," she said, "because I want so much to share it with you. I'm so happy, Sarah Ann, and I feel so free, don't you see? We've always been so close—I've been closer to you than to Father, I think—or at least differently." She had to qualify it, you see, because it wasn't true. But it still made me happy and I promised not to tell, and I was even glad for her because, as I've told you, I've always loved Olive.

I saw them together one day when I was coming home from school. They were walking together in the rain, holding hands like school children, and when Olive saw me from a distance she dropped his hand suddenly and then just as suddenly took it again.

"Hullo!" he said when she introduced us. "She does look like you!"

I want to be fair and honest with you—it is Olive's

dishonesty that still shocks me—and so I will say that I liked Mr. Dixon that day. But I thought even then how different he was from my father, and that should have warned me. He was a big man with a square face and sun-bleached hair. I could see a glimpse of his bright, speckled tie under his tan raincoat, and his laugh sounded warm and easy in the rain. I liked him, I suppose, for the very things I should have distrusted in him. I liked his ease and the way that he accepted me immediately, spontaneously and freely, without waiting—waiting for whatever people wait for when they hold themselves back (as I should have done) to find out more about you. I could almost understand what had made Olive, after five minutes, tell him how she wore her hair at night.

I am glad at least, that I begged Olive to tell my father about him. I couldn't understand why at first she refused. I think now that she was afraid of seeing them together, that she was afraid of seeing the difference. I have told you that my father is a gentleman. Even now you must be able to tell what sort of man Mr. Dixon was. My father knew at once, without even meeting him.

The weeks had passed and Olive told me that Mr. Dixon's business was completed but that his vacation was coming and he planned to spend it in Conkling. She said she would tell my father.

We were sitting on the porch after dinner. The evening had just begun to thicken and some children had wandered down the road, playing a game of pirates at the very edge of our lawn. One of them had a long paper sword and the others were waving tall sticks, and they were screaming. My father had to raise his voice to be heard.

"So this man whom you have been seeing behind my back is a traveling salesman for Miracle-wear soles."

"Surrender in the name of the King!"

"I am more than surprised at you, Olive. That hardly sounds like the kind of man you would want to be associated with."

"Why not?" said Olive. "Why not?"

"It's notorious, my dear. Men like that have no respect for a girl. They'll flatter her with slick words but

it doesn't mean anything. Just take my word for it, dear.
It may seem hard, but I know the world."

"Fight to the death! Fight to the death!"

"I can't hear you, my dear. Sarah Ann, ask the children to play their games somewhere else."

I went down the steps and across the lawn.

"Doctor Landis is trying to rest after a long day," I
explained. They nodded and vanished down the dusky
road, brandishing their silent swords.

"I am saying nothing of the extraordinary manner of
your meeting, not even of the deceitful way in which he
has carried on this—friendship."

It was dark on the porch. I switched on the yellow
overhead light, and the three of us blinked for a moment, rediscovering each other as the shadows leaped
back.

"The cheapness of it is so apparent it amazes me that
even in your innocence of the world—"

My father was fitting a cigarette into its black holder.
He turned it slowly to and fro until it was firm before
he struck a match and lit it. It is beautiful to watch him
do even the most trivial things. He is always in control of
himself and he never makes a useless gesture or thinks a
useless thought. If you met him you might believe at
first that he was totally relaxed, but because I have lived
with him so long I know that there is at all times a
tension controlling his body; you can feel it when you
touch his hand. Tension, I think, is the wrong word. It
is rather a self-awareness, as though not a muscle contracted without his conscious knowledge.

"You know it very well yourself, Olive. Could anything but shame have kept you from bringing this man
to your home?"

His voice is like the way he moves. It is clear and
considered and each word exists by itself. However common it may be, when he speaks it, it has become his, it
has dignity because he has chosen it.

"Father, all I ask is that you'll have him here—that
you will meet him. Surely that's not too much to ask
before you—judge him."

Olive sat on the step at my father's feet. Her hands
had been moving across her skirt, smoothing the folds
over her knees, but when she spoke she clasped them

tightly in her lap. She was trying to speak as he spoke, in that calm, certain voice, but it was a poor imitation.

"I'm afraid that it is too much to ask, Olive. I have seen too many of his kind to take any interest in seeing another."

"I think you should see him, Father." She spoke very softly. "I think I am in love with him."

"Olive!" I said. I had known it all along, of course, but when she spoke it, in that voice trying so childishly to sound sure, I knew its absurdity. How could she say it after Father had made it so clear? As soon as he had repeated after her, "A salesman for Miracle-wear soles," even the inflections of his voice showed me that it was ludicrous; I realized what I had known all along, the cheapness of it all for Olive—for Olive with her ideals.

I looked across at my father but he had not stirred. The moths brushed their wings against the light bulb. He flicked a long gray ash.

"Don't use that word lightly, Olive," he said. "That is a sacred word. Love is the word for what I felt for your mother—what I hope you feel for me and for your sister. You mustn't confuse it with innocent infatuation."

"But I do love him—how can you know? How can you know anything about it? I do love him." Her voice was shrill and not pleasant.

"Olive," said my father. "I must ask you not to use that word."

She sat looking up at his face and from his chair he looked back at her. Then she rose and went into the house. He did not follow her, even with his eyes. We sat for a long time before I went over to him and took his hand. I think he had forgotten me. He started and said nothing, and his hand did not acknowledge mine. I would rather he had slapped me. I left him and went into the house.

In our bedroom Olive was sitting before the dressing table in her nightgown, brushing her hair. You mustn't think I don't love her, that I didn't love her then. As I say, we were like twins, and when I saw her reflection in the tall, gilded mirror I might have been seeing my own eyes filled with tears. I tell you, I wanted to put my arms around her, but you must see that it was for her own sake that I didn't. She had done wrong, she had deceived my father and she had made me deceive him. It would have been wicked to give her sympathy then.

"It's hard, of course, Olive," I said gently. "But you know that Father's right."

She didn't answer. She brushed her hair in long strokes and it rose on the air. She did not turn even when the doorknob rattled and my father stood in the doorway and quietly spoke her name.

"Olive," he repeated. "Of course I must ask you not to see this—this man again."

Olive turned suddenly with her dark hair whirling about her head. She hurled the silver hairbrush at my father, and in that single moment when it leaped from her hand I felt an elation I have never known before. Then I heard it clatter to the floor a few feet from where he stood, and I knew that he was unhurt and that it was I, and not Olive, who had for that single moment meant it to strike him. I longed to throw my arms about him and beg his forgiveness.

He went over and picked up the brush and gave it to Olive. Then he left the room.

"How could you, Olive?" I whispered.

She sat with the brush in her hand. Her hair had fallen about her face and her eyes were dark and bright. The next morning at breakfast she did not speak to my father and he did not speak to her, although he sat looking at her so intensely that if I had been Olive I would have blushed. I thought, He loves her more now, this morning, than when he used to smile and say she was like Mother. I remember thinking, Why couldn't he love me like that? I would never hurt him.

Just before she left for work he went over to her and brushed her arm lightly with his hand.

"We'll talk it all over tonight, Olive," he said. "I know you will understand that this is best."

She looked down at his hand as though it were a strange animal and shook her head and hurried down the porch steps.

That night she called from a little town outside of Richmond to say that she was married. I stood behind my father in the shadowy little hallway as he spoke to her. I could hear her voice, higher-pitched than usual over the static of the wires, and I heard her say that they would come, that very evening, if he would see them.

I almost thought he hadn't understood her, his voice was so calm.

"I suppose you want my blessings. I cannot give them to deceit and cowardice. You will have to find them elsewhere if you can, my dear. If you can."

After he had replaced the receiver he still stood before the mouthpiece, talking into it.

"That she would give up all she has had—that she would stoop to a—for a—physical attraction—"

Then he turned to me. His eyes were dark.

"Why are you crying?" he said suddenly. "What are you crying for? She's made her choice. Am I crying? Do you think I would want to see her—now? If she—when she comes to see what she has done—but it's not a question of forgiveness. Even then it wouldn't be the same. She has made her choice."

He stood looking at me and I thought at first that what he saw was distasteful to him, but his voice was gentle when he spoke.

"Would you have done this to me, Sarah Ann? Would you have done it?"

"No," I said, and I was almost joyful, knowing it was true. "Oh, no."

That was a year ago. We never speak of Olive any more. At first letters used to come from her, long letters from New York and then from Chicago. Always she asked me about Father and whether he would read a letter if she wrote one. I wrote her long letters back and said that I would talk to him. But he wasn't well—even now he has to stay in bed for days at a time—and I knew that he didn't want to hear her name.

One morning he came into my room while I was writing to her. He saw me thrust the package of letters into a cubby-hole and I knew I had betrayed him again.

"Don't ally yourself with deception, Sarah Ann," he said quietly. "You did that once and you see what came of it."

"But if she writes to me—" I said. "What do you want me to do?"

He stood in the doorway in his long bathrobe. He had

been in bed and his hair was slightly awry from the pillows and his face was a little pale. I have taken good care of him and he still looks young—not more than forty—but his cheekbones worry me. They are sharp and white.

"I want you to give me her letters," he said. "To burn."

"Won't you read them, Father? I know that what she did was wrong, but she sounds happy—"

I don't know what made me say that except that, you see, I did love Olive.

He stared at me and came into the room.

"And you believe her? Do you think that happiness can come from deception?"

"But she's my sister," I said, and although I knew that he was right I began to cry. "And she's your daughter. And you love her so."

He came and stood beside my chair. This time he didn't ask me why I was crying.

He kneeled suddenly beside me and spoke very softly and quickly.

"We'll keep each other company, Sarah Ann, just the two of us. We can be happy that way, can't we? We'll always have each other, don't you know?" He put his hand on my hair.

I knew then that was the way it should be. I leaned my head on his shoulder, and when I had finished crying I smiled at him and gave him Olive's letters.

"You take them," I said. "I can't—"

He nodded and took them and then took my hand.

I know that when he took them he meant to burn them. I found them by chance yesterday in the back of his desk drawer, under a pile of old medical reports. They lay there like love letters from someone who had died or moved away. They were tied in a slim green hair ribbon—it was one of mine, but I suppose he had found it and thought it was Olive's.

I didn't wonder what to do. It wasn't fair, don't you see? He hadn't any right to keep those letters after he told me I was the only daughter he had left. He would always be secretly reading them and fingering them, and it wouldn't do him any good. I took them to the incinerator in the back yard and burned them carefully, one by one. His bed is by the window and I know that he was watching me, but of course he couldn't say anything.

Maybe you feel sorry for Father, maybe you think I was cruel. But I did it for his sake and I don't care what you think because you're all of you strangers, anyway, and you can't understand that there couldn't be two of us. As I said before, I don't hate Olive. But sometimes I think this is the way it was meant to be. First Mother died and left just the two of us to take care of Father. And yesterday when I burned Olive's letters I thought, Now there is only me.

Why, You Reckon?

Langston Hughes

Well, sir, I ain't never been mixed up in nothin'
wrong before nor since, and I don't intend to be
again, but I was hongry that night. Indeed, I was! Depression times before the war plants opened up and
money got to circulating again and that Second World
War had busted out.

I was goin' down a Hundred Thirty-third Street in
the snow when another colored fellow that looks hongry
sidetracks me and says, "Say buddy, you wanta make a
little jack?"

"Sure," I says. "How?"

"Stickin' up a guy," he says. "The first white guy what
comes out o' one o' these speakeasies and looks like
bucks, we gonna grab him!"

"Oh, no," says I.

"Oh yes, we will," says this other guy. "Man, ain't
you hongry? Didn't I see you down there at the charities
today, not gettin' nothin'—like me? You didn't get a
thing, did you? Hell, no! Well, you gotta take what you
want, that's all, reach out and *take* it," he says. "Even
if you are starvin', don't starve like a fool. You must be
in love with white folks or somethin'. Else scared. Do
you think they care anything about you?"

"No," I says.

"They sure don't," he says. "These here rich folks
comes up to Harlem spendin' forty or fifty bucks in the
night clubs and speakeasies and don't care nothin' 'bout
you and me out here in the street, do they? Huh? Well,
one of 'em's gonna give up some money tonight before
he gets home."

"What about the cops?"

"To hell with the cops!" said the other guy. "Now,
listen, now. I live right here, sleep on the ash pile back

of the furnace down in this basement. Don't nobody never come down there after dark. They let me stay here for keepin' the furnace goin' at night. Now, you grab this here guy we pick out, push him down to the basement door, right here, I'll pull him in, we'll drag him on back yonder to the furnace room and rob him, money, watch, clothes, and all. Then push him out in the rear court. If he hollers—and he sure will holler when that cold air hits him—folks'll just think he's some drunken white man. But by that time we'll be long gone. What do you say, boy?"

Well, sir, I'm tellin' you, I was so tired and hongry and cold that night I didn't hardly know what to say, so I said all right, and we decided to do it. Looked like to me 'bout that time a Hundred Thirty-third Street was just workin' with people, taxis cruisin', white folks from downtown lookin' for hot spots.

It were just midnight.

This guy's front basement door was right near the door of the Dixie Bar where that woman sings the kind of blues ofays is crazy about.

Well, sir! Just what we wanted to happen happened right off. A big party of white folks in furs and things come down the street. They musta parked their car on Lenox, 'cause they wasn't in no taxi! They was walkin' in the snow. And just when they got right by us, one o' them white women says, "Ed-*ward*," she said, "oh, darlin', don't you know I left my purse and cigarettes and compact in the car. Please go and ask the chauffeur to give 'em to you." And they went on in the Dixie. The boy started toward Lenox again.

Well, sir, Edward never did get back no more that evenin' to the Dixie Bar. No, pal, uh-hum! 'Cause we nabbed him. When he come back down the street in his evenin' clothes and all, with a swell black overcoat on that I wished I had, just a-tippin' so as not to slip up and fall on the snow, I grabbed him. Before he could say Jack Robinson, I pulled him down the steps to the basement door, the other fellow jerked him in, and by the time he knew where he was, we had that white boy back yonder behind the furnace in the coalbin.

"Don't you holler," I said on the way down.

There wasn't much light back there, just the raw gas

comin' out of a jet, kind of blue-like, blinkin' in the coal dust. Took a few minutes before we could see what he looked like.

"Ed-*ward*," the other fellow said, "don't you holler in this coalbin."

But Edward didn't holler. He just sat down on the coal. I reckon he was scared weak-like.

"Don't you throw no coal, neither," the other fellow said. But Edward didn't look like he was gonna throw coal.

"What do you want?" he asked by and by in a nice white-folks kind of voice. "Am I kidnaped?"

Well, sir, we never thought of kidnapin'. I reckon we both looked puzzled. I could see the other guy thinkin' maybe we *ought* to hold him for ransom. Then he musta decided that that weren't wise, 'cause he says to this white boy, "No, you ain't kidnaped," he says. "We ain't got no time for that. We's hongry right *now*, so, buddy, gimme your money."

The white boy handed out of his coat pocket amongst other things a lady's pretty white beaded bag that he'd been sent after. My partner held it up.

"Doggone," he said, "my gal could go for this. She likes purty things. Stand up and lemme see what else you got."

The white guy got up and the other fellow went through his pockets. He took out a wallet and a gold watch and a cigarette lighter, and he got a swell key ring and some other little things colored folks never use.

"Thank you," said the other guy when he got through friskin' the white boy, "I guess I'll eat tomorrow! And smoke right now," he said, opening up the white boy's cigarette case. "Have one," and he passed them swell fags around to me and the white boy, too. "What kind is these?" he wanted to know.

"Benson's Hedges," said the white boy, kinder scared-like, 'cause the other fellow was makin' an awful face over the cigarette.

"Well, I don't like 'em," the other fellow said, frownin' up. "Why don't you smoke decent cigarettes? Where do you get off, anyhow?" he said to the white boy standin' there in the coalbin. "Where do you get off comin' up here to Harlem with these kind of cigarettes?

Don't you know no colored folks smoke these kind of cigarettes? And what're you doin' bringin' a lot of purty rich women up here wearin' white fur coats? Don't you know it's more'n we colored folks can do to get a black fur coat, let alone a white one? I'm askin' you a question," the other fellow said.

The poor white fellow looked like he was gonna cry. "Don't you know," the colored fellow went on, "that I been walkin' up and down Lenox Avenue for three or four months tryin' to find some way to earn money to get my shoes half-soled? Here, look at 'em." He held up the palms of his feet for the white boy to see. There were sure big holes in his shoes. "Looka here!" he said to that white boy. "Still you got the nerve to come up here to Harlem all dressed up in a tuxedo suit with a stiff shirt on and diamonds shinin' out of the front of it, and a silk muffler on and a big heavy overcoat! Gimme that overcoat," the other fellow said.

He grabbed the white guy and took off his overcoat.

"We can't use that M.C. outfit you got on," he said, talking about the tux. "But we might be able to make earrings for our janes out of them studs. Take 'em off," he said to the white kid.

All this time I was just standin' there, wasn't doin' nothin'. The other fellow had taken all the stuff, so far, and had his arms full.

"Wearin' diamonds up here to Harlem, and me starvin'!" the other fellow said. "Damn!"

"I'm sorry," said the white fellow.

"Sorry?" said the other guy. "What's your name?"

"Edward Peedee McGill, III," said the white fellow.

"What third?" said the colored fellow. "Where's the other two?"

"My father and grandfather," said the white boy. "I'm the third."

"I had a father and a grandfather, too," said the other fellow, "but I ain't no third. I'm the first. Ain't never been one like me. I'm a new model." He laughed out loud.

When he laughed, the white boy looked real scared. He looked like he wanted to holler. He sat down in the coal again. The front of his shirt was all black where he took the diamonds out. The wind came in through a

broken pane above the coalbin and the white fellow sat
there shiverin'. He was just a kid—eighteen or twenty
maybe—runnin' around to night clubs.

"We ain't gonna kill you." The other fellow kept
laughin'. "We ain't got the time. But if you sit in that
coal long enough, white boy, you'll be black as me.
Gimme your shoes. I might maybe can sell 'em."

The white fellow took off his shoes. As he handed
them to the colored fellow, he had to laugh, hisself. It
looked so crazy handin' somebody else your shoes. We
all laughed.

"But I'm laughin' last," said the other fellow. "You
two can stay here and laugh if you want to, both of you,
but I'm gone. So long!"

And, man, don't you know he went on out from that
basement and took all that stuff! Left me standin' just
as empty-handed as when I come in there. Yes, sir! He
left me with that white boy standin' in the coal. He'd
done took the money, the diamonds, and everythin',
even the shoes! And me with nothin'! Was I stung? I'm
askin' you!

"Ain't you gonna gimme none?" I hollered, runnin'
after him down the dark hall. "Where's my part?"

I couldn't even see him in the dark—but I *heard* him.

"Get back there," he yelled at me, "and watch that
white boy till I get out o' here. Get back there," he
hollered, "or I'll knock your livin' gizzard out! I don't
know you."

I got back. And there me and that white boy was
standin' in a strange coalbin, him lookin' like a picked
chicken—and me *feelin'* like a fool. Well, sir, we both
had to laugh again.

"Say," said the white boy, "is he gone?"

"He ain't here," I said.

"Gee, this was exciting," said the white fellow, turning
up his tux collar. "This was thrilling!"

"What?" I says.

"This is the first exciting thing that's ever happened
to me," said the white guy. "This is the first time in my
life I've ever had a good time in Harlem. Everything
else has been fake, a show. You know, something you
pay for. This was real."

"Say, buddy," I says, "if I had your money, I'd be always having a good time."

"No, you wouldn't," said the white boy.

"Yes, I would, too," I said, but the white boy shook his head. Then he asked me if he could go home, and I said, "Sure! Why not?" So we went up the dark hall. I said, "Wait a minute."

I went up and looked, but there wasn't no cops or nobody much in the streets, so I said, "So long," to that white boy. "I'm glad you had a good time." And left him standin' on the sidewalk in his stocking feet, waitin' for a taxi.

I went on up the street hongrier than I am now. And I kept thinkin' about that boy with all his money. I said to myself, "What do you suppose is the matter with rich white folks? Why you reckon they ain't happy?"

A & P

John Updike

In walks these three girls in nothing but bathing suits. I'm in the third checkout slot, with my back to the door, so I don't see them until they're over by the bread. The one that caught my eye first was the one in the plaid green two-piece. She was a chunky kid, with a good tan and a sweet broad soft-looking can with those two crescents of white just under it, where the sun never seems to hit, at the top of the backs of her legs. I stood there with my hand on a box of HiHo crackers trying to remember if I rang it up or not. I ring it up again and the customer starts giving me hell. She's one of these cash-register-watchers, a witch about fifty with rouge on her cheekbones and no eyebrows, and I know it made her day to trip me up. She'd been watching cash registers for fifty years and probably never seen a mistake before.

By the time I got her feathers smoothed and her goodies into a bag—she gives me a little snort in passing, if she'd been born at the right time they would have burned her over in Salem—by the time I get her on her way the girls had circled around the bread and were coming back, without a pushcart, back my way along the counters, in the aisle between the checkouts and the Special bins. They didn't even have shoes on. There was this chunky one, with the two-piece—it was bright green and the seams on the bra were still sharp and her belly was still pretty pale so I guessed she just got it (the suit)—there was this one, with one of those chubby berry-faces, the lips all bunched together under her nose, this one, and a tall one, with black hair that hadn't quite frizzed right, and one of these sunburns right across under the eyes, and a chin that was too long—you know, the kind of girl other girls think is very "striking" and "attractive" but never quite makes it, as they very well know, which is why they like her so much—and then the third one, that wasn't quite so tall. She was the queen. She kind of led them, the other two peeking around and making their shoulders round. She didn't look around, not this queen, she just walked straight on slowly, on these long white prima-donna legs. She came down a little hard on her heels, as if she didn't walk in her bare feet that much, putting down her heels and then letting the weight move along to her toes as if she was testing the floor with every step, putting a little deliberate extra action into it. You never know for sure how girls' minds work (do you really think it's a mind in there or just a little buzz like a bee in a glass jar?) but you got the idea she had talked the other two into coming in here with her, and now she was showing them how to do it, walk slow and hold yourself straight.

She had on a kind of dirty-pink—beige maybe, I don't know—bathing suit with a little nubble all over it and, what got me, the straps were down. They were off her shoulders looped loose around the cool tops of her arms, and I guess as a result the suit had slipped a little on her, so all around the top of the cloth there was this shining rim. If it hadn't been there you wouldn't have known there could have been anything whiter than those shoulders. With the straps pushed off, there was nothing between the top of the suit and the top of her head except just *her*, this clean bare plane of the top of her chest down from the shoulder bones like a dented sheet of metal tilted in the light. I mean, it was more than pretty.

She had sort of oaky hair that the sun and salt had bleached, done up in a bun that was unraveling, and a kind of prim face. Walking into the A & P with your straps down, I suppose it's the only kind of face you *can* have. She held her head so high her neck, coming up out of those white shoulders, looked kind of stretched, but I didn't mind. The longer her neck was, the more of her there was.

She must have felt in the corner of her eye me and over my shoulder Stokesie in the second slot watching, but she didn't tip. Not this queen. She kept her eyes moving across the racks, and stopped, and turned so slow it made my stomach rub the inside of my apron, and buzzed to the other two, who kind of huddled against her for relief, and then they all three of them went up the cat-and-dog-food-breakfast-cereal-macaroni-rice-raisins-seasonings-spreads-spaghetti-soft-drinks-crackers-and-cookies aisle. From the third slot I look straight up this aisle to the meat counter, and I watched them all the way. The fat one with the tan sort of fumbled with the cookies, but on second thought she put the package back. The sheep pushing their carts down the aisle—the girls were walking against the usual traffic (not that we have one-way signs or anything)—were pretty hilarious. You could see them, when Queenie's white shoulders dawned on them, kind of jerk, or hop, or hiccup, but their eyes snapped back to their own baskets and on they pushed. I bet you could set off dynamite in an A & P and the people would by and large keep reaching and checking oatmeal off their lists and muttering "Let me see, there was a third thing, began with A, asparagus, no, ah, yes, applesauce!" or whatever it is they do mutter. But there was no doubt, this jiggled them. A few houseslaves in pin curlers even looked around after pushing their carts past to make sure what they had seen was correct.

You know, it's one thing to have a girl in a bathing suit down on the beach, where what with the glare nobody can look at each other much anyway, and another thing in the cool of the A & P, under the fluorescent lights, against all those stacked packages, with her feet paddling along naked over our checkerboard green-and-cream rubber-tile floor.

"Oh, Daddy," Stokesie said beside me. "I feel so faint."

"Darling," I said. "Hold me tight." Stokesie's married, with two babies chalked up on his fuselage already, but as far as I can tell that's the only difference. He's twenty-two, and I was nineteen this April.

"Is it done?" he asks, the responsible married man finding his voice. I forgot to say he thinks he's going to be manager some sunny day, maybe in 1990 when it's called the Great Alexandrov and Petrooshki Tea Company or something.

What he meant was, our town is five miles from a

beach, with a big summer colony out on the Point, but
we're right in the middle of town, and the women generally put on a shirt or shorts or something before they
get out of the car into the street. And anyway these
are usually women with six children and varicose veins
mapping their legs and nobody, including them, could
care less. As I say, we're right in the middle of town,
and if you stand at our front doors you can see two
banks and the Congregational church and the newspaper
store and three real-estate offices and about twenty-
seven old freeloaders tearing up Central Street because
the sewer broke again. It's not as if we're on the Cape;
we're north of Boston and there's people in this town
haven't seen the ocean for twenty years.

The girls had reached the meat counter and were asking McMahon something. He pointed, they pointed, and
they shuffled out of sight behind a pyramid of Diet Delight peaches. All that was left for us to see was old
McMahon patting his mouth and looking after them sizing up their joints. Poor kids, I began to feel sorry for
them, they couldn't help it.

Now here comes the sad part of the story, at least my
family says it's sad, but I don't think it's so sad myself.
The store's pretty empty, it being Thursday afternoon,
so there was nothing much to do except lean on the
register and wait for the girls to show up again. The
whole store was like a pinball machine and I didn't know
which tunnel they'd come out of. After a while they
come around out of the far aisle, around the light bulbs,
records at discount of the Caribbean Six or Tony Martin
Sings or some such gunk you wonder they waste the wax
on, sixpacks of candy bars, and plastic toys done up in
cellophane that fall apart when a kid looks at them anyway. Around they come, Queenie still leading the way,
and holding a little gray jar in her hand. Slots Three
through Seven are unmanned and I could see her wondering between Stokes and me, but Stokesie with his
usual luck draws an old party in baggy gray pants who
stumbles up with four giant cans of pineapple juice (what
do these bums *do* with all that pineapple juice? I've
often asked myself) so the girls come to me. Queenie
puts down the jar and I take it into my fingers icy cold.

Kingfish Fancy Herring Snacks in Pure Sour Cream: 49¢.
Now her hands are empty, not a ring or a bracelet, bare
as God made them, and I wonder where the money's
coming from. Still with that prim look she lifts a folded
dollar bill out of the hollow at the center of her nubbled
pink top. The jar went heavy in my hand. Really, I
thought that was so cute.

Then everybody's luck begins to run out. Lengel
comes in from haggling with a truck full of cabbages on
the lot and is about to scuttle into that door marked
MANAGER behind which he hides all day when the girls
touch his eye. Lengel's pretty dreary, teaches Sunday
school and the rest, but he doesn't miss that much. He
comes over and says, "Girls, this isn't the beach."

Queenie blushes, though maybe it's just a brush of
sunburn I was noticing for the first time, now that she
was so close. "My mother asked me to pick up a jar of
herring snacks." Her voice kind of startled me, the way
voices do when you see the people first, coming out so
flat and dumb yet kind of tony, too, the way it ticked
over "pick up" and "snacks." All of a sudden I slid right
down her voice into her living room. Her father and the
other men were standing around in ice-cream coats and
bow ties and the women were in sandals picking up herring snacks on toothpicks off a big glass plate and they
were all holding drinks the color of water with olives
and sprigs of mint in them. When my parents have somebody over they get lemonade and if it's a real racy affair
Schlitz in tall glasses with "They'll Do It Every Time"
cartoons stenciled on.

"That's all right," Lengel said. "But this isn't the
beach." His repeating this struck me as funny, as if it
had just occurred to him, and he had been thinking all
these years the A & P was a great big dune and he was
the head lifeguard. He didn't like my smiling—as I say
he doesn't miss much—but he concentrates on giving the
girls that sad Sunday-school-superintendent stare.

Queenie's blush is no sunburn now, and the plump
one in plaid, that I liked better from the back—a really
sweet can—pipes up, "We weren't doing any shopping.
We just came in for the one thing."

"That makes no difference," Lengel tells her, and I
could see from the way his eyes went that he hadn't

noticed she was wearing a two-piece before. "We want you decently dressed when you come in here."

"We *are* decent," Queenie says suddenly, her lower lip pushing, getting sore now that she remembers her place, a place from which the crowd that runs the A & P must look pretty crummy. Fancy Herring Snacks flashed in her very blue eyes.

"Girls, I don't want to argue with you. After this come in here with your shoulders covered. It's our policy." He turns his back. That's policy for you. Policy is what the kingpins want. What the others want is juvenile delinquency.

All this while, the customers had been showing up with their carts but, you know, sheep, seeing a scene, they had all bunched up on Stokesie, who shook open a paper bag as gently as peeling a peach, not wanting to miss a word. I could feel in the silence everybody getting nervous, most of all Lengel, who asks me, "Sammy, have you rung up their purchase?"

I thought and said "No" but it wasn't about that I was thinking. I go through the punches, 4, 9, GROC, TOT—it's more complicated than you think, and after you do it often enough, it begins to make a little song, that you hear words to, in my case "Hello (*bing*) there, you (*gung*) hap-py *pee*-pul (*splat*)!"—the *splat* being the drawer flying out. I uncrease the bill, tenderly as you may imagine, it just having come from between the two smoothest scoops of vanilla I had ever known were there, and pass a half and a penny into her narrow pink palm, and nestle the herrings in a bag and twist its neck and hand it over, all the time thinking.

The girls, and who'd blame them, are in a hurry to get out, so I say "I quit" to Lengel quick enough for them to hear, hoping they'll stop and watch me, their unsuspected hero. They keep right on going, into the electric eye; the door flies open and they flicker across the lot to their car, Queenie and Plaid and Big Tall Goony-Goony (not that as raw material she was so bad), leaving me with Lengel and a kink in his eyebrow.

"Did you say something, Sammy?"

"I said I quit."

"I thought you did."

"You didn't have to embarrass them."

"It was they who were embarrassing us."

I started to say something that came out "Fiddle-de-doo." It's a saying of my grandmother's, and I know she would have been pleased.

"I don't think you know what you're saying," Lengel said.

"I know you don't," I said. "But I do." I pull the bow at the back of my apron and start shrugging it off my shoulders. A couple customers that had been heading for my slot begin to knock against each other, like scared pigs in a chute.

Lengel sighs and begins to look very patient and old and gray. He's been a friend of my parents for years. "Sammy, you don't want to do this to your Mom and Dad," he tells me. It's true, I don't. But it seems to me that once you begin a gesture it's fatal not to go through with it. I fold the apron, "Sammy" stitched in red on the pocket, and put it on the counter, and drop the bow tie on top of it. The bow tie is theirs, if you've ever wondered. "You'll feel this for the rest of your life," Lengel says, and I know that's true, too, but remembering how he made that pretty girl blush makes me so scrunchy inside I punch the No Sale tab and the machine whirs "pee-pul" and the drawer splats out. One advantage to this scene taking place in summer, I can follow this up with a clean exit, there's no fumbling around getting your coat and galoshes, I just saunter into the electric eye in my white shirt that my mother ironed the night before, and the door heaves itself open, and outside the sunshine is skating around on the asphalt.

I look around for my girls, but they're gone, of course. There wasn't anybody but some young married screaming with her children about some candy they didn't get by the door of a powder-blue Falcon station wagon. Looking back in the big windows, over the bags of peat moss and aluminum lawn furniture stacked on the pavement, I could see Lengel in my place in the slot, checking the sheep through. His face was dark gray and his back stiff, as if he'd just had an injection of iron, and my stomach kind of fell as I felt how hard the world was going to be to me hereafter.

Distance

Grace Paley

You would certainly be glad to meet me. I was the lady who appreciated youth. Yes, all that happy time, I was not like some. It did not go by me like a flitting dream. Tuesdays and Wednesdays was as gay as Saturday nights.

Have I suffered since? No sir, we've had as good times as this country gives: cars, renting in Jersey summers, TV the minute it first came out, everything grand for the kitchen. I have no complaints worth troubling the manager about.

Still, it is like a long hopeless homesickness my missing those young days. To me, they're like my own place that I have gone away from forever, and I have lived all the time since among great pleasures but in a foreign town. Well, O.K. Farewell, certain years.

But that's why I have an understanding of that girl Ginny downstairs and her kids. They're runty, underdeveloped. No sun, no beef. Noodles, beans, cabbage. Well, my mother off the boat knew better than that.

Once upon a time, as they say, her house was the spit of mine. You could hear it up and down the air shaft, the singing from her kitchen, banjo playing in the parlor, she would admit it first, there was a tambourine in the bedroom. Her husband wasn't American. He had black hair—like Gypsies do.

And everything then was spotless, the kitchen was all inlay like broken-up bathroom tiles, pale lavender. Formica on all surfaces, everything bright. The shine of the pots and pans was turned to stun the eyes of company ... you could see it, the mischievousness of that family home.

Of course, on account of misery now, she's always

dirty. Crying crying crying. She would not let tap water touch her.

Five ladies on the block, old friends, nosy, me not included, got up a meeting and wrote a petition to Child Welfare. I already knew it was useless, as the requirement is more than dirt, drunkenness, and a little once-in-a-while whoring. That is probably something why the children in our city are in such a state. I've noticed it for years, though it's not my business. Mothers and fathers get up when they wish, half being snuggled in relief, go to bed in the afternoon with their rumpy bumpy sweethearts pumping away before 3 p.m. (So help me.) Child Welfare does not show its concern. No matter who writes them. People of influence, known in the district, even the district leader, my cousin Leonie, who put her all into electing the mayor, she doesn't get a reply if she sends in a note. So why should I, as I'm nothing but a Primary Day poll watcher?

Anyhow there are different kinds coming into this neighborhood, and I do not mean the colored people alone. I mean people like you and me, religious, clean, many of these have gone rotten. I go along with live and let live, but what of the children?

Ginny's husband ran off with a Puerto Rican girl who shaved between the legs. This is common knowledge and well known or I'd never say it. When Ginny heard that he was going around with this girl, she did it too, hoping to entice him back, but he got nauseated by her and that tipped the scales.

Men fall for terrible weirdos in a dumb way more and more as they get older; my old man, fond of me as he constantly was, often did. I never give it the courtesy of my attention. My advice to mothers and wives: Do not imitate the dimwit's girl friends. You will be damnfool-looking, what with your age and all. Have you heard the saying "Old dough won't rise in a new oven?"

Well, you know it, I knew it, even the punks and the queers that have wiggled their way into this building are in on the inside dope. John, my son, is a constant attendant now at that Ginny's poor grubby flat. Tired, who can blame him, of his Margaret's shiny face all pitted and potted by Jersey smog. My grandchildren, of which I have close to six, are pale, as the sun can't have a chance through the oil in Jersey. Even the leaves of the trees there won't turn a greenish green.

John! Look me in the eye once in a while! What a good little twig you were always, we did try to get you out with the boys and you did go when we asked you. After school when he was eight or so, we got him into a bunch of Cub Scouts, a very raw bunch with a jawful of curse words. All of them tough and wild, but at attention when the master came among them. Right turn! You would've thought the United States Marines was in charge they was that accurate in marching, and my husband on Tuesday nights taught them what he recalled from being a sergeant. Hup! two, three, four! I guess is what he knew. But John, good as his posture was, when he come home I give him a hug and a kiss and "What'd you do today at Scouts, son? Have a parade, darling?"

"Oh no, Mother," says he. "Mrs. McClennon was collecting money the whole time for the district-wide picnic, so I just got the crayons and I drew this here picture of Our Blessed Mother," he says.

That's my John. And if you come with a Polaroid Land camera, you couldn't snap much clearer.

People have asked and it's none of their business. Why didn't the two of you (meaning Jack and me—both working) send the one boy you had left to college?

Well now to be honest, he would have had only grief in college. Truth: he was not bright. His father was not bright, and he inherited his father's brains. Our Michael was clever. But Michael is dead. We had it all talked over, his father and me, the conclusion we come to: a trade. My husband Jack was well established in the union from its early struggle, he was strong and loyal. John just floated in on the ease of recommendation and being related. We were wise. It's proved.

For now (this very minute) he's a successful man with a wonderful name in the building trade, and he has a small side business in cement plaques, his own beautiful home, and every kid of his dressed like the priest's nephew.

But don't think I'm the only one that seen Ginny and John when they were the pearls of this pitchy pigsty block. Oh, there were many, and they are still around holding the picture in the muck under their skulls, like

crabs. And I am never surprised when they speak of it,
when they try to make something of it, that nice-looking
time, as though *I* was in charge of its passing.

"Ha," Jack said about twenty times that year, "she's
a wild little bird. Our Johnny's dying ... Watch her."

O.K. Wild enough, I guess. But no wilder than me
when I was seventeen, as I never told him, that whole
year, long ago, mashing the grass of Central Park with
Anthony Aldo. Why I'd put my wildness up against any
wildness of present day, though I didn't want Jack to
know. For he was a simple man ... Put in the hours of
a wop, thank God pulled the overtime of a decent American. I didn't like to worry worry worry him. He was
kindness itself, as they say.

He come home 6 p.m. I come home 6:15 p.m. from
where I was afternoon cashier. Put supper up. Seven
o'clock, we ate it up and washed the dishes; 7:45 p.m.
sharp, if there was no company present and the boy out
visiting, he liked his pussy. Quick and very neat. By 8:15
he had showered every bit of it away. I give him his
little whiskey. He tried that blabbermouth *Journal-
American* for news of the world. It was too much. Good
night, Mr. Raftery, my pal.

Leaving me, thank goodness, the cream of the TV and
a cup of sweet wine till midnight. Though I liked the
attentions as a man he daily give me as a woman, it
hardly seemed to tire me as it exhausted him. I could
stay with the Late Show not fluttering an eyelid till the
very end of the last commercial. My wildness as a girl is
my own life's business, no one else's.

Now: As a token for friendship under God, John'd
given Ginny his high school G.O. pin, though he was
already a working man. He couldn't of given her his
union card (that never got customary), though he did
take her to a famous dinner in honor of Klaus Schnauer:
thirty-five years at Camillo, the only heinie they ever
let into that American local; he was a disgusting fat-
bottomed Nazi so help me, he could've turned you into
a pink Commie, his ass, excuse me, was that fat. Well,
as usual for that young-hearted gang, Saturday night
went on and on, it give a terrible jolt to Sunday morning,
and John staggered in to breakfast, not shaved or any-

thing. (A man, husband, son, or lodger should be shaved at breakfast.) "Mother," he said, "I am going to ask Virginia to marry me."

"I told you so," said my husband and dropped the funnies on his bacon.

"You are?" I said.

"I am, and if God is good, she'll have me."

"No blasphemy intended," I said, "but He'll have to be off in the old country fishing if she says yes."

"Mother!" said John. He is a nice boy, loyal to friends and good.

"She'll go out with anyone at all," I said.

"Oh, Mother!" said John, meaning they weren't engaged, and she could do what she wanted.

"Go out is nothing," I said. "I seen her only last Friday night with Pete, his arm around her, going into Phelan's."

"Pete's like that, Mother," meaning it was no fault of hers.

"Then what of last Saturday night, you had to go to the show yourself as if there wasn't no one else in the Borough of Manhattan to take to a movie, and when you was gone I seen her buy two Cokes at Carlo's and head straight to the third floor to John Kameron's ..."

"So? So?"

"... and come out at 11 p.m. and *his* arm was around her."

"So?"

"... and his hand was well under her sweater."

"That's not so, Mother."

"It *is* so, and tell me, young man, how you'll feel married to a girl that every wild boy on the block has been leaning his thumbs on her titties like she was a Carvel dairy counter, tell me that?"

"Dolly!" says Jack. "You went too far."

John just looked at me as red and dumb as a baby's knees.

"I haven't gone far enough into the facts, and I'm not ready to come out yet, and you listen to me, Johnny Raftery, you're somebody's jackass, I'll tell you, you look out that front window and I bet you if you got yourself your dad's spyglass you would see some track of your little lady. I think there are evenings she don't get out of the back of that trailer truck parked over there and it's no trouble at all for Pete or Kameron's half-witted kid to get his way of her. Listen Johnny, there isn't a grown-up woman who was sitting on the stoop last Sunday when it was so damn windy that doesn't know that Ginny don't wear underpants."

"Oh, Dolly," says my husband, and plops his head into his hands.

"I'm going, Mother, that's libel, I'll have her sue you for libel," dopey John starts to holler out of his tomato-red face. "I'm going and I'll ask her and I love her and I don't care what you say. Truth or lies, I don't care."

"And if you go, Johnny," I said, calm as a dead fish, my eyes rolling up to pray and be heeded, "this is what I must do," and I took a kitchen knife, a bit blunt, and plunged it at least an eighth of an inch in the fat of my heart. I guess that the heart of a middle-aged lady is jammed in deeper than an eighth of an inch, for I am here to tell the tale. But some blood did come soon, to my son's staring; it touched my nightie and spread out on my bathrobe, and it was as red on my apron as a picture in an Italian church. John fell down on his knees and hid his head in my lap. He cried, "Mother, Mother, you've hurt yourself." My husband didn't say a word to me. He kept his madness in his teeth, but he told me later, Face it: the feelings in his heart was cracked.

I met Ginny the next morning in Carlo's store. She didn't look at me. Then she did. Then she said, "It's a nice day, Mrs. Raftery."

"Mm," I said. (It was.) "How can you tell the kind of day it is?" (I don't know what I meant by that.)

"What's wrong, Mrs. Raftery?" she said.

"Hah! wrong?" I asked.

"Well, you know, I mean, you act mad at me, you don't seem to like me this morning." She made a little laugh.

"I do. I like you a great deal," I said, outwitting her. "It's you, you know, you don't like Johnny. You don't."

"What?" she said, her head popping up to catch sight of that reply.

"Don't don't don't," I said. "Don't don't!" I hollered, giving Ginny's arm a tug. "Let's get out of here. Ginny, you don't like John. You'd let him court you, squeeze you, and he's very good, he wouldn't press you further."

"You ought to mind your business," says Ginny very soft, me being the elder (but with tears).

"My son is my business."

"No," she says, "he's his own."

"My son is my business. I have one son left, and he's my business."

"No," she says. "He's his own."

MY SON IS MY BUSINESS. BY LOVE AND DUTY.

"Oh no," she says. Soft because I am the older one, but very strong. (I've noticed it. All of a sudden they look at you, and then it comes to them, young people, they are bound to outlast you, so they temper up their icy steel and stare into about an inch away from you a lot. Have you noticed it?)

At home, I said, "Jack now, the boy needs guidance. Do you want him to spend the rest of his life in bed with an orphan on welfare?"

"Oh," said Jack. "She's an orphan, is she? It's just her mother that's dead. What has one thing to do with another? You're a pushy damn woman, Dolly. I don't know what use you are ..."

What came next often happens in a family, causing sorrow at the time. Looking back, it's a speck compared to life.

For: Following this conversation, Jack didn't deal with me at all, and he broke his many years' after-supper habits and took long walks. That's what killed him, I think, for he was a habitual person.

And: Alongside him on one of these walks was seen a skinny crosstown lady, known to many people over by Tompkins Square—wears a giant Ukrainian cross in and out of the tub, to keep from going down the drain, I guess.

"In that case, the hell with you" is what I said. "I don't care. Get yourself a cold-water flat on Avenue D."

"Why not? I'll go. O.K.," said Jack. I think he figured a couple of weeks' vacation with his little cuntski and her color television would cool his requirements.

"Stay off the block," I said, "you slippery relic. I'll send your shirts by the diaper-service man."

"Mother," said poor John, when he noticed his dad's

absence, "what's happening to you? The way you talk. To Dad. It's the wine, Mother. I know it."

"You're a bloated beer guzzler!" I said quietly. (People that drink beer are envious against the ones in favor of wine. Though my dad was a mick in cotton socks, in his house, we had a choice.)

"No, Mother, I mean you're not clear sometimes."

"Crazy, you mean, son. Huh? Split personality?"

"Something's wrong!" he said "Don't you want Dad back?" He was nervous to his fingernails.

"Mind your business, he'll be back, it's happened before, Mr. Two-Weeks-Old."

"What?" he said, horrified.

"You're blind as a bat, Mr. Just Born. Where was you three Christmases ago?"

"What! But Mother! Didn't you feel terrible? Terrible! How'd you stand for him acting that way? Dad!"

"Now quit it, John, you're a damnfool kid. Sure I don't want to look at his dumb face being pleased. That'd kill."

"Mother, it's not right."

"Phoo, go to work and mind your business, sonny boy."

"It is my business," he said, "and don't call me sonny."

About two months later, John came home with Margaret, both of them blistered from Lake Hopatcong at ninety-four degrees. I will be fair. She was not yet ruined by Jersey air, and she was not too terrible looking, at least to the eye of a clean-minded boy.

"This is Margaret," he says. "She's from Monmouth, Jersey."

"Just come over on the *Queen Mary*, dear?" I asked for the joke in it.

"I have to get her home for supper. Her father's strict."

"Sure," I said, "have a Coke first."

"Oh, thank you so much," says Margaret. "Thank you, thank you, thank you, Mrs. Raftery."

"Has she blood in her?" hollered Jack after his shower. He had come home by then, skinny and dissatisfied. Is there satisfaction anywhere in getting old?

John didn't inquire an O.K. of his dad or me, nor

answer to nobody Yes or No. He was that age that couldn't live without a wife. He had to use this Margaret.

It was his time to go forward like we all did once. And he has. Number One: She is kept plugged up with babies. Number Two: As people nowadays need a house, he has bought one and tangled it around in Latin bushes. Nobody but the principal at Holy Redeemer High knows what little tags on the twigs say. Every evening after hard work you can find him with a hose scrubbing down his lawn. His oldest kid is now fourteen and useless. The littlest one is four, and she reminds me of me with the flashiest eyes and a little tongue sharpened to a scrappy point.

"How come you never named one for *me*, Margaret?" I asked her straight in her face.

"Oh," she said, "there's only the two girls, Teresa, for my mother, and Cathleen, for my best sister. The very next'll be for you."

"What? Next! Are you trying to kill my son?" I asked her. "Why he has to be working nights as it is. You don't look well, you know. You ought to see a smart Jewish doctor and get your tubes tied up."

"Oh," she said, "never!"

I have to tease a little to grapple any sort of a reply out of her. But mostly it doesn't work. It is something like I am a crazy construction worker in conversation with fresh cement. Can there be more in the world like her? Don't answer. Time will pass in spite of her slow wits.

In fact it has, for here we are in the present, which is happening now, and I am a famous widow babysitter for whoever thinks I am unbalanced but within reason. I am a grand storybook reader to the little ones. I read like an actress, Joan Crawford or Maureen O'Sullivan, my voice is deeper than it was. So I do make a little extra for needs, though my Johnny sees to the luxuries I must have. I won't move away to strangers. This is my family street, and I don't need to.

And of course as friendship never ends, Johnny comes twice a week for his entertainment to Ginny. Ginny and I do not talk a word, though we often pass. She knows I am right as well as victorious. She's had it unusually lovely (most people don't)—a chance to be some years with a younger fellow like Blackie that gave her great rattling shivers, top to bottom, though it was all cut off before youth ended. And as for my Johnny, he now absolutely has her as orginally planned and desired, and she depends on him in all things. She requires him. Her children lean on him. They climb up his knees to his shoulder. They cry out the window for him, *John, John*, if his dumb Margaret keeps him home.

It's a pity to have become so right and Jack's off stalking the innocent angels.

I wait on the stoop steps to see John on summer nights, as he hasn't enough time to visit me and Ginny both, and I need the sight of him, though I don't know why. I like the street anyway, and the hot night when the ice-cream truck brings all the dirty kids and the big nifty boys with their hunting-around eyes. I put a touch of burgundy on my strawberry ice-cream cone as my father said we could on Sunday, which drives these sozzle-headed ladies up the brown brick wall, so help me Mary.

Now, some serious questions, so far unasked:

What the devil is it all about, the noisiness and the speediness, when it's no distance at all? How come John had to put all them courtesy calls into Margaret on his lifelong trip to Ginny? Also, Jack, what was his real nature? Was he for or against? And that Anthony, what *did* he have in mind as I knuckled under again and again (and I know I was the starter)? He did not get me pregnant as in books it happens at once. How come the French priest said to me, crying tears and against his order, "Oh no, Dolly, if you are *enceinte* (meaning pregnant), he will certainly marry you, poor child, now smile, poor child, for that is the Church's promise to infants born." To which, how come, tough and cheery as I used to be, all I could say before going off to live and die was: "No, Father, he doesn't love me."

DETACHED
AUTOBIOGRAPHY

Now we enter the more traditional range of the story-telling spectrum. From here on the narrators are as reliable and objective as they can ever be. They become guides for the readers, mediating between them and the characters.

True, these narrators are themselves still the main characters, because they are telling about what happened to them in the past. But each's frame of mind has changed greatly since the experience recounted, sometimes as a result of that experience itself, sometimes just as a result of general maturation. In fact, the autobiographical story is popular not only because a reliable narrator frames events and helps us interpret them but also because it is so often about the very process of growing up (which interests everyone). Many novels like Charles Dickens's David Copperfield, *Charlotte Brontë's* Jane Eyre, *Joseph Krumgold's* And Now Miguel, *Ralph Ellison's* Invisible Man, *and Thomas Mann's* Buddenbrooks *are bildungsromans or novels of growing up. For contrast with subjective narration, compare Holden Caulfield's account, narrated a year later while still "disturbed," with that of the middle-aged David Copperfield or with the adult Scout of Harper Lee's* To Kill a Mockingbird.

In the following stories the reader becomes less concerned with interpreting through *the narrator and more inclined to accept the narrator's interpretation of what happened. What meaning does the experiencer attach to his or her own experience, which vicariously we undergo also? Becoming detached about one's own life means that one splits into I-now and I-then. Looking on one's former self as someone else amounts to splitting oneself into a*

*first person and a third person. Whereas, then, the domi-
nant issue up to now has been the relation of the speaker
to an audience, from here on the chief issue is the relation
of the speaker to the third party who is the main subject.
In the case of autobiography—where storyteller and protagonist are the same—the distance between them is psychological, usually brought about by time. When the
protagonist becomes a person other than the narrator, the
issue is spatial distance, the actual separateness. For
the first, gaining distance is the challenge; for the second,
overcoming distance.*

   *But no story can be entirely about oneself. Even Rob-
inson Crusoe eventually found a footprint in the sand.
The stories here vary in how much they focus on the
speaker versus the other characters that make up the environment, supporting cast, or antagonists. Titles often indicate this focus very handily, along with the author's intent.
In the Bambara story, the girl's workplace, Johnson's
Drugs N Goods, provides the catalyzing agents for her
central experience. In "The Circuit" it is the seasonal mi-
gration of fruit pickers. In "A Coupla Scalped Indians"
the hero undergoes initiation with a buddy, with whom
he is also contrasted. The title of "The Passing" indicates
that the main character shares focus with another character from whom he receives something and with whom he
is identified. Joseph Conrad's novella "The Secret
Sharer" is a classic of this sort of alter ego or double
story, which serves as transition into memoir stories,
where the narrator features some other person.*

Christmas Eve at Johnson's Drugs N Goods

Toni Cade Bambara

I was probably the first to spot them cause I'd been watching the entrance to the store on the lookout for my daddy, knowing that if he didn't show soon, he wouldn't be coming at all. His new family would be expecting him to spend the holidays with them. For the first half of my shift, I'd raced the cleaning cart down the aisles doing a slapdash job on the signs and glass cages, eager to stay in view of the doorway. And look like Johnson's kept getting bigger, swelling, sprawling itself all over the corner lot, just to keep me from the door, to wear me out in the marathon vigil.

In point of fact, Johnson's Drugs N Goods takes up less than one-third of the block. But it's laid out funny in crisscross aisles so you get to feeling like a rat in an endless maze. Plus the ceilings are high and the fluorescents a blazing white. And Mrs. Johnson's got these huge signs sectioning off the spaces—TOBACCO DRUGS HOUSEWARES, etc.—like it was some big-time department store. The thing is, till the two noisy women came in, it felt like a desert under a blazing sun. Piper in Tobacco even had on shades. The new dude in Drugs looked like he was at the end of a wrong-way telescope. I got to feeling like a nomad with the cleaning cart, trekking across the sands with no end in sight, wandering. The overhead lights creating mirages and racing up my heart till I'd realize that wasn't my daddy in the parking lot, just the poster-board Santa Claus. Or that wasn't my daddy in the entrance way, just the Burma Shave man in a frozen stance. Then I'd tried to make out pictures of Daddy getting off the bus at the terminal, or driving a rented car past the Chamber of Commerce building, or sitting jammed-leg in one of them DC point-o-nine brand X planes, coming to see me.

By the time the bus pulled into the lot and the two women in their big-city clothes hit the door, I'd decided Daddy was already at the house waiting for me, knowing that for a mirage too, since Johnson's is right across from the railroad and bus terminals and the house is a dollar-sixty cab away. And I know he wouldn't feature going to the house on the off chance of running into Mama. Or even if he escaped that fate, having to sit in the parlor with his hat in his lap while Aunt Harriet looks him up and down grunting, too busy with the latest crossword puzzle contest to offer the man some supper. And Uncle Henry talking a blue streak bout how he outfoxed the city council or somethin and nary a cold beer in sight for my daddy.

But then the two women came banging into the store and I felt better. Right away the store stopped sprawling, got fixed. And we all got pulled together from our various zones to one focal point—them. Changing up the whole atmosphere of the place fore they even got into the store proper. Before we knew it, we were all smiling, looking halfway like you supposed to on Christmas Eve, even if you do got to work for ole lady Johnson, who don't give you no slack whatever the holiday.

"What the hell does this mean, Ethel?" the one in the fur coat say, talking loud and fast, yanking on the rails that lead the way into the store. "What are we, cattle? Being herded into the blankety-blank store and in my fur coat," she grumbles, boosting herself up between the rails, swinging her body along like the kids do in the park.

Me and Piper look at each other and smile. Then Piper moves down to the edge of the counter right under the Tobacco sign so as not to miss nothing. Madeen over in Housewares waved to me to ask what's up and I just shrug. I'm fascinated by the women.

"Look here," the one called Ethel say, drawing the words out lazy slow. "Do you got a token for this sucker?" She's shoving hard against the turnstile folks supposed to exit through. Pushing past and grunting, the turnstile crank cranking like it gonna bust, her Christmas corsage of holly and bells just ajingling and hanging by a thread. Then she gets through and stumbles toward the cigar counter and leans back against it, studying the turnstile hard. It whips back around in place, making scrunching noises like it's been abused.

"You know one thing," she say, dropping her face onto her coat collar so Piper'd know he's being addressed.

"Ma'am?"

"That is one belligerent bad boy, that thing right there."

Piper laughs his prizewinning laugh and starts touching the stacks of gift-wrapped stuff, case the ladies in the market for pipe tobacco or something. Two or three of the customers who'd been falling asleep in the magazines coming to life now, inching forward. Phototropism, I'd call it, if somebody asked me for a word.

The one in the fur coat's coming around now the right way—if you don't count the stiff-elbow rail-walking she was doing—talking about "Oh, my God, I can walk, I can walk, Ethel, praise de lawd."

The two women watching Piper touch the cigars, the humidors, the gift-wrapped boxes. Mostly he's touching himself, cause George Lee Piper love him some George Lee Piper. Can't blame him. Piper be fine.

"You work on commissions, young man?" Fur Coat asking.

"No, ma'am."

The two women look at each other. They look over toward the folks inching forward. They look at me gliding by with the cleaning cart. They look back at each other and shrug.

"So what's his problem?" Ethel says in a stage whisper. "Why he so hot to sell us something?"

"Search me." Fur Coat starts flapping her coat and frisking herself. "You know?" she asking me.

"It's a mystery to me," I say, doing my best to run ole man Samson over. He sneaking around trying to jump Madeen in Housewares. And it is a mystery to me how come Piper always so eager to make a sale. You'd think he had half interest in the place. He says it's because it's his job, and after all, the Johnsons are Black folks. I guess so, I guess so. Me, I just clean the place and stay busy in case Mrs. J is in the prescription booth, peeking out over the top of the glass.

When I look around again, I see that the readers are suddenly very interested in cigars. They crowding

around Ethel and Fur Coat. Piper kinda embarrassed by
all the attention, though fine as he is, he oughta be used
to it. His expression's cool but his hands give him away,
sliding around the counter like he shuffling a deck of
slippery cards. Fur Coat nudges Ethel and they bend
over to watch the hands, doing these chicken-head jerk-
ings. The readers take up positions just like a director
was hollering "Places" at em. Piper, never one to disappoint an audience, starts zipping around these invisible
walnut shells. Right away Fur Coat whips out a little red
change purse and slaps a dollar bill on the counter. Ethel
dips deep into her coat pocket, bending her knees and
being real comic, then plunks down some change. Ole
man Sampson tries to boost up on my cleaning cart to
see the shells that ain't there.

"Scuse me, Mr. Sampson," I say, speeding the cart up
sudden so that quite naturally he falls off, the dirty dog.

Piper is snapping them imaginary shells around like
nobody's business, one of the readers leaning over another's shoulder, staring pop-eyed.

"All right now, everybody step back," Ethel announces. She waves the crowd back and pushes up one
coat sleeve, lifts her fist into the air and jerks out one
stiff finger from the bunch, and damn if the readers don't
lift their heads to behold in amazement this wondrous
finger.

"That, folks," Fur Coat explains, "is what is known
as the indicator finger. The indicator is about to indicate
the indicatee."

"Say wha?" Dirty ole man Sampson decides he'd
rather sneak up on Madeen than watch the show.

"What's going on over there?" Miz Della asks me. I
spray the watch case and make a big thing of wiping it
and ignoring her. But then the new dude in Drugs hollers over the same thing.

"Christmas cheer gone to the head. A coupla vaude-
villians," I say. He smiles, and Miz Della says "Ohhh"
like I was talking to her.

"This one," Ethel says, planting a finger exactly one-
quarter of an inch from the countertop.

Piper dumb-shows a lift of the shell, turning his face
away as though he can't bear to look and find the elusive
pea ain't there and he's gonna have to take the ladies'

money. Then his eyes swivel around and sneak a peek and widen, lighting up his whole face in a prizewinning grin.

"You got it," he shouts.

The women grab each other by the coat shoulders and jump each other up and down. And I look toward the back cause I know Mrs. J got to be hearing all this carrying-on, and on payday if Mr. J ain't handing out the checks, she's going to give us some long lecture about decorum and what it means to be on board at Johnson's Drugs N Goods. I wheel over to the glass jars and punch bowls, wanting alibi distance just in case. And also to warn Madeen about Sampson gaining on her. He's ducking down behind the coffeepots, walking squat and shameless.

"Pay us our money, young man," Fur Coat is demanding, rapping her knuckles on the counter.

"Yeah, what kind of crooked shell game is you running here in this joint?" say Ethel, finding a good foil character to play.

"We should hate to have to turn the place out, young man."

"It out," echoes Ethel.

The women nod to the crowd and a coupla folks giggle. And Piper tap-taps on the cash register like he shonuff gonna give em they money. I'd rather they turned the place out myself. I want to call my daddy. Only way any of us are going to get home in time to dress for the Christmas dance at the center is for the women to turn it out. Like I say, Piper ain't too clear about the worker's interest versus management's, as the dude in Drugs would say it. So he's light-tapping and quite naturally the cash drawer does not come out. He's yanking some unseen dollar from the not-there drawer and handing it over. Damn if Fur Coat don't snatch it, deal out the bills to herself and her friend and then make a big production out of folding the money flat and jamming it in that little red change purse.

"I wanna thank you," Ethel says, strolling off, swinging her pocketbook so that the crowd got to back up and disperse. Fur Coat spreads her coat and curtsies.

"A pleasure to do business with you ladies," Piper says, tipping his hat, looking kinda disappointed that he didn't sell em something. Tipping his hat the way he tipped the shells, cause you know Mrs. J don't allow no hats indoors. I came to work in slacks one time and she sent me home to change and docked me too. I wear a gele some times just to mess her around, and you can tell she trying to figure out if she'll go for it or not. The woman is crazy. Not Uncle Henry type crazy, but Black property owner type crazy. She thinks this is a museum, which is why folks don't hardly come in here to shop. That's okay cause we all get to know each other well. It's not okay cause it's a drag to look busy. If you look like you ain't buckling under a weight of work, Mrs. J will have you count the Band-Aids in the boxes to make sure the company ain't pulling a fast one. The woman crazy.

Now Uncle Henry type crazy is my kind of crazy. The type crazy to get you a job. He march into the "saloon" as he calls it and tells Leon D that he is not an equal opportunity employer and that he, Alderman Henry Peoples, is going to put some fire to his ass. So soon's summer comes, me and Madeen got us a job at Leon D. Salon. One of them hushed, funeral type shops with skinny models parading around for customers corseted and strangling in their seats, huffin and puffin.

Madeen got fired right off on account of the pound of mascara she wears on each lash and them weird dresses she designs for herself (with less than a yard of cloth each if you ask me). I did my best to hang in there so's me and Madeen'd have hang-around money till Johnson started hiring again. But it was hard getting back and forth from the stockroom to this little kitchen to fix the espresso to the showroom. One minute up to your ass in carpet, the next skidding across white linoleum, the next making all this noise on ceramic tile and people looking around at you and all. Was there for two weeks and just about had it licked by stationing different kind of shoes at each place that I could slip into, but then Leon D stumbled over my bedroom slippers one afternoon.

But to hear Uncle Henry tell it, writing about it all to Daddy, I was working at a promising place making a name for myself. And Aunt Harriet listening to Uncle Henry read the letter, looking me up and down and grunting. She know what kind of name it must be, cause my name in the family is Miss Clumsy. Like if you got a glass-top coffee table with doodads on em, or a hurricane lamp sitting on a mantel anywhere near a door I got to come through, or an antique jar you brought all the way from Venice the time you won the crossword puzzle contest—you can rest assure I'll demolish them by and by. I ain't vicious, I'm just clumsy. It's my gawky stage, Mama says. Aunt Harriet cuts her eye at Mama and grunts.

My daddy advised me on the phone not to mention anything to the Johnsons about this gift of mine for disaster or the fact that I worked at Leon D. Salon. No sense the Johnsons calling up there to check on me and come to find I knocked over a perfume display two times in the same day. Like I say—it's a gift. So when I got to clean the glass jars and punch bowls at Johnson's, I take it slow and pay attention. Then I take up my station relaxed in Fabrics, where the worst that can happen is I upset a box of pins.

Mrs. J is in the prescription booth, and she clears her throat real loud. We all look to the back to read the smoke signals. She ain't paying Fur Coat and Ethel no attention. They over in Cosmetics messing with Miz Della's mind and her customers. Mrs. J got her eye on some young teen-agers browsing around Jewelry. The other eye on Piper. But this does not mean Piper is supposed to check the kids out. It means Madeen is. You got to know how to read Mrs. J to get along.

She always got one eye on Piper. Tries to make it seem like she don't trust him at the cash register. That may be part of the reason now, now that she's worked up this cover story so in her mind. But we all know why she watches Piper, same reason we all do. Cause Piper is so fine you just can't help yourself. Tall and built up, blue-black and smooth, got the nerve to have dimples, and wears this splayed-out push-broom mustache he's always raking in with three fingers. Got a big butt too that makes you wanna hug the customer that asks for the cartoons Piper keeps behind him, two shelfs down. Mercy. And when it's slow, or when Mrs. J comes bustling over for the count, Piper steps from behind the counter and shows his self. You get to see the whole

Piper from the shiny boots to the glistening fro and
every inch of him fine. Enough to make you holler.

Miz Della in Cosmetics, a sister who's been passing
for years but fooling nobody but herself, she always lolli-
gagging over to Tobacco talking bout are there any new
samples of those silver-tipped cigars for women. Piper
don't even squander energy to bump her off any more.
She mostly just ain't even there. At first he would get
mad when she used to act hinkty and had these white
men picking her up at the store. Then he got sorrowful
about it all, saying she was a pitiful person. Now that
she's going out with the blond chemist back there, he
just wiped her off the map. She tries to mess with him,
but Piper ain't heard the news she's been born. Sometimes his act slips, though, cause he does take a lot of
unnecessary energy to play up to Madeen whenever Miz
Della's hanging around. He's not consistent in his attentions, and that spurs Madeen the dress designer to madness. And Piper really oughta put brakes on that, cause
Madeen subject to walk in one day in a fishnet dress
and no underwear and then what he goin do about that?

Last year on my birthday my daddy got on us about
dressing like hussies to attract the boys. Madeen
shrugged it off and went about her business. It hurt my
feelings. The onliest reason I was wearing that tight
sweater and that skimpy skirt was cause I'd been to the
roller rink and that's how we dress. But my daddy didn't
even listen and I was really hurt. But then later that
night, I come through the living room to make some
cocoa and he apologized. He lift up from the couch
where he always sleeps when he comes to visit, lifted up
and whispered it—"Sorry." I could just make him out
by the light from the refrigerator.

"Candy," he calls to make sure I heard him. And I
don't want to close the fridge door cause I know I'll
want to remember this scene, figuring it's going to be
the last birthday visit cause he fixin to get married and
move outta state.

"Sir?"

He pat the couch and I come on over and just leave
the fridge door open so we can see each other. I forgot
to put the milk down, so I got this cold milk bottle in
my lap, feeling stupid.

"I was a little rough on you earlier," he say, picking something I can't see from my bathrobe. "But you're getting to be a woman now and certain things have to be said. Certain things have to be understood so you can decide what kind of woman you're going to be, ya know?"

"Sir," I nod. I'm thinking Aunt Harriet ought to tell me, but then Aunt Harriet prefers to grunt at folks, reserving words for the damn crossword puzzles. And my mama stay on the road so much with the band, when she do come home for a hot minute all she has to tell me is "My slippers're in the back closet" or "Your poor tired Ma'd like some coffee."

He takes my hand and don't even kid me about the milk bottle, just holds my hand for a long time saying nothing, just squeezes it. And I know he feeling bad about moving away and all, but what can he do, he got a life to lead. Just like Mama got her life to lead. Just like I got my life to lead and'll probably leave here myself one day and become an actress or a director. And I know I should tell him it's all right. Sitting there with that milk bottle chilling me through my bathrobe, the light from the refrigerator throwing funny shadows on the wall, I know that years later when I'm in trouble or something, or hear that my daddy died or something like that, I'm going to feel real bad that I didn't tell him— it's all right, Daddy, I understand. It ain't like he'd made any promises about making a home for me with him. So it ain't like he's gone back on his word. And if the new wife can't see taking in no half-grown new daughter, hell, I understand that. I can't get the words together, neither can he. So we just squeeze each other's hands. And that'll have to do.

"When I was a young man," he says after while, "there were girls who ran around all made up in sassy clothes. And they were okay to party with, but not the kind you cared for, ya know?" I nod and he pats my hand. But I'm thinking that ain't right, to party with a person you don't care for. How come you can't? I want to ask, but he's talking. And I was raised not to interrupt folk when they talking, especially my daddy. "You and Madeen cause quite a stir down at the barbershop." He tries to laugh it, but it comes out scary. "Got to make

up your mind now what kind of woman you're going to
be. You know what I'm saying?" I nod and he loosens
his grip so I can go make my cocoa.

I'm messing around in the kitchenette feeling dishon-
est. Things I want to say, I haven't said. I look back
over toward the couch and know this picture is going to
haunt me later. Going to regret the things left unsaid.
Like a coward, like a child maybe. I fix my cocoa and
keep my silence, but I do remember to put the milk
back and close the refrigerator door.

"Candy?"

"Sir?" I'm standing there in the dark, the fridge door
closed now and we can't even see each other.

"It's not about looks anyway," he says, and I hear
him settling down into the couch and pulling up the bedclothes. "And it ain't always about attracting some man
either . . . not necessarily."

I'm waiting to hear what it is about, the cup shaking
in the saucer and me wanting to ask him all over again
how it was when he and Mama first met in Central Park,
and how it used to be when they lived in Philly and had
me and how it was when the two of them were no longer
making any sense together but moved down here anyway and then split up. But I could hear that breathing
he does just before the snoring starts. So I hustle on
down the hall so I won't be listening for it and can't get
to sleep.

All night I'm thinking about this woman I'm going to
be. I'll look like Mama but don't wanna be no singer.
Was named after Grandma Candestine but don't wanna
be no fussy old woman with a bunch of kids. Can't see
myself turning into Aunt Harriet either, doing crossword
puzzles all day long. I look over at Madeen, all sprawled
out in her bed, tangled up in the sheets looking like the
alcoholic she trying to be these days, sneaking liquor
from Uncle Henry's closet. And I know I don't wanna
be stumbling down the street with my boobs out and my
dress up and my heels cracking off and all. I write for a
whole hour in my diary trying to connect with the future
me and trying not to hear my daddy snoring.

Fur Coat and Ethel in Housewares talking with Madeen. I know they must be cracking on Miz Della,

cause I hear Madeen saying something about equal opportunity. We used to say that Mrs. J was an equal opportunity employer for hiring Miz Della. But then she went and hired real white folks—a blond, crew-cut chemist and a pimply-face kid for the stockroom. If you ask me, that's running equal opportunity in the ground. And running the business underground cause don't nobody round here deal with no white chemist. They used to wrinkly old folks grinding up the herbs and bark and telling them very particular things to do and not to do working the roots. So they keep on going to Mama Drear down past the pond or Doc Jessup in back of the barbershop. Don't do a doctor one bit of good to write out a prescription talking about fill it at Johnson's, cause unless it's an emergency folk stay strictly away from a white root worker, especially if he don't tell you what he doing.

Aunt Harriet in here one day when Mama Drear was too sick to counsel and quite naturally she asks the chemist to explain what all he doing back there with the mortar and pestle and the scooper and the scales. And he say something about rules and regulations, the gist of which was mind your business, lady. Aunt Harriet dug down deep into her crossword-puzzle words and pitched a natural bitch. Called that man a bunch of choicest names. But the line that got me was—"Medication without explanation is obscene." And what she say that for, we ran that in the ground for days. Infatuation without fraternization is obscene. Insemination without obligation is tyranny. Fornication without contraception is obtuse, and so forth and so on. Madeen's best line came out the night we were watching a TV special about welfare. Sterilization without strangulation and hell's damnation is I-owe-you-one-crackers. Look like every situation called for a line like that, and even if it didn't, we made it fit.

Then one Saturday morning we were locked out and we standing around shivering in our sweaters and this old white dude jumps out a pickup truck hysterical, his truck still in gear and backing out the lot. His wife had given their child an overdose of medicine and the kid was out cold. Look like everything he said was grist for the mill.

"She just administered the medicine without even reading the label," he told the chemist, yanking on his jacket so the man couldn't even get out his keys. "She never even considered the fact it might be dangerous, the medicine so old and all." We follow the two down the aisle to the prescription booth, the old white dude talking a mile a minute, saying they tried to keep the kid awake, tried to walk him, but he wouldn't walk. Tried to give him an enema, but he wouldn't stay propped up. Could the chemist suggest something to empty his stomach out and sooth his inflamed ass and what all? And besides he was breathing funny and should he administer mouth-to-mouth resuscitation? The minute he tore out of there and ran down the street to catch up with his truck, we started in.

Administration without consideration is illiterate. Irrigation without resuscitation is evacuation without ambulation is inflammation without information is execution without restitution is. We got downright silly about the whole thing till Mrs. J threatened to fire us all. But we kept it up for a week.

Then the new dude in Drugs who don't never say much stopped the show one afternoon when we were trying to figure out what to call the street riots in the sixties and so forth. He say Revolution without Transformation is Half-assed. Took me a while to ponder that one, a whole day in fact just to work up to it. After while I would listen real hard whenever he opened his mouth, which wasn't often. And I jotted down the titles of the books I'd seen him with. And soon's I finish up the stack that's by my bed, I'm hitting the library. He started giving me some of the newspapers he keeps stashed in that blue bag of his we all at first thought was full of funky jockstraps and sneakers. Come to find it's full of carrots and oranges and books and stuff. Madeen say he got a gun in there too. But then Madeen all the time saying something. Like she saying here lately that the chemist's jerking off there behind the poisons and the goopher dust.

The chemist's name is Hubert Tarrly. Madeen tagged him Herbert Tareyton. But the name that stuck was Nazi Youth. Every time I look at him I hear Hitler barking out over the loudspeaker urging the youth to measure up and take over the world. And I can see these stark-eyed gray kids in short pants and suspenders doing jump-ups and scissor kicks and turning they mamas in to the Gestapo for listening to the radio. Chemist looks like he grew up like that, eating knockwurst and beating on Jews, rounding up gypsies, saying *Sieg heil* and shit. Mrs. J said something to him one morning and damn if he didn't click his heels. I like to die. She blushing all over her simple self talking bout that's Southern cavalier style. I could smell the gas. I could see the flaming cross too. Nazi Youth and then some. The dude in Drugs started calling him that too, the dude whose name I can never remember. I always wanna say Ali Baba when I talk about him with my girl friends down at the skating rink or with the older sisters at the arts center. But that ain't right. Either you call a person a name that says what they about or you call em what they call themselves, one or the other.

Now take Fur Coat, for instance. She is clearly about the fur coat. She moving up and down the aisles talking while Ethel in the cloth coat is doing all the work, picking up teapots, checking the price on the dust mops, clicking a bracelet against the punch bowl to see if it ring crystal, hollering to somebody about whether the floor wax need buffing or not. And it's all on account of the fur coat. Her work is something other than that. Like when they were in Cosmetics messing with Miz Della, some white ladies come up talking about what's the latest in face masks. And every time Miz Della pull something out the box, Ethel shake her head and say that brand is crap. Then Fur Coat trots out the sure-fire recipe for the face mask. What she tells the old white ladies is to whip us some egg white to peaks, pour in some honey, some oil of wintergreen, some oil of eucalyptus, the juice of a lemon and a half a teaspoon of arsenic. Now any fool can figure out what lemon juice do to arsenic, or how honey going make the concoction stick, and what all else the oil of this and that'll do to your face. But Fur Coat in her fur coat make you stand still and listen to this madness. Fur Coat an authority in her fur coat. The fur coat is an act of alchemy in itself, as Aunt Harriet would put it.

Just like my mama in her fur coat, same kind too—

Persian lamb, bought hot in some riot or other. Mama's
coat was part of the Turn the School Out Outfit. Hardly
ever came out of the quilted bag cept for that. Wasn't
for window-shopping, wasn't for going to rehearsal,
wasn't for church teas, was for working her show. She'd
flip a flap of that coat back over her hip when she
strolled into the classroom to get on the teacher's case
bout saying something out of the way about Black folks.
Then she'd pick out the exact plank, exact spot she'd
take her stand on, then plant one of them black suede
pumps from the I. Miller outlet she used to work at.
Then she'd lift her chin arrogant proud to start the rap,
and all us kids would lean forward and stare at the
cameo brooch visible now on the wide-wale wine plush
corduroy dress. Then she'd work her show in her outfit.
Bam-bam that black suede pocketbook punctuating the
points as Mama ticked off the teacher's offenses. And
when she got to the good part, and all us kids would
strain up off the benches to hear every word so we could
play it out in the schoolyard, she'd take both fists and
brush that fur coat way back past her hips and she'd
challenge the teacher to either change up and apologize
or meet her for a showdown at a school-board hearing.
And of course ole teacher'd apologize to all us Black
kids. Then Mama'd let the coat fall back into place and
she'd whip around, the coat draping like queen robes,
and march herself out. Mama was baad in her fur coat.

I don't know what-all Fur Coat do in her fur coat but
I can tell it's hellafyin whatever it all is. They came into
Fabrics and stood around a while trying to see what shit
they could get into. All they had in their baskets was a
teapot and some light bulbs and some doodads from the
special gift department, perfume and whatnot. I waited
on a few customers wanting braid and balls of macramé
twine, nothing where I could show my stuff. Now if
somebody wanted some of the silky, juicy cotton stuff I
could get into something fancy, yanking off the yards,
measuring it doing a shuffle-stick number, nicking it just
so, then ripping the hell out the shit. But didn't nobody
ask for that. Fur Coat and Ethel kinda finger some bolts
and trade private jokes, then they moved onto Drugs.

"We'd like to see the latest in rubberized fashions for
men, young man." Fur Coat is doing a super Lady Gran-

ville Whitmore the Third number. "If you would." She bows her head, fluttering her lashes.

Me and Madeen start messing around in the shoe-polish section so's not to miss nothing. I kind of favor Fur Coat, on account of she got my mama's coat on, I guess. On the other hand, I like the way Ethel drawl talk like she too tired and bored to go on. I guess I like em both cause they shopping the right way, having fun and all. And they got plenty of style. I wouldn't mind being like that when I am full-grown.

The dude in Drugs thinks on the request a while, sucking in his lips like he wanna talk to himself on the inside. He's looking up and down the counter, pauses at the plastic rain hats, rejects them, then squints hard at Ethel and Fur Coat. Fur Coat plants a well-heeled foot on the shelf with the tampons and pads and sighs. Something about that sigh I don't like. It's real rather than play snooty. The dude in Drugs always looks a little crumbled, a little rough dry, like he jumped straight out the hamper but not quite straight. But he got stuff to him if you listen rather than look. Seems to me ole Fur Coat is looking. She keeps looking while the dude moves down the aisle behind the counter, ducks down out of sight, reappears and comes back, dumping an armful of boxes on the counter.

"One box of Trojans and one box of Ramses," Ethel announces. "We want to do the comparison test."

"On the premises?" Lady G Fur says, planting a dignified hand on her collarbone.

"Egg-zack-lee."

"In your opinion, young man," Lady G Fur says, staying the arm of the brand tester, "which of the two is the best? Uhmm—the better of the two, that is. In your vast experience as lady-killer and cock hound, which passes the X test?" It's said kinda snotty. Me and Madeen exchange a look and dust around the cans of shoe polish.

"Well," the dude says, picking up a box in each hand, "in my opinion, Trojans have a snappier ring to em." He rattles the box against his ear, then lets Ethel listen. She nods approval. Fur Coat will not be swayed. "On the other hand, Ramses is a smoother smoke. Cooler on the throat. What do you say in your vast experience as— er—"

Ethel is banging down boxes of Kotex cracking up, screaming, "He gotcha. He gotcha that time. Old laundry bag got over on you, Helen."

Mrs J comes out of the prescription booth and hustles her bulk to the counter. Me and Madeen clamp down hard on giggles and I damn near got to climb in with the neutral shoe polish to escape attention. Ethel and Fur Coat don't give a shit, they paying customers, so they just roar. Cept Fur Coat's roar is phony, like she really mad and gonna get even with the dude for not turning out to be a chump. Meanwhile, the dude is standing like a robot, arms out at exactly the same height, elbows crooked just so, boxes displayed between thumb and next finger, the gears in the wrist click, turning. And not even cracking a smile.

"What's the problem here?" Mrs. J trying not to sound breathless or angry and ain't doing too good a job. She got to say it twice to be heard.

"No problem, Mrs. Johnson," the dude says straight-face. "The customers are buying condoms, I am selling condoms. A sale is being conducted, as is customary in a store."

Mrs. J looks down at the jumble of boxes and covers her mouth. She don't know what to do. I duck down, cause when folks in authority caught in a trick, the first they look for is a scapegoat.

"Well, honey," Ethel says, giving a chummy shove to Mrs. J's shoulder, "what do you think? I've heard that Trojans are ultrasensitive. They use a baby lamb brain, I understand."

"Membrane, dear, membrane," Fur Coat says down her nose. "They remove the intestines of a four-week-old lamb and use the membrane. Tough, resilient, sheer."

"Gotcha," says Ethel. "On the other hand, it is said by folks who should know that Ramses has a better box score."

"Box score," echoes Mrs. J in a daze.

"Box score. You know, honey—no splits, breaks, leaks, seeps."

"Seepage, dear, seepage," says Fur Coat, all nasal.

"Gotcha."

"The solution," says the dude in an almost robot

voice, "is to take one small box of each and do the comparison test as you say. A survey. A random sampling of your friends." He says this to Fur Coat, who is not enjoying it all nearly so much as Ethel, who is whooping and hollering.

Mrs. J backs off and trots to the prescription booth. Nazi Youth peeks over the glass and mumbles something soothing to Mrs J. He waves me and Madeen away like he somebody we got to pay some mind.

"We will take one super-duper, jumbo family size of each."

"Family size?" Fur Coat is appalled. "And one more thing, young man," she orders. "Wrap us a petite size for a small-size smart-ass acquaintance of mine. Gift-wrapped, ribbons and all."

It occurs to me that Fur Coat's going to present this to the dude. Right then and there I decide I don't like her. She's not discriminating with her stuff. Up till then I was thinking how much I'd like to trade Aunt Harriet in for either of these two, hang out with them, sit up all night while they drink highballs and talk about men they've known and towns they've been in. I always did want to hang out with women like this and listen to their stories. But they beginning to reveal themselves as not nice people, just cause the dude is rough dry on Christmas Eve. My Uncle Henry all the time telling me they different kinds of folks in the community, but when you boil it right down there's just nice and not nice. Uncle Henry say they folks who'll throw they mamas to the wolves if the fish sandwich big enough. They folks who won't whatever the hot sauce. They folks that're scared, folks that are dumb; folks that have heart and some with heart to spare. That all boils down to nice and not nice if you ask me. It occurs to me that Fur Coat is not nice. Fun, dazzling, witty, but not nice.

"Do you accept Christmas gifts, young man?" Fur Coat asking in icy tones she ain't masking too well.

"No. But I do accept Kwanza presents at the feast."

"Quan . . . hmm . . ."

Fur Coat and Ethel go into a huddle with the stage whispers. "I bet he thinks we don't know beans about Quantas . . . Don't he know we are The Ebony Jet Set . . . We never travel to kangaroo land except by . . ."

Fur Coat straightens up and stares at the dude. "Will you accept a whatchamacallit gift from me even though we are not feasting, as it were?"

"If it is given with love and respect, my sister, of course." He was sounding so sincere, it kinda got to Fur Coat.

"In that case . . ." She scoops up her bundle and sweeps out the place. Ethel trotting behind hollering, "He gotcha, Helen. Give the boy credit. Maybe we should hire him and do a threesome act." She spun the turnstile round three times for she got into the spin and spun out the store.

"Characters," says Piper on tiptoe, so we all can hear him. He laughs and checks his watch. Madeen slinks over to Tobacco to be in asking distance in case he don't already have a date to the dance. Miz Della's patting some powder on. I'm staring at the door after Fur Coat and Ethel, coming to terms with the fact that my daddy ain't coming. It's gonna be just Uncle Henry and Aunt Harriet this year, with maybe Mama calling on the phone between sets to holler in my ear, asking have I been a good girl, it's been that long since she's taken a good look at me.

"You wanna go to the Kwanza celebrations with me sometime this week or next week, Candy?"

I turn and look at the dude. I can tell my face is falling and right now I don't feel up to doing anything about it. Holidays are depressing. Maybe there's something joyous about this celebration he's talking about. Cause Lord knows Christmas is a drag. The sister who taught me how to wrap a gele asked me was I coming to the celebration down at the Black Arts Center, but I didn't know nothing bout it.

"Look here," I finally say, "would you please get a pencil and paper and write your name down for me. And write that other word down too so I can look it up."

He writes his name down and spins the paper around for me to read.

"Obatale."

"Right," he says, spinning it back. "But you can call me Ali Baba if you want to." He was leaning over too far writing out Kwanza for me to see if that was a smile on his face or a smirk. I figure a smile, cause Obatale nice people.

The Circuit

Francisco Jiménez

It was that time of year again. Ito, the strawberry share-cropper, did not smile. It was natural. The peak of the strawberry season was over and the last few days the workers, most of them braceros, were not picking as many boxes as they had during the months of June and July.

As the last days of August disappeared, so did the number of braceros. Sunday, only one—the best picker—came to work. I liked him. Sometimes we talked during our half-hour lunch break. That is how I found out he was from Jalisco, the same state in Mexico my family was from. That Sunday was the last time I saw him.

When the sun had tired and sunk behind the mountains, Ito signaled us that it was time to go home. "Ya esora," he yelled in his broken Spanish. Those were the words I waited for twelve hours a day, every day, seven days a week, week after week. And the thought of not hearing them again saddened me.

As we drove home Papá did not say a word. With both hands on the wheel, he stared at the dirt road. My older brother, Roberto, was also silent. He leaned his head back and closed his eyes. Once in a while he cleared from his throat the dust that blew in from outside.

Yes, it was that time of year. When I opened the front door to the shack, I stopped. Everything we owned was neatly packed in cardboard boxes. Suddenly I felt even more the weight of hours, days, weeks, and months of work. I sat down on a box. The thought of having to move to Fresno and knowing what was in store for me there brought tears to my eyes.

That night I could not sleep. I lay in bed thinking about how much I hated this move.

A little before five o'clock in the morning, Papá woke everyone up. A few minutes later, the yelling and screaming of my little brothers and sisters, for whom the move was a great adventure, broke the silence of dawn. Shortly, the barking of the dogs accompanied them.

While we packed the breakfast dishes, Papá went outside to start the "Carcanchita." That was the name Papá gave his old '38 black Plymouth. He bought it in a used-car lot in Santa Rosa in the winter of 1949. Papá was very proud of his little jalopy. He had a right to be proud of it. He spent a lot of time looking at other cars before buying this one. When he finally chose the "Carcanchita," he checked it thoroughly before driving it out of the car lot. He examined every inch of the car. He listened to the motor, tilting his head from side to side like a parrot, trying to detect any noises that spelled car trouble. After being satisfied with the looks and sounds of the car, Papá then insisted on knowing who the original owner was. He never did find out from the car salesman, but he bought the car anyway. Papá figured the original owner must have been an important man because behind the rear seat of the car he found a blue necktie.

Papá parked the car out in front and left the motor running. "Listo," he yelled. Without saying a word, Roberto and I began to carry the boxes out to the car. Roberto carried the two big boxes and I carried the two smaller ones. Papá then threw the mattress on top of the car roof and tied it with ropes to the front and rear bumpers.

Everything was packed except Mamá's pot. It was an old large galvanized pot she had picked up at an army surplus store in Santa María the year I was born. The pot had many dents and nicks, and the more dents and nicks it acquired the more Mamá liked it. "Mi olla," she used to say proudly.

I held the front door open as Mamá carefully carried out her pot by both handles, making sure not to spill the cooked beans. When she got to the car, Papá reached out to help her with it. Roberto opened the rear car door and Papá gently placed it on the floor behind the front seat. All of us then climbed in. Papá sighed, wiped the sweat off his forehead with his sleeve, and said wearily: "Es todo."

As we drove away, I felt a lump in my throat. I turned around and looked at our little shack for the last time.

At sunset we drove into a labor camp near Fresno. Since Papá did not speak English, Mamá asked the camp foreman if he needed any more workers. "We don't need no more," said the foreman, scratching his head. "Check with Sullivan down the road. Can't miss him. He lives in a big white house with a fence around it."

When we got there, Mamá walked up to the house. She went through a white gate, past a row of rose bushes, up the stairs to the front door. She rang the doorbell. The porch light went on and a tall husky man came out. They exchanged a few words. After the man went in, Mamá clasped her hands and hurried back to the car. "We have work! Mr. Sullivan said we can stay there the whole season," she said, gasping and pointing to an old garage near the stables.

The garage was worn out by the years. It had no windows. The walls, eaten by termites, strained to support the roof full of holes. The dirt floor, populated by earth worms, looked like a gray road map.

That night, by the light of a kerosene lamp, we unpacked and cleaned our new home. Roberto swept away the loose dirt, leaving the hard ground. Papá plugged the holes in the walls with old newspapers and tin can tops. Mamá fed my little brothers and sisters. Papá and Roberto then brought in the mattress and placed it in the far corner of the garage. "Mamá, you and the little ones sleep on the mattress. Roberto, Panchito, and I will sleep outside under the trees," Papá said.

Early next morning Mr. Sullivan showed us where his crop was, and after breakfast, Papá, Roberto, and I headed for the vineyard to pick.

Around nine o'clock the temperature had risen to almost one hundred degrees. I was completely soaked in sweat and my mouth felt as if I had been chewing on a handkerchief. I walked over to the end of the row, picked up the jug of water we had brought, and began drinking. "Don't drink too much; you'll get sick," Roberto shouted. No sooner had he said that than I felt sick to my stomach. I dropped to my knees and let the jug roll off my hands. I remained motionless with my eyes glued on the hot sandy ground. All I could hear was the drone of insects. Slowly I began to recover. I poured water over my face and neck and watched the dirty water run down my arms to the ground.

I still felt a little dizzy when we took a break to eat lunch. It was past two o'clock and we sat underneath a large walnut tree that was on the side of the road. While we ate, Papá jotted down the number of boxes we had picked. Roberto drew designs on the ground with a stick. Suddenly I noticed Papá's face turn pale as he looked down the road. "Here comes the school bus," he whispered loudly in alarm. Instinctively, Roberto and I ran and hid in the vineyards. We did not want to get in trouble for not going to school. The neatly dressed boys about my age got off. They carried books under their arms. After they crossed the street, the bus drove away. Roberto and I came out from hiding and joined Papá. "Tienen que tener cuidado," he warned us.

After lunch we went back to work. The sun kept beating down. The buzzing insects, the wet sweat, and the hot dry dust made the afternoon seem to last forever. Finally the mountains around the valley reached out and swallowed the sun. Within an hour it was too dark to continue picking. The vines blanketed the grapes, making it difficult to see the bunches. "Vámonos," said Papá, signaling to us that it was time to quit work. Papá then took out a pencil and began to figure out how much we had earned our first day. He wrote down numbers, crossed some out, wrote down some more. "Quince," he murmured.

When we arrived home, we took a cold shower underneath a waterhose. We then sat down to eat dinner around some wooden crates that served as a table. Mamá had cooked a special meal for us. We had rice and tortillas with "carne con chile," my favorite dish.

The next morning I could hardly move. My body ached all over. I felt little control over my arms and legs. This feeling went on every morning for days until my muscles finally got used to the work.

It was Monday, the first week of November. The grape season was over and I could now go to school. I woke up early that morning and lay in bed, looking at the stars and savoring the thought of not going to work and of starting sixth grade for the first time that year. Since I could not sleep, I decided to get up and join Papá and Roberto at breakfast. I did not want to look up and face him. I knew he was sad. He was not going to school today. He was not going tomorrow, or next week, or next month. He would not go until the cotton season was over, and that was sometime in February. I rubbed my hands together and watched the dry, acid stained skin fall to the floor in little rolls.

When Papá and Roberto left for work, I felt relief. I walked to the top of a small grade next to the shack and watched the "Carcanchita" disappear in the distance in a cloud of dust.

Two hours later, around eight o'clock, I stood by the side of the road waiting for school bus number twenty. When it arrived I climbed in. Everyone was busy either talking or yelling. I sat in an empty seat in the back.

When the bus stopped in front of the school, I felt very nervous. I looked out the bus window and saw boys and girls carrying books under their arms. I put my hands in my pockets and walked to the principal's office. When I entered I heard a woman's voice say: "May I help you?" I was startled. I had not heard English for months. For a few seconds I remained speechless. I looked at the lady who waited for an answer. My first instinct was to answer her in Spanish, but I held back. Finally, after struggling for English words, I managed to tell her that I wanted to enroll in the sixth grade. After answering many questions, I was led to the classroom.

Mr. Lema, the sixth grade teacher, greeted me and assigned me a desk. He then introduced me to the class. I was so nervous and scared at that moment when everyone's eyes were on me that I wished I were with Papá and Roberto picking cotton. After taking roll, Mr. Lema gave the class the assignment for the first hour. "The first thing we have to do this morning is finish reading the story we began yesterday," he said enthusiastically. He walked up to me, handed me an English book, and asked me to read. "We are on page 125," he said politely. When I heard this, I felt my blood rush to my head; I felt dizzy. "Would you like to read?" he asked hesitantly. I opened the book to page 125. My mouth was dry. My eyes began to water. I could not begin. "You can read later," Mr. Lema said understandingly.

For the rest of the reading period I kept getting angrier and angrier with myself. I should have read, I thought to myself.

During recess I went into the restroom and opened my English book to page 125. I began to read in a low voice, pretending I was in class. There were many words I did not know. I closed the book and headed back to the classroom.

Mr. Lema was sitting at his desk correcting papers. When I entered he looked up at me and smiled. I felt better. I walked up to him and asked if he could help me with the new words. "Gladly," he said.

The rest of the month I spent my lunch hours working on English with Mr. Lema, my best friend at school.

One Friday during lunch hour Mr. Lema asked me to take a walk with him to the music room. "Do you like music?" he asked me as we entered the building.

"Yes, I like corridos," I answered. He then picked up a trumpet, blew on it and handed it to me. The sound gave me goose bumps. I knew that sound. I had heard it in many corridos. "How would you like to learn how to play it?" he asked. He must have read my face because before I could answer, he added: "I'll teach you how to play it during our lunch hours."

That day I could hardly wait to get home to tell Papá and Mamá the great news. As I got off the bus, my little brothers and sisters ran up to meet me. They were yelling and screaming. I thought they were happy to see me, but when I opened the door to our shack, I saw that everything we owned was neatly packed in cardboard boxes.

First Confession

Frank O'Connor

All the trouble began when my grandfather died and my grandmother—my father's mother—came to live with us. Relations in the one house are a strain at the best of times, but, to make matters worse, my grandmother was a real old countrywoman and quite unsuited to the life in town. She had a fat, wrinkled old face, and, to Mother's great indignation went round the house in bare feet—the boots had her crippled, she said. For dinner she had a jug of porter and a pot of potatoes with—sometimes—a bit of salt fish, and she poured out the potatoes on the table and ate them slowly, with great relish, using her fingers by way of a fork.

Now, girls are supposed to be fastidious, but I was the one who suffered most from this. Nora, my sister, just sucked up to the old woman for the penny she got every Friday out of the old-age pension, a thing I could not do. I was too honest, that was my trouble; and when I was playing with Bill Connell, the sergeant major's son, and saw my grandmother steering up the path with the jug of porter sticking out from beneath her shawl I was mortified. I made excuses not to let him come into the house, because I could never be sure what she would be up to when we went in.

When Mother was at work and my grandmother made the dinner I wouldn't touch it. Nora once tried to make me, but I hid under the table from her and took the bread knife with me for protection. Nora let on to be very indignant (she wasn't, of course, but she knew Mother saw through her, so she sided with Gran) and came after me. I lashed out at her with the bread knife, and after that she left me alone. I stayed there till Mother came in from work and made my dinner, but when Father came in later Nora said in a shocked voice:

"Oh, Dadda, do you know what Jackie did at dinnertime?" Then, of course, it all came out; Father gave me a flaking; Mother interfered, and for days after that he didn't speak to me and Mother barely spoke to Nora. And all because of that old woman! God knows, I was heart-scalded.

Then, to crown my misfortunes, I had to make my first confession and communion. It was an old woman called Ryan who prepared us for these. She was about the one age with Gran; she was well-to-do, lived in a big house on Montenotte, wore a black cloak and bonnet, and came every day to school at three o'clock when we should have been going home, and talked to us of hell. She may have mentioned the other place as well, but that could only have been by accident, for hell had the first place in her heart.

She lit a candle, took out a new half crown, and offered it to the first boy who would hold one finger— only one finger!—in the flame for five minutes by the school clock. Being always very ambitious I was tempted to volunteer, but I thought it might look greedy. Then she asked were we afraid of holding one finger—only one finger!—in a little candle flame for five minutes and not afraid of burning all over in roasting hot furnaces for all eternity. "All eternity! Just think of that! A whole lifetime goes by and it's nothing, not even a drop in the ocean of your sufferings." The woman was really interesting about hell, but my attention was all fixed on the half crown. At the end of the lesson she put it back in her purse. It was a great disappointment; a religious woman like that, you wouldn't think she'd bother about a thing like a half crown.

Another day she said she knew a priest who woke one night to find a fellow he didn't recognize leaning over the end of his bed. The priest was a bit frightened— naturally enough—but he asked the fellow what he wanted, and the fellow said in a deep, husky voice that he wanted to go to confession. The priest said it was an awkward time and wouldn't it do in the morning, but the fellow said that last time he went to confession, there was one sin he kept back, being ashamed to mention it, and now it was always on his mind. Then the priest knew it was a bad case, because the fellow was after making a bad confession and committing a mortal sin. He got up to dress, and just then the cock crew in the yard outside, and—lo and behold!—when the priest looked round there was no sign of the fellow, only a smell of burning timber, and when the priest looked at his bed didn't he see the print of two hands burned in it? That was because the fellow had made a bad confession. This story made a shocking impression on me.

But the worst of all was when she showed us how to examine our conscience. Did we take the name of the Lord, our God, in vain? Did we honor our father and our mother? (I asked her did this include grandmothers and she said it did.) Did we love our neighbors as ourselves? Did we covet our neighbor's goods? (I thought of the way I felt about the penny that Nora got every Friday.) I decided that, between one thing and another, I must have broken the whole ten commandments, all on account of that old woman, and so far as I could see, so long as she remained in the house I had no hope of ever doing anything else.

I was scared to death of confession. The day the whole class went I let on to have a toothache, hoping my absence wouldn't be noticed; but at three o'clock, just as I was feeling safe, along comes a chap with a message from Mrs. Ryan that I was to go to confession myself on Saturday and be at the chapel for communion with the rest. To make it worse, Mother couldn't come with me and sent Nora instead.

Now, that girl had ways of tormenting me that Mother never knew of. She held my hand as we went down the hill, smiling sadly and saying how sorry she was for me, as if she were bringing me to the hospital for an operation.

"Oh, God help us!" she moaned. "Isn't it a terrible pity you weren't a good boy? Oh, Jackie, my heart bleeds for you! How will you ever think of all your sins? Don't forget you have to tell him about the time you kicked Gran on the shin."

"Lemme go!" I said, trying to drag myself free of her. "I don't want to go to confession at all."

"But sure, you'll have to go to confession, Jackie," she replied in the same regretful tone. "Sure, if you didn't, the parish priest would be up to the house, look-

ing for you. 'Tisn't, God knows, that I'm not sorry for
you. Do you remember the time you tried to kill me
with the bread knife under the table? And the language
you used to me? I don't know what he'll do with you at
all, Jackie. He might have to send you up to the bishop."

I remember thinking bitterly that she didn't know the
half of what I had to tell—if I told it. I knew I couldn't
tell it, and understood perfectly why the fellow in Mrs.
Ryan's story made a bad confession; it seemed to me a
great shame that people wouldn't stop criticizing him. I
remember that steep hill down to the church, and the
sunlit hillsides beyond the valley of the river, which I
saw in the gaps between the houses like Adam's last
glimpse of Paradise.

Then, when she had maneuvered me down the long
flight of steps to the chapel yard, Nora suddenly changed
her tone. She became the raging malicious devil she really was.

"There you are!" she said with a yelp of triumph,
hurling me through the church door. "And I hope he'll
give you the penitential psalms, you dirty little caffler."

I knew then I was lost, given up to eternal justice. The
door with the colored-glass panels swung shut behind
me, the sunlight went out and gave place to deep
shadow, and the wind whistled outside so that the silence
within seemed to crackle like ice under my feet. Nora
sat in front of me by the confession box. There were a
couple of old women ahead of her, and then a miserable-
looking poor devil came and wedged me in at the other
side, so that I couldn't escape even if I had the courage.
He joined his hands and rolled his eyes in the direction
of the roof, muttering aspirations in an anguished tone,
and I wondered had he a grandmother too. Only a
grandmother could account for a fellow behaving in that
heartbroken way, but he was better off than I, for he at
least could go and confess his sins; while I would make
a bad confession and then die in the night and be continually coming back and burning people's furniture.

Nora's turn came, and I heard the sound of something
slamming, and then her voice as if butter wouldn't melt
in her mouth, and then another slam, and out she came.
God, the hypocrisy of women. Her eyes were lowered,
her head was bowed, and her hands were joined very

low down on her stomach, and she walked up the aisle to the side altar looking like a saint. You never saw such an exhibition of devotion; and I remembered the devilish malice with which she had tormented me all the way from our door, and wondered were all religious people like that, really. It was my turn now. With the fear of damnation in my soul I went in, and the confessional door closed of itself behind me.

It was pitch dark and I couldn't see the priest or anything else. Then I really began to be frightened. In the darkness it was a matter between God and me, and He had all the odds. He knew what my intentions were before I even started; I had no chance. All I had ever been told about confession got mixed up in my mind, and I knelt to one wall and said: "Bless me, father, for I have sinned; this is my first confession." I waited for a few minutes, but nothing happened, so I tried it on the other wall. Nothing happened there either. He had me spotted all right.

It must have been then that I noticed the shelf at about one height with my head. It was really a place for grown-up people to rest their elbows, but in my distracted state I thought it was probably the place you were supposed to kneel. Of course, it was on the high side and not very deep, but I was always good at climbing and managed to get up all right. Staying up was the trouble. There was room only for my knees, and nothing you could get a grip on but a sort of wooden molding a bit above it. I held on to the molding and repeated the words a little louder, and this time something happened all right. A slide was slammed back; a little light entered the box, and a man's voice said: "Who's there?"

" 'Tis me, father," I said for fear he mightn't see me and go away again. I couldn't see him at all. The place the voice came from was under the molding, about level with my knees, so I took a good grip of the molding and swung myself down till I saw the astonished face of a young priest looking up at me. He had to put his head on one side to see me, and I had to put mine on one side to see him, so we were more or less talking to one another upside-down. It struck me as a queer way of hearing confessions, but I didn't feel it my place to criticize.

"Bless me, father, for I have sinned; this is my first confession," I rattled off all in one breath, and swung myself down the least shade more to make it easier for him.

"What are you doing up there?" he shouted in an angry voice, and the strain the politeness was putting on my hold of the molding, and the shock of being addressed in such an uncivil tone, were too much for me. I lost my grip, tumbled, and hit the door an unmerciful wallop before I found myself flat on my back in the middle of the aisle. The people who had been waiting stood up with their mouths open. The priest opened the door of the middle box and came out, pushing his biretta back from his forehead; he looked something terrible. Then Nora came scampering down the aisle.

"Oh, you dirty little caffler!" she said, "I might have known you'd do it. I might have known you'd disgrace me. I can't leave you out of my sight for one minute."

Before I could even get to my feet to defend myself she bent down and gave me a clip across the ear. This reminded me that I was so stunned I had even forgotten to cry, so that people might think I wasn't hurt at all, when in fact I was probably maimed for life. I gave a roar out of me.

"What's all this about?" the priest hissed, getting angrier than ever and pushing Nora off me. "How dare you hit the child like that, you little vixen?"

"But I can't do my penance with him, father," Nora cried, cocking an outraged eye up at him.

"Well, go and do it, or I'll give you more to do," he said, giving me a hand up. "Was it coming to confession you were, my poor man?" he asked me.

" 'Twas, father," said I with a sob.

"Oh," he said respectfully, "a big hefty fellow like you must have terrible sins. Is this your first?"

" 'Tis, father," said I.

"Worse and worse," he said gloomily. "The crimes of a lifetime. I don't know will I get rid of you at all today. You'd better wait now till I'm finished with these old ones. You can see by the looks of them they haven't much to tell."

"I will, father," I said with something approaching joy. The relief of it was really enormous. Nora stuck out her tongue at me from behind his back, but I couldn't even be bothered retorting. I knew from the very moment that man opened his mouth that he was intelligent above the ordinary. When I had time to think, I saw how right I was. It only stood to reason that a fellow confessing after seven years would have more to tell than people that went every week. The crimes of a lifetime, exactly as he said. It was only what he expected, and the rest was the cackle of old women and girls with their talk of hell, the bishop, and the penitential psalms. That was all they knew. I started to make my examination of conscience, and barring the one bad business of my grandmother it didn't seem so bad.

The next time, the priest steered me into the confession box himself and left the shutter back the way I could see him get in and sit down at the further side of the grille from me.

"Well, now," he said, "what do they call you?"

"Jackie, father," said I.

"And what's a-trouble to you, Jackie?"

"Father," I said, feeling I might as well get it over while I had him in good humor, "I had it all arranged to kill my grandmother."

He seemed a bit shaken by that, all right, because he said nothing for quite a while.

"My goodness," he said at last, "that'd be a shocking thing to do. What put that into your head?"

"Father," I said, feeling very sorry for myself, "she's an awful woman."

"Is she?" he asked. "What way is she awful?"

"She takes porter, father," I said, knowing well from the way Mother talked of it that this was a mortal sin, and hoping it would make the priest take a more favorable view of my case.

"Oh, my!" he said, and I could see he was impressed.

"And snuff, father," said I.

"That's a bad case, sure enough, Jackie," he said.

"And she goes round in her bare feet, father," I went on in a rush of self-pity, "and she knows I don't like her, and she gives pennies to Nora and none to me, and my dad sides with her and flakes me, and one night I was so heart-scalded I made up my mind I'd have to kill her."

"And what would you do with the body?" he asked with great interest.

"I was thinking I could chop that up and carry it away in a barrow I have," I said.

"Begor, Jackie," he said, "do you know you're a terrible child?"

"I know, father," I said, for I was just thinking the same thing myself. "I tried to kill Nora too with a bread knife under the table, only I missed her."

"Is that the little girl that was beating you just now?" he asked.

" 'Tis, father."

"Someone will go for her with a bread knife one day, and he won't miss her," he said rather cryptically. "You must have great courage. Between ourselves, there's a lot of people I'd like to do the same to but I'd never have the nerve. Hanging is an awful death."

"Is it, father?" I asked with the deeper interest—I was always very keen on hanging. "Did you ever see a fellow hanged?"

"Dozens of them," he said solemnly. "And they all died roaring."

"Jay!" I said.

"Oh, a horrible death!" he said with great satisfaction. "Lots of the fellows I saw killed their grandmothers too, but they all said 'twas never worth it."

He had me there for a full ten minutes talking, and then walked out the chapel yard with me. I was genuinely sorry to part with him, because he was the most entertaining character I'd ever met in the religious line. Outside, after the shadow of the church, the sunlight was like the roaring of waves on a beach; it dazzled me; and when the frozen silence melted and I heard the screech of trams on the road my heart soared. I knew now I wouldn't die in the night and come back, leaving marks on my mother's furniture. It would be a great worry to her, and the poor soul had enough.

Nora was sitting on the railing, waiting for me, and she put on a very sour puss when she saw the priest with me. She was mad jealous because a priest had never come out of the church with her.

"Well," she said coldly, after he left me, "what did he give you?"

"Three Hail Marys," I said.

"Three Hail Marys," she repeated incredulously. "You mustn't have told him anything."

"I told him everything," I said confidently.

"About Gran and all?"

"About Gran and all."

(All she wanted was to be able to go home and say I'd made a bad confession.)

"Did you tell him you went for me with the bread knife?" she asked with a frown.

"I did to be sure."

"And he only gave you three Hail Marys?"

"That's all."

She slowly got down from the railing with a baffled air. Clearly, this was beyond her. As we mounted the steps back to the main road she looked at me suspiciously.

"What are you sucking?" she asked.

"Bullseyes."

"Was it the priest gave them to you?"

" 'Twas."

"Lord God," she wailed bitterly, "some people have all the luck! 'Tis no advantage to anybody trying to be good. I might just as well be a sinner like you."

A Coupla Scalped Indians

Ralph Ellison

They had a small, loud-playing band, and as we moved through the trees, I could hear the notes of the horns bursting like bright metallic bubbles against the sky. It was a faraway and sparklike sound, shooting through the late-afternoon quiet of the hill; very clear now and definitely music, band music. I was relieved. I had been hearing it for several minutes as we moved through the woods, but the pain down there had made all my senses so deceptively sharp that I had decided that the sound was simply a musical ringing in my ears. But now I was doubly sure, for Buster stopped and looked at me, squinching up his eyes with his head cocked to one side. He was wearing a blue cloth headband with a turkey feather stuck over his ear, and I could see it flutter in the breeze.

"You hear what I hear, man?" he said.

"I *been* hearing it," I said.

"Damn! We better haul it outta these woods so we can see something. Why didn't you say something to a man?"

We moved again, hurrying along. Until suddenly we were out of the woods, standing at a point of the hill where the path dropped down to the town, our eyes searching. It was close to sundown, and below me I could see the red clay of the path cutting through the woods and moving past a white, lightning-blasted tree to join the river road, and the narrow road shifting past Aunt Mackie's old shack and on, beyond the road and the shack, I could see the dull, mysterious movement of the river. The horns were blasting brighter now, though still far away, sounding like somebody flipping bright handfuls of new small change against the sky. I listened and followed the river swiftly with my eyes as it wound through the trees and on past the buildings and houses of the town—until there, there at the farther edge of the town, past the tall smokestack and the great silver sphere of the gas storage tower, floated the tent, spread white and cloudlike with its bright ropes of fluttering flags.

That's when we started running. It was a dogtrotting Indian run, because we were both wearing packs and were tired from the tests we had been taking in the woods and in Indian Lake. But now the bright blare of the horns made us forget our tiredness and pain, and we bounded down the path like young goats in the twilight; our army-surplus mess kits and canteens rattling against us.

"We late, man," Buster said. "I told you we was gon' fool around and be late. But naw, you had to cook that damn sage hen with mud on him just like it says in the book. We coulda barbecued a damn elephant while we was waiting for a tough sucker like that to get done. . . ."

His voice grumbled on like a trombone with a big, fat, pot-shaped mute stuck in it, and I ran on without answering. We had tried to take the cooking test by using a sage hen instead of a chicken because Buster said Indians didn't eat chicken. So we'd taken time to flush a sage hen and kill him with a slingshot. Besides, he was the one who insisted that we try the running endurance test, the swimming test, *and* the cooking test all in one day. Sure it had taken time. I knew it would take time; especially with our having no Scout Master. We didn't even have a troop, only the Boy Scout's Handbook that Buster had found, and—as we'd figured—our hardest problem had been working out the tests for ourselves. He had no right to argue anyway, since he'd beaten me in all the tests—although I'd passed them, too. And he was the one who insisted that we start taking them today even though we were both still sore and wearing our bandages, and I was still carrying some of the catgut stitches around in me. I had wanted to wait a few days until I was healed, but Mister Know-it-all Buster challenged me by saying that a real stud Indian could take the tests even right after the doctor had just finished sewing on him. So, since we were more interested in being *Indian* scouts than simply *boy* scouts, here I was running toward the spring carnival instead of being already there. I wondered how Buster knew so much about what an Indian would do, anyway. We certainly hadn't read anything about what the doctor had done to us. He'd probably made it up, and I had let him urge me into going to the woods even though I had to slip out of the house. The doctor had told Miss Janey (she's the lady who takes care of me) to keep me quiet for a few days, and she dead-aimed to do it. You would've thought from the way she carried on that she was the one who had the operation—only that's one kind of operation no woman ever gets to brag about.

Anyway, Buster and me had been in the woods, and now we were plunging down the hill through the fast-falling dark to the carnival. I had begun to throb, and the bandage was chafing, but as we rounded a curve, I could see the tent and the flares and the gathering crowd. There was a breeze coming up the hill against us now, and I could almost smell that cotton candy, the hamburgers, and the kerosene smell of the flares. We stopped to rest, and Buster stood very straight and pointed down below, making a big sweep with his arm like an Indian chief in the movies when he's up on a hill telling his braves and the Great Spirit that he's getting ready to attack a wagon train.

"Heap big . . . teepee . . . down yonder," he said in Indian talk. "Smoke signal say . . . Blackfeet . . . make . . . heap much . . . stink, buck-dancing in tennis shoes!"

"Ugh," I said, bowing my suddenly war-bonneted head, "ugh!"

Buster swept his arm from east to west, his face impassive, "Smoke medicine say . . . heap . . . *Big* stink! Hot toe jam!" He struck his palm with his fist, and I looked at his puffed-out cheeks and giggled.

"Smoke medicine say you tell heap big lie," I said. "Let's get on down there."

We ran past some trees, Buster's canteen jangling. Around us it was quiet except for the roosting birds.

"Man," I said, "you making as much noise as a team of mules in full harness. Don't no Indian scout make all that racket when he runs."

"No scout-um now," he said. "Me go make heap much pow-wow at stinkydog carnival!"

"Yeah, but you'll get yourself scalped, making all that noise in the woods," I said. "Those other Indians don't give a damn 'bout no carnival—what does a carnival mean to them? They'll scalp the hell outta you!"

"Scalp?" he said, talking Colored now, "Hell, man—that damn doctor scalped me last week. Damn near took my whole head off!"

I almost fell with laughing. "Have mercy, Lord," I laughed, "we're just a coupla poor scalped Indians!"

We laughed. Buster stumbled about, grabbing a tree for support. The doctor had said that it would make us men, and Buster had said, hell, he was a man already—what he wanted was to be an Indian. We hadn't thought about it making us scalped ones.

"You right, man," Buster said. "Since he done scalped so much of my head away, I must be crazy as a fool. That's why I'm in such a hurry to get down yonder with the other crazy folks. I want to be right in the middle of 'em when they really start raising hell."

"Oh, you'll be there, Chief Baldhead," I said.

He looked at me blankly. "What you think ole Doc done with our scalps?"

"Made him a tripe stew, man."

"You nuts," Buster said, "he probably used 'em for fish bait."

"He did, I'm going to sue him for one trillion, zillion dollars, cash," I said.

"Maybe he gave 'em to ole Aunt Mackie, man. I bet with them she could work up some out*rageous* spells!"

"Man," I said, suddenly shivering, "don't talk about that old woman, she's evil."

"Hell, everybody's so scared of her. I just wish she'd mess with me or my daddy, I'd fix her."

I said nothing—I was afraid. For though I had seen the old woman about town all my life, she remained to me like the moon, mysterious in her very familiarity; and in the sound of her name there was terror:

Ho, Aunt Mackie, talker-with-spirits, prophetess-of-disaster, odd-dweller-alone in a riverside shack surrounded by sunflowers, morning-glories, and strange magical weeds (Yao, as Buster during our Indian phase, would have put it, Yao!); *Old Aunt Mackie, wizen-faced walker-with-a-stick, shrill-voiced ranter in the night,*

*round-eyed malicious one, given to dramatic trances and
fiery flights of rage; Aunt Mackie, preacher of wild ser-
mons on the busy streets of the town, hot-voiced chaser
of children, snuff-dipper, visionary; wearer of greasy
headrags, wrinkled gingham aprons, and old men's shoes;
Aunt Mackie, nobody's sister but still Aunt Mackie to us
all* (Ho, yao!); *teller of fortunes, concocter of powerful,
body-rending spells* (Yao, Yao!); *Aunt Mackie, the remote one though always seen about us; night-consulted
adviser to farmers on crops and cattle* (Yao!); *herb-
healer, root-doctor, and town-confounding oracle to wild-
cat drillers seeking oil in the earth*—(Yaaaah-Ho!). It was
all there in her name and before her name I shivered.
Once uttered, for me the palaver was finished; I resigned
it to Buster, the tough one.

Even some of the grown folks, both black and white,
were afraid of Aunt Mackie, and all the kids except Buster.
Buster lived on the outskirts of the town and was as unim-
pressed by Aunt Mackie as by the truant officer and others
whom the rest of us regarded with awe. And because I
was his buddy I was ashamed of my fear.

Usually I had extra courage when I was with him.
Like the time two years before when we had gone into
the woods with only our slingshots, a piece of fatback,
and a skillet and had lived three days on the rabbits we
killed and the wild berries we picked and the ears of
corn we raided from farmers' fields. We slept each rolled
in his quilt, and in the night Buster had told bright stories of the world we'd find when we were grown up and
gone from hometown and family. I had no family, only
Miss Janey, who took me after my mother died (I didn't
know my father), so that getting away always appealed
to me, and the coming time of which Buster liked to
talk loomed in the darkness around me rich with pastel
promise. And although we heard a bear go lumbering
through the woods nearby and the eerie howling of a
coyote in the dark, yes, and had been swept by the soft
swift flight of an owl, Buster was unafraid, and I had
grown brave in the grace of his courage.

But to me Aunt Mackie was a threat of a different
order, and I paid her the respect of fear.

"Listen to those horns," Buster said. And now the

sound came through the trees like colored marbles glinting in the summer sun.

We ran again. And now, keeping pace with Buster, I felt good; for I meant to be there, too, at the carnival; right in the middle of all that confusion and sweating and laughing and all the strange sights to see.

"Listen to 'em now, man," Buster said. "Those fools is starting to shout amazing grace on those horns. Let's step on the gas!"

The scene danced below us as we ran. Suddenly there was a towering Ferris wheel revolving slowly out of the dark, its red and blue lights glowing like drops of dew dazzling a big spider web when you see it in the early morning. And we heard the beckoning blare of the band now shot through with the small, insistent, buckshot voices of the barkers.

"Listen to that trombone, man," I said.

"Sounds like he's playing the dozens with the whole wide world."

"What's he saying, Buster?"

"He's saying, 'Ya'll's mamas don't wear 'em. Is strictly without 'em. Don't know nothing 'bout 'em. . . .' "

"Don't know about what, man?"

"Draw's, fool; he's talking 'bout draw's!"

"How you know, man?"

"I hear him talking, don't I?"

"Sure, but you been scalped, remember? You crazy. How he know about those peoples' mamas?" I said.

"Says he saw 'em with his great big ole eye."

"Damn! He must be a Peeping Tom. How about those other horns?"

"Now that there tuba's saying:

"They don't play 'em, I know they don't.
They don't play 'em, I know they won't.
They just don't play no nasty dirty twelves. . . ."

"Man, you *are* a scalped-headed fool. How about that trumpet?"

"Him? That fool's a soldier, he's really signifying. Saying,

"So ya'll don't play 'em, hey?
So ya'll *won't* play 'em, hey?

Well pat your feet and clap your hands.
'Cause I'm going to play 'em to the promised
land. . . ."

"Man, the white folks know what that fool is signifying on that horn, they'd run him clear on out the
world. Trumpet's got a real *nasty* mouth."

"Why you call him a soldier, man?" I said.

" 'Cause he's slipping 'em in the twelves and choosing
'em, all at the same time. Talking 'bout they mamas and
offering to fight 'em. Now he ain't like that old clarinet;
clarinet so sweet-talking he just *eases* you in the dozens."

"Say, Buster," I said, seriously now. "You know, we
gotta stop cussing and playing the dozens if we're going
to be boy scouts. Those white boys don't play that
mess."

"You doggone right they don't," he said, the turkey
feather vibrating above his ear. "Those guys can't take
it, man. Besides, who wants to be just like them? Me,
I'm gon' be a scout and play the twelves, too! You have
to, with some of these old jokers we know. You don't
know what to say when they start easing you, you never
have no peace. You have to outtalk 'em, outrun 'em, or
outfight 'em and I don't aim to be running and fighting
all the time. N'mind those white boys."

We moved on through the growing dark. Already I
could see a few stars, and suddenly there was the moon.
It emerged bladelike from behind a thin veil of cloud,
just as I heard a new sound and looked about me with
quick uneasiness. Off to our left I heard a dog, a big
one. I slowed, seeing the outlines of a picket fence and
the odd-shaped shadows that lurked in Aunt Mackie's
yard.

"What's the matter, man?" Buster said.

"Listen," I said. "That's Aunt Mackie's dog. Last year
I was passing here and he sneaked up and bit me
through the fence when I wasn't even thinking about
him. . . ."

"Hush, man," Buster whispered. "I hear the sonofa-
bitch back in there now. You leave him to me."

We moved by inches now, hearing the dog barking in
the dark. Then we were going past and he was throwing
his heavy body against the fence, straining at his chain.

We hesitated, Buster's hand on my arm. I undid my heavy canteen belt and held it, suddenly light in my fingers. In my right I gripped the hatchet which I'd brought along.

"We'd better go back and take the other path," I whispered.

"Just stand still, man," Buster said.

The dog hit the fence, again, barking hoarsely; and in the interval following the echoing crash I could hear the distant music of the band.

"Come on," I said, "let's go 'round."

"Hell, no! We're going straight! I ain't letting no damn dog scare me, Aunt Mackie or no Aunt Mackie. Come on!"

Trembling, I moved with him toward the roaring dog, then felt him stop again, and I could hear him removing his pack and taking out something wrapped in paper.

"Here," he said, "you take my stuff and come on."

I took his gear and went behind him, hearing his voice suddenly hot with fear and anger saying, "Here, you 'gator-mouthed egg-sucker, see how you like this sage hen," just as I tripped over the straps of his pack and went down. Then I was crawling frantically, trying to untangle myself and hearing the dog growling as he crunched something in his jaws. "Eat it, you buzzard," Buster was saying. "See if you tough as he is," as I tried to stand, stumbling and sending an old cooking range crashing in the dark. Part of the fence was gone, and in my panic I had crawled into the yard. Now I could hear the dog bark threateningly and leap the length of his chain toward me, then back to the sage hen; toward me, a swift leaping form snatched backwards by the heavy chain, turning to mouth savagely on the mangled bird. Moving away I floundered over the stove and pieces of crating, against giant sunflower stalks, trying to get back to Buster when I saw the lighted window and realized that I had crawled to the very shack itself. That's when I pressed against the weathered-satin side of the shack and came erect. And there, framed by the window in the lamp-lit room, I saw the woman.

A brown naked woman, whose black hair hung beneath her shoulders. I could see the long graceful curve of her back as she moved in some sort of slow dance, bending forward and back; her arms and body moving as though gathering in something which I couldn't see but which she drew to her with pleasure; a young, girlish body with slender, well-rounded hips. *But who?* flashed through my mind as I heard Buster's *Hey, man; where'd you go? You done run out on me?* from back in the dark. And I willed to move, to hurry away—but in that instant she chose to pick up a glass from a wobbly old round white table and to drink, turning slowly as she stood with backward-tilted head, slowly turning in the lamplight and drinking slowly as she turned, slowly; until I could see the full-faced glowing of her feminine form.

And I was frozen there, watching the uneven movement of her breasts beneath the glistening course of the liquid, spilling down her body in twin streams drawn by the easy tiding of her breathing. Then the glass came down and my knees flowed beneath me like water. The air seemed to explode soundlessly. I shook my head, but she, the image, would not go away, and I wanted suddenly to laugh wildly and to scream. For above the smooth shoulders of the girlish form I saw the wrinkled face of old Aunt Mackie.

Now I had never seen a naked woman before, only very little girls or once or twice a skinny one my own age who looked like a boy with the boy part missing. And even though I'd seen a few calendar drawings, they were not alive like this, nor images of someone you'd thought familiar through having seen them passing through the streets of the town; nor like this inconsistent, with wrinkled face mismatched with glowing form. So that mixed with my fear of punishment for peeping there was added the terror of her mystery. And yet I could not move away. I was fascinated, hearing the growling dog and feeling a warm pain grow beneath my bandage—along with the newly risen terror that this deceptive old woman could cause me to feel this way, that she could be so young beneath her old baggy clothes.

She was dancing again now, still unaware of my eyes, the lamplight playing on her body as she swayed and enfolded the air or invisible ghosts or whatever it was within her arms. Each time she moved, her hair, which was black as night now that it was no longer hidden beneath a greasy headrag, swung heavily about her shoulders. And as she moved to the side I could see the gentle tossing of her breasts beneath her upraised arms. *It just can't be,* I thought, *it just can't* and moved closer, determined to see and to know. But I had forgotten the hatchet in my hand until it struck the side of the house and I saw her turn quickly toward the window, her face evil as she swayed. I was rigid as stone, hearing the growling dog mangling the bird and knowing that I should run even as she moved toward the window, her shadow flying before her, her hair now wild as snakes writhing on a dead tree during a springtime flood. Then I could hear Buster's hoarse-voiced, *Hey, man! where in hell are you?* even as she pointed at me and screamed, sending me moving backwards and I was aware of the sickle-bladed moon flying like a lightning flash as I fell, still gripping my hatchet, and struck my head in the dark.

When I started out of it someone was holding me and I lay in light and looked up to see her face above me. Then it all flooded swiftly back, and I was aware again of the contrast between smooth body and wrinkled face and experienced a sudden warm yet painful thrill. She held me close. Her breath came to me, sweetly alcoholic as she mumbled something about, "Little devil, lips that touch wine shall never touch mine! That's what I told him, understand me? Never," she said loudly. "You understand?"

"Yes, ma'm."

"Never, never, NEVER!"

"No, ma'm," I said, seeing her study me with narrowed eyes.

"You young, but you young'uns understand, devilish as you is. What you doing messing 'round in my yard?"

"I got lost," I said. "I was coming from taking some boy scout tests and I was trying to get by your dog."

"So that's what I heard," she said. "He bite you?"

"No, ma'm."

"Course not, he don't bite on the new moon. No, I think you come in my yard to spy on me."

"No, ma'm, I didn't," I said. "I just happened to see the light when I was stumbling around trying to find my way."

"You got a pretty big hatchet there," she said, looking down at my hand. "What you plan to do with it?"

"It's a kind of boy scout axe," I said. "I used it to come through the woods...."

She looked at me dubiously. "So," she said, "you're a heavy hatchet man, and you stopped to peep. Well, what I want to know is, is you a drinking man? Have your lips ever touched wine?"

"Wine? No, ma'm."

"So you ain't a drinking man, but do you belong to church?"

"Yes, ma'm."

"And have you been saved and ain't no backslider?"

"Yessum."

"Well," she said, pursing her lips, "I guess you can kiss me."

"MA'M?"

"That's what I said. You passed all the tests, and you was peeping in my window...."

She was holding me there on a cot, her arms around me as though I were a three-year-old, smiling like a girl, I could see her fine white teeth and the long hairs on her chin, and it was like a bad dream. "You peeped," she said, "now you got to do the rest. I said kiss me, or I'll fix you...."

I saw her face come close and felt her warm breath and closed my eyes, trying to force myself. *It's just like kissing some sweaty woman at church,* I told myself, *some friend of Miss Janey's.* But it didn't help, and I could feel her drawing me, and I found her lips with mine. It was dry and firm and winey and I could hear her sigh. "Again," she said, and once more my lips found hers. And suddenly she drew me to her and I could feel her breasts soft against me as once more she sighed.

"That was a nice boy," she said, her voice kind, and I opened my eyes. "That's enough now, you're both too young and too old, but you're brave. A regular lil' chocolate hero."

And now she moved, and I realized for the first time that my hand had found its way to her breast. I moved it guiltily, my face flaming as she stood.

"You're a good brave boy," she said, looking at me from deep in her eyes, "but you forget what happened here tonight."

I sat up as she stood looking down upon me with a mysterious smile. And I could see her body up close now, in the dim yellow light; see the surprising silkiness of black hair mixed here and there with gray, and suddenly I was crying and hating myself for the compelling need. I looked at my hatchet lying on the floor now and wondered how she'd gotten me into the shack as the tears blurred my eyes.

"What's the matter, boy?" she said. And I had no words to answer.

"What's the matter, I say!"

"I'm hurting in my operation," I said desperately, knowing that my tears were too complicated to put into any words I knew.

"Operation? Where?"

I looked away.

"Where you hurting, boy?" she demanded.

I looked into her eyes and they seemed to flood through me, until reluctantly I pointed toward my pain.

"Open it, so's I can see," she said. "You know I'm a healer, don't you?"

I bowed my head, still hesitating.

"Well open it, then. How'm I going to see with all those clothes on you?"

My face burned like fire now and the pain seemed to ease as a dampness grew beneath the bandage. But she would not be denied and I undid myself and saw a red stain on the gauze. I lay there ashamed to raise my eyes.

"Hmmmmmmm," she said, "a fishing worm with a headache!" And I couldn't believe my ears. Then she was looking into my eyes and grinning.

"Pruned," she cackled in her high, old woman's voice, "pruned. Boy, you have been pruned. I'm a doctor but no tree surgeon— No, lay still a second."

She paused, and I saw her hand come forward, three clawlike fingers taking me gently as she examined the bandage.

And I was both ashamed and angry, and now I stared at her out of a quick resentment and a defiant pride. *I'm a man*, I said within myself. *Just the same I am a man!* But I could only stare at her face briefly as she looked at me with a gleam in her eyes. Then my eyes fell and I forced myself to look boldly at her now, very

brown in the lamplight, with all the complicated appara-
tus within the globular curvatures of flesh and vessel
exposed to my eyes. I was filled then with a deeper sense
of the mystery of it, too, for now it was as though the
nakedness was nothing more than another veil; much
like the old baggy dresses she always wore. Then across
the curvature of her stomach I saw a long, puckered,
crescent-shaped scar.

"How old are you, boy?" she said, her eyes suddenly round.

"Eleven," I said. And it was as though I had fired
a shot.

"Eleven! Git out of here," she screamed, stumbling
backwards, her eyes wide upon me as she felt for the
glass on the table to drink. Then she snatched an old
gray robe from a chair, fumbling for the tie cord which
wasn't there. I moved, my eyes upon her as I knelt for
my hatchet and felt the pain come sharp. Then I straightened, trying to arrange my knickers.

"You go now, you little rascal," she said. "Hurry and
git out of here. And if I ever hear of you saying anything
about me I'll fix your daddy and your mammy, too. I'll
fix 'em, you hear?"

"Yes, ma'm," I said, feeling that I had suddenly lost
the courage of my manhood, now that my bandage was
hidden and her secret body gone behind her old gray
robe. But how could she fix my father when I didn't
have one? Or my mother, when she was dead?

I moved, backing out of the door into the dark. Then
she slammed the door, and I saw the light grow intense
in the window, and there was her face looking out at
me, and I could not tell if she frowned or smiled, but in
the glow of the lamp the wrinkles were not there. I stumbled over the packs now and gathered them up, leaving.

This time the dog raised up, huge in the dark, his
green eyes glowing as he gave me a low disinterested
growl. *Buster really must have fixed you, I thought. But
where'd he go?* Then I was past the fence into the road.

I wanted to run but was afraid of starting the pain
again, and as I moved, I kept seeing her as she'd appeared with her back turned toward me, the sweet un-
drunken movements that she made. It had been like
someone dancing by herself and yet like praying without

kneeling down. Then she had turned, exposing her familiar face. I moved faster now, and suddenly all my senses seemed to sing alive. I heard a night bird's song, the lucid call of a quail arose. And from off to my right in the river there came the leap of a moon-mad fish and I could see the spray arch up and away. There was wisteria in the air and the scent of moonflowers. And now moving through the dark I recalled the warm, intriguing smell of her body and suddenly, with the shout of the carnival coming to me again, the whole thing became thin and dreamlike. The images flowed in my mind, became shadowy, no part was left to fit another. But still there was my pain, and here was I, running through the dark toward the small, loud-playing band. It was real, I knew, and I stopped in the path and looked back, seeing the black outlines of the shack and the thin moon above. Behind the shack the hill arose with the shadowy woods and I knew the lake was still hidden there, reflecting the moon. All was real.

And for a moment I felt much older, as though I had lived swiftly long years into the future and had been as swiftly pushed back again. I tried to remember how it had been when I kissed her, but on my lips my tongue found only the faintest trace of wine. But for that it was gone, and I thought forever, except the memory of the scraggly hairs on her chin. Then I was again aware of the imperious calling of the horns and moved again toward the carnival. Where was that other scalped Indian, where had Buster gone?

Birthday

David Wong Louie

There's a man outside the door. He pounds away at it with his fists, and that whole side of the room shakes. He can pound until the house falls. I don't care, it's his house; he can do with it what he pleases.

He talks to me through the door. His talk is nothing like his knock. His voice is gentle, soothing, contrite. I might even be tempted to say it's sweet, only he's a man, and the man that he is.

I came to see the boy. It's true I have no rights except those that come with love. And if I paid any attention to what the court says, I wouldn't be here. The court says the boy belongs to the man, the boy's father. This has been hard to take. After all, the boy calls us both by our first names, and as far as I'm concerned that means we're equals.

It's the boy's birthday, and back in the days when the world was cold and rainy and sane, back in the days when we still lived together, I had promised we'd go for an afternoon of baseball—sunshine, pop, hotdogs. I told the man I was coming. I kept calling his number, but no one answered. I left plenty of messages on his machine, detailing what I had planned for my date with the boy. No response. When the boy first moved into this house, I tried phoning him every couple of weeks. I just wanted to hear him say my name again, Wallace Wong—the clearest three syllables in his vocabulary when his mother introduced us. But all I ever got for my troubles was the man's recorded voice—until yesterday, that is, when he interrupted the message I was leaving to say, "Wong, why don't you leave us alone?"

I just hung up on him. I couldn't talk to someone who used that tone of voice.

The boy's mother is gone from the picture. She's in

New York; I say New York because that's where she's from originally, but she might be in Topeka for all I know. Losing the boy almost killed her. All those days in court for nothing. What did that black robe know about the weave of our three hearts? The man won custody. Perhaps he bribed the judge; it's happened before. More likely it's because he's making money now writing movies, and in this town that's everything. He had written a script based on their marriage and breakup, which was made into a film and did well at the box office, so now he's in big demand.

One day I came home from the shop, and she was gone. No note then, and not a word from her since. But I'm confident she'll come home once her heart's on the mend. Her disappearance wasn't a complete surprise. She's a quirky one. I've learned to expect such behavior. When we first started going out, she wanted me to prove that I really loved her. She was still recovering from the marriage then and didn't trust what anyone said about anything, especially love. So she said she needed proof. I told her okay, but for weeks she couldn't decide what she wanted me to do. Then one day while we were having lunch at a restaurant, she said, "This is it."

"What?"

"Steal his radio." She pointed across the street.

"You crazy?"

The radio went into a health club with a man built like a heavyweight boxer.

I crossed the street, and as I followed the radio into the building, I imagined the possible headline for tomorrow's paper: CHINESE ROMEO BITES GYM FLOOR. Having accepted the possibility of severe bodily injury, I found the actual theft of the radio surprisingly easy. I just hung around the locker room, watching him strip and flex, and when he got up to relieve himself, I snatched up the radio left sitting on the bench.

She met me on the street in front of the gym. "Keep it," she said. "A present from me to you."

This I didn't appreciate. I reminded her the size of that man's fist was bigger than my entire head.

"Frank," she said, laughing in a mean sort of way, "wouldn't hurt anyone he wasn't married to."

That's Frank out there, punching the door.

*   *   *

I'm sitting on a kiddie chair. My knees are pressed against the bottom of a table that's under two feet tall. It's as if I'm crammed in a crate. In front of me, I have a drawing pad and eight thick crayons. Sooner or later, the man will find the key to the lock or poke his fist through the door. Before that happens, I want to leave the boy a note, just to let him know I didn't forget his birthday. But unless he's learned to read in the past few months, words will be useless. So I have to say my piece with pictures, and I'm not much when it comes to pictures.

I take up the red crayon and draw a circle; then I put in some eyes. I'm trying for a self-portrait but it's sizing up more feline than *Homo sapien.* Soon I admit defeat and finish off the cat with a pair of triangles for ears.

The man calls my name. "Don't do anything funny while I'm away," he says. His footsteps go down the stairs.

I hurry to the window. The man's walking up the front path. He goes about halfway, turns, and looks back at the house. He catches my eyes and gestures with his hand, like an umpire thumbing a guy out.

I try a yellow crayon. I make another circle, but now I'm distracted by the man's absence. Can't draw with him there, can't draw without him. I go to the window. He's standing at the curb, waiting for the boy, or maybe he's called the police.

Back at the table again, I give my drawing some teeth, big yellow squares. My creation reminds me of my father, though no one else would make the connection.

"What good's a son that doesn't know who his own father is?" That's what my father said when I told my parents about the boy and how the three of us planned to set up housekeeping. He didn't care for the idea of his only son adopting a used family. He gritted his false teeth, which he does when he's mad, and said, "Wallace" (he never uses my American name), "don't be such a jerk. There are millions of available Chinese girls. And I'll tell you a secret. The basic anatomy's the same no matter where it comes from. Just say yes, and we'll go to China and find you a nice girl."

My mother nodded, her hair jet black from a beautician's bottle. She said, "Love between lions and sheep has but one consequence." She talks in aphorisms. I don't know if they're the real thing or if she makes them up.

My parents had their hearts set on Connie Chung. "Marry your mother a girl she can talk to without having to use her hands," said my father.

"What makes you think Connie Chung can even speak Chinese?" I said.

"Because she's smart; otherwise, she wouldn't be on TV," said my father.

My mother said, "Only a fool whistles into the wind." At this, even my father shot her a funny look.

On the drive over here I heard a story on the radio about California condors going extinct. I tried to imagine myself as a condor at the dead end of evolution. In my veins I felt the primordial soup bubbling, and my whole entropic bulk quaked as I gazed at the last females of my species. I knew I was supposed to mate, but I wasn't sure how. Yeah, I'd probably have to start by picking a partner. But which one? I looked them over, the last three in creation, she'd need to have good genes. Finally, after careful consideration, I chose—her, the bird with the blond tail feathers. Then I heard my father's voice: "No, not that one, that one."

I wonder if he might be right. Maybe I'd be wise to pack a few suitcases full of Maybelline and soft Italian shoes and go over to China. Plenty of women there in that lipstick-free society. Seduce them with bourgeois decadence, and they'll gladly surrender their governmentally mandated 1.2 children to me.

This morning I taped a sign on the door for my customers, saying that I had to attend a funeral. Even though Saturdays show my best profit, for the boy's birthday I didn't bother to open the shop. I operate an Italian-style café. I traffic in slow death: buttery eggs, pinguid coffee, and sweets on top of sweets. At first business was slow. People didn't believe a Chinaman could produce a decent cappuccino. I could hardly blame them. I'd shy away, too, from moo shu pork from a Sicilian's pan. But I do all right now, and take off when the need comes up.

So I drove over to the man's house, and when I first caught sight of it I was surprised by its size, its thick Greek columns, its funereal cypresses, its imposing terracotta roof.

Seated on a white cast-iron love seat by the front door, the man was hunched over a book in which he appeared to be writing. I walked up the long front path, flanked on both sides by enormous expanses of chipped white stone where there should've been grass. He acted as if I weren't there. He just kept on scribbling. This reminded me of his courtroom manner: done up in a pinstriped suit, he sat at his table, writing feverishly on a yellow legal pad, as if he were an agent of the law.

I hated that time. The boy and his mother stayed downtown in a hotel to be near the court building. Each night my father would call to ask who was winning. Of course he was rooting against us. My mother wanted to know if I was eating rice again, now that the girl was gone. I got so confused talking to them that I moved out of the house just to avoid their calls. I set up a cot in the café storeroom and slept next to egg cartons, milk crates, and hot exhaust from the refrigerator fan. Those nights I fell asleep listening to talk shows on the radio.

They were good company. So much misery on the airwaves, it was a comfort. I heard this one guy complaining about his chronic indigestion, and the radio doctor, without so much as laying a stethoscope on him, diagnosed that the caller had cancer. I listened to too many women with a similar story. The husband's a hitter, they'd say, and in the morning she's ready to hit back, but by then the bum's gone off somewhere, so she smacks the kids instead, and wants to know why she doesn't feel sorry for doing so. We were all half-crazed insomniacs, one big aching family.

I even called a radio psychologist the night of the day the boy's mother left me. The second I got through to the station I realized how desperate I was, and felt pretty silly. But I didn't hang up, I had a conversation with the show's producer. He said my story was too complex. He wanted me to simplify it. He advised me that if I wanted the listeners' sympathy I should consider dropping the "Chinese stuff." Before I listened to another word, I told him that I hoped one day he'd be lonesome and heartbroken in the back roads of China, thousands of miles from Western ears, and the nearest ones carved from stone.

"I've been expecting you," said the man. He motioned for me to sit next to him on the love seat. I held my ground. He crossed his legs and reopened his book to a page marked with a greeting card. "You like poetry?" he asked, then bowed his head and finished copying a poem from the book onto the card. "I read this one back in high school, so I guess it must be good." He handed me the card when he was through. His handwriting looked like ants set end to end, painfully tiny words crawling all over the place.

I said, "Would you mind calling the boy?"

"We should talk," he said, taking back the card and slipping it into a hot-pink envelope. "I don't know you from the Gang of Four, and here you are asking for Welby."

I had braced myself for that. Welby. I can hardly say it. Named the poor kid after a TV doctor. The boy's mother swears it was all the man's doing. When she comes home, and we're settled, we'll go to court and have his name changed.

"It's his birthday," I said. "We have plans. The ball game, remember?"

"And don't think he hasn't talked about seeing you," the man said.

"Well then, let's not disappoint the boy." I took a step forward and reached for the doorbell.

"That's not necessary," said the man, rising from his seat. "We're talking now."

He pushed back the cuff of his long-sleeved shirt and checked his watch. "Can you spare me a few minutes?" he said and, with a sweep of his hand, invited me to sit again. This time I did.

"The scene opens in a supermarket," he began. "Rows of fruits and vegetables. People, carts fill the aisle. Closeup on Welby; he's about eighteen months old, sitting in the kiddie seat. I go squeeze avocados. Reverse angle: Welby watches as I join the swarm of shoppers. Pan of aisle, finally zeroing in on a nice-looking lady, who parks her cart next to mine. Zoom in: she's talking to her own kid, who's too big for the kiddie seat and looks awkward and clumsy in it. His head's bowed, eyes dim and sad. His mother says, 'Here's another little boy,' and she disappears among the shoppers. Zoom in on me in the crowd. I look over at Welby. Cut back to kids. Welby's leaning across the cart and pats the new boy, nothing rough, just finding out what the other kid feels like. Twin shot: big boy freezes, letting Welby do his thing, the way people let mean dogs sniff all they want, instead of trying to get away. I return to the cart. See the kid's crying, no noise, just these tears on his cheeks. Mom comes back. I apologize. Closeup on Mom: she's eating a candy bar right in front of her kid's face. You know something's wrong with the picture, but you can't figure out what. It takes a few seconds, but then you realize the kid's blind. Fade out."

"Scene from a new movie?" I asked.

"No, from real life."

"Oh. Look, we have to get going." I stood up and stepped away from the door. "So what's your point?"

He looked at his watch again. "Look, she left me, she left you. On that score, we're dead even." He came up behind me and put his hand on my shoulder. "Say, what kind of car you driving?" He gave me the gentlest push, and we started walking up the front path. "You know what Welby thought when he came to live here? He thought he was being punished for breaking up our marriage. How do you think that made me feel? We all do things we don't mean, and end up hurting people. I hurt her, she hurt me; now you're hurt."

We were still walking toward the curb. The man nudged me whenever my feet slowed down.

"Frank, look, thanks for the talk."

"Sure," he said. "It's about time we had a man-to-man." He touched me on the shoulder again.

"But you're forgetting something—where's Welby? We really should hit the road. I promised him batting practice."

"Say, that reminds me, what kind of tickets you buy? I'll reimburse you for them."

We reached the curb. He opened the driver-side door and rolled down the window. "The ballpark express," he said, sweeping his hand past the opening, like a model on a game show showing off a prize.

I slid in behind the wheel. "Okay. Now call Welby."

He shut the door and crouched, his big forearms resting against the bottom of the window. "Listen to me," Frank said. "To Welby, you're big time. You're like a living, breathing video game. There've been times I couldn't stand being around him. He'd tell stories. 'One day me and Wallace Wong' did this, did that. I'm never in any of his stories." The man looked into the side-view mirror and fixed his hair. "But I'm his father, right? Come on, give me a chance. Leave us alone, okay? He's starting to get used to me."

It was obvious he wasn't going to hand the boy over. So I proposed a trade: I'd do what he wanted, but in exchange I'd get the boy for the afternoon. We'd have so much fun, the man would need all of geologic time to chase those nine innings from the boy's memory.

He drummed his fingers against the door and looked at his watch. "It's late," he said. "You better get rolling." He reached across my body and pointed at the ignition switch.

My equal and opposite reaction: I leaned on the horn. I got in two long blasts before he stopped my hand. "The people in this neighborhood are still sleeping," he said. "Now listen up, friend, I'm telling you for your own good—you don't want to be here."

"So get the boy," I said. I brought my fist down on the dashboard to show I meant business. The glove compartment flew open. Things spilled onto the passenger seat.

"Hey, my radio," said the man.

"Your what? What do you mean, your radio?" I had brought it along so we could listen to the play-by-play in the stands.

"That's her. Zenith eight transistor with a crack in back where the battery goes."

I shook my head.

"Don't be that way," he said. "I know all about it. Sylvie told me she made you steal it."

"She what?"

"Sylvie always was a touch *loco en la cabeza*." He tapped his finger against his temple. "She always had funny ideas, don't you think so?"

"Here," I said, "take the radio."

"No, you keep her."

"I don't want it. I never did."

"No, keep her," he said. "Must feel like she belongs to you now anyway."

He stood up from his crouch and checked the time. "We need to stop fooling around. I have an appointment in a few minutes with someone. So, if you don't mind—"

"You mean like a date, Frank? You have a girlfriend?"

He didn't answer.

"Well, don't let me stand in the way of romance. Just call the boy, and we'll be off. Think of me as his sitter. Then you two will have the whole afternoon free to yourselves."

The man put his hands on his hips and arched his back. "Nothing's clicking with you, is it? Come with me," he said. "I have something to show you."

We walked up the front path, and I followed him into the kitchen. "Smell that?" he said. "Welby's birthday cake. My first ever, and I'm doing it from scratch. Fudge swirl topped with chocolate mousse frosting." He caught my eye and grinned. He was proud of his achievement. The place was a mess—bowls, spoons, measuring cups, cookbook, batter, eggshells, flour scattered and smeared everywhere. The cake layers were cooling on racks. "I'm trying my best," he said.

I was standing in an archway that separated the kitchen from the dining area. Past the round glass table, the wall of glass bricks, the giant earthenware horse, just to the left of the dwarf lemon tree, I spotted the staircase to the second floor. I had a clear path, an easy dash, and I'd be upstairs where the boy was waiting for me.

"Say, you cook in a restaurant," he said, picking the cookbook off the counter. "Maybe you can help. What do they mean by fold egg mixture into the chocolate?" he asked. "Am I supposed to pour the whole thing out and fold it with my hands?" He had his nose in the book and reread the passage.

I didn't hang around to give my expert advice.

The boy's room was the second off the hallway. I locked the door. Why there was a lock on the boy's door, I'll never know. But I was glad it was there. At first, I thought I had the wrong room. It didn't look like a child's room. At least not one the boy's age. The walls were covered with posters of TV starlets. So much cleavage and bare thigh couldn't be good for someone that young. I wondered what a social worker would think if I sent one up here.

The man knocked on the door. "Can't you see," he said, "Welby's not home? I sent him to a friend's for the night so I can bake his cake. It's a surprise."

It was my surprise. "He has to come home sometime," I said.

"Get out of there!" he shouted. "You can still make the game if you leave now."

I didn't answer. The man then started to pound on the door. I went over and inspected the boy's toy shelves. I couldn't tell if the boy had chosen the toys or, like the posters, they were a reflection of the man's tastes. There was such an emphasis on angles, gadgetry, and intimidation. Very high-tech stuff. Mostly robots, rockets, and spaceguns. So much plastic and chrome. Do kids instinctively gravitate to these materials? Whatever happened to animal love, the considerate petting of fur? I searched for the stuffed rabbit I had given him back in the good times. It was nowhere in sight. I wanted to believe it had accompanied him on the overnight but knew that wasn't likely. Then I tried to imagine the boy playing with these contraptions. I tried to hear the accompanying narrative as he sailed the toys through outer space. But I couldn't remember his voice. It was lost to me, just as my own boyhood voice is forever gone, tumbling across light-years and, like radio signals, bouncing off the four corners of the universe.

I watch the man coming toward the house. I hear him climb the stairs. He goes past my room. Then, a few minutes later, he knocks at my door. "You're in there now," he says. "So stay put. Got it?" He hurries downstairs. I go to the window. He's in a sports coat now, as he jogs to the curb. In one hand is a bunch of flowers wrapped in pink paper, in the other the greeting card. I don't know what to think. First killer robots and now poetry and roses?

The man runs off the curb. He surveys the sun-washed street, checks his watch once more, and then looks back at me.

Soon a car pulls up behind mine. I look for the boy in the backseat. If I do seventy all the way, we can still catch the first pitch.

The driver gets out: a woman with coral-red hair, cropped close to her scalp, earrings like a set of handcuffs, and miles of doodads around her neck. She's wearing a sleeveless purple jumpsuit that shifts like leather. I try my best to see into the car. But there's no sign of life.

The woman adjusts her sunglasses and throws her arms around the man. He crushes the flowers against the small of her back. I had forgotten about her coming. Quite a change from the boy's mother. But that's none of my business.

I return to the little table and look at what I've drawn. I wish I had some talent. At least a bit of imagination. On the page is a flock of animals, ones the boy used to ask me to draw. "How about a horse," he'd say, handing me a crayon. And no matter how the drawing turned out, I'd say, "That's a horse," and he'd generously say, "That's a horse."

I don't know if he'll still be so generous, now that he's abandoned rabbits for ray guns, but he'll know who did the drawings. It troubles me, though, that I haven't said what I want to say, that no matter how hard I try, I'm stuck doing the same old things in the same old ways. What have I accomplished but a page full of nouns —a camel, a dog, a cat, a cow, a bird, and my famous horse. Sure, I can try adopting a new vocabulary, sketch in a rocket ship, a rectangle, and a few well-placed triangles. That shouldn't be too hard. But that's not how he knows me. Ours was a simpler world. He must be a different boy now. The universe he knows has expanded, just as his palette broadened during our time together. This is inevitable. But in this expansion have I been eclipsed? Am I like a rattle, once a favorite toy, then—not so much discarded, but neglected with the discovery of blocks and things with wheels? I wish there was some way for me to know what he's up to, the way my father came home one day from Sears with a bat and ball and glove for me. There he was, son of China's great famines, who knew nothing of earned-run averages or the number of homers Mantle hit in '56, but somehow he anticipated my next step. With the boy, I didn't know what to think. Will the drawings delight him? That's what I mean—I should know.

I look out at the street. The trunk of the woman's car is open, and there's a ton of luggage stacked on the sidewalk. She must be here on an extended visit or else she's moving in. None of that's my business either, but she better not think she can take the boy's mother's place.

The woman goes over to my car. It's just an old VW square-back, but she's really checking it over. She does a lap around it, then sticks her head in the driver's window. She holds the radio up in her hand. The man's saying things that don't seem to please her. She spins away from him and starts up the front path. The man points at the house. She flips up her sunglasses. She sees me; I see her, too. I've waited a long time for this day. But it isn't how I've imagined it would feel when Sylvie finally came home.

The man catches her halfway up the front walk. They argue, but I can't hear them. About a minute later, they move slowly toward the street, turn at her luggage, and keep walking until they're gone from sight. It's plain they're giving me a chance to leave.

I go downstairs. The house is still sweet with baking. I reach the foyer but then make a U-turn and go to the kitchen. The layers of cake have cooled nicely.

What else is there for me to do? It is his birthday.

I crack an egg and separate the yolk from the whites. I repeat this three more times. I add sugar to the yolks and beat them with a whisk. This feels good. Then I heat up a pan of water and melt the chocolate in a second pan. In the meantime I beat the egg whites. I'm not thinking now. The whites hold their peaks perfectly. I mix the chocolate with the sugar and the yolks. Then I fold in the whipped whites.

I work briskly. And for the first time in a long time, perhaps for the first time ever, I feel at peace. I'm not familiar with this recipe, but I know what I need to do.

I spread the mousse on the layers of cake. I spread it on thick. This, I know, the boy will like.

The Passing

Durango Mendoza

Ever since Mama married Miguel we had lived in the country. He had built a tall, single-walled, two-room house on the land of his family above the big bend of Fish Creek, and it stood there, lean and unpainted among the trees back from the road. Even after Mama and I came to live there it remained unpainted. It was built of unfinished sawmill planks and had two stovepipe chimneys sticking through its green Sheetrock roof. Right across the road was the Indian church.

The house stood above a steep, boulder-littered and heavily wooded slope and the creek that ran below. I had developed a swimming hole there, and across the creek on the wooded slopes I played at hunting. It had been almost two years since we had settled there, and I had already explored the surrounding countryside for miles in winter and summer so that I now usually stayed close to the house. Summer had grown old, and I was becoming restless.

One evening as I played cars with pieces of wood in the dust beside the house, Mama saw the boy coming along the road. She stopped gathering the clothes from the line and took the clothespins from her mouth. I looked after her gaze and beyond. Through the shadows and trees I saw how the road curved and disappeared quickly into the dusk and woods. I looked back to her when she spoke.

"Sonny, there goes Joe Willow," she said. Then she paused and put the shirt she was holding into the basket at her feet. "He sure does work hard. I hope old Jimmy Bear and Fannie appreciate it, those two."

She shook her head and began to gather the rest of the clothes. I sat back on my heels and wondered at the tone of her voice. I had never really noticed Joe Willow

298

before, but I knew the rest of the family from church meetings. And once I had seen where they lived.

It was about a mile beyond the curve, far back from the road and reached by a rutted drive that skirted the Indian graveyard. I knew the graveyard because near it were some pecan trees from which I gathered the nuts each fall. Their house was very old and unpainted. It sat low and gray under a group of large blackjack oaks and within a grassless yard that was pressed closely by the thick, surrounding woods.

Joe Willow's mother, Fannie, was a short, round woman with mottled brown skin and a high, shiny forehead that wrinkled when she laughed. Jimmy Bear was her second husband, and they used to pass our house often, going to the beer joint in town or to stomp dances. They had once driven an old Dodge, but it no longer ran, and it now sat lopsided and windowless among the weeds beside their lane. Jimmy Bear was a skinny man, but he had a round, protruding belly and wore his belt under it so that it looked as if he carried a basketball inside. He had gaps in his teeth and a rough guttural laugh and walked with a shuffle. Mama told me that Fannie had once had land money but that they had long since used it up.

I remembered the young worker's brother and sister; his sister because of what she had once said when she met me on the path to the toilet at church. "Been to the OUT-house?" she had asked. I only knew his brother on sight though, and noticed that he always seemed to keep his black boots shiny and his long hair greased. Mama said he went with Jimmy Bear and Fannie to stomp dances.

The next evening when the young worker passed the gate I got up and ran to hang on it as I watched him pass on up the road. The sun, being low and to his back, sent a long finger of shadow ahead of him. I could hear the crunch and whisper of his footsteps between the squeaks of the bucket he carried until they began to fade alongside the road. The bucket creaked faintly and the breeze dropped for a moment.

I called to him.

"Hello, Joe Willow," I said.

In the stillness my voice carried, and he turned, his

shadow pointing into the woods, and lifted his hand. He squinted into the sun and smiled. I waved, and he turned back up the road and soon faded against the shadow and trees.

I watched where the road curved into the woods and knew that to the right the land dropped down to the part of the creek I seldom visited because I had heard that some wolves had been seen there. Beyond it the woods stretched for miles, and the creek merged finally with the river. I remembered once finding a pair of women's underpants, rotten and clinging to some brush near the water there, and scattered among the leaves and twigs were some old, empty beer bottles. The air always seemed heavy there, and the stillness under the drooping trees disturbed me.

I sat on the gate for a while until a deeper darkness crept from the woods and began to fuse with the trees. I heard the trees begin to sigh and settle down for the night, the lonely cooing of a dove, and from somewhere across the creek the hoot of an owl. Then I hurried back to the house in the new coolness and stood near my mom for a while as she moved about the warm iron cookstove preparing supper.

Almost every evening of August that summer the young Indian passed along the road in front of our gate. I saw him several times a week as he came up from the bridge, always carrying a small, empty lard bucket whose handle squeaked faintly as he passed by and out of sight. He walked like someone who is used to walking, slowly, without spirit, but with the strength seen in a young workhorse.

He would come up from the hill, the sun to his back, and his skin, a very reddish brown, would be covered with a fine dust, making his brows appear lighter and thicker than they were. His hair was cut short, but it lacked the uniformity of a regular barbershop haircut, and he wore no hat.

Many evenings I swung back and forth on the gate and waited for him to come by. I had no brothers or sisters as yet, but Mama was expecting Miguel's first child before spring. Miguel was my stepfather, and since he said very little to me and because I couldn't be around Mama all the time, I waited for Joe Willow to

pass by, although I seldom spoke except to reply to his
greetings. Often I didn't even show myself at all and
only sat among the grapevines next to the gate until the
darkness sent me home.

I remembered one of the last times I saw him. It was
early in September, and I was sitting on the gate watching the sun caught on the treetops, noticing how the
leaves looked like embers across its face as it settled into
them, when Joe Willow appeared like a moving post
upon the road. I had just gotten down from the gate and
sat on the large rock that propped up our mailbox when
Miguel called for me to eat supper. Instead, I began to
sift sand into little conical piles as I waited. I looked
down the road past the young worker to where the sun
had fallen behind the trees. It looked trapped. The wind
was very soft and smelled of smoke and dust. A few
birds chuckled above me in the trees, and the insects of
the evening buzzed in the weeds below.

Miguel called again and I looked up.

"Howdy, Joe Willow," I said. "You coming home
from work?"

He stopped and grinned.

"That's right," he said. He leaned on the mailbox, and
we said nothing for a few moments until he spoke again.
"You're Miguel's boy, aren't you?"

"Huh-uh. I belong to Rosa."

"Oh." He squatted down. "You know what? I'm the
same way. Everybody calls me Jimmy Bear's boy, but
I'm not. He's not my daddy."

We both shifted around and watched where the sun
had gone down.

"You see what happens when the sun goes down?"
He pointed to the evening star and motioned toward the
other stars that had appeared in the east. "When the
daddy goes to bed, all the little children come out." His
teeth gleamed in the gathering darkness, and I smiled,
too.

We had watched the stars for only a moment when
Miguel called again.

"You better get on home," Joe Willow said. "That's
your daddy calling you."

"I'm Rosa's boy," I said.

"I know," he said, "but you better get on back." He

looked up again at the deepening sky and laughed softly. "I'll see you some other time — 'Rosa's boy.' "

Mama and Miguel were already eating when I stepped quietly into the kitchen. I washed my hands and climbed into my chair. Miguel frowned.

"You hear me callin' you?"

I nodded and looked at Mama.

"Eat now, Sonny," she said.

"He better mind me," Miguel said.

After September came, I started to school and no longer saw Joe Willow pass our gate. One day I asked Mama about him, and she said that he had gone to the free Indian boarding school in the northern part of the state, just south of the Kansas line. And it was when winter was just melting into spring, a few weeks after Mama had returned from the hospital with my baby brother, that I remembered him again.

Just before supper Miguel came into the kitchen, stamping the bits of dirty snow from his overshoes.

"Jimmy Bear's boy's been killed by the Santa Fe train at Chillocco," he said. "But they say they ain't sure how it happened." He warmed his hands over the stove and sat down.

I looked at Mama. She said nothing and rocked the baby. On the stove the beans bubbled softly, and their smell filled the room. I watched the lid on the pot jiggle as the steam escaped, and I heard the wind rattle gently at the window. Miguel struggled with his overshoes and continued:

"Fannie tol' me a railroad man was down the first thing and said they was willin' to pay." He grunted and shoved the overshoes near the stove. "The funeral's Tuesday," he said.

Mama nodded and handed me the baby and got up to put the food on the table. She touched my head, and we sat down to supper.

At the funeral Joe Willow's family cried, and old Fannie even fainted at the grave site when they started to cover him. Jimmy Bear had to struggle to keep her from falling. The dirt sounded on the wooden vault, and the little houses over the older graves looked gray and damp with the people standing among them. I went over to the pecan trees and kicked among the damp mulch looking for good nuts, but I couldn't find any.

That evening after supper I stepped out onto the back stoop to go to the bathroom, and the yellow lamplight behind me threw my shadow onto the patches of snow and earth, enclosing it in the rectangle that the doorway formed. I looked up. The spotty clouds looked like bits of melting snow pressed into the darkness, and the stars were out, sprinkled into the stillness beyond. The black trees swayed, and the cold wind was familiar.

Behind me Mama moved around the kitchen, and I heard the chink and gentle clatter of the plates and pans as she put those things away. I shivered. And I knew that soon, as it did every spring, the clouds would come and it would begin to rain, a cold, heavy drizzle, and the land would turn to mud.

MEMOIR, OR
OBSERVER NARRATION

These stories shift focus onto characters other than the speaker, who becomes more observer than participant, starting with "The Voice from the Wall," which is arguably still autobiographical in focus. How much is the story about the narrator's mother and neighbors and how much about what they catalyzed for her?

If these stories are really about a "third" person, one could ask why the authors chose to tell them through the eyes of a peripheral first person. Examples give the answer, the titles again provide an artistic clue. The hero of Scott Fitzgerald's The Great Gatsby *is great perhaps only as perceived and purveyed to us by his acquaintance and occasional confidant Nick. Joseph Conrad's* Lord Jim *and Alain-Fournier's* Le Grand Meaulnes *are also told by someone who knew their story and resonated with it to the point of mythifying their heroes. This resonance is the key to why one person tells another's story. Consider other stories titled for characters who are not the narrator—Willa Cather's* My Àntonia, *Guy de Maupassant's "Mademoiselle Pearl," John Steinbeck's "Johnny Bear," Herman Melville's "Bartleby the Scrivener," Sondra Spratt's "Hoods I Have Known," O. Henry's "A Municipal Report," and Robert Penn Warren's* All the King's Men. *Consider too how different the effect would be of the Sherlock Holmes stories if not narrated by Dr. Watson (a device that A. Conan Doyle borrowed from Edgar Allan Poe along with the very genre of the detective story itself).*

As the O. Henry title suggests, observer narration mimics real-life reportage, or, as the Cather and Spratt titles suggest, memoir. But if the speaker was not at the center

*of the experience, how does she or he know what hap-
pened and what the events meant to the protagonist? The
stories selected for this group demonstrate some of the
different relationships observer narrators may have to
events and to main characters and how these relationships
determine what they know. An observer may be a confidant of the protagonist, an eyewitness to the action, or a
member of some community in which the protagonist is
known, comparable to the chorus in Greek drama. Confidant, eyewitness, and chorus roles furnish knowledge,
respectively, of inner life, specific incidents, and background information.*

*The following stories vary according to which of these
roles the narrator plays and therefore according to the
distance in one sense or another that he or she stood from
the principals at the time of events. Generally, the degree
of involvement scales off from a family relationship in
the first through that of lover, friend, proprietor, and, in
the last, casual witness. So the confidant role, paramount
at first, increasingly yields to the more distant roles of
eyewitness and chorus.*

*Memoir, or observer narration, is the hinge between
autobiography and biography, first-person and third-
person storytelling. In it we can see clearly the channels
of information and the personal involvement that disappear from the text once narrators no longer identify themselves. But, fortunately, affinity and empathy, attraction
and fascination, are not so easy to hide.*

The Voice from the Wall
Amy Tan

When I was little, my mother told me my great-grandfather had sentenced a beggar to die in the worst possible way, and that later the dead man came back and killed my great-grandfather. Either that, or he died of influenza one week later.

I used to play out the beggar's last moments over and over again in my head. In my mind, I saw the executioner strip off the man's shirt and lead him into the open yard. "This traitor," read the executioner, "is sentenced to die the death of a thousand cuts." But before he could even raise the sharp sword to whittle his life away, they found the beggar's mind had already broken into a thousand pieces. A few days later, my great-grandfather looked up from his books and saw this same man looking like a smashed vase hastily put back together. "As the sword was cutting me down," said the ghost, "I thought this was the worst I would ever have to endure. But I was wrong. The worst is on the other side." And the dead man embraced my great-grandfather with the jagged pieces of his arm and pulled him through the wall, to show him what he meant.

I once asked my mother how he really died. She said, "In bed, very quickly, after being sick for only two days."

"No, no, I mean the other man. How was he killed? Did they slice off his skin first? Did they use a cleaver to chop up his bones? Did he scream and feel all one thousand cuts?"

"Annh! Why do you Americans have only these morbid thoughts in your mind?" cried my mother in Chinese. "That man has been dead for almost seventy years. What does it matter how he died?"

I always thought it mattered, to know what is the

worst possible thing that can happen to you, to know how you can avoid it, to not be drawn by the magic of the unspeakable. Because, even as a young child, I could sense the unspoken terrors that surrounded our house, the ones that chased my mother until she hid in a secret dark corner of her mind. And still they found her. I watched, over the years, as they devoured her, piece by piece, until she disappeared and became a ghost.

As I remember it, the dark side of my mother sprang from the basement in our old house in Oakland. I was five and my mother tried to hide it from me. She barricaded the door with a wooden chair, secured it with a chain and two types of key locks. And it became so mysterious that I spent all my energies unraveling this door, until the day I was finally able to pry it open with my small fingers, only to immediately fall headlong into the dark chasm. And it was only after I stopped screaming—I had seen the blood of my nose on my mother's shoulder—only then did my mother tell me about the bad man who lived in the basement and why I should never open the door again. He had lived there for thousands of years, she said, and was so evil and hungry that had my mother not rescued me so quickly, this bad man would have planted five babies in me and then eaten us all in a six-course meal, tossing our bones on the dirty floor.

And after that I began to see terrible things. I saw these things with my Chinese eyes, the part of me I got from my mother. I saw devils dancing feverishly beneath a hole I had dug in the sandbox. I saw that lightning had eyes and searched to strike down little children. I saw a beetle wearing the face of a child, which I promptly squashed with the wheel of my tricycle. And when I became older, I could see things that Caucasian girls at school did not. Monkey rings that would split in two and send a swinging child hurtling through space. Tether balls that could splash a girl's head all over the playground in front of laughing friends.

I didn't tell anyone about the things I saw, not even my mother. Most people didn't know I was half Chinese, maybe because my last name is St. Clair. When people first saw me, they thought I looked like my father, English-

Irish, big boned and delicate at the same time. But if they looked really close, if they knew that they were there, they could see the Chinese parts. Instead of having cheeks like my father's sharp-edged points, mine were smooth as beach pebbles. I didn't have his straw-yellow hair or his white skin, yet my coloring looked too pale, like something that was once darker and had faded in the sun.

And my eyes, my mother gave me my eyes, no eyelids, as if they were carved on a jack-o'-lantern with two swift cuts of a short knife. I used to push my eyes in on the sides to make them rounder. Or I'd open them very wide until I could see the white parts. But when I walked around the house like that, my father asked me why I looked so scared.

I have a photo of my mother with this same scared look. My father said the picture was taken when Ma was first released from Angel Island Immigration Station. She stayed there for three weeks, until they could process her papers and determine whether she was a War Bride, a Displaced Person, a Student, or the wife of a Chinese-American citizen. My father said they didn't have rules for dealing with the Chinese wife of a Caucasian citizen. Somehow, in the end, they declared her a Displaced Person, lost in a sea of immigration categories.

My mother never talked about her life in China, but my father said he saved her from a terrible life there, some tragedy she could not speak about. My father proudly named her in her immigration papers: Betty St. Clair, crossing out her given name of Gu Ying-ying. And then he put down the wrong birth year, 1916 instead of 1914. So, with the sweep of a pen, my mother lost her name and became a Dragon instead of a Tiger.

In this picture you can see why my mother looks displaced. She is clutching a large clam-shaped bag, as though someone might steal this from her as well if she is less watchful. She has on an ankle-length Chinese dress with modest vents at the side. And on top she is wearing a Westernized suit jacket, awkwardly stylish on my mother's small body, with its padded shoulders, wide lapels, and oversize cloth buttons. This was my mother's wedding dress, a gift from my father. In this outfit she looks as if she were neither coming from nor going to someplace. Her chin is bent down and you can see the precise part in her hair, a neat white line drawn from above her left brow then over the black horizon of her head.

And even though her head is bowed, humble in defeat, her eyes are staring up past the camera, wide open.

"Why does she look scared?" I asked my father.

And my father explained: It was only because he said "Cheese," and my mother was struggling to keep her eyes open until the flash went off, ten seconds later.

My mother often looked this way, waiting for something to happen, wearing this scared look. Only later she lost the struggle to keep her eyes open.

"Don't look at her," said my mother as we walked through Chinatown in Oakland. She had grabbed my hand and pulled me close to her body. And of course I looked. I saw a woman sitting on the sidewalk, leaning against a building. She was old and young at the same time, with dull eyes as though she had not slept for many years. And her feet and her hands—the tips were as black as if she had dipped them in India ink. But I knew they were rotted.

"What did she do to herself?" I whispered to my mother.

"She met a bad man," said my mother. "She had a baby she didn't want."

And I knew that was not true. I knew my mother made up anything to warn me, to help me avoid some unknown danger. My mother saw danger in everything, even in other Chinese people. Where we lived and shopped, everyone spoke Cantonese or English. My mother was from Wushi, near Shanghai. So she spoke Mandarin and a little bit of English. My father, who spoke only a few canned Chinese expressions, insisted my mother learn English. So with him, she spoke in moods and gestures, looks and silences, and sometimes a combination of English punctuated by hesitations and Chinese frustration: "*Shwo buchulai*"—Words cannot come out. So my father would put words in her mouth.

"I think Mom is trying to say she's tired," he would whisper when my mother became moody.

"I think she's saying we're the best darn family in the

country!'' he'd exclaim when she had cooked a wonderfully fragrant meal.

But with me, when we were alone, my mother would speak in Chinese, saying things my father could not possibly imagine. I could understand the words perfectly, but not the meanings. One thought led to another without connection.

"You must not walk in any direction but to school and back home," warned my mother when she decided I was old enough to walk by myself.

"Why?" I asked.

"You can't understand these things," she said.

"Why not?"

"Because I haven't put it in your mind yet."

"Why not?"

"Aii-ya! Such questions! Because it is too terrible to consider. A man can grab you off the streets, sell you to someone else, make you have a baby. Then you'll kill the baby. And when they find this baby in a garbage can, then what can be done? You'll go to jail, die there."

I knew this was not a true answer. But I also made up lies to prevent bad things from happening in the future. I often lied when I had to translate for her, the endless forms, instructions, notices from school, telephone calls. "*Shemma yisz?*"—What meaning?—she asked me when a man at a grocery store yelled at her for opening up jars to smell the insides. I was so embarrassed I told her that Chinese people were not allowed to shop there. When the school sent a notice home about a polio vaccination, I told her the time and place, and added that all students were now required to use metal lunch boxes, since they had discovered old paper bags can carry polio germs.

"We're moving up in the world," my father proudly announced, this being the occasion of his promotion to sales supervisor of a clothing manufacturer. "Your mother is thrilled."

And we did move up, across the bay to San Francisco and up a hill in North Beach, to an Italian neighborhood, where the sidewalk was so steep I had to lean into the slant to get home from school each day. I was ten and

I was hopeful that we might be able to leave all the old fears behind in Oakland.

The apartment building was three stories high, two apartments per floor. It had a renovated façade, a recent layer of white stucco topped with connected rows of metal fire-escape ladders. But inside it was old. The front door with its narrow glass panes opened into a musty lobby that smelled of everybody's life mixed together. Everybody meant the names on the front door next to their little buzzers: Anderson, Giordino, Hayman, Ricci, Sorci, and our name, St. Clair. We lived on the middle floor, stuck between cooking smells that floated up and feet sounds that drifted down. My bedroom faced the street, and at night, in the dark, I could see in my mind another life. Cars struggling to climb the steep, fog-shrouded hill, gunning their deep engines and spinning their wheels. Loud, happy people, laughing, puffing, gasping: "Are we almost there?" A beagle scrambling to his feet to start his yipping yowl, answered a few seconds later by fire truck sirens and an angry woman hissing, "Sammy! Bad dog! Hush now!" And with all this soothing predictability, I would soon fall asleep.

My mother was not happy with the apartment, but I didn't see that at first. When we moved in, she busied herself with getting settled, arranging the furniture, unpacking dishes, hanging pictures on the wall. It took her about one week. And soon after that, when she and I were walking to the bus stop, she met a man who threw her off balance.

He was a red-faced Chinese man, wobbling down the sidewalk as if he were lost. His runny eyes saw us and he quickly stood up straight and threw out his arms, shouting, "I found you! Suzie Wong, girl of my dreams! Hah!" And with his arms and mouth wide open, he started rushing toward us. My mother dropped my hand and covered her body with her arms as if she were naked, unable to do anything else. In that moment as she let go, I started to scream, seeing this dangerous man lunging closer. I was still screaming after two laughing men grabbed this man and, shaking him, said, "Joe, stop it, for Chrissake. You're scaring that poor little girl and her maid."

The rest of the day—while riding on the bus, walking

in and out of stores, shopping for our dinner—my
mother trembled. She clutched my hand so tightly it
hurt. And once when she let go of my hand to take her
wallet out of her purse at the cash register, I started to
slip away to look at the candy. She grabbed my hand
back so fast I knew at that instant how sorry she was
that she had not protected me better.

As soon as we got home from grocery shopping, she
began to put the cans and vegetables away. And then,
as if something were not quite right, she removed the
cans from one shelf and switched them with the cans on
another. Next she walked briskly into the living room
and moved a large round mirror from the wall facing
the front door to a wall by the sofa.

"What are you doing?" I asked.

She whispered something in Chinese about "things not
being balanced," and I thought she meant how things
looked, not how things felt. And then she started to
move the larger pieces: the sofa, chairs, end tables, a
Chinese scroll of goldfish.

"What's going on here?" asked my father when he
came home from work.

"She's making it look better," I said.

And the next day, when I came home from school, I
saw she had again rearranged everything. Everything
was in a different place. I could see that some terrible
danger lay ahead.

"Why are you doing this?" I asked her, afraid she
would give me a true answer.

But she whispered some Chinese nonsense instead:
"When something goes against your nature, you are not
in balance. This house was built too steep, and a bad
wind from the top blows all your strength back down
the hill. So you can never get ahead. You are always
rolling backward."

And then she started pointing to the walls and doors
of the apartment. "See how narrow this doorway is, like
a neck that has been strangled. And the kitchen faces
this toilet room, so all your worth is flushed away."

"But what does it mean? What's going to happen if
it's not balanced?" I asked my mother.

My father explained it to me later. "Your mother is

just practicing her nesting instincts," he said. "All mothers get it. You'll see when you're older."

I wondered why my father never worried. Was he blind? Why did my mother and I see something more?

And then a few days later, I found out that my father had been right all along. I came home from school, walked into my bedroom, and saw it. My mother had rearranged my room. My bed was no longer by the window but against a wall. And where my bed once was—now there stood a used crib. So the secret danger was a ballooning stomach, the source of my mother's imbalance. My mother was going to have a baby.

"See," said my father as we both looked at the crib. "Nesting instincts. Here's the nest. And here's where the baby goes." He was so pleased with this imaginary baby in the crib. He didn't see what I later saw. My mother began to bump into things, into table edges as if she forgot her stomach contained a baby, as if she were headed for trouble instead. She did not speak of the joys of having a new baby; she talked about a heaviness around her, about things being out of balance, not in harmony with one another. So I worried about that baby, that it was stuck somewhere between my mother's stomach and this crib in my room.

With my bed against the wall, the nighttime life of my imagination changed. Instead of street sounds, I began to hear voices coming from the wall, from the apartment next door. The front door buzzer said a family called the Sorcis lived there.

That first night I heard the muffled sound of someone shouting. A woman? A girl? I flattened my ear against the wall and heard a woman's angry voice, then another, the higher voice of a girl shouting back. And now, the voices turned toward me, like fire sirens turning onto our street, and I could hear the accusations fading in and out: *Who am I to say!* ... *Why do you keep buggin' me?* ... *Then get out and stay out!* ... *rather die rather be dead!* ... *Why doncha then!*

Then I heard scraping sounds, slamming, pushing and shouts and then *whack! whack! whack!* Someone was killing. Someone was being killed. Screams and shouts, a mother had a sword high above a girl's head and was starting to slice her life away, first a braid, then her scalp, an eyebrow, a toe, a thumb, the point of her cheek, the slant of her nose, until there was nothing left, no sounds.

I lay back against my pillow, my heart pounding at what I had just witnessed with my ears and my imagination. A girl had just been killed. I hadn't been able to stop myself from listening. I wasn't able to stop what happened. The horror of it all.

But the next night, the girl came back to life with more screams, more beating, her life once more in peril. And so it continued, night after night, a voice pressing against my wall telling me that this was the worst possible thing that could happen: the terror of not knowing when it would ever stop.

Sometimes I heard this loud family across the hallway that separated our two apartment doors. Their apartment was by the stairs going up to the third floor. Ours was by the stairs going down to the lobby.

"You break your legs sliding down that banister, I'm gonna break your neck," a woman shouted. Her warnings were followed by the sounds of feet stomping on the stairs. "And don't forget to pick up Pop's suits!"

I knew this terrible life so intimately that I was startled by the immediacy of seeing her in person for the first time. I was pulling the front door shut while balancing an armload of books. And when I turned around, I saw her coming toward me just a few feet away and I shrieked and dropped everything. She snickered and I knew who she was, this tall girl whom I guessed to be about twelve, two years older than I was. Then she bolted down the stairs and I quickly gathered up my books and followed her, careful to walk on the other side of the street.

She didn't seem like a girl who had been killed a hundred times. I saw no traces of bloodstained clothes; she wore a crisp white blouse, a blue cardigan sweater, and a blue-green pleated skirt. In fact, as I watched her, she seemed quite happy, her two brown braids bouncing jauntily in rhythm to her walk. And then, as if she knew that I was thinking about her, she turned her head. She gave me a scowl and quickly ducked down a side street and walked out of my sight.

Every time I saw her after that, I would pretend to look down, busy rearranging my books or the buttons on my sweater, guilty that I knew everything about her.

My parents' friends Auntie Su and Uncle Canning picked me up at school one day and took me to the hospital to see my mother. I knew this was serious because everything they said was unnecessary but spoken with solemn importance.

"It is now four o'clock," said Uncle Canning, looking at his watch.

"The bus is never on time," said Auntie Su.

When I visited my mother in the hospital, she seemed half asleep, tossing back and forth. And then her eyes popped open, staring at the ceiling.

"My fault, my fault. I knew this before it happened," she babbled. "I did nothing to prevent it."

"Betty darling, Betty darling," said my father frantically. But my mother kept shouting these accusations to herself. She grabbed my hand and I realized her whole body was shaking. And then she looked at me, in a strange way, as if she were begging me for her life, as if I could pardon her. She was mumbling in Chinese.

"Lena, what's she saying?" cried my father. For once, he had no words to put in my mother's mouth.

And for once, I had no ready answer. It struck me that the worst possible thing had happened. That what she had been fearing had come true. They were no longer warnings. And so I listened.

"When the baby was ready to be born," she murmured, "I could already hear him screaming inside my womb. His little fingers, they were clinging to stay inside. But the nurses, the doctor, they said to push him out, make him come. And when his head popped out, the nurses cried, His eyes are wide open! He sees everything! Then his body slipped out and he lay on the table, steaming with life.

"When I looked at him, I saw right away. His tiny legs, his small arms, his thin neck, and then a large head so terrible I could not stop looking at it. This baby's eyes were open and his head—it was open too! I could see all the way back, to where his thoughts were supposed to be, and there was nothing there. No brain, the doctor shouted! His head is just an empty eggshell!

"And then this baby, maybe he heard us, his large head seemed to fill with hot air and rise up from the table. The head turned to one side, then to the other. It looked right through me. I knew he could see everything inside me. How I had given no thought to killing my other son! How I had given no thought to having this baby!"

I could not tell my father what she had said. He was so sad already with this empty crib in his mind. How could I tell him she was crazy?

So this is what I translated for him: "She says we must all think very hard about having another baby. She says she hopes this baby is very happy on the other side. And she thinks we should leave now and go have dinner."

After the baby died, my mother fell apart, not all at once, but piece by piece, like plates falling off a shelf one by one. I never knew when it would happen, so I became nervous all the time, waiting.

Sometimes she would start to make dinner, but would stop halfway, the water running full steam in the sink, her knife poised in the air over half-chopped vegetables, silent, tears flowing. And sometimes we'd be eating and we would have to stop and put our forks down because she had dropped her face into her hands and was saying "*Mei gwansyi*"—It doesn't matter. My father would just sit there, trying to figure out what it was that didn't matter this much. And I would leave the table, knowing it would happen again, always a next time.

My father seemed to fall apart in a different way. He tried to make things better. But it was as if he were running to catch things before they fell, only he would fall before he could catch anything.

"She's just tired," he explained to me when we were eating dinner at the Gold Spike, just the two of us, because my mother was lying like a statue on her bed. I knew he was thinking about her because he had this worried face, staring at his dinner plate as if it were filled with worms instead of spaghetti.

At home, my mother looked at everything around her with empty eyes. My father would come home from work, patting my head, saying, "How's my big girl," but always looking past me, toward my mother. I had such fears inside, not in my head but in my stomach. I could no longer see what was so scary, but I could feel it. I could feel every little movement in our silent house. And at night, I could feel the crashing loud fights on the other side of my bedroom wall, this girl being beaten to death. In bed, with the blanket edge lying across my neck, I used to wonder which was worse, our side or theirs? And after thinking about this for a while, after feeling sorry for myself, it comforted me somewhat to think that this girl next door had a more unhappy life.

But one night after dinner our doorbell rang. This was curious, because usually people rang the buzzer downstairs first.

"Lena, could you see who it is?" called my father from the kitchen. He was doing the dishes. My mother was lying in bed. My mother was now always "resting" and it was as if she had died and become a living ghost.

I opened the door cautiously, then swung it wide open with surprise. It was the girl from next door. I stared at her with undisguised amazement. She was smiling back at me, and she looked ruffled, as if she had fallen out of bed with her clothes on.

"Who is it?" called my father.

"It's next door!" I shouted to my father. "It's . . ."

"Teresa," she offered quickly.

"It's Teresa!" I yelled back to my father.

"Invite her in," my father said almost the same moment that Teresa squeezed past me and into our apartment. Without being invited, she started walking toward my bedroom. I closed the front door and followed her two brown braids that were bouncing like whips beating the back of a horse.

She walked right over to my window and began to open it. "What are you doing?" I cried. She sat on the window ledge, looked out on the street. And then she looked at me and started to giggle. I sat down on my bed watching her, waiting for her to stop, feeling the cold air blow in from the dark opening.

"What's so funny?" I finally said. It occurred to me that perhaps she was laughing at me, at my life. Maybe

she had listened through the wall and heard nothing, the
stagnant silence of our unhappy house.

"Why are you laughing?" I demanded.

"My mother kicked me out," she finally said. She
talked with a swagger, seeming to be proud of this fact.
And then she snickered a little and said, "We had this
fight and she pushed me out the door and locked it. So
now she thinks I'm going to wait outside the door until
I'm sorry enough to apologize. But I'm not going to."

"Then what are you going to do?" I asked breath-
lessly, certain that her mother would kill her for good
this time.

"I'm going to use your fire escape to climb back into
my bedroom," she whispered back. "And she's going to
wait. And when she gets worried, she'll open the front
door. Only I won't be there! I'll be in my bedroom, in
bed." She giggled again.

"Won't she be mad when she finds you?"

"Nah, she'll just be glad I'm not dead or something.
Oh, she'll pretend to be mad, sort of. We do this kind
of stuff all the time." And then she slipped through my
window and soundlessly made her way back home.

I stared at the open window for a long time, wondering about her. How could she go back? Didn't she see
how terrible her life was? Didn't she recognize it would
never stop?

I lay down on my bed waiting to hear the screams and
shouts. And late at night I was still awake when I heard
the loud voices next door. Mrs. Sorci was shouting and
crying. *You stupida girl. You almost gave me a heart
attack.* And Teresa was yelling back, *I coulda been killed.
I almost fell and broke my neck.* And then I heard them
laughing and crying, crying and laughing, shouting with
love.

I was stunned. I could almost see them hugging and
kissing one another. I was crying for joy with them, because I had been wrong.

And in my memory I can still feel the hope that beat
in me that night, I clung to this hope, day after day,
night after night, year after year. I would watch my
mother lying in her bed, babbling to herself as she sat
on the sofa. And yet I knew that this, the worst possible

thing, would one day stop. I still saw bad things in my mind, but now I found ways to change them. I still heard Mrs. Sorci and Teresa having terrible fights, but I saw something else.

I saw a girl complaining that the pain of not being seen was unbearable. I saw the mother lying in bed in her long flowing robes. Then the girl pulled out a sharp sword and told her mother, "Then you must die the death of a thousand cuts. It is the only way to save you."

The mother accepted this and closed her eyes. The sword came down and sliced back and forth, up and down, *whish! whish! whish!* And the mother screamed and shouted, cried out in terror and pain. But when she opened her eyes, she saw no blood, no shredded flesh.

The girl said, "Do you see now?"

The mother nodded: "Now I have perfect understanding. I have already experienced the worst. After this, there is no worst possible thing."

And the daughter said, "Now you must come back, to the other side. Then you can see why you were wrong."

And the girl grabbed her mother's hand and pulled her through the wall.

Country

Jayne Anne Phillips

We went down there because she was easy. She was always easy, watching us later across the stubbled field, dried-out West Virginia winter and she stood by the window braiding that long swatch of hair that smelled of smoke and fruit, of burnt apples. Sixteen, she was sixteen, moving on you, rolling flat and hard against you like some aging waitress. Feeling that hard scissored grip, you smelled her mechanical musk; her mouth on your face opened and her soft sounds spilled out empty and sugared in that filthy room. Her sheets were gray with men's dust, heavy black dust of the tunnels, and sweats mixed on her skin.

Shifts changed, that long empty whistle howling like a dog. Wizard dog, empty whirling dog. The light was flat, broken on the hills. We walked to the truck and burned up that dirt road to her house. House so close the mine she heard that doggy moan and waiting for us on the porch, knife in her hand, she peeled potatoes around and around. Eyed skins dropping limp and curled on faded boards. She thin-legged in her man's boots. Budded breasts and that dark, high-boned face. Mouth petulant but its hardness in it, behind it. Looking at that mouth you felt her teeth in you, hard white negroid teeth, and the town looked on the whole family as niggers. This in '59, dark beauties taunted in schools. In that old brick school on dented river land, governor's picture in the hall smelled of river sop and the dark tiger-eyed were taunted as they are, I guess, still, in those towns. She had that gaunt full-hipped Appalachian stance till she opened those lips and spoke, moving in flimsy cotton dresses, her voice singsong like she was sleeping. She moving smooth-bellied in fields, swell-

320

thighed, and the harsh nettled grass gone bleached behind her.

He, Billy, found her first. Said she was down at the company store with her pap and a string of brats. Said she was standing sucking her scarf, them hauling those thirty-pound bags of staples to the truck. Flour filmed in her napped hair and he said he like to burn up looking at her. Billy and me came down from Youngstown when the mills closed. For months I watched Billy grind at pouty women in gritted Ohio bars, us working those hot mills too long, going lean in a nothing town. Him a city boy working steel and ships, tired of going back broke to married girl friends, Lower East Side sweat-handed girls afraid of their dockworker husbands. Said he had an uncle, mine boss in the South, and when the mills laid off we came down in his truck, me having sold my junk car to get him out of jail. Drunken Billy ended his good-bye bender smashing windows and the jaws of some fat Puerto Rican pimp. We rolled all night into no-man's-land West Virginia, and gas pumps alone by the side of the road went gray. Winter then. Deserted early-morning towns dusted gauzy; wooden-eyed perpetual thirties and Mail Pouch barns. This ain't the South, Billy muttered, hung over, his head in his arms on the steering wheel. This is the goddamn past. And passing, just passing through, rolls you like a smoke train. Those heaped mountains lower the sky and roll you like some slow-limbed heavenly whore. And she, Billy said, that day at the store, carried bags a man would feel. Her face was hard and passive, the sensual hard of those women. He looked at her, thinking *half-breed* and sexual tales. She knew it, seeing him look as men look.

Her pap worked the Century mine down at Hundred, worked the swing shift. Billy said he stood in the woods at the edge of their fifteen acres of farm, waited, watched him swing his pail and hat up the seat of that broken bed truck. Truck started up and her pap just sat there in the shaking cab, a brawny-armed man near fifty touching his sandy hair. Billy said he watched him there so long he forgot the girl in the house. Something about the way he only sat, fingers edging his face. They lived,

she told us later, in Detroit a few years when he tried
to leave the mines. Said he came home from the Chevy
plant stretched tight those nights. She cooked whatever
she could get for the kids, his woman having left him by
then. The mines, he told her, has got that dust settled
in you and the black in your gut down deep. You work
in small light to tear the wall, chink it out, then suddenly
comes the monster clack of the cars. And when they're
gone, coal-heavy, the picks make the same hard ticking
up and down the rails, ticking the muffled black. In Detroit that factory city oil smelled all night, motors on the
assembly line going till there's no rest from it. Nothing
has a weight there on the line. Just smooth whir of motors in your head. He told her this, kneading his big
hands, late nights drunk in their neon-windowed place.
Touching her, saying, Them lines gets tight, thin cat
gut lines like ties off bellies. Them workers in line by
the belts got such nothing in their chests, after a while
even the black coal dust, stealing air, is a relief. That
way he could see, he said, his years leaving him—at
least he could feel them going. He felt it mornings in
his broken truck, listening. Hounds bayed the light and
field smoke rose off the frost. The truck caught low
and rumbled and he in the shaking cab touched his
face. Like something pulled his hand and its laced
black cuts to his face.

Her mother was mulatto but she was gone. The grandmother, sometimes crazy, turned circles in the floor. We
heard her outside the bedroom door, chanting, or she
walked through the house holding eggs in her hands.
Old woman at the foot of the bed motioning us to come
butta butta butta. She talked nonsense but all of them,
seven kids and others drifted in from up and down the
road, they watched her. Some days, boiling jimson in a
pot, she hung wild dope in a shed they'd used to keep
hogs. Shit walked to a powder on the warped floor. She
walked sometimes all day back and forth. Billy laughed,
called her Ole Lady Mindbender. Hey looka that, he
said, his thin lips curled, and she traced eights in the air.
Gnarled fingers jabbing close, she cackled. I kept seeing
their faces together, the old woman and the girl. The

old woman cackling and she, young, with her beige
Negro face, had those same gold-irised eyes, but paler
against her dark skin.

Later she talked of her thin brown mother leaving
those mines her pap worked, him a doghole miner then,
so poor his wife took three of the kids and went to D.C.
They rode buses, riding to bars where her mother sang
for hamburgers and band's donations. Finally she
whored out of Baltimore hotels, the kids waiting outside
on the stoop. Ten-dollar tricks and swarthy short-order
cooks. Movie house janitors' nicotined fingers and
doughy thighs of the satin-haired dago cops. Most nights
the kids slept below in alley porno shop, warmer there,
and Baker, black faggot, kept mattresses in back. Baker,
his moony bagged eyes, his old bottles in windows, gave
them white gravy and bread at 3 A.M. Alley feet stumbled by his grilled basement windows, size of tomato
boxes. It was '49 and he talked about the war, hiding
his knobby hands. Sunk easy in a flushed barbiturate
high, he gave the kids Japanese fans GIs had traded for
pinups. Filmy cataracts liquid as spaniel's eyes, he said
he 'got to move dis place up da street, up dere woan
hafta burn dese lights all day.' She and her brothers stole
opiated cough syrup he heated in a pan. They stole tuna
and steak from the grocery and they ate good some days,
upstairs not so cold come spring. Then it was hot, so hot
they breathed their own sweat. Their mother laughed,
broad mouth stretched tight, eating on carton table in
empty grime city rooms. Fans on full, she wore a bra
and panties, fed them beer and fried meat. Brown
woman, her black hair kerchiefed or pulled back in a
knot. High-cheeked opal face, thick-browed, her smell
raw in rooms. The heat that summer, and at the hotel
there was backed-up plumbing, sad junkies on the roof,
hot-summer Baltimore hepatitis. Their mother taken
from mattress on floor not talking. At the crowded hospital, they were separated, beds on different floors, white
wards, and she, seven years old, thought it was because
someone knew they had stolen the food. She and the
brother left were sent back to the country, where their
father had a woman, more sons.

*   *   *

She had an older brother at Moundsville, sent up I
guess for car theft, big-time state-pen theft. She wrote
him letters on schoolgirl's lined paper, careful not to
smudge pencil sketches of the hounds she kept for him.
Billy making her laugh would kiss the dogs passionate,
holding them tackled in his arms until she ran to him.
The dogs jumped, yelping their womanish sounds. Working with her pap on their truck, we drank Dickel, and
the dogs, five big loose hounds, nuzzled our hands with
their pink snouts. Billy went back to town in the late
evening. The rest of them left through the woods to the
mission church where the grandmother spoke in tongues
and translated what they called the Word. That full-
mooned night her pap and me had the engine out in the
quiet. We worked together and the church sounded faint
through the trees, a distanced animal music come to
echo by the house. Don't like my kids going, he said.
It's hypnosis, some part don't no one need see. And the
women raving, he said, Jesus no lover for a woman. He
said it low, corners of his mouth gone soft, his hard face
naked. He looked at me, and I thought for the first time
that he must have been with her, not now, but long
before, and more than once. He seeing me know stood
confused and then brought his big arms down fisted. We
rolled in the yard and I felt her in his arms in that Detroit room. I tried to say it was all right, I thought she
would be all right, but I hit him because he wanted me
to. He wanted to be hit, beaten, but he came at me so
hard I fell under him, then saw his brutal face go sad.
We said nothing, sat there in patched snow.

Toward spring, Billy left for the last time. Billy in New
York with his East Side girls laughed no doubt then
seriously talked of this cool-faced girl in her miner father's house. You're the good boy here, he told me. I
go, he said, you stay. When I first went there alone (that
is, everything was changed), we stood in the yard. She
feeding chickens made a ck ck ck sound, sucking her
cheeks. I watched her lips move, feeling oddly freaked
there in the mud yard near the scraggly chickens and
their round soulless eyes. Their washed yellow beaks
were faded and sharp and her mouth moved, talking
them close with some gentle sexual sound. I felt like I'd

never slept with her, like both of us, Billy and me, had really only watched her, watched her strange small house and the dirt-scratched farm in big fields, watched the crouched mountains. At first it was like she said, no one around here going anywhere. Then things started moving, sliding; she got to us. When she talked, her curved-edged words ran together, her voice coming low in her throat. There in the yard, early daylight flattened space between us. Seemed I'd never seen her in such light. Always before it was pale. Subdued winter midnights till 6 A.M., the one big bed. Coal stove going and kids asleep in the house. One or two up in the night came in to sleep with us, whimpering. Billy got up first and sat in the chair, reading Revelations out loud drunkenly to himself and she slept close to me. I watched windows in by-then late winter, trees wobbly and the shack buildings pale through the plastic-covered windows.

Or I saw her in dim lights, warm, like in the pool hall in town those afternoons, dark, and the balls cracking sides under one low light hung from ceiling. She on flat stool by the bar talked maybe to Lowry, the owner, whose breath smelled always of black beans, whom she knew well, having helped his old lady midwife in the county since she was a kid. Solemn by steaming cunts of cousins and her father's women, she held pans for the hamlike hands of Elva Lowry. Telling me later (long after chickens in cold spring), once they went clear to Pickens in Elva's Ford, a not-bright woman whooing like a cow for two days. Her one-armed man in the kitchen yelled Shut that up now, and finally the baby birthed breech. Elva, sweating, wrapped it, he frying fat in a shallow pan in the kitchen where she went to wash it. Elva was gone and the woman blathered about jams, about crookberries. Get out there at the pump now, Elva said. Get water, ain nobody finished here. Another baby came. It was blue, its head dented. Elva laid it down. There, she said, let the poor thing go. Women, she said, got the sense of camels.

In the poolroom Lowry told stories. Elva, he said, was a good doctor till she died her own self. Ain't that the way. He laughed in the rosy light and wiped glasses with

a rag. Behind him the cheap beer signs threw shadows
and made his head big on the wall. In that light she was
easy to look at, her crossed legs shiny in dollar nylons,
her head bent in her hair. Making a shot she never
smiled, just chalked her stick and waited. Billy guzzled
cold beer and sharpened in the fuzzy room. He sharpened, his face seemed clearer in those half-lights (he said
to me in private even then, I got to get out of this).
Afterward we'd give her a ride to her place with the
groceries. The town looked abandoned with its slope-
roofed buildings, even old men on stoops sat alone.
Those late afternoons everyone was gone to the mines
or to the Carbide plant. Me and Billy full of male laughter told tales, entertaining her but really gaming each
other. She scratched her nails slow on the coarse bags
in her lap. Billy, mock serious, said he was going to paint
this truck in red letters, name it The Triangle. The whole
truck smelled of him and beer. His shirt open he howled
Hoo Whee, the peddler the priest and the miner's
daughter. She laughed, all of us suddenly sweating. That
spring turned hot before he left. He poured cold beer
down his neck, in his hair, saying Why does he have to
drive this bus Why the hell does he always have to drive.
She said Why Billy because you're the only one got
sense enough not to ask questions. All of us got drunk
on beer and Cutty Sark and then lay in the creek to
sober in cold water.

She told me later (Billy running coke in the Bowery,
heisting TVs in sad-faced apartments for bucks) she'd
heard Billy talking. She said sometimes he'd get so
drunk she'd find him in the woods outside the house,
unconscious, open-eyed, unable to move and mumbling
terrified about avenues and sharks. Early spring in the
yard that morning it was still cool but the sun was a
glassy promised heat. Billy's eyes were gone but they
were close—I felt them in her dress, where she held feed
aproned in the cloth, her sounding ck ck ck and the
stupid staccato chickens. Going in the house she tripped,
the chickens clouding her feet. She called one of the kids
in from the woods. He was the youngest, the rest were
in school by then. Bubby, she yelled. Come on back
here. But he stood still in the yellow field. We started

for him and he came, dragging what we thought was rope but as he came closer we saw it was a big black-snake gaping its harmless mouth. He held it up and we saw its eggs rounded under the hide. He touched its end on the ground and an egg eased out on the grass. The snake, elastic around the shell, tried to coil. The boy looked at us, seemed to forget the snake and left it there on the steps. She stared at it in a way that scared me. I pulled her into the kitchen and she began filling up every pan and kettle in the house with water. The old woman caught on and hauled buckets from the pump. The kid, crowing, hitched up his pants and ran, following her, scuttling in the dirt. The woodburning stove was fired up and thickened the air. The sun got hotter, rubbing on the glass. We opened windows and doors, both of us seeing the swollen snake still on the porch. We moved the big tub to the center of the floor and she burned her hands lugging the heavy kettles. I moved behind her to take them and pressed against her by the wooden tub. The water steamed and I felt her skin under flannel. She was so familiar, the granted smell of her, the dark hay smell. Seeing her firm full-lipped face, I was frightened again by the old stare in her eyes as she'd watched the snake, her stare as she'd watched pitted windows in Billy's rainy truck. Stopping for gas the day before he left, we'd talked past her and she watched numbers turn on the pumps. Listened. Harsh rake of the nozzle, clunk of its handling.

I got in the water with her, the big tub smelling of soaked pine. The old woman turned garden outside and the woods were overgrown already (was it April?). We bathed each other, soaped her black-nippled breasts, and the little boy between us was slippery, shivering against us. She rose, dripping water. The wet floor was shaded dark. She wrapped the boy in blankets and put him in a chair. All of it everything, so slow. Seeming we are in the water for hours, her kinky hair pasted to her back and face in tight curls, she stepping over dogs alseep on the damp floor and me dreaming of us alone in some Southwest, some Canada. She dried me with her hands in bed, her mouth on my eyes. Kunk of old woman's hoe at the side of the house. We had each other slow,

looking at ourselves. Like when he and I came from the
mine that first time she took our clothes, put her face
to our white stomachs. We drank cheap hot whiskey,
kissed her whiskied mouth and she laughed. Our black
faces rubbed her shoulders gray. And it gets confused,
she, her face on me, silent, oh god easing into her we're
in the dark.

Scales

Louise Erdrich

I was sitting before my third or fourth Jellybean—which is anisette, grain alcohol, a lit match, and a small, wet explosion in the brain. On my left sat Gerry Nanapush of the Chippewa Tribe. On my right sat Dot Adare of the has-been, of the never-was, of the what's-in-front-of-me people. Still in her belly and tensed in its fluids coiled the child of their union, the child we were waiting for, the child whose name we were making a strenuous and lengthy search for in a cramped and littered bar at the very edge of that Dakota town.

Gerry had been on the wagon for thirteen years. He was drinking a tall glass of tonic water in which a crescent of soiled lemon bobbed, along with a maraschino cherry or two. He was thirty-six years old and had been in prison, or out of prison and on the run, for exactly half of those years. He was not in the clear yet nor would he ever be; that is why the yellow tennis player's visor was pulled down to the rim of his eyeglass frames. The bar was dimly lit and smoky; his glasses were very dark. Poor visibility must have been the reason Officer Lovchik saw him first.

Lovchik started toward us with his hand on his hip, but Gerry was over the backside of the booth and out the booth before Lovchik got close enough to make a positive identification.

"Siddown with us," said Dot to Lovchik when he neared our booth. "I'll buy you a drink. It's so dead here. No one's been through all night."

Lovchik sighed, sat, and ordered a blackberry brandy.

"Now tell me," she said, staring at him, "honestly. What do you think of the name Ketchup Face?"

It was through Gerry that I first met Dot, and in a bar like that one, only denser with striving drinkers, con-

329

struction crews in town because of the highway. I sat
down by Gerry early in the evening and we struck up a
conversation, during the long course of which we became friendly enough for Gerry to put his arm around
me. Dot entered at exactly the wrong moment. She was
quick-tempered anyway, and being pregnant (Gerry had
gotten her that way on a prison visit five months previ-
ous) increased her irritability. It was only natural then,
I guess, that she would pull the barstool out from under
me and threaten my life. Only I didn't know she was
threatening my life at the time. I didn't know anyone
else like Dot, so I didn't know she was serious.

"I'm gonna bend you out of shape," she said, flexing
her hands over me. Her hands were small, broad, capable, with pointed nails. I used to do the wrong thing
sometimes when I was drinking, and that time I did the
wrong thing even though I was stretched out on the floor
beneath her. I started laughing at her because her hands
were so small (though strong and determined looking, I
should have been more conscious of that). She was
about to dive on top of me, five-month belly and all, but
Gerry caught her in mid-air and carried her, yelling, out
the door. The next day I reported to work. It was my
first day on the job, and the only other woman on the
construction site besides me was Dot Adare.

The first day Dot just glared toward me from a distance. She worked in the weighshack and I was hired to
press buttons on the conveyor belt. All I had to do was
adjust the speeds on the belt for sand, rocks, or gravel,
and make sure it was aimed toward the right pile. There
was a pyramid of each type of material, which was used
to make hot-mix and cement. Across the wide yard, I
saw Dot emerge from the little white shack from time
to time. I couldn't tell whether she recognized me and
thought, by the end of the day, that she probably didn't.
I found out differently the next morning when I went to
the company truck for coffee.

She got me alongside of the truck somehow, away
from the men. She didn't say a word, just held a buck
knife out where I could see it, blade toward me. She
jiggled the handle and the tip waved like the pointy head
of a pit-viper. Blind. Heat-seeking. I was completely as-

tonished. I had just put the plastic cover on my coffee and it steamed between my hands.

"Well I'm sorry I laughed," I said. She stepped back. I peeled the lid off my coffee, took a sip, and then I said the wrong thing again.

"And I wasn't going after your boyfriend."

"Why not!" she said at once. "What's wrong with him!"

I saw that I was going to lose this argument no matter what I said, so for once, I did the right thing. I threw my coffee in her face and ran. Later on that day Dot came out of the weighshack and yelled "Okay, then!" I was close enough to see that she even smiled. I waved. From then on things were better between us, which was lucky, because I turned out to be such a good button presser that within two weeks I was promoted to the weighshack, to help Dot.

It wasn't that Dot needed help weighing trucks, it was just a formality for the State Highway Department. I never quite understood, but it seems Dot had been both the truck-weigher and the truck-weight-inspector for a while, until someone caught wind of this. I was hired to actually weigh the trucks then, for the company, and Dot was hired by the State to make sure I recorded accurate weights. What she really did was sleep, knit, or eat all day. Between truckloads I did the same. I didn't even have to get off my stool to weigh the trucks, because the arm of the scale projected through a rectangular hole and the weights appeared right in front of me. The standard back dumps, belly-dumps, and yellow company trucks eased onto a platform built over the arm next to the shack. I wrote their weight on a little pink slip, clipped the paper in a clothes-pin attached to a broom handle, and handed it up to the driver. I kept a copy of the pink slip on a yellow slip that I put in a metal file-box—no one ever picked up the filebox, so I never knew what the yellow slips were for. The company paid me very well.

It was early July when Dot and I started working together. At first I sat as far away from her as possible and never took my eyes off her knitting needles, although it made me a little dizzy to watch her work. It wasn't long

before we came to an understanding though, and after
this I felt perfectly comfortable with Dot. She was nothing but direct, you see, and told me right off that only
three things made her angry. Number one was someone
flirting with Gerry. Number two was a cigarette leech
(someone who was always quitting but smoking yours).
Number three was a piss-ant. I asked her what that was.
"A piss-ant," she said, "is a man with fat buns who tries
to sell you things, a Jaycee, an Elk, a Kiwanis." I always
knew where I stood with Dot, so I trusted her. I knew
that if I fell out of her favor she would threaten me and
give me time to run before she tried anything physical.

By mid-July our shack was unbearable, for it drew
heat in from the bare yard and held it. We sat outside
most of the time, moving around the shack to catch what
shade fell, letting the raw hot wind off the beetfield suck
the sweat from our armpits and legs. But the seasons
change fast in North Dakota. We spent the last day of
August jumping from foot to numb foot before Hadji,
the foreman, dragged a little column of bottled gas into
the shack. He lit the spoked wheel on its head, it
bloomed, and from then on we huddled close to the
heater—eating, dozing, or sitting blankly in its small ra-
dius of warmth.

By that time Dot weighed over 200 pounds, most of
it peanut-butter cups and egg salad sandwiches. She was
a short, broad-beamed woman with long yellow eyes and
spaces between each of her strong teeth. When we began
working together, her hair was cropped close. By the
cold months it had grown out in thick quills—brown at
the shank, orange at the tip. The orange dye-job had not
suited her coloring. By that time, too, Dot's belly was
round and full, for she was due in October. The child
rode high, and she often rested her forearms on it while
she knitted. One of Dot's most peculiar feats was trans-
forming that gentle task into something perverse. She
knit viciously, jerking the yarn around her thumb until
the tip whitened, pulling each stitch so tightly that the
little garments she finished stood up by themselves like
miniature suits of mail.

But I thought that the child would need those tight
stitches when it was born. Although Dot, as expecting
mother, lived a fairly calm life, it was clear that she

had also moved loosely among dangerous elements. The child, for example, had been conceived in a visiting room at the state prison. Dot had straddled Gerry's lap, in a corner the closed circuit TV did not quite scan. Through a hole ripped in her pantyhose and a hole ripped in Gerry's jeans they somehow managed to join and, miraculously, to conceive. When Dot was sure she was pregnant, Gerry escaped from the prison to see her. Not long after my conversation with Gerry in the bar, he was caught. That time he went back peacefully, and didn't put up a fight. He was mainly in the penitentiary for breaking out of it, anyway, since for his crime (assault and battery when he was eighteen) he had received three years and time off for good behavior. He just never managed to serve those three years or behave well. He broke out time after time, and was caught each time he did it, regular as clockwork.

Gerry was talented at getting out, that's a fact. He boasted that no steel or concrete shitbarn could hold a Chippewa, and he had eel-like properties in spite of his enormous size. Greased with lard once, he squirmed into a six-foot thick prison wall and vanished. Some thought he had stuck there, immured forever, and that he would bring luck like the bones of slaves sealed in the wall of China. But Gerry rubbed his own belly for luck and brought luck to no one else, for he appeared suddenly at Dot's door and she was hard-pressed to hide him.

She managed for nearly a month. Hiding a six-foot-plus, two hundred and fifty pound Indian in the middle of a town that doesn't like Indians in the first place isn't easy. A month was quite an accomplishment, when you know what she was up against. She spent most of her time walking to and from the grocery store, padding along on her swollen feet, astonishing the neighbors with the size of what they thought was her appetite. Stacks of pork-chops, whole fryers, thick steaks disappeared overnight, and since Gerry couldn't take the garbage out by day, sometimes he threw the bones out the windows, where they collected, where dogs soon learned to wait for a hand-out and fought and squabbled over whatever there was.

The neighbors finally complained, and one day, while Dot was at work, Lovchik knocked on the door of the

trailerhouse. Gerry answered, sighed, and walked over
to their car. He was so good at getting out of the joint
and so terrible at getting caught. It was as if he couldn't
stay out of their hands. Dot knew his problem, and told
him that he was crazy to think he could walk out of
prison, and then live like a normal person. Dot told him
that didn't work. She told him to get lost for a while on
the reservation, any reservation, to change his name and,
although he couldn't grow a beard, to at least let the
straggly hairs above his lip form a kind of mustache that
would slightly disguise his face. But Gerry wouldn't do
that. He simply knew he did not belong in prison, although he admitted it had done him some good at eighteen, when he hadn't known how to be a criminal and
so had taken lessons from professionals. Now that he
knew all there was to know, however, he couldn't see
the point of staying in a prison and taking the same
lessons over and over. "A hate-factory," he called it
once, and said it manufactured black poisons in his stomach that he couldn't get rid of, although he poked a
finger down his throat and retched and tried to be a
clean and normal person in spite of everything. Gerry's
problem, you see, was he believed in justice, not laws.
He felt he had paid for his crime, which was done in a
drunk heat and to settle the question with a cowboy of
whether a Chippewa was also a nigger. Gerry said that
the two had never settled it between them, but that the
cowboy at least knew that if a Chippewa was a nigger
he was sure also a hell of a mean and lowdown fighter.
For Gerry did not believe in fighting by any rules but
reservation rules, which is to say the first thing Gerry did
to the cowboy, after they squared off, was kick his balls.

It hadn't been much of a fight after that, and since
there were both white and Indian witnesses Gerry
thought it would blow over if it ever reached court. But
there is nothing more vengeful and determined in this
world than a cowboy with sore balls, and Gerry soon
found this out. He also found that white people are good
witnesses to have on your side, since they have names,
addresses, social security numbers, and work phones.
But they are terrible witnesses to have against you, almost as bad as having Indians witness for you.

Not only did Gerry's friends lack all forms of identification except their band cards, not only did they disappear (out of no malice but simply because Gerry was tried during powwow time), but the few he did manage to get were not interested in looking judge or jury in the eye. They mumbled into their laps. Gerry's friends, you see, had no confidence in the United States Judicial System. They did not seem comfortable in the courtroom, and this increased their unreliability in the eyes of judge and jury. If you trust the authorities, they trust you better back, it seems. It looked that way to Gerry anyhow.

A local doctor testified on behalf of the cowboy's testicles, and said his fertility might be impaired. Gerry got a little angry at that, and said right out in court that he could hardly believe he had done that much damage since the cowboy's balls were very small targets, it had been dark, and his aim was off anyway because of three, or maybe it was only two, beers. That made matters worse, of course, and Gerry was socked with a heavy sentence for an eighteen-year-old, but not for an Indian. Some said he got off lucky.

Only one good thing came from the whole experience, said Gerry, and that was maybe the cowboy would not have any little cowboys, although, Gerry also said, he had nightmares sometimes that the cowboy did manage to have little cowboys, all born with full sets of grinning teeth, stetson hats, and little balls hard as plum pits.

So you see, it was difficult for Gerry, as in Indian, to retain the natural good humor of his ancestors in these modern circumstances. He tried though, and since he believed in justice, not laws, Gerry knew where he belonged (out of prison, in the bosom of his new family). And in spite of the fact that he was untrained in the honest life, he wanted it. He was even interested in getting a job. It didn't matter what kind of job. "Anything for a change," Gerry said. He wanted to go right out and apply for one, in fact, the moment he was free. But of course Dot wouldn't let him. And so, because he wanted to be with Dot, he stayed hidden in her trailerhouse even though they both realized, or must have, that it wouldn't be long before the police came asking around or the neighbors wised up and Gerry Nanapush would be back at square one again. So it happened. Lovchik came for him. And Dot now believed she would have to go through the end of her pregnancy and the delivery all by herself.

Dot was angry about having to go through it alone, and besides that, she loved Gerry with a deep and true love—that was clear. She knit his absence into thick little suits for the child, suits that would have stopped a truck on a dark road with their colors—bazooka pink, bruise blue, the screaming orange flagmen wore.

The child was as restless a prisoner as his father, and grew more anxious and unruly as his time of release neared. As a place to spend a nine-month sentence in, Dot wasn't much. Her body was inhospitable. Her skin was slack, sallow, and draped like upholstery fabric over her short, boardlike bones. Like the shack we spent our days in, she seemed jerry-built, thrown into the world with loosely nailed limbs and lightly puttied joints. Some pregnant women's bellies look like they always have been there. But Dot's stomach was an odd shape, almost square, and had the tacked-on air of a new and unpainted bay window. The child was clearly ready for a break and not interested in earning his parole, for he kept her awake all night by pounding reasonlessly at her inner walls, or beating against her bladder until she swore. "He wants out, bad," poor Dot would groan. "You think he might be premature?" From the outside, anyway, the child looked big enough to stand and walk and maybe even run straight out of the maternity ward the moment he was born.

The sun, at the time, rose around seven and we got to the weighshack while the frost was still thick on the gravel. Each morning I started the gas heater, turning the nozzle and standing back, flipping the match at it the way you would feed a fanged animal. Then one morning I saw the red bud through the window, lit already. But when I opened the door the shack was empty. There was, however, evidence of an overnight visitor— cigarette stubs, a few beer cans crushed to flat disks— I swept these things out and didn't say a word about them to Dot when she arrived.

She seemed to know something was in the air, however; her face lifted from time to time all that morning.

She sniffed, and even I could smell the lingering odor of sweat like sour wheat, the faint reek of slept-in clothes and gasoline. Once, that morning, Dot looked at me and narrowed her long, hooded eyes. "I got pains," she said, "every so often. Like it's going to come sometime soon. Well all I can say is he better drag ass to get here, that Gerry." She closed her eyes then, and went to sleep.

Ed Rafferty, one of the drivers, pulled in with a load. It was overweight, and when I handed him the pink slip he grinned. There were two scales, you see, on the way to the cement plant, and if a driver got past the state-run scale early, before the state officials were there, the company would pay for whatever he got away with. But it was not illicit gravel that tipped the wedge past the red mark on the balance. When I walked back inside I saw the weight had gone down to just under the red. Ed drove off, still laughing, and I assumed that he had leaned on the arm of the scale, increasing the weight.

"That Ed," I said, "got me again."

But Dot stared past me, needles poised in her fist like a picador's lances. It gave me a start, to see her frozen in such a menacing pose. It was not the sort of pose to turn your back on, but I did turn, following her gaze to the door that a man's body filled suddenly.

Gerry, of course it was Gerry. He'd tipped the weight up past the red and leapt down, cat-quick for all his mass, and silent. I hadn't heard his step. Gravel crushed, evidently, but did not roll beneath his tight, thin boots.

He was bigger than I remembered from the bar, or perhaps it was just that we'd been living in that dollhouse of a weighshack so long I saw everything else as huge. He was so big that he had to hunker one shoulder beneath the lintel and back his belly in, pushing the doorframe wider with his long, soft hands. It was the hands I watched as Gerry filled the shack. His plump fingers looked so graceful and artistic against his smooth mass. He used them prettily. Revolving agile wrists, he reached across the few inches left between himself and Dot. Then his littlest fingers curled like a woman's at tea, and he disarmed his wife. He drew the needles out

of Dot's fists, and examined the little garment that hung
like a queer fruit beneath.

" 'S very, very nice," he said, scrutinizing the tiny,
even stitches. " 'S for the kid?"

Dot nodded solemnly and dropped her eyes to her
lap. It was an almost tender moment. The silence lasted
so long that I got embarrassed and would have left, had
I not been wedged firmly behind his hip in one corner.

Gerry stood there, smoothing black hair behind his
ears. Again, there was a queer delicacy about the way
he did this. So many things Gerry did might remind you
of the way that a beautiful woman, standing naked before a mirror, would touch herself—lovingly, conscious
of her attractions. He nodded encouragingly. "Let's go
then," said Dot.

Suave, grand, gigantic, they moved across the parking
lot and then, by mysterious means, slipped their bodies
into Dot's compact car. I expected the car to belly down,
thought the muffler would scrape the ground behind
them. But instead they flew, raising a great spume of
dust that hung in the air a long time after they were out
of sight.

I went back into the weighshack when the air behind
them had settled. I was bored, dead bored. And since
one thing meant about as much to me as another, I
picked up her needles and began knitting, as well as I
could anyway, jerking the yarn back after each stitch,
becoming more and more absorbed in my work until, as
it happened, I came suddenly to the end of the garment,
snipped the yarn, and worked the loose ends back into
the collar of the thick little suit.

I missed Dot in the days that followed, days so alike
they welded seamlessly to one another and took your
mind away. I seemed to exist in a suspension and spent
my time sitting blankly at the window, watching nothing
until the sun went down, bruising the whole sky as it
dropped, clotting my heart. I couldn't name anything I
felt anymore, although I knew it was a kind of boredom.
I had been living the same life too long. I did jumping
jacks and push-ups and stood on my head in the little
shack to break the tedium, but too much solitude rots
the brain. I wondered how Gerry had stood it. Some-

times I grabbed drivers out of their trucks and talked loudly and quickly and inconsequentially as a mad-woman. There were other times I couldn't talk at all because my tongue had rusted to the roof of my mouth.

Sometimes I daydreamed about Dot and Gerry. I had many choice daydreams, but theirs was my favorite. I pictured them in Dot's long tan and aqua trailerhouse, both hungry. Heads swaying, clasped hands swinging be-tween them like hooked trunks, they moved through the kitchen feeding casually from boxes and bags on the counters, like ponderous animals alone in a forest. When they fed, they moved on to the bedroom and settled themselves upon Dot's kingsize and sateen-quilted spread. They rubbed together, locked and unlocked their parts. They set the trailer rocking on its cement block and plywood foundation and the tremors spread, causing cups to fall, plates to shatter in the china hutches of their more established neighbors.

But what of the child there, suspended between them. Did he know how to weather such tropical storms? It was a week past the week he was due, and I expected the good news to come any moment. I was anxious to hear the outcome, but still I was surprised when Gerry rumbled to the weighshack door on a huge and ancient, rust-pocked, untrustworthy-looking machine that was like no motorcycle I'd ever seen before.

"She asst for you," he hissed. "Quick, Get on!"

I hoisted myself up behind him, although there wasn't room on the seat. I clawed his smooth back for a hand-hold and finally perched, or so it seemed, on the rim of his heavy belt. Fly-like, glued to him by suction, we rode as one person, whipping a great wind around us. Cars scattered, the lights blinked and flickered on the main street. Pedestrians swiveled to catch a glimpse of us—a mountain tearing by balanced on a toy, and clinging to the sheer northwest face, a young and scrawny girl howl-ing something that dopplered across the bridge and faded out, finally, in the parking lot of the Saint Fran-cis Hospital.

In the waiting room we settled on chairs molded of orange plastic. The spike legs splayed beneath Gerry's

mass, but managed to support him the four hours we
waited. Nurses passed, settling like field gulls among reports and prescriptions, eyeing us with reserved hostility.
Gerry hardly spoke. He didn't have to. I watched his
ribs and the small of his back darken with sweat, for
that well-lighted tunnel, the waiting room, the tin rack
of magazines, all were the props and inevitable features
of institutions. From time to time Gerry paced in the
time-honored manner of the prisoner or expectant father. He made lengthy trips to the bathroom. All the
quickness and delicacy of his movements had disappeared, and he was only a poor weary fat man in those
hours, a husband worried about his wife, menaced, tired
of getting caught.

The gulls emerged finally, and drew Gerry in among
them. He visited Dot for perhaps half an hour, and then
came out of her room. Again he settled; the plastic chair
twitched beneath him. He looked bewildered and silly
and a little addled with what he had seen. The shaded
lenses of his glasses kept slipping down his nose. Beside
him, I felt the aftermath of the shockwave, traveling
from the epicenter deep in his flesh, outward from part
of him that had shifted along a crevice. The tremors
moved in widening rings. When they reached the very
surface of him, and when he began trembling, Gerry
stood suddenly. "I'm going after cigars," he said, and
walked quickly away.

His steps quickened to a near run as he moved down
the corridor. Waiting for the elevator, he flexed his nimble fingers. Dot told me she had once sent him to the
store for a roll of toilet paper. It was eight months before she saw him again, for he'd met the local constabu-
lary on the way. So I knew, when he flexed his fingers,
that he was thinking of pulling the biker's gloves over
his knuckles, of running. It was perhaps the very first
time in his life he had something to run for.

It seemed to me, at that moment, that I should at least
let Gerry know it was all right for him to leave, to run
as far and fast as he had to now. Although I felt heavy,
my body had gone slack, and my lungs ached with
smoke, I jumped up. I signaled him from the end of the
corridor. Gerry turned, unwillingly turned. He looked
my way just as two of our local police—Officers Lovchik

and Harris, pushed open the firedoor that sealed off the staircase behind me. I didn't see them, and was shocked at first that my wave caused such an extreme reaction in Gerry.

His hair stiffened. His body lifted like a hot-air balloon filling suddenly. Behind him there was a wide, tall window. Gerry opened it and sent the screen into thin air with an elegant, chorus-girl kick. Then he followed the screen, squeezing himself unbelievably through the frame like a fat rabbit disappearing down a hole. It was three stories down to the cement and asphalt parking lot.

Officers Lovchik and Harris gained the window. The nurses followed. I slipped through the fire exit and took the back stairs down into the parking lot, believing I would find him stunned and broken there.

But Gerry had chosen his window with exceptional luck, for the officers had parked their car directly underneath. Gerry landed just over the driver's seat, caving the roof into the steering wheel. He bounced off the hood of the car and then, limping, a bit dazed perhaps, straddled his bike. Out of duty, Lovchik released several rounds into the still trees below him. The reports were still echoing when I reached the front of the building.

I was just in time to see Gerry Nanapush, emboldened by his godlike leap and recovery, pop a wheelie and disappear between the neat shrubs that marked the entrance to the hospital.

Two weeks later Dot and her boy, who was finally named Jason, like most boys born that year, came back to work at the scales. Things went on as they had before, except that Jason kept us occupied during the long hours. He was large, of course, and had a sturdy pair of lungs he used often. When he cried, Jason screwed his face into fierce baby wrinkles and would not be placated with sugar tits or pacifiers. Dot unzipped her parka halfway, pulled her blouse up, and let him nurse for what seemed like hours. We could scarcely believe his appetite. Dot was a diligent producer of milk, however. Her breasts, like overfilled innertubes, strained at her nylon blouses. Sometimes, when she thought no one was looking, Dot rose and carried them in the crooks of her arms, for her shoulders were growing bowed beneath their weight.

The trucks came in on the hour, or half hour. I heard the rush of airbrakes, gears grinding only inches from my head. It occurred to me that although I measured many tons every day, I would never know how heavy a ton was unless it fell on me. I wasn't lonely now that Dot had returned. The season would end soon, and we wondered what had happened to Gerry.

There were only a few weeks left of work when we heard that Gerry was caught again. He'd picked the wrong reservation to hide on—Pine Ridge. At the time it was overrun with Federal Agents and armored vehicles. Weapons were stashed everywhere and easy to acquire. Gerry got himself a weapon. Two men tried to arrest him. Gerry would not go along and when he started to run and the shooting started Gerry shot and killed a clean-shaven man with dark hair and light eyes, a Federal Agent, a man whose picture was printed in all the papers.

They sent Gerry to prison in Marion, Illinois. He was placed in the control unit. He receives his visitors in a room where no touching is allowed, where the voice is carried by phone, glances meet through sheets of plexiglass, and no children will ever be engendered.

Dot and I continued to work the last weeks together. Once we weighed baby Jason. We unlatched his little knit suit, heavy as armor, and bundled him in a light, crocheted blanket. Dot went into the shack to adjust the weights. I stood there with Jason. He was such a solid child, he seemed heavy as lead in my arms. I placed him on the ramp between the wheelsights and held him steady for a moment, then took my hands slowly away. He stared calmly into the rough, distant sky. He did not flinch when the wind came from every direction, wrapping us tight enough to squeeze the very breath from a stone. He was so dense with life, such a powerful distillation of Dot and Gerry, it seemed he might weigh about as much as any load. But that was only a thought, of course. For as it turned out, he was too light and did not register at all.

The Bridle

Raymond Carver

This old station wagon with Minnesota plates pulls into a parking space in front of the window. There's a man and woman in the front seat, two boys in the back. It's July, temperature's one hundred plus. These people look whipped. There are clothes hanging inside; suitcases, boxes, and such piled in back. From what Harley and I put together later, that's all they had left after the bank in Minnesota took their house, their pickup, their tractor, the farm implements, and a few cows.

The people inside sit for a minute, as if collecting themselves. The air-conditioner in our apartment is going full blast. Harley's around in back cutting grass. There's some discussion in the front seat, and then she and him get out and start for the front door. I pat my hair to make sure that it's in place and wait till they push the doorbell for the second time. Then I go to let them in. "You're looking for an apartment?" I say. "Come on in here where it's cool." I show them into the living room. The living room is where I do business. It's where I collect the rents, write the receipts, and talk to interested parties. I also do hair. I call myself a *stylist*. That's what my cards say. I don't like the word *beautician*. It's an old-time word. I have the chair in a corner of the living room, and a dryer I can pull up to the back of the chair. And there's a sink that Harley put in a few years ago. Alongside the chair, I have a table with some magazines. The magazines are old. The covers are gone from some of them. But people will look at anything while they're under the dryer.

The man says his name.

"My name is Holits."

He tells me she's his wife. But she won't look at me. She looks at her nails instead. She and Holits won't sit

343

down, either. He says they're interested in one of the furnished units.

"How many of you?" But I'm just saying what I always say. I know how many. I saw the two boys in the back seat. Two and two is four.

"Me and her and the boys. The boys are thirteen and fourteen, and they'll share a room, like always."

She has her arms crossed and is holding the sleeves of her blouse. She takes in the chair and the sink as if she's never seen their like before. Maybe she hasn't.

"I do hair," I say.

She nods. Then she gives my prayer plant the once-over. It has exactly five leaves to it.

"That needs watering," I say. I go over and touch one of its leaves. "Everything around here needs water. There's not enough water in the air. It rains three times a year if we're lucky. But you'll get used to it. We had to get used to it. But everything here is air-conditioned."

"How much is the place?" Holits wants to know.

I tell him and he turns to her to see what she thinks. But he may as well have been looking at the wall. She won't give him back his look. "I guess we'll have you show us," he says. So I move to get the key for 17, and we go outside.

I hear Harley before I see him.

Then he comes into sight between the buildings. He's moving along behind the power mower in his Bermudas and T-shirt, wearing the straw hat he bought in Nogales. He spends his time cutting grass and doing the small maintenance work. We work for a corporation, Fulton Terrace, Inc. They own the place. If anything major goes wrong, like air-conditioning trouble or something serious in the plumbing department, we have a list of phone numbers.

I wave. I have to. Harley takes a hand off the mower handle and signals. Then he pulls the hat down over his forehead and gives his attention back to what he's doing. He comes to the end of his cut, makes his turn, and starts back toward the street.

"That's Harley," I have to shout it. We go in at the side of the building and up some stairs. "What kind of work are you in, Mr. Holits?" I ask him.

"He's a farmer," she says.

"No more."

"Not much to farm around here." I say it without thinking.

"We had us a farm in Minnesota. Raised wheat. A few cattle. And Holits knows horses. He knows everything there is about horses."

"That's all right, Betty."

I get a piece of the picture then. Holits is unemployed. It's not my affair, and I feel sorry if that's the case—it is, it turns out—but as we stop in front of the unit, I have to say something. "If you decide, it's first month, last month, and one-fifty as security deposit." I look down at the pool as I say it. Some people are sitting in deck chairs, and there's somebody in the water.

Holits wipes his face with the back of his hand. Harley's mower is clacking away. Farther off, cars speed by on Calle Verde. The two boys have got out of the station wagon. One of them is standing at military attention, legs together, arms at his sides. But as I watch, I see him begin to flap his arms up and down and jump, like he intends to take off and fly. The other one is squatting down on the driver's side of the station wagon, doing knee bends.

I turn to Holits.

"Let's have a look," he says.

I turn the key and the door opens. It's just a little two-bedroom furnished apartment. Everybody has seen dozens. Holits stops in the bathroom long enough to flush the toilet. He watches till the tank fills. Later, he says, "This could be our room." He's talking about the bedroom that looks out over the pool. In the kitchen, the woman takes hold of the edge of the drainboard and stares out the window.

"That's the swimming pool," I say.

She nods. "We stayed in some motels that had swimming pools. But in one pool they had too much chlorine in the water."

I wait for her to go on. But that's all she says. I can't think of anything else, either.

"I guess we won't waste any more time. I guess we'll take it." Holits looks at her as he says it. This time she meets his eyes. She nods. He lets out breath through his

teeth. Then she does something. She begins snapping her
fingers. One hand is still holding the edge of the drainboard, but with her other hand she begins snapping her
fingers. Snap, snap, snap, like she was calling her dog,
or else trying to get somebody's attention. Then she
stops and runs her nails across the counter.

I don't know what to make of it. Holits doesn't either.
He moves his feet.

"We'll walk back to the office and make things official," I say. "I'm glad."

I *was* glad. We had a lot of empty units for this time of
year. And these people seemed like dependable people.
Down on their luck, that's all. No disgrace can be
attached to that.

Holits pays in cash—first, last, and the one-fifty deposit. He counts out bills of fifty-dollar denomination
while I watch. U. S. Grants, Harley calls them, though
he's never seen many. I write out the receipt and give
him two keys. "You're all set."

He looks at the keys. He hands her one. "So, we're
in Arizona. Never thought you'd see Arizona, did you?"

She shakes her head. She's touching one of the prayer-
plant leaves.

"Needs water," I say.

She lets go of the leaf and turns to the window. I go
over next to her. Harley is still cutting grass. But he's
around in front now. There's been this talk of farming,
so for a minute I think of Harley moving along behind
a plow instead of behind his Black and Decker power
mower.

I watch them unload their boxes, suitcases, and
clothes. Holits carries in something that has straps hanging from it. It takes a minute, but then I figure out it's
a bridle. I don't know what to do next. I don't feel like
doing anything. So I take the Grants out of the cashbox.
I just put them in there, but I take them out again.
The bills have come from Minnesota. Who knows where
they'll be this time next week? They could be in Las
Vegas. All I know about Las Vegas is what I see on
TV—about enough to put into a thimble. I can imagine
one of the Grants finding its way out to Waikiki Beach,
or else some other place. Miami or New York City, New

Orleans. I think about one of those bills changing hands
during Mardi Gras. They could go anyplace, and anything could happen because of them. I write my name
in ink across Grant's broad old forehead: MARGE. I print
it. I do it on every one. Right over his thick brows.
People will stop in the midst of their spending and wonder. Who's this Marge? That's what they'll ask themselves, Who's this Marge?

Harley comes in from outside and washes his hands
in my sink. He knows it's something I don't like him to
do. But he goes ahead and does it anyway.

"Those people from Minnesota," he says. "The
Swedes. They're a long way from home." He dries his
hands on a paper towel. He wants me to tell him what
I know. But I don't know anything. They don't look like
Swedes and they don't talk like Swedes.

"They're not Swedes," I tell him. But he acts like he
doesn't hear me.

"So what's he do?"

"He's a farmer."

"What do you know about that?"

Harley takes his hat off and puts it on my chair. He
runs a hand through his hair. Then he looks at the hat
and puts it on again. He may as well be glued to it.
"There's not much to farm around here. Did you tell
him that?" He gets a can of soda pop from the fridge
and goes to sit in his recliner. He picks up the remote-
control, pushes something, and the TV sizzles on. He
pushes some more buttons until he finds what he's looking for. It's a hospital show. "What else does the Swede
do? Besides farm?"

I don't know, so I don't say anything. But Harley's
already taken up with his program. He's probably forgotten he asked me the question. A siren goes off. I hear
the screech of tires. On the screen, an ambulance has
come to a stop in front of an emergency-room entrance,
its red lights flashing. A man jumps out and runs around
to open up the back.

The next afternoon the boys borrow the hose and
wash the station wagon. They clean the outside and the
inside. A little later I notice her drive away. She's wearing high heels and a nice dress. Hunting up a job, I'd

say. After a while, I see the boys messing around the pool in their bathing suits. One of them springs off the board and swims all the way to the other end underwater. He comes up blowing water and shaking his head. The other boy, the one who'd been doing knee bends the day before, lies on his stomach on a towel at the far side of the pool. But this one boy keeps swimming back and forth from one end of the pool to the other, touching the wall and turning back with a little kick.

There are two other people out there. They're in lounge chairs, one on either side of the pool. One of them is Irving Cobb, a cook at Denny's. He calls himself Spuds. People have taken to calling him that, Spuds, instead of Irv or some other nickname. Spuds is fifty-five and bald. He already looks like beef jerky, but he wants more sun. Right now, his new wife, Linda Cobb, is at work at the K Mart. Spuds works nights. But him and Linda Cobb have it arranged so they take their Saturdays and Sundays off. Connie Nova is in the other chair. She's sitting up and rubbing lotion on her legs. She's nearly naked—just this little two-piece suit covering her. Connie Nova is a cocktail waitress. She moved in here six months ago with her so-called fiancé, an alcoholic lawyer. But she got rid of him. Now she lives with a long-haired student from the college whose name is Rick. I happen to know he's away right now, visiting his folks. Spuds and Connie are wearing dark glasses. Connie's portable radio is going.

Spuds was a recent widower when he moved in, a year or so back. But after a few months of being a bachelor again, he got married to Linda. She's a red-haired woman in her thirties. I don't know how they met. But one night a couple of months ago Spuds and the new Mrs. Cobb had Harley and me over to a nice dinner that Spuds fixed. After dinner, we sat in their living room drinking sweet drinks out of big glasses. Spuds asked if we wanted to see home movies. We said sure. So Spuds set up his screen and his projector. Linda Cobb poured us more of that sweet drink. Where's the harm? I asked myself. Spuds began to show films of a trip he and his dead wife had made to Alaska. It began with her getting on the plane in Seattle. Spuds talked as he ran the projector. The deceased was in her fifties, good-looking, though maybe a little heavy. Her hair was nice.

"That's Spuds's first wife," Linda Cobb said. "That's the first Mrs. Cobb."

"That's Evelyn," Spuds said.

The first wife stayed on the screen for a long time. It was funny seeing her and hearing them talk about her like that. Harley passed me a look, so I know he was thinking something, too. Linda Cobb asked if we wanted another drink or a macaroon. We didn't. Spuds was saying something about the first Mrs. Cobb again. She was still at the entrance to the plane, smiling and moving her mouth even if all you could hear was the film going through the projector. People had to go around her to get on the plane. She kept waving at the camera, waving at us there in Spuds's living room. She waved and waved. "There's Evelyn again," the new Mrs. Cobb would say each time the first Mrs. Cobb appeared on the screen.

Spuds would have shown films all night, but we said we had to go. Harley made the excuse.

I don't remember what he said.

Connie Nova is lying on her back in the chair, dark glasses covering half of her face. Her legs and stomach shine with oil. One night, not long after she moved in, she had a party. This was before she kicked the lawyer out and took up with the long-hair. She called her party a housewarming. Harley and I were invited, along with a bunch of other people. We went, but we didn't care for the company. We found a place to sit close to the door, and that's where we stayed till we left. It wasn't all that long, either. Connie's boyfriend was giving a door prize. It was the offer of his legal services, without charge, for the handling of a divorce. Anybody's divorce. Anybody who wanted to could draw a card out of the bowl he was passing around. When the bowl came our way, everybody began to laugh. Harley and I swapped glances. I didn't draw. Harley didn't draw, either. But I saw him look in the bowl at the pile of cards. Then he shook his head and handed the bowl to the person next to him. Even Spuds and the new Mrs. Cobb drew cards. The winning card had something written across the back. "Entitles bearer to one free uncontested divorce," and

the lawyer's signature and the date. The lawyer was a
drunk, but I say this is no way to conduct your life.
Everybody but us had put his hand into the bowl, like
it was a fun thing to do. The woman who drew the winning card clapped. It was like one of those game shows.
"Goddamn, this is the first time I ever won anything!"
I was told she had a husband in the military. There's no
way of knowing if she still has him, or if she got her
divorce, because Connie Nova took up with a different
set of friends after she and the lawyer went their separate ways.

We left the party right after the drawing. It made such
an impression we couldn't say much, except one of us
said, "I don't believe I saw what I think I saw."

Maybe I said it.

A week later Harley asks if the Swede—he means
Holits—has found work yet. We've just had lunch, and
Harley's in his chair with his can of pop. But he hasn't
turned his TV on. I say I don't know. And I don't. I
wait to see what else he has to say. But he doesn't say
anything else. He shakes his head. He seems to think
about something. Then he pushes a button and the TV
comes to life.

She finds a job. She starts working as a waitress in an
Italian restaurant a few blocks from here. She works a
split shift, doing lunches and then going home, then back
to work again in time for the dinner shift. She's meeting
herself coming and going. The boys swim all day, while
Holits stays inside the apartment. I don't know what he
does in there. Once, I did her hair and she told me a
few things. She told me she did waitressing when she
was just out of high school and that's where she met
Holits. She served him some pancakes in a place back
in Minnesota.

She'd walked down that morning and asked me could
I do her a favor. She wanted me to fix her hair after her
lunch shift and have her out in time for her dinner shift.
Could I do it? I told her I'd check the book. I asked
her to step inside. It must have been a hundred degrees already.

"I know it's short notice," she said. "But when I came
in from work last night, I looked in the mirror and saw

my roots showing. I said to myself, 'I need a treatment.'
I don't know where else to go."

I find Friday, August 14. There's nothing on the page.

"I could work you in at two-thirty, or else at three
o'clock," I say.

"Three would be better," she says. "I have to run for
it now before I'm late. I work for a real bastard. See
you later."

At two-thirty, I tell Harley I have a customer, so he'll
have to take his baseball game into the bedroom. He
grumps, but he winds up the cord and wheels the set
out back. He closes the door. I make sure everything I
need is ready. I fix up the magazines so they're easy to
get to. Then I sit next to the dryer and file my nails. I'm
wearing the rose-colored uniform that I put on when I
do hair. I go on filing my nails and looking up at the
window from time to time.

She walks by the window and then pushes the doorbell. "Come on in," I call. "It's unlocked."

She's wearing the black-and-white uniform from her
job. I can see how we're both wearing uniforms. "Sit
down, honey, and we'll get started." She looks at the
nail file. "I give manicures, too," I say.

She settles into the chair and draws a breath.

I say, "Put your head back. That's it. Close your eyes
now, why don't you? Just relax. First I'll shampoo you
and touch up these roots here. Then we'll go from there.
How much time do you have?"

"I have to be back there at five-thirty."

"We'll get you fixed up."

"I can eat at work. But I don't know what Holits and
the boys will do for their supper."

"They'll get along fine without you."

I start the warm water and then notice Harley's left
me some dirt and grass. I wipe up his mess and start
over.

I say, "If they want, they can just walk down the street
to the hamburger place. It won't hurt them."

"They won't do that. Anyway, I don't want them to
have to go there."

It's none of my business, so I don't say any more. I
make up a nice lather and go to work. After I've done
the shampoo, rinse, and set, I put her under the dryer.

Her eyes have closed. I think she could be asleep. So I take one of her hands and begin.

"No manicure." She opens her eyes and pulls away her hand.

"It's all right, honey. The first manicure is always no charge."

She gives me back her hand and picks up one of the magazines and rests it in her lap. "They're his boys," she says. "From his first marriage. He was divorced when we met. But I love them like they were my own. I couldn't love them any more if I tried. Not even if I was their natural mother."

I turn the dryer down a notch so that it's making a low, quiet sound. I keep on with her nails. Her hand starts to relax.

"She lit out on them, on Holits and the boys, on New Year's Day ten years ago. They never heard from her again." I can see she wants to tell me about it. And that's fine with me. They like to talk when they're in the chair. I go on using the file. "Holits got the divorce. Then he and I started going out. Then we got married. For a long time, we had us a life. It had its ups and downs. But we thought we were working toward something." She shakes her head. "But something happened. Something happened to Holits, I mean. One thing happened was he got interested in horses. This one particular race horse, he bought it, you know—something down, something each month. He took it around to the tracks. He was still up before daylight, like always, still doing the chores and such. I thought everything was all right. But I don't know anything. If you want the truth, I'm not so good at waiting tables. I think those wops would fire me at the drop of a hat, if I gave them a reason. Or for no reason. What if I got fired? Then what?"

I say, "Don't worry, honey. They're not going to fire you."

Pretty soon she picks up another magazine. But she doesn't open it. She just holds it and goes on talking. "Anyway, there's this horse of his. Fast Betty. The Betty part is a joke. But he says it can't help but be a winner if he names it after me. A big winner, all right. The fact is, wherever it ran, it lost. Every race. Betty Longshot—

that's what it should have been called. In the beginning,
I went to a few races. But the horse always ran ninety-
nine to one. Odds like that. But Holits is stubborn if
he's anything. He wouldn't give up. He'd bet on the
horse and bet on the horse. Twenty dollars to win. Fifty
dollars to win. Plus all the other things it costs for keeping a horse. I know it don't sound like a large amount.
But it adds up. And when the odds were like that—
ninety-nine to one, you know—sometimes he'd buy a
combination ticket. He'd ask me if I realized how much
money we'd make if the horse came in. But it didn't,
and I quit going."

I keep on with what I'm doing. I concentrate on her
nails. "You have nice cuticles," I say. "Look here at
your cuticles. See these little half-moons? Means your
blood's good."

She brings her hand up close and looks. "What do
you know about that?" She shrugs. She lets me take her
hand again. She's still got things to tell. "Once, when I
was in high school, a counselor asked me to come to her
office. She did it with all the girls, one of us at a time.
'What dreams do you have?' this woman asked me.
'What do you see yourself doing in ten years? Twenty
years?' I was sixteen or seventeen. I was just a kid. I
couldn't think what to answer. I just sat there like a
lump. This counselor was about the age I am now. I
thought she was *old*. She's old, I said to myself. I knew
her life was half over. And I felt like I knew something
she didn't. Something she'd never know. A secret. Something nobody's supposed to know, or ever talk about. So
I stayed quiet. I just shook my head. She must've written
me off as a dope. But I couldn't say anything. You know
what I mean? I thought I knew things she couldn't guess
at. Now, if anybody asked me that question again, about
my dreams and all, I'd tell them."

"What would you tell them, honey?" I have her other
hand now. But I'm not doing her nails. I'm just holding
it, waiting to hear.

She moves forward in the chair. She tries to take her
hand back.

"What would you tell them?"

She sighs and leans back. She lets me keep the hand.
"I'd say, 'Dreams, you know, are what you wake up

from.' That's what I'd say." She smooths the lap of her
skirt. "If anybody asked, that's what I'd say. But they
won't ask." She lets out her breath again. "So how much
longer?" she says.

"Not long," I say.

"You don't know what it's like."

"Yes, I do," I say. I pull the stool right up next to
her legs. I'm starting to tell how it was before we moved
here, and how it's still like that. But Harley picks right
then to come out of the bedroom. He doesn't look at
us. I hear the TV jabbering away in the bedroom. He
goes to the sink and draws a glass of water. He tips his
head back to drink. His Adam's apple moves up and
down in his throat.

I move the dryer away and touch the hair at both
sides of her head. I lift one of the curls just a little.

I say, "You look brand-new, honey."

"Don't I wish."

The boys keep on swimming all day, every day, till
their school starts. Betty keeps on at her job. But for
some reason she doesn't come back to get her hair done.
I don't know why this is. Maybe she doesn't think I did
a good job. Sometimes I lie awake, Harley sleeping like
a grindstone beside me, and try to picture myself in Betty's shoes. I wonder what I'd do then.

Holits sends one of his sons with the rent on the first
of September, and on the first of October, too. He still
pays in cash. I take the money from the boy, count the
bills right there in front of him, and then write out the
receipt. Holits has found work of some sort. I think so,
anyway. He drives off every day with the station wagon.
I see him leave early in the morning and drive back late
in the afternoon. She goes past the window at ten-thirty
and comes back at three. If she sees me, she gives me a
little wave. But she's not smiling. Then I see Betty again
at five, walking back to the restaurant. Holits drives in
a little later. This goes on till the middle of October.

Meanwhile, the Holits couple acquainted themselves
with Connie Nova and her long-hair friend, Rick. And
they also met up with Spuds and the new Mrs. Cobb.
Sometimes, on a Sunday afternoon, I'd see all of them
sitting around the pool, drinks in their hands, listening

to Connie's portable radio. One time Harley said he saw them all behind the building, in the barbecue area. They were in their bathing suits then, too. Harley said the Swede had a chest like a bull. Harley said they were eating hot dogs and drinking whiskey. He said they were drunk.

It was Saturday, and it was after eleven at night. Harley was asleep in his chair. Pretty soon I'd have to get up and turn off the set. When I did that, I knew he'd wake up. "Why'd you turn it off? I was watching that show." That's what he'd say. That's what he always said. Anyway, the TV was going, I had the curlers in, and there's a magazine on my lap. Now and then I'd look up. But I couldn't get settled on the show. They were all out there in the pool area—Spuds and Linda Cobb, Connie Nova and the long-hair, Holits and Betty. We have a rule against anyone being out there after ten. But this night they didn't care about rules. If Harley woke up, he'd go out and say something. I felt it was all right for them to have their fun, but it was time for it to stop. I kept getting up and going over to the window. All of them except Betty had on bathing suits. She was still in her uniform. But she had her shoes off, a glass in her hand, and she was drinking right along with the rest of them. I kept putting off having to turn off the set. Then one of them shouted something, and another one took it up and began to laugh. I looked and saw Holits finish off his drink. He put the glass down on the deck. Then he walked over to the cabana. He dragged up one of the tables and climbed onto that. Then—he seemed to do it without any effort at all—he lifted up onto the roof of the cabana. It's true, I thought; he's strong. The long-hair claps his hands, like he's all for this. The rest of them are hooting Holits on, too. I know I'm going to have to go out there and put a stop to it.

Harley's slumped in his chair. The TV's still going. I ease the door open, step out, and then push it shut behind me. Holits is up on the roof of the cabana. They're egging him on. They're saying, "Go on, you can do it." "Don't belly-flop, now." "I double-dare you." Things like that.

Then I hear Betty's voice. "Holits, think what you're

doing." But Holits just stands there at the edge. He looks down at the water. He seems to be figuring how much of a run he's going to have to make to get out there. He backs up to the far side. He spits in his palm and rubs his hands together. Spuds calls out, "That's it, boy! You'll do it now."

I see him hit the deck. I hear him, too.

"Holits!" Betty cries.

They all hurry over to him. By the time I get there, he's sitting up. Rick is holding him by the shoulders and yelling into his face. "Holits! Hey, man!"

Holits has this gash on his forehead, and his eyes are glassy. Spuds and Rick help him into a chair. Somebody give him a towel. But Holits holds the towel like he doesn't know what he's supposed to do with it. Somebody else hands him a drink. But Holits doesn't know what to do with that, either. People keep saying things to him. Holits brings the towel up to his face. Then he takes it away and looks at the blood. But he just looks at it. He can't seem to understand anything.

"Let me see him." I get around in front of him. It's bad. "Holits, are you all right?" But Holits just looks at me, and then his eyes drift off. "I think he'd best go to the emergency room." Betty looks at me when I say this and begins to shake her head. She looks back at Holits. She gives him another towel. I think she's sober. But the rest of them are drunk. Drunk is the best that can be said for them.

Spuds picks up what I said. "Let's take him to the emergency room."

Rick says, "I'll go, too."

"We'll all go," Connie Nova says.

"We better stick together," Linda Cobb says.

"Holits." I say his name again.

"I can't go it," Holits says.

"What'd he say?" Connie Nova asks me.

"He says he can't go it," I tell her.

"Go what? What's he talking about?" Rick wants to know.

"Say again?" Spuds says. "I didn't hear."

"He says he can't go it. I don't think he knows what he's talking about. You'd best take him to the hospital," I say. Then I remember Harley and the rules. "You

shouldn't have been out here. Any of you. We have
rules. Now go on and take him to the hospital."

"Let's take him to the hospital," Spuds says like it's
something he's just thought of. He might be farther gone
than any of them. For one thing, he can't stand still. He
weaves. And he keeps picking up his feet and putting
them down again. The hair on his chest is snow white
under the overhead pool lights.

"I'll get the car." That's what the long-hair says.
"Connie, let me have the keys."

"I can't go it," Holits says. The towel has moved down
to his chin. But the cut is on his forehead.

"Get him that terry-cloth robe. He can't go to the
hospital that way." Linda Cobb says that. "Holits! Holits, it's us." She waits and then she takes the glass of
whiskey from Holits's fingers and drinks from it.

I can see people at some of the windows, looking
down on the commotion. Lights are going on. "Go to
bed!" someone yells.

Finally, the long-hair brings Connie's Datsun from behind the building and drives it up close to the pool. The
headlights are on bright. He races the engine.

"For Christ's sake, go to bed!" the same person yells.
More people come to their windows. I expect to see
Harley come out any minute, wearing his hat, steaming.
Then I think, No, he'll sleep through it. Just forget
Harley.

Spuds and Connie Nova get on either side of Holits.
Holits can't walk straight. He's wobbly. Part of it's because he's drunk. But there's no question he's hurt himself. They get him into the car, and they all crowd inside,
too. Betty is the last to get in. She has to sit on somebody's lap. Then they drive off. Whoever it was that has
been yelling slams the window shut.

The whole next week Holits doesn't leave the place.
And I think Betty must have quit her job, because I
don't see her pass the window anymore. When I see the
boys go by, I step outside and ask them, point-blank:
"How's your dad?"

"He hurt his head," one of them says.

I wait in hopes they'll say some more. But they don't.
They shrug and go on to school with their lunch sacks

and binders. Later, I was sorry I hadn't asked after their stepmom.

When I see Holits outside, wearing a bandage and standing on his balcony, he doesn't even nod. He acts like I'm a stranger. It's like he doesn't know me or doesn't want to know me. Harley says he's getting the same treatment. He doesn't like it. "What's with him?" Harley wants to know. "Damn Swede. What happened to his head? Somebody belt him or what?" I don't tell Harley anything when he says that. I don't go into it at all.

Then that Sunday afternoon I see one of the boys carry out a box and put it in the station wagon. He goes back upstairs. But pretty soon he comes back down with another box, and he puts that in, too. It's then I know they're making ready to leave. But I don't say what I know to Harley. He'll know everything soon enough.

Next morning, Betty sends one of the boys down. He's got a note that says she's sorry but they have to move. She gives me her sister's address in Indio where she says we can send the deposit to. She points out they're leaving eight days before their rent is up. She hopes there might be something in the way of a refund there, even though they haven't given the thirty days' notice. She says, "Thanks for everything. Thanks for doing my hair that time." She signs the note, "Sincerely, Betty Holits."

"What's your name?" I ask the boy.

"Billy."

"Billy, tell her I said I'm real sorry."

Harley reads what she's written, and he says it will be a cold day in hell before they see any money back from Fulton Terrace. He says he can't understand these people. "People who sail through life like the world owes them a living." He asks me where they're going. But I don't have any idea where they're going. Maybe they're going back to Minnesota. How do I know where they're going? But I don't think they're going back to Minnesota. I think they're going someplace else to try their luck.

Connie Nova and Spuds have their chairs in the usual places, one on either side of the pool. From time to time, they look over at the Holits boys carrying things out to the station wagon. Then Holits himself comes out with

some clothes over his arm. Connie Nova and Spuds holler and wave. Holits looks at them like he doesn't know
them. But then he raises up his free hand. Just raises it,
that's all. They wave. Then Holits is waving. He keeps
waving at them, even after they've stopped. Betty comes
downstairs and touches his arm. She doesn't wave. She
won't even look at these people. She says something to
Holits, and he goes on to the car. Connie Nova lies back
in her chair and reaches over to turn up her portable
radio. Spuds holds his sunglasses and watches Holits and
Betty for a while. Then he fixes the glasses over his ears.
He settles himself in the lounge chair and goes back to
tanning his leathery old self.

Finally, they're all loaded and ready to move on. The
boys are in the back, Holits behind the wheel, Betty in
the seat right up next to him. It's just like it was when
they drove in here.

"What are you looking at?" Harley says.

He's taking a break. He's in his chair, watching the
TV. But he gets up and comes over to the window.

"Well, there they go. They don't know where they're
going or what they're going to do. Crazy Swede."

I watch them drive out of the lot and turn onto the
road that's going to take them to the freeway. Then I
look at Harley again. He's settling into his chair. He has
his can of pop, and he's wearing his straw hat. He acts
like nothing has happened or ever will happen.

"Harley?"

But, of course, he can't hear me. I go over and stand
in front of his chair. He's surprised. He doesn't know
what to make of it. He leans back, just sits there looking
at me.

The phone starts ringing.

"Get that, will you?" he says.

I don't answer him. Why should I?

"Then let it ring," he says.

I go find the mop, some rags, S.O.S. pads, and a
bucket. The phone stops ringing. He's still sitting in his
chair. But he's turned off the TV. I take the passkey, go
outside and up the stairs to 17. I let myself in and walk
through the living room to their kitchen—what used to
be their kitchen.

The counters have been wiped down, the sink and

cupboards are clean. It's not so bad. I leave the cleaning things on the stove and go take a look at the bathroom. Nothing there a little steel wool won't take care of. Then I open the door to the bedroom that looks out over the pool. The blinds are raised, the bed is stripped. The floor shines. "Thanks," I say out loud. Wherever she's going, I wish her luck. "Good luck, Betty." One of the bureau drawers is open and I go to close it. Back in a corner of the drawer I see the bridle he was carrying in when he first came. It must have been passed over in their hurry. But maybe it wasn't. Maybe the man left it on purpose.

"Bridle," I say. I hold it up to the window and look at it in the light. It's not fancy, it's just an old dark leather bridle. I don't know much about them. But I know that one part of it fits in the mouth. That part's called the bit. It's made of steel. Reins go over the head and up to where they're held on the neck between the fingers. The rider pulls the reins this way and that, and the horse turns. It's simple. The bit's heavy and cold. If you had to wear this thing between your teeth, I guess you'd catch on in a hurry. When you felt it pull, you'd know it was time. You'd know you were going somewhere.

The Eggs of the World
Toshio Mori

Almost everyone in the community knew Sessue
Matoi as the heavy drinker. There was seldom a
time when one did not see him staggering full of drink.
The trouble was that people did not know when he was
sober or drunk. He was very clever when he was drunk
and also very clever when sober. The people were afraid
to touch him. They were afraid of this man, sober or
drunk, for his tongue and brains. They dared not coax
him too solicitously or make him look ridiculous as they
would treat the usual tipsy gentleman. The people may
have had only contempt for him, but they were afraid
and silent. And Sessue Matoi did little work. We always
said he practically lived on sake and wit. And that was
not far from truth.

I was at Mr. Hasegawa's when Sessue Matoi staggered
in the house with several drinks under his belt. About
the only logical reason I could think of for his visit that
night was that Sessue Matoi must have known that Mr.
Hasegawa carried many bottles of Japan-imported sake.
There was no other business why he should pay a visit
to Hasegawa's. I knew Mr. Hasegawa did not tolerate
drinking bouts. He disliked riotous scenes and people.

At first I thought Mr. Hasegawa might have been
afraid of this drinker, and Sessue Matoi had taken advantage of it. But this was not the case. Mr. Hasegawa
was not afraid of Sessue Matoi. As I sat between the
two that night, I knew I was in the fun, and as likely as
any minute something would explode.

"I came to see you on a very important matter, Hasegawa," Sessue Matoi said without batting an eye. "You
are in a very dangerous position. You will lose your
life."

"What are you talking about?" Mr. Hasegawa said.

"You are in an egg," Sessue Matoi said. "You have seen nothing but the inside of an egg, and I feel sorry for you. I pity you."

"What are you talking about? Are you crazy?" Mr. Hasegawa said.

"I am not crazy. I see you very clearly in an egg," Sessue Matoi said. "That is very bad. Pretty soon you will be rotten."

Mr. Hasegawa was a serious fellow, not taking to laughter and gaiety. But he laughed out loud. This was ridiculous. Then he remembered Sessue Matoi was drunk.

"What about this young fellow?" Mr. Hasegawa said, pointing at me.

Sessue Matoi looked me over quizzically. He appeared to study me from all angles. Then he said, "His egg is forming. Pretty soon he must break the shell of his egg or little later will find himself too weak to do anything about it."

I said nothing. Mr. Hasegawa sat with a twinkle in his eyes.

"What about yourself, Sessue Matoi?" he said. "Do you live in an egg?"

"No," Sessue Matoi said. "An egg is when you are walled in, a prisoner within yourself. I am free; I have broken the egg long ago. You see me as I am. I am not hidden beneath a shell, and I am not enclosed in one either. I am walking on this earth with my good feet, and also I am drinking and enjoying, but am sad on seeing so many eggs in the world, unbroken, untasted, and rotten."

"Are you insulting the whole world, or are you just insulting me?" Mr. Hasegawa said.

"I am insulting no one. Look, look me in the eye, Hasegawa. See how sober I am," he said. "I am not insulting you. I love you. I love the whole world, and sober or drunk it doesn't make a bit of difference. But when I say an egg's an egg, I mean it. You can't very well break the eggs I see."

"Couldn't you break the eggs for us?" Mr. Hasegawa said. "You seem to see the eggs very well. Couldn't you go around and break the shells and make this world the hatching ground?"

"No, no!" Sessue Matoi said. "You have me wrong! I cannot break the eggs. You cannot break the eggs. You can break an egg, though."

"I don't get you," said Mr. Hasegawa.

"An egg is broken from within," said Sessue Matoi. "The shell of an egg melts by itself through heat or warmth, and it's natural and independent."

"This is ridiculous," said Mr. Hasegawa. "An egg can be broken from outside. You know very well an egg may be broken by a rap from outside."

"You can rape and assault, too," said Sessue Matoi.

"This is getting to be fantastic," Mr. Hasegawa said. "This is silly! Here we are getting all burned up over a little egg, arguing over nonsense."

"This is very important to me," Sessue Matoi said. "Probably the only thing I know about. I study egg culture twenty-four hours. I live for it."

"And for sake," Mr. Hasegawa said.

"And for sake," Sessue Matoi said.

"Shall we study about sake tonight? Shall we taste the sake and you tell me about the flavor?" Mr. Hasegawa said.

"Fine, fine, fine!" said Mr. Matoi.

Mr. Hasegawa went back in the kitchen, and we heard him moving about. Pretty soon he came back with a steaming bottle of sake. "This is Hakushika," he said.

"Fine, fine," Sessue Matoi said. "All brands are the same to me; all flavors match my flavor. When I drink, I am drinking my flavor."

Mr. Hasegawa poured him several cups, which Sessue Matoi promptly gulped down. Sessue Matoi gulped down several more. "Ah, when I drink sake, I think of the eggs in the world," he said. "All the unopened eggs in the world."

"Just what are you going to do with all these eggs lying about? Aren't you going to do something about it? Can't you put some of the eggs aside and heat them up or warm them and help break the shells from within?" Mr. Hasegawa said.

"No," Sessue Matoi said. "I am doing nothing of the sort. If I do all you think I should do, then I will have no time to sit and drink. And I must drink. I cannot go a day without drinking, because when I drink, I am really going outward, not exactly drinking, but expressing myself outwardly, talking very much and saying little, sadly and pathetically."

"Tell me, Sessue Matoi," said Mr. Hasegawa. "Are you sad at this moment? Aren't you happy in your paganistic fashion, drinking and laughing through twenty-four hours?"

"Now, you are feeling sorry for me, Hasegawa," Sessue Matoi said. "You are getting sentimental. Don't think of me in that manner. Think of me as the mess I am. I am a mess. Then laugh very hard; keep laughing very hard. Say, oh, what an egg he has opened up! Look at the shells; look at the drunk without a bottle."

"Why do you say these things?" Mr. Hasegawa said. "You are very bitter."

"I am not bitter; I am not mad at anyone," Sessue Matoi said. "But you are still talking through the eggshell."

"You are insulting me again," Mr. Hasegawa said. "Do not allow an egg to come between us."

"That is very absurd," Sessue Matoi said, rising from his chair. "You are very absurd, sir. An egg is the most important and the most disturbing thing in the world. Since you are an egg, you do not know an egg. That is sad. I say, good night, gentlemen."

Sessue Matoi in all seriousness bowed formally and then tottered to the door.

"Wait, Sessue Matoi," said Mr. Hasegawa. "You didn't tell me what you thought of the flavor of my sake."

"I did tell you," Sessue Matoi said. "I told you the flavor right along."

"That's the first time I ever heard you talking about the flavor of sake tonight," said Mr. Hasegawa.

"You misunderstand me again," said Sessue Matoi. "When you wish to taste the flavor of sake which I drank, then you must drink the flavor which I have been spouting all evening. Again, good night, gentlemen."

Again he bowed formally at the door and staggered out of the house.

I was expecting to see Mr. Hasegawa burst out laughing the minute Sessue Matoi stepped out of the house. He didn't. "I suppose he will be around in several days to taste your sake. This must happen every time he comes to see you," I said.

"No," Mr. Hasegawa said. "Strangely, this is the first time he ever walked out like that. I cannot understand him. I don't believe he will be back for a long time."

"Was he drunk or sober tonight?" I said.

"I really don't know," said Mr. Hasegawa. "He must be sober and drunk at the same time."

"Do you really think we will not see him for a while?" I said.

"Yes, I am very sure of it. To think that an egg would come between us!"

ANONYMOUS NARRATION—
SINGLE CHARACTER
POINT OF VIEW

This technique is no doubt the most commonly employed because it enables authors to convey most fully both the inside and outside views of a protagonist, something that fictional autobiography and memoir provide only together. Most stories feature an individual, and anonymous narrators can deploy the most resources because they do not have to account for how they know what they tell.

Not having to refer to oneself licenses a narrator to convey the combined knowledge of eyewitness, confidant, and chorus as she or he sees fit for a given subject and purpose. The stories here vary in the amount an author plays the eyewitness role for scenic depiction and the chorus role for "offstage" or background information. They vary, too, in how much the author plays chorus in another sense—as interpreter and commentator. What the stories have in common is the presentation of the protagonist's thoughts, feelings, values, and vantage point, as if author and reader were confidants.

"Single character point of view" means that the author takes us essentially only where a certain character goes and permits us to know only what that character is thinking and feeling. Readers see the world as that chosen person sees it, but they also see it as the author understands it, for the hidden narrator may be paraphrasing what the character thinks as well as organizing and perhaps commenting on the material. Hidden or not, where there is a narrative there is a narrator. Everything from selecting and sequencing incidents to naming and phrasing particulars can convey the author's view. In fact, it is this binocular perspective created by author and character together that typifies third-person stories with one or more inner points of view. A binocular prose results from the various alternating, grafting, and fusing of author and character voices that critic Mikhail Bahktin has exhaustively analyzed in "Discourse in the Novel."

But why only one character point of view? And why this character? Answering these questions for themselves may carry readers to the heart of the author's matter. It may also help understand why authors choose sometimes to enter more than one character's mind or none at all.

The Five-Forty-Eight

John Cheever

When Blake stepped out of the elevator, he saw her. A few people, mostly men waiting for girls, stood in the lobby watching the elevator doors. She was among them. As he saw her, her face took on a look of such loathing and purpose that he realized she had been waiting for him. He did not approach her. She had no legitimate business with him. They had nothing to say. He turned and walked toward the glass doors at the end of the lobby, feeling that faint guilt and bewilderment we experience when we by-pass some old friend or classmate who seems threadbare, or sick, or miserable in some other way. It was five-eighteen by the clock in the Western Union office. He could catch the express. As he waited his turn at the revolving doors, he saw that it was still raining. It had been raining all day, and he noticed now how much louder the rain made the noises of the street. Outside, he started walking briskly east toward Madison Avenue. Traffic was tied up, and horns were blowing urgently on a crosstown street in the distance. The sidewalk was crowded. He wondered what she had hoped to gain by a glimpse of him coming out of the office building at the end of the day. Then he wondered if she was following him.

Walking in the city, we seldom turn and look back. The habit restrained Blake. He listened for a minute—foolishly—as he walked, as if he could distinguish her footsteps from the worlds of sound in the city at the end of a rainy day. Then he noticed, ahead of him on the other side of the street, a break in the wall of buildings. Something had been torn down; something was being put up, but the steel structure had only just risen above the sidewalk fence and daylight poured through the gap. Blake stopped opposite here and looked into a store window. It was a decorator's or an auctioneer's. The window was arranged like a room in which people live and entertain their friends. There were cups on the coffee table, magazines to read, and flowers in the vases, but the flowers were dead and the cups were empty and the guests had not come. In the plate glass, Blake saw a clear reflection of himself and the crowds that were passing, like shadows, at his back. Then he saw her image—so close to him that it shocked him. She was standing only a foot or two behind him. He could have turned then and asked her what she wanted, but instead of recognizing her, he shied away abruptly from the reflection of her contorted face and went along the street. She might be meaning to do him harm—she might be meaning to kill him.

The suddenness with which he moved when he saw the reflection of her face tipped the water out of his hatbrim in such a way that some of it ran down his neck. It felt unpleasantly like the sweat of fear. Then the cold water falling into his face and onto his bare hands, the rancid smell of the wet gutters and pavings, the knowledge that his feet were beginning to get wet and that he might catch cold—all the common discomforts of walking in the rain—seemed to heighten the menace of his pursuer and to give him a morbid consciousness of his own physicalness and of the ease with which he could be hurt. He could see ahead of him the corner of Madison Avenue, where the lights were brighter. He felt that if he could get to Madison Avenue he would be all right. At the corner, there was a bakery shop with two entrances, and he went in by the door on the crosstown street, bought a coffee ring, like any other commuter, and went out the Madison Avenue door. As he started down Madison Avenue, he saw her waiting for him by a hut where newspapers were sold.

She was not clever. She would be easy to shake. He could get into a taxi by one door and leave by the other. He could speak to a policeman. He could run—although he was afraid that if he did run, it might precipitate the violence he now felt sure she had planned. He was approaching a part of the city that he knew well and where the maze of street-level and underground passages, elevator banks, and crowded lobbies made it easy for a man to lose a pursuer. The thought of this, and a whiff of sugary warmth from the coffee ring, cheered him. It was absurd to imagine being harmed on a crowded street. She was foolish, misled, lonely perhaps—that was all it could amount to. He was an insignificant man, and there was no point in anyone's following him from his office to the station. He knew no secrets of any consequence. The reports in his brief case had no bearing on war, peace, the dope traffic, the hydrogen bomb, or any of the other international skulduggeries that he associated with pursuers, men in trench coats, and wet sidewalks. Then he saw ahead of him the door of a men's bar. Oh, it was so simple!

He ordered a Gibson and shouldered his way in between two other men at the bar, so that if she should be watching from the window she would lose sight of him. The place was crowded with commuters putting down a drink before the ride home. They had brought in on their clothes—on their shoes and umbrellas—the rancid smell of wet dusk outside, but Blake began to relax as soon as he tasted his Gibson and looked around at the common, mostly not-young faces that surrounded him and that were worried, if they were worried at all, about tax rates and who would be put in charge of merchandising. He tried to remember her name—Miss Dent, Miss Bent, Miss Lent—and he was surprised to find that he could not remember it, although he was proud of the retentiveness and reach of his memory and it had only been six months ago.

Personnel had sent her up one afternoon—he was looking for a secretary. He saw a dark woman—in her twenties, perhaps—who was slender and shy. Her dress was simple, her figure was not much, one of her stockings was crooked, but her voice was soft and he had been willing to try her out. After she had been working for him a few days, she told him that she had been in the hospital for eight months and that it had been hard after this for her to find work, and she wanted to thank him for giving her a chance. Her hair was dark, her eyes were dark; she left him with a pleasant impression of darkness. As he got to know her better, he felt that she was oversensitive and, as a consequence, lonely. Once, when she was speaking to him of what she imagined his life to be—full of friendships, money, and a large and loving family—he had thought he recognized a peculiar feeling of deprivation. She seemed to imagine the lives of the rest of the world to be more brilliant than they were. Once, she had put a rose on his desk, and he had dropped it into the wastebasket. "I don't like roses," he told her.

She had been competent, punctual, and a good typist, and he had found only one thing in her that he could object to—her handwriting. He could not associate the crudeness of her handwriting with her appearance. He would have expected her to write a rounded backhand, and in her writing there were intermittent traces of this, mixed with clumsy printing. Her writing gave him the feeling that she had been the victim of some inner—some emotional—conflict that had in its violence broken the continuity of the lines she was able to make on paper. When she had been working for him three weeks—no longer—they stayed late one night and he offered, after work, to buy her a drink. "If you really want a drink," she said, "I have some whiskey at my place."

She lived in a room that seemed to him like a closet. There were suit boxes and hatboxes piled in a corner, and although the room seemed hardly big enough to hold the bed, the dresser, and the chair he sat in, there was an upright piano against one wall, with a book of Beethoven sonatas on the rack. She gave him a drink and said that she was going to put on something more comfortable. He urged her to; that was, after all, what he had come for. If he had had any qualms, they would have been practical. Her diffidence, the feeling of deprivation in her point of view, promised to protect him from any consequences. Most of the many women he had known had been picked for their lack of self-esteem.

When he put on his clothes again, an hour or so later, she was weeping. He felt too contented and warm and sleepy to worry much about her tears. As he was dressing, he noticed on the dresser a note she had written to a cleaning woman. The only light came from the bathroom—the door was ajar—and in this half light the hideously scrawled letters again seemed entirely wrong for her, and as if they must be the handwriting of some other and very gross woman. The next day, he did what he felt was the only sensible thing. When she was out for lunch, he called personnel and asked them to fire her. Then he took the afternoon off. A few days later, she came to the office, asking to see him. He told the switchboard girl not to let her in. He had not seen her again until this evening.

Blake drank a second Gibson and saw by the clock that he had missed the express. He would get the local— the five-forty-eight. When he left the bar the sky was still light; it was still raining. He looked carefully up and down the street and saw that the poor woman had gone. Once or twice, he looked over his shoulder, walking to the station, but he seemed to be safe. He was still not quite himself, he realized, because he had left his coffee ring at the bar, and he was not a man who forgot things. This lapse of memory pained him.

He bought a paper. The local was only half full when he boarded it, and he got a seat on the river side and took off his raincoat. He was a slender man with brown hair—undistinguished in every way, unless you could have divined in his pallor or his gray eyes his unpleasant tastes. He dressed—like the rest of us—as if he admitted the existence of sumptuary laws. His raincoat was the pale buff color of a mushroom. His hat was dark brown; so was his suit. Except for the few bright threads in his necktie, there was a scrupulous lack of color in his clothing that seemed protective.

He looked around the car for neighbors: Mrs. Compton was several seats in front of him, to the right. She smiled, but her smile was fleeting. It died swiftly and horribly. Mr. Watkins was directly in front of Blake. Mr. Watkins needed a haircut, and he had broken the sumptuary laws; he was wearing a corduroy jacket. He and Blake had quarreled, so they did not speak.

The swift death of Mrs. Compton's smile did not affect Blake at all. The Comptons lived in the house next to the Blakes, and Mrs. Compton had never understood the importance of minding her own business. Louise Blake took her troubles to Mrs. Compton, Blake knew, and instead of discouraging her crying jags, Mrs. Compton had come to imagine herself a sort of confessor and had developed a lively curiosity about the Blakes' intimate affairs. She had probably been given an account of their most recent quarrel. Blake had come home one night, overworked and tired, and had found that Louise had done nothing about getting supper. He had gone into the kitchen, followed by Louise, and he had pointed out to her that the date was the fifth. He had drawn a circle around the date on the kitchen calendar. "One week is the twelfth," he had said. "Two weeks will be the nineteenth." He drew a circle around the nineteenth. "I'm not going to speak to you for two weeks," he had said. "That will be the nineteenth." She had wept, she had protested, but it had been eight or ten years since she had been able to touch him with her entreaties. Louise had got old. Now the lines in her face were ineradicable, and when she clapped her glasses onto her nose to read the evening paper she looked to him like an unpleasant stranger. The physical charms that had been her only attraction were gone. It had been nine years since Blake had built a bookshelf in the doorway that connected their rooms and had fitted into the bookshelf wooden doors that could be locked, since he did not want the children to see his books. But their prolonged estrangement didn't seem remarkable to Blake. He had quarreled with his wife, but so did every other man born of woman. It was human nature. In any place where you can hear their voices—a hotel courtyard, an air shaft, a street on a summer evening—you will hear harsh words.

The hard feeling between Blake and Mr. Watkins also had to do with Blake's family, but it was not as serious or as troublesome as what lay behind Mrs. Compton's fleeting smile. The Watkinses rented. Mr. Watkins broke the sumptuary laws day after day—he once went to the eight-fourteen in a pair of sandals—and he made his living as a commercial artist. Blake's oldest son—Charlie was fourteen—had made friends with the Watkins boy. He had spent a lot of time in the sloppy rented house where the Watkinses lived. The friendship had affected his manners and his neatness. Then he had begun to take some meals with the Watkinses, and to spend Saturday nights there. When he had moved most of his possessions over to the Watkinses' and had begun to spend more than half his nights there, Blake had been forced to act. He had spoken not to Charlie but to Mr. Watkins, and had, of necessity, said a number of things that must have sounded critical. Mr. Watkins' long and dirty hair and his corduroy jacket reassured Blake that he had been in the right.

But Mrs. Compton's dying smile and Mr. Watkins' dirty hair did not lessen the pleasure Blake took in settling himself in an uncomfortable seat on the five-forty-eight deep underground. The coach was old and smelled oddly like a bomb shelter in which whole families had spent the night. The light that spread from the ceiling down onto their heads and shoulders was dim. The filth on the window glass was streaked with rain from some other journey, and clouds of rank pipe and cigarette smoke had begun to rise from behind each newspaper, but it was a scene that meant to Blake that he was on a safe path, and after his brush with danger he even felt a little warmth toward Mrs. Compton and Mr. Watkins.

The train traveled up from underground into the weak daylight, and the slums and the city reminded Blake vaguely of the woman who had followed him. To avoid speculation or remorse about her, he turned his attention to the evening paper. Out of the corner of his eye he could see the landscape. It was industrial and, at that hour, sad. There were machine sheds and warehouses, and above these he saw a break in the clouds—a piece of yellow light. "Mr. Blake," someone said. He looked up. It was she. She was standing there holding one hand on the back of the seat to steady herself in the swaying coach. He remembered her name then—Miss Dent. "Hello, Miss Dent," he said.

"Do you mind if I sit here?"

"I guess not."

"Thank you. It's very kind of you. I don't like to inconvenience you like this. I don't want to . . ." He had been frightened when he looked up and saw her, but her timid voice rapidly reassured him. He shifted his hams—that futile and reflexive gesture of hospitality—and she sat down. She sighed. He smelled her wet clothing. She wore a formless black hat with a cheap crest stitched onto it. Her coat was thin cloth, he saw, and she wore gloves and carried a large pocketbook.

"Are you living out in this direction now, Miss Dent?"

"No."

She opened her purse and reached for her handkerchief. She had begun to cry. He turned his head to see if anyone in the car was looking, but no one was. He had sat beside a thousand passengers on the evening train. He had noticed their clothes, the holes in their gloves; and if they fell asleep and mumbled he had wondered what their worries were. He had classified almost all of them briefly before he buried his nose in the paper. He had marked them as rich, poor, brilliant or dull, neighbors or strangers, but no one of the thousands had ever wept. When she opened her purse, he remembered her perfume. It had clung to his skin the night he went to her place for a drink.

"I've been very sick," she said. "This is the first time I've been out of bed in two weeks. I've been terribly sick."

"I'm sorry that you've been sick, Miss Dent," he said in a voice loud enough to be heard by Mr. Watkins and Mrs. Compton. "Where are you working now?"

"What?"

"Where are you working now?"

"Oh, don't make me laugh," she said softly.

"I don't understand."

"You poisoned their minds."

He straightened his back and braced his shoulders. These wrenching movements expressed a brief—and hopeless—longing to be in some other place. She meant trouble. He took a breath. He looked with deep feeling at the half-filled, half-lighted coach to affirm his sense of actuality, of a world in which there was not very much bad trouble after all. He was conscious of her heavy breathing and the smell of her rain-soaked coat. The train stopped. A nun and a man in overalls got off. When it started again, Blake put on his hat and reached for his raincoat.

"Where are you going?" she said.

"I'm going up to the next car."

"Oh, no," she said. "No, no, no." She put her white face so close to his ear that he could feel her warm breath on his cheek. "Don't do that," she whispered. "Don't try and escape me. I have a pistol and I'll have to kill you and I don't want to. All I want to do is talk

with you. Don't move or I'll kill you. Don't, don't,
don't!"

Blake sat back abruptly in his seat. If he had wanted
to stand and shout for help, he would not have been
able to. His tongue had swelled to twice its size, and
when he tried to move it, it stuck horribly to the roof
of his mouth. His legs were limp. All he could think of
to do then was to wait for his heart to stop its hysterical
beating, so that he could judge the extent of his danger.
She was sitting a little sidewise, and in her pocketbook
was the pistol, aimed at his belly.

"You understand me now, don't you?" she said. "You
understand that I'm serious?" He tried to speak but he
was still mute. He nodded his head. "Now we'll sit quietly for a little while," she said. "I got so excited that
my thoughts are all confused. We'll sit quietly for a little
while, until I can get my thoughts in order again."

Help would come, Blake thought. It was only a question of minutes. Someone, noticing the look on his face
or her peculiar posture, would stop and interfere, and it
would all be over. All he had to do was to wait until
someone noticed his predicament. Out of the window he
saw the river and the sky. The rain clouds were rolling
down like a shutter, and while he watched, a streak of
orange light on the horizon became brilliant. Its bril-
liance spread—he could see it move—across the waves
until it raked the banks of the river with a dim firelight.
Then it was put out. Help would come in a minute, he
thought. Help would come before they stopped again;
but the train stopped, there were some comings and goings, and Blake still lived on, at the mercy of the woman
beside him. The possibility that help might not come
was one that he could not face. The possibility that his
predicament was not noticeable, that Mrs. Compton
would guess that he was taking a poor relation out to
dinner at Shady Hill, was something he would think
about later. Then the saliva came back into his mouth
and he was able to speak.

"Miss Dent?"

"Yes."

"What do you want?"

"I want to talk with you."

"You can come to my office."

"Oh, no. I went there every day for two weeks."

"You could make an appointment."

"No," she said. "I think we can talk here. I wrote you a letter but I've been too sick to go out and mail it. I've put down all my thoughts. I like to travel. I like trains. One of my troubles has always been that I could never afford to travel. I suppose you see this scenery every night and don't notice it any more, but it's nice for someone who's been in bed a long time. They say that He's not in the river and the hills but I think He is. 'Where shall wisdom be found,' it says. 'Where is the place of understanding? The depth saith it is not in me; the sea saith it is not with me. Destruction and death say we have heard the force with our ears.'

"Oh, I know what you're thinking," she said. "You're thinking that I'm crazy, and I have been very sick again but I'm going to be better. It's going to make me better to talk with you. I was in the hospital all the time before I came to work for you but they never tried to cure me, they only wanted to take away my self-respect. I haven't had any work now for three months. Even if I did have to kill you, they wouldn't be able to do anything to me except put me back in the hospital, so you see I'm not afraid. But let's sit quietly for a little while longer. I have to be calm."

The train continued its halting progress up the bank of the river, and Blake tried to force himself to make some plans for escape, but the immediate threat to his life made this difficult, and instead of planning sensibly, he thought of the many ways in which he could have avoided her in the first place. As soon as he had felt these regrets, he realized their futility. It was like regretting his lack of suspicion when she first mentioned her months in the hospital. It was like regretting his failure to have been warned by her shyness, her diffidence, and the handwriting that looked like the marks of a claw. There was no way now of rectifying his mistakes, and he felt—for perhaps the first time in his mature life— the full force of regret. Out of the window, he saw some men fishing on the nearly dark river, and then a ramshackle boat club that seemed to have been nailed together out of scraps of wood that had been washed up on the shore.

Mr. Watkins had fallen asleep. He was snoring. Mrs. Compton read her paper. The train creaked, slowed, and halted infirmly at another station. Blake could see the southbound platform, where a few passengers were waiting to go into the city. There was a workman with a lunch pail, a dressed-up woman, and a man with a suitcase. They stood apart from one another. Some advertisements were posted on the wall behind them. There was a picture of a couple drinking a toast in wine, a picture of a Cat's Paw rubber heel, and a picture of a Hawaiian dancer. Their cheerful intent seemed to go no farther than the puddles of water on the platform and to expire there. The platform and the people on it looked lonely. The train drew away from the station into the scattered lights of a slum and then into the darkness of the country and the river.

"I want you to read my letter before we get to Shady Hill," she said. "It's on the seat. Pick it up. I would have mailed it to you, but I've been too sick to go out. I haven't gone out for two weeks. I haven't had any work for three months. I haven't spoken to anybody but the landlady. Please read my letter."

He picked up the letter from the seat where she had put it. The cheap paper felt abhorrent and filthy to his fingers. It was folded and refolded. "Dear Husband," she had written, in that crazy, wandering hand, "they say that human love leads us to divine love, but is this true? I dream about you every night. I have such terrible desires. I have always had a gift for dreams. I dreamed on Tuesday of a volcano erupting with blood. When I was in the hospital they said they wanted to cure me but they only wanted to take away my self-respect. They only wanted me to dream about sewing and basketwork but I protected my gift for dreams. I'm clairvoyant. I can tell when the telephone is going to ring. I've never had a true friend in my whole life. . . ."

The train stopped again. There was another platform, another picture of the couple drinking a toast, the rubber heel, and the Hawaiian dancer. Suddenly she pressed her face close to Blake's again and whispered in his ear. "I know what you're thinking. I can see it in your face. You're thinking you can get away from me in Shady Hill, aren't you? Oh, I've been planning this for weeks.

It's all I've had to think about. I won't harm you if you'll
let me talk. I've been thinking about devils. I mean if
there are devils in the world, if there are people in the
world who represent evil, is it our duty to exterminate
them? I know that you always prey on weak people. I
can tell. Oh, sometimes I think that I ought to kill you.
Sometimes I think you're the only obstacle between me
and my happiness. Sometimes . . ."

She touched Blake with the pistol. He felt the muzzle
against his belly. The bullet, at that distance, would
make a small hole where it entered, but it would rip out
of his back a place as big as a soccer ball. He remembered the unburied dead he had seen in the war. The
memory came in a rush: entrails, eyes, shattered bone,
ordure, and other filth.

"All I've ever wanted in life is a little love," she said.
She lightened the pressure of the gun. Mr. Watkins still
slept. Mrs. Compton was sitting calmly with her hands
folded in her lap. The coach rocked gently, and the coats
and mushroom-colored raincoats that hung between the
windows swayed a little as the car moved. Blake's elbow
was on the window sill and his left shoe was on the
guard above the steampipe. The car smelled like some
dismal classroom. The passengers seemed asleep and
apart, and Blake felt that he might never escape the
smell of heat and wet clothing and the dimness of the
light. He tried to summon the calculated self-deceptions
with which he sometimes cheered himself, but he was
left without any energy for hope or self-deception.

The conductor put his head in the door and said
"Shady Hill, next, Shady Hill."

"Now," she said. "Now you get out ahead of me."

Mr. Watkins waked suddenly, put on his coat and hat,
and smiled at Mrs. Compton, who was gathering her
parcels to her in a series of maternal gestures. They went
to the door. Blake joined them, but neither of them
spoke to him or seemed to notice the woman at his back.
The conductor threw open the door, and Blake saw on
the platform of the next car a few other neighbors who
had missed the express, waiting patiently and tiredly in
the wan light for their trip to end. He raised his head
to see through the open door the abandoned mansion
outside of town, a NO TRESPASSING sign nailed to a tree,

and then the oil tanks. The concrete abutments of the bridge passed, so close to the open door that he could have touched them. Then he saw the first of the lamp-posts on the northbound platform, the sign SHADY HILL in black and gold, and the little lawn and flower bed kept up by the Improvement Association, and then the cab stand and a corner of the old-fashioned depot. It was raining again; it was pouring. He could hear the splash of water and see the lights reflected in puddles and in the shining pavement, and the idle sound of splashing and dripping formed in his mind a conception of shelter, so light and strange that it seemed to belong to a time of his life that he could not remember.

He went down the steps with her at his back. A dozen or so cars were waiting by the station with their motors running. A few people got off from each of the other coaches; he recognized most of them, but none of them offered to give him a ride. They walked separately or in pairs—purposefully out of the rain to the shelter of the platform, where the car horns called to them. It was time to go home, time for a drink, time for love, time for supper, and he could see the lights on the hill—lights by which children were being bathed, meat cooked, dishes washed—shining in the rain. One by one, the cars picked up the heads of families, until there were only four left. Two of the stranded passengers drove off in the only taxi the village had. "I'm sorry, darling," a woman said tenderly to her husband when she drove up a few minutes later. "All our clocks are slow." The last man looked at his watch, looked at the rain, and then walked off into it, and Blake saw him go as if they had some reason to say good-by—not as we say good-by to friends after a party but as we say good-by when we are faced with an inexorable and unwanted parting of the spirit and the heart. The man's footsteps sounded as he crossed the parking lot to the sidewalk, and then they were lost. In the station, a telephone began to ring. The ringing was loud, plaintive, evenly spaced, and unanswered. Someone wanted to know about the next train to Albany, but Mr. Flanagan, the stationmaster, had gone home an hour ago. He had turned on all his lights before he went away. They burned in the empty waiting room. They burned, tin-shaded, at intervals up and down the platform and with the peculiar sadness of dim and purposeless light. They lighted the Hawaiian dancer, the couple drinking a toast, the rubber heel.

"I've never been here before," she said. "I thought it would look different. I didn't think it would look so shabby. Let's get out of the light. Go over there."

His legs felt sore. All his strength was gone. "Go on," she said.

North of the station there were a freight house and a coalyard and an inlet where the butcher and the baker and the man who ran the service station moored the dinghies from which they fished on Sundays, sunk now to the gunwales with the rain. As he walked toward the freight house, he saw a movement on the ground and heard a scraping sound, and then he saw a rat take its head out of a paper bag and regard him. The rat seized the bag in its teeth and dragged it into a culvert.

"Stop," she said. "Turn around. Oh, I ought to feel sorry for you. Look at your poor face. But you don't know what I've been through. I'm afraid to go out in the daylight. I'm afraid the blue sky will fall down on me. I'm like poor Chicken-Licken. I only feel like myself when it begins to get dark. But still and all I'm better than you. I still have good dreams sometimes. I dream about picnics and Heaven and the brotherhood of man, and about castles in the moonlight and a river with willow trees all along the edge of it and foreign cities, and after all I know more about love than you."

He heard from off the dark river the drone of an outboard motor, a sound that drew slowly behind it across the dark water such a burden of clear, sweet memories of gone summers and gone pleasures that it made his flesh crawl, and he thought of dark in the mountains and the children singing. "They never wanted to cure me," she said. "They . . ." The noise of a train coming down from the north drowned out her voice, but she went on talking. The noise filled his ears, and the windows where people ate, drank, slept, and read flew past. When the train had passed beyond the bridge, the noise grew distant, and he heard her screaming at him, "*Kneel down!* Kneel down! Do what I say. *Kneel down!*"

He got to his knees. He bent his head. "There," she said. "You see, if you do what I say, I won't harm you,

because I really don't want to harm you, I want to help
you, but when I see your face it sometimes seems to me
that I can't help you. Sometimes it seems to me that if
I were good and loving and sane—oh, much better than
I am—sometimes it seems to me that if I were all these
things and young and beautiful, too, and if I called to
show you the right way, you wouldn't heed me. Oh, I'm
better than you, I'm better than you, and I shouldn't
waste my time or spoil my life like this. Put your face
in the dirt. *Put your face in the dirt!* Do what I say. Put
your face in the dirt."

He fell forward in the filth. The coal skinned his face.
He stretched out on the ground, weeping. "Now I feel
better," she said. "Now I can wash my hands of you, I
can wash my hands of all this, because you see there is
some kindness, some saneness in me that I can find again
and use. I can wash my hands." Then he heard her footsteps go away from him, over the rubble. He heard the
clearer and more distant sound they made on the hard
surface of the platform. He heard them diminish. He
raised his head. He saw her climb the stairs of the
wooden footbridge and cross it and go down to the other
platform, where her figure in the dim light looked small,
common, and harmless. He raised himself out of the
dust—warily at first, until he saw by her attitude, her
looks, that she had forgotten him; that she had completed what she had wanted to do, and that he was safe.
He got to his feet and picked up his hat from the ground
where it had fallen and walked home.

The Stone Boy
Gina Berriault

Arnold drew his overalls and raveling gray sweater over his naked body. In the other narrow bed his brother Eugene went on sleeping, undisturbed by the alarm clock's rusty ring. Arnold, watching his brother sleeping, felt a peculiar dismay; he was nine, six years younger than Eugie, and in their waking hours it was he who was subordinate. To dispel emphatically his uneasy advantage over his sleeping brother, he threw himself on the hump of Eugie's body.

"Get up! Get up!" he cried.

Arnold felt his brother twist away and saw the blankets lifted in a great wing, and, all in an instant, he was lying on his back under the covers with only his face showing, like a baby, and Eugie was sprawled on top of him.

"Whassa matter with you?" asked Eugie in sleepy anger, his face hanging close.

"Get up," Arnold repeated. "You said you'd pick peas with me."

Stupidly, Eugie gazed around the room as if to see if morning had come into it yet. Arnold began to laugh derisively, making soft, snorting noises, and was thrown off the bed. He got up from the floor and went down the stairs, the laughter continuing, like hiccups, against his will. But when he opened the staircase door and entered the parlor, he hunched up his shoulders and was quiet because his parents slept in the bedroom downstairs.

Arnold lifted his .22-caliber rifle from the rack on the kitchen wall. It was an old lever-action Winchester that his father had given him because nobody else used it any more. On their way down to the garden he and Eugie would go by the lake, and if there were any ducks

on it he'd take a shot at them. Standing on the stool
before the cupboard, he searched on the top shelf in the
confusion of medicines and ointments for man and beast
and found a small yellow box of .22 cartridges. Then he
sat down on the stool and began to load his gun.

It was cold in the kitchen so early, but later in the
day, when his mother canned the peas, the heat from
the wood stove would be almost unbearable. Yesterday
she had finished preserving the huckleberries that the
family had picked along the mountains, and before that
she had canned all the cherries his father had brought
from the warehouse in Corinth. Sometimes, on these
summer days, Arnold would deliberately come out from
the shade where he was playing and make himself as
uncomfortable as his mother was in the kitchen by standing in the sun until the sweat ran down his body.

Eugie came clomping down the stairs and into the
kitchen, his head drooping with sleepiness. From his
perch on the stool Arnold watched Eugie slip on his
green knit cap. Eugie didn't really need a cap; he hadn't
had a haircut in a long time and his brown curls grew
thick and matted, close around his ears and down his
neck, tapering there to a small whorl. Eugie passed his
left hand through his hair before he set his cap down
with his right. The very way he slipped his cap on was
an announcement of his status; almost everything he did
was a reminder that he was eldest—first he, then Nora,
then Arnold—and called attention to how tall he was
(almost as tall as his father), how long his legs were,
how small he was in the hips, and what a neat dip above
his buttocks his thick-soled logger's boots gave him. Arnold never tired of watching Eugie offer silent praise
unto himself. He wondered, as he sat enthralled, if when
he got to be Eugie's age he would still be undersized
and his hair still straight.

Eugie eyed the gun. "Don't you know this ain't duck
season?" he asked gruffly, as if he were the sheriff.

"No, I don't know," Arnold said with a snigger.

Eugie picked up the tin washtub for the peas, un-
bolted the door with his free hand and kicked it open.
Then, lifting the tub to his head, he went clomping down
the back steps. Arnold followed, closing the door behind him.

The sky was faintly gray, almost white. The mountains behind the farm made the sun climb a long way to show itself. Several miles to the south, where the range opened up, hung an orange mist, but the valley in which the farm lay was still cold and colorless.

Eugie opened the gate to the yard and the boys passed between the barn and the row of chicken houses, their feet stirring up the carpet of brown feathers dropped by the molting chickens. They paused before going down the slope to the lake. A fluky morning wind ran among the shocks of wheat that covered the slope. It sent a shimmer northward across the lake, gently moving the rushes that formed an island in the center. Killdeer, their white markings flashing, skimmed the water, crying their shrill, sweet cry. And there at the south end of the lake were four wild ducks, swimming out from the willows into open water.

Arnold followed Eugie down the slope, stealing, as his brother did, from one shock of wheat to another. Eugie paused before climbing through the wire fence that divided the wheatfield from the marshy pasture around the lake. They were screened from the ducks by the willows along the lake's edge.

"If you hit your duck, you want me to go in after it?" Eugie said.

"If you want," Arnold said.

Eugie lowered his eyelids, leaving slits of mocking blue. "You'd drown 'fore you got to it, them legs of yours are so puny," he said.

He shoved the tub under the fence and, pressing down the center wire, climbed through into the pasture.

Arnold pressed down the bottom wire, thrust a leg through and leaned forward to bring the other leg after. His rifle caught on the wire and he jerked at it. The air was rocked by the sound of the shot. Feeling foolish, he lifted his face, baring it to an expected shower of derision from his brother. But Eugie did not turn around. Instead, from his crouching position, he fell to his knees and then pitched forward onto his face. The ducks rose up crying from the lake, cleared the mountain background and beat away northward across the pale sky.

Arnold squatted beside his brother. Eugie seemed to

be climbing the earth, as if the earth ran up and down, and when he found he couldn't scale it he lay still.

"Eugie?"

Then Arnold saw it, under the tendril of hair at the nape of the neck—a slow rising of bright blood. It had an obnoxious movement, like that of a parasite.

"Hey, Eugie," he said again. He was feeling the same discomfort he had felt when he had watched Eugie sleeping; his brother didn't know that he was lying face-down in the pasture.

Again he said, "Hey, Eugie," an anxious nudge in his voice. But Eugie was as still as the morning about them.

Arnold set his rifle on the ground and stood up. He picked up the tub and, dragging it behind him, walked along by the willows to the garden fence and climbed through. He went down on his knees among the tangled vines. The pods were cold with the night, but his hands were strange to him, and not until some time had passed did he realize that the pods were numbing his fingers. He picked from the top of the vine first, then lifted the vine to look underneath for pods and then moved on to the next.

It was a warmth on his back, like a large hand laid firmly there, that made him raise his head. Way up the slope the gray farmhouse was struck by the sun. While his head had been bent the land had grown bright around him.

When he got up his legs were so stiff that he had to go down on his knees again to ease the pain. Then, walking sideways, he dragged the tub, half full of peas, up the slope.

The kitchen was warm now; a fire was roaring in the stove with a closed-up, rushing sound. His mother was spooning eggs from a pot of boiling water and putting them into a bowl. Her short brown hair was uncombed and fell forward across her eyes as she bent her head. Nora was lifting a frying pan full of trout from the stove, holding the handle with a dish towel. His father had just come in from bringing the cows from the north pasture to the barn, and was sitting on the stool, unbuttoning his red plaid Mackinaw.

"Did you boys fill the tub?" his mother asked.

"They ought of by now," his father said. "They went out of the house an hour ago. Eugie woke me comin' downstairs. I heard you shootin'—did you get a duck?"

"No," Arnold said. They would want to know why Eugie wasn't coming in for breakfast, he thought. "Eugie's dead," he told them.

They stared at him. The pitch cracked in the stove.

"You kids playin' a joke?" his father asked.

"Where's Eugene?" his mother asked scoldingly. She wanted, Arnold knew, to see his eyes, and when he had glanced at her she put the bowl and spoon down on the stove and walked past him. His father stood up and went out the door after her. Nora followed them with little skipping steps, as if afraid to be left alone.

Arnold went into the barn, down along the foddering passage past the cows waiting to be milked, and climbed into the loft. After a few minutes he heard a terrifying sound coming toward the house. His parents and Nora were returning from the willows, and sounds sharp as knives were rising from his mother's breast and carrying over the sloping fields. In a short while he heard his father go down the back steps, slam the car door and drive away.

Arnold lay still as a fugitive, listening to the cows eating close by. If his parents never called him, he thought, he would stay up in the loft forever, out of the way. In the night he would sneak down for a drink of water from the faucet over the trough and for whatever food they left for him by the barn.

The rattle of his father's car as it turned down the lane recalled him to the present. He heard voices of his Uncle Andy and Aunt Alice as they and his father went past the barn to the lake. He could feel the morning growing heavier with sun. Someone, probably Nora, had let the chickens out of their coops and they were cackling in the yard.

After a while another car turned down the road off the highway. The car drew to a stop and he heard the voices of strange men. The men also went past the barn and down to the lake. The undertakers, whom his father must have phoned from Uncle Andy's house, had ar-

rived from Corinth. Then he heard everybody come back
and heard the car turn around and leave.

"Arnold!" It was his father calling from the yard.

He climbed down the ladder and went out into the
sun, picking wisps of hay from his overalls.

Corinth, nine miles away, was the county seat. Arnold
sat in the front seat of the old Ford between his father,
who was driving, and Uncle Andy; no one spoke. Uncle
Andy was his mother's brother, and he had been fond
of Eugie because Eugie had resembled him. Andy had
taken Eugie hunting and had given him a knife and a
lot of things, and now Andy, his eyes narrowed, sat tall
and stiff beside Arnold.

Arnold's father parked the car before the courthouse.
It was a two-story brick building with a lamp on each
side of the bottom step. They went up the wide stone
steps, Arnold and his father going first, and entered the
darkly paneled hallway. The shirt-sleeved man in the
sheriff's office said that the sheriff was at Carlson's Parlor examining the Curwing boy.

Andy went off to get the sheriff while Arnold and his
father waited on a bench in the corridor. Arnold felt his
father watching him, and he lifted his eyes with painful
casualness to the announcement, on the opposite wall,
of the Corinth County Annual Rodeo, and then to the
clock with its loudly clucking pendulum. After he had
come down from the loft his father and Uncle Andy had
stood in the yard with him and asked him to tell them
everything, and he had explained to them how the gun
had caught on the wire. But when they had asked him
why he hadn't run back to the house to tell his parents,
he had had no answer—all he could say was that he had
gone down into the garden to pick the peas. His father
had stared at him in a pale, puzzled way, and it was then
that he had felt his father and the others set their cold,
turbulent silence against him. Arnold shifted on the
bench, his only feeling a small one of compunction imposed by his father's eyes.

At a quarter past nine Andy and the sheriff came in.
They all went into the sheriff's private office, and Arnold
was sent forward to sit in the chair by the sheriff's desk;

his father and Andy sat down on the bench against the wall.

The sheriff lumped down into his swivel chair and swung toward Arnold. He was an old man with white hair like wheat stubble. His restless green eyes made him seem not to be in his office but to be hurrying and bobbing around somewhere else.

"What did you say your name was?" the sheriff asked.

"Arnold," he replied; but he could not remember telling the sheriff his name before.

"Curwing?"

"Yes."

"What were you doing with a .22, Arnold?"

"It's mine," he said.

"Okay. What were you going to shoot?"

"Some ducks," he replied.

"Out of season?"

He nodded.

"That's bad," said the sheriff. "Were you and your brother good friends?"

What did he mean—good friends? Eugie was his brother. That was different from a friend, Arnold thought. A best friend was your own age, but Eugie was almost a man. Eugie had had a way of looking at him, slyly and mockingly and yet confidentially, that had summed up how they both felt about being brothers. Arnold had wanted to be with Eugie more than with anybody else but he couldn't say they had been good friends.

"Did they ever quarrel?" the sheriff asked his father.

"Not that I know," his father replied. "It seemed to me that Arnold cared a lot for Eugie."

"Did you?" the sheriff asked Arnold.

If it seemed so to his father, then it was so. Arnold nodded.

"Were you mad at him this morning?"

"No."

"How did you happen to shoot him?"

"We was crawlin' through the fence."

"Yes?"

"An' the gun got caught on the wire."

"Seems the hammer must of caught," his father put in.

"All right, that's what happened," said the sheriff.

"But what I want you to tell me is this. Why didn't you go back to the house and tell your father right away? Why did you go and pick peas for an hour?"

Arnold gazed over his shoulder at his father, expecting his father to have an answer for this also. But his father's eyes, larger and even lighter blue than usual, were fixed upon him curiously. Arnold picked at a callus in his right palm. It seemed odd now that he had not run back to the house and wakened his father, but he could not remember why he had not. They were all waiting for him to answer.

"I come down to pick peas," he said.

"Didn't you think," asked the sheriff, stepping carefully from word to word, "that it was more important for you to go tell your parents what had happened?"

"The sun was gonna come up," Arnold said.

"What's that got to do with it?"

"It's better to pick peas while they're cool."

The sheriff swung away from him, laid both hands flat on his desk. "Well, all I can say is," he said across to Arnold's father and Uncle Andy, "he's either a moron or he's so reasonable that he's way ahead of us." He gave a challenging snort. "It's come to my notice that the most reasonable guys are mean ones. They don't feel nothing."

For a moment the three men sat still. Then the sheriff lifted his hand like a man taking an oath. "Take him home," he said.

Andy uncrossed his legs. "You don't want him?"

"Not now," replied the sheriff. "Maybe in a few years."

Arnold's father stood up. He held his hat against his chest. "The gun ain't his no more," he said wanly.

Arnold went first through the hallway, hearing behind him the heels of his father and Uncle Andy striking the floorboards. He went down the steps ahead of them and climbed into the back seat of the car. Andy paused as he was getting into the front seat and gazed back at Arnold, and Arnold saw that his uncle's eyes had absorbed the knowingness from the sheriff's eyes. Andy and his father and the sheriff had discovered what made him go down into the garden. It was because he was cruel, the sheriff had said, and didn't care about his brother. Was that the reason? Arnold lowered his eye-lids meekly against his uncle's stare.

The rest of the day he did his tasks around the farm, keeping apart from the family. At evening, when he saw his father stomp tiredly into the house, Arnold did not put down his hammer and leave the chicken coop he was repairing. He was afraid that they did not want him to eat supper with them. But in a few minutes another fear that they would go to the trouble of calling him and that he would be made conspicuous by his tardiness made him follow his father into the house. As he went through the kitchen he saw the jars of peas standing in rows on the workbench, a reproach to him.

No one spoke at supper, and his mother, who sat next to him, leaned her head in her hand all through the meal, curving her fingers over her eyes so as not to see him. They were finishing their small, silent supper when the visitors began to arrive, knocking hard on the back door. The men were coming from their farms now that it was growing dark and they could not work any more. Old Man Matthews, gray and stocky, came first, with his two sons, Orion, the elder, and Clint, who was Eugie's age. As the callers entered the parlor, where the family ate, Arnold sat down in a rocking chair. Even as he had been undecided before supper whether to remain outside or take his place at the table, he now thought that he should go upstairs, and yet he stayed to avoid being conspicuous by his absence. If he stayed, he thought, as he always stayed and listened when visitors came, they would see that he was only Arnold and not the person the sheriff thought he was. He sat with his arms crossed and his hands tucked into his armpits and did not lift his eyes.

The Matthews men had hardly settled down around the table, after Arnold's mother and Nora had cleared away the dishes, when another car rattled down the road and someone else rapped on the back door. This time it was Sullivan, a spare and sandy man, so nimble of gesture and expression that Arnold had never been able to catch more than a few of his meanings. Sullivan, in dusty jeans, sat down in the other rocker, shot out his skinny legs and began to talk in his fast way, recalling every-

thing that Eugene had ever said to him. The other men
interrupted to tell of occasions they remembered, and
after a time Clint's young voice, hoarse like Eugene's
had been, broke in to tell about the time Eugene had
beat him in a wrestling match.

Out in the kitchen the voices of Orion's wife and of
Mrs. Sullivan mingled with Nora's voice but not, Arnold
noticed, his mother's. Then dry little Mr. Cram came,
leaving large Mrs. Cram in the kitchen, and there was
no chair left for Mr. Cram to sit in. No one asked Arnold
to get up and he was unable to rise. He knew that the
story had got around to them during the day about how
he had gone and picked peas after he had shot his
brother, and he knew that although they were talking
only about Eugie they were thinking about him and if
he got up, if he moved even his foot, they would all be
alerted. Then Uncle Andy arrived and leaned his tall,
lanky body against the doorjamb and there were two
men standing.

Presently Arnold was aware that the talk had stopped.
He knew without looking up that the men were watching him.

"Not a tear in his eye," said Andy, and Arnold knew
that it was his uncle who had gestured the men to
attention.

"He don't give a hoot, is that how it goes?" asked
Sullivan, trippingly.

"He's a reasonable fellow," Andy explained. "That's
what the sheriff said. It's us who ain't reasonable. If we'd
of shot our brother, we'd of come runnin' back to the
house, cryin' like a baby. Well, we'd of been unreasonable. What would of been the use of actin' like that? If
your brother is shot dead, he's shot dead. What's the
use of gettin' emotional about it? The thing to do is go
down to the garden and pick peas. Am I right?"

The men around the room shifted their heavy, satisfying weight of unreasonableness.

Matthews' son Orion said: "If I'd of done what he
done, Pa would've hung my pelt by the side of that big
coyote's in the barn."

Arnold sat in the rocker until the last man had filed
out. While his family was out in the kitchen bidding the
callers good night and the cars were driving away down

the dirt lane to the highway, he picked up one of the
kerosene lamps and slipped quickly up the stairs. In his
room he undressed by lamplight, although he and Eugie
had always undressed in the dark, and not until he was
lying on his bed did he blow out the flame. He felt nothing, not any grief. There was only the same immense
silence and crawling inside of him; it was the way the
house and fields felt under a merciless sun.

He awoke suddenly. He knew that his father was out
in the yard, closing the doors of the chicken houses so
that the chickens could not roam out too early and fall
prey to the coyotes that came down from the mountains
at daybreak. The sound that had wakened him was the
step of his father as he got up from the rocker and went
down the back steps. And he knew that his mother was
awake in her bed.

Throwing off the covers, he rose swiftly, went down
the stairs and across the dark parlor to his parents'
room. He rapped on the door.

"Mother?"

From the closed room her voice rose to him, a seeking
and retreating voice. "Yes?"

"Mother?" he asked insistently. He had expected her
to realize that he wanted to go down on his knees by
her bed and tell her that Eugie was dead. She did not
know it yet, nobody knew it, and yet she was sitting up
in bed, waiting to be told, waiting for him to confirm
her dread. He had expected her to tell him to come in,
to allow him to dig his head into her blankets and tell
her about the terror he had felt when he had knelt beside Eugie. He had come to clasp her in his arms and,
in his terror, to pommel her breasts with his head. He
put his hand upon the knob.

"Go back to bed, Arnold," she called sharply.

But he waited.

"Go back! Is night when you get afraid?"

At first he did not understand. Then, silently, he left
the door and for a stricken moment stood by the rocker.
Outside everything was still. The fences, the shocks of
wheat seen through the window before him were so still
it was as if they moved and breathed in the daytime and
had fallen silent with the lateness of the hour. It was a

silence that seemed to observe his father, a figure moving alone around the yard, his lantern casting a circle of light by his feet. In a few minutes his father would enter the dark house, the lantern still lighting his way.

Arnold was suddenly aware that he was naked. He had thrown off his blankets and come down the stairs to tell his mother how he felt about Eugie, but she had refused to listen to him and his nakedness had become unpardonable. At once he went back up the stairs, fleeing from his father's lantern.

At breakfast, he kept his eyelids lowered as if to deny the humiliating night. Nora, sitting at his left, did not pass the pitcher of milk to him and he did not ask for it. He would never again, he vowed, ask them for anything, and he ate his fried eggs and potatoes only because everybody ate meals—the cattle ate, and the cats; it was customary for everybody to eat.

"Nora, you gonna keep that pitcher for yourself?" his father asked.

Nora lowered her head unsurely.

"Pass it on to Arnold," his father said.

Nora put her hands in her lap.

His father picked up the metal pitcher and set it down at Arnold's plate.

Arnold, pretending to be deaf to the discord, did not glance up but relief rained over his shoulders at the thought that his parents recognized him again. They must have lain awake after his father had come in from the yard: had they realized together why he had come down the stairs and knocked at their door?

"Bessie's missin' this morning," his father called out to his mother, who had gone into the kitchen. "She went up the mountain last night and had her calf, most likely. Somebody's got to go up and find her 'fore the coyotes get the calf."

That had been Eugie's job, Arnold thought. Eugie would climb the cattle trails in search of a newborn calf and come down the mountain carrying the calf across his back, with the cow running down along behind him, mooing in alarm.

Arnold ate the few more forkfuls of his breakfast, put his hands on the edge of the table and pushed back his chair. If he went for the calf he'd be away from the farm all morning. He could switch the cow down the mountain slowly, and the calf would run along at its mother's side.

When he passed through the kitchen his mother was setting a kettle of water on the stove. "Where you going?" she asked awkwardly.

"Up to get the calf," he replied, averting his face.

"Arnold?"

At the door he paused reluctantly, his back to her, knowing that she was seeking him out, as his father was doing, and he called upon his pride to protect him from them.

"Was you knocking at my door last night?"

He looked over his shoulder at her, his eyes narrow and dry.

"What'd you want?" she asked humbly.

"I didn't want nothing," he said flatly.

Then he went out the door and down the back steps, his legs trembling from the fright his answer gave him.

Doby's Gone

Ann Petry

When Doby first came into Sue Johnson's life her family were caretakers on a farm way up in New York State. And because Sue had no one else to play with, the Johnsons reluctantly accepted Doby as a member of the family.

The spring that Sue was six they moved to Wessex, Connecticut—a small New England town whose neat colonial houses cling to a group of hills overlooking the Connecticut River. All that summer Mrs. Johnson had hoped that Doby would vanish long before Sue entered school in the fall. He would only complicate things in school.

For Doby wasn't real. He existed only in Sue's mind. He had been created out of her need for a friend of her own age—her own size. And he had gradually become an escape from the very real world that surrounded her. She first started talking about him when she was two and he had been with her ever since. He always sat beside her when she ate and played with her during the day. At night he slept in a chair near her bed so that they awoke at the same time in the morning. A place had to be set for him at mealtime. A seat had to be saved for him on trains and buses.

After they moved to Wessex, he was still her constant companion just as he had been when she was three and four and five.

On the morning that Sue was to start going to school she said, "Doby has a new pencil, too. And he's got a red plaid shirt just like my dress."

"Why can't Doby stay home?" Mrs. Johnson asked.

"Because he goes everywhere I go," Sue said in amazement. "Of course he's going to school. He's going to sit right by me."

Sue watched her mother get up from the breakfast table and then followed her upstairs to the big front bedroom. She saw with surprise that her mother was putting on her going-out clothes.

"You have to come with me, Mommy?" she asked anxiously. She had wanted to go with Doby. Just the two of them. She had planned every step of the way since the time her mother told her she would start school in the fall.

"No, I don't have to, but I'm coming just the same. I want to talk to your teacher." Mrs. Johnson fastened her coat and deftly patted a loose strand of hair in place.

Sue looked at her and wondered if the other children's mothers would come to school, too. She certainly hoped so because she wouldn't want to be the only one there who had a mother with her.

Then she started skipping around the room holding Doby by the hand. Her short black braids jumped as she skipped. The gingham dress she wore was starched so stiffly that the hemline formed a wide circular frame for her sturdy dark brown legs as she bounced up and down.

"Ooh," she said suddenly. "Doby pulled off one of my hair ribbons." She reached over and picked it up from the floor and came to stand in front of her mother while the red ribbon was retied into a crisp bow.

Then she was walking down the street hand in hand with her mother. She held Doby's hand on the other side. She decided it was good her mother had come. It was better that way. The street would have looked awfully long and awfully big if she and Doby had been by themselves, even though she did know exactly where the school was. Right down the street on this side. Past the post office and town hall that sat so far back with green lawn in front of them. Past the town pump and the old white house on the corner, past the big empty lot. And there was the school.

It had a walk that went straight down between the green grass and was all brown-yellow gravel stuff—coarser than sand. One day she had walked past there with her mother and stopped to finger the stuff the walk was made of, and her mother had said, "It's gravel."

She remembered how they'd talk about it. "What's gravel?" she asked.

"The stuff in your hand. It's like sand, only coarser. People use it for driveways and walks," her mother had said.

Gravel. She liked the sound of the word. It sounded like pebbles. Gravel. Pebble. She said the words over to herself. You gravel and pebble. Pebble said to gravel. She started making up a story. Gravel said to pebble, "You're a pebble." Pebble said back, "You're a gravel."

"Sue, throw it away. It's dirty and your hands are clean," her mother said.

She threw it down on the sidewalk. But she kept looking back at it as she walked along. It made a scattered yellow, brown color against the rich brown-black of the dirt-path.

She held on to Doby's hand a little more tightly. Now she was actually going to walk up that long gravel walk to the school. She and Doby would play there every day when school was out.

The school yard was full of children. Sue hung back a little looking at them. They were playing ball under the big maple trees near the back of the yard. Some small children were squatting near the school building, letting gravel trickle through their fingers.

"I want to play, too." She tried to free her hand from her mother's firm grip.

"We're going inside to see your teacher first." And her mother went on walking up the school steps holding on to Sue's hand.

Sue stared at the children on the steps. "Why are they looking so hard?" she asked.

"Probably because you're looking at them so hard. Now come on," and her mother pulled her through the door. The hall inside was dark and very long. A neat white sign over a door to the right said FIRST GRADE in bold black letters.

Sue peered inside the room while her mother knocked on the door. A pretty lady with curly yellow hair got up from a desk and invited them in. While the teacher and her mother talked grown-up talk, Sue looked around. She supposed she'd sit at one of those little desks. There were a lot of them and she wondered if there would be a child at each desk. If so then Doby would have to squeeze in beside her.

"Sue, you can go outside and play. When the bell rings you must come in," the teacher said.

"Yes, teacher," Sue started out the door in a hurry.

"My name is Miss Whittier," the teacher said. "You must call me that."

"Yes, Miss Whittier. Good-bye, Mommy," she said, and went quickly down the hall and out the door.

"Hold my hand, Doby," she said softly under her breath.

Now she and Doby would play in the gravel. Squeeze it between their fingers, pat it into shapes like those other children were doing. Her short starched skirt stood out around her legs as she skipped down the steps. She watched the children as long as she could without saying anything.

"Can we play, too?" she asked finally.

A boy with a freckled face and short stiff red hair looked up at her and frowned. He didn't answer but kept ostentatiously patting at a little mound of gravel.

Sue walked over a little closer, holding Doby tightly by the hand. The boy ignored her. A little girl in a blue and white checked dress stuck her tongue out.

"Your legs are black," she said suddenly. And then when the others looked up she added, "Why, look, she's black all over. Looky, she's black all over."

Sue retreated a step away from the building. The children got up and followed her. She took another backward step and they took two steps forward. The little girl who had stuck her tongue out began a chant, "Look, look. Her legs are black. Her legs are black."

The children were all saying it. They formed a ring around her and they were dancing up and down and screaming. "Her legs are black. Her legs are black."

She stood in the middle of the circle completely bewildered. She wanted to go home where it was safe and quiet and where her mother would hold her tight in her arms. She pulled Doby nearer to her. What did they mean her legs were black? Of course they were. Not black but dark brown. Just like these children were white some other children were dark like her. Her mother said so. But her mother hadn't said anyone would make her feel bad about being a different color. She didn't know what to do; so she just stood there watching them come closer and closer to her—their faces red with excitement, their voices hoarse with yelling.

Then the school bell rang. And the children suddenly plunged toward the building. She was left alone with Doby. When she walked into the school room she was crying.

"Don't you mind, Doby," she whispered. "Don't you mind. I won't let them hurt you."

Miss Whittier gave her a seat near the front of the room. Right near her desk. And she smiled at her. Sue smiled back and carefully wiped away the wet on her eyelashes with the back of her hand. She turned and looked around the room. There were no empty seats. Doby would have to stand up.

"You stand right close to me and if you get tired just sit on the edge of my seat," she said.

She didn't go out for recess. She stayed in and helped Miss Whittier draw on the blackboard with colored chalk—yellow and green and red and purple and brown. Miss Whittier drew the flowers and Sue colored them. She put a small piece of crayon out for Doby to use. And Miss Whittier noticed it. But she didn't say anything, she just smiled.

"I love her," Sue thought. "I love my teacher." And then again, "I love Miss Whittier, my teacher."

At noon the children followed her halfway home from school. They called after her and she ran so fast and so hard that the pounding in her ears cut off the sound of their voices.

"Go faster, Doby," she said. "You have to go faster." And she held his hand and ran until her legs ached.

"How was school, Sue?" asked her mother.

"It was all right," she said slowly. "I don't think Doby likes it very much. He likes Miss Whittier though."

"Do you like her?"

"Oh, yes," Sue let her breath come out with a sigh.

"Why are you panting like that?" her mother asked.

"I ran all the way home," she said.

Going back after lunch wasn't so bad. She went right in to Miss Whittier. She didn't stay put in the yard and wait for the bell.

When school was out, she decided she'd better hurry right home and maybe the children wouldn't see her.

She walked down the gravel path taking quick little looks over her shoulder. No one paid any attention and she was so happy that she gave Doby's hand a squeeze.

And then she saw that they were waiting for her right by the vacant lot. She hurried along trying not to hear what they were saying.

"My mother says you're a little nigger girl," the boy with the red hair said.

And then they began to shout: "Her legs are black. Her legs are black."

It changed suddenly. "Run. Go ahead and run." She looked over her shoulder. A boy was coming toward her with a long switch in his hand. He raised it in a threatening gesture and she started running.

For two days she ran home from school like that. Ran until her short legs felt as though they couldn't move another step.

"Sue," her mother asked anxiously, watching her try to catch her breath on the front steps, "what makes you run home from school like this?"

"Doby doesn't like the other children very much," she said panting.

"Why?"

"I don't think they understand about him," she said thoughtfully. "But he loves Miss Whittier."

The next day the children waited for her right where the school's gravel walk ended. Sue didn't see them until she was close to them. She was coming slowly down the path hand in hand with Doby trying to see how many of the big pebbles they could step on without stepping on any of the finer, sandier gravel.

She was in the middle of the group of children before she realized it. They started off slowly at first. "How do you comb that kind of hair?" "Does that black color wash off?" And then the chant began and it came faster and faster: "Her legs are black. Her legs are black."

A little girl reached out and pulled one of Sue's braids. Sue tried to back away and the other children closed in around her. She rubbed the side of her head— it hurt where her hair had been pulled. Someone pushed her. Hard. In the middle of her back. She was suddenly outraged. She planted her feet firmly on the path. She started hitting out with her fists. Kicking. Pulling hair.

Tearing at clothing. She reached down and picked up handfuls of gravel and aimed it at eyes and ears and noses.

While she was slapping and kicking at the small figures that encircled her, she became aware that Doby had gone. For the first time in her life he had left her. He had gone when she started to fight.

She went on fighting—scratching and biting and kicking—with such passion and energy that the space around her slowly cleared. The children backed away. And she stood still. She was breathing fast as though she had been running.

The children ran off down the street—past the big empty lot, past the old white house with the green shutters. Sue watched them go. She didn't feel victorious. She didn't feel anything except an aching sense of loss. She stood there panting, wondering about Doby.

And then, "Doby," she called softly. Then louder, "Doby! Doby! Where are you?"

She listened—cocking her head on one side. He didn't answer. And she felt certain he would never be back because he had never left her before. He had gone for good. And then she didn't know why. She decided it probably had something to do with growing up. And she looked down at her legs hoping to find they had grown as long as her father's. She saw instead that her dress was torn in three different places, her socks were down around her ankles, there were long angry scratches on her legs and her arms. She felt for her hair—the red hair ribbons were gone and her braids were coming undone.

She started looking for the hair ribbons. And as she looked she saw that Daisy Bell, the little girl who had stuck her tongue out that first day of school, was leaning against the oak tree at the end of the path.

"Come on, let's walk home together," Daisy Bell said matter-of-factly.

"All right," Sue said.

As they started past the empty lot, she was conscious that someone was tagging along behind them. It was Jimmie Piebald, the boy with the stiff red hair. When she looked back he came up and walked on the other side of her.

They walked along in silence until they came to the

town pump. They stopped and looked deep down into the well. And spent a long time hallooing down into it and listening delightedly to the hollow funny sound of their voices.

It was much later than usual when Sue got home. Daisy Bell and Jimmie walked up to the door with her. Her mother was standing on the front steps waiting for her.

"Sue," her mother said in a shocked voice. "What's the matter? What happened to you?"

Daisy Bell put her arm around Sue. Jimmie started kicking at some stones in the path.

Sue stared at her mother, trying to remember. There was something wrong but she couldn't think what it was. And then it came to her. "Oh," she wailed, "Doby's gone. I can't find him anywhere."

Act of Faith

Irwin Shaw

"Present it in a pitiful light," Olson was saying, as they picked their way through the mud toward the orderly room tent. "Three combat-scarred veterans, who fought their way from Omaha Beach to—what was the name of the town we fought our way to?"

"Konigstein," Seeger said.

"Konigstein." Olson lifted his right foot heavily out of a puddle and stared admiringly at the three pounds of mud clinging to his overshoe. "The backbone of the army. The noncommissioned officer. We deserve better of our country. Mention our decorations in passing."

"What decorations should I mention?" Seeger asked. "The marksman's medal?"

"Never quite made it," Olson said. "I had a cross-eyed scorer at the butts. Mention the Bronze Star, the Silver Star, the Croix de Guerre, with palms, the unit citation, the Congressional Medal of Honor."

"I'll mention them all." Seeger grinned. "You don't think the CO'll notice that we haven't won most of them, do you?"

"Gad, sir," Olson said with dignity, "do you think that one southern military gentleman will dare doubt the word of another southern military gentleman in the hour of victory?"

"I come from Ohio," Seeger said.

"Welch comes from Kansas," Olson said, coolly staring down a second lieutenant who was passing. The lieutenant made a nervous little jerk with his hand as though he expected a salute, then kept it rigid, as a slight superior smile of scorn twisted at the corner of Olson's mouth. The lieutenant dropped his eyes and splashed on through the mud. "You've heard of Kansas," Olson said. "Magnolia-scented Kansas."

"Of course," said Seeger. "I'm no fool."

"Do your duty by your men, Sergeant." Olson stopped to wipe the rain off his face and lectured him. "Highest ranking noncom present took the initiative and saved his comrades, at great personal risk, above and beyond the call of you-know-what, in the best traditions of the American army."

"I will throw myself in the breach," Seeger said.

"Welch and I can't ask more," said Olson, approvingly.

They walked heavily through the mud on the streets between the rows of tents. The camp stretched drearily over the Rheims plain, with the rain beating on the sagging tents. The division had been there over three weeks by now, waiting to be shipped home, and all the meager diversions of the neighborhood had been sampled and exhausted, and there was an air of watchful suspicion and impatience with the military life hanging over the camp now, and there was even reputed to be a staff sergeant in C Company who was laying odds they would not get back to America before July Fourth.

"I'm redeployable," Olson sang. "It's so enjoyable ..." It was a jingle he had composed to no recognizable melody in the early days after the victory in Europe, when he had added up his points and found they only came to 63. "Tokyo, wait for me ..."

They were going to be discharged as soon as they got back to the States, but Olson persisted in singing the song, occasionally adding a mournful stanza about dengue fever and brown girls with venereal disease. He was a short, round boy who had been flunked out of air cadets' school and transferred to the infantry, but whose spirits had not been damaged in the process. He had a high, childish voice and a pretty baby face. He was very good-natured, and had a girl waiting for him at the University of California, where he intended to finish his course at government expense when he got out of the army, and he was just the type who is killed off early and predictably and sadly in motion pictures about the war, but he had gone through four campaigns and six major battles without a scratch.

Seeger was a large lanky boy, with a big nose, who had been wounded at Saint Lô, but had come back to his outfit in the Siegfried Line, quite unchanged. He was cheerful and dependable, and he knew his business and had broken in five or six second lieutenants who had been killed or wounded and the CO had tried to get him commissioned in the field, but the war had ended while the paperwork was being fumbled over at headquarters.

They reached the door of the orderly tent and stopped. "Be brave, Sergeant," Olson said. "Welch and I are depending on you."

"O.K.," Seeger said, and went in.

The tent had the dank, army-canvas smell that had been so much a part of Seeger's life in the past three years. The company clerk was reading a July, 1945, issue of the *Buffalo Courier-Express,* which had just reached him, and Captain Taney, the company CO, was seated at a sawbuck table he used as a desk, writing a letter to his wife, his lips pursed with effort. He was a small, fussy man, with sandy hair that was falling out. While the fighting had been going on, he had been lean and tense and his small voice had been cold and full of authority. But now he had relaxed, and a little pot belly was creeping up under his belt and he kept the top button of his trousers open when he could do it without too public a loss of dignity. During the war Seeger had thought of him as a natural soldier, tireless, fanatic about detail, aggressive, severely anxious to kill Germans. But in the past few months Seeger had seen him relapsing gradually and pleasantly into a small-town wholesale hardware merchant, which he had been before the war, sedentary and a little shy, and, as he had once told Seeger, worried, here in the bleak champagne fields of France, about his daughter, who had just turned twelve and had a tendency to go after the boys and had been caught by her mother kissing a fifteen-year-old neighbor in the hammock after school.

"Hello, Seeger," he said, returning the salute in a mild, offhand gesture. "What's on your mind?"

"Am I disturbing you, sir?"

"Oh, no. Just writing a letter to my wife. You married, Seeger?" He peered at the tall boy standing before him.

"No, sir."

"It's very difficult," Taney sighed, pushing dissatisfiedly at the letter before him. "My wife complains I don't

tell her I love her often enough. Been married fifteen
years. You'd think she'd know by now." He smiled at
Seeger. "I thought you were going to Paris," he said. "I
signed the passes yesterday."

"That's what I came to see you about, sir."

"I suppose something's wrong with the passes." Taney
spoke resignedly, like a man who has never quite got
the hang of army regulations and has had requisitions,
furloughs, requests for court-martial returned for correc-
tion in a baffling flood.

"No, sir," Seeger said. "The passes're fine. They start
tomorrow. Well, it's just ..." He looked around at the
company clerk, who was on the sports page.

"This confidential?" Taney asked.

"If you don't mind, sir."

"Johnny," Taney said to the clerk, "go stand in the
rain some place."

"Yes, sir," the clerk said, and slowly got up and
walked out.

Taney looked shrewdly at Seeger, spoke in a secret
whisper. "You pick up anything?" he asked.

Seeger grinned. "No, sir, haven't had my hands on a
girl since Strasbourg."

"Ah, that's good." Taney leaned back, relieved, happy
he didn't have to cope with the disapproval of the Medical Corps.

"It's—well," said Seeger, embarrassed, "it's hard to
say—but it's money."

Taney shook his head sadly. "I know."

"We haven't been paid for three months, sir, and ..."

"Damn it!" Taney stood up and shouted furiously. "I
would like to take every bloody chair-warming old lady
in the Finance Department and wring their necks."

The clerk stuck his head into the tent. "Anything
wrong? You call for me, sir?"

"No," Taney shouted. "Get out of here."

The clerk ducked out.

Taney sat down again. "I suppose," he said, in a more
normal voice, "they have their problems. Outfits being
broken up, being moved all over the place. But it is
rugged."

"It wouldn't be so bad," Seeger said. "But we're going

to Paris tomorrow, Olson, Welch and myself. And you
need money in Paris."

"Don't I know it." Taney wagged his head. "Do you
know what I paid for a bottle of champagne on the Place
Pigalle in September ...?" He paused significantly. "I
won't tell you. You won't have any respect for me the
rest of your life."

Seeger laughed. "Hanging," he said, "is too good for
the guy who thought up the rate of exchange."

"I don't care if I never see another franc as long as I
live." Taney waved his letter in the air, although it had
been dry for a long time.

There was silence in the tent and Seeger swallowed a
little embarrassedly, watching the CO wave the flimsy
sheet of paper in regular sweeping movements. "Sir," he
said, "the truth is, I've come to borrow some money for
Welch, Olson and myself. We'll pay it back out of the
first pay we get, and that can't be too long from now. If
you don't want to give it to us, just tell me and I'll
understand and get the hell out of here. We don't like
to ask, but you might just as well be dead as be in
Paris broke."

Taney stopped waving his letter and put it down
thoughtfully. He peered at it, wrinkling his brow, looking
like an aged bookkeeper in the single gloomy light that
hung in the middle of the tent.

"Just say the word, Captain," Seeger said, "and I'll
blow ..."

"Stay where you are, son," said Taney. He dug in his
shirt pocket and took out a worn, sweat-stained wallet.
He looked at it for a moment. "Alligator," he said, with
automatic, absent pride. "My wife sent it to me when
we were in England. Pounds don't fit in it. However ..."
He opened it and took out all the contents. There was
a small pile of francs on the table in front of him. He
counted them. "Four hundred francs," he said. "Eight
bucks."

"Excuse me," Seeger said humbly. "I shouldn't have
asked."

"Delighted," Taney said vigorously. "Absolutely delighted." He started dividing the francs into two piles.
"Truth is, Seeger, most of my money goes home in allot-
ments. And the truth is, I lost eleven hundred francs in

a poker game three nights ago, and I ought to be ashamed of myself. Here . . ." he shoved one pile toward Seeger. "Two hundred francs."

Seeger looked down at the frayed, meretricious paper, which always seemed to him like stage money, anyway. "No, sir," he said, "I can't take it."

"Take it," Taney said. "That's a direct order."

Seeger slowly picked up the money, not looking at Taney. "Some time, sir," he said, "after we get out, you have to come over to my house and you and my father and my brother and I'll go on a real drunk."

"I regard that," Taney said, gravely, "as a solemn commitment."

They smiled at each other and Seeger started out.

"Have a drink for me," said Taney, "at the Café de la Paix. A small drink." He was sitting down to write his wife he loved her when Seeger went out of the tent.

Olson fell into step with Seeger and they walked silently through the mud between the tents.

"Well, *mon vieux*?" Olson said finally.

"Two hundred francs," said Seeger.

Olson groaned. "Two hundred francs! We won't be able to pinch a whore's behind on the Boulevard des Capucines for two hundred francs. That miserable, penny-loving Yankee!"

"He only had four hundred," Seeger said.

"I revise my opinion," said Olson.

They walked disconsolately and heavily back toward their tent.

Olson spoke only once before they got there. "These raincoats," he said, patting his. "Most ingenious invention of the war. Highest saturation point of any modern fabric. Collect more water per square inch, and hold it, than any material known to man. All hail the quartermaster!"

Welch was waiting at the entrance of their tent. He was standing there peering excitedly and short-sightedly out at the rain through his glasses, looking angry and tough, like a big-city hack driver, individual and incorruptible even in the ten-million colored uniform. Every time Seeger came upon Welch unexpectedly, he couldn't help smiling at the belligerent stance, the harsh stare through the steel-rimmed GI glasses, which had nothing at all to do with the way Welch really was. "It's a family inheritance," Welch had once explained. "My whole family stands as though we were getting ready to rap a drunk with a beer glass. Even my old lady." Welch had six brothers, all devout, according to Welch, and Seeger from time to time idly pictured them standing in a row, on Sunday mornings in church, seemingly on the verge of general violence, amid the hushed Latin and Sabbath millinery.

"How much?" Welch asked loudly.

"Don't make us laugh," Olson said, pushing past him into the tent.

"What do you think I could get from the French for my combat jacket?" Seeger said. He went into the tent and lay down on his cot.

Welch followed them in and stood between the two of them, a superior smile on his face. "Boys," he said, "on a man's errand."

"I can just see us now," Olson murmured, lying on his cot with his hands clasped behind his head, "painting Montmartre red. Please bring on the naked dancing girls. Four bucks worth."

"I am not worried," Welch announced.

"Get out of here." Olson turned over on his stomach.

"I know where we can put our hands on sixty-five bucks." Welch looked triumphantly first at Olson, then at Seeger.

Olson turned over slowly and sat up. "I'll kill you," he said, "if you're kidding."

"While you guys are wasting your time," Welch said, "fooling around with the infantry, I used my head. I went into Reems and used my head."

"Rance," Olson said automatically. He had had two years of French in college and he felt, now that the war was over, that he had to introduce his friends to some of his culture.

"I got to talking to a captain in the air force," Welch said eagerly. "A little fat old paddle-footed captain that never got higher off the ground than the second floor of the Com Z headquarters, and he told me that what he would admire to do more than anything else is to take home a nice shiny German Luger pistol with him to show to the boys back in Pacific Grove, California."

Silence fell on the tent and Welch and Olson looked tentatively at Seeger.

"Sixty-five bucks for a Luger, these days," Olson said, "is a very good figure."

"They've been sellin' for as low as thirty-five," said Welch hesitantly. "I'll bet," he said to Seeger, "you could sell yours now and buy another one back when you get some dough, and make a clear twenty-five on the deal."

Seeger didn't say anything. He had killed the owner of the Luger, an enormous SS major, in Coblenz, behind some paper bales in a warehouse, and the major had fired at Seeger three times with it, once nicking his helmet, before Seeger hit him in the face at twenty feet. Seeger had kept the Luger, a long, heavy, well-balanced gun, very carefully since then, lugging it with him, hiding it at the bottom of his bedroll, oiling it three times a week, avoiding all opportunities of selling it, although he had been offered as much as a hundred dollars for it and several times eighty and ninety, while the war was still on, before German weapons became a glut on the market.

"Well," said Welch, "there's no hurry. I told the captain I'd see him tonight around 8 o'clock in front of the Lion d'Or Hotel. You got five hours to make up your mind. Plenty of time."

"Me," said Olson, after a pause. "I won't say anything."

Seeger looked reflectively at his feet and the other two men avoided looking at him. Welch dug in his pocket. "I forgot," he said. "I picked up a letter for you." He handed it to Seeger.

"Thanks," Seeger said. He opened it absently, thinking about the Luger.

"Me," said Olson, "I won't say a bloody word. I'm just going to lie here and think about that nice fat air force captain."

Seeger grinned a little at him and went to the tent opening to read the letter in the light. The letter was from his father, and even from one glance at the handwriting, scrawly and hurried and spotted, so different from his father's usual steady, handsome, professorial script, he knew that something was wrong.

"Dear Norman," it read, "sometime in the future, you must forgive me for writing this letter. But I have been holding this in so long, and there is no one here I can talk to, and because of your brother's condition I must pretend to be cheerful and optimistic all the time at home, both with him and your mother, who has never been the same since Leonard was killed. You're the oldest now, and although I know we've never talked very seriously about anything before, you have been through a great deal by now, and I imagine you must have matured considerably, and you've seen so many different places and people.... Norman, I need help. While the war was on and you were fighting, I kept this to myself. It wouldn't have been fair to burden you with this. But now the war is over, and I no longer feel I can stand up under this alone. And you will have to face it some time when you get home, if you haven't faced it already, and perhaps we can help each other by facing it together...."

"I'm redeployable," Olson was singing softly, on his cot. "It's so enjoyable. In the Pelilu mud, With the tropical crud ..." He fell silent after his burst of song.

Seeger blinked his eyes, at the entrance of the tent, in the wan rainy light, and went on reading his father's letter, on the stiff white stationery with the University letterhead in polite engraving at the top of each page.

"I've been feeling this coming on for a long time," the letter continued, "but it wasn't until last Sunday morning that something happened to make me feel it in its full force. I don't know how much you've guessed about the reason for Jacob's discharge from the army. It's true he was pretty badly wounded in the leg at Metz, but I've asked around, and I know that men with worse wounds were returned to duty after hospitalization. Jacob got a medical discharge, but I don't think it was for the shrapnel wound in his thigh. He is suffering now from what I suppose you call combat fatigue, and he is subject to fits of depression and hallucinations. Your mother and I thought that as time went by and the war and the army receded, he would grow better. Instead, he is growing worse. Last Sunday morning when I came down into the living room from upstairs he was crouched in his old uniform, next to the window, peering out ..."

"What the hell," Olson was saying, "if we don't get the sixty-five bucks we can always go to the Louvre. I understand the Mona Lisa is back."

"I asked Jacob what he was doing," the letter went on, "He didn't turn around. 'I'm observing,' he said. 'V-1's and V-2's. Buzz-bombs and rockets. They're coming in by the hundreds.' I tried to reason with him and he told me to crouch and save myself from flying glass. To humor him I got down on the floor beside him and tried to tell him the war was over, that we were in Ohio, 4,000 miles away from the nearest spot where bombs had fallen, that America had never been touched. He wouldn't listen. 'These're the new rocket bombs,' he said, 'for the Jews.' "

"Did you ever hear of the Pantheon?" Olson asked loudly.

"No," said Welch.

"It's free."

"I'll go," said Welch.

Seeger shook his head a little and blinked his eyes before her went back to the letter.

"After that," his father went on, "Jacob seemed to forget about the bombs from time to time, but he kept saying that the mobs were coming up the street armed with bazookas and Browning automatic rifles. He mumbled incoherently a good deal of the time and kept walking back and forth saying, 'What's the situation? Do you know what the situation is?' And he told me he wasn't worried about himself, he was a soldier and he expected to be killed, but he was worried about Mother and myself and Leonard and you. He seemed to forget that Leonard was dead. I tried to calm him and get him back to bed before your mother came down, but he refused and wanted to set out immediately to rejoin his division. It was all terribly disjointed and at one time he took the ribbon he got for winning the Bronze Star and threw it in the fireplace, then he got down on his hands and knees and picked it out of the ashes and made me pin it on him again, and he kept repeating, 'This is when they are coming for the Jews.' "

"The next war I'm in," said Olson, "they don't get me under the rank of colonel."

It had stopped raining by now and Seeger folded the

unfinished letter and went outside. He walked slowly down to the end of the company street, and facing out across the empty, soaked French fields, scarred and neglected by various armies, he stopped and opened the letter again.

"I don't know what Jacob went through in the army," his father wrote, "that has done this to him. He never talks to me about the war and he refuses to go to a psychoanalyst, and from time to time he is his own bouncing, cheerful self, playing in tennis tournaments, and going around with a large group of girls. But he has devoured all the concentration camp reports, and I have found him weeping when the newspapers reported that a hundred Jews were killed in Tripoli some time ago.

"The terrible thing is, Norman, that I find myself coming to believe that it is not neurotic for a Jew to behave like this today. Perhaps Jacob is the normal one, and I, going about my business, teaching economics in a quiet classroom, pretending to understand that the world is comprehensible and orderly, am really the mad one. I ask you once more to forgive me for writing you a letter like this, so different from any letter or any conversation I've ever had with you. But it is crowding me, too. I do not see rockets and bombs, but I see other things.

"Wherever you go these days—restaurants, hotels, clubs, trains—you seem to hear talk about the Jews, mean, hateful, murderous talk. Whatever page you turn to in the newspapers you seem to find an article about Jews being killed somewhere on the face of the globe. And there are large, influential newspapers and well-known columnists who each day are growing more and more outspoken and more popular. The day that Roosevelt died I heard a drunken man yelling outside a bar, 'Finally, they got the Jew out of the White House.' And some of the people who heard him merely laughed and nobody stopped him. And on V-E Day, in celebration, hoodlums in Los Angeles savagely beat a Jewish writer. It's difficult to know what to do, whom to fight, where to look for allies.

"Three months ago, for example, I stopped my Thursday night poker game, after playing with the same men for over ten years. John Reilly happened to say that the Jews were getting rich out of this war, and when I demanded an apology, he refused, and when I looked around at the faces of the men who had been my friends for so long, I could see they were not with me. And when I left the house no one said good night to me. I know the poison was spreading from Germany before the war and during it, but I had not realized it had come so close.

"And in my economics class, I find myself idiotically hedging in my lectures. I discover that I am loath to praise any liberal writer or any liberal act and find myself somehow annoyed and frightened to see an article of criticism of existing abuses signed by a Jewish name. And I hate to see Jewish names on important committees, and hate to read of Jews fighting for the poor, the oppressed, the cheated and hungry. Somehow, even in a country where my family has lived a hundred years, the enemy has won this subtle victory over me—he has made me disfranchise myself from honest causes by calling them foreign, Communist, using Jewish names connected with them as ammunition against them.

"And, most hateful of all, I find myself looking for Jewish names in the casualty lists and secretly being glad when I discover them there, to prove that there at least, among the dead and wounded, we belong. Three times, thanks to you and your brothers, I have found our name there, and, may God forgive me, at the expense of your blood and your brother's life, through my tears, I have felt that same twitch of satisfaction. . . .

"When I read the newspapers and see another story that Jews are still being killed in Poland, or Jews are requesting that they be given back their homes in France, or that they be allowed to enter some country where they will not be murdered, I am annoyed with them, I feel they are boring the rest of the world with their problems, they are making demands upon the rest of the world by being killed, they are disturbing everyone by being hungry and asking for the return of their property. If we could all fall through the crust of the earth and vanish in one hour, with our heroes and poets and prophets and martyrs, perhaps we would be doing the memory of the Jewish race a service. . . .

"This is how I feel today, son. I need some help. You've been to the war, you've fought and killed men, you've seen the people of other countries. Maybe you understand things that I don't understand. Maybe you see some hope somewhere. Help me. Your loving father."

Seeger folded the letter slowly, not seeing what he was doing because the tears were burning his eyes. He walked slowly and aimlessly across the dead autumn grass of the empty field, away from the camp.

He tried to wipe away his tears, because with his eyes full and dark, he kept seeing his father and brother crouched in the old-fashioned living room in Ohio and hearing his brother, dressed in the old, discarded uniform, saying, "These're the new rocket bombs. For the Jews."

He sighed, looking out over the bleak, wasted land. Now, he thought, now I have to think about it. He felt a slight, unreasonable twinge of anger at his father for presenting him with the necessity of thinking about it. The army was good about serious problems. While you were fighting, you were too busy and frightened and weary to think about anything, and at other times you were relaxing, putting your brain on a shelf, postponing everything to that impossible time of clarity and beauty after the war. Well, now, here was the impossible, clear, beautiful time, and here was his father, demanding that he think. There are all sorts of Jews, he thought, there are the sort whose every waking moment is ridden by the knowledge of Jewishness, who see signs against the Jew in every smile on a streetcar, every whisper, who see pogroms in every newspaper article, threats in every change of the weather, scorn in every handshake, death behind each closed door. He had not been like that. He was young, he was big and healthy and easy-going and people of all kinds had seemed to like him all his life, in the army and out. In America, especially, what was going on in Europe had seemed remote, unreal, unrelated to him. The chanting, bearded old men burning in the Nazi furnaces, and the dark-eyed women screaming prayers in Polish and Russian and German as they were pushed naked into the gas chambers had seemed as shadowy and almost as unrelated to him as he trotted out onto the stadium field for a football game, as they must have been to the men named O'Dwyer and Wick-ersham and Poole who played in the line beside him.

They had seemed more related in Europe. Again and again in the towns that had been taken back from the Germans, gaunt, gray-faced men had stopped him hum-bly, looking searchingly at him, and had asked, peering at his long, lined, grimy face, under the anonymous hel-met, "Are you a Jew?" Sometimes they asked it in En-glish, sometimes French, or Yiddish. He didn't know French or Yiddish, but he learned to recognize the phrase. He had never understood exactly why they had asked the question, since they never demanded anything from him, rarely even could speak to him, until, one day in Strasbourg, a little bent old man and a small, shape-less woman had stopped him, and asked, in English, if he was Jewish.

"Yes," he said, smiling at them.

The two old people had smiled widely, like children. "Look," the old man had said to his wife. "A young American soldier. A Jew. And so large and strong." He had touched Seeger's arm reverently with the tips of his fingers, then had touched the Garand he was carrying. "And such a beautiful rifle . . ."

And there, for a moment, although he was not particu-larly sensitive, Seeger got an inkling of why he had been stopped and questioned by so many before. Here, to these bent, exhausted old people, ravaged of their fami-lies, familiar with flight and death for so many years, was a symbol of continuing life. A large young man in the uniform of the liberator, blood, as they thought, of their blood, but not in hiding, not quivering in fear and helplessness, but striding secure and victorious down the street, armed and capable of inflicting terrible destruc-tion on his enemies.

Seeger had kissed the old lady on the cheek and she had wept and the old man had scolded her for it, while shaking Seeger's hand fervently and thankfully before saying goodby.

And, thinking back on it, it was silly to pretend that, even before his father's letter, he had been like any other American soldier going through the war. When he had stood over the huge dead SS major with the face blown in by his bullets in the warehouse in Coblenz, and had taken the pistol from the dead hand he had tasted a strange little extra flavor of triumph. How many Jews, he'd thought, has this man killed, how fitting it is that I've killed him. Neither Olson nor Welch, who were like his brothers, would have felt that in picking up the Luger, its barrel still hot from the last shots its owner had fired before dying. And he had resolved that he was going to make sure to take this gun back with him to America, and plug it and keep it on his desk at home, as a kind of vague, half-understood sign to himself that justice had once been done and he had been its instrument.

Maybe, he thought, maybe I'd better take it back with me, but not as a memento. Not plugged, but loaded. America by now was a strange country for him. He had been away a long time and he wasn't sure what was waiting for him when he got home. If the mobs were coming down the street toward his house, he was not going to die singing and praying.

When he was taking basic training he'd heard a scrawny, clerk-like-looking soldier from Boston talking at the other end of the PX bar, over the watered beer. "The boys at the office," the scratchy voice was saying, "gave me a party before I left. And they told me one thing. 'Charlie,' they said, 'hold onto your bayonet. We're going to be able to use it when you get back. On the Yids.'"

He hadn't said anything then, because he'd felt it was neither possible nor desirable to fight against every random overheard voice raised against the Jews from one end of the world to another. But again and again, at odd moments, lying on a barracks cot, or stretched out trying to sleep on the floor of a ruined French farmhouse, he had heard that voice, harsh, satisfied, heavy with hate and ignorance, saying above the beery grumble of apprentice soldiers at the bar, "Hold onto your bayonet. . . ."

And the other stories—Jews collected stories of hatred and injustice and inklings of doom like a special, lunatic kind of miser. The story of the naval officer, commander of a small vessel off the Aleutians, who, in the officers' wardroom, had complained that he hated the Jews be-cause it was the Jews who had demanded that the Germans be beaten first and the forces in the Pacific had been starved in consequence. And when one of his junior officers, who had just come aboard, had objected and told the commander that he was a Jew, the commander had risen from the table and said, "Mister, the Constitution of the United States says I have to serve in the same navy with Jews, but it doesn't say I have to eat at the same table with them." In the fogs and the cold, swelling Arctic seas off the Aleutians, in a small boat, subject to sudden, mortal attack at any moment . . .

And the two young combat engineers in an attached company on D Day, when they were lying off the coast right before climbing down into the landing barges. "There's France," one of them had said.

"What's it like?" the second one had asked, peering out across the miles of water toward the smoking coast.

"Like every place else," the first one had answered. "The Jews've made all the dough during the war."

"Shut up!" Seeger had said, helplessly thinking of the dead, destroyed, wandering, starving Jews of France. The engineers had shut up, and they'd climbed down together into the heaving boat, and gone into the beach together.

And the million other stories. Jews, even the most normal and best adjusted of them, became living treasuries of them, scraps of malice and bloodthirstiness, clever and confusing and cunningly twisted so that every act by every Jew became suspect and blameworthy and hateful. Seeger had heard the stories, and had made an almost conscious effort to forget them. Now, holding his father's letter in his hand, he remembered them all.

He stared unseeingly out in front of him. Maybe, he thought, maybe it would've been better to have been killed in the war, like Leonard. Simpler. Leonard would never have to face a crowd coming for his mother and father. Leonard would not have to listen and collect these hideous, fascinating little stories that made of every Jew a stranger in any town, on any field, on the face of the earth. He had come so close to being killed so many times, it would have been so easy, so neat and final.

Seeger shook his head. It was ridiculous to feel like that, and he was ashamed of himself for the weak moment. At the age of twenty-one, death was not an answer.

"Seeger!" It was Olson's voice. He and Welch had sloshed silently up behind Seeger, standing in the open field. "Seeger, *mon vieux*, what're you doing—grazing?"

Seeger turned slowly to them. "I wanted to read my letter," he said.

Olson looked closely at him. They had been together so long, through so many things, that flickers and hints of expression on each other's faces were recognized and acted upon. "Anything wrong?" Olson asked.

"No," said Seeger. "Nothing much."

"Norman," Welch said, his voice young and solemn. "Norman, we've been talking, Olson and me. We decided—you're pretty attached to that Luger, and maybe—if you—well . . ."

"What he's trying to say," said Olson, "is we withdraw the request. If you want to sell it, O.K. If you don't, don't do it for our sake. Honest."

Seeger looked at them, standing there, disreputable and tough and familiar. "I haven't made up my mind yet," he said.

"Anything you decide," Welch said oratorically, "is perfectly all right with us. Perfectly."

They walked aimlessly and silently across the field, away from camp. As they walked, their shoes making a wet, sliding sound in the damp, dead grass, Seeger thought of the time Olson had covered him in the little town outside Cherbourg, when Seeger had been caught going down the side of a street by four Germans with a machine gun on the second story of a house on the corner and Olson had had to stand out in the middle of the street with no cover at all for more than a minute, firing continuously, so that Seeger could get away alive. And he thought of the time outside Saint Lô when he had been wounded and had lain in a mine field for three hours and Welch and Captain Taney had come looking for him in the darkness and had found him and picked him up and run for it, all of them expecting to get blown up any second.

And he thought of all the drinks they'd had together and the long marches and the cold winter together, and all the girls they'd gone out with together, and he thought of his father and brother crouching behind the window in Ohio waiting for the rockets and the crowds armed with Browning automatic rifles.

"Say," he stopped and stood facing them. "Say, what do you guys think of the Jews?"

Welch and Olson looked at each other, and Olson glanced down at the letter in Seeger's hand.

"Jews?" Olson said finally. "What're they? Welch, you ever hear of the Jews?"

Welch looked thoughtfully at the gray sky. "No," he said. "But remember, I'm an uneducated fellow."

"Sorry, Bud," Olson said, turning to Seeger. "We can't help you. Ask us another question. Maybe we'll do better."

Seeger peered at the faces of his friends. He would have to rely upon them, later on, out of uniform, on their native streets, more than he had ever relied on them on the bullet-swept street and in the dark mine field in France. Welch and Olson stared back at him, troubled, their faces candid and tough and dependable.

"What time," Seeger asked, "did you tell that captain you'd meet him?"

"Eight o'clock," Welch said. "But we don't have to go. If you have any feeling about that gun . . ."

"We'll meet him," Seeger said. "We can use that sixty-five bucks."

"Listen," Olson said, "I know how much you like that gun and I'll feel like a heel if you sell it."

"Forget it," Seeger said, starting to walk again. "What could I use it for in America?"

Come Out the Wilderness

James Baldwin

Paul did not yet feel her eyes on him. She watched him. He went to the window, peering out between the slats in the Venetian blinds. She could tell from his profile that it did not look like a pleasant day. In profile, all of the contradictions that so confounded her seemed to be revealed. He had a boy's long, rather thin neck, but it supported a head that seemed even more massive than it actually was because of its plantation of thickly curling black hair, hair that was always a little too long or else, cruelly, much too short. His forehead was broad and high, but this austerity was contradicted by a short, blunt, almost ludicrously upturned nose. And he had a large mouth and very heavy, sensual lips, which suggested a certain wry cruelty when turned down but looked like the mask of comedy when he laughed. His body was really excessively black with hair, which proved, she said, since Negroes were generally less hairy than whites, which race, in fact, had moved farthest from the ape. Other people did not see his beauty, which always mildly astonished her—it was like thinking that the sun was ordinary. He was sloppy about the way he stood and sat, that was true, and so his shoulders were already beginning to be round. And he was a poor man's son, a city boy, and so his body could not really remind anyone of a Michelangelo statue as she—"fantastically," he said—claimed; it did not have that luxury or that power. It was economically tense and hard and testified only to the agility of the poor, who are always dancing one step ahead of the devil.

He stepped away from the window, looking worried. Ruth closed her eyes. When she opened them, he was disappearing away from her down the short, black hall that led to the bathroom. She wondered what time he had come in last night; she wondered if he had a hangover; she heard the water running. She thought that he had probably not been home long. She was very sensitive to his comings and goings and had often found herself abruptly upright and wide awake a moment after he, restless at two-thirty in the morning, had closed the door behind him. Then there was no more sleep for her. She lay there on a bed that inexorably became a bed of ashes and hot coals, while her imagination dwelt on every conceivable disaster, from his having forsaken her for another woman to his having somehow ended up in the morgue. And as the night faded from black to gray to daylight, the telephone began to seem another presence in the house, sitting not far from her like a great, malevolent black cat that might, at any moment, with one shrill cry, scatter her life like dismembered limbs all over this tiny room. There were places she could have called, but she would have died first. After all—he had only needed to point it out once, he would never have occasion to point it out again—they were not married. Often she had pulled herself out of bed, her loins cold and all her body trembling, and gotten dressed and had coffee and gone to work without seeing him. But he would call her in the office later in the day. She would have had several stiff drinks at lunch and so could be very offhand over the phone, pretending that she had only supposed him to have gotten up a little earlier than herself that morning. But the moment she put the receiver down she hated him. She made herself sick with fantasies of how she would be revenged. Then she hated herself; thinking into what an iron maiden of love and hatred he had placed her, she hated him even more. She could not help feeling that he treated her this way because of her color, because she was a colored girl. Then her past and her present threatened to engulf her. She knew she was being unfair; she could not help it; she thought of psychiatry; she saw herself transformed, at peace with the world, herself, her color, with the male of indeterminate color she would have found. Always, this journey 'round her skull ended with tears, resolutions, prayers, with Paul's face, which then had the power to reconcile her even to the lowest circle of hell.

After work, on the way home, she stopped for another

drink, or two or three; bought Sen-Sen to muffle the odor; wore the most casually glowing of smiles as he casually kissed her when she came through the door.

She knew that he was going to leave her. It was in his walk, his talk, his eyes. He wanted to go. He had already moved back, crouching to leap. And she had no rival. He was not going to another woman. He simply wanted to go. It would happen today, tomorrow, three weeks from today; it was over, she could do nothing about it; neither could she save herself by jumping first. She had no place to go; she only wanted him. She had tried hard to want other men, and she was still young, only twenty-six, and there was no real lack of opportunity. But all she knew about other men was that they were not Paul.

Through the gloom of the hallway he came back into the room and, moving to the edge of the bed, lit a cigarette. She smiled up at him.

"Good morning," she said. "Would you light one for me, too?"

He looked down at her with a sleepy and slightly shame-faced grin. Without a word he offered her his freshly lit cigarette, lit another, and then got into bed, shivering slightly.

"Good morning," he said then. "Did you sleep well?"

"Very well," she said lightly. "Did you? I didn't hear you come in."

"Ah, I was very quiet," he said teasingly, curling his great body toward her and putting his head on her breast. "I didn't want to wake you up. I was afraid you'd hit me with something."

She laughed. "What time *did* you come in?"

"Oh"—he raised his head, dragging on his cigarette, and half-frowned, half-smiled—"about an hour or so ago."

"What did you do? Find a new after-hours joint?"

"No. I ran into Cosmo. We went over to his place to look at a couple new paintings he's done. He had a bottle, we sat around."

She knew Cosmo and distrusted him. He was about forty, and he had had two wives; he did not think women were worth much. She was sure that Cosmo had been giving Paul advice as to how to be rid of her; she could imagine, or believed she could, how he had spoken about her, and she felt her skin tighten. At the same moment she became aware of the warmth of Paul's body.

"What did you talk about?" she asked.

"Oh. Painting. His paintings, my paintings, all God's chillun's paintings."

During the day, while she was at work, Paul painted in the back room of this cramped and criminally expensive Village apartment where the light was bad and where there was not really room enough for him to step back and look at his canvas. Most of his paintings were stored with a friend. Still, there were enough, standing against the wall, piled on top of the closet and on the table, for a sizable one-man show. "If they were any good," said Paul, who worked very hard. She knew this despite the fact that he said so rather too often. She knew, by his face, his distance, his quality, frequently, of seeming to be like a spring, unutterably dangerous to touch. And by the exhaustion, different in kind from any other, with which he sometimes stretched out in bed.

She thought—of course—that his paintings were very good, but he did not take her judgment seriously. "You're sweet, funnyface," he sometimes said, "but, you know, you aren't really very bright." She was scarcely at all mollified by his adding, "Thank heaven. I hate bright women."

She remembered, now, how stupid she had felt about music all the time she had lived with Arthur, a man of her own color who had played a clarinet. She was still finding out today, so many years after their breakup, how much she had learned from him—not only about music, unluckily. If I stay on this merry-go-round, she thought, I'm going to become very accomplished, just the sort of girl no man will ever marry.

She moved closer to Paul, the fingers of one hand playing with his hair. He lay still. It was very silent.

"Ruth," he said finally, "I've been thinking . . ."

At once she was all attention. She drew on her cigarette, her fingers still drifting through his hair, as though she were playing with water.

"Yes?" she prompted.

She had always wondered, when the moment came, if she would make things easy for him or difficult. She still did not know. He leaned up on one elbow, looking down at her. She met his eyes, hoping that her own eyes reflected nothing but calm curiosity. He continued to stare at her and put one hand on her short, dark hair. Then, "You're a nice girl," he said irrelevantly, and leaned down and kissed her.

With a kiss! she thought.

"My father wouldn't think so," she said, "if he could see me now. What is it you've been thinking?"

He still said nothing but only looked down at her, an expression in his eyes that she could not read.

"I've been thinking," he said, "that it's about time I got started on that portrait of you. I ought to get started right away."

She felt, very sharply, that his nerve had failed him. But she felt, too, that his decision now to do a portrait of her was a means of moving far enough away from her to be able to tell her the truth. Also, he had always said that he could do something wonderful with her on canvas—it would be foolish to let the opportunity pass. Cosmo had probably told him this. She had always been flattered by his desire to paint her, but now she hoped that he would suddenly go blind.

"Anytime," she said, and could not resist, "Am I to be part of a gallery?"

"Yeah. I'll probably be able to sell you for a thousand bucks," he said, and kissed her again.

"That's not a very nice thing to say," she murmured.

"You're a funny girl. What's not nice about a thousand dollars?" He leaned over her to put out his cigarette in the ash tray near the bed; then took hers and put it out, too. He fell back against her and put his hand on her breast.

She said tentatively: "Well, I suppose if you do it often enough, I could stop working."

His arms tightened, but she did not feel that this was due entirely to desire; it might be said that he was striving now to distract her. "If I do *what* enough?" he grinned.

"Now, now," she smiled, "you just said that I was a nice girl."

"You're one of the nicest girls I ever met," said Paul soberly. "Really you are. I often wonder . . ."

"You often wonder what?"

"What's going to become of you."

She felt like a river trying to run two ways at once: she felt herself shrinking from him, yet she flowed toward him, too; she knew he felt it. "But as long as you're with me," she said, and she could not help herself, she felt she was about to cry; she held his face between her hands, pressing yet closer against him. "As long as you're with me." His face was white, his eyes glowed; there was a war in him, too. Everything that divided them charged, for an instant, the tiny space between them. Then the veils of habit and desire covered both their eyes.

"Life is very long," said Paul at last. He kissed her. They both sighed. And slowly she surrendered, opening up before him like the dark continent, made mad and delirious and blind by the entry of a mortal as bright as the morning, as white as milk.

When she left the house, he was sleeping. Because she was late for work and because it was raining, she dropped into a cab and was whirled out of the streets of the Village—which still suggested, at least, some faint memory of the individual life—into the grim publicities of midtown Manhattan. Blocks and squares and exclamation marks, stone and steel and glass as far as the eye could see; everything towering, lifting itself against, though by no means into, heaven. The people, so surrounded by heights that they had lost any sense of what heights were, rather resembled, nevertheless, these gray rigidities and also resembled, in their frantic motion, people fleeing a burning town. Ruth, who was not so many years removed from trees and earth, had felt in the beginning that she would never be able to live on an island so eccentric; she had, for example, before she arrived, dreamed of herself as walking by the river. But apart from the difficulties of realizing this ambition, which were not inconsiderable, it turned out that a lone girl walking by the river was simply asking to be victimized by both the disturbers and the defenders of the public peace. She retreated into the interior, and this dream was abandoned—along with others. For her as for most of Manhattan, trees and water ceased to be realities; the nervous, trusting landscape of the city

began to be the landscape of her mind. And soon her
mind, like life on the island, seemed to be incapable of
flexibility, of moving outward, could only shriek upward
into meaningless abstractions or drop downward into
cruelty and confusion.

She worked for a life insurance company that had only
recently become sufficiently progressive to hire Negroes.
This meant that she worked in an atmosphere so positively electric with interracial good will that no one ever
dreamed of telling the truth about anything. It would
have seemed, and it quite possibly would have been, a
spiteful act. The only other Negro there was a male, a
Mr. Davis, who was very highly placed. He was an expert, it appeared, in some way about Negroes and life
insurance, from which Ruth had ungenerously concluded
that he was the company's expert on how to cheat more
Negroes out of more money and not only remain within
the law but also be honored with a plaque for good race
relations. She often—but not always—took dictation
from him. The other girls, manifesting a rough, girl-
scoutish camaraderie that made the question of their
sincerity archaic, found him "marvelous" and wondered
if he had a wife. Ruth found herself unable to pursue
these strangely overheated and yet eerily impersonal
speculations with anything like the indicated vehemence.
Since it was extremely unlikely that any of these girls
would ever even go dancing with Mr. Davis, it was impossible to believe that they had any ambition to share
his couch, matrimonial or otherwise, and yet, lacking this
ambition, it was impossible to account for their avidity.
But they were all incredibly innocent and made her
ashamed of her body. At the same time it demanded,
during their maddening coffee breaks, a great deal of
will power not to take Paul's photograph out of her wallet and wave it before them, saying, *"You'll never lay a
finger on Mr. Davis. But look what I took from you!"*
Her face at such moments allowed them to conclude that
she was planning to ensnare Mr. Davis herself. It was
perhaps this assumption, despite her phone calls from
Paul, that allowed them to discuss Mr. Davis so freely
before her, and they also felt, in an incoherent way, that
these discussions were proof of their democracy. She did
not find Mr. Davis "marvelous," though she thought him

good looking enough in a square, stocky, gleaming, black-boyish sort of way.

Near her office, visible from her window and having the air of contraband in Caesar's market place, was a small gray chapel. An ugly neon cross jutted out above the heads of passers-by, proclaiming "Jesus Saves." Today, as the lunch hour approached and she began, as always, to fidget, debating whether she should telephone Paul or wait for Paul to telephone her, she found herself staring in some irritation at this cross, thinking about her childhood. The telephone rang and rang, but never for her; she began to feel the need of a drink. She thought of Paul sleeping while she typed and became outraged, then thought of his painting and became maternal; thought of his arms and paused to light a cigarette, throwing the most pitying of glances toward the girl who shared her office, who still had a crush on Frank Sinatra. Nevertheless, the sublimatory tube still burning, the smoke tickling her nostrils and the typewriter bell clanging at brief intervals like signals flashing by on a railroad track, she relapsed into bitterness, confusion, fury: for she was trapped. Paul was a trap. She wanted a man of her own, and she wanted children, and all she could see for herself today was a lifetime of typing while Paul slept or a lifetime of typing with no Paul. And she began rather to envy the stocky girl with the crush on Frank Sinatra since she would settle one day, obviously, for a great deal less, and probably turn out children as Detroit turned out cars and never sigh for an instant for what she had missed, having indeed never, and especially with a lifetime of moviegoing behind her, missed anything.

"Jesus Saves." She began to think of the days of her innocence. These days had been spent in the South, where her mother and father and older brother remained. She had an older sister, married and with several children, in Oakland, and a baby sister who had become a small-time night club singer in New Orleans. There were relatives of her father's living in Harlem, and she was sure that they wrote to him often complaining that she never visited them. They, like her father, were earnest churchgoers, though, unlike her father, their religion was strongly mixed with an opportunistic

respectability and with ambitions to better society and
their own place in it, which her father would have
scorned. Their ambitions vitiated in them what her father called the "true" religion, and what remained of
this religion, which was principally vindictiveness, pre-
vented them from understanding anything whatever
about those concrete Northern realities that made them
at once so obsequious and so venomous.

Her innocence. It was many years ago. She remembered their house, so poor and plain, standing by itself,
apart from other houses, as nude and fragile on the
stony ground as an upturned cardboard box. And it was
nearly as dark inside as it might have been beneath a
box, it leaked when the rain fell, froze when the wind
blew, could scarcely be entered in July. They tried to
coax sustenance out of a soil that had long ago gone out
of the business. As time went on, they grew to depend
less and less on the soil and more on the oyster boats,
and on the wages and leftovers brought home by their
mother, and then herself, from the white kitchens in
town. And her mother still struggled in these white
kitchens, humming sweet hymns, tiny, mild-eyed, and
bent, her father still labored on the oyster boats; after a
lifetime of labor, should they drop dead tomorrow, there
would not be a penny for their burial clothes. Her
brother, still unmarried, nearing thirty now, loitered
through the town with his dangerous reputation, drinking and living off the women he murdered with his love-
making. He made her parents fearful, but they reiterated
in each letter that they had placed him, and all of their
children, in the hands of God. Ruth opened each letter
in guilt and fear, expecting each time to be confronted
with the catastrophe that had at last overtaken her kin;
anticipating, too, with a selfish annoyance that added to
her guilt, the enforced and necessary journey back to
her home in mourning; the survivors gathered together
to do brief honor to the dead, whose death was certainly,
in part, attributable to the indifferences of the living.
She often wrote her brother asking him to come North,
and asked her sister in Oakland to second her in this
plea. But she knew that he would not come North—
because of her. She had shamed him and embittered
him, she was one of the reasons he drank.

Her mother's song, which she, doubtless, still hummed each evening as she walked the old streets homeward, began with the question, *How did you feel when you come out the wilderness?*

And she remembered her mother, half-humming, half-singing, with a steady, tense beat that would have made any blues singer sit up and listen (though she thought it best not to say this to her mother):

Come out the wilderness,
Come out the wilderness.
How did you feel when you
    come out the wilderness,
Leaning on the Lord?

And the answers were many: *Oh, my soul felt happy!* or, *I shouted hallelujah!* or, *I do thank God!*

Ruth finished her cigarette, looking out over the stone-cold, hideous New York streets, and thought with a strange new pain of her mother. Her mother had once been no older than she, Ruth, was today, she had probably been pretty, she had also wept and trembled and cried beneath the rude thrusting that was her master and her life, and children had knocked in her womb and split her as they came crying out. Out, and into the wilderness: she had placed them in the hands of God. She had known nothing but labor and sorrow, she had had to confront, every day of her life, the everlasting, nagging, infinitesimal details, it had clearly all come to nothing, how could she be singing still?

"Jesus Saves." She put out her cigarette, and a sense of loss and disaster wavered through her like a mist. She wished, in that moment, from the bottom of her heart, that she had never left home. She wished that she had never met Paul. She wished that she had never been touched by his whiteness. She should have found a great, slow, black man, full of laughter and sighs and grace, a man at whose center there burned a steady, smokeless fire. She should have surrendered to him and been a woman, and had his children, and found, through being irreplaceable, despite whatever shadows life might cast, peace that would enable her to endure.

She had left home practically by accident: it had been

partly due to her brother. He had grown too accustomed to thinking of her as his prized, adored little sister to recognize the changes that were occurring within her. This had had something to do with the fact that his own sexual coming of age had disturbed his peace with her—he would, in good faith, have denied this, which did not make it less true. When she was seventeen, her brother had surprised her alone in a barn with a boy. Nothing had taken place between herself and this boy, though there was no saying what might not have happened if her brother had not come in. She, guilty though she was in everything but the act, could scarcely believe and had not, until today, ever quite forgiven his immediate leap to the obvious conclusion. She began screaming before he hit her, her father had had to come running to pull her brother off the boy. And she had shouted their innocence in a steadily blackening despair, for the boy was too badly beaten to be able to speak, and it was clear that no one believed her. She bawled at last: "Goddamit, I wish I had, I wish I had. I might as well of done it!" Her father slapped her. Her brother gave her a look and said: "You dirty ... you dirty ... you black and dirty—" Then her mother had had to step between her father and her brother. She turned and ran and sat down for a long time in the darkness on a hillside, by herself, shivering. And she felt dirty, she felt that nothing would ever make her clean.

After this she and her brother scarcely spoke. He had wounded her so deeply she could not face his eyes. Her father dragged her to church to make her cry repentance, but she was as stubborn as her father, she told him she had nothing to repent. And she avoided them all, which was exactly the most dangerous thing that could have happened, for when she met the musician, Arthur, who was more than twenty years older than she, she ran away to New York with him. She lived with him for more than four years. She did not love him all that time. She simply did not know how to escape his domination. He had never made the big-time himself, and he therefore wanted her to become a singer; and perhaps she had ceased to love him when it became clear that she had no talent whatever. He was very disappointed, but he was also very proud, and he made her go to school to study shorthand and typing, and made her self-conscious about her accent and her grammar, and took great delight in dressing her. Through him, she got over feeling that she was black and unattractive, and as soon as this happened, she was able to leave him. In fleeing Harlem and her relatives there, she drifted downtown to the Village where, eventually, she found employment as a waitress in one of those restaurants with candles on the tables. Here, after a year or so and several increasingly disastrous and desperate liaisons, she met Paul.

The telephone rang several desks away from her and, at the same instant she was informed that Mr. Davis wanted her in his office. She was sure that it was Paul telephoning, but she picked up her pad and walked into Mr. Davis's cubbyhole. Someone picked up the receiver cutting off the bell, and she closed the door of Mr. Davis's office behind her.

"Good morning," she said.

"Good morning," he answered. He looked out of his window. "Though, between you and me, I've seen better mornings. This morning ain't half trying."

They both laughed, self-consciously amused and relieved by his "ain't."

She sat down, her pencil poised, looking at him questioningly.

"How do you like your job?" he asked her.

She had not expected his question, which she immediately distrusted and resented, suspecting him, on no evidence whatever, of acting now as a company spy.

"It's quite pleasant," she said in a guarded, ladylike tone, and stared hypnotically at him as though she believed that he was about to do her mischief by magical means and she had to resist his spell.

"Are you intending to be a career girl?"

He was giving her more attention this morning than he ever had before, with the result that she found herself reciprocating. A tentative friendliness wavered in the air between them. She smiled. "I guess I ought to say that it depends on my luck."

He laughed—perhaps rather too uproariously, though, more probably, she had merely grown unaccustomed to his kind of laughter. Her brother bobbed briefly to the surface of her mind.

"Well," he said, "does your luck seem likely to take you out of this office anytime in the near future?"

"No," she said, "it certainly doesn't look that way," and they laughed again. But she wondered if he would be laughing if he knew about Paul.

"If you don't mind my saying so, then," he said. "*I'm* lucky." He quickly riffled some papers on his desk, putting on a business air as rakishly as she had seen him put on his hat. "There's going to be some changes made around here—I reckon you have heard that." He grinned. Then, briskly: "I'm going to be needing a secretary. Would you like it? You get a raise"—he coughed—"in salary, of course."

"Why, I'd love it," she heard herself saying before she had had time for the bitter reflection that this professional advance probably represented the absolute extent of her luck. And she was ashamed of the thought, which she could not repress, that Paul would probably hang on a little longer if he knew she was making more money.

She resolved not to tell him and wondered how many hours this resolution would last.

Mr. Davis looked at her with an intentness almost personal. There was a strained, brief silence, "Good," he said at last. "There are a few details to be worked out, like getting me more office space"—they both smiled—"but you'll be hearing directly in a few days. I only wanted to sound you out first." He rose and held out his hand. "I hope you're going to like working with me," he said. "I think I'm going to like working with you."

She rose and shook his hand, bewildered to find that something in his simplicity had touched her very deeply. "I'm sure I will," she said gravely. "And thank you very much." She reached backward for the doorknob.

"Miss Bowman," he said sharply—and paused. "Well, if I were you, I wouldn't mention it yet to"—he waved his hand uncomfortably—"the girls out there." Now he really did look rather boyish. "It looks better if it comes from the front office."

"I understand," she said quickly.

"Also, I didn't ask you out of any—racial—considerations," he said. "You just seemed the most *sensible* girl available."

"I understand," she repeated; they were both trying not to smile. "And thank you again." She closed the door of his office behind her.

"A man called you," said the stocky girl. "He said he'd call back."

"Thank you," Ruth said. She could see that the girl wanted to talk, so she busily studied some papers on her desk and retired behind the noise of her typewriter.

The stocky girl had gone out to lunch, and Ruth was reluctantly deciding that she might as well go, too, when Paul called again.

"Hello. How's it going up there?"

"Dull. How are things down there? Are you out of bed already?"

"What do you mean, already?" He sounded slightly nettled and was trying not to sound that way, the almost certain signal that a storm was coming. "It's nearly one o'clock. I got work to do, too, you know."

"Yes. I know." But neither could she quite keep the sardonic edge out of her voice.

There was a silence.

"You coming straight home from work?"

"Yes. Will you be there?"

"Yeah. I got to go uptown with Cosmo this afternoon, talk to some gallery guy. Cosmo thinks he might like my stuff."

"Oh"—thinking *Damn Cosmo!*—"that's wonderful, Paul. I hope something comes of it."

Nothing whatever would come of it. The gallery owner would be evasive—*if* he existed, if they ever got to his gallery—and then Paul and Cosmo would get drunk. She would hear, while she ached to be free, to be anywhere else, *with* anyone else, from Paul, all about how stupid art dealers were, how incestuous the art world had become, how impossible it was to *do* anything—his eyes, meanwhile, focusing with a drunken intensity, his eyes at once arrogant and defensive.

Well. Most of what he said was true, and she knew it, it was not his fault.

Not his fault. "Yeah. I sure hope so. I thought I'd take

up some of my water colors, some small sketches—you know, all the most *obvious* things I've got."

This policy did not, empirically, seem to be as foolproof as everyone believed, but she did not know how to put her uncertain objections into words. "That sounds good. What time have you got to be there?"

"Around three. I'm meeting Cosmo now for lunch."

"Oh"—lightly—"why don't you two, just this once, order your lunch before you order your cocktails?"

He laughed, too, and was clearly no more amused than she. "Well, Cosmo'll be buying, he'll have to, so I guess I'll leave it up to him to order."

Touché. Her hand, holding the receiver, shook. "Well, I hope you two make it to the gallery without falling flat on your faces."

"Don't worry." Then, in a rush, she recognized the tone before she understood the words, it was his you-can't-say-I-haven't-been-honest-with-you tone: "Cosmo says the gallery owner's got a daughter."

I hope to God she marries you, she thought. I hope she marries you and takes you off to Istanbul forever where I will never have to hear of you again, so I can get a breath of air, so I can get out from under.

They both laughed, a laugh conspiratorial and sophisticated, like the whispered, whisky laughter of a couple in a night club. "Oh?" she said. "Is she pretty?"

"She's probably a pig. She's had two husbands already, both artists."

She laughed again. "Where has she buried the bodies?"

"Well"—really amused this time but also rather grim—"one of them ended up in the booby hatch and the other turned into a fairy and was last seen dancing with some soldiers in Majorca."

Now they laughed together, and the wires between them hummed, almost, with the stormless friendship they both hoped to feel for each other someday. "A powerful pig. Maybe you *better* have a few drinks."

"You see what I mean? But Cosmo says she's not such a fool about painting."

"She doesn't seem to have much luck with painters. Maybe you'll break the jinx."

"Maybe. Wish me luck. It sure would be nice to un-load some of my stuff on somebody."

You're doing just fine, she thought. "Will you call me later?"

"Yeah. Around three-thirty, four o'clock, as soon as I get away from there."

"Right. Be good."

"You, too. Good-by."

"Good-by."

She put down the receiver, still amused and still trembling. After all, he had called her. But he would probably not have called her if he were not actually nourishing the hope that the gallery owner's daughter might find him interesting; in that case he would have to tell Ruth about her, and it was better to have the way prepared. Paul was always preparing the way for one unlikely exploit or flight or another, it was the reason he told Ruth "everything." To tell everything is a very effective means of keeping secrets. Secrets hidden at the heart of midnight are simply waiting to be dragged to the light, as, on some unlucky high noon, they always are. But secrets shrouded in the glare of candor are bound to defeat even the most determined and agile inspector, for the light is always changing and proves that the eye cannot be trusted. So Ruth knew about Paul nearly all there was to know, knew him better than any-one else on earth ever had or probably ever would, only—she did not know him well enough to stop him from being Paul.

While she was waiting for the elevator, she realized, with mild astonishment, that she was actually hoping that the gallery owner's daughter would take Paul away. This hope resembled the desperation of someone suffering from a toothache who, in order to bring the toothache to an end, was almost willing to jump out of a window. But she found herself wondering if love really ought to be like a toothache. Love ought—she stepped out of the elevator, really wondering for a moment which way to turn—to be a means of being released from guilt and terror. But Paul's touch would never release her. He had power over her not because she was free but because she was guilty. To enforce his power over her he had only to keep her guilt awake. This did not demand mal-

ice on his part, it scarcely demanded perception—it only
demanded that he have, as, in fact, he overwhelmingly
did have, an instinct for his own convenience. His touch,
which should have raised her, lifted her roughly only to
throw her down hard; whenever he touched her, she became blacker and dirtier than ever; the loneliest place
under heaven was in Paul's arms.

And yet—she went into his arms with such eagerness
and such hope. She had once thought herself happy. Was
this because she had been proud that he was white?
But—it was she who was insisting on these colors. Her
blackness was not Paul's fault. Neither was her guilt. She
was punishing herself for something, a crime she could
not remember. *You dirty . . . you black and dirty . . .*

She bumped into someone as she passed the cigar
stand in the lobby and, looking up to murmur, "Excuse
me," recognized Mr. Davis. He was stuffing cigars into
his breast pocket—though the gesture was rather like
that of a small boy stuffing his pockets with cookies, she
was immediately certain that they were among the most
expensive cigars that could be bought. She wondered
what he spent on his clothes—it looked like a great deal.
From the crown of rakishly tilted, deafeningly conservative hat to the tips of his astutely dulled shoes, he glowed
with a very nearly vindictive sharpness. There were no
flies on Mr. Davis. He would always be the best-dressed
man in *any*body's lobby.

He was just about the last person she wanted to see.
But perhaps his lunch hour was over and he was coming in.

"Miss Bowman!" He gave her a delighted grin. "Are
you just going to lunch?"

He made her want to laugh. There was something so
incongruous about finding that grin behind all that manner and under all those clothes.

"Yes," she said. "I guess you've had your lunch?"

"*No*, I ain't had no lunch," he said. "I'm hungry just
like you." He paused. "I be delighted to have your company, Miss Bowman."

Very courtly, she thought, amused, and the smile is
extremely wicked. Then she realized that she was
pleased that a man was *being* courtly with her, even if
only for an instant in a crowded lobby, and at the same

instant made the discovery that what was so widely referred to as a "wicked" smile was really only the smile, scarcely ever to be encountered anymore, of a man who was not afraid of women.

She thought it safe to demur. "Please don't think you have to be polite."

"I'm never polite about food," he told her. "Almost drove my mamma crazy." He took her arm. "I know a right nice place nearby." His stride and his accent made her think of home. She also realized that he, like many Negroes of his uneasily rising generation, kept in touch, so to speak, with himself by deliberately affecting, whenever possible, the illiterate speech of his youth. "We going to get on real well, you'll see. Time you get through being *my* secretary, you likely to end up with Alcoholics Anonymous."

The place "nearby" turned out to be a short taxi ride away, but it was, as he had said, "right nice." She doubted that Mr. Davis could possibly eat there every day, though it was clear that he was a man who liked to spend money.

She ordered a dry Martini and he a bourbon on the rocks. He professed himself astonished that she knew what a dry Martini was. "I thought you was a country girl."

"I *am* a country girl," she said.

"No, no," he said, "no more. You a country girl who came to the city, and that's the dangerous kind. Don't know if it's safe, having you for my secretary."

Underneath all this chatter she felt him watching her, sizing her up.

"Are you afraid your wife will object?" she asked.

"You ought to be able to look at me," he said, "and tell that I ain't got a wife."

She laughed. "So you're *not* married. I wonder if I should tell the girls in the office?"

"I don't care what you tell them," he said. Then: "How do you get along with them?"

"We get along fine," she said. "We don't have much to talk about except whether or not you're married, but that'll probably last until you *do* get married, and then we can talk about your wife."

But thinking for God's sake let's get off *this* subject,

she added, before he could say anything: "You called me a country girl. Aren't you a country boy?"

"I am," he said, "but *I* didn't *change* my drinking habits when I come North. If bourbon was good enough for me down yonder, it's good enough for me up here."

"*I* didn't have any drinking habits to change, Mr. Davis," she told him. "I was too young to be drinking when I left home."

His eyes were slightly questioning, but he held his peace, while she wished that she had held hers. She concentrated on sipping her Martini, suddenly remembering that she was sitting opposite a man who knew more about why girls left home than could be learned from locker-room stories. She wondered if he had a sister and tried to be amused at finding herself still so incorrigibly old-fashioned. But he did not, really, seem to be much like her brother. She met his eyes again.

"Where I come from," he said, with a smile, "*nobody* was too young to be drinking. Toughened them up for later life," and he laughed.

By the time lunch was over she had learned that he was from a small town in Alabama, was the youngest of three sons (but had no sisters), had gone to college in Tennessee, was a reserve officer in the Air Force. He was thirty-two. His mother was living, his father was dead. He had lived in New York for two years but was beginning, now, to like it less than he had in the beginning.

"At first," he said, "I thought it would be fun to live in a city where didn't nobody know you and you didn't know nobody and where, look like, you could do just anything you was big and black enough to do. But you get tired not knowing nobody, and there ain't really that many things you want to do alone."

"Oh, but you must have friends," she said, "uptown."

"I don't live uptown. I live in Brooklyn. Ain't *nobody* in Brooklyn got friends."

She laughed with him but distrusted the turn the conversation was taking. They were walking back to the office. He walked slowly as though in deliberate opposition to the people around them, although they were already a little late—at least *she* was late, but since she was with one of her superiors, it possibly didn't matter.

"Where do you live?" he asked her. "Do you live uptown?"

"No," she said, "I live downtown on Bank Street." And after a moment: "That's in the Village, Greenwich Village."

He grinned. "Don't tell me you studying to be a writer or a dancer or something?"

"No. I just found myself there. It used to be cheap."

He scowled. "Ain't nothing cheap in this town no more, not even the necessities."

His tone made clear to which necessities he referred, and she would have loved to tease him a little, just to watch him laugh. But she was beginning, with every step they took, to be a little afraid of him. She was responding to him with parts of herself that had been buried so long she had forgotten they existed. In his office that morning, when he shook her hand, she had suddenly felt a warmth of affection, of nostalgia, of gratitude even—and again in the lobby—he had somehow made her feel safe. It was his friendliness that was so unsettling. She had grown used to unfriendly people.

Still, she did not *want* to be friends with him; still less did she desire that their friendship should ever become anything more. Sooner or later he would learn about Paul. He would look at her differently then. It would not be—so much—because of Paul as a man, perhaps not even Paul as a white man. But it would make him bitter, it would make her ashamed for him to see how she was letting herself be wasted—for Paul, who did not love her.

This was the reason she was ashamed and wished to avoid the scrutiny of Mr. Davis. She was doing something to herself—out of shame?—that he would be right in finding indefensible. She was punishing herself. For what? She looked sideways at his black Sambo profile under the handsome lightweight Dobbs hat and wished she could tell him about it, that he would turn his head, holding it slightly to one side, and watch her with those eyes that had seen and that had learned to hide so much. Eyes that had seen so many girls like her taken beyond the hope of rescue, while all the owner of the eyes could do—perhaps she wore Paul the way Mr. Davis wore his hat. And she looked away from him, half-smiling and yet near tears, over the furious streets on which, here and there, like a design, colored people also hurried, thinking, *And we were slaves here once.*

"Do you like music?" he asked her abruptly. "I don't necessarily mean Carnegie Hall."

Now was the time to stop him. She had only to say, "Mr. Davis, I'm living with someone." It would not be necessary to say anything more than that.

She met his eyes. "Of course I like music," she said faintly.

"Well, I know a place I'd like to take you one of these evenings after work. Not going to be easy, being *my* secretary."

His smile forced her to smile with him. But, "Mr. Davis," she said, and stopped. They were before the entrance to their office building.

"What's the matter?" he asked. "You forget something?"

"No." She looked down, feeling big, black, and foolish. "Mr. Davis," she said, "you don't know anything about me."

"You don't know anything about me, either," he said.

"That's not what I mean," she said.

He sounded slightly angry. "I ain't asked you nothing yet," he said. "Why can't you wait till you're asked?"

"Well," she stammered, "it may be too late by then."

They stared at each other for a moment. "Well," he said, "if it turns out to be too late, won't be nobody to blame but me, will it?"

She stared at him again, almost hating him. She blindly felt that he had no right to do this to her, to cause her to feel such a leap of hope, if he was only, in the end, going to give her back all of her shame.

"You know what they say down home," she said slowly. "If you don't know what you doing, you better ask somebody." There were tears in her eyes.

He took her arm. "Come on in this house, girl," he said. "We got insurance to sell."

They said nothing to each other in the elevator on the way upstairs. She wanted to laugh, and she wanted to cry. He, ostentatiously, did not watch her; he stood next to her, humming *Rocks In My Bed.*

She waited all afternoon for Paul to telephone, but

although, perversely enough, the phone seemed never to cease ringing, it never rang for her. At five-fifteen, just before she left the office, she called the apartment. Paul was not there. She went downstairs to a nearby bar and ordered a drink and called again at a quarter to six. He was not there. She resolved to have one more drink and leave this bar, which she did, wandering a few blocks north to a bar frequented by theatre people. She sat in a booth and ordered a drink and at a quarter to seven called again. He was not there.

She was in a reckless, desperate state, like flight. She knew that she could not possibly go home and cook supper and wait in the empty apartment until his key turned in the lock. He would come in, breathless and contrite—or else, truculently, *not* contrite—probably a little drunk, probably quite hungry. He would tell her where he had been and what he had been doing. Whatever he told her would probably be true—there are so many ways of telling the truth! And whether it was true or not did not matter, and she would not be able to reproach him for the one thing that *did* matter: that he had left her sitting in the house alone. She could not make this reproach because, after all, leaving women sitting around in empty houses had been the specialty of all men for ages. And, for ages, when the men arrived, women bestirred themselves to cook supper—luckily, it was not yet common knowledge that many a woman had narrowly avoided committing murder by calmly breaking a few eggs.

She wondered where it had all gone to—the ease, the pleasure they had had together once. At one time their evenings together, sitting around the house, drinking beer or reading or simply laughing and talking, had been the best part of all their days. Paul, reading or walking about with a can of beer in his hand, talking, gesturing, scratching his chest; Paul, stretched out on the sofa, staring at the ceiling; Paul, cheerful, with that lowdown, cavernous chuckle and that foolish grin; Paul, grim, with his mouth turned down and his eyes burning; Paul doing anything whatever. Paul with his eyelids sealed in sleep, drooling and snoring. Paul lighting her cigarette, touching her elbow, talking, talking, talking, in his million ways, to her, had been the light that lighted up her world. Now it was all gone, it would never come again, and that face which was like the heavens was darkening against her.

These present days, after supper, when the chatter each used as a cover began to show dangerous signs of growing thinner, there would be no choice but sleep. She might, indeed, have preferred a late movie or a round of the bars, lights, noise, other people, but this would scarcely be Paul's desire, already tired from his day. Besides—after all, she had to face the office in the morning. Eventually, therefore, bed; perhaps he or she or both of them might read awhile; perhaps there would take place between them what had sometimes been described as the act of love. Then sleep, black and dreadful, like a drugged state, from which she would be rescued by the scream of the alarm clock or the realization that Paul was no longer in bed.

Ah. Her throat ached with tears of fury and despair. In the days before she had met Paul men had taken her out, she laughed a lot, she had been young. She had not wished to spend her life protecting herself, with laughter, against men she cared nothing about; but she could not go on like this, either, drinking in random bars because she was afraid to go home; neither could she guess what life might bring her when Paul was gone.

She wished that she had never met him. She wished that he, or she, or both of them were dead. And for a moment she really wished it, with a violence that frightened her. Perhaps there was always murder at the very heart of love; the strong desire to murder the beloved so that one could at last be assured of privacy and peace and be as safe and unchanging as the grave. Perhaps this was why disasters, thicker and more malevolent than bees, circled Paul's head whenever he was out of her sight. Perhaps in those moments when she had believed herself willing to lay down her life for him she had not only been presenting herself with a metaphor for her peace, his death; death, which would be an inadequate revenge for the color of his skin, for his failure, by not loving her, to release her from the prison of her own.

The waitress passed her table, and Ruth ordered another drink. After this drink she would go. The bar was beginning to fill up, mostly, as she judged, with theatre people, some of them, possibly, on their way to work, most of them drawn here by habit and hope. For the past few moments, without realizing it, she had been watching a lean, pale boy at the bar, whose curly hair leaned electrically over his forehead like a living, awry crown. Something about him, his stance, his profile, or his grin, prodded painfully at her attention. But it was not that he reminded her of Paul. He reminded her of a boy she had known briefly a few years ago, a very lonely boy who was now a merchant seaman, probably, wherever he might be on the globe at this moment, whoring his unbearably unrealized, mysteriously painful life away. She had been fond of him, but loneliness in him had been like a cancer, it had really unfitted him for human intercourse, and she had not been sorry to see him go. She had not thought of him for years; yet, now, this stranger at the bar, whom she was beginning to recognize as an actor of brief but growing reputation, abruptly brought him back to her; brought him back encrusted, as it were, with the anguish of the intervening years. She remembered things she had forgotten and wished that she had been wiser then—then she smiled at herself, wishing she were wiser now.

Once, when he had done something to hurt her, she told him, trying to be calm but choked and trembling with rage: "Look. This is the twentieth century. We're not down on a plantation, you're not the master's son, and I'm not the black girl you can just sleep with when you want to and kick about as you please!"

His face, then, had held something, held many things—bitterness, amusement, fury; but the startling element was pain, his pain, with which she now invested the face of the actor at the bar. It made her wish that she had held her tongue.

"Well," he said at last, "I guess I'll get on back to the big house and leave you down here with the pickaninnies."

They had seen each other a few times thereafter, but that was really the evening on which everything had ended between them.

She wondered if that boy had ever found a home.

The actor at the bar looked toward her briefly, but she knew he was not seeing her. He looked at his watch,

frowned, she saw that he was not as young as he looked;
he ordered another drink and looked downward, leaning
both elbows on the bar. The dim lights played on the
crown of his hair. He moved his head slightly, with impatience, upward, his mouth slightly open, and in that instant, somehow, his profile was burned into her mind.
He reminded her then of Paul, of the vanished boy, of
others she had seen and never touched, of an army of
boys—boys forever!—an army she feared and hated and
loved. In that gesture, that look upward, with the light
so briefly on his face, she saw the bones that held his
face together and the sorrow beginning to corrode his
brow, the blood beating like butterfly wings against the
cage of his heavy neck. But there was no name for something blind, cruel, lustful, lost, intolerably vulnerable in
his eyes and mouth. She knew that in spite of everything,
his color, his power, or his coming fame, he was lost. He
did not know what had happened to his life. And never
would. This was the pain she had seen on the face of
that boy so long ago, and it was this that had driven
Paul into her arms, and now away. The sons of the mas-
ters were roaming the world, looking for arms to hold
them. And the arms that might have held them—could
not forgive.

A sound escaped her; she was astonished to realize it
was a sob. The waitress looked at her sharply. Ruth put
some money on the table and hurried out. It was dark
now, and the rain that had been falling intermittently all
day spangled the air and glittered all over the street. It
fell against her face and mingled with her tears and she
walked briskly through the crowds to hide from them
and from herself the fact that she did not know where
she was going.

ANONYMOUS NARRATION—
DUAL CHARACTER
POINT OF VIEW

The narrators of the next four stories continue to offer the kinds of knowledge that a confidant, eyewitness, or chorus might supply, but they expand the confidant's role by presenting the inner life of two characters. This addition is not a mere matter of numbers; a double character vision signals a particular purpose. In two of these stories, the dual points of view are alternated and given equal time because both characters are protagonists and the play-off between their perspectives is the story. In the other two stories, one character dominates but is illuminated by being perceived for a while through another character.

Because this technique is reserved for such specific purposes, it is not commonly used. Other examples are Sherwood Anderson's "Unlighted Lamps," the lamps being a father and daughter whose feelings about each other become known to the reader but—the point of the story— not to each other, and D. H. Lawrence's "The Shadow in the Rose Garden," where the alternating viewpoints of husband and wife document and dramatize the antagonism of a doomed marriage.

Sinking House

T. Coraghessan Boyle

When Monty's last breath caught somewhere in the
back of his throat with a sound like the tired
wheeze of an old screen door, the first thing she did was
turn on the water. She leaned over him a minute to
make sure, then she wiped her hands on her dress and
shuffled into the kitchen. Her fingers trembled as she
jerked at the lever and felt the water surge against the
porcelain. Steam rose in her face; a glitter of liquid leapt
for the drain. Croak, that's what they called it. Now she
knew why. She left the faucet running in the kitchen and
crossed the gloomy expanse of the living room, swung
down the hallway to the guest bedroom, and turned on
both taps in the bathroom there. It was almost as an
afterthought that she decided to fill the tub too.

For a long while she sat in the leather armchair in the
living room. The sound of running water—pure, baptis-
mal, as uncomplicated as the murmur of a brook in Vermont or a toilet at the Waldorf—soothed her. It trickled
and trilled, burbling from either side of the house and
driving down the terrible silence that crouched in the
bedroom over the lifeless form of her husband.

The afternoon was gone and the sun plunging into the
canopy of the big eucalyptus behind the Finkelsteins'
when she finally pushed herself up from the chair. Head
down, arms moving stiffly at her sides, she scuffed out
the back door, crossed the patio, and bent to turn on
the sprinklers. They sputtered and spat—not enough
pressure, that much she understood—but finally came to
life in halfhearted umbrellas of mist. She left the hose
trickling in the rose garden, then went back into the house,
passed through the living room, the kitchen, the master
bedroom—not even a glance for Monty, no: she wouldn't
look at him, not yet—and on into the master bath. The

taps were weak, barely a trickle, but she left them on anyway, then flushed the toilet and pinned down the float with the brick Monty had used as a doorstop. And then finally, so weary she could barely lift her arms, she leaned into the stall and flipped on the shower.

Two weeks after the ambulance came for the old man next door, Meg Terwilliger was doing her stretching exercises on the prayer rug in the sunroom, a menthol cigarette glowing in the ashtray on the floor beside her, the new CD by Sandee and the Sharks thumping out of the big speakers in the corners. Meg was twenty-three, with the fine bones and haunted eyes of a poster child. She wore her black hair cut close at the temples, long in front, and she used a sheeny black eyeshadow to bring out the hunger in her eyes. In half an hour she'd have to pick up Tiffany at nursery school, drop off the dog at the veterinarian's, take Sonny's shirt to the cleaner's, buy a pound and a half of thresher shark, cilantro, and flour tortillas at the market, and start the burritos for supper. But now, she was stretching.

She took a deep drag on the cigarette, tugged at her right foot, and brought it up snug against her buttocks. After a moment she released it and drew back her left foot in its place. One palm flat on the floor, her head bobbing vaguely to the beat of the music, she did half a dozen repetitions, then paused to relight her cigarette. It wasn't until she turned over to do her straight-leg lifts that she noticed the dampness in the rug.

Puzzled, she rose to her knees and reached behind her to rub at the twin wet spots on the seat of her sweats. She lifted the corner of the rug, suspecting the dog, but there was no odor of urine. Looking closer, she saw that the concrete floor was a shade darker beneath the rug, as if it were bleeding moisture as it sometimes did in the winter. But this wasn't winter, this was high summer in Los Angeles and it hadn't rained for months. Cursing Sonny—he'd promised her ceramic tile and though she'd run all over town to get the best price on a nice Italian floral pattern, he still hadn't found the time to go look at it—she shot back the sliding door and stepped into the yard to investigate.

Immediately, she felt the Bermuda grass squelch be-

neath the soles of her aerobic shoes. She hadn't taken
three strides—the sun in her face, Queenie yapping frantically from the fenced-in pool area—and her feet were
wet. Had Sonny left the hose running? Or Tiffany? She
slogged across the lawn, the pastel Reeboks spattered
with wet, and checked the hose. It was innocently coiled
on its tender, the tap firmly shut. Queenie's yapping
went up an octave. The heat—it must have been ninety-
five, a hundred—made her feel faint. She gazed up into
the cloudless sky, then bent to check each of the sprinklers in succession.

She was poking around in the welter of bushes along
the fence, looking for an errant sprinkler, when she
thought of the old lady next door—Muriel, wasn't that
her name? What with her husband dying and all, maybe
she'd left the hose running and forgotten all about it.
Meg rose on her tiptoes to peer over the redwood fence
that separated her yard from the neighbors' and found
herself looking into a glistening, sunstruck garden, with
banks of impatiens, bird of paradise, oleander, and lo-
quat, roses in half a dozen shades. The sprinklers were
on and the hose was running. For a long moment Meg
stood there, mesmerized by the play of light through the
drifting fans of water; she was wondering what it would
be like to be old, thinking of how it would be if Sonny
died and Tiffany were grown up and gone. She'd probably forget to turn off the sprinklers too.

The moment passed. The heat was deadening, the dog
hysterical. Meg knew she would have to do something
about the sodden yard and wet floor in the sunroom,
but she dreaded facing the old woman. What would she
say—I'm sorry your husband died but could you turn off
the sprinklers? She was thinking maybe she'd phone—
or wait till Sonny got home and let him handle it—when
she stepped back from the fence and sank to her ankles
in mud.

When the doorbell rang, Muriel was staring absently
at the cover of an old *National Geographic* which lay
beneath a patina of dust on the coffee table. The cover
photo showed the beige and yellow sands of some distant desert, rippled to the horizon with corrugations that
might have been waves on a barren sea. Monty was dead

and buried. She wasn't eating much. Or sleeping much either. The sympathy cards sat unopened on the table in the kitchen, where the tap overflowed the sink and water plunged to the floor with a pertinacity that was like a redemption. When it was quiet—in the early morning or late at night—she could distinguish the separate taps, each with its own voice and rhythm, as they dripped and trickled from the far corners of the house. In those suspended hours she could make out the comforting gurgle of the toilet in the guest room, the musical wash of the tub as water cascaded over the lip of its porcelain dam, the quickening rush of the stream in the hallway as it shot like a miniature Niagara down the chasm of the floor vent ... she could hear the drip in the master bedroom, the distant hiss of a shower, and the sweet eternal sizzle of the sprinklers on the back lawn.

But now she heard the doorbell.

Wearily, gritting her teeth against the pain in her lower legs and the damp lingering aches of her feet, she pushed herself up from the chair and sloshed her way to the door. The carpet was black with water, soaked through like a sponge—and in a tidy corner of her mind she regretted it—but most of the runoff was finding its way to the heating vents and the gaps in the corners where Monty had miscalculated the angle of the baseboard. She heard it dripping somewhere beneath the house and for a moment pictured the water lying dark and still in a shadowy lagoon that held the leaking ship of the house poised on its trembling surface. The doorbell sounded again. "All right, all right," she muttered, "I'm coming."

A girl with dark circles round her eyes stood on the doorstep. She looked vaguely familiar, and for a moment Muriel thought she recognized her from a TV program about a streetwalker who rises up to kill her pimp and liberate all the other leather-clad, black-eyed streetwalkers of the neighborhood, but the the girl spoke and Muriel realized her mistake. "Hi," the girl said, and Muriel saw that her shoes were black with mud, "I'm your neighbor? Meg Terwilliger?"

Muriel was listening to the bathroom sink. She said nothing. The girl looked down at her muddy shoes. "I, uh, just wanted to tell you that we're, uh—Sonny and I,

I mean—he's my husband?—we're sorry about your trouble and all, but I wondered if you knew your sprinklers were on out back?"

Muriel attempted a smile—surely a smile was appropriate at this juncture, wasn't it?—but managed only to lift her upper lip back from her teeth in a sort of wince or grimace.

The girl was noticing the rug now, and Muriel's sodden slippers. She looked baffled, perhaps even a little frightened. And young. So young. Muriel had had a young friend once, a girl from the community college who used to come to the house before Monty got sick. She had a tape recorder, and she would ask them questions about their childhood, about the days when the San Fernando Valley was dirt roads and orange groves. Oral history, she called it. "It's all right," Muriel said, trying to reassure her.

"I just—is it a plumbing problem?" the girl said, backing away from the door. "Sonny . . ." she said, but didn't finish the thought. She ducked her head and retreated down the steps, but when she reached the walk she wheeled around. "I mean you really ought to see about the sprinklers," she blurted, "the whole place is soaked, my sunroom and everything—"

"It's all right," Muriel repeated, and then the girl was gone and she shut the door.

"She's nuts, she is. Really. I mean she's out of her gourd."

Meg was searing chunks of thresher shark in a pan with green chilies, sweet red pepper, onion, and cilantro. Sonny, who was twenty-eight and so intoxicated by real estate he had to forgo the morning paper till he got home at night, was slumped in the breakfast nook with a vodka tonic and the sports pages. His white-blond hair was cut fashionably, in what might once have been called a flattop, though it was thinning, and his open, appealing face, with its boyish look, had begun to show signs of wear, particularly around the eyes, where years of escrow had taken their toll. Tiffany was in her room, playing quietly with a pair of six-inch dolls that had cost sixty-five dollars each.

"Who?" Sonny murmured, tugging unconsciously at the gold chain he wore around his neck.

"Muriel. The old lady next door. Haven't you heard a thing I've been saying?" With an angry snap of her wrist, Meg cut the heat beneath the saucepan and clapped a lid over it. "The floor in the sunroom is flooded, for god's sake," she said, stalking across the kitchen in her bare feet till she stood poised over him. "The rug is ruined. Or almost is. And the yard—"

Sonny slapped the paper down on the table. "All right! Just let me relax a minute, will you?"

She put on her pleading look. It was a look compounded of pouty lips, tousled hair, and those inevitable eyes, and it always had its effect on him. "One minute," she murmured. "That's all it'll take. I just want you to see the backyard."

She took him by the hand and led him through the living room to the sunroom, where he stood a moment contemplating the damp spot on the concrete floor. She was surprised herself at how the spot had grown—it was three times what it had been that afternoon, and it seemed to have sprouted wings and legs like an enormous Rorschach. She pictured a butterfly. Or no, a hovering crow or bat. She wondered what Muriel would have made of it.

Outside, she let out a little yelp of disgust—all the earthworms in the yard had crawled up on the step to die. And the lawn wasn't merely spongy now, it was soaked through, puddled like a swamp. "Jesus Christ," Sonny muttered, sinking in his wingtips. He cakewalked across the yard to where the fence had begun to sag, the post leaning drunkenly, the slats bowed. "Will you look at this?" he shouted over his shoulder. Squeamish about the worms, Meg stood at the door to the sunroom. "The goddam fence is falling down!"

He stood there a moment, water seeping into his shoes, a look of stupefaction on his face. Meg recognized the look. It stole over his features in moments of extremity, as when he tore open the phone bill to discover mysterious twenty-dollar calls to Billings, Montana, and Greenleaf, Mississippi, or when his buyer called on the day escrow was to close to tell him he'd assaulted the seller and wondered if Sonny had five hundred dollars for bail. These occasions always took him by surprise. He was shocked anew each time the crisply surveyed, neatly kept world he so cherished rose up to confront him with all its essential sloppiness, irrationality, and bad business sense. Meg watched the look of disbelief turn to one of injured rage. She followed him through the house, up the walk, and into Muriel's yard, where he stalked up to the front door and pounded like the Gestapo.

There was no response.

"Son of a bitch," he spat, turning to glare over his shoulder at her as if it were her fault or something. From inside they could hear the drama of running water, a drip and gurgle, a sough and hiss. Sonny turned back to the door, hammering his fist against it till Meg swore she could see the panels jump.

It frightened her, this sudden rage. Sure, there was a problem here and she was glad he was taking care of it, but did he have to get violent, did he have to get crazy? "You don't have to beat her door down," she called, focusing on the swell of his shoulder and the hammer of his fist as it rose and fell in savage rhythm. "Sonny, come on. It's only water, for god's sake."

"Only?" he snarled, spinning round to face her. "You saw the fence—next thing you know the foundation'll shift on us. The whole damn house—" he never finished. The look on her face told him that Muriel had opened the door.

Muriel was wearing the same faded blue housecoat she'd had on earlier, and the same wet slippers. Short, heavyset, so big in front it seemed as if she were about to topple over, she clung to the doorframe and peered up at Sonny out of a stony face. Meg watched as Sonny jerked round to confront her and then stopped cold when he got a look at the interior of the house. The plaster walls were stained now, drinking up the wet in long jagged fingers that clawed toward the ceiling, and a dribble of coffee-colored liquid began to seep across the doorstep and puddle at Sonny's feet. The sound of rushing water was unmistakable, even from where Meg was standing. "Yes?" Muriel said, the voice withered in her throat. "Can I help you?"

It took Sonny a minute—Meg could see it in his eyes: this was more than he could handle, willful destruction

of a domicile, every tap in the place on full, the floors
warped, plaster ruined—but then he recovered himself.
"The water," he said. "You—our fence—I mean you
can't, you've got to stop this—"

The old woman drew herself up, clutching the belt of
her housedress till her knuckles bulged with the tension.
She looked first at Meg, still planted in the corner of
the yard, and then turned to Sonny. "Water?" she said.
"What water?"

The young man at the door reminded her, in a way, of
Monty. Something about the eyes or the set of the ears—or
maybe it was the crisp high cut of the sideburns ... Of
course, most young men reminded her of Monty. The
Monty of fifty years ago, that is. The Monty who'd
opened up the world to her over the shift lever of his
Model-A Ford, not the crabbed and abrasive old man
who called her bonehead and dildo and cuffed her like
a dog. Monty. When the stroke brought him down, she
was almost glad. She saw him pinned beneath his tubes
in the hospital and something stirred in her; she brought
him home and changed his bedpan, peered into the
vaults of his eyes, fed him Gerber's like the baby she'd
never had, and she knew it was over. Fifty years. No
more drunken rages, no more pans flung against the
wall, never again his sour flesh pressed to hers. She was
on top now.

The second young man—he was a Mexican, short,
stocky, with a mustache so thin it could have been pen-
ciled on and wicked little red-flecked eyes—almost reminded her of Monty. Not so much in the way he looked
as in the way he held himself, the way he swaggered and
puffed out his chest. And the uniform too, of course.
Monty had worn a uniform during the war.

"Mrs. Burgess?" the Mexican asked.

Muriel stood at the open door. It was dusk, the heat
cut as if there were a thermostat in the sky. She'd been
sitting in the dark. The electricity had gone out on her—
something to do with the water and the wires. She nodded her head in response to the policeman's question.

"We've had a complaint," he said.

Little piggy eyes. A complaint. *We've had a complaint.*
He wasn't fooling her, not for a minute. She knew what

they wanted, the police, the girl next door, and the boy she was married to—they wanted to bring Monty back. Prop him up against the bedframe, stick his legs back under him, put the bellow back in his voice. Oh, no, they weren't fooling her.

She followed the policeman around the darkened house as he went from faucet to faucet, sink to tub to shower. He firmly twisted each of the taps closed and drained the basins, then crossed the patio to kill the sprinklers and the hose too. "Are you all right?" he kept asking. "Are you all right?"

She had to hold her chin in her palm to keep her lips from trembling. "If you mean am I in possession of my faculties, yes, I am, thank you. I am all right."

They were back at the front door now. He leaned nonchalantly against the doorframe and dropped his voice to a confidential whisper. "So what's this with the water then?"

She wouldn't answer him. She knew her rights. What business was it of his, or anybody's, what she did with her own taps and her own sprinklers? She could pay the water bill. Had paid it, in fact. Eleven hundred dollars' worth. She watched his eyes and shrugged.

"Next of kin?" he asked. "Daughter? Son? Anybody we can call?"

Now her lips held. She shook her head.

He gave it a moment, then let out a sigh. "Okay," he said, speaking slowly and with exaggerated emphasis, as if he were talking to a child, "I'm going now. You leave the water alone—wash your face, brush your teeth, do the dishes. But no more of this." He swaggered back from her, fingering his belt, his holster, the dead weight of his nightstick. "One more complaint and we'll have to take you into custody for your own good. You're endangering yourself and the neighbors too. Understand?"

Smile, she told herself, smile. "Oh, yes," she said softly. "Yes, I understand."

He held her eyes a moment, threatening her—just like Monty used to do, just like Monty—and then he was gone.

She stood there on the doorstep a long while, the night deepening around her. She listened to the cow-birds, the wild parakeets that nested in the Murtaughs' palm, the whoosh of traffic from the distant freeway. After a while, she sat on the step. Behind her, the house was silent: no faucet dripped, no sprinkler hissed, no toilet gurgled. It was horrible. Insupportable. In the pit of that dry silence she could hear him, Monty, treading the buckled floors, pouring himself another vodka, cursing her in a voice like sandpaper.

She couldn't go back in there. Not tonight. The place was deadly, contaminated, sick as the grave—after all was said and done, it just wasn't clean enough. If the rest of it was a mystery—oral history, fifty years of Monty, the girl with the blackened eyes—that much she understood.

Meg was watering the cane plant in the living room when the police cruiser came for the old lady next door. The police had been there the night before and Sonny had stood out front with his arms folded while the officer shut down Muriel's taps and sprinklers. "I guess that's that," he said, coming up the walk in the oversized Hawaiian shirt she'd given him for Father's Day. But in the morning, the sprinklers were on again and Sonny called the local substation three times before he left for work. She's crazy, he'd hollered into the phone, irresponsible, a threat to herself and the community. He had a four-year-old daughter to worry about, for christ's sake. A dog. A wife. His fence was falling down. Did they have any idea what that amount of water was going to do to the substrata beneath the house?

Now the police were back. The patrol car stretched across the window and slid silently into the driveway next door. Meg set down the watering can. She was wearing her Fila sweats and a new pair of Nikes and her hair was tied back in a red scarf. She'd dropped Tiffany off at nursery school, but she had the watering and her stretching exercises to do and a pasta salad to make before she picked up Queenie at the vet's. Still, she went directly to the front door and then out onto the walk.

The police—it took her a minute to realize that the shorter of the two was a woman—were on Muriel's front porch, looking stiff and uncertain in their razor-creased uniforms. The man knocked first—once, twice, three times. Nothing happened. Then the woman knocked.

Still nothing. Meg folded her arms and waited. After a minute, the man went around to the side gate and let himself into the yard. Meg heard the sprinklers die with a wheeze, and then the officer was back, his shoes heavy with mud.

Again he thumped at the door, much more violently now, and Meg thought of Sonny. "Open up," the woman called in a breathy contralto she tried unsuccessfully to deepen, "police."

It was then that Meg saw her, Muriel, at the bay window on the near side of the door. "Look," she shouted before she knew what she was saying, "she's there, there in the window!"

The male officer—he had a mustache and pale, fine hair like Sonny's—leaned out over the railing and gestured impatiently at the figure behind the window. "Police," he growled. "Open the door." Muriel never moved. "All right," he grunted, cursing under his breath, "all right," and he put his shoulder to the door. There was nothing to it. The frame splintered, water dribbled out, and both officers disappeared into the house.

Meg waited. She had things to do, yes, but she waited anyway, bending to pull the odd dandelion the gardener had missed, trying to look busy. The police were in there an awful long time—twenty minutes, half an hour—and then the woman appeared in the doorway with Muriel.

Muriel seemed heavier than ever, her face pouchy, arms swollen. She was wearing white sandals on her old splayed feet, a shapeless print dress, and a white straw hat that looked as if it had been dug out of a box in the attic. The woman had her by the arm; the man loomed behind her with a suitcase. Down the steps and up the walk, she never turned her head. But then, just as the policewoman was helping her into the backseat of the patrol car, Muriel swung round as if to take one last look at her house. But it wasn't the house she was looking at: it was Meg.

The morning gave way to the heat of afternoon. Meg finished the watering, made the pasta salad—bow-tie twists, fresh salmon, black olives, and pine nuts—ran her errands, picked up Tiffany, and put her down for a nap. Somehow, though, she just couldn't get Muriel out of her head. The old lady had stared at her for five seconds maybe, and then the policewoman was coaxing her into the car. Meg had felt like sinking into the ground. But then she realized that Muriel's look wasn't vengeful at all—it was just sad. It was a look that said this is what it comes to. Fifty years and this is what it comes to.

The backyard was an inferno, the sun poised directly overhead. Queenie, defleaed, shampooed, and with her toenails clipped, was stretched out asleep in the shade beside the pool. It was quiet. Even the birds were still. Meg took off her Nikes and walked barefoot through the sopping grass to the fence, or what was left of it. The post had buckled overnight, canting the whole business into Muriel's yard. Meg never hesitated. She sprang up onto the plane of the slats and dropped to the grass on the other side.

Her feet sank in the mud, the earth like pudding, like chocolate pudding, and as she lifted her feet to move toward the house the tracks she left behind her slowly filled with water. The patio was an island. She crossed it, dodging potted plants and wicker furniture, and tried the back door; finding it locked, she moved to the window, shaded her face with her hands, and peered in. The sight made her catch her breath. The plaster was crumbling, wallpaper peeling, the rug and floors ruined: she knew it was bad, but this was crazy, this was suicide.

Grief, that's what it was. Or was it? And then she was thinking of Sonny again—what if he was dead and she was old like Muriel? She wouldn't be so fat, of course, but maybe like one of those thin and elegant old ladies in Palm Springs, the ones who'd done their stretching all their lives. Or what if she wasn't an old lady at all— the thought swooped down on her like a bird out of the sky—what if Sonny was in a car wreck or something? It could happen.

She stood there gazing in on the mess through her own wavering reflection. One moment she saw the wreckage of the old lady's life, the next the fine mouth and expressive eyes everyone commented on. After a while, she turned away from the window and looked out on the yard as Muriel must have seen it. There were the roses, gorged with water and flowering madly, the impatiens, rigid as sticks, oleander drowning in their own yellowed leaves—and there, poking innocuously from the bushes at the far corner of the patio, was the steel wand that controlled the sprinklers. Handle, neck, prongs: it was just like theirs.

And then it came to her. She'd turn them on—the sprinklers—just for a minute, to see what it felt like. She wouldn't leave them on long—it could threaten the whole foundation of her house.

That much she understood.

The Only Rose

Sarah Orne Jewett

I.

Just where the village abruptly ended, and the green mowing fields began, stood Mrs. Bickford's house, looking down the road with all its windows, and topped by two prim chimneys that stood up like ears. It was placed with an end to the road, and fronted southward; you could follow a straight path from the gate past the front door and find Mrs. Bickford sitting by the last window of all in the kitchen, unless she were solemnly stepping about, prolonging the stern duties of her solitary housekeeping.

One day in early summer, when almost every one else in Fairfield had put her house plants out of doors, there were still three flower pots on a kitchen window sill. Mrs. Bickford spent but little time over her rose and geranium and Jerusalem cherry-tree, although they had gained a kind of personality born of long association. They rarely undertook to bloom, but had most courageously maintained life in spite of their owner's unsympathetic but conscientious care. Later in the season she would carry them out of doors, and leave them until the time of frosts, under the shade of a great appletree, where they might make the best of what the summer had to give.

The afternoon sun was pouring in, the Jerusalem cherry-tree drooped its leaves in the heat and looked pale, when a neighbor, Miss Pendexter, came in from the next house but one to make a friendly call. As she passed the parlor with its shut blinds, and the sitting-room, also shaded carefully from the light, she wished, as she had done many times before, that somebody beside the owner might have the pleasure of living in and using so good and pleasant a house. Mrs. Bickford always complained of having so much care, even while she

461

valued herself intelligently upon having the right to do
as she pleased with one of the best houses in Fairfield.
Miss Pendexter was a cheerful, even gay little person,
who always brought a pleasant flurry of excitement, and
usually had a genuine though small piece of news to tell,
or some new aspect of already received information.

Mrs. Bickford smiled as she looked up to see this
sprightly neighbor coming. She had no gift at entertaining herself, and was always glad, as one might say, to be
taken off her own hands.

Miss Pendexter smiled back, as if she felt herself to
be equal to the occasion.

"How be you to-day?" the guest asked kindly, as she
entered the kitchen. "Why, what a sight o' flowers, Mis'
Bickford! What be you goin' to do with 'em all?"

Mrs. Bickford wore a grave expression as she glanced
over her spectacles. "My sister's boy fetched 'em over,"
she answered. "You know my sister Parsons's a great
hand to raise flowers, an' this boy takes after her. He
said his mother thought the gardin never looked hand-
somer, and she picked me these to send over. They was
sendin' a team to Westbury for some fertilizer to put on
the land, an' he come with the men, an' stopped to eat
his dinner 'long o' me. He's been growin' fast, and looks
peakëd. I expect sister 'Liza thought the ride, this pleasant day, would do him good. 'Liza sent word for me to
come over and pass some days next week, but it ain't
so that I can."

"Why, it's a pretty time of year to go off and make a
little visit," suggested the neighbor encouragingly.

"I ain't got my sitting-room chamber carpet taken up
yet," sighed Mrs. Bickford. "I do feel condemned. I
might have done it to-day, but 't was all at end when I
saw Tommy coming. There, he's a likely boy, an' so
relished his dinner; I happened to be well prepared. I
don't know but he's my favorite o' that family. Only
I've been sittin' here thinkin', since he went, an' I can't
remember that I ever was so belated with my spring
cleaning."

" 'Twas owin' to the weather," explained Miss Pendexter. "None of us could be so smart as common this
year, not even the lazy ones that always get one room

done the first o' March, and brag of it to others' shame, and then never let on when they do the rest."

The two women laughed together cheerfully. Mrs. Bickford had put up the wide leaf of her large table between the windows and spread out the flowers. She was sorting them slowly into three heaps.

"Why, I do declare if you haven't got a rose in bloom yourself!" exclaimed Miss Pendexter abruptly, as if the bud had not been announced weeks before, and its progress regularly commented upon. "Ain't it a lovely rose? Why, Mis' Bickford!"

"Yes'm, it's out to-day," said Mrs. Bickford, with a somewhat plaintive air. "I'm glad you come in so as to see it."

The bright flower was like a face. Somehow, the beauty and life of it were surprising in the plain room, like a gay little child who might suddenly appear in a doorway. Miss Pendexter forgot herself and her hostess and the tangled mass of garden flowers in looking at the red rose. She even forgot that it was incumbent upon her to carry forward the conversation. Mrs. Bickford was subject to fits of untimely silence which made her friends anxiously sweep the corners of their minds in search of something to say, but any one who looked at her now could easily see that it was not poverty of thought that made her speechless, but an overburdening sense of the inexpressible.

"Goin' to make up all your flowers into bo'quets? I think the short-stemmed kinds is often pretty in a dish," suggested Miss Pendexter compassionately.

"I thought I should make them into three bo'quets. I wish there wa'n't quite so many. Sister Eliza's very lavish with her flowers; she's always been a kind sister, too," said Mrs. Bickford vaguely. She was not apt to speak with so much sentiment, and as her neighbor looked at her narrowly she detected unusual signs of emotion. It suddenly became evident that the three nosegays were connected in her mind with her bereavement of three husbands, and Miss Pendexter's easily roused curiosity was quieted by the discovery that her friend was bent upon a visit to the burying-ground. It was the time of year when she was pretty sure to spend an afternoon there, and sometimes they had taken the walk in company. Miss Pendexter expected to receive the usual invitation, but there was nothing further said at the moment, and she looked again at the pretty rose.

Mrs. Bickford aimlessly handled the syringas and flowering almond sprays, choosing them out of the fragrant heap only to lay them down again. She glanced out of the window; then gave Miss Pendexter a long expressive look.

"I expect you're going to carry 'em over to the burying-ground?" inquired the guest, in a sympathetic tone.

"Yes 'm," said the hostess, now well started in conversation and in quite her every-day manner. "You see I was goin' over to my brother's folks to-morrow in South Fairfield, to pass the day; they said they were goin' to send over to-morrow to leave a wagon at the blacksmith's, and they'd hitch that to their best chaise, so I could ride back very comfortable. You know I have to avoid bein' out in the mornin' sun?"

Miss Pendexter smiled to herself at this moment; she was obliged to move from her chair at the window, the May sun was so hot on her back, for Mrs. Bickford always kept the curtains rolled high up, out of the way, for fear of fading and dust. The kitchen was a blaze of light. As for the Sunday chaise being sent, it was well known that Mrs. Bickford's married brothers and sisters comprehended the truth that she was a woman of property, and had neither chick nor child.

"So I thought 't was a good opportunity to just stop an' see if the lot was in good order,—last spring Mr. Wallis's stone hove with the frost; an' so I could take these flowers." She gave a sigh. "I ain't one that can bear flowers in a close room,—they bring on a headache; but I enjoy 'em as much as anybody to look at, only you never know what to put 'em in. If I could be out in the mornin' sun, as some do, and keep flowers in the house, I should have me a gardin, certain," and she sighed again.

"A garden's a sight o' care, but I don't begrudge none o' the care I give to mine. I have to scant on flowers so's to make room for pole beans," said Miss Pendexter gayly. She had only a tiny strip of land behind her house, but she always had something to give away, and made riches out of her narrow poverty. "A few flowers gives me just as much pleasure as more would," she added. "You get acquainted with things when you've only got one or two roots. My sweet-williams is just like folks."

"Mr. Bickford was partial to sweet-williams," said Mrs. Bickford. "I never knew him to take notice of no other sort of flowers. When we'd be over to Eliza's, he'd walk down her gardin, an' he'd never make no comments until he come to them, and then he'd say, 'Those is sweet-williams.' How many times I've heard him!"

"You ought to have a sprig of 'em for his bo'quet," suggested Miss Pendexter.

"Yes, I've put a sprig in," said her companion.

At this moment Miss Pendexter took a good look at the bouquets, and found that they were as nearly alike as careful hands could make them. Mrs. Bickford was evidently trying to reach absolute impartiality.

"I don't know but you think it's foolish to tie 'em up this afternoon," she said presently, as she wound the first with a stout string. "I thought I could put 'em in a bucket o' water out in the shed, where there's a draught o' air, and then I should have all my time in the morning. I shall have a good deal to do before I go. I always sweep the setting-room and front entry Wednesdays. I want to leave everything nice, goin' away for all day so. So I meant to get the flowers out o' the way this afternoon. Why, it's most half past four, ain't it? But I sha'n't pick the rose till mornin'; 't will be blowed out better then."

"The rose?" questioned Miss Pendexter. "Why, are you goin' to pick that, too?"

"Yes, I be. I never like to let 'em fade on the bush. There, that's just what's a-troublin' me," and she turned to give a long, imploring look at the friend who sat beside her. Miss Pendexter had moved her chair before the table in order to be out of the way of the sun. "I don't seem to know which of 'em ought to have it," said Mrs. Bickford despondently. "I do so hate to make a choice between 'em; they all had their good points, especially Mr. Bickford, and I respected 'em all. I don't know but what I think of one on 'em 'most as much as I do of the other."

"Why, 't is difficult for you, ain't it?" responded Miss Pendexter. "I don't know 's I can offer advice."

"No, I s'pose not," answered her friend slowly, with a shadow of disappointment coming over her calm face. "I feel sure you would if you could, Abby."

Both of the women felt as if they were powerless before a great emergency.

"There's one thing,—they're all in a better world now," said Miss Pendexter, in a self-conscious and constrained voice; "they can't feel such little things or take note o' slights same 's we can."

"No; I suppose 't is myself that wants to be just," answered Mrs. Bickford. "I feel under obligations to my last husband when I look about and see how comfortable he left me. Poor Mr. Wallis had his great projects, an' perhaps if he'd lived longer he'd have made a record; but when he died he'd failed all up, owing to that patent cornsheller he'd put everything into, and, as you know, I had to get along 'most any way I could for the next few years. Life was very disappointing with Mr. Wallis, but he meant well, an' used to be an amiable person to dwell with, until his temper got spoilt makin' so many hopes an' havin' 'em turn out failures. He had consider'ble of an air, an' dressed very handsome when I was first acquainted with him, Mr. Wallis did. I don't know's you ever knew Mr. Wallis in his prime?"

"He died the year I moved over here from North Denfield," said Miss Pendexter, in a tone of sympathy. "I just knew him by sight. I was to his funeral. You know you lived in what we call the Wells house then, and I felt it wouldn't be an intrusion, we was such near neighbors. The first time I ever was in your house was just before that, when he was sick, an' Mary 'Becca Wade an' I called to see if there was anything we could do."

"They used to say about town that Mr. Wallis went to an' fro like a mail-coach an' brought nothin' to pass," announced Mrs. Bickford without bitterness. "He ought to have had a better chance than he did in this little neighborhood. You see, he had excellent ideas, but he never'd learned the machinist's trade, and there was somethin' the matter with every model he contrived. I used to be real narrow-minded when he talked about moving 'way up to Lowell, or some o' them places; I hated to think of leaving my folks; and now I see that I never done right by him. His ideas was good. I know once he was on a jury, and there was a man stopping to the tavern where he was, near the court house, a man that traveled for a firm to Lowell; and they engaged in talk, an' Mr. Wallis let out some o' his notions an' contrivances, an' he said that man wouldn't hardly stop to eat, he was so interested, an' said he'd look for a chance for him up to Lowell. It all sounded so well that I kind of begun to think about goin' myself. Mr. Wallis said we'd close the house here, and go an' board through the winter. But he never heard a word from him, and the disappointment was one he never got over. I think of it now different from what I did then. I often used to be kind of disapproving to Mr. Wallis; but there, he used to be always tellin' over his great projects. Somebody told me once that a man by the same name of the one he met while he was to court had got some patents for the very things Mr. Wallis used to be workin' over; but 't was after he died, an' I don't know's 't was in him to ever really set things up so other folks could ha' seen their value. His machines always used to work kind of rickety, but folks used to come from all round to see 'em; they was curiosities if they wa'n't nothin' else, an' gave him a name."

Mrs. Bickford paused a moment, with some geranium leaves in her hand, and seemed to suppress with difficulty a desire to speak even more freely.

"He was a dreadful notional man," she said at last, regretfully, and as if this fact were a poor substitute for what had just been in her mind. "I recollect one time he worked all through the early winter over my churn, an' got it so it would go three quarters of an hour all of itself if you wound it up; an' if you 'll believe it, he went an' spent all that time for nothin' when the cow was dry, an' we was with difficulty borrowin' a pint o' milk a day somewheres in the neighborhood just to get along with." Mrs. Bickford flushed with displeasure, and turned to look at her visitor. "Now what do you think of such a man as that, Miss Pendexter?" she asked.

"Why, I don't know but 't was just as good for an invention," answered Miss Pendexter timidly; but her friend looked doubtful, and did not appear to understand.

"Then I asked him where it was, one day that spring

when I'd got tired to death churnin', an' the butter wouldn't come in a churn I'd had to borrow, and he'd gone an' took ours all to pieces to get the works to make some other useless contrivance with. He had no sort of a business turn, but he was well meanin', Mr. Wallis was, an' full o' divertin' talk; they used to call him very good company. I see now that he never had no proper chance. I've always regretted Mr. Wallis," said she who was now the widow Bickford.

"I'm sure you always speak well of him," said Miss Pendexter. "'T was a pity he hadn't got among good business men, who could push his inventions an' do all the business part."

"I was left very poor an' needy for them next few years," said Mrs. Bickford mournfully; "but he never'd give up but what he should die worth his fifty thousand dollars. I don't see now how I ever did get along them next few years without him; but there, I always managed to keep a pig, an' sister Eliza gave me my potatoes, and I made out somehow. I could dig me a few greens, you know, in spring, and then 't would come strawberry-time, and other berries a-followin' on. I was always decent to go to meetin' till within the last six months, an' then I went in bad weather, when folks wouldn't notice; but 't was a rainy summer, an' I managed to get considerable preachin' after all. My clothes looked proper enough when 't was a wet Sabbath. I often think o' them pinched days now, when I'm left so comfortable by Mr. Bickford."

"Yes'm, you've everything to be thankful for," said Miss Pendexter, who was as poor herself at that moment as her friend had ever been, and who could never dream of venturing upon the support and companionship of a pig. "Mr. Bickford was a very personable man," she hastened to say, the confidences were so intimate and interesting.

"Oh, very," replied Mrs. Bickford; "there was something about him that was very marked. Strangers would always ask who he was as he come into meetin'. His words counted; he never spoke except he had to. 'T was a relief at first after Mr. Wallis's being so fluent; but Mr. Wallis was splendid company for winter evenings,— 'twould be eight o'clock before you knew it. I didn't use to listen to it all, but he had a great deal of information. Mr. Bickford was dreadful dignified; I used to be sort of meechin' with him along at the first, for fear he'd disapprove of me; but I found out 't wa'n't no need; he was always just that way, an' done everything by rule an' measure. He hadn't the mind of my other husbands, but he was a very dignified appearing man; he used 'most always to sleep in the evenin's, Mr. Bickford did."

"Them is lovely bo'quets, certain!" exclaimed Miss Pendexter. "Why, I couldn't tell 'em apart; the flowers are comin' out just right, aren't they?"

Mrs. Bickford nodded assent, and then, startled by sudden recollection, she cast a quick glance at the rose in the window.

"I always seem to forget about your first husband, Mr. Fraley," Miss Pendexter suggested bravely. "I've often heard you speak of him, too, but he'd passed away long before I ever knew you."

"He was but a boy," said Mrs. Bickford. "I thought the world was done for me when he died, but I've often thought since 't was a mercy for him. He come of a very melancholy family, and all his brothers an' sisters enjoyed poor health; it might have been his lot. Folks said we was as pretty a couple as ever come into church; we was both dark, with black eyes an' a good deal o' color,—you wouldn't expect it to see me now. Albert was one that held up his head, and looked as if he meant to own the town, an' he had a good word for everybody. I don't know what the years might have brought."

There was a long pause. Mrs. Bickford leaned over to pick up a heavy-headed Guelder-rose that had dropped on the floor.

"I expect 't was what they call fallin' in love," she added, in a different tone; "he wa'n't nothin' but a boy, an' I wa'n't nothin' but a girl, but we was dreadful happy. He didn't favor his folks,—they all had hay-colored hair and was faded-looking, except his mother; they was alike, and looked alike, an' set everything by each other. He was just the kind of strong, hearty young man that goes right off if they get a fever. We was just settled on a little farm, an' he'd have done well if he'd had time; as it was, he left debts. He had a hasty temper, that was his great fault, but Albert had a lovely voice to

sing; they said there wa'n't no such tenor voice in this
part o' the State. I could hear him singin' to himself
right out in the field a-ploughin' or hoein', an' he didn't
know it half o' the time, no more 'n a common bird
would. I don't know's I valued his gift as I ought to, but
there was nothin' ever sounded so sweet to me. I ain't
one that ever had much fancy, but I knowed Albert had
a pretty voice."

Mrs. Bickford's own voice trembled a little, but she
held up the last bouquet and examined it critically. "I
must hurry now an' put these in water," she said, in a
matter of fact tone. Little Miss Pendexter was so quiet
and sympathetic that her hostess felt no more embarrassed than if she had been talking only to herself.

"Yes, they do seem to droop some; 't is a little warm
for them here in the sun," said Miss Pendexter; "but
you'll find they'll all come up if you give them their fill
o' water. They'll look very handsome to-morrow; folks'll
notice them from the road. You've arranged them very
tasty, Mis' Bickford."

"They do look pretty, don't they?" Mrs. Bickford regarded the three in turn. "I want to have them all pretty.
You may deem it strange, Abby."

"Why, no, Mis' Bickford," said the guest sincerely,
although a little perplexed by the solemnity of the occasion. "I know how 'tis with friends,—that having one
don't keep you from wantin' another; 't is just like havin'
somethin' to eat, and then wantin' somethin' to drink
just the same. I expect all friends find their places."

But Mrs. Bickford was not interested in this figure,
and still looked vague and anxious as she began to brush
the broken stems and wilted leaves into her wide calico
apron. "I done the best I could while they was alive,"
she said, "and mourned 'em when I lost 'em, an' I feel
grateful to be left so comfortable now when all is over.
It seems foolish, but I'm still at a loss about that rose."

"Perhaps you'll feel sure when you first wake up in the
morning," answered Miss Pendexter solicitously. "It's a
case where I don't deem myself qualified to offer you
any advice. But I'll say one thing, seeing's you've been
so friendly spoken and confiding with me. I never was
married myself, Mis' Bickford, because it wa'n't so that
I could have the one I liked."

"I suppose he ain't livin', then? Why, I wan't never aware you had met with a disappointment, Abby," said Mrs. Bickford instantly. None of her neighbors had ever suspected little Miss Pendexter of a romance.

"Yes'm, he's livin'," replied Miss Pendexter humbly. "No'm, I never have heard that he died."

"I want to know!" exclaimed the woman of experience. "Well, I'll tell you this, Abby: you may have regretted your lot, and felt lonesome and hardshipped, but they all have their faults, and a single woman's got her liberty, if she ain't got other blessin's."

" 'T wouldn't have been my choice to live alone," said Abby, meeker than before. "I feel very thankful for my blessin's, all the same. You've always been a kind neighbor, Mis' Bickford."

"Why can't you stop to tea?" asked the elder woman, with unusual cordiality; but Miss Pendexter remembered that her hostess often expressed a dislike for unexpected company, and promptly took her departure after she had risen to go, glancing up at the bright flower as she passed outside the window. It seemed to belong most to Albert, but she had not liked to say so. The sun was low; the green fields stretched away southward into the misty distance.

II.

Mrs. Bickford's house appeared to watch her out of sight down the road, the next morning. She had lost all spirit for her holiday. Perhaps it was the unusual excitement of the afternoon's reminiscences, or it might have been simply the bright moonlight night which had kept her broad awake until dawn, thinking of the past, and more and more concerned about the rose. By this time it had ceased to be merely a flower, and had become a definite symbol and assertion of personal choice. She found it very difficult to decide. So much of her present comfort and well-being was due to Mr. Bickford; still, it was Mr. Wallis who had been most unfortunate, and to whom she had done least justice. If she owed recognition to Mr. Bickford, she certainly owed amends to Mr. Wallis. If she gave him the rose, it would be for the sake of affectionate apology. And then there was Albert, to whom she had no thought of being either indebted or forgiving. But she could not escape from the terrible feeling of indecision.

It was a beautiful morning for a drive, but Mrs. Bickford was kept waiting some time for the chaise. Her nephew, who was to be her escort, had found much social advantage at the blacksmith's shop, so that it was after ten when she finally started with the three large flat-backed bouquets, covered with a newspaper to protect them from the sun. The petals of the almond flowers were beginning to scatter, and now and then little streams of water leaked out of the newspaper and trickled down the steep slope of her best dress to the bottom of the chaise. Even yet she had not made up her mind; she had stopped trying to deal with such an evasive thing as decision, and leaned back and rested as best she could.

"What an old fool I be!" she rebuked herself from time to time, in so loud a whisper that her companion ventured a respectful "What, ma'am?" and was astonished that she made no reply. John was a handsome young man, but Mrs. Bickford could never cease thinking of him as a boy. He had always been her favorite among the younger members of the family, and now returned this affectionate feeling, being possessed of an instinctive confidence in the sincerities of his prosaic aunt.

As they drove along, there had seemed at first to be something unsympathetic and garish about the beauty of the summer day. After the shade and shelter of the house, Mrs. Bickford suffered even more from a contracted and assailed feeling out of doors. The very trees by the roadside had a curiously fateful, trying way of standing back to watch her, as she passed in the acute agony of indecision, and she was annoyed and startled by a bird that flew too near the chaise in a moment of surprise. She was conscious of a strange reluctance to the movement of the Sunday chaise, as if she were being conveyed against her will; but the companionship of her nephew John grew every moment to be more and more a reliance. It was very comfortable to sit by his side, even though he had nothing to say; he was manly and cheerful, and she began to feel protected.

"Aunt Bickford," he suddenly announced, "I may's well out with it! I've got a piece o' news to tell you, if you won't let on to nobody. I expect you'll laugh, but you know I've set everything by Mary Lizzie Gifford ever since I was a boy. Well, sir!"

"Well, sir!" exclaimed Aunt Bickford in her turn, quickly roused into most comfortable self-forgetfulness. "I am really pleased. She'll make you a good, smart wife, John. Ain't all the folks pleased, both sides?"

"Yes, they be," answered John soberly, with a happy, important look that became him well.

"I guess I can make out to do something for you to help along, when the right time comes," said Aunt Bickford impulsively, after a moment's reflection. "I've known what it is to be starting out in life with plenty o' hope. You ain't calculatin' on gettin' married before fall,—or be ye?"

"'Long in the fall," said John regretfully. "I wish t' we could set up for ourselves right away this summer. I ain't got much ahead, but I can work well as anybody, an' now I'm out o' my time."

"She 's a nice, modest, pretty girl. I thought she liked you, John," said the old aunt. "I saw her over to your mother's, last day I was there. Well, I expect you'll be happy."

"Certain," said John, turning to look at her affectionately, surprised by this outspokenness and lack of embarrassment between them. "Thank you, aunt," he said simply; "you're a real good friend to me;" and he looked away again hastily, and blushed a fine scarlet over his sun-browned face. "She's coming over to spend the day with the girls," he added. "Mother thought of it. You don't get over to see us very often."

Mrs. Bickford smiled approvingly. John's mother looked for her good opinion, no doubt, but it was very proper for John to have told his prospects himself, and in such a pretty way. There was no shilly-shallying about the boy.

"My gracious!" said John suddenly. "I'd like to have drove right by the burying-ground. I forgot we wanted to stop."

Strange as it may appear, Mrs. Bickford herself had not noticed the burying-ground, either, in her excitement and pleasure; now she felt distressed and responsible again, and showed it in her face at once. The young man leaped lightly to the ground, and reached for the flowers.

"Here, you just let me run up with 'em," he said kindly. " 'T is hot in the sun to-day, an' you'll mind it risin' the hill. We'll stop as I fetch you back to-night, and you can go up comfortable an' walk the yard after sundown when it's cool, an' stay as long as you're a mind to. You seem sort of tired, aunt."

"I don't know but what I will let you carry 'em," said Mrs. Bickford slowly.

To leave the matter of the rose in the hands of fate seemed weakness and cowardice, but there was not a moment for consideration. John was a smiling fate, and his proposition was a great relief. She watched him go away with a terrible inward shaking, and sinking of pride. She had held the flowers with so firm a grasp that her hands felt weak and numb, and as she leaned back and shut her eyes she was afraid to open them again at first for fear of knowing the bouquets apart even at that distance, and giving instructions which she might regret. With a sudden impulse she called John once or twice eagerly; but her voice had a thin and piping sound, and the meditative early crickets that chirped in the fresh summer grass probably sounded louder in John's ears. The bright light on the white stones dazzled Mrs. Bickford's eyes; and then all at once she felt light-hearted, and the sky seemed to lift itself higher and wider from the earth, and she gave a sigh of relief as her messenger came back along the path. "I know who I do hope's got the right one," she said to herself. "There, what a touse I be in! I don't see what I had to go and pick the old rose for, anyway."

"I declare, they did look real handsome, aunt," said John's hearty voice as he approached the chaise. "I set 'em up just as you told me. This one fell out, an' I kept it. I don't know's you'll care. I can give it to Lizzie."

He faced her now with a bright, boyish look. There was something gay in his buttonhole,—it was the red rose.

Aunt Bickford blushed like a girl. "Your choice is easy made," she faltered mysteriously, and then burst out laughing, there in front of the burying-ground. "Come, get right in, dear," she said. "Well, well! I guess the rose was made for you; it looks very pretty in your coat, John."

She thought of Albert, and the next moment the tears came into her old eyes. John was a lover, too.

"My first husband was just such a tall, straight young man as you be," she said as they drove along. "The flower he first give me was a rose."

Strong Horse Tea

Alice Walker

Rannie Toomer's little baby boy Snooks was dying from double pneumonia and whooping cough. She sat away from him, gazing into the low fire, her long crusty bottom lip hanging. She was not married. Was not pretty. Was not anybody much. And he was all she had.

"Lawd, why don't that doctor come on here?" she moaned, tears sliding from her sticky eyes. She had not washed since Snooks took sick five days ago and a long row of whitish snail tracks laced her ashen face.

"What you ought to try is some of the old home remedies," Sarah urged. She was an old neighboring lady who wore magic leaves round her neck sewed up in possumskin next to a dried lizard's foot. She knew how magic came about, and could do magic herself, people said.

"We going to have us a doctor," Rannie Toomer said fiercely, walking over to shoo a fat winter fly from her child's forehead. "I don't believe in none of that swamp magic. All the old home remedies I took when I was a child come just short of killing me."

Snooks, under a pile of faded quilts, made a small gravelike mound in the bed. His head was like a ball of black putty wedged between the thin covers and the dingy yellow pillow. His little eyes were partly open, as if he were peeping out of his hard wasted skull at the chilly room, and the forceful pulse of his breathing caused a faint rustling in the sheets near his mouth like the wind pushing damp papers in a shallow ditch.

"What time you reckon that doctor'll git here?" asked Sarah, not expecting Rannie Toomer to answer her. She sat with her knees wide apart under many aprons and long dark skirts heavy with stains. From time to time she reached long cracked fingers down to sweep her damp skirts away from the live coals. It was almost spring, but the winter cold still clung to her bones and she had to almost sit in the fireplace to be warm. Her deep sharp eyes set in the rough leather of her face had aged a moist hesitant blue that gave her a quick dull stare like a hawk's. Now she gazed coolly at Rannie Toomer and rapped the hearthstones with her stick.

"White mailman, white doctor," she chanted skeptically, under her breath, as if to banish spirits.

"They gotta come see 'bout this baby," Rannie Toomer said wistfully. "Who'd go and ignore a little sick baby like my Snooks?"

"Some folks we don't know so well as we thinks we do might," the old lady replied. "What you want to give that boy of yours is one or two of the old home remedies; arrowsroot or sassyfras and cloves, or a sugar tit soaked in cat's blood."

Rannie Toomer's face went tight.

"We don't need none of your witch's remedies," she cried, grasping her baby by his shrouded toes, trying to knead life into him as she kneaded limberness into flour dough.

"We going to git some of them shots that makes peoples well, cures 'em of all they ails, cleans 'em out and makes 'em strong all at the same time."

She spoke upward from her son's feet as if he were an altar. "Doctor'll be here soon, baby," she whispered to him, then rose to look out the grimy window. "I done sent the mailman." She rubbed her face against the glass, her flat nose more flattened as she peered out into the rain.

"Howdy, Rannie Mae," the red-faced mailman had said pleasantly as he always did when she stood by the car waiting to ask him something. Usually she wanted to ask what certain circulars meant that showed pretty pictures of things she needed. Did the circulars mean that somebody was coming around later and would give her hats and suitcases and shoes and sweaters and rubbing alcohol and a heater for the house and a fur bonnet for her baby? Or, why did he always give her the pictures if she couldn't have what was in them? Or, what

did the words say ... especially the big word written in
red: "S-A-L-E!"?

He would explain shortly to her that the only way she
could get the goods pictured on the circulars was to buy
them in town and that town stores did their advertising
by sending out pictures of their goods. She would listen
with her mouth hanging open until he finished. Then she
would exclaim in a dull amazed way that *she* never *had*
any money and he could ask anybody. *She* couldn't ever
buy any of the things in the pictures—so why did the
stores keep sending them to her?

He tried to explain to her that *everybody* got the circulars, whether they had any money to buy with or not.
That this was one of the laws of advertising and he could
do nothing about it. He was sure she never understood
what he tried to teach her about advertising, for one day
she asked him for any extra circulars he had and when
he asked what she wanted them for—since she couldn't
afford to buy any of the items advertised—she said she
needed them to paper the inside of her house to keep
out the wind.

Today he thought she looked more ignorant than
usual as she stuck her dripping head inside his car. He
recoiled from her breath and gave little attention to what
she was saying about her sick baby as he mopped up the
water she dripped on the plastic door handle of the car.

"Well, never *can* keep 'em dry, I mean *warm* enough,
in rainy weather like this here," he mumbled absently,
stuffing a wad of circulars advertising hair driers and
cold creams into her hands. He wished she would stand
back from his car so he could get going. But she clung
to the side gabbing away about "Snooks" and "NEW-
monia" and "shots" and how she wanted a "REAL
doctor."

"That right?" he injected sympathetically from time
to time, and from time to time he sneezed, for she was
letting in wetness and damp, and he felt he was coming
down with a cold. Black people as black as Rannie Mae
always made him uneasy, especially when they didn't
smell good, and when you could tell they didn't right
away. Rannie Mae, leaning in over him out of the rain,
smelt like a wet goat. Her dark dirty eyes clinging to his
face with such hungry desperation made him nervous.

Why did colored folks always want you to do something for them?

Now he cleared his throat and made a motion forward as if to roll up his window. "Well, ah, *mighty* sorry to hear 'bout that little fella," he said, groping for the window crank. "We'll see what we can do!" He gave her what he hoped was a big friendly smile. God! He didn't want to hurt her feelings! She looked so pitiful hanging there in the rain. Suddenly he had an idea.

"Whyn't you try some of old Aunt Sarah's home remedies?" he suggested brightly, still smiling. He half believed with everybody else in the county that the old blue-eyed black woman possessed magic. Magic that if it didn't work on whites probably would on blacks. But Rannie Mae almost turned the car over shaking her head and body with an emphatic "NO!" She reached in a wet crusted hand to grasp his shoulder.

"We wants a doctor, a real doctor!" she screamed. She had begun to cry and drop her tears on him. "You git us a doctor from town," she bellowed, shaking the solid shoulder that bulged under his new tweed coat.

"Like I say," he drawled lamely although beginning to be furious with her, "we'll do what we can!" And he hurriedly rolled up the window and sped down the road, cringing from the thought that she had put her hands on him.

"Old home remedies! Old home remedies!" Rannie Toomer cursed the words while she licked at the hot tears that ran down her face, the only warmth about her. She turned back to the trail that led to her house, trampling the wet circulars under her feet. Under the fence she went and was in a pasture, surrounded by dozens of fat white folks' cows and an old gray horse and a mule or two. Animals lived there in the pasture all around her house, and she and Snooks lived in it.

It was less than an hour after she had talked to the mailman that she looked up expecting the doctor and saw old Sarah tramping through the grass on her walking stick. She couldn't pretend she wasn't home with the smoke climbing out the chimney, so she let her in, making her leave her bag of tricks on the front porch.

Old woman old as that ought to forgit trying to cure other people with her nigger magic . . . ought to use some of it on herself, she thought. She would not let her lay a finger on Snooks and warned her if she tried she would knock her over the head with her own cane.

"He coming all right," Rannie Toomer said firmly, looking, straining her eyes to see through the rain.

"Let me tell you, child," the old woman said almost gently, "he ain't." She was sipping something hot from a dish. When would this one know, she wondered, that she could only depend on those who would come.

"But I *told* you," Rannie Toomer said in exasperation, as if explaining something to a backward child. "I asked the mailman to bring a doctor for my Snooks!"

Cold wind was shooting all around her from the cracks in the window framing, faded circulars blew inward from the walls. The old woman's gloomy prediction made her tremble.

"He done fetched the doctor," Sarah said, rubbing her dish with her hand. "What you reckon brung me over here in this here flood? Wasn't no desire to see no rainbows, I can tell you."

Rannie Toomer paled.

"I's the doctor, child." Sarah turned to Rannie with dull wise eyes. "That there mailman didn't git no further with that message than the road in front of my house. Lucky he got good lungs—deef as I is I had myself a time trying to make out what he was yellin'."

Rannie began to cry, moaning.

Suddenly the breathing of Snooks from the bed seemed to drown out the noise of the downpour outside. Rannie Toomer could feel his pulse making the whole house tremble.

"Here," she cried, snatching up the baby and handing him to Sarah. "Make him well. *O my lawd*, make him well!"

Sarah rose from her seat by the fire and took the tiny baby, already turning a purplish blue around the eyes and mouth.

"Let's not upset this little fella unnessarylike," she said, placing the baby back on the bed. Gently she began to examine him, all the while moaning and humming some thin pagan tune that pushed against the sound of the wind and rain with its own melancholy power. She stripped him of all his clothes, poked at his fibreless baby ribs, blew against his chest. Along his tiny flat back she ran her soft old fingers. The child hung on in deep rasping sleep, and his small glazed eyes neither opened fully nor fully closed.

Rannie Toomer swayed over the bed watching the old woman touching the baby. She thought of the time she had wasted waiting for the real doctor. Her feeling of guilt was a stone.

"I'll do anything you say do, Aunt Sarah," she cried, mopping at her nose with her dress. "Anything. Just, please God, make him git better!"

Old Sarah dressed the baby again and sat down in front of the fire. She stayed deep in thought for several moments. Rannie Toomer gazed first into her silent face and then at the baby, whose breathing seemed to have eased since Sarah picked him up.

Do something quick, she urged Sarah in her mind, wanting to believe in her powers completely. Do something that'll make him rise up and call his mama!

"The child's dying," said Sarah bluntly, staking out beforehand some limitation to her skill. "But there still might be something we can do. . . ."

"What, Aunt Sarah, what?" Rannie Toomer was on her knees before the old woman's chair, wringing her hands and crying. She fastened hungry eyes on Sarah's lips.

"What can I *do*?" she urged fiercely, hearing the faint labored breathing from the bed.

"It's going to take a strong stomach," said Sarah slowly. "A *mighty* strong stomach. And most you young peoples these days don't have 'em."

"Snooks got a strong stomach," said Rannie Toomer, looking anxiously into the old serious face.

"It ain't him that's got to have the strong stomach," Sarah said, glancing down at Rannie Toomer. "*You* the one got to have a strong stomach . . . he won't know *what* it is he's drinking."

Rannie Toomer began to tremble way down deep in her stomach. It sure was weak, she thought. Trembling like that. But what could she mean her Snooks to drink? Not cat's blood—! And not some of the messes with bat's wings she'd heard Sarah mixed for people sick in the head? . . .

"What is it?" she whispered, bringing her head close to Sarah's knee. Sarah leaned down and put her toothless mouth to her ear.

"The only thing that can save this child now is some good strong horse tea," she said, keeping her eyes on the girl's face. "The *only* thing. And if you wants him out of that bed you better make tracks to git some."

Rannie Toomer took up her wet coat and stepped across the porch into the pasture. The rain fell against her face with the force of small hailstones. She started walking in the direction of the trees where she could see the bulky lightish shapes of cows. Her thin plastic shoes were sucked at by the mud, but she pushed herself forward in search of the lone gray mare.

All the animals shifted ground and rolled big dark eyes at Rannie Toomer. She made as little noise as she could and leaned against a tree to wait.

Thunder rose from the side of the sky like tires of a big truck rumbling over rough dirt road. Then it stood a split second in the middle of the sky before it exploded like a giant firecracker, then rolled away again like an empty keg. Lightning streaked across the sky, setting the air white and charged.

Rannie Toomer stood dripping under her tree, hoping not to be struck. She kept her eyes carefully on the behind of the gray mare, who, after nearly an hour, began nonchalantly to spread her muddy knees.

At that moment Rannie Toomer realized that she had brought nothing to catch the precious tea in. Lightning struck something not far off and caused a crackling and groaning in the woods that frightened the animals away from their shelter. Rannie Toomer slipped down in the mud trying to take off one of her plastic shoes to catch the tea. And the gray mare, trickling some, broke for a clump of cedars yards away.

Rannie Toomer was close enough to catch the tea if she could keep up with the mare while she ran. So alternately holding her breath and gasping for air she started after her. Mud from her fall clung to her elbows and streaked her frizzy hair. Slipping and sliding in the mud she raced after the mare, holding out, as if for alms, her plastic shoe.

In the house Sarah sat, her shawls and sweaters tight around her, rubbing her knees and muttering under her breath. She heard the thunder, saw the lightning that lit up the dingy room and turned her waiting face to the bed. Hobbling over on stiff legs she could hear no sound; the frail breathing had stopped with the thunder, not to come again.

Across the mud-washed pasture Rannie Toomer stumbled, holding out her plastic shoe for the gray mare to fill. In spurts and splashes mixed with rainwater she gathered her tea. In parting, the old mare snorted and threw up one big leg, knocking her back into the mud. She rose, trembling and crying, holding the shoe, spilling none over the top but realizing a leak, a tiny crack at her shoe's front. Quickly she stuck her mouth there, over the crack, and ankle deep in the slippery mud of the pasture and freezing in her shabby wet coat, she ran home to give the still warm horse tea to her baby Snooks.

Uglypuss

Margaret Atwood

Joel hates November. As far as he's concerned they could drop it down the chute and he wouldn't complain. Drizzle and chill, everyone depressed, and then the winter to go through afterwards. The landlord has turned down the heat again, which means Joel has to either let his buns solidify and break off or use the electric heater, which means more money, because the electricity's extra. The landlord does this to spite him, Joel, personally. Just for that, Joel refuses to move. He tells other people he likes the building, which he does: it's a golden oldie, a mansion that's seen better days, with an arched entrance-way and stained glass. But also he won't give the old rent-gouger the satisfaction. Becka could handle him, when she was still living here. All she'd had to do was lean over the banister while the old bugger was standing below, and use her good voice, the furry one, and up went the temperature; a trick that's not possible for Joel.

He'd like to be someplace warm, but who can afford it? Too bad they made grants taxable, not that he's likely to get another one the ways things are going.

Things are not going too well. He's beginning to think street theatre should stay in California: up here you can only do it three months of the year, and some of that is too hot, they steam inside those outsize masks. Even directing is no picnic. Last summer he got a sunburn, on the top of his head, where he's beginning to go bald. It was right after this that Becka caught him in the bathroom, standing with his back to the mirror, looking at his head from behind with a plastic violet-framed hand mirror, hers. She wouldn't let up on that for weeks. "Checked out your manly beauty this morning?" "Thought about Hair-Weeve?" "You'd look cute as a

blonde. It would go with the skull." "Chest wigs yet?"
"You could cut off some of your beard and glue it on
the top, right?" Maybe he had it coming; he remembered getting onto her about spending twenty-five dollars at the hairdresser's once, soon after she'd moved in
with him. It was her twenty-five dollars, but they were
supposed to be sharing expenses. He'd called it an indulgence. She remembered that he remembered, of course.
She has a memory like a rat-trap: full of rats.

Joel's fingers are cold. The apartment is like a football
game in the rain. He puts down the black Bic ball-point
with which he hasn't written anything for the past half
hour, stretches, scratches his head. He recalls, for an
instant and with irritation, the Italian calligraphy pen
Becka affected for a while: an affectation that has gone
the way of all the others. Then he turns back to square
one.

The piece they're working on is for two weeks from
now: the Crucifixion according to Solemate Sox, with
management as Judas. They're going to do it right beside
the picket lines, which will cheer the picketers up, or
that was the general idea. Joel isn't too sure about this
piece, and there's been a certain amount of debate about
it within the group. The concept was Becka's: she justi-
fied it by saying they should pick symbolism the workers
can tune into, and most of these workers are Portuguese,
they'll know all about Judas, you only have to look at
the statues on their lawns, all those bleeding plaster Je-
suses and Virgin Marys with their creepy-looking babies.
Though for the same reason some of the others felt that
Christ as a large knitted sock, in red and white stripes,
might turn out to be too much for them. There could
be a communications breakdown. Joel himself had been
uneasy, but he'd voted on Becka's side, because they'd
still been trying to work it out then and he knew what
hell there would be to pay if he'd come out against her.
Just another example, she would have said, of how he
would never let her express herself.

He hopes it won't rain: if it does, the giant sock will
get waterlogged, among other things. Maybe they should
scrap it, try for another approach. Whatever they do,
though, they'll probably have the assistant manager and
the old boy himself coming outside and accusing them

of anti-Semitism. This happens to Joel a lot; it's escalated after the piece on Lebanon and arms sales to South Africa they did outside the Beth Tzedec on Yom Kippur. Possibly the portable canvas mass grave, filled with baby dolls and splashed with red paint, had been going too far. A couple of the troupe members had wondered whether it was in bad taste, but Joel had said that bad taste was just an internalized establishment enforcer.

Joel doesn't believe in pulling punches. And if you punch, they punch back. It's getting so he can hardly go to parties any more. Though it's not all parties he should avoid, only certain kinds, the kinds where he will find his own second cousins and men he went to *shul* with, who are now dentists or have gone into business. Even before the Lebanon piece, they were none too polite. At the last party, a woman he didn't know at all, an older woman, came up to him and said, "Instead of shaking your hand I should kick you in the stomach."

"What for?" said Joel.

"You know what for," the woman said. "You've got a nerve. Eating our food. Better you should choke."

"Don't you think there should be an open discussion of the situation?" said Joel. "Like they do in Israel?"

"Goys have no right," said the woman.

"So who's a goy?" said Joel.

"You," said the woman. "You're not a real Jew."

"All of a sudden you're some kind of self-appointed committee on racial purity?" said Joel. "Anyway, read the Torah. They used to stone the prophets."

"Shmuck," said the woman.

Joel tries not to let it get to him: he's got his credentials ready. You want murdered relatives? he'll tell them. I've got.

Then how can you betray them? they'll say. Spitting on the dead.

You think they'd agree with what's happening? he'll say. Two wrongs don't make a right.

Then there's a silence in him, because that's a thing no one will ever know.

Joel's head hurts. He gets up from his desk, sits down in the chair he thinks in, which is like the one at home that his father used to lie in to read the paper, a La-Z-

Boy recliner, covered in black Naugahyde. Joel bought his at least third-hand from the Goodwill, out of nostalgia and a wish for comfort; though Becka said he did it to affront her. She could never stand any of his furniture, especially the Ping-Pong table; she was always lobbying for a real dining-room table, though, as Joel would point out with great reasonableness, it wouldn't have a double function.

"You're always talking about bourgeois," she'd say, which wasn't true. "But that chair is the essence. Eau de bourgeois." She pronounced it in three syllables: *boor-joo-ice.* Maybe she did this on purpose, to get at him by mutilating the word, though the only time he'd corrected her (the *only* time, he's sure of that), she'd said, "Well, excuse me for living." Could he help it if he'd spent a year in Montreal? And she hadn't. He couldn't help any of the things that he had and she hadn't.

Early on, he thought they'd been engaging in a dialogue, out of which, sooner or later, a consensus would emerge. He thought they'd been involved in a process of mutual adjustment and counter-adjustment. But viewed from here and now, it was never a dialogue. It was merely a degrading squabble.

Joel decides not to brood any more about boring personal shit. There are more important things in the world. He picks up this morning's paper, from where it lies in segments on the floor, in which he knows he will read distorted and censored versions of some of them; but just as he's settling down to the purblind and moronic "Letters to the Editor" section, the phone rings. Joel hesitates before answering it: maybe it will be Becka, and he never knows which angle she'll be coming at him from. But curiosity wins, as it often does where Becka is concerned.

It isn't Becka though. "I'm going to cut your nuts off," says a male voice, almost sensuously, into his ear.

"To whom do you wish to speak?" says Joel, doing his best imitation of an English butler from a thirties film. Joel watches a lot of late movies.

This isn't the first phone call like this he's had. Sometimes they're anti-Semites, wanting to cut his Jewish nuts off; sometimes they're Jews, wanting to cut his nuts off because they don't think he's Jewish enough. In either case the message is the same: his nuts must go. Maybe he should introduce the two sides and they could cut each other's nuts off; that seems to be their shtick. He likes his where they are.

Joel's elocution throws the guy and he mumbles something about dirty Commie bastards. Joel tells him that Mr. Murgatroyd is not home at the moment; would he care to leave his name and number? The coward hangs up, and so does Joel. He's sweating all over. He didn't when this first started happening, but the ones at two A.M. have been getting to him.

Joel doesn't want to turn into one of those paranoids who dive under the sofa every time there's a knock at the door. No Gestapo here, he tells himself. What he needs is some food. He goes out to the kitchen and rummages through the refrigerator, finding not much. Of the two of them, it was Becka who'd done most of the shopping. Without her, he's reverted to his old habits: pizza, Kentucky Fried, doughnuts from the Dunkin' Doughnuts. He knows it's unhealthy, but he indulges in unhealth as a kind of perverse rebellion against her. He used to justify his tastes by saying that this was what the average worker eats, but he knew even at the time that he was using ideology to cover for addiction. He must be getting middle-aged though, because he's still taking the vitamin pills Becka used to foist on him, threatening him with beri-beri, constipation, and scurvy if he dodged. He recalls with some pain her roughage phase.

The truth is that even Becka's normal cooking, good though it was, made him nervous. He always felt he was in the wrong house, not his, since he'd never associated home with edible food. His mother had been such a terrible cook that he'd left the dinner table hungry more evenings than not. At midnight he would prowl through his mother's apartment, stomach growling so loud you'd have thought it would wake her up, on bare criminal feet into the kitchen. Then followed the hunt for the only remotely digestible objects in the place, which were always baked goods from stores like Hunt's or Woman's Bakery, apple turnovers, muffins, cupcakes, cookies. She used to hide them on him; they'd never be in the refrigerator or the breadbox, not once she'd figured out that

it was him who'd been eating them at night. Carefully,
like a safe-cracker turning a sensitive combination lock,
he'd dismantle the kitchen, moving one pot at a time,
one stack of dishes. Sometimes she'd go so far as to
stash them in the living room; once, even in the bathroom, under the sink. That was stooping pretty low. He
remembers the sense of challenge, the mounting excitement, the triumph when he would finally uncover those
familiar sweet oily brown-paper bags with their tightly
screwed tops and their odour, faintly stale. He has an
image of himself, in his pyjamas, crouching beside the
cache he's just dragged out from under the easy chair,
cramming in the Chelsea buns, gloating. Next day she'd
never mention it. Once or twice he failed, but only once
or twice. She never mentioned that, either.

Now, prodding the shambles in his own refrigerator,
Joel can't find anything to eat. There's half a pint of
yoghurt, but it's left over from Becka and, by now, ques-
tionable. He decides to go out. He locates his jacket
finally, which is in the nest of clothing at the bottom of
the hall closet. Things somehow don't stay hung up when
he hangs them. The jacket has *Bluejays* across the back
and is ravelling at the cuffs; it has grease on it from
where he crawled under the car, years ago, trying to
prove to someone or other that he knew why it was
leaking; a futile exercise. The car had been completely
irrational; there was never a plausible explanation for
any of the things it did, any of the parts that fell off it.
Joel felt that driving it was like thumbing your nose at
the car establishment, at car snobbery, at the Platonic
idea of cars; he refused to trade it in. This was the car
that finally got stolen. "They were doing us all a favour,"
said Becka.

Becka once threatened to burn his Bluejays jacket.
She said if he had to wear a stupid macho label, at least
he could pick a winner; which goes to show how much
she knows about it. Expos she could live with. By that
time he'd started ignoring her; the text anyway, not the
subtext. In so far as that was possible.

As he's doing up the zipper the phone rings. Joel
thinks it may be another nut-cutter; he should get a
telephone-answering machine, the kind you can listen in
on. But this time it really is Becka. The small sad voice

tonight, the one he never trusts. She's more believable when she's being loud.

"Hi, Becka," he says, carefully neutral. "How are things going?" She was the one who walked out, though "walked" is too mild a description of it, so if there's conciliation to be done she can do it. "You want something?" he adds.

"Don't be like that," she says, after a short evaluating pause.

"Like what?" he says. "What am I being like that's so terrible?"

She sighs. He's familiar with these sighs of hers: she sighs over the phone better than any woman he's ever known. If he hadn't been sighed at by her so often, if he didn't know the hidden costs, he'd fall for it. She dodges his question, though; once she'd have met it head-on. "I thought maybe I could come over," she says. "So we could talk about it."

"Sure," says Joel, sliding into an old habit: he's never refused an offer to talk about it. But also he knows where talking about it leads. He pictures Becka's body, which she always holds back as the clincher; which is what he calls lush and she calls fat. Some of their first arguments were over this difference of opinion. "I'll be here," he says. If it's an offer, why turn it down?

But after he puts down the phone he regrets his easy acquiescence. So they go to bed. So what? What's it expected to prove? Is she working up to another move, back in? He's not sure he feels like going through the whole wash and spin cycle once again. Anyway, he's hungry. He types out a note—writing would be too intimate—saying he's been called out suddenly, to an important meeting, and he'll talk to her later. He doesn't say *see*. He opens the back door, which is the one she'll use, and tapes the note to it, noticing as he does so that someone has thrown an egg at his door: the remains are oozing down the paintwork, partly solidified, the broken shell is on the sidewalk.

Joel goes back in, closes the door. It's dark out there. Someone has taken a lot of trouble, going around to the back like that; someone who knows exactly who lives behind his door. It wasn't just a random shot, someone who happened to be passing by with an egg in his hand and got a sudden urge to hurl it. He has choices: maybe it's one of the nut-slicers, an idea he doesn't relish. Maybe it's the landlord: that's what he thought last week, when he found a nail hammered through the back tire of his bicycle. He doesn't think it's anyone official. He's suspected the RCMP of bugging his phone, more than once, he knows that squeaky-clean sound on the line, and no doubt he's on their list, most people who do anything at all in this country are. But eggs they wouldn't bother with.

Or maybe it's Becka. Throwing an egg at his door, then phoning him to make up because she feels guilty about something she'll never confess to him she's done, that's her style. "What egg?" she'll say to him if he asks, making her innocent chipmunk eyes, and how will he ever know? Once, when they were at a party together, they heard a gossipy story about a woman who'd recently split up with a man they both knew. She'd gone to the post office and filled out a change-of-address card in his name, redirecting all his mail to a town somewhere in the middle of Africa. At the time, and because he didn't like the guy much, Joel had found this hilarious. Becka hadn't, though she'd listened to the story more carefully than he had, and had asked questions. It strikes him now that she'd been filing it away for future reference. Now he tries to remember the rest of the story, the other things the woman had done: intercepting the man's shirts on the way back from the laundry and cutting off all the buttons, sending funeral wreaths to his new girl friend. Joel is safe on both counts: no laundered shirts, no new girl friend. It's just the mail he'll have to watch.

Now he's wondering whether going out is such a good idea. Becka still has a key, which he'll have to do something about pretty soon. Maybe she'll be in his apartment, waiting for him, when he gets back. He decides to take his chances. When she finds he isn't there, she can stay or she can go, it's up to her. (Leaving it up to her has always been one of his best tactics. It drives her mad.) Either way, he's made his move. He's shown her he's not eager. Any effort put out this time around is going to be hers.

As he searches for his wallet in the jumble of paper backs, papers, and socks beside the bed, Uglypuss brushes against his legs, purring. He scratches her between the ears and pulls her up slowly by the tail, which he's convinced cats like. ("Cut that out, you'll break its spine," Becka would protest. But Uglypuss was his goddamn cat, to begin with.)

"Uglypuss," he says. He's had her almost as long as he's had his La-Z-Boy recliner and his Ping-Pong table: she's been through a lot with him. She turns her odd face up at him, half orange, half black, divided down the nose, a Yin and Yang cat, as Becka used to say during her organic-cereal and body-mind-energy phase.

She follows him to the door, the front one this time; he'll leave through the communal vestibule, walk down the steps, where there are street lights. She meows, but he doesn't want her going out, not at night. Even though she's spayed, she wanders, and sometimes gets into fights. Maybe the toms can't tell she's a girl; or maybe they think she is, but she disagrees. He used to make pointed analyses of Uglypuss's sexual hang-ups, to Becka, over breakfast. Whatever the reason, she gets herself messed up: her ears are nicked, and he's had it with the antibiotic ointment, which she licks off anyway. He thinks of distracting her with food, but he's out of cat kibble, which is one more reason for going out. He takes the container of dubious yoghurt out of the refrigerator and leaves it on the floor, opened for her.

Joel wipes his mouth, pushes the plate away. He's stuffed down everything: Wiener schnitzel, home fries, the lot. Now he's full and lazy. The back room of the Blue Danube used to be one of his favourite places to eat, before he moved in with Becka, or rather, she moved in with him. It's inexpensive and you get a lot for your money, good quality too. It has another advantage: other people who want cheap food come here, art students, in pairs or singly, out-of-work actors or actresses, those on the prowl but not desperate or rich or impervious enough to go to singles bars. Joel wouldn't want to pick up the kind of girl who would go to singles bars.

Becka never liked this place, so he gradually eased

out of the habit of coming here. The last time they ate together it was here, though: a sure sign, for both of them, that the tide had turned.

Becka had come back from the washroom and plunked herself down opposite him, as though she'd just made an earth-shattering discovery. "Guess what's written in the women's can?" she'd asked.

"I'll bite," said Joel.

"Women make love. Men make war," she said.

"So?" Joel said. "Is the lipstick pink or red?"

"So it's true."

"That's supposed to be an insight?" said Joel. "It's not *men* that make war. It's *some* men. You think those young working-class guys want to march off and be slaughtered? It's the generals, it's the . . ."

"But it's not women, is it?" said Becka.

"That's got nothing to do with anything," Joel said, exasperated.

"That's what I mean about you," said Becka. "It's only your goddamned point of view that's valid, right?"

"Bullshit," he said. "We aren't talking about points of view. We're talking about *history*."

As he said this, the futility of what he was trying to do swept over him, as it sometimes does: what's the point of continuing, in a society like this one, where it's always two steps forward and two back? The frustration, the lack of money, the indifference, and on top of that the incessant puerile bickering on the left over who's more pure. If there was a real fight (he thinks "guns" but not "war"), if it was out in the open, things would be clearer; but this too can be seen as a temptation, the impulse to romanticize other people's struggles. It's hard to decide what form of action is valid. Do you have to be dead to be authentic, as the purists seem to believe? Though he hasn't noticed any of them actually lining up for the firing squads. Maybe he's chosen the wrong mode; maybe street theatre doesn't fit in up here, where the streets are so neat and clean and nobody lives on them, in shacks or storm sewers or laid out on mats along the sidewalks. Sometimes he thinks maybe they're all just play-acting, indulging in a game of adult dress-up that accomplishes nothing in the end.

But these moods of his seldom last long. "Wars are

fought so those in power can stay there," he said to
Becka, trying to be patient.

"You don't think you're ever going to *win*, do you?"
Becka said softly. She can read his mind, but only at
bad times.

"It's not about winning," Joel said. "I know whose
side I'd rather be on, that's all."

"How about being on mine?" Becka said. "For a
change."

"What the shit are you talking about?" said Joel.

"I'm not hungry," said Becka. "Let's go home."

It's the word *home* that echoes in the air here for Joel
now, plaintively, in a minor key. Home isn't a place,
Becka said once, it's a feeling. Maybe that's what's the
matter with it, Joel answered. For him, when he was
growing up, home was the absence of a thing that should
have been there. Going home was going into nothing-
ness. He'd rather be out.

He looks around the room, which is smoke-filled,
bare-walled, his gaze passing over couples, resting longer
on women by themselves. Why not admit it? He's come
out tonight because he's looking for it, as so many times
before: someone to go home with, to her home, not his,
in the hope that this unknown place, yet another unknown place, will finally contain something he wants to
have. It's Becka's phone call that's done it: she has that
effect on him. Every move to encircle him, pin him
down, force him into a corner, only makes him more
desperate to escape. She never came right out and said
so, but what she wanted was permanence, commitment,
monogamy, the works. Forty years of the same thing
night after night was a long time to contemplate.

He sees a girl he knows slightly, remembers from the
summer, when they were doing the Cannibal Monster
Tomato play down near Leamington, for the itinerant
harvesters. (Cold-water shacks. Insecticides in the lungs.
No medical protection. Intimidation. It was a good
piece.) The girl was a minor player, someone who carried a sign. As he recalls, she was getting laid by one of
the troupe; that was the only explanation he could think
of at the time for her presence among them. He hopes
he was right, he hopes she's not too political. Becka
wasn't political when he first met her. In those days she

was doing art therapy at one of the nuthouses, helping the loonies to express themselves with wet newspaper and glue. She'd had a calmness, a patience that he's since realized was only a professional veneer, but at the time he'd settled into it like a hammock. He'd enjoyed trying to educate her, and she'd gotten into it to parrot him or please him. What a mistake.

In recent years, he's come to realize that the kind of women that ought to turn him on—left-leaning intellectual women who can hold up their end of a debate, who believe in fifty-fifty, who can be good pals—aren't the kind that actually do. He's not ashamed of this discovery, as he would have been once. He prefers women who are soft-spoken and who don't live all the time in their heads, who don't take everything with deadly seriousness. What he needs is someone who won't argue about whether he's too macho, whether he should or shouldn't encourage the capitalists by using under-arm deodorant, whether the personal is political or the political is personal, whether he's anti-Semitic, anti-female, anti-anything. Someone who won't argue.

He pushes back his chair and walks over, ready for rejection. They can always tell him to go away. He doesn't mind that much, he never tries to force the issue. There's no sense in being obnoxious, and he doesn't want to be with anyone who doesn't want to be with him. He's never seen the point of rape.

This girl has reddish hair, parted in the middle and drawn back. She's crouched over her noodles, pretending to be absorbed in a large but paperbacked book that's propped open beside her plate. Joel goes through the openers: "Hi, good to see you again. Mind if I join you?"

She glances up, with that little frown he's seen on their faces so often, that coming-out-of-the-trance face, *Oh, you startled me*, as if she hasn't been aware of his approach. She's been aware. She recognizes him, hesitates, deciding; then she smiles. She's grateful, he sees, for the company: it must be all over with what's-his-name. Relieved, he sits down. Even though he knows no one is really watching him, it still makes him feel like an idiot to be sent away, like a puppy that's made a mess.

Now for the book: that's always a good way in. He

turns it so he can see the title. *Quilt-Making Through History.* That's a hard one; he knows nothing and cares less about quilt-making. He guesses that she's the kind of girl who would read about it but would never actually do it; though opening up with a statement to this effect would be far too aggressive. It's a mistake to begin by putting them down.

"Like a beer," he says, "or are you a vegetarian?"

"As a matter of fact I am," she says, with that superior tight mini-smile they give you. She hasn't got the joke. Joel sighs; they're off to a roaring start.

"Then I guess you mind if I smoke?" he says.

She relents; evidently she doesn't want to drive him away. "You go ahead," she says. "It's a big room." She doesn't add that it's full of smoke already, and he likes her better.

He thinks of saying, "Live around here?" but he can't, not again. "Tell me about yourself" is out too. Instead he finds himself shifting almost immediately, much sooner than he usually does, into social realism. "This day has been total shit," he says. He feels this, it's not fake, the day *has* been total shit; but on another level he knows he wants sympathy, and on yet another one he's aware it's a useful ploy; if they feel sorry for you, how can they turn you down?

Becka used to accuse him of having a detachable prick. In her version, he unscrewed it, put it on a leash, and took it out for walks, like a dachshund without legs or a kind of truffle-hunting pig (her metaphor). According to her, it would stick itself into any hole or crevice it could find, anything vaguely funnel-shaped, remotely female. In her more surrealistic inventions (when she was still trying to live with what she called this habit of his, before she switched to *compulsion*, when she was still trying to be humorous about it), he'd find himself stuck somewhere, in a mouse-hole or a dead tree or an outside faucet, unable to get loose, because his prick had made a mistake. What could you expect, she said, from a primitive animal with no eyes?

"If I got you a sheep and a pair of rubber boots, would you stay home more?" she said. "We could keep it in the garage. If we had a garage. If it wasn't too boor-joo-ice to have a garage."

But she was wrong, it isn't the sex he's after. It isn't only the sex. Sometimes he thinks, in the middle of it, that really he'd rather be jogging around the block or watching a movie or playing Ping-Pong. Sex is merely a social preliminary, the way a handshake used to be; it's the first step in getting to know someone. Once it's out of the way, you can concentrate on the real things; though without it, somehow you can't. He likes women, he likes just talking with them sometimes. The ones he likes talking with, having a laugh with, these are the ones that become what he refers to privately as "repeaters."

"How come I'm not enough for you?" Becka said, soon after the first two or three, when she'd figured it out. He wasn't a very good liar; he resented having to conceal things.

"It's not important," he said, trying to comfort her; she was crying. He still loved her in a simple way then. "It's no more important than sneezing. It's not an emotional commitment. You're an emotional commitment."

"If it's not important, why do you do it?" she said.

He wasn't able to answer that. "This is just the way I am," he said finally. "It's part of me. Can't you accept it?"

"But this is just the way *I* am," she said, crying even more. "You make me feel like nothing. You make me feel I'm worth nothing to you. I'm not even worth any more than a sneeze."

"That's blackmail," he said, pulling away. He couldn't stand to have love and fidelity extracted from him, like orange juice or teeth. No squeezers. No pliers. She should have known she was the central relationship: he'd told her often enough.

This girl's name, which he's forgotten but which he digs out of her by pretending to almost remember it, is Amelia. She works, of course, in a bookstore. Looking more closely, he can see she's not quite as young as he first thought. There are tiny shrivellings beginning around her eyes, a line forming from the nostril to the corner of her mouth; later it will extend down to her chin, which is small and pointed, and she will develop that peevish, starved look. Redheads have delicate skin, they age early. She has a chain around her neck, with a glass pendant on it containing dried flowers. He guesses she'll be the kind of girl who has prisms hanging in her window and a poster of a whale over the bed, and when they get to her place, she does.

Amelia turns out to be one of the vocal kind, which he likes: it's a tribute, in a way. He's surprised, too: you couldn't have told it by looking at her, that almost prissy restraint and decorum, the way she tightened her little bum, moved it away when he put his hand on it as she was unlocking the door. Joel doesn't know why he always expects girls with pierced ears and miniature gold stars in them, high cheekbones and frail rib cages, to be quiet in bed. It's some antiquated notion he has about good taste, though he should know by now that the thin ones have more nerve-endings per square inch.

Afterwards she goes back to being subdued, as if she's faintly ashamed of herself for those groans, for having clutched him like that, as if he's not a semi-stranger after all. He wonders how many times she's gone home with someone she barely knows; he's curious, he'd like to ask, "You do this often?" But he knows from past experience they're likely to find this insulting, some kind of obscure slur on their moral standards; even if, like himself, they do. Sometimes, especially when they're younger, he feels he ought to tell them they shouldn't behave like this. Not all men are good risks, even the ones who eat at the Blue Danube. They could be violent, into whips or safety pins, perverts, murderers, not like him. But any interference from him could be interpreted as patriarchal paternalism: he knows that from experience too. It's their own lookout; anyway, why should he complain?

Amelia lies against him, head on his biceps, red hair spilling across his arm, her mouth relaxed; he's grateful for her simple physical presence, the animal warmth. Women don't like the term "muff," he knows that; but for him it's both descriptive and affectionate: something furry that keeps you warm. This is the kind of thing he needs to get him through November. She's even being friendly, in a detached sort of way. He can't always depend on them to be friendly afterwards. They've been known to hold it against him, as if it's something he's done all by himself, to them instead of with them; as if they've had nothing to do with it.

*   *   *

He likes this one well enough to suggest that maybe
they could watch the late show on TV, which isn't an
experience he'd want to share with just anyone. Sex yes,
late movies no. He wonders if she's got any food in the
house, some cake maybe, which they could eat right off
the plate while watching, licking the icing from each other's fingers. He's hungry again, but more than that, he
wants the feeling of comfort this would bring. There's
something about lemon icing in a dark room. But when
she says without any undertones that, no, she'd like
some sleep, she needs to get up early to go to her fitness
class before work, that's all right with him too. He puts
on his clothes, lighthearted; this whole thing has cheered
him up a lot. He has that secret feeling of having gotten
away with it again, in the bedroom window and out
again without being caught: no sticky flypaper here. He
remembers, briefly, the day he figured out his mother
was hiding the cookies, not so he wouldn't find them,
but so he would, and how enraged, how betrayed he'd
been. He'd seen the edge of her green chenille bathrobe
whisking back around the corner; she'd been standing in
the hall outside the kitchen, listening to him eat. She
must have known what a rotten cook she was, and this
was her backhanded way of making sure he got at least
some food into him. That's what he thinks now, but at
the time he merely felt he'd been controlled, manipu-
lated by her all along. Maybe that was when he started
to have his first doubts about free will.

Amelia has turned on her side and is almost asleep.
He kisses her, says he'll let himself out. He wonders if
he likes her well enough to see her again, decides he
probably doesn't. Nevertheless he makes a note of her
phone number, memorizing it off the bedside phone;
he'll jot it down later, out in the kitchen, where she
won't notice. He never knows when a thing like that will
come in handy. Any port in a storm, and when he's at
a low point, a trough in the graph, he needs to be with
someone and it doesn't much matter who, within limits.

He pisses into her toilet, flushes it, noting the antinuke
sticker on the mirror, the pots of herbs struggling for
existence on the windowsill. Then he goes into the kitchenette and turns on the light, taking a quick peek into

the refrigerator in passing, on the off-chance she's got something unhealthy and delicious in there. But she's a tofu girl, and reluctantly he's out the door.

He's not thinking about Becka. He doesn't remember her till his key's in the lock, when he has a sudden image of her, waiting on the other side, black hair falling around her face like something in a Lorca play, large wounded eyes regarding him, some deadly instrument in her hand: a corkscrew, a potato peeler, or, more historically, an ice-pick, though he doesn't own one. Cautiously he opens the door, eases through, is relieved when nothing happens. Maybe it's finally over, after all. It occurs to him that he's forgotten to buy cat food.

His relief lasts until he hits the living room. She's been here, all right. He gazes at the innards of his La-Z-Boy, strewn across the floor, its wiry guts protruding from what's left of the frame, at the hunks of soft foam from the sofa washing against the fireplace as if it's a shore, as if Becka has been a storm, a hurricane. In another corner he finds all his Ping-Pong balls, lined up in a row and stomped on; they look like hatched-out turtle eggs. Some of his underwear is lying in the fireplace, charred around the edges, still smouldering.

He shrugs. Histrionic bitch, he thinks. So he'll replace it: there's nothing here that can't be duplicated. She won't get to him that easily. She hasn't touched the typewriter, though: she knows exactly how far she can go.

Then he sees the note. *Want Uglypuss back? It's in a garbage can. Start looking.* The note is pinned to the big orange art-shop candle on the mantelpiece, one of the first things she gave him. It's as if he's finally had a visit from Santa Claus, who has turned out to be the monster his mother was always warning him against when he showed symptoms of wanting a Christmas like some of the other kids on the block. *Santa Claus brings you lumps of coal and rotten potatoes. What do you need it for?*

But this was no Santa Claus, it was Becka, who knows just where to slide in the knife. Dead or alive, she doesn't say. She's never exactly loved Uglypuss, but surely she wouldn't murder. He fears the worst, but he can't assume it. He'll have to go and see. He hears the claws scrabbling on metal, the plaintive wails, the mounting panic, as he does up his zipper again. Finally he knows she'll stop at nothing.

He walks in a widening circle through the streets around his house, opening every can, digging through the bags, listening for faint meows. He shouldn't be spending time on something this trivial, this personal; he should be conserving his energy for the important things. What he needs is perspective. This is Becka controlling him again. Maybe she was lying, maybe Uglypuss is safe and sound at her new place, purring beside the hot-air register. Maybe Becka is making him go through all this for nothing, hoping he'll arrive on her doorstep and she can torture him or reward him, whichever she feels like at the moment.

"Uglypuss!" he calls. He tells himself he's in a state of shock, it will hit him tomorrow, when the full implications of a future without Uglypuss will sink in. At the moment though he's thinking: *Why did I have to give it that dumb name?*

Becka walks along the street. She has often walked along this particular street. She tells herself there is nothing unusual about it.

Both of her hands are bare, and there's blood on the right one and four thin lines of it across her cheek. In her right hand she's carrying an axe. Actually it's smaller than an axe, it's a hatchet, the one Joel keeps beside the fireplace to split the kindling when he lights the fire. Once she liked to make love with him on the rug in front of the fireplace, in the orange glow from the candle. That was until he said there was always a draft and he'd rather be in bed, where it was warmer. After a while she figured out that he didn't really like being looked at; he had an odd sort of modesty, as if he felt his body belonged to him alone. Once she tried flattering him about it, but this was a bad move, you weren't supposed to compare. So then it was under the covers, like a married couple. Before that she used to bug him about keeping the axe in the living room, she wanted him to leave it on the back porch and split the kindling out there instead; she told him she didn't like getting splinters.

It was looking at the axe that finally did it. Joel was gone when he said he'd be there. She didn't know ex-

Margaret Atwood

actly where he'd gone but she knew in general. He was always doing that to her. She waited for an hour and a half, pacing, reading his magazines, surrounded by a space that used to be hers and still felt like it. The heat was off, which meant Joel had been antagonizing the landlord again. She thought about lighting a fire. Uglypuss came and rubbed against her legs and complained, and when she went into the kitchen to put out some food, there was the yoghurt she'd bought herself, opened on the floor.

She asked herself how long she was going to wait. Even if he came back soon, he'd have that smug look and the smell of it still on him. She'd have the choice of ignoring it, in which case he won, or saying something, in which case he won also, because then he could accuse her of intruding on his privacy. It would be just another example, he'd say, of why things couldn't work out. That would make her angry—they could, they could work out if he'd only try—and then he would criticize her for being angry. Her anger would be a demonstration of the power he still holds over her. She knows it, but she can't control it. This time was once too often. It was always once too often.

Becka walks quickly, head a little down and forward, as if she has to push to make her way through the air. Her hair blows back in the wind. It's beginning to drizzle. In her left hand she's carrying a green plastic garbage bag, screwed shut and knotted at the top. The street she's on is Spadina, a street she remembers from childhood as the place where she would be taken by her grandfather when he wanted to pay visits to some of his old cronies. She'd be shown off by him, and given things to eat. That was before the Chinese mostly took over. It's well enough lighted, even at this time of night, bamboo furniture, wholesale clothing, restaurants, ethnic as they say; but she's not buying or eating, she's just looking, thanks, for a garbage can, someplace to dump the bag. An ordinary garbage can is all she asks; why can't she find one?

She can't believe she's done what she's just done. What horrifies her is that she enjoyed it, the axe biting into the black Naugahyde of that ratty chair of his, into the sofa, the stuffing she'd pulled out and thrown

around, it might as well have been Joel. Though if he'd
been there he would have stopped her. Just by being
there, by looking at her as if to say, *You mean you really
can't think of anything more important to do?*

This is what he's turned me into, she thinks. I was
never this mean before, I used to be a nice person, a
nice girl. Didn't I?

Today, before calling him, she'd been sick of the taste
of the inside of her own mouth. She'd had enough of
solitude, enough freedom. A woman without a man is
like a fish without a bicycle. Brave words, she'd said
them once herself. That was before she figured out she
wasn't a fish. Today she thought she still loved him, and
love conquers all, doesn't it? Where there's love there's
hope. Maybe they could get it back, together. Now, she
doesn't know.

She thinks about stuffing the garbage bag into a mailbox, the parcel kind, or a newspaper stand. She could
put in the quarter, open the box, take out the newspaper, leave the bag. Someone would find it quicker that
way. She is not heartless.

But suddenly there's a garbage can, not a plastic one
but old-style metal, in front of a Chinese fruit-and-vege-
table store. She goes over to it, leans the hatchet against
it, sets down the bag, tries to lift the lid. Either it's stuck
or her hands are numb. She bangs it against a telephone
pole; several people look at her. At last the lid comes
loose. Luckily the can is half empty. She drops the bag
in. Not a sound: she sprayed in some boot water-proofer,
which was about the only thing she could think of:
breathing the fumes makes you dizzy. Kids at high
school used to get high on it. The stupid cat clawed its
way through the first two garbage bags, before she
thought of tying it up in one of Joel's shirts and spraying
it with boot water-proofer to quiet it down. She doesn't
know if it went unconscious; maybe it just couldn't get
through Joel's shirt and decided not to fight a losing
battle. Maybe it's catatonic. To coin a phrase. She hopes
she hasn't killed it. She pokes the bag a little: there's a
wiggle. She's relieved, but she doesn't relent and let it
loose. Why should she have all the grief? Let him have
some, for a change.

This is what will really get to him, she knows: this

theft. His kidnapped child, the one he wouldn't let her have. *We're not ready yet* and all that crap. Crap! He'd always thought more of the cat than he did of her. It used to make her sick, to watch the way he'd pick it up by the tail and run it through his hands, like sand, and the cat loved it, like the nauseating masochist it was. It was the kind of cat that drooled when you stroked it. It fawned all over him. Maybe the real reason she couldn't stand it was that it was a grotesque and stunted furry little parody of herself. Maybe this was what she looked like, to other people, when she was with him. Maybe this was what she looked like to him. She thinks of herself lying with her eyes closed and her mouth slack and open. Did he remember what she looked like at those moments, when he was with others?

She doesn't close the lid on the garbage can. She leaves the hatchet where it is, walks away. She feels smaller, diminished, as if something's been sucking on her neck. Anger is supposed to be liberating, so goes the mythology, but her anger has not freed her in any way that she can see. It's only made her emptier, flowing out of her like this. She doesn't want to be angry; she wants to be comforted. She wants a truce.

She can remember, just barely, having had confidence in herself. She can't recall where she got it from. Go through life with your mouth open, that used to be her motto. Live in the now. Encounter experience fully. Hold out your arms in welcome. She once thought she could handle anything.

Tonight she feels dingy, old. Soon she will start getting into the firming cream; she will start worrying about her eyelids. Beginning again is supposed to be exciting, a challenge. Beginning again is fine as an idea, but what with? She's used it all up; she's used up.

Still, she would like to be able to love someone; she would like to feel inhabited again. This time she wouldn't be so picky, she'd settle for a man maybe a little worn around the edges, a second, with a few hairline cracks, a few pulled threads, something from a fire sale, someone a little damaged. Like those ads for adoptable children in the *Star*: "Today's Child." Today's lover. A man in a state of shock, a battered male. She'd take a divorced one, an older one, someone who could only get it up for kinky sex, anything, as long as he'd be grateful. That's what she wants, when it comes right down to it: a gratitude equal to her own. But even in this she's deluding herself. Why should such a man be any different from the rest? They're all a little damaged. Anyway, she'd be clutching at a straw, and who wants to be a straw?

She should never have called him. She should know by now that over is over, that when it says *The End* at the end of a book it means there isn't any more; which she can never quite believe. The problem is that she's invested so much suffering in him, and she can't shake the notion that so much suffering has to be worth something. Maybe unhappiness is a drug, like any other: you could develop a tolerance to it, and then you'd want more.

People came to the end of what they had to say to one another, Joel told her once, during one of their many sessions about whether they should stay together or not; the time he was trying for wisdom. After that point, he said, it was only repetition. But Becka protested; Becka hadn't come to the end of what she had to say, or so she thought. That was the trouble: she never came to the end of what she had to say. He'd push her too far and she'd blurt things out, things she couldn't retrieve, she would make clumsy mistakes of a kind she never made with other people, the landlord for instance, with whom she was a miracle of tact. But with Joel, the irrevocable is always happening.

He once told her he wanted to share his life with her. He said he'd never asked anyone that before. How she melted over that, how she lapped it up! But he never said he wanted her to share her life with him, which, when it happened, turned out to be a very different thing.

What now, now that she's done it? Time will go on. She'll walk back to the row house in Cabbagetown she shares with two other women. This is about all she can afford; at least she has her own room. She hardly ever sees the other two women; she knows them mostly by their smells, burnt toast in the mornings, incense (from one of them, the one with the lay-over boy friend) at night. The situation reeks of impermanence. She got the place by answering an ad in the paper, *Third woman needed, share kitchen, no drugs or freaks*, after moving out of the apartment she still thinks of as her own, and after a miserable week with her mother, who thought but did not say that it served her right for not insisting on marriage. What did she expect anyway, from a man like that? Not a real job. Not a real Jew. Not real.

When she gets to the house she'll be worn out, her adrenaline high gone, replaced by a flat grey fatigue. She'll put on her most penitential nightgown, blue-flowered flannelette, the one Joel hates because it reminds him of landladies. She'll fix herself a hot-water bottle and climb into a bed which does not yet smell like hers and feel sorry for herself. Maybe she should go out hunting, sit in a bar, something she's never done, though there's always a first time. But she needs her sleep. Tomorrow she has to go to work, at her new job, her old job, mixing poster paints for the emotionally disturbed, a category that right now includes her. It doesn't pay well and there are hazards, but these days she's lucky to have it.

She couldn't stay with the troupe, even though she'd done such a good job of the headless corpses for the El Salvador piece in the spring, even though it was her who'd come up with Christ as a knitted sock. It would be disruptive for the troupe, they both agreed on that, to have her there; the tension, the uneven balance of conflicting egos. Or words to that effect. He was so good at that bullshit, the end result of which was that she'd been out of a job and he hadn't, and for a while she'd even felt noble about it.

Becka's four blocks away from the garbage can now, and it's raining in earnest. She stands under an awning, waiting for the rain to slow down, trying to decide whether or not to give in and take the streetcar. She wants to walk all the way back, to get rid of this furious energy.

It's time for Joel to be coming home. She pictures him opening the door, throwing his jacket on the floor; she sees what he will find. Now she feels as if she's committed a sacrilege. Why should she feel that way? Because for at least two years she thought he was God.

He isn't God. She can see him, in his oily Bluejays

jacket, running through the streets, panting because he'll be out of breath, he'll have eaten too much for dinner, with whatever slut he'd picked up, plunging his hands into chilly garbage, calling like a fool: *Uglypuss!* People will think he's crazy. But he will only be mad with grief.

Like her, leaning her forehead against the cold shop window, staring through the dark glass, yellowed by those plastic things they put there to keep the sun from fading the colours, at the fur-coated woman inside, tears oozing down her cheeks. She can't even remember now which garbage can she put the damn thing in, she couldn't find it again if she looked. She should have taken it home with her. It was her cat too, more or less, once. It purred and drooled for her, too. It kept her company. How could she have done that to it? Maybe the boot spray will make it feeble-minded. That's all he'll need, a feeble-minded cat. Not that anyone will be able to tell the difference.

In her either, if she goes on like this. She wipes her nose and eyes on her damp sleeve, straightens. When she gets home she'll do some Yogic breathing and concentrate on the void for a while, trying once more for serenity, and take a bath. *My heart does not bleed*, she tells herself. But it does.

ANONYMOUS NARRATION— MULTIPLE CHARACTER POINT OF VIEW

Traditionally, three may stand for any number over three, and so it does here. Once beyond two character points of view, the number makes little difference insofar as choice of technique is concerned. Entering the minds of several or many people obviously expands considerably the perspective of a story. Not surprisingly, one finds more novels than short stories written in this technique. Interplaying multiple viewpoints, especially more than three, requires greater scope than most short fiction can accommodate. It better befits the societal cyclorama of novels like William Thackeray's Vanity Fair, *Leo Tolstoy's* War and Peace, *and Katherine Anne Porter's* Ship of Fools, *the titles of which announce their ambitious intention. Also, how "omniscient" does an author feel she or he is or ought to pretend to be?*

The three stories here show the limited effect of this technique in a small compass but hint at what the corresponding novel can do. "Fever Flower" adds to the multiple viewpoints the rare device of previewing the future of the characters, the combined effect being to create an uncommonly broad perspective on a common domestic situation. The longest of the stories, "The Suicides of Private Greaves," enters many minds to build up a composite portrait of the army as social microcosmos. Interestingly enough for our journey through storytelling, all three stories go into the minds of every significant character except the one referred to in the title, a central figure whose vacuum pulls in the others.

Fever Flower

Shirley Ann Grau

Summers, even the dew is hot. The big heavy drops, tadpole-shaped, hang on leaves and stems and grass, lie on the face of the earth like sweat, until the spongy sun cleans them away. That is why summer mornings are always steamy. The windows of the Cadillacs parked in carports are frosted with mist. By ten the dew is gone and the steam with it, and the day settles down to burn itself out in dry heat.

In the houses air-conditioning units buzz twenty-four hours a day. And colored laundresses grumble at the size of washes. And colored cooks work with huck towels tied around their necks and large wet spots on their black linen uniforms—until by mid-July they refuse to come in the mornings and fix any sort of breakfast. It is a mass movement. None of the white people can do anything about it. But then it is not serious. No one needs breakfast in summer. Most people simply skip the meal; the men, those of them who have strict bosses, grumble through the mornings empty-stomached or gulp hasty midmorning coffee; the women lie in bed late— until it is lunch time and the cooks have come. Nurses feed children perfunctory breakfasts: cold cereals and juices at eleven o'clock. Summer mornings no one gets up early.

By eight-thirty Katherine Fleming was sitting alone in the efficient white and yellow tiled kitchen at breakfast: orange juice and instant coffee. She had somehow spilled the juice and she was idly mopping up the liquid from the stainless-steel counter top when the phone rang. Her hands were sticky when she picked up the receiver.

"Why, Jerry—" She swallowed the last of the coffee.

"I really didn't think you'd be up this early. . . . Sure I'm all right."

She leaned her elbow on the counter, remembered the spilled juice and lifted her arm hastily, as she listened. She shook her head. "Let's not try lunch, honey. I'm supposed to run out and say hello to Mamma."

She listened another moment, frowning a bit with the beginnings of irritation. "Don't tease me, honey. I'm going because she's lonesome for me. I ought to, you know. Even if I'd rather be with you. And, anyway, there's tonight."

She listened a moment more, said good-by, and stood up, irritably ruffling the back of her hair with one hand.

It always annoyed her to lie. But it would never have done to tell Jerry Stevenson to his face that she did not want to see him; she felt she owed him that much, because he had been fun the night before. Last night she had adored him; this morning all that was left was a feeling of well-being. She stretched, arching her back. She felt wonderful, soft and rested and fine. He was part of last night; he would be part of tonight. But this sudden intrusion into the morning left her vaguely annoyed, though she knew she could forget about him.

Katherine Fleming went upstairs and dressed quickly: a summer suit of white linen, a pale green blouse that would bring out the color of her eyes. She finished her makeup and studied herself in the mirror, nodding just a bit in approval: nice brown hair, very nice gray eyes, a figure Grable needn't have been ashamed of. And furthermore, she told herself, she had years in her favor. She was twenty-five: she looked twenty-two. She picked up her handbag and went quickly down the hall to tell her daughter good-by.

Four years ago Katherine had been married; two years ago she had been divorced. A house that was new and very modern, a daughter whose name was Maureen, and a sizable check that came every month on the third: these were left of her marriage.

She did not regret anything. She did not look back on her marriage with anger or any feeling stronger than a kind of vague relief that it was finished at last. She was not angry with Hugh; she had never been. Not even when she heard of his remarriage to one of her college friends. Not even that last time when they had called it quits.

Hugh had sat quietly in the armchair over by the window and listened while she told him that nothing between them was ever going to work. He sat facing her, his eyes lifted a little and focused on the spot of wall slightly above her head, so that he was at once looking at her and not seeing her. He had gray eyes, large ones, with lashes for a man ridiculously long and curly. In the light from the window the gray eyes turned shiny as silver and as hard. When she had finished, he got up and left without a word. He hadn't even stopped to pack. The next morning he called and told the maid to send his things to the hotel. Katherine remembered that the only thing she had felt was a kind of wonder that it had all been so easy.

She had never seen him again. But she was sure that had they met, she could have talked amicably with him. He, however, made very certain that they did not meet. Even on the one day a week when he came to see his daughter, she was not allowed to be in the house. His lawyers had insisted on that during the settlement. She was to have the child and a regular check; he was to have the one day a week when she would not be in the house.

Katherine Fleming walked quickly down the hall to tell her daughter good-by, her bag swinging idly from her fingers. A stupid arrangement, she thought, but then Hugh had been a strange fellow, full of odd ideas. One time he had got fascinated by sculpture. He had even considered lessons from Vittorio Manale, who was making a name for himself as one of the moderns. Hugh would always have the best of everything. But Hugh was also a practical man. He never could quite convince himself that money spent for lessons would have been well spent, so he never took any. But he never quite gave up the idea. He spent his Saturday afternoons—just about the only free time he had—in the museums, walking around and around the figures that interested him, figures in white marble, in polished brown granite. He stared at them with his eyes half-shut, trying to imagine how they had been done.

He couldn't work in marble, of course: he couldn't

have used a chisel. But he always had been a marvelous whittler—he kept a row of different knives in his desk drawer—so he went to work in soap. That was when Katherine first knew him, the summer she finished college. The first piece he did was a dog, with the ears of a spaniel and the body of a terrier. He had given the little bit of carved soap to her mother. (Her mother still kept it on the whatnot shelves along with the other things of china and straw and the little basket of true Italian marble that they had sent her from Naples on their honeymoon.)

Katherine thought the whole thing was more than a little silly. A grown man, in his late thirties, and as handsome as Hugh Fleming, ought not to be whittling like a boy. But there were many things about him that were boyish: his clothes dropped all over the room at night (even four years in the navy had not cured him of that habit); the quick brushing back of his hair when he was angry; the open joy in new money or a new car or a new house or a new and beautiful wife. Or his whittling. But then Katherine had to admit that some of the things he made were lovely. As he caught the knack, his products came to have the look of marble; one in particular, a woman's head. He said it was she; he had her sit as a model for him, while he worked, but it did not look much like her. She was not that beautiful: her features were somewhat irregular, her eyes not large enough to be so striking, her hair not so perfectly waved. His work had the perfection of line and contour of the face on a cameo. Perhaps, though, he really saw her like that. After all, by the time the figure was completed they were engaged. In any case, that bit of her was undoubtedly the finest thing he ever did. After they had separated she dropped the head into a pan of water and watched its slow disintegration, which took several days.

A crazy idea, Katherine thought, having me leave the house. But like him, she admitted. She went into her daughter's room. Maureen was three, but the room in which she slept was not a nursery. It was a young girl's room with pale blue ruffled organdy curtains and an organdy skirt around the vanity table and a blue-chintz-lined closet; a long mirror on one wall—the extra wide kind in which one surveys an evening dress's lacy folds;

small colored balls of perfume atomizers: red and gold, empty and waiting for the scent their owner would choose when she got old enough to care for such things.

Katherine had insisted that the room be furnished in this manner a few months ago. She did not quite realize why, why it had seemed very necessary to her that the changes be made at once. Perhaps it was only her longing to get through the awkward growing years, the child years.

Perhaps an unconscious admission that the only real contact between herself and Maureen would come during the four or five years of the girl's first beauty, years that would be terminated by her marriage. They would not see each other very often: Maureen must go away to college; at home her time would be occupied by her friends. Yet for mother and daughter it would be the happiest time, although an uneasy one, for they would both realize that they did not really like each other very much.

Katherine leaned over and kissed her daughter. "I'm leaving now, honey."

Maureen stared at her solemnly. " 'By." She had been drinking orange juice (briefly Katherine recalled her own breakfast): her upper lip with the soft invisible hairs now sported an orange mustache.

"Messy." Katherine picked up a napkin from the tray beside the bed. "Now wipe your mouth."

Solemnly Maureen scrubbed the napkin across her lips, then turned her attention to the bowl of cereal in front of her.

"She's eating, ma'am," Annie said, rolling pale blue eyes behind her rimless glasses. "And it isn't easy to get her to eat in the morning."

Katherine shrugged. She had come in at the wrong time; she admitted the mistake to herself. "I'm glad her appetite's better," she said sweetly. "I was worried."

"Yes, ma'am," Annie said. Her voice had no inflection to give the words a second and ironic meaning.

She's angry, Katherine thought, because I interrupted the routine. And now she's thinking I don't care a bit what happens to my daughter. But I do. I do.

Then because she did not quite believe herself, she
leaned over and kissed Maureen on top of the head.
"Good-by, honey. I'll see you tonight, I reckon."

She did not say good-by to Annie. She turned and
picked up her gloves and bag from the chair and left
quickly.

There was nothing else to do. She had to be out of
the house. And she didn't like going downtown: shopping, eating lunch alone, going to a movie. And she
didn't like to go with any of the women she knew. What
they thought showed so plainly on their stupid faces (and
Katherine was not stupid by any means). And what they
thought was a combination of admiration and pity: she
has got rid of her husband; she looks happy over it; and
today by court order she cannot go home; it is her husband's house again. Katherine saw these things plainly
in their faces and she did not go out with these women
who were her best friends and whom she liked on other
days of the week.

It was not that she minded being out. Not at all. Her
friends and her club work took up all her time. But she
could have gone home, had she wanted. On these days
she could not, not and keep the settlement. Hugh would
be strict on that point, she knew. Katherine was furious,
but she was too sensible to object. So she usually drove
the thirty-five miles over to Barksfield and visited her
mother. It seemed the best thing to do.

After a few more years she would find that she much
preferred a solitary day in town. After a few years she
would find a positive pleasure in being alone.

Perhaps that was why she never remarried. Not that
she did not have a chance to. She was a very beautiful
woman. She dressed superbly; she went out a great deal
and had hundreds of friends. She could have remarried
a dozen times, but she said, No, thank you, in a polite
way that left no room for argument or doubt. She did
not take lovers either, except in the first few years after
the divorce, for she was confused then and afraid of
loneliness. But she freed herself from them when she
realized she could be happiest alone. Each day she experienced a great pleasure when she woke to her beautifully appointed house, her beautiful daughter. Her own
lovely body delighted her. She liked to lie in the tub and

feel the water move over her and pour half a vial of bath oil over her shoulders. She also found that it was a delicious pleasure to walk around her room naked and feel her body move. She had a perfect body; she was a superb animal. But she was not quite human. She did not need anyone.

Hugh Fleming unlocked the front door and came into the hall. He still kept his door key, though he used it only one day in the week. He kept it in the leather case along with his other keys—the car, the office, the other house. It was a silver key with his initials on the head, the sort that had to be specially made. Katherine had given it to him for Christmas the first year of their marriage. He folded up the leather case, put it in his pocket, and went upstairs to see his daughter. He was earlier than usual: she was just finishing her breakfast.

"I have not done a thing to getting her dressed, Mr. Fleming," Annie told him, lifting her eyebrows in polite annoyance. "You came on us a bit early."

Hugh picked up his daughter, who hugged him delightedly, one hand grabbing his ear, the other holding his tie. "How's my girl?" he said. "How's my big girl?"

She giggled in her thin high-pitched voice and reached for his coat pocket where he always kept a present for her. She let herself hang limp across his arm while she reached into his left-hand pocket, then straightened up, triumphantly holding a green and white bead necklace.

"Now, that is pretty for sure," Annie said. "And isn't he a nice daddy to be remembering you?"

Hugh brushed the rumpled brown hair with his fingertips and twisted it into ringlets. He was holding his daughter, he thought. It was hard to realize that sometimes, she looked so much like her mother.

The awkward squarish child body in his arms squirmed and shifted; a little hand dug into the cloth of his coat as Maureen climbed up to sit atop his shoulder. Tenderness, a great protecting tenderness, burst its soft petals. "I'll give her the bath, Annie. You go start the water."

"Sure, she splashes like a baby whale, Mr. Fleming," Annie said warningly. "And you'll be ruining your suit."

"She's my daughter." He hugged Maureen tighter and

she squealed a little at the sudden pressure. "To hell with the suit. I want to."

Annie lifted her eyebrows slightly. She would have given Mr. Fleming the same lecture on blaspheming and evil words that she gave her nephews but for one fact: he paid her salary. So she went and filled the tub and spread the towels and handed Mr. Fleming Maureen's slip and panties. "I will leave her dress on the bed." She spoke with dignity, her conscience still smarting under his affront. "It would only be wilting up in the steaming bathroom."

"Okay," said Hugh, not noticing the iciness of her tone. "Come on, honey," he told Maureen, "your old man's going to give you a bath."

Contrary to Annie's dour prediction, Maureen did not splash in the tub. She was a bit awed at the unaccustomed turn of events and sat very still, staring up into her father's face with neither anger nor friendliness but only a kind of surprise. Hugh washed his baby carefully, an aching pleasant tenderness in his heart. It was not a usual feeling for him; he had not experienced it often before and it never lasted long. It would fade and be replaced by the vaguely angry, dissatisfied stirring with which he usually viewed his daughter. It was not that he disliked her. Not at all. He was being a very good father to her; he was supporting her well. And that was the point—although Hugh would never have admitted it. He was a businessman, one of the shrewdest; he knew a good deal when he saw one. He was spending quite a bit of money on his daughter and he could not quite convince himself that it was worth it.

Of course, it was, in the long run. Maureen turned out to be a lovely young woman. She had a truly magnificent wedding, and Hugh, circulating among the guests, his head buzzing a little from the champagne, finally realized how fine an investment his daughter had been. After all, it was none of his fault that the man she married turned out to be no good, even though he was handsome and came from a fine family.

At her wedding Hugh could be happy in his investment, and it was a great satisfaction to him.

But it was not the same sort of pleasure he felt that morning when against the sour disapproving looks of Annie he bathed and dressed his daughter. And that emotion, perhaps because more rare, is more precious.

They went to the park that particular morning. "Just like I promised you last week," he reminded her. She stared at him without understanding, her dark eyes puzzled: she had long ago forgotten his promise. For a moment he was annoyed that she had not looked forward to it, as he had done. Then he laughed and told her: "You're only a baby yet," and hugged her soft little body. And all day he was very careful of her.

Toward the end of the afternoon, just as they were walking back to the parked car, they passed the tropical gardens. Through the glass door Maureen caught sight of the huge silver reflecting globe and pointed to it with an insistent nod.

"You don't want to go in here, honey," Hugh told her. But she was already hanging on the chrome handle, trying to pull open the glass door.

They went inside. Hugh had always found the air too humid to be comfortable; he found himself taking shallow quick breaths, panting almost. But Maureen loved the heat and the dampness. She smiled up at him, her dark eyes impish and full of life. She tugged at his hand and would have run off, had he not tightened his grip. Finally she stood on tiptoe, swaying back and forth, her nose crinkling with the heavy scents.

He walked slowly up and down the paths with her, past broad wax-leaved plants dripping moisture, and heavy pollened red flowers, and vines carefully propagated by hand and bound up with straw. And then the orchids, a whole wall of them with their great spreading petals reaching into the heat. "See," Hugh told Maureen. "Pretty. Just the color of your dress." The blooms were forced to grow to gigantic size in half the time; they were beautiful and exotic and they did not last.

"Now let's go," Hugh said, for he was beginning to be very tired himself. He picked up Maureen and carried her to the car. She protested, crying, and then suddenly fell asleep. He watched her with faint stirrings of the tenderness whose great upsurge he had experienced that morning.

And it was the last time he would have such a joy in his daughter, Maureen. That afternoon his wife, his second wife, whose name was Sylvia, decided not to go for a drive as she usually did. Even with a cape she thought she looked just too big; and with the anxiety of the novice, she was desperately afraid that her baby would come on her suddenly and indecently in a field or on a road. In the late afternoon she called Hugh and asked him to come home.

By that time Hugh's pleasant affection for his daughter had worn off and had left only the sense of viewing a not particularly successful venture. They had just come back and were still in the front hall when the phone rang. Hugh shifted Maureen to his left arm and answered it himself, saying yes quickly.

Maureen was still dozing. He carried her upstairs to the room her mother had designed with expensive good taste. Then he left quickly, calling out a brief good-by to Annie, and thinking only of Sylvia, wondering if anything could go wrong. (Sylvia bore him three more children: three boys after the first girl. All of them grew up prosperous and healthy. She was a very fine wife for him. And after his death—she found him one evening, sitting on the porch, erect but not breathing—she discovered that she did not want to live either.)

Annie left Maureen to sleep undisturbed in her clothes. The house was very quiet and empty: Hugh had gone and Katherine had not returned. (She would be just now beginning the drive back, her face white and strained from the effect of being polite, her make-up a little streaked by the heat.) Outside on the dry lawns sprinklers were beginning to throw out fan-shaped streams of water.

Annie went down the hall to her own room, leaving the door ajar in case Maureen should call. She opened the blinds and sat down by the window, the late afternoon heat against her face, and, taking a stiff bound Bible from the table, began to read. She was a very religious woman and read in the Bible every day for a half-hour. She did not like the Old Testament; she could never quite convince herself that its heroes (with their bloody swords and many wives) were men of God. And although she always began the New Testament at the Gospel of St. Matthew—she felt that she should begin at the beginning—she found that she preferred the epistles. (She could make no sense of the Apocalypse at all.) Today it was Paul to the Galatians. "Walk in the spirit and you shall not fulfil the lusts of the flesh. . . . The fruit of the Spirit is joy." She heard the front door open, then slam shut, as Katherine came home.

Annie stood up. Joy. The lusts of the flesh. The chaff which shall be cast in the fire. Hell fire. Which was like summer sun, but stronger seven times. In her mind she saw clearly: Katherine and Hugh revolving slowly in a great sputtering, leaping fire while she stood on the edge, watching, dressed in some sort of luminous stuff which all the righteous wore in the hereafter, holding Maureen by the hand.

(Annie died while Maureen was on her honeymoon, just a week after there'd been a card from Hawaii signed: "Love from your little girl, Maureen.")

No one suspected then that Maureen's husband would turn into the sort of fellow he did. No one guessed that she would have two more ex-husbands when, as a middle-aged, strikingly handsome woman, she took a very beautiful, very expensive apartment for one on the west coast. . . .

Annie found Katherine sprawled on the couch in the living room. "Is something wrong, ma'am?" she asked politely.

"I've had some day," Katherine said. "Lord, but my head aches."

"Maureen is sleeping." Annie stood with her hands in the pockets of her white apron, holding herself stiffly erect. "She is very tired."

"That's fine," Katherine said. "I knew her father would take good care of her." She rubbed her temples gently. "Annie, go get me an aspirin. What a day I've had!"

"Yes, ma'am," Annie said.

Katherine stretched herself on the couch, one arm

across her eyes. "You damn old Puritan," she said. "See
if the air-conditioner's working. It's hot as hell."

Later that evening Maureen woke, fretful, and began
to cry. Lying on her bed in the orchid pinafore she had
worn to the park, she began to cry—softly at first, then
louder so that Annie could hear.

"You eat something wrong, lamb?" Annie asked.
"Did that father of yours feed you something wrong?"

Maureen spread out her arms and legs and stretched,
as if she would grow suddenly, grow to fill the bed, which
was too big for her.

"We'll take off your dress, lamb. And you'll rest
better."

But Maureen shook her head and dug her fingers into
the bed. The orchid dress was wet through in spots
with perspiration.

"Annie won't move you, then, lamb. But we'll cool
off this old room for you." She walked over to the door
and glanced at the thermostat dial: it was as low as it
could go. "You're running a fever, lamb."

Annie stood looking down at her. "My pretty little
one. My pretty, pretty one."

Annie rubbed her hands together slowly. "Sure," she
said, "and you look like a young lady already, there."

Maureen did not answer. She lay on the bed, staring
up at the ceiling, her eyes wide.

"Don't look like that, lamb." Annie moved over and
sat on the edge of the bed. Half under her breath she
began a lullaby, a soft, plaintive little air, with a wide
tonal range—too wide, for her voice faltered on the high
notes. But the Gaelic words came out soft and clear:

> *"My little lady, sleep*
> *And I will wish for you: A love to have,*
> *A true heart,*
> *A true mind,*
> *And strong arms to carry you away."*

Her fingers brushed away the hair from Maureen's
forehead: it was damp and sticking to the skin in little
wisps. The child pulled away. The sun had left her
cheeks flushed—bright color, high across the cheek-

bones. Fever sparkled her eyes and enlarged them. Tiredness gave lines to her face and shadows and the illusion of age.

"Sure," Annie repeated, "and you look like a young lady, a lovely young lady already, there."

Maureen lay on her side, the clear lines of her profile showing against the pink spread. She did not turn again: she had stopped crying. And lay there, beautiful and burning.

The Suicides
of Private Greaves

James Moffett

A savage beating against wood of something below caused the men on the second floor to look up at each other from their dismantled rifles strewn across their laps and bunks. One man leaped up and bounded off so quickly that the small parts on his bunk sprang up after him. Then everyone started running down the loose barracks floor toward the stairs in a flapping of unbuttoned fatigue shirts. Rifle barrels fell on spread blankets, with the cleaning rod half in the muzzle. The tips of untied boot laces popped along the floor.

During the jolting descent someone said, "I thought the downstairs squads were policing outside." The stairs ended facing the rear screen door and on the passage to the latrine adjacent. As the flood spilled onto the passage and swirled around the hairpin turn, left toward the main section, one fellow was caught and channeled right on out through the screen door. "This way, Milt." Craning and crowding, the mob of trainees rounded the rifle racks, halted and telescoped.

"Might have known it was Greaves."

Two men who had been downstairs in the latrine, and had arrived almost immediately after the noise, were kneeling on either side of a small figure against the front of a footlocker. Greaves was a round-headed boy sitting with an expression of shock on his soft formless features. His chest pumped as he sucked and blew air in animal-like fashion. A fat Italian boy was loosening a knotted leather boot thong from Greaves' neck. The cut end hung down the front. His partner, a tall beardless youth, sat on his heels, knees down. He stretched his palms out in an explicative gesture. "We hear this terrific racket, come tearing in and there he is kicking the hell out of the locker trying to get back on it."

"Here," said the Italian to the other. "I ain't got no fingernails at all. You try it awhile. He can breathe all right but I can't untie the knot." He squatted back on his heels and rubbed his fingertips against his palms. "You should have seen him at first," he said to the crowd. "With that round head of his he looked like the reddest tomato you ever saw. And fighting—Je-sus Christ! He was turning and twisting and wrestling himself all over the place."

A second wave of trainees burst in—the police call returning. There were startled faces, openmouthed queries, grudged explanations from those on the fringe who could not see well anyway, and glances of impatience from the old witnesses.

Greaves' left leg was bent back and to the side as it had naturally folded when they had lowered him to the floor. It pushed with the slow sporadic movement of a lizard in throes. His coloring and breathing were becoming normal, though his face was still fixed in shock. There was no communication apparent between face and leg.

"I can't undo that damn knot," said the tall youth, straightening up and nursing his fingers. He leaned around to the eyes still in eternity: "You're a great big pain in the ass, Greaves. Do you know that?" He appealed to the crowd. "He don't care—there's always somebody to do his dirty work for him. How come he wasn't policing with you guys, anyway—he bug out again?"

"Sure he bugged out again."

"You mean he really tried to hang himself?" asked a latecomer.

"Naw," said the Italian, "he just got that beam up there mixed in while he was tying his boots." Some laughed eagerly. Everybody looked up and saw the long thin remnant of thong hanging down.

"Course he might have used his tent rope and done a better job."

"Maybe he didn't really want to kill himself."

The tall youth said, "Yeah, but you guys didn't see him when he was still doing his little dance up there."

"That footlocker is pretty low for a gallows, isn't it?" Some laughed and others joined in.

"Besides that, he knew you guys were right upstairs. That's typical of him, to expect others to get him out of a mess."

"I'm telling you, the guy *could* have killed himself. If we hadn't just happened to be in the latrine talking it might have been too late."

"To hell with them," said the Italian. "If they'd seen his tongue sticking out they would know."

Greaves' elbows hooked the edge of the locker behind him and the leg still pushed sporadically. He seemed cognizant now of people around him. His two saviors pulled him to a sitting position on top of the locker. He moved his head a little, then straightened his back into a stiff and stuffed attitude. It looked like dignity. One man began to clap and they all applauded.

"Why didn't you tell us you wanted to do it, Greaves? We would have rigged up something nice for you." Greaves' numb face turned in the direction of the speaker. The Italian and his friend had backed into the crowd.

"Yeah, you got buddies, you know." Greaves turned his face slowly to that one too.

"Look at him—he's still punchy. Trying to remember where he is."

Someone too far back to participate said, "Hey, has anyone thought to send for Sgt. Clinton?" In a sudden change of tone everyone tried to show by a few mumbled words his sincerity about summoning Sgt. Clinton. A man near the front door ran out into the quadrangle on earnest mission as someone hollered for him to try the day room and as two others, outdistanced, retraced their steps.

Sgt. Clinton was a Negro in his mid-twenties. His long body hung low out over the billiard table as he poked the cue tentatively at the ball, sliding the stick forward in a sure glide on the back of his thumb and drawing it swiftly to the rear in simulated recoil. The toe of one boot mirrored the stout, blond table leg, and his starched fatigues broke into only two neat wrinkles when the pendulous swing changed the angle of his elbow. Suddenly the cue drove home with a satisfying contact that showed force and control. Sgt. Clinton remained in the position of completed stroke, laughing in a way that shook his chest and jingled the ID tag he wore close to his throat instead of down in his shirt. It swung just under his Adam's apple and bounced off the brilliantly white wedge of T-shirt at his chocolate throat.

"Now, cat, if you could shoot like that I would not be here. I would be afraid to play with you." He enunciated each syllable with the finest care.

A stocky red-haired cook in soiled whites grinned and said "Sh-i-it" and moved around an opposite corner of the table, preparing to shoot.

At that moment the trainee pushed open the door. "Sgt. Clinton, Greaves has just tried to kill himself. You better come over and see him."

"Is he hurt?" he asked, laying the cue down with such quiet rapidity that the movement seemed slow.

"Well, he's all right now. . . ." Emptied of his dramatic burden, the boy stood emptied himself.

Sgt. Clinton said "Damn!" and started running across the cindered quadrangle in a long-legged gait that favored his right leg.

He entered the barracks and saw the focusing of the crowd on Greaves. He squinted with exaggeration at his watch as he walked down the aisle. "Gentlemen, if I remember correctly, you have exactly fifteen minutes to finish these rifles." His voice was not loud but the clarity of the exquisite enunciation carried strongly. His facial expression understated the situation. By the time Sgt. Clinton reached him, Greaves was no longer the center of interest but only the unnatural part of a routine atmosphere.

His body was still galvanized, but his eyes had followed Sgt. Clinton, registering full consciousness for the first time. With irresistible matter-of-factness, Sgt. Clinton placed his long brown palm on the back of Greaves' neck and started moving off, not saying anything and already looking to the door at the front where he would lead him. The boy rose and followed.

The cadre room by the front door contained two bunks and a folding camp table with a snowy towel spread over it as a cover. An electric cord ran from a double socket in the center of the ceiling to a radio sitting on the towel, near several copies of *Ebony* and *Jet.* Hanging on a rigged section of broomstick were five sets of khakis and three suits of fatigues, stiffly starched, the sleeve creases hanging parallel.

They each took a bunk, facing, with their knees almost touching in the small space. "Has anyone been making it difficult for you in the platoon here?" Greaves readily shook his head, No.

"Now don't be afraid to tell me. You know I don't tolerate any rough stuff in my platoon." Greaves shook his head again.

Sgt. Clinton blinked, thinking. "Have you received any bad news from home?" Greaves had his palms flat on the bunk behind him, leaning back on his straight arms.

"No." He looked past the sergeant at some roto-gravure portraits of Negro baseball players and enter-tainers pinned to the wooden wall. "We don't write," he added, refocusing his eyes to the face before him. But the eyes opposite were absorbed.

Then Sgt. Clinton smiled and said, "Maybe you're just homesick." The boy stiffened and looked away, remote. He stared at the creases on the khaki sleeves that bi-sected the shoulder insignia and sergeant chevrons. With a movement fast for him, he moved his gaze to the snowy wedge of T-shirt, dropped it to the miraculously polished boots.

Sgt. Clinton was straining for reasons, trying to under-stand by sheer dint of mental and visual confrontation. Then without realizing it he was remembering his mother saying, "They's helpless—alla them white chil-lun. It's always us that gotta take care of their chillun for them. And when they's growed up, what happen? They turns on us—tha's what happen, after we done took care of them when they was soft and helpless." She was old-fashioned—a Southern Negro. He had never missed a promotion in the army because he was colored. If you live and talk like a slave, that's how they will treat you.

He caught Greaves' gaze resting on the rotogravures behind him and followed his eyes as they fell on the *Ebony.* He saw that Greaves was unconsciously curious now, and he felt like a Negro and knew it was his own fault and missed the feeling of paternal patronage. The boy was gone now. He thought of that day on the range when the grenade had gone off on the end of the kid's—that other white kid's—rifle, and how he had put his arm, still stinging with bits of metal, around the kid's shoulders and had led him off, soothing his fear and silencing the raging accusations of Sgt. Frennell, who was trying to blame the boy when it was not his fault. But *this* kid *wanted* to die. Why?

Sgt. Clinton shook himself inwardly to regain his poise. "Look, Greaves. Wouldn't you rather tell me the trouble and let me try to keep the whole business in the platoon? You know how Sgt. Brodder handles trainees,"—he saw that other Negro sitting at the First Sergeant's desk in the orderly room, solving all issues by being a first-class bastard to everybody, white or colored—"but if I have an explanation ahead of time, make him feel it's all more or less settled, he won't have an excuse to screw around with you so much."

A flicker of fear passed over Greaves' face.

"Why did you do it?" It cost him to have to ask, finally, so directly. But he needed the relief of resolution.

"I don't know." Greaves looked full at him. He had said it as a child will say anything meaningless to temporize.

They sat with their knees almost touching, Sgt. Clinton blinking slowly and thus belying his natural intelligent expression. His mind stood in stupid contemplation before the synthetic wall of "I don't know." Then it turned away and he became smoothed and indifferent. He had done all he could.

"I guess it really was the fellows—they were after me until I thought I couldn't stand it."

It was a patent lie, a last-minute bid for something—to be spared the ordeal of Sgt. Brodder, thought Clinton. His only reply was an understated glance at Greaves with a tilt of the head. But he forgave the white child.

When he stood up he was confident again. The gleaming boots moved toward the door, the brown palm pressing Greaves' back, and he ushered the figure in disorderly fatigues out of his room.

The First Sergeant, Master Sergeant Brodder, already knew about Greaves' suicide. The mail clerk, passing through the barracks to the latrine, had learned from the trainees and brought the story back to the orderly room. Sgt. Brodder was a powerful Negro with arms that seemed long because, due to his short waist, they hung nearly to his knees. He had a beautiful broad forehead and sculptured temples. He was at his desk when the mail clerk told him and he just continued looking down at his hands folded on the desk. "Where is he now?"

"In Sgt. Clinton's room."

Sgt. Brodder looked up with a grin so sparkling and winning that no one could have believed it was not genuine. "In the chaplain's office, huh? Sgt. Clinton trying to make him feel good 'cause he tried to kill hisself." The grin lasted a moment longer while he reared in his chair. Then he brought his elbows down on the desk and sobered. "If Sgt. Clinton had his way, this comp'ny'd be nothing but a *ho*tel and the cadre'd do nothing but buhp them and pat their asses for them." His speech was unhurried, and everything he did was extraordinarily deliberate, as if form were all.

The mail clerk darted into his mail cage, his face gleeful with anticipation. Sgt. Brodder thought a minute, staring at his folded hands, then looked over at the company clerk seated to his right, who, like the mail clerk, was a draftee, a pfc.

"Ain't Greaves one of them that's been riding the sick book lately?"

"Sure," said the company clerk, without interrupting his rapid typing. "You turned him down on sick call this morning."

"Oh, is that Greaves? That scrawngy little dodo? With the grapefruit head? Yeah, I know which one you mean." He leaned back and looked at the ceiling, silent for a while.

"I don't understand this suicide business. In the Old Army we had to stop them from killing each other. Now they want to kill themselves. Like that Rawlings we had there a while back. I don't get this crop. What do a man want to kill hisself for? I can see wanting to beat up on another guy—and maybe carve on his throat a little. But these guys that's always trying to hang themselves . . . there's something inhuman about that. Course this here whole New Army don't make sense to me. This camp here's more like one of them finishing schools than an army." The clerk smiled to himself.

Sgt. Brodder sat silent again, looking at his hands, then he swung quarter around in his swivel chair: "Do you understand it?"

"What?" The clerk was sunk in concentration.

"A man like that Greaves trying to hang hisself."

The clerk pushed the carriage over and started a new line without breaking rhythm. His voice was somnolescent, issuing from distraction: "No gratification."

"What are you talking about—'gratification'? He ain't here to be gratified."

"True, true," the clerk said, as if he did not know he was speaking.

"There he comes now," said Sgt. Brodder, lifting a little out of his chair. "And Big Brother along with him," he added.

He sat down. "I reckon our little friend has been through the usual *it*inerary—the chaplain and the I.G. and Mental Hygiene. I know he went to Mental Hygiene. . . ." He shuffled through papers on his desk.

The clerk was rolling a new sheet into the typewriter. "Upper left-hand corner of the pad."

"Yeah." He squared himself, as if confronting an old foe, and began to read the slip as Sgt. Clinton and Greaves reached the steps outside. " 'Recommend close observation during basic and later assignment to clerk-typist. Probably emotionally unreliable in stress situations, which should be avoided.' Says he shows signs of unhappy family life. That don't mean nothing—I can show them kind of signs, too, all over my back where my old man used to beat me. Didn't make a maniac out of me. . . . 'Stress situations'—like fighting a war maybe."

Sgt. Clinton led his charge across the orderly room and up to the desk. Sgt. Brodder continued staring at the paper, head down, a full minute while the two stood before him. Finally Sgt. Clinton said, "I have company business here, Sergeant."

He looked up and his eyes lighted into that winning grin. "What has you dragged into my office, Sgt. Clinton?" He looked all merriment. "Is this one of them things been lying around 'neath your barracks over there? 'Bout time you had him change his oil, ain't it?"

Even through the brown skin a flush could be seen in Clinton's face.

"I'm bringing this man in here to see that he gets taken care of. He needs some *professional* help. He's all twisted up." His enunciation was at its most exquisite, his voice clear and controlled. The firmness of his look equaled Brodder's.

"Yeah, I can see his clothes is all twisted around him. We'll have to get that man some *pee*jamas so he won't have to sleep in his duty clothes."

"He's one of my boys and I intend—"

Brodder's brow shifted up and his eyes lighted all over again. "My, you got a powerful lot of chillun, ain't you?" His eyes flitted to the white boy and back. "Why, I didn't even know you's married."

"As First Sergeant in a training unit, you should remember that you are only an *administrator*"—the corners of his mouth diverged and he lifted his chin—"and not anything but a chair-borne receptionist for our commanding officer."

Brodder's face became sober. He dipped his head ironically. "Thank you, Sergeant, that'll be all for you now. You may go and take charge of your *platoon*."

The clerk had long since stopped typing. He sat looking down at his fingers resting on the keys. The mail clerk was avidly leaning on the half-door of his cage. Greaves had stood perfectly still between the two sergeants, looking straight ahead. Now he shifted uneasily as he bore for the first time the full personal force of Sgt. Brodder.

"*What's* your name, soldier?" The ritual began.

Greaves looked down. "Private Greaves, Sergeant."

Sgt. Brodder raised up carefully and peered over the front of his desk. "I don't see anybody down there. Who you talking to, soldier?"

"You, Sergeant."

"Then *look* at me!" Greaves began to tremble as if the vocal vibrations actually had shaken his frame.

"You'se shifty-eyed, ain't you?" He tilted his head and looked into Greaves' face. The movement had an element of play in it, yet the withering reality of the man emanated from the eyes and fixed Greaves with an inescapable exaction. "Ain't you a man? Well, *ain't* you?" Greaves shook more, straining in every tissue to keep his eyes level. Brodder made the chair squeak by shifting back, broke his gaze, then posed leaning on his forearm at the right side of his desk, his back straight.

"How old are you?" At the same time he cocked his eye at him formally, without moving his head and pressing his right palm flat down.

"Seventeen."

Brodder looked past him a moment. "Just a punk, ain't you? Don't know nothing, ain't good for nothing, or to nobody, are you? *Are* you?" That intolerable demand turned on Greaves again. He tottered. His eyes watered as though he were looking into an overwhelming beam. "*Look* at me!"

"No."

Like a wrathful god momentarily appeased, Brodder released him by looking half to the side. His face put on the theatrical mask "disgust" for a few seconds. Then he rose slowly, walked around the corner of the desk, and stood at a relaxed "attention," facing the boy's profile, long enough for Greaves to become anxious and turn his head, then: "Nobody told you to look around!" Inspecting Greaves' clothes, he snapped his glance up, then snapped it down. He leaned around the boy's face with his feet still together, making a twisting motion that would have been awkward if he had had less muscular control or if he did not always move in that highly stylized manner.

"*Filthy!*" he said into his face. He had his indignation mask on. "These clothes is *filthy*." His bottom lip exploded from behind his teeth when he pronounced the *f*. Next he walked behind Greaves and tugged rapidly at his loose shirt. "Have you cleaned them boots since the Civil Wah?" He walked completely around him and lifted the end of the thong. "That to remind you to do something?" Suddenly a thunderous roar burst from him, right into Greaves' ear. "*Stand* up straight!" And the trembling form nearly collapsed.

Brodder walked back and sat down. He just sat looking up at Greaves, the splendid mahogany temples gleaming.

"It's a court-martial offense to commit suicide. Did you know that?" He lit a cigarette and gave the appear-

ance of being confidential, by dropping his deliberate-
ness. "Did you?

"Don't"—Greaves jumped—"wag your head like a
dog. You're a man." He smiled scornfully. Another
mask. "You could get the death sentence for suicide.
Attempted suicide. You ain't got the right to kill yourself, trooper. You'se U.S. government property, you
don't own yourself. I don't know why, but they wants
you. Only one who's got the right to kill you is the
enemy."

While he was talking, another Master Sergeant, the
Field First Sergeant, walked in. He was small, lean, and
wiry and had the most alert expression conceivable. His
eyes, his entire face, suggested in their raptness the sharp
muzzle and keen ears of a hunting dog. Though not out
of his twenties, he had a conspicuous blending of gray
in his black hair. His face was chiseled out of bone. He
glanced at Greaves and appraised him completely. Then
walking to a side position he stood with his legs planted
apart, thumbs hooked in his pockets, and cocked his
head and watched with narrowed eyes. Even standing so
squarely he looked ready to spin or pivot if a leaf fell
behind him.

"Now suppose you just pretend I'm your father and
tell me why you caused all this trouble, draping yourself
all over our barracks with a shoestring. Huh? How come
you did that?"

"I don't—"

"You know." Greaves crumpled a little more.

"I don't . . . like it here."

Brodder put on a splendid frown. "Now I don't understand that. I see by your serial number that you's RA.
That mean Reg'lar Army, don't it? And that mean you
wanted to be here, you volunteered your services. Now
if you was just another old draftee they hauled in off the
streets, that'd be different. But you, it was your *desire* to
be a soldier.

"You know what I think? I think you joined up to
get a little *pres*teedge with the girls. Thought a uniform
would—"

"I didn't like home." Brodder searched Greaves' face
in the wake of the ripple that had broken his taut
impassivity.

"You don't like *no* place, do you? I bet you don't even like yourself. *I* wouldn't if I was—"

"I hate soldiers," Greaves blurted.

All the game went out of Brodder's manner. The other sergeant leaned forward on his planted feet and his eyes narrowed more.

Brodder let the realization of what Greaves had done dawn on him. He looked silently at him, for the first time devoid of style or play, for the first time personally involved. Greaves began to cringe.

"You playing crazy, Greaves, but it won't do no good. You'll never get out of the army as long as I'm in it. You didn't even *try* to kill yourself, did you? *Did* you?" His voice blasted with stunning effect. "*Look* at me, God damn it!" Greaves was trying to raise his eyes by raising his head, until his chin was pointing upward. But the eyes could not meet Brodder's. They tugged like muscles straining against tremendous weight.

The veins in the mahogany temples stood in relief, breaking the round polished surfaces. "*Look* at me!"

The clerk jumped from nervousness.

Greaves' lids fluttered, his eyes showed all white for a moment, then he collapsed to the floor. The other sergeant had just turned to drop a match into an ashtray; a jerk of the head and his whole being was gathered in the alarm of his face—which relaxed, however, immediately after. Brodder was already motioning to two trainee runners sitting along the wall. "*Get* that man off my floor. I can't have no trainees sacked out in here cluttering up my office. I don't care *where* you put him. Put him in a chair over there in the corner and hold his head down till he come to. And turn him to the wall. I'm tired of looking at that meathead."

He rose. "Sgt. Krita, you want to watch the place for a minute, while I get a cup of coffee? This boy's disturbed my peace of mind this morning."

The clerk supported himself on the typewriter, collecting himself. He noticed the mail clerk leaning over the half-door, trying to see Greaves around the corner of the wall. "You've got the most shit-eating grin I ever saw," he said. Sgt. Krita, too, looked at the mail clerk, then made a leering imitation of his gawking, grinning curiosity. "You're nothing but an overgrown punk yourself," Krita said to him. His voice was rough and irritable. He took his eyes slowly from the mail clerk with a lingering look of scorn.

Sitting down on the edge of an empty desk, he began reading a newspaper with inviolate concentration. Sometimes his jaw sagged, and he looked brutish then.

Twice he glanced over the top of the paper and checked on Greaves, who was sitting awake now but slumped and tired. Finally Krita walked in front of Greaves and stood with his palms pressed to his upper buttocks, his feet apart and the thin lithe body bent backward from the hips. It was the stance of a much larger man but natural for him.

He spoke to Greaves in a low-keyed voice. "Do you know what that means when you can't look a man in the eye? It means you're ashamed. You know he's right, don't you? You are a punk." He lit another cigarette. "I hate punks." It was venomous, and Greaves looked up for the first time. "Sit up—you ain't sick." Krita took a long, even draw on the cigarette, looking coolly at Greaves. The clerk was typing again.

"Do you know what I mean when I say 'punk'? A punk is a guy that's got no pride. He don't do his job right, he don't stand by his buddies, he don't *give* a shit. He just looks after himself. Me! Me! Me!" He was striking his chest, and suddenly his lower teeth stood out in detail, fine and tiny, stained with nicotine around the gums and crevices. "I seen them in combat."

He drew on the cigarette, tilting his head to avoid the smoke that rose straight up. He stared to the side, pouting.

"You ain't home with your mummy any more." He leaned forward and rolled his head from side to side in Greaves' face, mocking. "When you join the army you ain't got a mummy any more. You got to be a man even if you're only a kid." The light glinted from the bristly gray hairs on his closely cut sideburns.

"*Sit* up, God damn it!" Greaves shuffled in the chair and half straightened, casting a glance of hot, helpless hatred at him as he did.

With incredible suddenness Greaves' head was slammed sickeningly into the wall behind him, bounced, and left him staring stunned before him. Krita's hand

was back on his upper buttock before Greaves knew
what had happened.

The typewriter stopped. Krita twisted slowly around
without breaking his stance and waited for the mail clerk
to pop his head out. When he appeared Krita flapped
his hand at him and commanded, "Crawl back into your
hole, you big fart-sniffer." He did.

Meanwhile the company clerk was walking out the
door. Krita flicked his head around and looked thoughtfully after him. He shrugged and turned back to
Greaves. Taking hold of the dangling end of the thong
at Greaves' breast, he let his hand swing slightly there.
"I don't give a damn for you—you can go hang yourself
after the sixteenth week. But while you're a trainee in
my company you'll soldier." He tugged on the thong,
but not hard. "Do you hear that? When I take this company out in the field, they train, and when I graduate
them they're soldiers, men." He released the thong with
a flip. "I don't give a damn for you, but I don't want
nobody spoiling my company."

He straightened up into his stance again. "Sgt. Brodder here," he nodded toward his desk, "he'll bullshit
around with you half a day playing games. I don't. I
mean business. If I ever think for one minute you're
trying to bug out . . . well, you *better* go hang yourself. I've
straightened out more than one trainee and the I.G.
never proved nothing on me yet."

He pivoted, walked over to an ashtray and crushed
out the butt.

Greaves opened a jackknife and, staring dumbly at his
palm on his knee, pulled the blade slowly across his
wrist, where a red line appeared as if the knife had
sketched it. He changed the knife from one hand to the
other, but stopped then. The blood welled up fast. He
got excited and the knife shook in his hand. Hearing a
quick movement from Krita he pulled it hastily across
his other wrist. Then the lightning swoop of Krita's
cupped hand sent the knife clattering away.

Before Krita knew it, his thumbs were pressing at the
cuts and he was holding Greaves' arms over their heads,
apparently having jerked him to his feet and wrestled
him into position in one movement. They stood locked
face to face.

Krita transformed. He began to shudder violently from head to foot. Instinctively he wanted to kill the boy for wanting to kill himself. But for once his will was twisted on itself and locked. Killing Greaves was a futile punishment for his not wanting to live. To let him die was to abet suicide, to answer death with death, which was a contradiction of the law that he must keep him alive to face. The law that says you must preserve and defend your existence, in whatever pain, at whatever odds, to the extremity of nerve and blood and heart.

And others' existence. Scabs were torn from the flesh of his mind, revealing raw and tender images. Again crouched in that hole in Korea with three dying men, sobbing because he had not hands enough to tend them and at the same time to spray the slope with his carbine, not faculties enough to keep aware of all there was to know about each of these three men and himself and the Chinese moving somewhere around him. And now, once again, to care so desperately, to be made to care like that, all over again to care so much, betrayed by his reflexes at the sudden scent of blood into engaging himself for this kid—whom he hated for tearing him open again and reducing his life to its hard and bitter start.

Crucified on the rack of this other's body, prisoner of the thing he held, he glared with red-eyed rage at the round head before him, until surely he would kill him yet, seeing the dazed apathy of Greaves beside his own uncontrollable caring. The strain of holding his arms up and pressing his thumbs into the boy's flesh increased the shuddering of his frustration.

The mail clerk came up with two tourniquets he had got from a desk drawer. His face was white and horrified. Krita did not remember having told him to get them. Now, as he directed how to put them on, having seated Greaves, he became calmer, and finally released the wrists with a fling of his dripping hands. They laid him on the floor and the mail clerk knelt and held the twisted tourniquets.

Krita sat down at Brodder's desk. His hands he held before him, up off the desk. His hands: the very mark and brand of his immersion in other life, of his blasted unity, the stigma that gave the lie to mere prideful efficiency and condescending involvement. Then the unnecessary cruelty of guilt, as he stared at the primal symbol of his bloody agent parts. His mind fought the sense of implication, but he was breached and could not shrug it off. His brow lowered as if to hide the sanctum behind the eyes. He was pouting again. The clipped bristles of premature gray hair stood out singly against the redness of the skin clogged with blood.

"Hey, I'm getting tired of holding these things."

Krita's voice rasped with irritation. "Quit your bellyaching and hold them." He smoked a cigarette, sitting motionless, building himself up out of silence and stillness. When he had finished the cigarette he reached down to the bottom drawer and got out two compresses and a roll of tape. Then he went to Greaves and bandaged the wrists, working steadily without looking at his face. He removed the sticks from the tourniquets but left the bands tied half-tight around the upper arms.

As he was finishing, the screen door slapped shut and Sgt. Brodder walked in with the company commander, a captain in his thirties, who was wearing the CO's red and white helmet liner and fatigues that were not well pressed. Though tall and broad-shouldered, he walked with mincing steps. And his knees seemed to bend backward like a dog's, due to the loose-jointed way he swung, instead of placed, his feet forward. The general impression was that he was walking backward and forward at the same time. He stopped in the middle of the floor and looked at Greaves from the altitude of his back-tilted head. A cigarette dangled from his mouth and his eyes were practically shut trying to avoid the smoke. He stood still and his ankles nestled together.

Sgt. Krita said, "He cut his wrists. I got to him before he lost any blood." Sgt. Brodder had alerted as soon as he entered. A flicker of confusion, of guilt, showed. For a moment he could not form his face or movements. Then he examined Greaves and said, "He look all right, suh, but I guess we better send him to the hospital so there won't be no trouble later."

The captain said in a voice unconvincingly peremptory, "No, he's all right. I want to talk to him."

"I'se just thinking though, suh, you know how they come around checking up later."

The captain walked over to Greaves with the peculiar

retrograde progression. "That's all right, Sergeant, I'll handle that." Brodder stood behind his desk, with Krita sitting near him on the clerk's desk top. Krita was rapt, with just the same curl of scorn to his mouth that Brodder had. The captain pulled Greaves to his feet and led him back across the orderly room to his private office. Passing the reviewing stand of the sergeants he kept a self-conscious "eyes front" that curled even more the lips of Brodder and Krita.

When the two were by themselves, Brodder, still standing, looked at the other. "Sergeant, you didn't do nothing to make that boy try to kill hisself, did you?" Krita gave a derisive snort, leaving his mouth half-open afterward, scorn still there.

Brodder looked at the ceiling. "Well, it's just that I know you ain't above sorta nu-u-dging a trainee now and then." He cut his eyes theatrically. Krita's face had not changed. Brodder sobered. "You know, I getting tired of covering for you with the I.G," he said. Krita snorted.

The captain seated Greaves in his office and stood over him with his hands on his hips. Greaves was actually looking up at him.

"Now, son, I know the army's hard to take sometimes, and I know you're pretty young and a little bewildered by it all. But why didn't you come to me before and tell me your troubles instead of ... of taking such drastic action?"

"They wouldn't let me see you before."

"Well, if I had known, I flatter myself I could have helped you. These fellows are rough old soldiers, these cadre, and—well, they're not very well educated." The captain started trying to button the flap of Greaves' shirt pocket. He watched his own fingers distractedly as they fumbled slowly with the button. "We're not all like that in the army. Myself, I've been to college and I could have had another career. But—" His voice slowed almost to a halt. His attention was so divided between speaking and buttoning that both acts seemed unconscious. Greaves' hand moved toward the button, but since the captain obviously intended to finish and Greaves would contact his fingers, he let the hand fall and shifted in the chair. "But—uh—I like the army because—uh—that's where you find real men." He grew conscious and twisted the button into place.

"But I want to find out about you." He straightened up and popped his heavy lids, which habitually covered half his protruding eyeballs. "Now a suicidal tendency generally indicates that the subject has some conflict that he can't resolve—you know, take care of." He glanced at Greaves a moment, then up at the ceiling. "Well, no. More likely he's obsessed by some feeling about himself that he can't get rid of. May even have hallucinations." He gave Greaves an intendedly casual glance that was shrewd instead. "He may have long periods of depression—you know, feels the world's against him. Of course everybody feels this way sometimes. I've had spells myself. You know, feeling gloomy, and things look uncertain and the world seems chaotic and you wonder about yourself."

Greaves looked uncomfortable. A gleam of success came into the captain's eyes. He lit a cigarette, shifted his weight to one leg, and looked at the ceiling again. "I was telling my wife the other night about some of the tough times. We haven't been married very long. Yeah, sometimes you feel you've failed and you lose your nerve. You feel like a worm and there's nothing to do but kill yourself.

"But stick it out"—he looked down at Greaves, who looked away—"and one day it works out. I'm married and got a pretty wife—blond—and a captain's rank means something. You'll understand that after you've been in a while. No, the army's not a bad place, but you've got to toughen up, son. An army's got to be tough. I'm being nice to you now because you need special help, but ordinarily I'm tough in the field. You've probably noticed that, during training, and wondered, 'Why is the old man such a mean bastard?' Well, we have to be. We leaders have the responsibility of preparing you kids for a time when you may have to fight. To make men out of trainees it takes leaders who are men, to set the example."

Holding his spent cigarette cautiously to save the long ash, the captain looked at an ashtray on his desk, looked at one on the Executive Officer's empty desk equidistant, and back at the one on his desk, his legs starting for it while he glanced rapidly, trunk twisted, back to the other desk. The result was that he tripped himself, in a confused movement that he eventually straightened out by walking briskly to the Executive Officer's desk. Heading back, he caught Greaves' expression of objective curiosity.

He placed himself before Greaves again, folded his arms, and lifted his head haughtily. "Now, young man, suppose you tell me why you wanted to kill yourself. Or maybe you didn't really try to. Maybe you think you can get out of the army that way. You knew Krita would save you, didn't you?" He smiled sardonically. "And that boot lace . . ." He took hold of the dangling end, toyed with it, then let his fingers creep up to the knot, and held the knot with his fist. His knuckles rested against Greaves' chest. "Well, you won't get away with it." He leaned down to Greaves' face. Greaves did not avoid his eyes, because they did not really focus on him, but somewhere behind him, as if his head were transparent.

"We've handled a lot of cases like you—guys playing crazy. They're like alcoholics—good actors, and cunning." The captain revolved his fist, and the thong alternately tightened and loosened at the sides of Greaves' neck. "They think they're clever but they're *sick*. You have to be crazy to want to play crazy. Don't you see? That means you can't adjust, you can't face reality. Then you're sick . . . sick. That's true of *you*, isn't it?" The lids of his eyes were raised. "Well, *isn't* it?"

"I don't know, sir."

The captain released the thong and straightened up. "What did Mental Hygiene tell you?"

"The guy was real nice—"

"Yes, but what did he say?"

"He said something about depression. Same as you did, sir."

"Well, you get to recognize these things after a while. A CO has to be something of a psychiatrist in this army.

"Tell you what, Greaves. Let's glide over this whole thing. Give you a new start." He was sliding a little calendar back and forth on his desk. "You go back to your platoon, try to be a good soldier and adjust to this life, for your own sake. And I promise to keep all this off your record and not bring any disciplinary action against you. I think a good start would be for you to go right on out to training now. I just heard Sgt. Krita's whistle for the formation. We have an hour of map reading before lunch, nothing strenuous, and it won't hurt you to go out. That'll make you feel that nothing has happened. Okay, that's all, Greaves."

A few moments later, the captain emerged from his office and stood in the middle of the floor thinking, his ankles together and one knee bent.

"Sgt. Brodder."

"Yes, suh." Brodder stood up behind his desk. Both clerks looked up at the captain.

"You've been on this post a long time. Do you know anybody who handles furniture for dependents' quarters?"

"No, suh, not very well."

"Well, when we moved into these quarters they told us we'd have to take twin beds for the time being. My wife doesn't like twin beds and she's after me to get them changed for a double."

The two clerks wrestled with smiles, but Brodder's eyes were hard. "No, suh," he said.

After marching three blocks of regimental streets, the company turned onto a vast meadow flanked by woods at the low horizon. A red-and-white checkered water tower squatted like a monstrous make-believe toadstool, dwarfing the men halting near it. The enormous sky was cloudless and brilliant with sun. A constellation of flowers sparkled in the field of green.

Standing in ranks before a wooden bleachers, the company dissolved momentarily in the confusion of stacking arms, then rapidly crystallized, leaving neat rows of three-rifled cones, like a shadow of the men's formation.

After a lieutenant had briefed the trainees in the bleachers, five or six corporals and pfc's in the blue and white helmet liners of the Faculty appeared, trailing a final stream of cigarette smoke from nostrils or the corners of mouths, and each took a group into the field. Turning and shaking compasses, the trainees scattered and became minute in the immense meadow, a loose nucleus forming here and there around a glint of blue. Beneath the imminence of the over-sized toadstool stood the deserted rifle stacks like the skeletal huts of grass insects.

Off in the meadow the antenna of an arm rippled toward the tower. Tiny, high cries broke out. From where Greaves leaned against the circular iron rail, with the bulge of the tank at his back, he saw the miniature herds begin to arrange in an arc at his feet. A red and white flower near the stands moved, broke into a run toward the tower, intercepted a trainee and dispatched him down the road. Greaves walked around the balcony of the tower, revolving the cyclorama of the entire camp—the platitude of ranged barracks identically built, the mutation of a ruddy brick building flying flags, the shrunken flare of the parade field, the bonewhite spires of chapels pricking in isolated verticality. Level wooded reaches, then the wastes, the dunes of the ranges, each with its own close atmosphere of gun smoke. The regiment again.

The arc of spectators had shifted on the circle in the direction Greaves had followed. He smiled.

"God damn that little son of a bitch!" said the captain, prancing back and forth.

"Did you tell that trainee to have Sgt. Brodder call the fire wagon, sir?" said Sgt. Krita. "They got a net."

The captain lowered his bright gaze from the tower to Sgt. Krita. "They couldn't really catch him with one of those, could they?"

Krita shrugged. "Looks good to have one of them around, though." He called over a trainee, instructed him and sent him off. Then he called after him, "Go to Regimental Headquarters—it's closer."

"Regimental!" The captain stopped prancing. "The colonel and everybody else will be over here."

Krita snorted out of the side of his mouth. "Can't hide all this." He gestured liberally around him, then watched the growing terror in the captain's face.

"I could kill him myself," said the captain.

"There's going to be trouble over those bandaged wrists anyway when they find out he wasn't sent to the hospital."

"I knew what I was doing! They better not try to give me trouble over that, too."

A raspberry-colored Buick pulled up on the road, and Sgt. Brodder started walking toward them, his eyes fixed on the tower.

The captain called Sgt. Clinton. Loping over, favoring his right leg, Sgt. Clinton ran with one eye cocked on Greaves. He stopped in mid-stride. Greaves had a leg hooked over the rail. But he stopped there and appeared to be merely seeking a new position to stand in.

"Do you really think he'll do it this time?" the captain asked Sgt. Clinton.

"I couldn't tell you, sir."

"Well, don't you know anything about him? He's one of your men."

"Sir, I don't understand any better than you do what goes on in the head of a suicidal man." Krita smiled but turned away so that Clinton would not have the satisfaction.

Sgt. Brodder joined the group. "I called the meat wagon, suh," he said. "They ought to be here any minute."

"Sgt. Clinton, maybe you could go and talk to the damn fool," said the captain.

"Sir, what makes you think I can help him?"

"You ought to be able to handle your own men—you're . . ." Sgt. Clinton started walking toward the ladder of the tower. When the crowd saw where he was headed they alternately looked after him and at Greaves, who had both feet back on the platform and was leaning over the rail trying to see who was coming, looking like a kid on a holiday at a tourist observation point.

A white ambulance pulled up the road and parked. A moment later the colonel's glistening olive-drab staff car pulled behind it. The captain ran to welcome the colonel.

Sgt. Clinton climbed up about twenty feet, then leaned back as far as he could and looked to the balcony. Greaves, who could recognize him at that distance, did not move until Clinton swung back to look at him and he could see his face. Evidently Clinton did not become real to him before then. Greaves crouched quickly under the rail, his knees sticking out over the edge of the platform, grasping the rail above his head with both hands, monkey-fashion. People shouted and motioned to Clinton. He had seen, too, and came down. He walked away and did not look back.

The captain and the colonel, having halted to watch the outcome of the attempt, moved toward the tower. Though portly, the colonel carried himself well. He was gray-haired, in his middle fifties. He looked weary and harassed.

"The damned kid has been nothing but trouble since he came into my company," said the captain. The colonel looked over at him, examined him with a frown. "And he's tried suicide before this."

"When?"

"Today, sir."

"Good God, Captain, and you mean you had him out training?"

"Well, sir, he had already been to Mental Hygiene, then I talked with him and he seemed capable of carrying on."

"You talked with him. Don't you know by now what to do with men like that? Get rid of them, wash your hands of them. Let the hospital take care of them. Tell them you think he needs observation. Then they'll probably discharge him sooner or later." They neared the tower now, both watching the figure on the balcony. A long, brilliantly red fire truck parked along the road.

"How did he try to kill himself before?"

"Hanging, then cutting his wrists."

"Good Lord! Twice? Didn't anyone try to *watch* him after the first time?"

"It was so fast, sir. They had him waiting for me in the orderly room when he cut his wrists."

"With his wrists cut he should have been sent to the hospital immediately. There was the perfect chance to get rid of him. Now look at this mess. Don't you think this regiment's hot enough without more scandals like this? And none of them my fault, but because of some damn company commander with no judgment." Then he added, "Besides, those wrists could open up again very easily, you ought to know that."

"Sir, since it was just an easy class in map reading I thought it would be good for him."

The colonel moved his eyes from the balcony to the

captain's face and scanned it critically. Suddenly his own face relaxed in an inward dismissal of the captain, beyond anger or disgust. "You better go take charge of your company."

Six civilian firemen were holding the net in readiness. Stray soldiers in khaki or fatigues, clerks, off-duty men and inexplicables had joined the loose semicircle of spectators.

"If he ever hit that net, he going to bounce right over the moon," said Sgt. Brodder. The colonel approached him and Sgt. Krita and they all saluted.

"What's this man's background anyway, Sergeant Brodder?"

"Seventeen-year-old RA, sir. We sent him to Mental Hygiene and they said he showed signs of a disturbed family. But I think he's prob'ly playing crazy."

"Why do you think so?"

Brodder shuffled. "Well, sir, I ain't sure—I don't know no *psychology* or nothing—but he never go off by hisself to pull these things."

"How did he know he might not die, though?" He glanced at the sergeant. His face no longer looked harassed, but absorbed. He spoke in a familiar tone.

"I don't know, sir. Maybe he figure if somebody save him, that's all right, and if nobody save him, that's all right too." He twisted and watched two MPs step out of a patrol car that they had just parked behind the raspberry Buick and white ambulance and staff car and fire engine.

The colonel strained to make out something of Greaves' features. He became lost in his absorption, no longer conscious of his bearing and the many stares that his presence drew. Suddenly Greaves came to attention and snapped his hand to a salute. The brusqueness of the gesture just as the colonel was concentrating intently on the figure evoked the old response: His feet were together and his hand was level with his shoulder before he stopped himself, made a fist of the hand, and turned away swearing.

He walked for a while among the crowd. *Extraordinary! No wonder it got my goat so. Just Ralph's impudence. Just like his imitations of Point men, standing in the living room that day.*

"All right, I can't force you to stay at the Academy, but why do you hate the army so?"

"Maybe it's because my father's a soldier."

"Do you really hate me so?"

"I couldn't say that, sir. It would be disrespect to an officer." And where are you now, Ralph?

The MPs approached, in fine male feather, tall and erect, resplendent in burnished leather and snowy braid. They saluted the colonel, who was too deep in himself to comprehend their presence at first, though he saw them well enough. Holding the salute for his reply, they became annoyed. Finally he relieved them.

"Anything we can do to help, sir?" one of them asked in his deepest timbre.

"No. Well, go keep order in the crowd over there—anywhere—somewhere over there."

They exchanged sour smiles walking off. "Old geezer like that ought to be selling poppies on street corners."

Am I afraid for two young jackasses to hear my voice unsteady and see my face worked up? The colonel doesn't look very military, they think. Is a man less a man because he has something inside that moves every now and then? My own father's idea, that. But I've got to break through to this kid, think of something these non-coms and that stupid captain haven't thought of. They're all wondering what the colonel's going to do.

The crowd became more excited. Greaves was standing at the break in the rail where the ladder started down. It was the only place where he could jump from a standing position. People shifted. The net was brought around. With a hand grasping each end of the rail, he had placed himself at the very edge of the platform.

Suddenly he let his body fall forward, still holding the ends of the rail, freezing in a swan-dive position. A unanimous outcry arose from the crowd. Sgt. Krita, who had been watching alertly, broke stance and dashed forward several yards in sheer neural response before he caught up with himself. He pivoted and started walking back to the road. His face was a cloud of fury and despair.

Greaves swung back to a standing position. In a voice pitched unnaturally to carry, he screamed out, "Sick—lame—and cra-zy." It carried surprisingly far, even back to the road where Clinton stood, and hushed the crowd, and rang like an anathema in the ears of all. It shook Krita as he was walking away from the tower pouting at the ground. The phrase was the one he used at least twice a week when he asked for sick call at reveille. He snarled over his shoulder at the tower, like a dog that cannot rid itself of something. The captain danced as if he were standing on flames. Brodder winced. Even the MPs seemed disconcerted.

Greaves took off his cartridge belt with its paraphernalia and flung it out into the air. All eyes followed it down.

A gesture of defiance, thought the colonel. *Like Ralph. Is he playing with us or himself? But the game will wear out soon and he will have to decide. Perhaps he is thinking of what it would be like to return and he is feeling that he can't bear more of what he has already known. It must be the conviction that nothing will change that persuades you to commit suicide. That you will take things the way you have always taken them and you will never be different. Someone ruined him as I ruined Ralph.*

Greaves' helmet liner came sailing down.

He's getting ready to jump! That's the way you prepare yourself when you think you're going to die. Imagine a loose, banging death with canteen and helmet on. Could I stop him if I hollered to him? But Ralph never came back when I called. But the kid may die in a minute. Greaves was rocking on the edge of the platform, between his hands on the ends of the rail.

"Don't, my boy, *don't!"* It was a hoarse and ragged cry. The bystanders glanced swiftly at him, then at Greaves, then back at the colonel. A half-minute passed.

A full bird colonel and I can't do any more than all the others he's passed through today. The more I try the worse it'll look. He'll die anyway and I'll just be the butt of every gaping yardbird, and more stories on top of the scandals. While his mind went on chattering, some part of him that his own unpremeditated cry had liberated mounted the tower and looked down as Greaves was doing. He saw a couple of hundred olive-drab figures, foreshortened, dotted and clumped about the field as if some unit had recently broken ranks. But mainly he saw helmets—red, blue, and olive-drab helmets. A field of tipped shells.

Greaves stood motionless on the edge. An almost palpable tension bound the crowd, as when a diver holds poised after all preliminaries.

The colonel, too, hung in balance. Then again he acted before he knew it, this time as if his arm were tied to and obeying his vision and not himself. Abruptly, his forearm skipped off the side of his head and tumbled his helmet to the ground. The reaction of the crowd was shock. He too felt an inner gasp, like sudden sin, as the air cooled his damp hair. It had been untold years since he had gone bareheaded outdoors. He almost expected some reprisal from on high. But on high was Greaves, and the colonel stood steadfast in his difficult exposure, his head feeling as naked and damp and tender as a suddenly unbandaged wound.

Waiting a moment to see that he had not jumped, the colonel began moving to the foot of the ladder. Without looking up again, he walked unabashed through the gaping trainees and staring cadre and then across the spot where Greaves would have hit. He felt like a full bird colonel.

"You watch," said one MP to the other, hitching his holster. "That kid's just playing with the old man and halfway down he'll go back up."

The colonel stood on the underside of the ladder with a hand on each upright bar. Presently he saw the shapeless, half-created boy between the rungs.

Inez

Merle Hodge

Mrs. Henry was ready to call the police. The children and the dogs had to get breakfast, she and Henry had to have their coffee, and the confounded girl was ten minutes late. And she had warned her, two years ago when she started, that if she ever came late, every minute would be deducted from her wages. This was the first time but it would also be the last.

And to think that the facety girl had, just the day before, put God out of her thoughts and asked for an advance on her week's pay. In the middle of the week!

"Only five dollars, ma'am."

"Five dollars! But that is half your pay—you can't get half your pay in the middle of the week!"

When the clock struck eight, Mrs. Henry was seized with panic. Suppose she had been fool enough to give her the five dollars! She had no idea where the girl lived, she knew nothing about her, she would just have disappeared like that with her five dollars.

Mrs. Henry now wanted to phone Matilda's Corner Police Station and report an attempted robbery.

The roll call revealed twelve absences. Praise be, sighed the teacher, God forgive my thoughts. But see my trial if all fifty-five of them turn up here one morning. And thank you, Jesus, Carlton didn't find his way to school today again (forgive me, Lord). He must be in the Plaza begging five cents, or his mother must be catch him up there yesterday and break his foot (I not wishing it on him, Lord).

But where is Maxine?

Maxine was very rarely absent, or late. She always arrived shining clean, her hair neat, her uniform well ironed, although it had long lost its colour. Maxine with a wisdom beyond her years. She was bright, bright, and would learn rapidly, if there was more time to teach her.

Yesterday Maxine had inquired of the teacher whether there was any way she could turn into a boy.

It was because the Baby-Father had said to her mother that the Last One still didn't look much like him, so he wasn't bringing one cent more, she could get his father to support him, and furthermore he wasn't bringing a cent more for Audrey either, though he wouldn't say it wasn't his pickney, but God strike him dead if he was going raise any gal-pickney, for gal-pickney grow into woman, and woman is a curse, don't the Bible say so? All woman bad like Satan.

So Maxine wanted to turn into a boy as soon as possible.

Afterwards, Miss Williams had gone into the Principal's office and looked into the records, just to make sure. But she was not mistaken, Maxine's date of birth made her seven years at her last birthday.

Where was Maxine today? The teacher felt a vague uneasiness. Then her heart sank, oh God! Suppose . . .

Maxine had related to her how the Baby-Father had tried to box her mother (Maxine wasn't too sure why), and how when she picked up the kitchen knife he left, swearing he would bring the police for her.

The father of Maxine, Donovan and Junie had posted his guard at the gate, as usual, for it was the last day of the month. But the boy had not yet raised the alarm. Almost two hours and his spar Nelson was still on standby, ready to take over his domino hand for him when he would have to make a hasty exit.

There had been one false alarm. Out of the corner of his eye he had seen the little boy coming into the yard and had sprung up from the bench—dominoes flying left and right—reached round the side of the house and dived into Wally's room. But David had only come in to use the toilet.

Malcolm was beginning to relax—maybe the miserable woman wasn't coming this month to hold out her hand. How was a man supposed to feed himself and *three* pickney out of what he got at the end of the month? He had told her to give the children to the Government, and that was final. Let the Government feed them, they had money to buy thousand-dollar suit from England for the Governor-General, so they must can feed the pickney them.

Presently David came back into the yard, reported that the Baby-Mother was still nowhere in sight, and collected his ten cents.

It was dark now, she never came this late. Nice, thought Malcolm. She must be decide to rest me. She must be decide to carry the pickney them go give the Government.

Cho, she no just haffe box-down one of them, break them hand, for police to come charge her for ill-treatment and carry-way the whole of them?

The landlord arrived, punctual as doom. The tenants paid, or tendered their excuses, and Mr. James was waiting for Inez. It was seven o'clock and none of the tenants had any idea where she was. The room was empty, and not a single one of her children was to be seen either. The yard neighbour who kept an eye on them in the daytime had not seen them all day.

Inez owed three months' rent. The door of the room was not locked. Mr. James opened it and stood, dejected, looking in. He shook his head wrily. It was a detestable business, what he was going to have to do. For if he didn't, his wife would come down and personally carry out the operation, and then it would be even more unpleasant.

Mrs. James had no use for sluttish women who spent their lives breeding bastard children and then expected you to feel sorry for them when they couldn't pay their debts. She was always willing to teach them a lesson.

He was all for selling the damn properties so he would never have to walk into a tenement yard again, stepping over dusty, snotty children to confront the stone-faced hostility of their parents. He would gladly sell all the properties. But over her dead body.

Now once again they were going to have to evict, seize . . . seize what? The Klim tin sitting smoky and awry in the dead coals? The low, lumpy bed with the deep well in the middle?

He wished with all his might that Inez could come

through the gate this very minute, bringing even part of the rent; then he could give her some more time—Mrs. James might not object to that. Otherwise ... it was a scene which he had never got used to; each time made him years older. A shouting swearing woman, her children screaming, crashing of kitchen utensils, crowd gathering, police ...

The nurse on her way out noticed the same silent knot of children still sitting on the bench. The waiting room was nearly empty now, most of the day's crowd had been seen to, there were not many numbers left.

She stepped back and went over to them. The younger ones drew closer round the girl who sat clutching a paper bag and an empty rum bottle.

"Where is your mother?"

"She soon come, ma'am," said the girl, without conviction.

"You have a number? One of you sick?"

"No, ma'am."

"Then what you doing here?"

The children stared, mute. Maxine lowered her eyes. "Don' know, ma'am," she whispered.

The nurses fed them, bought them ice-cream, put the two youngest ones to sleep on an examining table.

When the police came, Nurse Johnson asked one of the officers what they were going to do. He threw her a glance of part weariness and part scorn as though she had asked a naïve and unnecessary question.

"Look for the mother, ma'am," he explained in a long-suffering voice, "and charge her with abandonment."

The dogs had been barking at the edge of the gully for a full hour, an ominous, nerve-racking sound, for it echoed down the gully and from the caves on the other side.

But now there seemed to be another noise that chilled your spine—a long scream or a baby crying; and now it was all the dogs in the neighbourhood barking, shrieking at the edge of the gully.

Mrs. Campbell pulled in her children, locked the doors and the windows, and sent the maid down to the gully to look.

The maid flew back holding her head and screaming. Before she reached the house, Mrs. Campbell was on the phone to the police.

She lay on the bottom of the gully, face downwards. The Last One lay cosy in the crook of her dead arm, but he was crying now because his bottle had rolled away from him, his bottle of corn meal and water.

ANONYMOUS NARRATION—
NO CHARACTER
POINT OF VIEW

Anyone who has taken the journey this far will understand our logic in counting 1, 2, 3 . . . 0. By staying outside the minds of all the characters, a narrator drops the role of confidant and relies entirely on eyewitness and chorus knowledge alone. Stories of this sort that emphasize the eyewitness role tend toward scripts that include virtually nothing a bystander would not see and hear, like the first story here, which could be easily filmed. Narratives combining eyewitness with a strong chorus role may tend to resemble the other two stories, which are surreal because the chorus component of "The Lottery" takes the form of folkloric background, that of "Powerhouse," the form of poetic interpretation.

So our spectrum ends in legend, myth, and folk tale, where deeds speak for feelings and characters are archetypal. Since readers are expected to fill in the inner life empathically, the spokesperson narrator does not go into the characters. This type of story rests on assumptions of some communal consciousness or even universal unconscious. But then maybe all stories do, and only the degree of explicitness differs. If so, this most external technique represents the most implicit of storytelling as well as the most transpersonal. These are what make it the most mythopoetic. But of course such stories are individual creations in our day, rather than distillations of folk imagination. Unfilled characters can in fact allow the most personal projection of the author's perception and imagination, as in the phantasmagorical "Powerhouse."

Narrators who drop the role of eyewitness as well as confidant become mere members of a chorus dealing in only generalized, publicly digested information. So this is where the range of fiction ends. The rest—synoptic and depersonalized—is history.

A New Window Display

Nicholosa Mohr

On a cold, bleak Monday morning early in January, Hannibal and Joey walked along the avenue. They were on their way to school. But first, as usual, they stopped in front of the FUNERARIA ORTIZ and looked at the new window display. Sometimes the other kids would be there waiting, but this morning Hannibal and Joey were the first to arrive.

"Man," said Hannibal, "it sure is cold today. Maybe it'll snow."

"I hope so," said Joey. "A whole lotta snow, and we can build some forts. . . . Neat! Huh, Hannibal?"

Hannibal nodded and turned to look at the storefront. "They got a new one today, but it's an old man."

"Again?" Joey asked.

Every Monday, the funeral chapel had a new window display of color photographs showing the recently deceased from different angles, including close-ups. The inscription on every wreath was clearly visible. Hannibal pointed to a large photograph of an older man in a white-satin-lined coffin. His grey hair was neatly combed back, showing a receding hairline. His face was a dark orange, with a pinkish red spot on each cheek, and his lips were a deep purple-red, pushed back into a fixed smile. His eyes were shut. He wore a dark-blue suit and a clean white shirt with a black tie. His hands were folded over the lower part of his chest. They appeared very pale in contrast to his face; almost a greyish white. He wore a plain gold wedding band.

"They got a new one?" someone asked. Hannibal and Joey turned and saw Ramona, Mary, and Casilda.

"Well?" asked Ramona.

"They got an old man," answered Hannibal.

Ramona and the two girls stepped up and looked inside the storefront window. "Again?" Ramona asked.

"Yeah, all they got is old mens," Mary said.

"This guy got a mess of flowers. Look at all them decorations," said Joey. "Let's start reading them, O.K., Hannibal? Or ... maybe we should wait for Papo and Little Ray." Joey looked at Hannibal, waiting for him to make the final decision.

"He's late, man, and it's cold. I say we start reading," Hannibal replied.

"Maybe we should wait a little bit. You know Papo always has to bring his cousin to school...." Ramona said.

"No!" Hannibal said. "Let's read now." He looked at Ramona defiantly. She shrugged her shoulders.

"To our dear departed—" Hannibal began to read the inscription on one of the wreaths.

"Wait!" Ramona interrupted. "You going first again. You went first the last time."

"I don't remember going first last time," Hannibal said.

"Oh, yes! Right? Ask anybody." Ramona looked at the two girls standing beside her. They both nodded silently.

"What do you think, Joey? Do you think I went first before?"

"I don't remember. I don't think so," Joey replied quickly.

"You see?" Hannibal said to Ramona. "Now let me read!"

Ramona made a face and whispered something.

"What?" asked Hannibal. "What did you say, girl?"

"Nothing," Ramona said, sighing. "Go on."

"To our dear departed Uncle Felix," Hannibal read, "from his loving niece and husband and children, Rojelia and Esteban Martínez, Gilberto, María Patricia and Consuelo."

"Para un gran amigo," Joey read from another wreath. "Felix Umberto Cordero. De la familia Jiménez, 5013 Kelly Street, Bronx, New York."

"From your loving sister, María Elena Martínez and ..." Ramona took the next turn. Then Mary and Casilda read. It usually went in that order unless Papo and Little

Ray were there. Then the girls would be the last ones. Papo was a year younger than the others, and his little cousin was almost two years younger than Papo. Little Ray and his parents had arrived a few months ago from Puerto Rico. They always saved one inscription written in Spanish for him, because he read Spanish better than English.

The children finished reading all the inscriptions. "I guess they are real late, or they ain't coming. We better split or we are gonna be late," said Hannibal.

The group started once more toward school. They walked quickly, feeling the cold wind against their faces and bodies. They turned the corner of Prospect Avenue and headed down Longwood Avenue toward P.S. 39.

Except for a term in the second grade and once in the fourth grade, the group had been in the same classes since kindergarten. This term, they were all in the fifth grade except Papo, who was in the fourth. New in the group, he had become their friend when he moved to the Bronx about a year ago.

Little Ray was always with Papo, who had to look after him. In the four months since he had arrived, he had become the group's favorite. At first he had spoken no English, but now he was almost fluent. He spoke with an accent, which amused the other children, and he would get back at them by correcting their Spanish.

"That's not the way you say it." Little Ray would smile and gently correct them, giving them the proper pronunciation. They would laugh at him, but they could not help being impressed with his ability to speak so well.

"Man . . . Little Ray talks Spanish as good as my grandmother and parents and everybody!" Joey had said.

"Yeah," Ramona agreed. "He sure knows a lot for such a little kid."

The group had become protective of Little Ray, and they soon included him in everything they did. They were always anxious to see and hear his reaction to something different, or new, that he had never seen before.

"¡Qué fenomenal!" Little Ray would always shout with excitement. Everyone laughed and giggled. After a while, it got to be a game; they would wait for Little Ray to react, and then in unison they echoed, "Phenomenal!"

It was Little Ray's favorite word.

"He may be little but he's got a lotta heart, man. He's phenomenal! . . . And no squealer either," Hannibal had said admiringly, the day that they had all decided to take some potatoes from the vegetable stand in the outdoor market on Union Avenue.

Little Ray and Casilda were assigned to keep the man at the stand busy while the rest of them stuffed their pockets with roasting potatoes. Later, in an empty lot, they skewered the potatoes on long, thin pieces of wood, roasting them over an open fire, waiting for the skin to turn black and the inside soft and hot.

As they ate, a superintendent from one of the nearby tenements came over and began to question Little Ray suspiciously in Spanish. He assured the man, speaking to him in Spanish, that they had all brought the potatoes with them from home. After the man left, they laughed.

"He's the best little kid in El Bronx!" Ramona had said. "Right?"

"Phenomenal!" everyone had shouted in agreement.

Hannibal and Joey rushed on ahead, almost running, and left the girls a few yards behind.

"What do you mean the most flowers?" Hannibal argued with Joey.

"Yeah . . . today that man had the most decorations I seen so far."

"Get out, Joey. Remember the old lady with the wig that time? And the little baby—remember him? Now he had like a hundred decorations."

"Oh yeah, that's right," said Joey. "Do you think that was a real baby?"

"Of course it was! What do you think it was, a dummy?"

"No, but maybe . . . it was like a doll," Joey said.

"It was no doll. Man, Joey, what's the matter with you? Why they gonna give all them flowers to a doll and everything?"

"Well," Joey said. "Anyway, that was no hundred decorations he had. Wasn't even fifty!"

"Well, maybe not a whole hundred. But it was more

than fifty and more than that old guy today got. . . ." Hannibal continued trying to convince Joey as they raced to reach school before the late bell rang.

"To Our Dear Departed Brother and Uncle, Carlos Rodríguez . . ." read Hannibal.

"Rest in Peace, Co-Worker. From . . ." read Joey. As usual, they all stood together looking at another new window display. This Monday morning, the weather was quite pleasant, unseasonably warm; and the sun shone brightly. Then it was Papo's turn.

"I'm gonna read the one in Spanish for Little Ray, even though he ain't here today," Papo said. "Querido Esposo, Padre, y Abuelo . . ." he finished reading.

"This guy didn't have so many decorations," said Casilda.

"Yeah, not like the last guy," Joey said. "Look, even the coffin ain't so fancy."

"Yeah."

"Uh huh."

"That's right."

"How is Little Ray?" asked Hannibal. "He ain't been around now for about almost two weeks, right?"

"Yeah . . . well," Papo answered, "I think he's gotta go back to P.R."

"Puerto Rico?" asked Joey. "No kidding?"

"He got something in his chest, like—and they say it's the bad weather here that causes it. It's real bad and he's very sick. They say he gotta go back."

"Aww man, that's too bad!" said Hannibal.

"That's terrible," said Mary.

"When does he gotta leave?" asked Ramona.

"As soon as he gets better, so he can travel," answered Papo. "And he don't like the idea at all, let me tell you. Little Ray says they are very strict down there and that here he is much more free. He likes to hang out with us and play and everything."

"Do you think, Papo, that if he gets really well and all better, that maybe they will let him stay here?" asked Ramona.

"I don't know." Papo shrugged his shoulders. "His parents definitely say he gotta go back and stay with his aunt and uncle down there."

"Too bad," said Casilda. "He's nice."

"He's a real good kid," Hannibal agreed.

"Yeah."

"Uh huh."

The mildness in the air and the bright sun put the children in high spirits. They all walked to school at a slow pace, enjoying the January thaw.

"What a drag," Hannibal said; "going to school on such a day. It feels like springtime. How about cutting today?"

"Get out, Hannibal!" Ramona said quickly. "You better not start that business again and get into trouble. And you better not listen to him, Joey."

"Goody Two-Shoes," Hannibal said, making a face at Ramona.

Ramona stuck her tongue out at Hannibal.

"Whew . . . qué fea . . ." he said good-naturedly. "Ugly as sin." Ramona responded by shrugging her shoulders. Neither of them could really feel angry this morning.

The group strolled along and turned the corner onto Longwood Avenue.

"Hey . . . maybe if the weather changes and it keeps on being warm, they will let Little Ray stay. Then he can come back to school and stick around with us," said Joey.

"I sure hope so," said Papo, smiling. "Except after he gets well, then I hope it snows. He's never really seen snow—he's only seen like a little bit. Like flurries, so far. But I mean a real big storm. This way we could all build a fort, and have snowball fights and everything, you know. . . ."

"Yeah," said Mary, "that's right. Remember, we told Little Ray all about it. He was looking forward to it."

"Right now, let's just hope it stays warm," said Ramona. "That way he can come back and be with us real soon."

"Sure."

"Right."

"Absolutely."

A whole month had passed since Little Ray was buried. Many neighbors had attended the funeral mass. The group did not go, except for Papo. However, the members of the group had gone once to the funeral chapel with their families to pay their respects to Little Ray and his family. By now, things had gone back to normal except that the children no longer met in front of the storefront window of the FUNERARIA ORTIZ on Monday mornings. They just walked past the new window display on their way to school, not looking or stopping. No one ever spoke about it.

This morning, wet snow melted instantly as it hit the concrete pavement and black-tar streets. Hannibal and Joey rushed to school feeling cold and damp. As they approached the funeral chapel, they saw Papo, Ramona, Mary, and Casilda standing right in front of the storefront window.

"Hannibal, Joey—look!" Ramona called out, pointing to the new window display. "Papo told us."

Hannibal and Joey looked inside the storefront window and saw many photographs of Little Ray. There were so many floral wreaths that the small coffin was hardly visible. A large close-up showed him in a powder-blue, silk-lined coffin. His dark curly hair was oiled, combed and parted on the side. Little Ray's eyes were shut and his face was colored a light pink. Each cheek had a dark pink spot. His lips were bright orange and slightly parted. He looked like he was smiling, dreaming a pleasant dream. He wore his dark-blue First Holy Communion suit, with a white satin sash tied on his left sleeve, a white starched shirt, and a dark-blue tie. His small pale hands held a white missal and a set of white rosary beads with a gold cross.

"I thought we should stop. . . ." Papo hesitated. "My parents told me last night, and I figured that it would only be right . . . for us to come here. For Little Ray."

The group remained silent for a while.

"Wow!" Hannibal said, breaking the silence. "He sure looks different, don't he?"

"Yeah," Joey said. "I never even seen him with his hair combed before. He even looks healthy, like he got a sunburn."

"My father says they do a good job here," said Papo, nodding. "They made him look like he was making his Communion again. They made everything perfect."

"He looks nice," Mary said.

"Oh ... yeah, he does," said Casilda. "Like a little angel. Right?"

"He sure does." Ramona nodded.

"Now," Hannibal said. "He's the one that got the most flowers of anybody I ever seen!"

"That's right!" said Joey. "Even more than that little baby."

"Uh huh."

"The most!"

"Absolutely."

The children stood quietly and looked into the storefront window. The wet snow continued to fall. They were all damp and chilly, but no one moved. After a while, Papo asked, "Do you think we should read?"

The children looked at each other and shrugged. Then everyone turned to look at Hannibal.

"O.K.," Hannibal said, "who's gonna go first?" Everyone was surprised. Hannibal had never asked anyone to be first before.

"You go first," said Ramona. "Like you always do." Hannibal opened his mouth to protest, but Ramona stared at him and, folding her arms, said quickly, "Go on!" Hannibal read slowly.

"To the Santiago family in their Hour of Bereavement ..." He read on, looking at Joey when he finished.

"Beloved Son, Ramon Luis ..." Joey read.

Each took a turn. There were so many wreaths that they went twice around, and Hannibal and Joey had to read a third time. Finally they were all finished.

"I still miss him, you know," Papo said. "I never even minded taking care of him ... like he was no bother. Other little kids, man, you know, they can really be pests. But not him."

"He was really a good kid," said Hannibal.

"It's kinda funny, because like I know he's not gonna be around no more, yet like I can't believe he's gone." Papo paused for a moment, then continued, "Anyway, my parents ordered some of them pictures and this way we can remember him like he looked."

They walked silently toward school. It began to snow harder, and large snowflakes stuck to the pavement, piling up. Areas of sidewalk were covered by a soft white blanket. The children felt the soft crunch under their feet, so different from the familiar hard concrete.

"Hey!" yelled Joey. "We got us a real big snowstorm!"

"Hurray!"

The group shouted, sliding and turning.

"Oh, boy, imagine if Little Ray were here and seen this!" said Papo excitedly.

"Oh man! He would be so happy!" Hannibal smiled. "And we all know what he would say. . . ."

"Phenomenal!" everyone shouted.

The Lottery

Shirley Jackson

The morning of June 27th was clear and sunny, with the fresh warmth of a full-summer day; the flowers were blossoming profusely and the grass was richly green. The people of the village began to gather in the square, between the post office and the bank, around ten o'clock; in some towns there were so many people that the lottery took two days and had to be started on June 26th, but in this village, where there were only about three hundred people, the whole lottery took less than two hours, so it could begin at ten o'clock in the morning and still be through in time to allow the villagers to get home for noon dinner.

The children assembled first, of course. School was recently over for the summer, and the feelings of liberty sat uneasily on most of them; they tended to gather together quietly for a while before they broke into boisterous play, and their talk was still of the classroom and the teacher, of books and reprimands. Bobby Martin had already stuffed his pockets full of stones, and the other boys soon followed his example, selecting the smoothest and roundest stones; Bobby and Harry Jones and Dickie Delacroix—the villagers pronounced this name "Dellacroy"—eventually made a great pile of stones in one corner of the square and guarded it against the raids of the other boys. The girls stood aside, talking among themselves, looking over their shoulders at the boys, and the very small children rolled in the dust or clung to the hands of their older brothers or sisters.

Soon the men began to gather, surveying their own children, speaking of the planting and rain, tractors and taxes. They stood together, away from the pile of stones in the corner, and their jokes were quiet and they smiled rather than laughed. The women, wearing faded house dresses and sweaters, came shortly after their menfolk. They greeted one another and exchanged bits of gossip as they went to join their husbands. Soon the women, standing by their husbands, began to call to their children, and the children came reluctantly, having to be called four or five times. Bobby Martin ducked under his mother's grasping hand and ran, laughing, back to the pile of stones. His father spoke up sharply, and Bobby came quickly and took his place between his father and his oldest brother.

The lottery was conducted—as were the square dances, the teen-age club, the Halloween program—by Mr. Summers, who had time and energy to devote to civic activities. He was a round-faced, jovial man and he ran the coal business, and people were sorry for him, because he had no children and his wife was a scold. When he arrived in the square, carrying the black wooden box, there was a murmur of conversation among the villagers, and he waved and called, "Little late today, folks." The postmaster, Mr. Graves, followed him, carrying a three-legged stool, and the stool was put in the center of the square and Mr. Summers set the black box down on it. The villagers kept their distance, leaving a space between themselves and the stool, and when Mr. Summers said, "Some of you fellows want to give me a hand?" there was a hesitation before two men, Mr. Martin and his oldest son, Baxter, came forward to hold the box steady on the stool while Mr. Summers stirred up the papers inside it.

The original paraphernalia for the lottery had been lost long ago, and the black box now resting on the stool had been put into use even before Old Man Warner, the oldest man in town, was born. Mr. Summers spoke frequently to the villagers about making a new box, but no one liked to upset even as much tradition as was represented by the black box. There was a story that the present box had been made with some pieces of the box that had preceded it, the one that had been constructed when the first people settled down to make a village here. Every year, after the lottery, Mr. Summers began talking again about a new box, but every year the subject was allowed to fade off without anything's being done. The black box grew shabbier each year; by now it was no longer completely black but splintered badly along one side to show the original wood color, and in some places faded or stained.

Mr. Martin and his oldest son, Baxter, held the black box securely on the stool until Mr. Summers had stirred the papers thoroughly with his hand. Because so much of the ritual had been forgotten or discarded, Mr. Summers had been successful in having slips of paper substituted for the chips of wood that had been used for generations. Chips of wood, Mr. Summers had argued, had been all very well when the village was tiny, but now that the population was more than three hundred and likely to keep on growing, it was necessary to use something that would fit more easily into the black box. The night before the lottery, Mr. Summers and Mr. Graves made up the slips of paper and put them in the box, and it was then taken to the safe of Mr. Summers' coal company and locked up until Mr. Summers was ready to take it to the square next morning. The rest of the year the box was put away, sometimes one place, sometimes another; it had spent one year in Mr. Graves's barn and another year underfoot in the post office, and sometimes it was set on a shelf in the Martin grocery and left there.

There was a great deal of fussing to be done before Mr. Summers declared the lottery open. There were the lists to make up—of heads of families, heads of households in each family, members of each household in each family. There was the proper swearing-in of Mr. Summers by the postmaster, as the official of the lottery; at one time, some people remembered, there had been a recital of some sort, performed by the official of the lottery, a perfunctory, tuneless chant that had been rattled off duly each year; some people believed that the official of the lottery used to stand just so when he said or sang it, others believed that he was supposed to walk among the people, but years and years ago this part of the ritual had been allowed to lapse. There had been, also, a ritual salute, which the official of the lottery had had to use in addressing each person who came up to draw from the box, but this also had changed with time, until now it was felt necessary only for the official to speak to each person approaching. Mr. Summers was very good at all this; in his clean white shirt and blue jeans, with one hand resting carelessly on the black box, he seemed very proper and important as he talked interminably to Mr. Graves and the Martins.

Just as Mr. Summers finally left off talking and turned to the assembled villagers, Mrs. Hutchinson came hurriedly along the path to the square, her sweater thrown over her shoulders, and slid into place in the back of the crowd. "Clean forgot what day it was," she said to Mrs. Delacroix, who stood next to her, and they both laughed softly. "Thought my old man was out back stacking wood," Mrs. Hutchinson went on, "and then I looked out the window and the kids was gone, and then I remembered it was the twenty-seventh and came a-running." She dried her hands on her apron, and Mrs. Delacroix said, "You're in time, though. They're still talking away up there."

Mrs. Hutchinson craned her neck to see through the crowd and found her husband and children standing near the front. She tapped Mrs. Delacroix on the arm as a farewell and began to make her way through the crowd. The people separated good-humoredly to let her through; two or three people said, in voices just loud enough to be heard across the crowd, "Here comes your Missus, Hutchinson," and "Bill, she made it after all." Mrs. Hutchinson reached her husband, and Mr. Summers, who had been waiting, said cheerfully, "Thought we were going to have to get on without you, Tessie." Mrs. Hutchinson said, grinning, "Wouldn't have me leave m'dishes in the sink, now, would you, Joe?," and soft laughter ran through the crowd as the people stirred back into position after Mrs. Hutchinson's arrival.

"Well, now," Mr. Summers said soberly, "guess we better get started, get this over with, so's we can go back to work. Anybody ain't here?"

"Dunbar," several people said. "Dunbar, Dunbar."

Mr. Summers consulted his list. "Clyde Dunbar," he said. "That's right. He's broke his leg, hasn't he? Who's drawing for him?"

"Me, I guess," a woman said, and Mr. Summers turned to look at her. "Wife draws for her husband," Mr. Summers said. "Don't you have a grown boy to do it for you, Janey?" Although Mr. Summers and everybody else in the village knew the answer perfectly well, it was the business of the official of the lottery to ask such questions formally. Mr. Summers waited with an expression of polite interest while Mrs. Dunbar answered.

"Horace's not but sixteen yet," Mrs. Dunbar said regretfully. "Guess I gotta fill in for the old man this year."

"Right," Mr. Summers said. He made a note on the list he was holding. Then he asked, "Watson boy drawing this year?"

A tall boy in the crowd raised his hand. "Here," he said. "I'm drawing for m'mother and me." He blinked his eyes nervously and ducked his head as several voices in the crowd said things like "Good fellow, Jack," and "Glad to see your mother's got a man to do it."

"Well," Mr. Summers said, "guess that's everyone. Old Man Warner make it?"

"Here," a voice said, and Mr. Summers nodded.

A sudden hush fell on the crowd as Mr. Summers cleared his throat and looked at the list. "All ready?" he called. "Now, I'll read the names—heads of families first—and the men come up and take a paper out of the box. Keep the paper folded in your hand without looking at it until everyone has had a turn. Everything clear?"

The people had done it so many times that they only half listened to the directions; most of them were quiet, wetting their lips, not looking around. Then Mr. Summers raised one hand high and said, "Adams." A man disengaged himself from the crowd and came forward. "Hi, Steve," Mr. Summers said, and Mr. Adams said, "Hi, Joe." They grinned at one another humorlessly and nervously. Then Mr. Adams reached into the black box and took out a folded paper. He held it firmly by one corner as he turned and went hastily back to his place in the crowd, where he stood a little apart from his family, not looking down at his hand.

"Allen," Mr. Summers said. "Anderson . . . Bentham."

"Seems like there's no time at all between lotteries any more," Mrs. Delacroix said to Mrs. Graves in the back row. "Seems like we got through with the last one only last week."

"Time sure goes fast," Mrs. Graves said.

"Clark. . . . Delacroix."

"There goes my old man," Mrs. Delacroix said. She held her breath while her husband went forward.

"Dunbar," Mr. Summers said, and Mrs. Dunbar went steadily to the box while one of the women said, "Go on, Janey," and another said, "There she goes."

"We're next," Mrs. Graves said. She watched while Mr. Graves came around from the side of the box, greeted Mr. Summers gravely, and selected a slip of paper from the box. By now, all through the crowd there were men holding the small folded papers in their large hands, turning them over and over nervously. Mrs. Dunbar and her two sons stood together, Mrs. Dunbar holding the slip of paper.

"Harburt. . . . Hutchinson."

"Get up there, Bill," Mrs. Hutchinson said, and the people near her laughed.

"Jones."

"They do say," Mr. Adams said to Old Man Warner, who stood next to him, "that over in the north village they're talking of giving up the lottery."

Old Man Warner snorted. "Pack of crazy fools," he said. "Listening to the young folks, nothing's good enough for *them*. Next thing you know, they'll be wanting to go back to living in caves, nobody work any more, live *that* way for a while. Used to be a saying about 'Lottery in June, corn be heavy soon.' First thing you know, we'd all be eating stewed chickweed and acorns. There's *always* been a lottery," he added petulantly. "Bad enough to see young Joe Summers up there joking with everybody."

"Some places have already quit lotteries," Mrs. Adams said.

"Nothing but trouble in *that*," Old Man Warner said stoutly. "Pack of young fools."

"Martin." And Bobby Martin watched his father go forward. "Overdyke. . . . Percy."

"I wish they'd hurry," Mrs. Dunbar said to her older son. "I wish they'd hurry."

"They're almost through," her son said.

"You get ready to run tell Dad," Mrs. Dunbar said.

Mr. Summers called his own name and then stepped

forward precisely and selected a slip from the box. Then he called, "Warner."

"Seventy-seventh year I been in the lottery," Old Man Warner said as he went through the crowd. "Seventy-seventh time."

"Watson." The tall boy came awkwardly through the crowd. Someone said, "Don't be nervous, Jack," and Mr. Summers said, "Take your time, son."

"Zanini."

After that, there was a long pause, a breathless pause, until Mr. Summers, holding his slip of paper in the air, said, "All right, fellows." For a minute, no one moved, and then all the slips of paper were opened. Suddenly, all the women began to speak at once, saying, "Who is it?," "Who's got it?," "Is it the Dunbars?," "Is it the Watsons?" Then the voices began to say, "It's Hutchinson. It's Bill," "Bill Hutchinson's got it."

"Go tell your father," Mrs. Dunbar said to her older son.

People began to look around to see the Hutchinsons. Bill Hutchinson was standing quiet, staring down at the paper in his hand. Suddenly, Tessie Hutchinson shouted to Mr. Summers, "You didn't give him time enough to take any paper he wanted. I saw you. It wasn't fair!"

"Be a good sport, Tessie," Mrs. Delacroix called, and Mrs. Graves said, "All of us took the same chance."

"Shut up, Tessie," Bill Hutchinson said.

"Well, everyone," Mr. Summers said, "that was done pretty fast, and now we've got to be hurrying a little more to get done in time." He consulted his next list. "Bill," he said, "you draw for the Hutchinson family. You got any other households in the Hutchinsons?"

"There's Don and Eva," Mrs. Hutchinson yelled. "Make *them* take their chance!"

"Daughters draw with their husbands' families, Tessie," Mr. Summers said gently. "You know that as well as anyone else."

"It wasn't *fair*," Tessie said.

"I guess not, Joe," Bill Hutchinson said regretfully. "My daughter draws with her husband's family, that's only fair. And I've got no other family except the kids."

"Then, as far as the drawing for families is concerned,

it's you," Mr. Summers said in explanation, "and as far as drawing for households is concerned, that's you, too. Right?"

"Right," Bill Hutchinson said.

"How many kids, Bill?" Mr. Summers asked formally.

"Three," Bill Hutchinson said. "There's Bill, Jr., and Nancy, and little Dave. And Tessie and me."

"All right, then," Mr. Summers said. "Harry, you got their tickets back?"

Mr. Graves nodded and held up the slips of paper. "Put them in the box, then," Mr. Summers directed. "Take Bill's and put it in."

"I think we ought to start over," Mrs. Hutchinson said, as quietly as she could. "I tell you it wasn't *fair*. You didn't give him time enough to choose. *Every*body saw that."

Mr. Graves had selected the five slips and put them in the box, and he dropped all the papers but those onto the ground, where the breeze caught them and lifted them off.

"Listen, everybody," Mrs. Hutchinson was saying to the people around her.

"Ready, Bill?" Mr. Summers asked, and Bill Hutchinson, with one quick glance around at his wife and children, nodded.

"Remember," Mr. Summers said, "take the slips and keep them folded until each person has taken one. Harry, you help little Dave." Mr. Graves took the hand of the little boy, who came willingly with him up to the box. "Take a paper out of the box, Davy," Mr. Summers said. Davy put his hand into the box and laughed. "Take just *one* paper," Mr. Summers said. "Harry, you hold it for him." Mr. Graves took the child's hand and removed the folded paper from the tight fist and held it while little Dave stood next to him and looked up at him wonderingly.

"Nancy next," Mr. Summers said. Nancy was twelve, and her school friends breathed heavily as she went forward, switching her skirt, and took a slip daintily from the box. "Bill, Jr.," Mr. Summers said, and Billy, his face red and his feet overlarge, nearly knocked the box over as he got a paper out. "Tessie," Mr. Summers said. She hesitated for a minute, looking around defiantly, and then set her lips and went up to the box. She snatched a paper out and held it behind her.

"Bill," Mr. Summers said, and Bill Hutchinson reached into the box and felt around, bringing his hand out at last with the slip of paper in it.

The crowd was quiet. A girl whispered, "I hope it's not Nancy," and the sound of the whisper reached the edges of the crowd.

"It's not the way it used to be," Old Man Warner said clearly. "People ain't the way they used to be."

"All right," Mr. Summers said. "Open the papers. Harry, you open little Dave's."

Mr. Graves opened the slip of paper and there was a general sigh through the crowd as he held it up and everyone could see that it was blank. Nancy and Bill, Jr., opened theirs at the same time, and both beamed and laughed, turning around to the crowd and holding their slips of paper above their heads.

"Tessie," Mr. Summers said. There was a pause, and then Mr. Summers looked at Bill Hutchinson, and Bill unfolded his paper and showed it. It was blank.

"It's Tessie," Mr. Summers said, and his voice was hushed. "Show us her paper, Bill."

Bill Hutchinson went over to his wife and forced the slip of paper out of her hand. It had a black spot on it, the black spot Mr. Summers had made the night before with the heavy pencil in the coal-company office. Bill Hutchinson held it up, and there was a stir in the crowd.

"All right, folks," Mr. Summers said. "Let's finish quickly."

Although the villagers had forgotten the ritual and lost the original black box, they still remembered to use stones. The pile of stones the boys had made earlier was ready; there were stones on the ground with the blowing scraps of paper that had come out of the box. Mrs. Delacroix selected a stone so large she had to pick it up with both hands and turned to Mrs. Dunbar. "Come on," she said. "Hurry up."

Mrs. Dunbar had small stones in both hands, and she said, gasping for breath, "I can't run at all. You'll have to go ahead and I'll catch up with you."

The children had stones already, and someone gave little Davy Hutchinson a few pebbles.

Tessie Hutchinson was in the center of a cleared space by now, and she held her hands out desperately as the villagers moved in on her. "It isn't fair," she said. A stone hit her on the side of the head.

Old Man Warner was saying, "Come on, come on, everyone." Steve Adams was in the front of the crowd of villagers, with Mrs. Graves beside him.

"It isn't fair, it isn't right," Mrs. Hutchinson screamed, and then they were upon her.

Powerhouse

Eudora Welty

Powerhouse is playing!

He's here on tour from the city—"Powerhouse and His Keyboard"—"Powerhouse and His Tasmanians"—think of the things he calls himself! There's no one in the world like him. You can't tell what he is. "Nigger man?"—he looks more Asiatic, monkey, Jewish, Babylonian, Peruvian, fanatic, devil. He has pale gray eyes, heavy lids, maybe horny like a lizard's, but big glowing eyes when they're open. He has African feet of the greatest size, stomping, both together, on each side of the pedals. He's not coal black—beverage colored—looks like a preacher when his mouth is shut, but then it opens—vast and obscene. And his mouth is going every minute: like a monkey's when it looks for something. Improvising, coming on a light and childish melody—*smooch*—he loves it with his mouth.

Is is possible that he could be this! When you have him there performing for you, that's what you feel. You know people on a stage—and people of a darker race—so likely to be marveolous, frightening.

This is a white dance. Powerhouse is not a show-off like the Harlem boys, not drunk, not crazy—he's in a trance; he's a person of joy, a fanatic. He listens as much as he performs, a look of hideous, powerful rapture on his face. Big arched eyebrows that never stop traveling, like a Jew's—wandering-Jew eyebrows. When he plays he beats down piano and seat and wears them away. He is in motion every moment—what could be more obscene? There he is with his great head, fat stomach, and little round piston legs, and long yellow-sectioned strong big fingers, at rest about the size of bananas. Of course you know how he sounds—you've heard him on records—but still you need to see him. He's going all the time, like skating around the skating rink or rowing a boat. It makes everybody crowd around, here in the shadowless steel-trussed hall with the rose-like posters of Nelson Eddy and the testimonial for the mind-reading horse in handwriting magnified five hundred times. Then all quietly he lays his fingers on a key with the promise and serenity of a sibyl touching the book.

Powerhouse is so monstrous he sends everybody into oblivion. When any group, any performers, come to town, don't people always come out and hover near, leaning inward about them, to learn what it is? What is it? Listen. Remember how it was with the acrobats. Watch them carefully, hear the least word, especially what they say to one another, in another language—don't let them escape you; it's the only time for hallucination, the last time. They can't stay. They'll be somewhere else this time tomorrow.

Powerhouse has as much as possible done by signals. Everybody, laughing as if to hide a weakness, will sooner or later hand him up a written request. Powerhouse reads each one, studying with a secret face: that is the face which looks like a mask—anybody's; there is a moment when he makes a decision. Then a light slides under his eyelids, and he says, "92!" or some combination of figures—never a name. Before a number the band is all frantic, misbehaving, pushing, like children in a schoolroom, and he is the teacher getting silence. His hands over the keys, he says sternly, "You-all ready? You-all ready to do some serious walking?"—waits—then, STAMP. Quiet. STAMP, for the second time. This is absolute. Then a set of rhythmic kicks against the floor to communicate the tempo. Then, O Lord! say the distended eyes from beyond the boundary of the trumpets, Hello and good-by, and they are all down the first note like a waterfall.

This note marks the end of any known discipline. Powerhouse seems to abandon them all—he himself seems lost—down in the song, yelling up like somebody in a whirlpool—not guiding them—hailing them only. But he knows, really. He cries out, but he must know exactly. "Mercy! . . . What I say! . . . Yeah!" And then drifting, listening—"Where that skin beater?"—wanting drums, and starting up and pouring it out in the greatest

delight and brutality. On the sweet pieces such a leer
for everybody! He looks down so benevolently upon all
our faces and whispers the lyrics to us. And if you could
hear him at this moment on "Marie, the Dawn Is Breaking"! He's going up the keyboard with a few fingers in
some very derogatory triplet routine, he gets higher and
higher, and then he looks over the end of the piano, as
if over a cliff. But not in a show-off way—the song
makes him do it.

He loves the way they all play, too—all those next to
him. The far section of the band is all studious, wearing
glasses, every one—they don't count. Only those playing
around Powerhouse are the real ones. He has a bass fiddler
from Vicksburg, black as pitch, named Valentine, who
plays with his eyes shut and talking to himself, very young:
Powerhouse has to keep encouraging him. "Go on, go on,
give it up, bring it on out there!" When you heard him
like that on records, did you know he was really pleading?

He calls Valentine out to take a solo.

"What you going to play?" Powerhouse looks out
kindly from behind the piano; he opens his mouth and
shows his tongue, listening.

Valentine looks down, drawing against his instrument,
and says without a lip movement, " 'Honeysuckle Rose.' "

He has a clarinet player named Little Brother, and
loves to listen to anything he does. He'll smile and say,
"Beautiful!" Little Brother takes a step forward when
he plays and stands at the very front, with the whites of
his eyes like fishes swimming. Once when he played a
low note, Powerhouse muttered in dirty praise, "He
went clear downstairs to get that one!"

After a long time, he holds up the number of fingers
to tell the band how many choruses still to go—usually
five. He keeps his directions down to signals.

It's a bad night outside. It's a white dance, and nobody
dances, except a few straggling jitterbugs and two elderly
couples. Everybody just stands around the band and
watches Powerhouse. Sometimes they steal glances at
one another, as if to say, Of course, you know how it is
with *them*—Negroes—band leaders—they would play
the same way, giving all they've got, for an audience of
one.... When somebody, no matter who, gives everything, it makes people feel ashamed for him.

* * *

Late at night they play the one waltz they will ever consent to play—by request, "Pagan Love Song." Powerhouse's head rolls and sinks like a weight between his waving shoulders. He groans, and his fingers drag into the keys heavily, holding on to the notes, retrieving. It is a sad song.

"You know what happened to me?" says Powerhouse.

Valentine hums a response, dreaming at the bass.

"I got a telegram my wife is dead," says Powerhouse, with wandering fingers.

"Uh-huh?"

His mouth gathers and forms a barbarous O while his fingers walk up straight, unwillingly, three octaves.

"Gypsy? Why how come her to die, didn't you just phone her up in the night last night long distance?"

"Telegram say—here the words: Your wife is dead." He puts 4/4 over the 3/4.

"Not but four words?" This is the drummer, an unpopular boy named Scoot, a disbelieving maniac.

Powerhouse is shaking his vast cheeks. "What the hell was she trying to do? What was she up to?"

"What name has it got signed, if you got a telegram?" Scoot is spitting away with those wire brushes.

Little Brother, the clarinet player, who cannot now speak, glares and tilts back.

"Uranus Knockwood is the name signed." Powerhouse lifts his eyes open. "Ever heard of him?" A bubble shoots out on his lip like a plate on a counter.

Valentine is beating slowly on with his palm and scratching the strings with his long blue nails. He is fond of a waltz. Powerhouse interrupts him.

"I don't know him. Don't know who he is." Valentine shakes his head with the closed eyes.

"Say it agin."

"Uranus Knockwood."

"That ain't Lenox Avenue."

"It ain't Broadway."

"Ain't ever seen it wrote out in any print, even for horse racing."

"Hell, that's on a star, boy, ain't it?" Crash of the cymbals.

"What the hell was she up to?" Powerhouse shudders.

"Tell me, tell me, tell me." He makes triplets, and begins a new chorus. He holds three fingers up.

"You say you got a telegram." This is Valentine, patient and sleepy, beginning again.

Powerhouse is elaborate. "Yas, the time I go out, go way downstairs along a long cor-ri-dor to where they puts us: coming back along the cor-ri-dor: steps out and hands me a telegram: Your wife is dead."

"Gypsy?" The drummer like a spider over his drums.

"Aaaaaaaaa!" shouts Powerhouse, flinging out both powerful arms for three whole beats to flex his muscles, then kneading a dough of bass notes. His eyes glitter. He plays the piano like a drum sometimes—why not?

"Gypsy? Such a dancer?"

"Why you don't hear it straight from your agent? Why it ain't come from headquarters? What you been doing, getting telegrams in the *corridor*, signed nobody?"

They all laugh. End of that chorus.

"What time is it?" Powerhouse calls. "What the hell place is this? Where is my watch and chain?"

"I hang it on you," whimpers Valentine. "It still there."

There it rides on Powerhouse's great stomach, down where he can never see it.

"Sure did hear some clock striking twelve while ago. Must be *midnight*."

"It going to be intermission," Powerhouse declares, lifting up his finger with the signet ring.

He draws the chorus to an end. He pulls a big Northern hotel towel out of the deep pocket in his vast, special-cut tux pants and pushes his forehead into it.

"If she went and killed herself!" he says with a hidden face. "If she up and jumped out that window!" He gets to his feet, turning vaguely, wearing the towel on his head.

"Ha, ha!"

"Sheik, sheik!"

"She wouldn't do that." Little Brother sets down his clarinet like a precious vase, and speaks. He still looks like an East Indian queen, implacable, divine, and full of snakes. "You ain't going to expect people doing what they says over long distance."

"Come on!" roars Powerhouse. He is already at the

back door, he has pulled it wide open, and with a wild, gathered-up face is smelling the terrible night.

Powerhouse, Valentine, Scoot and Little Brother step outside into the drenching rain.

"Well, they emptying buckets," says Powerhouse in a mollified voice. On the street he holds his hands out and turns up the blanched palms like sieves.

A hundred dark, ragged, silent, delighted Negroes have come around from under the eaves of the hall, and follow wherever they go.

"Watch out Little Brother don't shrink," says Powerhouse. "You just the right size now, clarinet don't suck you in. You got a dry throat, Little Brother, you in the desert?" He reaches into the pocket and pulls out a paper of mints. "Now hold 'em in your mouth—don't chew 'em. I don't carry around nothing without limit."

"Go in that joint and have beer," says Scoot, who walks ahead.

"Beer? Beer? You know what beer is? What do they say is beer? What's beer? Where I been?"

"Down yonder where it say World Café—that do?" They are in Negrotown now.

Valentine patters over and holds open a screen door warped like a sea shell, bitter in the wet, and they walk in, stained darker with the rain and leaving footprints. Inside, sheltered dry smells stand like screens around a table covered with a red-checkered cloth, in the center of which flies hang onto an obelisk-shaped ketchup bottle. The midnight walls are checkered again with admonishing "Not Responsible" signs and black-figured, smoky calendars. It is a waiting, silent, limp room. There is a burned-out-looking nickelodeon and right beside it a long-necked wall instrument labeled "Business Phone, Don't Keep Talking." Circled phone numbers are written up everywhere. There is a worn-out peacock feather hanging by a thread to an old, thin, pink, exposed light bulb, where it slowly turns around and around, whoever breathes.

A waitress watches.

"Come here, living statue, and get all this big order of beer we fixing to give."

"Never seen you before anywhere." The waitress

moves and comes forward and slowly shows little gold
leaves and tendrils over her teeth. She shoves up her
shoulders and breasts. "How I going to know who you
might be? Robbers? Coming in out of the black of night
right at midnight, setting down so big at my table?"

"Boogers," says Powerhouse, his eyes opening lazily
as in a cave.

The girl screams delicately with pleasure. O Lord, she
likes talk and scares.

"Where you going to find enough beer to put out on
this here table?"

She runs to the kitchen with bent elbows and sliding
steps.

"Here's a million nickels," says Powerhouse, pulling
his hand out of his pocket and sprinkling coins out, all
but the last one, which he makes vanish like a magician.

Valentine and Scoot take the money over to the nickelodeon, which looks as battered as a slot machine, and
read all the names of the records out loud.

"Whose 'Tuxedo Junction'?" asks Powerhouse.

"You know whose."

"Nickelodeon, I request you please to play 'Empty
Bed Blues' and let Bessie Smith sing."

Silence: they hold it like a measure.

"Bring me all those nickels on back here," says Powerhouse. "Look at that! What you tell me the name of
this place?"

"White dance, week night, raining, Alligator, Mississippi, long ways from home."

"Uh-huh."

"Sent For You Yesterday and Here You Come
Today" plays.

The waitress, setting the tray of beer down on a back
table, comes up taut and apprehensive as a hen. "Says
in the kitchen, back there putting their eyes to little hole
peeping out, that you is Mr. Powerhouse.... They
knows from a picture they seen."

"They seeing right tonight, that is him," says Little
Brother.

"You him?"

"That is him in the flesh," says Scoot.

"Does you wish to touch him?" asks Valentine. "Because he don't bite."

"You passing through?"

"Now you got everything right."

She waits like a drop, hands languishing together in front.

"Little-Bit, ain't you going to bring the beer?"

She brings it, and goes behind the cash register and smiles, turning different ways. The little fillet of gold in her mouth is gleaming.

"The Mississippi River's here," she says once.

Now all the watching Negroes press in gently and bright-eyed through the door, as many as can get in. One is a little boy in a straw sombrero which has been coated with aluminum paint all over.

Powerhouse, Valentine, Scoot and Little Brother drink beer, and their eyelids come together like curtains. The wall and the rain and the humble beautiful waitress waiting on them and the other Negroes watching enclose them.

"Listen!" whispers Powerhouse, looking into the ketchup bottle and slowly spreading his performer's hands over the damp, wrinkling cloth with the red squares. "Listen how it is. My wife gets missing me. Gypsy. She goes to the window. She looks out and sees you know what. Street. Sign saying Hotel. People walking. Somebody looks up. Old man. She looks down, out the window. Well? . . . *Ssssst! Plooey!* What she do? Jump out and bust her brains all over the world."

He opens his eyes.

"That's it," agrees Valentine. "You gets a telegram."

"Sure she misses you," Little Brother adds.

"No, it's night time." How softly he tells them! "Sure. It's the night time. She say, What do I hear? Footsteps walking up the hall? That him? Footsteps go on off. It's not me. I'm in Alligator, Mississippi, she's crazy. Shaking all over. Listens till her ears and all grow out like old music-box horns but still she can't hear a thing. She says, All right! I'll jump out the window then. Got on her nightgown. I know that nightgown, and her thinking there. Says, Ho hum, all right, and jumps out the window. Is she mad at me! Is she crazy! She don't leave *nothing* behind her!"

"Ya! Ha!"

"Brains and insides everywhere, Lord, Lord."

All the watching Negroes stir in their delight, and to their higher delight he says affectionately, "Listen! Rats in here."

"That must be the way, boss."

"Only, naw, Powerhouse, that ain't true. That sound too *bad*."

"Does? I even know who finds her," cries Powerhouse. "That no-good pussyfooted crooning creeper, that creeper that follow around after me, coming up like weeds behind me, following around after me everything I do and messing around on the trail I leave. Bets my numbers, sings my songs, gets close to my agent like a Betsy-bug; when I going out he just coming in. I got him now! I got my eye on him."

"Know who he is?"

"Why it's that old Uranus Knockwood!"

"Ya! Ha!"

"Yeah, and he coming now, he going to find Gypsy. There he is, coming around that corner, and Gypsy ka-doodling down, oh-oh, watch out! *Sssst! Plooey!* See, there she is in her little old nightgown, and her insides and brains all scattered round."

A sigh fills the room.

"Hush about her brains. Hush about her insides."

"Ya! Ha! You talking about her brains and insides— old Uranus Knockwood," says Powerhouse, "look down and say Jesus! He say, Look here what I'm walking round in!"

They all burst into halloos of laughter. Powerhouse's face looks like a big hot iron stove.

"Why, he picks her up and carries her off!" he says.

"Ya! Ha!"

"Carries her *back* around the corner...."

"Oh, Powerhouse!"

"You know him."

"Uranus Knockwood!"

"Yeahhh!"

"He take our wives when we gone!"

"He come in when we goes out!"

"Uh-huh!"

"He go out when we comes in!"

"Yeahhh!"

"He standing behind the door!"

"Old Uranus Knockwood."

"You know him."

"Middle-size man."

"Wears a hat."

"That's him."

Everybody in the room moans with pleasure. The little boy in the fine silver hat opens a paper and divides out a jelly roll among his followers.

And out of the breathless ring somebody moves forward like a slave, leading a great logy Negro with bursting eyes, and says, "This here is Sugar-Stick Thompson, that dove down to the bottom of July Creek and pulled up all those drowned white people fall out of a boat. Last summer, pulled up fourteen."

"Hello," says Powerhouse, turning and looking around at them all with his great daring face until they nearly suffocate.

Sugar-Stick, their instrument, cannot speak; he can only look back at the others.

"Can't even swim. Done it by holding his breath," says the fellow with the hero.

Powerhouse looks at him seekingly.

"I his half brother," the fellow puts in.

They step back.

"Gypsy say," Powerhouse rumbles gently again, looking at *them,* " 'What is the use? I'm gonna jump out so far—so far. . . .' *Sssst—/*"

"Don't, boss, don't do it agin," says Little Brother.

"It's awful," says the waitress. "I hates that Mr. Knockwoods. All that the truth?"

"Want to see the telegram I got from him?" Powerhouse's hand goes to the vast pocket.

"Now wait, now wait, boss." They all watch him.

"It must be the real truth," says the waitress, sucking in her lower lip, her luminous eyes turning sadly, seeking the windows.

"No, babe, it ain't the truth." His eyebrows fly up, and he begins to whisper to her out of his vast oven mouth. His hand stays in his pocket. "Truth is something worse, I ain't said what, yet. It's something hasn't come to me, but I ain't saying it won't. And when it does, then want me to tell you?" He sniffs all at once, his eyes come open and turn up, almost too far. He is dreamily smiling.

"Don't, boss, don't, Powerhouse!"

"Oh!" the waitress screams.

"Go on git out of here!" bellows Powerhouse, taking his hand out of his pocket and clapping after her red dress.

The ring of watchers breaks and falls away.

"*Look* at that! Intermission is up," says Powerhouse.

He folds money under a glass, and after they go out, Valentine leans back in and drops a nickel in the nickelodeon behind them, and it lights up and begins to play "The Goona Goo." The feather dangles still.

"Take a telegram!" Powerhouse shouts suddenly up into the rain over the street. "Take a answer. Now what was that name?"

They get a little tired.

"Uranus Knockwood."

"You ought to know."

"Yas? Spell it to me."

They spell it all the ways it could be spelled. It puts them in a wonderful humor.

"Here's the answer. I got it right here. 'What in the hell you talking about? Don't make any difference: I gotcha.' Name signed: Powerhouse."

"That going to reach him, Powerhouse?" Valentine speaks in a maternal voice.

"Yas, yas."

All hushing, following him up the dark street at a distance, like old rained-on black ghosts, the Negroes are afraid they will die laughing.

Powerhouse throws back his vast head into the steaming rain, and a look of hopeful desire seems to blow somehow like a vapor from his own dilated nostrils over his face and bring a mist to his eyes.

"Reach him and come out the other side."

"That's it, Powerhouse, that's it. You got him now."

Powerhouse lets out a long sigh.

"But ain't you going back there to call up Gypsy long distance, the way you did last night in that other place? I seen a telephone. . . . Just to see if she there at home?"

There is a measure of silence. That is one crazy drummer that's going to get his neck broken some day.

"No," growls Powerhouse. "No! How many thousand times tonight I got to say No?"

He holds up his arm in the rain.

"You sure-enough unroll your voice some night, it about reach up yonder to her," says Little Brother, dismayed.

They go on up the street, shaking the rain off and on them like birds.

Back in the dance hall, they play "San" (99). The jitterbugs start up like windmills stationed over the floor, and in their orbits—one circle, another, a long stretch and a zigzag—dance the elderly couples with old smoothness, undisturbed and stately.

When Powerhouse first came back from intermission, no doubt full of beer, they said, he got the band tuned up again in his own way. He didn't strike the piano keys for pitch—he simply opened his mouth and gave falsetto howls—in A, D and so on—they tuned by him. Then he took hold of the piano, as if he saw it for the first time in his life, and tested it for strength, hit it down in the bass, played an octave with his elbow, lifted the top, looked inside, and leaned against it with all his might. He sat down and played it for a few minutes with outrageous force and got it under his power—a bass deep and coarse as a sea net—then produced something glimmering and fragile, and smiled. And who could ever remember any of the things he says? They are just inspired remarks that roll out of his mouth like smoke.

They've requested "Somebody Loves Me," and he's already done twelve or fourteen choruses, piling them up nobody knows how, and it will be a wonder if he ever gets through. Now and then he calls and shouts, " 'Somebody loves me! Somebody loves me, I wonder who!' " His mouth gets to be nothing but a volcano. "I wonder who!"

"Maybe . . ." He uses all his right hand on a trill.

"Maybe . . ." He pulls back his spread fingers and looks out upon the place where he is. A vast, impersonal and yet furious grimace transfigures his wet face.

". . . Maybe it's you!"

Afterword

Afterword

About a hundred years ago, Henry James established the concept of a central intelligence in fiction who filters the experience of a story. Discussions of point of view since then have recognized four or five general storytelling techniques—so-called omniscient third-person, third-person limited to one character's point of view, retrospective autobiography, first-person observer narration, and sometimes a subjective or unreliable narration.

Without a unified theory, these categories appear to be based on mixed principles—on distinctions, for example, between whether the character or the author is filtering the experience, or on whether the narrator is reliable or not. Besides omitting other important distinctions, this classification can lead to a great deal of confusion. One omniscient narrator may be more omniscient than another, and no third-person narration can really be limited to the point of view of a character. While interior and dramatic monologues, letters and diaries, may be recognized as ways of telling complete stories, they seldom figure in considerations of point of view. Some stories may be indiscriminately called "monologues" in one discussion and described as first-person or subjective in another.

Unless all techniques are placed in continuity with one another, they do not reveal their distinctions as alternatives in an author's repertory. This is a loss not only to teachers and literary critics but also to general readers. Anyone interested in stories at all has to be interested, consciously or not, in connections between form and content or between narrative art and everyday expression. This book makes available to anyone a comprehensive, unified theory of narrative by embodying it in a scaled array of illustrative stories.

Any piece of fiction one might name falls somewhere along this point-of-view spectrum or represents some combination—however subtly or intricately blended—of the techniques illustrated in it. This anthology provides a sampling of the whole range of narrative techniques, in the belief that someone who has become acquainted with all the forms will naturally be a more perceptive and sophisticated reader. Familiarity with the storyteller's full repertory makes more meaningful an author's choice of form for a particular story.

What a story is about is partly a question of *how* it is told. You cannot separate the tale from the telling. Beneath the content of every message is intent. Form embodies that intent. Intuitively or not, an author chooses techniques according to meaning. Spontaneously heeding form will tell the reader more about what an author is doing and saying than will direct analysis of meaning, which may break the spell and spoil the pleasure.

To appreciate the connection between form and subject, just imagine William Thackeray's *Vanity Fair* told by one of its characters instead of by the all-knowing author, who alone can give us a wide-angle view of the whole society. Or imagine Scott Fitzgerald's *The Great Gatsby* narrated by Gatsby himself instead of by the peripheral Nick, who can better turn him into an enigmatic and legendary figure. An anonymous narrator of Charles Dickens's *Great Expectations* who went beyond just Pip's thoughts to reveal the thoughts of the other characters would tell us another story, not immerse us in Pip's world as he knew it.

In *Points of View* the reader independently discovers the changes in intent, effect, meaning, and theme that occur as the technique changes. Through arrangement alone the stories illuminate each other. The techniques of fiction imitate everyday recording and reporting. The stories in the first two groups (interior monologue, dramatic monologue) purport to be actual discourse going on "now"—somebody thinking, somebody talking. The reader tunes in on a stream of thought or speech. The stories of the next five groups purport to be documents written by characters in the stories—letters, diaries, autobiographies, or memoirs. The remaining stories mimic third-person documents—biographies, case histories, or chronicles. Of course, art implies artifice; readers will appreciate for themselves how these fictional forms differ from their real-life counterparts.

The stories in the first five groups force us to pay attention to motive and attitude and style and tone, because we naturally scrutinize these for clues to offset the unreliability of these fallible narrators. Such stories feature all those qualities of speakers and their language that come through easily in everyday conversation but that become subtler on the page, especially in the techniques of anonymous narration later on in the spectrum. Third-person stories look deceptively bland: we take the hidden speaker's guidance for granted, and we easily forget that, third-person or not, each story is being told by *somebody,* by an individual just as influential as any character *I.*

Every story is first-person, whether the speaker is identified or not. Interior monologues, dramatic monologues, letters, diaries, and subjective narrations keep alive the drama of the narrating act: they put speakers on display so that we cannot ignore or forget the way they talk, the kind of logic they use, and the organization they impose on experience. Although Mark Twain himself tells the story of Tom Sawyer, instead of ventriloquizing through a character *I,* as he does in *Huckleberry Finn,* he has ways of organizing and setting down his material just as idiosyncratic as Huck's. Wolfgang Goethe and Samuel Richardson are essentially in the same position when they tell their tales as Goethe's young Werther is when recording his sorrows in his diary or Richardson's Clarissa Harlowe is when confiding in letters her plans to avert seduction. The difference is that the monologues of Huck, Werther, and Clarissa are spontaneous, vernacular, and private whereas the monologues of Twain, Goethe, and Richardson are composed, literary, and public. The spectrum is made up of distinctions like this. After listening to the everyday voices of characters caught in the open with all their prejudices showing, it is easier to detect and appreciate the less obvious rhetoric of the detached professional writer.

There is another way in which the earlier techniques

in the spectrum prepare for the later ones. Interior and dramatic monologues, letters, diaries, and other first-person stories are some of the building blocks of the larger, less limited techniques. Most novels contain some directly quoted thoughts and dialogue. Many novels, like those in Lawrence Durrell's *Alexandria Quartet,* incorporate the texts of letters and diaries. Herman Melville's *Moby Dick* touches every part of the discourse spectrum; there are the soliloquies of Ahab, dramatic monologue and dialogue by other characters, autobiography and observer narration by Ishmael, and broad anonymous narration by the author. (This prodigious work goes off the narrative scale completely into exposition and essay, encompassing both this volume and its nonfiction companion.) A reader familiar with stories consisting entirely of a monologue or personal document is better prepared for the hubbub of character voices mixed with the author's that make up fiction purporting to be memoir, biography, or chronicle.

Moreover, if you read, as usual, from front to back in this book, each technique in this spectrum, regarded as reportage of real life, becomes more comprehensive and abstract, takes in more territory. This is due to the narrator's increasingly complicated job of compiling and assimilating material from more and more remote sources, incorporating and digesting, quoting and paraphrasing. A social worker, for example, would have to summarize much more material to tell the story of a client or group of clients than one of them would need to include in a diary or autobiography.

Throughout the spectrum, the narrator becomes less and less confined to a particular time and place of telling and being listened to while also becoming farther and farther removed from the time and place of the events narrated. She floats more and more freely, regardless of the concreteness of her language, and her broadening vantage point implies greater and greater selectivity and reorganization of her original information. At the same time, her more public audience demands a more universal style, rhetoric, and logic. All these features correspond to expanding points of view.

The Development of Discourse

So arrayed, narrative techniques tend to recapitulate the course followed by any child in developing powers of speech, and to some extent the course adults follow in refining any raw subject matter through increasingly abstract stages of discourse. That is, the basic communication trio consists of sender, receiver, and subject—I, you, and it/he/she/they—or, in other words, teller, told-to, and told-about. When I talk to myself about myself, I am all three "persons," as in some interior monologue. This is the first solo discourse of the child, who does not distinguish between speaking to oneself and speaking to another, or between talking about oneself and talking about other people or things.

According to the great psychologist of child development, Jean Piaget, who called this discourse "egocentric speech," the very young child thinks aloud, talks to the air, not expecting others to pay attention or respond. Talk is an accompaniment to whatever else she or he is doing at the time. According to Piaget's Russian counterpart, Lev Vygotsky, egocentric speech "goes underground" and becomes the "inner speech" or thinking of the older person.

So play prattle is the starting point of monologue not only because it is the first solo speech to appear in the child but also because it is the speech of adults least adapted to others. "Persons" evolve from this genesis like three circles moving out from a common center, overlapping for a long time until finally they merely touch each other. Small children are not aware of the overlapping and blurring of speaker, listener, and subject. As one moves toward adulthood and tries to accommodate increasingly remote audiences and subjects, one continues to push these three circles apart. *You* is born from the rib of *I* in the form of a listener who is actually another person. Dramatic monologue represents the second stage of solo speech, which Piaget calls "socialized" because the speaker adapts her discourse to a second person whom she wishes to influence and by whom she is willing to be influenced.

Letters represent a further stage, dialogue at a distance, when separation in space or time requires that persons communicate in writing. Diary marks the transition between correspondence and publication. It is addressed to a personal but dimly envisioned listener, some persona introjected into oneself or oneself projected onto a persona, in any case neither a specific individual who can respond nor a large remote audience. Conversation and correspondence may consist of questions, retorts, entreaties, and commands, but diaries and publications are directed to an audience that cannot respond in kind, and the writer is reduced to declarative statement. The result is that the drama of *I*-and-*you* recedes in favor of the narrative of *he, she,* or *it*.

After these stages of verbalization to oneself, vocalization to others, and informal writing, the growing person arrives at public discourse written for a large, remote audience. The relation of speaker to audience now stands at maximum distance. Colloquial improvisation is replaced by literary composition, though the individuality of authors will always make the degree of distance vary some.

From here on, the main issue is essentially the speaker's relation to the *subject*. This works out in autobiography as the deliberate splitting of the speaker into *I-now* and *I-then,* into *virtually* distinct first and third persons. In memoir the speaker becomes observer rather than protagonist and focuses on some truly "other" person or people of whom at one time she or he had direct knowledge. The narrators of biography and chronicle no longer refer to themselves, usually because they have not had, or purport not to have had, any direct relation to the persons or events they refer to; they speak as if from second-knowledge.

So long as the speaker is talking about her own experience, her perspective depends on time distance between her past and present selves. But as soon as she begins to talk of others' experience, her perspective depends on how close she was to such events; she must overcome her distance from them in time and space through outside channels of information. Observer-narrators like Nick in *The Great Gatsby* or Marlowe in Joseph Conrad's *Lord Jim* identify themselves and tell us how they got their information. They can report only (1) what was confided to them, (2) what they saw and heard, and (3) background information picked up through membership in the same group or community in which Gatsby or Jim moved and was known.

These three sources provide information about the inner life of characters like Gatsby and Jim, specific acts and scenes in their lives, and their general circumstances. The confidant, like Nick or Marlowe, has the greatest possible intimacy with the main character(s). The eyewitness, like Art Croft in Walter Van Tilburg Clark's *The Ox-Bow Incident,* is further removed from them. The member of a chorus, like the narrator in Bret Harte's "Tennessee's Partner," is least privy to character and specific events. The stories included under Observer Narration show these roles, or information channels, in various combinations. This technique is the hinge between first- and third-person narrative; one can see clearly all the roles that anonymous narrators play even though, unlike identified narrators, they do not reveal their channels of information or their relation to the protagonists of the stories they tell.

The distance between a third-person narrator and her characters is reflected in the number of roles, and which of these roles, she plays as speaker. This is also her information system. If she relays to us the thoughts of the characters as a confidant, she remains close; indeed, she would have to have some empathy for the character even to imagine the thoughts. If the narrator is not a confidant, and reports only scenes and background information, as in the last group of stories (Anonymous Narration, No Character Point of View), she achieves the greatest separation from her subject possible in fiction. To drop the eyewitness role as well, and report only general information, is to pass beyond the spectrum of fiction into that more abstract narrative known as history. The third person loses its "personal" quality when we attempt to tell what many people did over a long period of time.

Beginning by listening to herself, the speaker gradually addresses a larger and larger audience, an audience necessarily spread over more and more time and space. At each stage of distance she must adapt language, logic, rhetoric, and organization to what her audience can understand and respond to. *What* the developing person discourses about becomes more and more a distilled "subject," accessible to this person only through an increasingly far-flung information system of communal knowledge. Necessarily, the subject generalizes as it progresses across the spectrum from relative, individual realities to a single, consensual reality. This is why the spectrum ends in mythic stories, which condense cultural experience.

I gradually disentangle myself from my sole point of view and learn to speak about myself, first, as if I were another person (objectification), then about others as if they were myself (identification), and finally about others without reference to myself (transpersonalization). Put another way, I evolve from passion to compassion to dispassion.

The Learning Process

The development of discourse corresponds closely to the human learning process. What hinders the growth of understanding in the child, Piaget says, is an unconscious preference for a limited local point of view. Learning is a matter of "decentering." We break through our egocentricity to other points of view not merely determined by our physical vantage point in time and space, by our cultural heritage, or by other partialities such as gender and emotional penchants. We achieve decentering by adapting ourselves to things and people outside ourselves and by adopting points of view initially foreign to us. This simultaneous accommodation to the world and assimilation of it amounts to expanding one's perspective. One does not become less oneself, but one's ego expands from a point to an ever broadening area. This is why the last two groups of stories jump from multiple character viewpoints to no character viewpoint: by hearing out the world, the narrator is centered in the middle of the community consciousness.

If we imagine a primary moment of experience such as interior monologue may record on the spot, we may think of the other sections of the spectrum as stages in the processing of this experience—as ways of combining it with other experiences, forms in which it is talked about, vantage points from which it is viewed, and levels to which it is abstracted. These are all different aspects of decentering and may demonstrate how this difficult and lifelong learning comes about. It makes a difference whether the primary moment of experience has just happened or happened a long time ago, whether it has happened to the speaker or to someone else, and whether one is confiding it to an acquaintance or broadcasting it to a larger audience. The stories at the end of the spectrum are not, of course, superior to earlier ones. What is important are the different modes of representing experience and what they correspond to in real life.

In the reader's own learning process, comprehension and appreciation best take place while spontaneously responding to the text rather than during vivisections and postmortems. Intuitions are swift and deep, and intuitions can be developed. The best means to such understanding may be through what learning psychologist Jerome Bruner has called "structure" and what Alfred North Whitehead long ago called "seeing the woods by means of the trees." That is, any field one might care to consider is a field because of certain basic relations that operate throughout it, lines of force that magnetize it. This set of relations shifts, because the field is dynamic. When a course of reading is structured to bring out such fundamental relations, readers gain perspective on the woods as they move through the trees. The spectacle of gradually shifting shapes permits beholders to grasp intuitively, for themselves, the facts of the field. Real learning does not consist of accepting statements of the sort appearing in this essay but rather of revising constantly one's own inner field so as to achieve some correspondence with the field being contemplated. To make the stories magnetize each other, *Points of View* is organized to highlight the relations of the fictional field generated by the basic structure of discourse, the trinity of persons.

This organization attempts to breathe new life into the truism that life and literature illumine each other. The interplay between reality and imagination is both more precise and more organic than is commonly understood by this truism. Fiction holds up a mirror not only to human behavior, in what it says, but to human modes of learning and communicating, in how it says it. Moving freely back and forth among the three realms of fiction, discourse, and growth, via a common structure, brings each to bear on the others for the greater illumination of all. Stories both *are* systems of communication and knowledge and are *about* such systems, inasmuch as the very subject matter of fiction tends to concern the making and breaking of communication among people, someone's learning or failure to learn, or something about discrepancies and adjustments of perspective. Art, as we all know, weds form to content, either through the dissonance of irony or the consonance of harmony. We can celebrate such weddings in fiction because the apprehending and sharing of experience are themselves a crucial part of what we call experience.

Art in-forms experience, but where do these forms come from if not from nature? Forms of storytelling derive from human nature, as in the relations among speaker, listener, and subject, but this communication triad derives in turn from interaction between organism and environment and the dynamics of time and space, mind and matter.

The History of Fiction

Now let's reverse the direction of the spectrum. Someone reading this book back to front relives in rough fashion the history of fictional art. The dominant genres of made-up stories have shifted over the centuries from objective to subjective, from universal to particular, at the same time that the scale of the hero or heroine has—as Northrop Frye put it—correspondingly diminished. The main characters of myth are gods or other immortal personages who represent aspects of the cosmos. Epics like *Odysseus, Gilgamesh,* and *Beowulf* feature demigods or mortals of high station gifted with superhuman powers and supernatural contacts who represent aspects of culture. Romances and folk tales begin to blend the actual and the magical as people with common human motives interact with sorcerers and spirits; all represent the potentialities of human experience in a culture still open to forces from beyond itself. Deriving, significantly, from mock epics like Cervantes's *Don Quixote* and developing through the picaresque, burlesque rogue and road stories like Paul Scarron's seventeenth-century *Le Roman Comique* and Alain-René Lesage's eighteenth-century *Gil Blas*, the novel arose as a vehicle of bourgeois realism. It represents people cut off from cosmic or supernatural forces and living in a culturally determined environment. Finally, the heroes of fiction become antiheroes like those of Dostoevsky and Kafka, Céline and Becket, representing individuals cut off even from society and festering in their own particularity.

Like the stories at the end of this book, myths are told by anonymous communal narrators who do not go into the thoughts of any of the characters, because the archetypal minds and actions of cosmic and cultural beings need no inner point of view. Even the mortal personages in these symbolic stories are usually so elemental that we can know them from their words and deeds alone, without access to their thoughts and feelings. Legends amplified and idealized the lives of certain saints and martyrs or of other historical figures such as King Arthur and Charlemagne, Robin Hood and William Tell. Like actual chronicles and history, these were told in third person, almost always without a character's point of view. Motives are obvious, the inner life generic, as in *Everyman*. In common with fables and parables and other folk literature, myths, epics, and legends condense and transmit a heritage of knowledge and wisdom, the public domain of collective consciousness, or unconsciousness.

But as fictional characters evolved during the Middle Ages and Renaissance from types into the individualized people of Chaucer and Shakespeare, they had to speak more and more for themselves. At first their thoughts and feelings were paraphrased by an anonymous and sometimes omniscient narrator privileged to know their inner life, but increasingly they became narrators themselves. The tellers of romances and folk tales occasionally go into the minds of the characters and often settle into the point of view held by a principal character with whom the reader travels and shares adventures, as in Chrétien de Troyes' *Perceval*. Departing from the assumption of a universal perspective, narrative broke down into a multiplicity of individual vantage points that became more and more idiosyncratic in the matter and manner of the stories.

Thus third person reigned in fiction until the seventeenth century or so, when personal stories began to pass into it from the monologues and soliloquies of drama, from first-person oral accounts like confessions and depositions, and from first-person texts like journals and memoirs. That is, first-person stories first occurred in literature as parts of plays or of third-person narratives but did not themselves constitute whole stories. They were interludes interpolated into epics, romances, and plays whenever some character had to inform others of events he or she had engaged in or witnessed. It is as if even when personal experiences and voices became recognized, they still had to be framed within a consensual or communal utterance. This utterance the characters created jointly with each other and the narrator but remained submerged within, as in the next to last category of the spectrum, Anonymous Narrator—Multiple Character Point of View.

The more personal emphasis of the Renaissance and the Romantic period extended fictional techniques beyond the third-person range into the first-person. Many of the earliest first-person works of fiction posed as diaries, correspondences, other found documents, or, like Jonathan Swift's *Gulliver's Travels,* as the popular accounts of voyages to exotic places. Other eighteenth-century stories such as Daniel Defoe's *Moll Flanders* or Abbé Prévost's *Manon Lescaut* simply imitated autobiography, which grew out of published confessions, for which St. Augustine had set an early precedent.

Only the rise of the short story in the nineteenth century would permit the further development of first-person narration, since the limited viewpoints of such techniques as diaries, monologues, and subjective autobiography make it difficult to sustain them successfully for the length of a novel. A sequence of diary entries, for example, became in the hands of Guy de Maupassant or Nikolai Gogol a way of registering some gradual descent into madness, as Daniel Keyes was later to trace shifting mental states in "Flowers for Algernon" through the diary of a retarded man turned genius. Monologues that used to punctuate older third-person stories, sometimes taking up whole chapters in episodic novels, could now be crafted as independent stories.

Dostoevsky may have been the first to make use of the technique we have called Subjective Autobiography. In novellas ("Notes from Underground" and "The Double") and in short stories ("White Nights" and "The Dream of a Ridiculous Man") he gave voice, along with other introspective French and Russian writers, to the underground man or antihero of the modern era. After the precedent of *Huck Finn, subjective* narration merged with vernacular narration, encouraged by the short story and the populist spirit of democracy. Between the world wars, American writers with a fine ear for common speech and the dialects and languages of particular milieux—Ring Lardner, John O'Hara, Langston Hughes, Sherwood Anderson, Dorothy Parker, Sinclair Lewis, George Milburn—gave us the first short story monologues at the same time that James Joyce, Virginia Woolf, and William Faulkner were adapting interior monologue to the novel, first attempted apparently by Édouard Dujarden in *We'll to the Woods No More.*

The Evolution of Consciousness

The history of fiction charts the evolution of consciousness and culture. Between mythic stories and interior monologues humankind moved not only from collective to personal consciousness, as Richard Bucke, Julian Jaynes, and Rudolf Steiner have variously described, but from monarchical theocracy to secular democracy. Individualism occurred both psychologically, as people developed different inner lives, and socially, as they demanded freedom from the state and from group rules of behavior. Literature separated itself from scripture and liturgy as its subject matter shifted from the divine comedy to the human comedy and its viewpoint modulated from objective omniscience into subjective and limited perspectives.

As the matter and manner of literature moved from sacred to profane, poetry became prose, and the language shifted from some imperial "classical" language like Hebrew, Greek, or Latin, in which the scripture had been written, to national languages like English, French, Italian, or German. Today storytellers frequently set aside even the national literary language to adopt some kind of colloquial speech that suits their purpose. In the spirit of democracy and individualism, this purpose is often to let the characters speak for themselves even if they betray themselves. Subjective narrations are democratic also in the sense that the author does not intervene to explain but allows readers to assess and interpret for themselves.

The master trait that seems to characterize this coevolution of culture and consciousness is the breaking down of some original unity into fragments, just as, reading backward, narrative in this book splinters off from a central intelligence beyond the characters to the diversity of increasingly claustrophobic viewpoints of the characters themselves. Fragmentation corresponds to alienation, freedom to anxiety. Psychological breakdowns in personality result from materialistic breakdown of experience by the analytical mind that accompanies self-consciousness. The shift from sacred to secular, from unity to disintegration, from hero to antihero, from omnipotence and omniscience to impotence and myopia, can seem a descent into materialistic hell, but it is also a journey of maturation precisely because it is a growth in consciousness. Pilgrimage is paradoxical.

Children start by lumping themselves together with others and then develop toward a self-conscious differentiation of themselves as physically and mentally distinct from the environment. They feel at one at first with other people and nature then gradually separate themselves as their consciousness becomes personal. Perceiving oneself as separate from other people and things initiates the breaking down of reality that characterizes the mental activity of analysis. It also sets in motion the pursuit of self-realization that can lead to reintegration with the world.

At first children prefer stories about people and places remote from their own lives—an imagined world where anything is possible because nothing is necessary or determined. This unconditioned state defines spiritual freedom. If children are indeed born "trailing clouds of glory" from a spiritual world, as Wordsworth described in his ode "Intimations of Immortality from Recollections of Childhood," they may long for and remember a former unconditioned state, like that of dreams. That state may account for their love of highly imaginative stories with personages and settings very different from their everyday life. In any case, into this world of there-then they seem to project their fantasies of power and unlimited possibility, which contrast with their actual limitation and dependence.

Only gradually do children withdraw this projection and move from hero to antihero, from there-then to here-now, from cosmic possibility to local confinement. It may be, as Wordsworth says, that "Shades of the prison-house begin to close/ upon the growing Boy" because "thy Soul shall have her earthly freight,/ and custom lie upon thee with a weight ..." until finally the adult perceives the vision "die away, and fade into the light of common day ... "?

Of course as children acquire knowledge and power, they need less to fantasize about omniscience and omnipotence. And as they become self-aware and acknowledge their fears and desires, they become more willing to deal with these directly in real life and need less to symbolize them unconsciously. As both child and human race, we identify first with animals, fantastic creatures, folk heroes, and epic and legendary figures. Then gradually we shrink our fantasies toward our own particular here-now. Slowly, the bell tolls us back to our sole self.

But always, even as grown-ups, we need to project into stories some aspects of our inner life of which we are still unconscious. Hence adult art, which allows us to externalize the inner life, as stories do, so that indirectly we can know it and respond to it. This reflexiveness eventually brings on self-awareness—the loss of innocence—the being at one with the world symbolized by the Edenic Tree of Life. But this loss purchases the raised consciousness required for self-realization, the Tree of Knowledge. This is a necessary step for both the species and the child.

But the tale isn't over. Only when we consider forward and backward directions of the book together do we get the whole story. People grow both ways at once. What is a descent from one viewpoint is an ascent from another. Once out of the womb, we have to differentiate ourselves from the world to defend ourselves in it, and we have to break down our thought to match the social and material breakdowns of the outer world that we have to make our way in. Trailing clouds of glory or not, we resort to egocentricity in order to survive. But this egocentricity must also mature by expanding across the culture, to accommodate our humanity, and eventually across the cosmos, to accommodate our divinity. Otherwise, we survive materially only but not psychologically or spiritually. We have to develop both a first-hand, first-person view in order to stand up for ourselves in the world and to fulfill our particular potential, meaning, or karma. The reverse direction of the spectrum shows this successive narrowing of contexts. At the same time, we must build ourselves ever more stately mansions, like Ralph Waldo Emerson's chambered nautilus, by successively enlarging the contexts in which we perceive and interpret action, as exemplified in the movement from monologues and personal documents through increasingly more inclusive second-hand, third-person stories to myth.

Esoteric teachings say that mankind is going through a cycle of, first, involution, of increasing involvement with matter that reaches a nadir in a descent into hell. Then from this painfully acquired understanding the human being begins to evolve back out of materialism toward a new oneness. This time, unity is based not on unconscious membership in a herd mind, like animals, but on fully articulated individual selfhood. In the fiction of Gabriel Marquez, Salman Rushdie, Thomas Pynchon, and Alice Walker we can see the return to the universal and supernatural but in a new fusion with individualistic realism.

One returns to the beginning but on another plane where all paradoxes are resolved. The adult becomes as a child again by maturing most fully as an adult. One returns home to the fold but as a self-reliant, self-realized individual who has outgrown egocentricity and ethnocentricity and become a citizen of the universe. Subjectivity and objectivity interpenetrate as in William Butler

Yeats' esoteric vision. Inner and outer are perceived as vanishing vantage points. The sum of all points of view creates a meta-perspective in the real world as it does in the fictional. The Tree of Life and the Tree of Knowledge become one. The human comedy coincides with the divine comedy as consciousness expands in both of the directions that make-believe faithfully reflects.

References

Bakhtin, Mikhail. "Discourse in the Novel" from Michael Holquist, ed., *The Dialogic Imagination*. Austin: University of Texas Press, 1981.

Bruner, Jerome. *The Process of Education*. Cambridge, Mass: Harvard University Press, 1960.

Bucke, Richard. *Cosmic Consciousness: A Study in the Evolution of the Human Mind*. New York: Viking/Penguin, 1901, 1991.

Frye, Northrop. *Anatomy of Criticism*. Princeton: Princeton University Press, 1957.

James, Henry. *The Art of the Novel: Critical Prefaces*. New York: Charles Scribner's Sons, 1934.

Jaynes, Julian. *The Origin of Consciousness in the Breakdown of the Bicameral Mind*. Boston: Houghton Mifflin, 1976.

Piaget, Jean. *The Language and Thought of the Child*. New York: Humanities Press, 1959.

————. "Comments on Vygotsky's Critical Remarks Concerning *The Language and Thought of the Child*," supplement to *Thought and Language*, Cambridge, Mass: Massachusetts Institute of Technology Press, 1962.

Steiner, Rudolf. *Aspects of Human Evolution*. Hudson, N.Y.: Anthroposophic Press, 1917, 1987.

————. *The Evolution of Consciousness*. Hudson, N.Y.: Anthroposophic Press, 1923, 1987.

Vygotsky, Lev. *Thought and Language*. Cambridge, Mass.: Massachusetts Institute of Technology Press, 1962.

Whitehead, Alfred North. *The Aims of Education*. New York: New American Library/Dutton, 1949.

Related Works By James Moffett

Student-Centered Language Arts, K-12, with Betty Jane Wagner, methods textbook and teacher handbook. Boynton/Cook Heinemann, 4th edition, 1992.

Teaching the Universe of Discourse, foreword by Harvard psychologist Roger Brown. Boynton/Cook Heinemann, 1968.

Active Voice: A Writing Program Across the Curriculum. Boynton/Cook Heinemann, revised edition 1992.

Coming on Center: Essays in English Education. Boynton/Cook Heinemann, revised edition 1988.

Harmonic Learning: Keynoting School Reform, Boynton/Cook Heinemann, 1992.

The Universal Schoolhouse: Spiritual Awakening Through Education. San Francisco: Jossey-Bass, 1994.

Other anthologies:

Points of Departure: An Anthology of Nonfiction. New York: New American Library/Dutton, 1985.

Active Voices. I–IV, student writing from elementary school through college, edited with others. Boynton/Cook Heinemann, 1985–87.

Acknowledgments